The Tindalos Cycle

THE HIPPOCAMPUS PRESS MYTHOS LIBRARY

Robert M. Price (editor), *Tales out of Dunwich* (2005)
W. H. Pugmire, *The Fungal Stain and Others* (2006)
Franklyn Searight, *Lair of the Dreamer* (2007)

THE TINDALOS CYCLE

Edited by Robert M. Price

Hippocampus Press

New York

Published by Hippocampus Press
P.O. Box 641, New York, NY 10156.
http://www.hippocampuspress.com

First Edition
1 3 5 7 9 8 6 4 2
ISBN 978-0-9814888-5-1

Contents

Chock Full o' Mutts

I once had the privilege of asking Frank Belknap Long how he intended us to pronounce *Tindalos,* the name of his fictive creepy breed. As I remember, he emphasized the first syllable: *Tin´*-dah-los. Okay, it's pedantic. Brian Lumley laughs at me for even wanting to know such things. (Is that enough name-dropping for you?) But as long as you've got Long on hand (and we don't anymore) you might as well settle the big questions for posterity. Likewise, S. T. Joshi once asked Long where he got the name "Tindalos" to begin with. He said that, one day while shaving, he was thinking about his hypothetical Hounds and wanted something that would sound "strong." "Tindalos" is what popped into his head. Where, I wonder, did it pop in from?

We have asked the same question about certain blasphemous names that came mysteriously to H. P. Lovecraft in his dreams, like *Necronomicon* and Nyarlathotep. He didn't consciously create either one of them, but we can very likely point out where he may have picked up the bits and pieces his mythopoeic subconscious cobbled into the final products which it then whispered into his sleeping ear. The *Necronomicon* was probably suggested by the ancient *Astronomica,* an astronomy text by Manilius. Nyarlathotep is probably based on two Dunsanian names: Mynarthitep the god and Alhireth-hotep the prophet. It makes me wonder if Tindalos, too, was a subconscious borrowing by Frank Long, this time from Robert H. Codrington's researches into primitive religious conceptions as evidenced by the islanders of Melanesia. I don't know what books in particular the inquisitive young intellectual Long used to read, but Codrington is surely the sort of thing he read. And Codrington wrote of such matters as *tabu* (the ceremonially forbidden) and *mana* (the potent luck-force that accounted for one islander having a greater fortune in pigs than his neighbor). The Melanesians called the human soul a *tarunga.* According to their anthropological conceptions, at death a man's *tarunga* became a ghost. And their word for that was *tindalo.* Are Long's hounds, then, "ghost hounds"? Maybe so. Consider this.

It is pretty clear even from a casual reading of "The Hounds of Tindalos" that two principal influences upon Long were Ambrose Bierce's "The Death of Halpin Frayser" and Robert W. Chambers's "The Maker of Moons." In fact, the protagonist of Long's tale is named "Halpin Chalmers," an amalgam of "Halpin Frayser" and "Robert Chambers." The two names are properly linked because of Chambers's momentous development of Bierce's intriguing myth-bits Hastur and Hali. Well, I believe Frank Long got the idea for the Hounds of Tindalos from the mysterious "Yeth Hounds" who appear in "The Maker of Moons." As explained there, the Yeth Hounds are headless dogs embodying the souls of murdered children. This notion Chambers seems in turn to have adapted from the eschatological beliefs of the English West Country. In Dartmoor they whispered of the Whisht Hounds, in Devon of the frightful Yeth Hounds. These were sometimes conceived as the souls of unbaptized infants, hounding their negligent parents, sometimes as spectral visitants pursuing the hapless souls of unbaptized babes.

In turn, this legend would seem to be a popular corruption of a common church architectural motif of "Christ the Huntsman," often depicted on baptismal fonts. The hunting Christ's pack of heavenly hounds pursued the souls of the unredeemed (or, again, of unbaptized babes), seeking to win them for his flock. This conception seems to be a Christianized version of an older pagan myth of the Hunt of Arawn, King of Annwn (the Netherworld), who hunts a stag, only to lose it to Pwyll, Prince of Dyfed, who then nonetheless makes a pact with his infernal counterpart.

And yet the fundamental mytheme back of the Hounds of Tindalos is something else. Isn't it obvious that the major prototype for the story is Cerberus, the guard dog of Hades? That Hell-hound was one but had three heads; Long has made the dogs themselves plural. Cerberus kept interlopers out of Hell (I guess they're dying to get in) until their time. And that's what Long's Hounds of Tindalos, his Ghost Hounds, do, too. For what is the link between Halpin Chalmers's retreat into the past and his fatally attracting the Hounds? Is there a link at all? If not, it's a pretty mechanical premise. But it isn't. As time-travelers, the Hounds guard the infinite reservoir of the Past, which is the same thing, basically, as Hades, for isn't Hades precisely the repository of the Past? Past deeds, the old souls who did them, all are there, relived and reliving. Hell is a memory bank, and Halpin Chalmers, like his prototype Halpin Frayser, had arrived to make a deposit.

Frank Long wrote three stories involving, to one degree or another, the Hounds of Tindalos, and all are included here. Another tale, less directly related, but definitely and explicitly linked nonetheless, is the novella "The Horror from the Hills." The star of the show in this one was another myth-based monster, one Chaugnar Faugn. He is famously described as roughly elephantine in appearance: flaring bat-wing ears and a tentacular proboscis. One feels the resemblance to earth's pachyderms is supposed to be merely fortuitous; Chaugnar is no more an elephant than Cthulhu is an octopus. Perhaps this is why Long dropped his working title "The Elephant God of Leng."

Whence Chaugnar Faugn? His origin is a direct borrowing, or inspiration. Young Long once chanced upon a decorative statue of the Hindu deity Ganesha. Doing a double-take, Long was much impressed with the divine effigy: a pot-bellied, four-armed human body crowned with an elephant head. For such is the Son of Siva. Long resolved to employ the unearthly figure in a more sinister context, Chaugnar Faugn being the result.

Did Long intend the theological connection that many readers now take for granted, that the Hounds of Tindalos and Chaugnar Faugn are members of the pantheon of the Lovecraftian Old Ones? I doubt that he did, for the simple reason that, when he was writing these stories, the Mythos was not really in anyone's mind as a system. Long no doubt did consider himself to be working in a Lovecraftian vein, writing the general sort of stuff Howard was writing, and that's close enough. Lovecraft seemed pleased to adopt Long's creations into his myth-cycle, once he realized he had created one. In "The Whisperer in Darkness" he has Wilmarth and Akeley discuss the Hounds of Tindalos among a catalogue of monsters derived from his own stories and from those of Dunsany, Bierce, Chambers, etc. The induction became official, however, in the revision tale "The Horror in the Museum," where we learn that the mad curator Rogers (who I'm pretty sure must have looked quite similar to Vincent Price or Lionel Atwill) has hunted down *and bagged* "proboscidian Chaugnar" and immobilized him inside a waxen shell, along with the likes of a diminutive Cthulhu and other once-Cyclopean entities. Chaugnar has joined the club. In the same story, Rogers curses his nemesis, the narrator: "Son of the dogs that howl in the Maelstrom of Azathoth!" (Now that's getting personal!) I have always assumed that Lovecraft here intended a reference to the Hounds of Tindalos. Azathoth dwells "beyond angled space," while we are told the Hounds travel the time-stream along angles, curves being anathema to them.

Of Long's Lovecraftian creations, Chaugnar has attracted rather less attention than the Tind'losi Hounds. This last designation is Brian Lumley's version of the name, intended, I would guess, to render the name more Semitic-sounding, to fit in with most other Lovecraftian names. Lumley has them dog the time-traveling heels of his Gulliver-like hero Titus Crow as if he were a cosmic postman. Roger Zelazny takes the pooches out for an interstellar walk, too. And you will find them nuzzling you on several pages of the present anthology as well.

The Hounds of Tindalos exploit the fundamental cheat of time-travel fiction, treating time as if it were space. Thus it is no surprise to observe the close analogy between the Hounds and the invisible predators in Long's "The Space-Eaters." The latter's medium of invasion is overtly spatial, not covertly as in "The Hounds of Tindalos." But the Hounds have truly traveled through time after all, haven't they? Because they continue to inspire and to appear in imaginative fiction to this day, over seventy years after their first appearance. So beware of dogs: They are lean and athirst!

ROBERT M. PRICE
Hierophant of the Horde

The Tindalos Cycle

The Maker of Moons
Robert W. Chambers

I have elsewhere discussed R. W. Chambers's "The Maker of Moons" as an influence on the work of H. P. Lovecraft. You will have no trouble recognizing numerous items that struck Lovecraft's imagination. Here are the prototypes for Lovecraft's eighteenth *Fungi from Yuggoth* sonnet "The Gardens of Yin," his underground civilization of scientist-sorcerers K'n-yan (in "The Mound"), his forbidden city Yian-Ho (in "The Diary of Alonzo Typer" and "The Whisperer in Darkness"). In addition, let me now point out what I judge to be the source of the mysterious golden jewelry of Innsmouth, really of Y'ha-n'thlei, in "The Shadow over Innsmouth." Like the strange golden ball in "The Maker of Moons," the Innsmouth tiara is inscribed with the writhing forms of archaic and unknown sea-leviathans. There is even the possibility that the Deep Ones make the metal themselves, as do the hidden Kuen-Yuin in "The Maker of Moons," since Lovecraft drops the hint that the Innsmouth gold has a peculiar silvery cast. (Interestingly, Chambers's conceit of gold not being a true element also occurs in John Taine's *The Time Stream*. Was it a current pseudo-science theory?) The sale of the artifact to a local museum even made it directly into "The Shadow over Innsmouth."

I have already explained my theory that the Yeth Hounds in "The Maker of Moons" were the immediate inspiration for the Hounds of Tindalos, but is it possible that "Yeth" was also the source for the name of Lovecraft's alien planet "Yith"? In a sense it might have been. Remember, the name was originally coined by Lovecraft's collaborator Duane Rimel as "Yid" for his poem sequence "Dreams from Yid," and Lovecraft advised him to change it since some readers would not be able to suppress the ethnic slur "Yid" (i.e., *'Jude*, German for Jew") when they read it, and it would spoil the desired mood. So why not change it to, oh, say, "Yith"? But who knows? Maybe in casting about for something else starting with a Y, Lovecraft thought of Yeth and combined it with the despised "Yid." (One wonders if Rimel had been thinking of "Dreams from the Id," dreams that arise from the psychic depths.)

Finally, don't you think Frank Long probably derived the name of his Liao drug from the name of Chambers's alchemist Yue-Laou? And it's not just the name: he doesn't just say the drug is from China; it is made by Chinese alchemists!

"The Maker of Moons" first appeared in Chambers's collection of the same title in 1896.

"I have heard what the Talkers were talking,—the talk
Of the beginning and the end;
But I do not talk of the beginning or the end."

I.

Concerning Yue-Laou and the Xin I know nothing more than you shall know. I am miserably anxious to clear the matter up. Perhaps what I write may save the United States Government money and lives, perhaps it may arouse the scientific world to action; at any rate it will put an end to the terrible suspense of two people. Certainty is better than suspense.

If the Government dares to disregard this warning and refuses to send a thoroughly equipped expedition at once, the people of the State may take swift vengeance on the whole region and leave a blackened devastated waste where to-day forest and flowering meadow land border the lake in the Cardinal Woods.

You already know part of the story; the New York papers have been full of alleged details. This much is true: Barris caught the "Shiner," red handed, or rather yellow handed, for his pockets and boots and dirty fists were stuffed with lumps of gold. I say gold, advisedly. You may call it what you please. You also know how Barris was—but unless I begin at the beginning of my own experiences you will be none the wiser after all.

On the third of August of this present year I was standing in Tiffany's, chatting with George Godfrey of the designing department. On the glass counter between us lay a coiled serpent, an exquisite specimen of chiselled gold.

"No," replied Godfrey to my question, "it isn't my work; I wish it was. Why, man, it's a masterpiece!"

"Whose?" I asked.

"Now I should be very glad to know also," said Godfrey. "We bought it from an old jay who says he lives in the country somewhere about the Cardinal Woods. That's near Starlit Lake, I believe——"

"Lake of the Stars?" I suggested.

"Some call it Starlit Lake,—it's all the same. Well, my rustic Reuben says that he represents the sculptor of this snake for all practical and business purposes. He got his price too. We hope he'll bring us something more. We have sold this already to the Metropolitan Museum."

I was leaning idly on the glass case, watching the keen eyes of the artist in precious metals as he stooped over the gold serpent.

"A masterpiece!" he muttered to himself, fondling the glittering coil; "look at the texture! whew!" But I was not looking at the serpent. Something was moving,—crawling out of Godfrey's coat pocket,—the pocket nearest to me,—something soft and yellow with crab-like legs all covered with coarse yellow hair.

"What in Heaven's name," said I, "have you got in your pocket? It's crawling out—it's trying to creep up your coat, Godfrey!"

He turned quickly and dragged the creature out with his left hand.

I shrank back as he held the repulsive object dangling before me, and he laughed and placed it on the counter.

"Did you ever see anything like that?" he demanded.

"No," said I truthfully, "and I hope I never shall again. What is it?"

"I don't know. Ask them at the Natural History Museum—they can't tell you. The Smithsonian is all at sea too. It is, I believe, the connecting link between a sea-urchin, a spider, and the devil. It looks venomous but I can't find either fangs or mouth. Is it blind? These things may be eyes but they look as if they were painted. A Japanese sculptor might have produced such an impossible beast, but it is hard to believe that God did. It looks unfinished too. I have a mad idea that this creature is only one of the parts of some larger and more grotesque organism,—it looks so lonely, so hopelessly dependent, so cursedly unfinished. I'm going to use it as a model. If I don't out-Japanese the Japs my name isn't Godfrey."

The creature was moving slowly across the glass case towards me. I drew back.

"Godfrey," I said, "I would execute a man who executed any such work as you propose. What do you want to perpetuate such a reptile for? I can stand the Japanese grotesque but I can't stand that—spider—"

"It's a crab."

"Crab or spider or blind-worm—ugh! What do you want to do it for? It's a nightmare—it's unclean!"

I hated the thing. It was the first living creature that I had ever hated.

For some time I had noticed a damp acrid odour in the air, and Godfrey said it came from the reptile.

"Then kill it and bury it," I said; "and by the way, where did it come from?"

"I don't know that either," laughed Godfrey; "I found it clinging to the box that this gold serpent was brought in. I suppose my old Reuben is responsible."

"If the Cardinal Woods are the lurking places for things like this," said I, "I am sorry that I am going to the Cardinal Woods."

"Are you?" asked Godfrey; "for the shooting?"

"Yes, with Barris and Pierpont. Why don't you kill that creature?"

"Go off on your shooting trip, and let me alone," laughed Godfrey.

I shuddered at the "crab," and bade Godfrey good-bye until December.

That night, Pierpont, Barris, and I sat chatting in the smoking-car of the Quebec Express when the long train pulled out of the Grand Central Depot. Old David had gone forward with the dogs; poor things, they hated to ride in the baggage car, but the Quebec and Northern road provides no sportsman's cars, and David and the three Gordon setters were in for an uncomfortable night.

Except for Pierpont, Barris, and myself, the car was empty. Barris, trim, stout, ruddy, and bronzed, sat drumming on the window ledge, puffing a short fragrant pipe. His gun-case lay beside him on the floor.

"When *I* have white hair and years of discretion," said Pierpont languidly, "I'll not flirt with pretty serving-maids; will you, Roy?"

"No," said I, looking at Barris.

"You mean the maid with the cap in the Pullman car?" asked Barris.

"Yes," said Pierpont.

I smiled, for I had seen it also.

Barris twisted his crisp grey moustache, and yawned.

"You children had better be toddling off to bed," he said. "That lady's-maid is a member of the Secret Service."

"Oh," said Pierpont, "one of your colleagues?"

"You might present us, you know," I said; "the journey is monotonous."

Barris had drawn a telegram from his pocket, and as he sat turning it over and over between his fingers he smiled. After a moment or two he handed it to Pierpont who read it with slightly raised eyebrows.

"It's rot,—I suppose it's cipher," he said; "I see it's signed by General Drummond——"

"Drummond, Chief of the Government Secret Service," said Barris.

"Something interesting?" I enquired, lighting a cigarette.

"Something so interesting," replied Barris, "that I'm going to look into it myself——"

"And break up our shooting trio——"

"No. Do you want to hear about it? Do you, Billy Pierpont?"

"Yes," replied that immaculate young man.

Barris rubbed the amber mouth-piece of his pipe on his handkerchief, cleared the stem with a bit of wire, puffed once or twice, and leaned back in his chair.

"Pierpont," he said, "do you remember that evening at the United States Club when General Miles, General Drummond, and I were examining that gold nugget that Captain Mahan had? You examined it also, I believe."

"I did," said Pierpont.

"Was it gold?" asked Barris, drumming on the window.

"It was," replied Pierpont.

"I saw it too," said I; "of course, it was gold."

"Professor La Grange saw it also," said Barris; "he said it was gold."

"Well?" said Pierpont.

"Well," said Barris, "it was not gold."

After a silence Pierpont asked what tests had been made.

"The usual tests," replied Barris. "The United States Mint is satisfied that it is gold, so is every jeweller who has seen it. But it is not gold,—and yet—it is gold."

Pierpont and I exchanged glances.

"Now," said I, "for Barris' usual coup-de-théâtre: what was the nugget?"

"Practically it was pure gold; but," said Barris, enjoying the situation intensely, "really it was not gold. Pierpont, what is gold?"

"Gold's an element, a metal——"

"Wrong! Billy Pierpont," said Barris coolly.

"Gold was an element when I went to school," said I.

"It has not been an element for two weeks," said Barris; "and, except General Drummond, Professor La Grange, and myself, you two youngsters are the only people, except one, in the world who know it,—or have known it."

"Do you mean to say that gold is a composite metal?" said Pierpont slowly.

"I do. La Grange has made it. He produced a scale of pure gold day before yesterday. That nugget was manufactured gold."

Could Barris be joking? Was this a colossal hoax? I looked at Pierpont. He muttered something about that settling the silver question, and turned his head to Barris, but there was that in Barris' face which forbade jesting, and Pierpont and I sat silently pondering.

"Don't ask me how it's made," said Barris, quietly; "I don't know. But I do know that somewhere in the region of the Cardinal Woods there is a gang of people who do know how gold is made, and who make it. You understand the danger this is to every civilized nation. It's got to be stopped of course. Drummond and I have decided that I am the man to stop it. Wherever and whoever these people are—these gold makers,— they must be caught, every one of them,—-caught or shot."

"Or shot," repeated Pierpont, who was owner of the Cross-Cut Gold Mine and found his income too small; "Professor La Grange will of course be prudent;—science need not know things that would upset the world!"

"Little Willy," said Barris laughing, "your income is safe."

"I suppose," said I, "some flaw in the nugget gave Professor La Grange the tip."

"Exactly. He cut the flaw out before sending the nugget to be tested. He worked on the flaw and separated gold into its three elements."

"He is a great man," said Pierpont, "but he will be the greatest man in the world if he can keep his discovery to himself."

"Who?" said Barris.

"Professor La Grange."

"Professor La Grange was shot through the heart two hours ago," replied Barris slowly.

II.

We had been at the shooting box in the Cardinal Woods five days when a telegram was brought to Barris by a mounted messenger from the nearest telegraph station, Cardinal Springs, a hamlet on the lumber railroad which joins the Quebec and Northern at Three Rivers Junction, thirty miles below.

Pierpont and I were sitting out under the trees, loading some special shells as experiments; Barris stood beside us, bronzed, erect, holding his pipe carefully so that no sparks should drift into our powder box. The beat of hoofs over the grass aroused us, and when the lank messenger drew bridle before the door, Barris stepped forward and took the sealed telegram. When he had torn it open he went into the house and presently reappeared, reading something that he had written.

"This should go at once," he said, looking the messenger full in the face.

"At once, Colonel Barris," replied the shabby countryman.

Pierpont glanced up and I smiled at the messenger who was gathering his bridle and settling himself in his stirrups. Barris handed him the written reply and nodded good-bye: there was a thud of hoofs on the greensward, a jingle of bit and spur across the gravel, and the messenger was gone. Barris' pipe went out and he stepped to windward to relight it.

"It is queer," said I, "that your messenger—a battered native,—should speak like a Harvard man."

"He is a Harvard man," said Barris.

"And the plot thickens," said Pierpont; "are the Cardinal Woods full of your Secret Service men, Barris?"

"No," replied Barris, "but the telegraph stations are. How many ounces of shot are you using, Roy?"

I told him, holding up the adjustable steel measuring cup. He nodded. After a moment on two he sat down on a camp-stool beside us and picked up a crimper.

"That telegram was from Drummond," he said; "the messenger was one of my men as you two bright little boys divined. Pooh! If he had spoken the Cardinal County dialect you wouldn't have known."

"His make-up was good," said Pierpont.

Barris twirled the crimper and looked at the pile of loaded shells. Then he picked up one and crimped it.

"Let 'em alone," said Pierpont, "you crimp too tight."

"Does his little gun kick when the shells are crimped too tight?" enquired Barris tenderly; "well, he shall crimp his own shells then,—where's his little man?"

"His little man" was a weird English importation, stiff, very carefully scrubbed, tangled in his aspirates, named Howlett. As valet, gilly, gun-bearer, and crimper, he aided Pierpont to endure the ennui of existence, by doing for him everything except breathing. Lately, however, Barris' taunts had driven Pierpont to do a few things for himself. To his astonishment he found that cleaning his own gun was not a bore, so he timidly loaded a shell or two, was much pleased with himself, loaded some more, crimped them, and went to breakfast with an appetite. So when Barris asked where "his little man" was, Pierpont did not reply but dug a cupful of shot from the bag and poured it solemnly into the half filled shell.

Old David came out with the dogs and of course there was a pow-wow when "Voyou," my Gordon, wagged his splendid tail across the loading table and sent a dozen unstopped cartridges rolling oven the grass, vomiting powder and shot.

"Give the dogs a mile on two," said I; "we will shoot over the Sweet Fern Covert about four o'clock, David."

"Two guns, David," added Barris.

"Are you not going?" asked Pierpont, looking up, as David disappeared with the dogs.

"Bigger game," said Barris shortly. He picked up a mug of ale from the tray which Howlett had just set down beside us and took a long pull. We did the same, silently. Pierpont set his mug on the turf beside him and returned to his loading.

We spoke of the murder of Professor La Grange, of how it had been concealed by the authorities in New York at Drummond's request, of the certainty that it was one of the gang of gold-makers who had done it, and of the possible alertness of the gang.

"Oh, they know that Drummond will be after them sooner or later," said Barris, "but they don't know that the mills of the gods have already begun to grind. Those smart New York papers builded better than they knew when their ferret-eyed reporter poked his red nose into the house on 58th Street and sneaked off with a column on his cuffs about the 'suicide' of Professor La Grange. Billy Pierpont, my revolver is hanging in your room; I'll take yours too———"

"Help yourself," said Pierpont.

"I shall be gone over night," continued Barris; "my poncho and some bread and meat are all I shall take except the 'barkers.'"

"Will they bark to-night?" I asked.

"No, I trust not for several weeks yet. I shall nose about a bit. Roy, did it ever strike you how queer it is that this wonderfully beautiful country should contain no inhabitants?"

"It's like those splendid stretches of pools and rapids which one finds on every trout river and in which one never finds a fish," suggested Pierpont.

"Exactly,—and Heaven alone knows why," said Barris; "I suppose this country is shunned by human beings for the same mysterious reasons."

"The shooting is the better for it," I observed.

"The shooting is good," said Barris, "have you noticed the snipe on the meadow by the lake? Why it's brown with them! That's a wonderful meadow."

"It's a natural one," said Pierpont, "no human being even cleaned that land."

"Then it's supernatural," said Barris; "Pierpont, do you want to come with me?"

Pierpont's handsome face flushed as he answered slowly, "It's awfully good of you,—if I may."

"Bosh," said I, piqued because he had asked Pierpont, "what use is little Willy without his man?"

"True," said Barris gravely, "you can't take Howlett, you know."

Pierpont muttered something which ended in "d—n."

"Then," said I, "there will be but one gun on the Sweet Fern Covert this afternoon. Very well, I wish you joy of your cold supper and colder bed. Take your night-gown, Willy, and don't sleep on the damp ground."

"Let Pierpont alone," retorted Barris, "you shall go next time, Roy."

"Oh, all right,—you mean when there's shooting going on?"

"And I?" demanded Pierpont, grieved.

"You too, my son; stop quarrelling! Will you ask Howlett to pack our kits— lightly mind you,—no bottles,—they clink."

"My flask doesn't," said Pierpont, and went off to get ready for a night's stalking of dangerous men.

"It is strange," said I, "that nobody ever settles in this region. How many people live in Cardinal Springs, Barris?"

"Twenty counting the telegraph operator and not counting the lumbermen; they are always changing and shifting. I have six men among them."

"Where have you no men? In the Four Hundred?"

"I have men there also,—chums of Billy's only he doesn't know it. David tells me that there was a strong flight of woodcock last night. You ought to pick up some this afternoon."

Then we chatted about alder-cover and swamp until Pierpont came out of the house and it was time to part.

"Au revoir," said Barris, buckling on his kit, "come along, Pierpont, and don't walk in the damp grass."

"If you are not back by to-morrow noon," said I, "I will take Howlett and David and hunt you up. You say your course is due north?"

"Due north," replied Barris, consulting his compass.

"There is a trail for two miles and a spotted lead for two more, said Pierpont.

"Which we won't use for various reasons," added Barris pleasantly; "don't worry, Roy, and keep your confounded expedition out of the way; there's no danger."

He knew, of course, what he was talking about and I held my peace.

When the tip end of Pierpont's shooting coat had disappeared in the Long Covert, I found myself standing alone with Howlett. He bore my gaze for a moment and then politely lowered his eyes.

"Howlett," said I, "take these shells and implements to the gun room, and drop nothing. Did Voyou come to any harm in the briers this morning?"

"No 'arm, Mr. Cardenhe, sir," said Howlett.

"Then be careful not to drop anything else," said I, and walked away leaving him decorously puzzled. For he had dropped no cartridges. Poor Howlett!

III.

About four o'clock that afternoon I met David and the dogs at the spinney which leads into the Sweet Fern Covert. The three setters, Voyou, Gamin, and Mioche, were in fine feather,—David had killed a woodcock and a brace of grouse over them that morning,—and they were thrashing about the spinney at short range when I came up, gun under arm and pipe lighted.

"What's the prospect, David," I asked, trying to keep my feet in the tangle of wagging, whining dogs; "hello, what's amiss with Mioche?"

"A brier in his foot sir; I drew it and stopped the wound but I guess the gravel's got in. If you have no objection, sir, I might take him back with me."

"It's safer," I said; "take Gamin too, I only want one dog this afternoon. What is the situation?"

"Fair sir; the grouse lie within a quarter of a mile of the oak second-growth. The woodcock are mostly on the alders. I saw any number of snipe on the meadows. There's something else in by the lake,—I can't just tell what, but the wood-duck set up a clatter when I was in the thicket and they come dashing through the wood as if a dozen foxes was snappin' at their tail feathers."

"Probably a fox," I said; "leash those dogs,—they must learn to stand in. I'll be back by dinner time."

"There is one more thing sir," said David, lingering with his gun under his arm.

"Well," said I.

"I saw a man in the woods by the Oak Covert,—at least I think I did."

"A lumberman?"

"I think not sir—at least,—do they have Chinamen among them?"

"Chinese? No. You didn't see a Chinaman in the woods here?"

"I—I think I did sir,—I can't say positively. He was gone when I ran into the covert."

"Did the dogs notice it?"

"I can't say—exactly. They acted queer like. Gamin here lay down an' whined—it may have been colic—and Mioche whimpered,—perhaps it was the brier."

"And Voyou?"

"Voyou, he was most remarkable sir, and the hair on his back stood up. I did see a groundhog makin' for a tree near by."

"Then no wonder Voyou bristled. David, your Chinaman was a stump or tussock. Take the dogs now."

"I guess it was sir; good afternoon sir," said David, and walked away with the Gordons leaving me alone with Voyou in the spinney.

I looked at the dog and he looked at me.

"Voyou!"

The dog sat down and danced with his fore feet, his beautiful brown eyes sparkling.

"You're a fraud," I said; "which shall it be, the alders or the upland? Upland? Good!—now for the grouse,—heel, my friend, and show your miraculous self-restraint."

Voyou wheeled into my tracks and followed close, nobly refusing to notice the impudent chipmunks and the thousand and one alluring and important smells which an ordinary dog would have lost no time in investigating.

The brown and yellow autumn woods were crisp with drifting heaps of leaves and twigs that crackled under foot as we turned from the spinney into the forest. Every silent little stream hurrying toward the lake was gay with painted leaves afloat, scarlet maple or yellow oak. Spots of sunlight fell upon the pools, searching the brown depths, illuminating the gravel bottom where shoals of minnows swam to and fro, and to and fro again, busy with the purpose of their little lives. The crickets were chirping in the long brittle grass on the edge of the woods, but we left them far behind in the silence of the deeper forest.

"Now!" said I to Voyou.

The dog sprang to the front, circled once, zigzagged through the ferns around us and, all in a moment, stiffened stock still, rigid as sculptured bronze. I stepped forward, raising my gun, two paces, three paces, ten perhaps, before a great cock-grouse blundered up from the brake and burst through the thicket fringe toward the deeper growth. There was a flash and puff from my gun, a crash of echoes among the low wooded cliffs, and through the faint veil of smoke something dark dropped from mid-air amid a cloud of feathers, brown as the brown leaves under foot.

"Fetch!"

Up from the ground sprang Voyou, and in a moment he came galloping back, neck arched, tail stiff but waving, holding tenderly in his pink mouth a mass of mottled bronzed feathers. Very gravely he laid the bird at my feet and crouched close beside it, his silky ears across his paws, his muzzle on the ground.

I dropped the grouse into my pocket, held for a moment a silent caressing communion with Voyou, then swung my gun under my arm and motioned the dog on.

It must have been five o'clock when I walked into a little opening in the woods and sat down to breathe. Voyou came and san down in front of me.

"Well?" I enquired.

Voyou gravely presented one paw which I took.

"We will never get back in time for dinner," said I, "so we might as well take it easy. It's all your fault, you know. Is there a brier in your foot?—let's see,—there! it's out my friend and you are free to nose about and lick it. If you loll your tongue out you'll get it all over twigs and moss. Can't you lie down and try to pant less? No, there is no use in sniffing and looking at that fern patch, for we are going to smoke a little, doze a little, and go home by moonlight. Think what a big dinner we will have! Think of Howlett's despair when we are not in time! Think of all the stories you will have to tell to Gamin and Mioche! Think what a good dog you have been! There—you are tired old chap; take forty winks with me."

Voyou was a little tired. He stretched out on the leaves at my feet but whether or not he really slept I could not be certain, until his hind legs twitched and I knew he was dreaming of mighty deeds.

Now I may have taken forty winks, but the sun seemed to be no lower when I sat up and unclosed my lids. Voyou raised his head, saw in my eyes that I was not going yet, thumped his tail half a dozen times on the dried leaves, and settled back with a sigh.

I looked lazily around, and for the first time noticed what a wonderfully beautiful spot I had chosen for a nap. It was an oval glade in the heart of the forest, level and carpeted with green grass. The trees that surrounded it were gigantic; they formed one towering circular wall of verdure, blotting out all except the turquoise blue of the sky-oval above. And now I noticed that in the centre of the greensward lay a pool of water, crystal clear, glimmering like a mirror in the meadow grass, beside a block of granite. It scarcely seemed possible that the symmetry of tree and lawn and lucent pool could have been one of nature's accidents. I had never before seen this glade nor had I ever heard it spoken of by either Pierpont or Barris. It was a marvel, this diamond clean basin, regular and graceful as a Roman fountain, set in the gem of turf. And these great trees,—they also belonged, not in America but in some legend-haunted forest of France, where moss-grown marbles stand neglected in dim glades, and the twilight of the forest shelters fairies and slender shapes from shadow-land.

I lay and watched the sunlight showering the tangled thicket where masses of crimson Cardinal-flowers glowed, or where one long dusty sunbeam tipped the edge of the floating leaves in the pool, running them to palest gilt. There were birds too, passing through the dim avenues of trees like jets of flame,—the gorgeous Cardinal-Bird in his deep stained crimson robe,—the bird that gave to the woods, to the village fifteen miles away, to the whole country, the name of Cardinal.

I rolled over on my back and looked up at the sky. How pale,—paler than a robin's egg,—it was. I seemed to be lying at the bottom of a well, walled with verdure, high towering on every side. And, as I lay, all about me the air became sweet scented. Sweeter and sweeter and more penetrating grew the perfume, and I wondered what stray breeze, blowing oven acres of lilies, could have brought it. But there was no breeze; the air was still. A gilded fly alighted on my hand,—a honey-fly. It was as troubled as I by the scented silence.

Then, behind me, my dog growled.

I sat quite still at first, hardly breathing, but my eyes were fixed on a shape that moved along the edge of the pool among the meadow grasses. The dog had ceased growling and was now staring, alert and trembling.

At last I rose and walked rapidly down to the pool, my dog following close to heel.

The figure, a woman's, turned slowly toward us.

IV.

She was standing still when I approached the pool. The forest around us was so silent that when I spoke the sound of my own voice startled me.

"No," she said,—and her voice was smooth as flowing water, "I have not lost my way. Will he come to me, your beautiful dog?"

Before I could speak, Voyou crept to her and laid his silky head against her knees.

"But surely," said I, "you did not come here alone."

"Alone? I did come alone."

"But the nearest settlement is Cardinal, probably nineteen miles from where we are standing."

"I do not know Cardinal," she said.

"Ste. Croix in Canada is forty miles at least,—how did you come into the Cardinal Woods?" I asked amazed.

"Into the woods?" she repeated a little impatiently.

"Yes."

She did not answer at first but stood caressing Voyou with gentle phrase and gesture.

"Your beautiful dog I am fond of, but I am not fond of being questioned," she said quietly. "My name is Ysonde and I came to the fountain here to see your dog."

I was properly quenched. After a moment or two I did say that in another hour it would be growing dusky, but she neither replied nor looked at me.

"This," I ventured, "is a beautiful pool,—you call it a fountain,—a delicious fountain: I have never before seen it. It is hard to imagine that nature did all this."

"Is it?" she said.

"Don't you think so?" I asked.

"I haven't thought; I wish when you go you would leave me your dog."

"My—my dog?"

"If you don't mind," she said sweetly, and looked at me for the first time in the face.

For an instant our glances met, then she grew grave, and I saw that her eyes were fixed on my forehead. Suddenly she rose and drew nearer, looking intently at my forehead. There was a faint mark there, a tiny crescent, just over my eyebrow. It was a birthmark.

"Is that a scar?" she demanded drawing nearer.

"That crescent shaped mark? No."

"No? Are you sure?" she insisted.

"Perfectly," I replied, astonished.

"A—a birthmark?"

"Yes,—may I ask why?"

As she drew away from me, I saw that the color had fled from her cheeks. For a second she clasped both hands over her eyes as if to shut out my face, then slowly dropping her hands, she sat down on a long square block of stone which half encircled the basin, and on which to my amazement I saw carving. Voyou went to her again and laid his head in her lap.

"What is your name?" she asked at length.

"Roy Cardenhe."

"Mine is Ysonde. I carved these dragon-flies on the stone, these fishes and shells and butterflies you see."

"You! They are wonderfully delicate,—but those are not American dragon-flies—"

"No—they are more beautiful. See, I have my hammer and chisel with me."

She drew from a queer pouch at her side a small hammer and chisel and held them toward me.

"You are very talented," I said, "where did you study?"

"I? I never studied,—I knew how. I saw things and cut them out of stone. Do you like them? Some time I will show you other things that I have done. If I had a great lump of bronze I could make your dog, beautiful as he is."

Her hammer fell into the fountain and I leaned over and plunged my arm into the water to find it.

"It is there, shining on the sand," she said, leaning over the pool with me.

"Where," said I, looking at our reflected faces in the water. For it was only in the water that I had dared, as yet, to look her long in the face.

The pool mirrored the exquisite oval of her head, the heavy hair, the eyes. I heard the silken rustle of her girdle, I caught the flash of a white arm, and the hammer was drawn up dripping with spray.

The troubled surface of the pool grew calm and again I saw her eyes reflected.

"Listen," she said in a low voice, "do you think you will come again to my fountain?"

"I will come," I said. My voice was dull; the noise of water filled my ears.

Then a swift shadow sped across the pool; I rubbed my eyes. Where her reflected face had bent beside mine there was nothing mirrored but the rosy evening sky with one pale star glimmering. I drew myself up and turned. She was gone. I saw the faint star twinkling above me in the afterglow, I saw the tall trees motionless in the still evening air, I saw my dog slumbering at my feet.

The sweet scent in the air had faded, leaving in my nostrils the heavy odor of fern and forest mould. A blind fear seized me, and I caught up my gun and sprang into the darkening woods. The dog followed me, crashing through the undergrowth at my side. Duller and duller grew the light, but I strode on, the sweat pouring from my face and hair, my mind a chaos. How I reached the spinney I can hardly tell. As I turned up the path I caught a glimpse of a human face peering at me from the darkening thicket,—a horrible human face, yellow and drawn with high-boned cheeks and narrow eyes.

Involuntarily I halted; the dog at my heels snarled. Then I sprang straight at it, floundering blindly through the thicket, but the night had fallen swiftly and I found myself panting and struggling in a maze of twisted shrubbery and twining vines, unable to see the very undergrowth that ensnared me.

It was a pale face, and a scratched one that I carried to a lane dinner that night. Howlett served me, dumb reproach in his eyes, for the soup had been standing and the grouse was juiceless.

David brought the dogs in after they had had their supper, and I drew my chair before the blaze and set my ale on a table beside me. The dogs curled up at my feet, blinking gravely at the sparks that snapped and flew in eddying showers from the heavy birch logs.

"David," said I, "did you say you saw a Chinaman today?"

"I did sir."

"What do you think about it now?"

"I may have been mistaken sir——"

"But you think not. What sort of whiskey did you put in my flask today?"

"The usual sir."

"Is there much gone?"

"About three swallows sir, as usual."

"You don't suppose there could have been any mistake about that whiskey,—no medicine could have gotten into it for instance."

David smiled and said, "No sir."

"Well," said I, "I have had an extraordinary dream."

When I said "dream," I felt comforted and reassured. I had scarcely dared to say it before, even to myself.

"An extraordinary dream," I repeated; "I fell asleep in the woods about five o'clock, in that pretty glade where the fountain—I mean the pool is. You know the place?"

"I do not sir."

I described it minutely, twice, but David shook his head.

"Carved stone did you say sir? I never chanced on it. You don't mean the New Spring——"

"No, no! This glade is way beyond that. Is it possible that any people inhabit the forest between here and the Canada line?"

"Nobody short of Ste. Croix; at least I have no knowledge of any."

"Of course," said I, "when I thought I saw a Chinaman, it was imagination. Of course I had been more impressed than I was aware of by your adventure. Of course you saw no Chinaman, David."

"Probably not sir," replied David dubiously.

I sent him off to bed, saying I should keep the dogs with me all night; and when he was gone, I took a good long draught of ale, "just to shame the devil," as Pierpont said, and lighted a cigar. Then I thought of Barris and Pierpont, and their cold bed, for I knew they would not dare build a fire, and, in spite of the hot chimney corner and the crackling blaze, I shivered in sympathy.

"I'll tell Barris and Pierpont the whole story and take them to see the carved stone and the fountain," I thought to myself; "what a marvelous dream it was— Ysonde,—if it was a dream."

Then I went to the mirror and examined the faint white mark above my eyebrow.

V.

About eight o'clock next morning, as I sat listlessly eyeing my coffee cup which Howlett was filling, Gamin and Mioche set up a howl, and in a moment more I heard Barris' step on the porch.

"Hello, Roy," said Pierpont, stamping into the dining room, "I want my breakfast by jingo! Where's Howlett,—none of your *café au lait* for me,—I want a chop and some eggs. Look at that dog, he'll wag the hinge off his tail in a moment——"

"Pierpont," said I, "this loquacity is astonishing but welcome. Where's Barris? You are soaked from neck to ankle."

Pierpont sat down and tore off his stiff muddy leggings.

"Barris is telephoning to Cardinal Springs,—I believe he wants some of his men,—down! Gamin, you idiot! Howlett, three eggs poached and more toast,— what was I saying? Oh, about Barris; he's struck something or other which he hopes will locate these gold-making fellows. I had a jolly time,—he'll tell you about it."

"Billy! Billy!" I said in pleased amazement, "you are learning to talk! Dear me! You load your own shells and you carry your own gun and you fire it yourself— hello! here's Barris all over mud. You fellows really ought to change your rig— whew! what a frightful odor!"

"It's probably this," said Barris tossing something onto the hearth where it shuddered for a moment and then began to writhe; "I found it in the woods by the lake. Do you know what it can be, Roy?"

To my disgust I saw it was another of those spidery wormy crablike creatures that Godfrey had in Tiffany's.

"I thought I recognized that acrid odor," I said; "for the love of the Saints take it away from the breakfast table, Barris!"

"But what is it?" he persisted, unslinging his field-glass and revolver.

"I'll tell you what I know after breakfast," I replied firmly. "Howlett, get a broom and sweep that thing into the road.—What are you laughing at, Pierpont?"

Howlett swept the repulsive creature out and Barris and Pierpont went to change their dew-soaked clothes for dryer raiment. David came to take the dogs for an airing and in a few minutes Barris reappeared and sat down in his place at the head of the table.

"Well," said I, "is there a story to tell?"

"Yes, not much. They are near the lake on the other side of the woods,—I mean these gold-makers. I shall collar one of them this evening. I haven't located the main gang with any certainty,—shove the toast rack this way will you, Roy,— no, I am not at all certain, but I've nailed one anyway. Pierpont was a great help, really,—and, what do you think, Roy? He wants to join the Secret Service!"

"Little Willy!"

"Exactly. Oh I'll dissuade him. What sort of a reptile was that I brought in? Did Howlett sweep it away?"

"He can sweep it back again for all I care," I said indifferently. "I've finished my breakfast."

"No," said Barris, hastily swallowing his coffee, "it's of no importance; you can tell me about the beast—"

"Serve you right if I had it brought it on toast," I returned.

Pierpont came in radiant, fresh from the bath.

"Go on with your story, Roy," he said; and I told them about Godfrey and his reptile pet.

"Now what in the name of common sense can Godfrey find interesting in that creature?" I ended, tossing my cigarette into the fireplace.

"It's Japanese, don't you think?" said Pierpont.

"No," said Barris, "it is not artistically grotesque, it's vulgar and horrible,—it looks cheap and unfinished——"

"Unfinished,—exactly," said I, "like an American humorist——"

"Yes," said Pierpont, "cheap. What about that gold serpent?"

"Oh, the Metropolitan Museum bought it; you must see it, it's marvellous."

Barris and Pierpont had lighted their cigarettes and, after a moment, we all rose and strolled out to the lawn, where chains and hammocks were placed under the maple trees.

David passed, gun under arm, dogs heeling.

"Three guns on the meadows at four this afternoon," said Pierpont.

"Roy," said Barris as David bowed and started on, "what did you do yesterday?"

This was the question that I had been expecting. All night long I had dreamed of Ysonde and the glade in the woods, where, at the bottom of the crystal fountain, I saw the reflection of her eyes. All the morning while bathing and dressing I had been persuading myself that the dream was not worth recounting and that a search for the glade and the imaginary stone carving would be ridiculous. But now, as Barris asked the question, I suddenly decided to tell him the whole story.

"See here, you fellows," I said abruptly, "I am going to tell you something queer. You can laugh as much as you please too, but first I want to ask Barris a question or two. You have been in China, Barris?"

"Yes," said Barris, looking straight into my eyes.

"Would a Chinaman be likely to turn lumberman?"

"Have you seen a Chinaman?" he asked in a quiet voice.

"I don't know; David and I both imagined we did."

Barris and Pierpont exchanged glances.

"Have you seen one also?" I demanded, turning to include Pierpont.

"No," said Barris slowly; "but I know that there is, or has been, a Chinaman in these woods."

"The devil!" said I.

"Yes," said Barris gravely; "the devil, if you like,—a devil,—a member of the Kuen-Yuin."

I drew my chair close to the hammock where Pierpont lay at full length, holding out to me a ball of pure gold.

"Well?" said I, examining the engraving on its surface, which represented a mass of twisted creatures,—dragons, I supposed.

"Well," repeated Barris, extending his hand to take the golden ball, "this globe of gold engraved with reptiles and Chinese hieroglyphics is the symbol of the Kuen-Yuin."

"Where did you get it?" I asked, feeling that something startling was impending.

"Pierpont found it by the lake at sunrise this morning. It is the symbol of the Kuen-Yuin," he repeated, "the terrible Kuen-Yuin, the sorcerers of China, and the most murderously diabolical sect on earth."

We puffed our cigarettes in silence until Barris rose, and began to pace backward and forward among the trees, twisting his grey moustache.

"The Kuen-Yuin are sorcerers," he said, pausing before the hammock where Pierpont lay watching him; "I mean exactly what I say,—sorcerers. I've seen them,—I've seen them at their devilish business, and I repeat to you solemnly, that as there are angels above, there is a race of devils on earth, and they are sorcerers. Bah!" he cried, "talk to me of Indian magic and Yogis and all that clap-trap! Why, Roy, I tell you that the Kuen-Yuin have absolute control of a hundred millions of people, mind and body, body and soul. Do you know what goes on in the interior of China? Does Europe know,—could any human being conceive of the condition of that gigantic hell-pit? You read the papers, you hear diplomatic twaddle about Li Hung Chang and the Emperor, you see accounts of battles on sea and land, and you know that Japan has raised a toy tempest along the jagged edge of the great unknown. But you never before heard of the Kuen-Yuin; no, nor has any European except a stray missionary or two, and yet I tell you that when the fires from this pit of hell have eaten through the continent to the coast, the explosion will inundate half a world,—and God help the other half."

Pierpont's cigarette went out; he lighted another, and looked hard at Barris.

"But," resumed Barris quietly, "'sufficient unto the day,' you know,—I didn't intend to say as much as I did,—it would do no good,—even you and Pierpont will forget it,—it seems so impossible and so far away,—like the burning out of the sun. What I want to discuss is the possibility or probability of a Chinaman,—a member of the Kuen-Yuin, being here, at this moment, in the forest."

"If he is," said Pierpont, "possibly the gold-makers owe their discovery to him."

"I do not doubt it for a second," said Barris earnestly.

I took the little golden globe in my hand, and examined the characters engraved upon it.

"Barris," said Pierpont, "I can't believe in sorcery while I am wearing one of Sanford's shooting suits in the pocket of which rests an uncut volume of the 'Duchess.'"

"Neither can I," I said, "for I read the *Evening Post*, and I know Mr. Godkin would not allow it. Hello! What's the matter with this gold ball?"

"What is the matter?" said Barris grimly.

"Why—why—it's changing color—purple, no, crimson—no, it's green I mean—good Heavens! these dragons are twisting under my fingers——"

"Impossible!" muttered Pierpont, leaning oven me; "those are not dragons——"

"No!" I cried excitedly; "they are pictures of that reptile that Barris brought back—see—see how they crawl and turn——"

"Drop it!" commanded Barris; and I threw the ball on the turf. In an instant we had all knelt down on the grass beside it, but the globe was again golden, grotesquely wrought with dragons and strange signs.

Pierpont, a little red in the face, picked it up, and handed it to Barris. He placed it on a chair, and sat down beside me.

"Whew!" said I, wiping the perspiration from my face, "how did you play us that trick, Barris?"

"Trick?" said Barris contemptuously.

I looked at Pierpont, and my heart sank. If this was not a trick, what was it? Pierpont returned my glance and colored, but all he said was, "It's devilish queer," and Barris answered, "Yes, devilish." Then Barris asked me again to tell my story, and I did, beginning from the time I met David in the spinney to the moment when I sprang into the darkening thicket where than yellow mask had grinned like a phantom skull.

"Shall we try to find the fountain?" I asked after a pause.

"Yes,—and—er—the lady," suggested Pierpont vaguely.

"Don't be an ass," I said a little impatiently, "you need not come, you know."

"Oh, I'll come," said Pierpont, "unless you think I am indiscreet——"

"Shut up, Pierpont," said Barris, "this thing is serious; I never heard of such a glade or such a fountain, but it's true that nobody knows this forest thoroughly. It's worth while trying for; Roy, can you find your way back to it?"

"Easily," I answered; "when shall we go?"

"It will knock our snipe shooting on the head," said Pierpont, "but then when one has the opportunity of finding a live dream-lady——"

I rose, deeply offended, but Pierpont was not very penitent and his laughter was irresistible.

"The lady's yours by right of discovery," he said. "I'll promise not to infringe on your dreams,—I'll dream about other ladies——"

"Come, come," said I, "I'll have Howlett put you to bed in a minute. Barris, if you are ready——we can get back to dinner——"

Barris had risen and was gazing at me earnestly.

"What's the matter?" I asked nervously, for I saw that his eyes were fixed on my forehead, and I thought of Ysonde and the white crescent scar.

"Is that a birthmark?" said Barris.

"Yes—why, Barris?"

"Nothing,—an interesting coincidence——"

"What!—for Heaven's sake!"

"The scar,—on rather the birthmark. It is the print of the dragon's claw,—the crescent symbol of Yue-Laou—"

"And who the devil is Yue-Laou?" I said crossly.

"Yue-Laou, the Moon Maker, Dzil-Nbu of the Kuen-Yuin;—it's Chinese Mythology, but it is believed that Yue-Laou has returned to rule the Kuen-Yuin—"

"The conversation," interrupted Pierpont, "smacks of peacock's feathers and yellow-jackets. The chicken-pox has left its card on Roy, and Barris is guying us. Come on, you fellows, and make your call on the dream-lady. Barris, I hear galloping; here come your men."

Two mud splashed riders clattered up to the porch and dismounted at a motion from Barris. I noticed that both of them carried repeating rifles and heavy Colt's revolvers.

They followed Barris, deferentially, into the dining-room, and presently we heard the tinkle of plates and bottles and the low hum of Barris' musical voice.

Half an hour later they came out again, saluted Pierpont and me, and galloped away in the direction of the Canadian frontier. Ten minutes passed, and, as Barris did not appear, we rose and went into the house, to find him. He was sitting silently before the table, watching the small golden globe, now glowing with scarlet and orange fire, brilliant as a live coal. Howlett, mouth ajar, and eyes starting from the sockets, stood petrified behind him.

"Are you coming," asked Pierpont, a little startled. Barris did not answer. The globe slowly turned to pale gold again,—but the face that Barris raised to ours was white as a sheet. Then he stood up, and smiled with an effort which was painful to us all.

"Give me a pencil and a bit of paper," he said.

Howlett brought it. Barris went to the window and wrote rapidly. He folded the paper, placed it in the top drawer of his desk, locked the drawer, handed me the key, and motioned us to precede him.

When again we stood under the maples, he turned to me with an impenetrable expression. "You will know when to use the key," he said: "Come, Pierpont, we must try to find Roy's fountain."

VI.

At two o'clock that afternoon, at Barris' suggestion, we gave up the search for the fountain in the glade and cut across the forest to the spinney where David and Howlett were waiting with our guns and the three dogs.

Pierpont guyed me unmercifully about the "dream-lady" as he called her, and, but for the significant coincidence of Ysonde's and Barris' questions concerning the white scar on my forehead, I should long ago have been perfectly persuaded that I had dreamed the whole thing. As it was, I had no explanation to offer. We had not been able to find the glade although fifty times I came to landmarks which convinced me that we were just about to enter it. Barris was quiet, scarcely uttering a word to either of us during the entire search. I had never before seen him depressed in spirits. However, when we came in sight of the spinney where a cold bit of grouse and a bottle of Burgundy awaited each, Barris seemed to recover his habitual good humor.

"Here's to the dream-lady!" said Pierpont, raising his glass and standing up.

I did not like it. Even if she was only a dream, it irritated me to hear Pierpont's mocking voice. Perhaps Barris understood,—I don't know, but he bade Pierpont drink his wine without further noise, and that young man obeyed with a childlike confidence which almost made Barris smile.

"What about the snipe, David," I asked; "the meadows should be in good condition."

"There is not a snipe on the meadows, sir," said David solemnly.

"Impossible," exclaimed Barris, "they can't have left."

"They have, sir," said David in a sepulchral voice which I hardly recognized.

We all three looked at the old man curiously, waiting for his explanation of this disappointing but sensational report.

David looked at Howlett and Howlett examined the sky.

"I was going," began the old man, with his eyes fastened on Howlett, "I was going along by the spinney with the dogs when I heard a noise in the covert and I seen Howlett come walkin' very fast toward me. In fact," continued David, "I may say he was runnin'. Was you runnin', Howlett?"

Howlett said "Yes," with a decorous cough.

"I beg pardon," said David, "but I'd rather Howlett told the rest. He saw things which I did not."

"Go on, Howlett," commanded Pierpont, much interested.

Howlett coughed again behind his large red hand.

"What David says is true sir," he began; "I h'observed the dogs at a distance 'ow they was a workin' sir, and David stood a lightin' of 's pipe be'ind the spotted beech when I see a 'ead pop up in the covert 'oldin a stick like 'e was h'aimin' at the dogs sir"——

"A head holding a stick?" said Pierpont severely.

"The 'ead 'ad 'ands, sir," explained Howlett, "'ands that 'eld a painted stick,—like that, sir. 'Owlett, thinks I to meself, this 'ere's queer, so I jumps it an' runs, but the beggar 'e seen me an' w'en I comes alongside of David, 'e was gone. "Ello 'Owlett,' sez David, 'what the 'ell'—I beg pardon, sir,—'ow did you come 'ere,' sez 'e very loud. 'Run!' sez I, 'the Chinaman is harryin' the dawgs!' 'For Gawd's sake wot Chinaman?' sez David, h'aimin' 'is gun at every bush. Then I thinks I see 'im an' we run an' run, the dawgs a boundin' close to heel sir, but we don't see no Chinaman."

"I'll tell the rest," said David, as Howlett coughed and stepped in a modest corner behind the dogs.

"Go on," said Barris in a strange voice.

"Well sir, when Howlett and I stopped chasin', we was on the cliff overlooking the south meadow. I noticed that there was hundreds of birds there, mostly yellow-legs and plover, and Howlett seen them too. Then before I could say a word to Howlett, something out in the lake gave a splash—a splash as if the whole cliff had fallen into the water. I was that scared that I jumped straight into the bush and Howlett he sat down quick, and all those snipe wheeled up——there was hundreds,—all a squeelin' with fright, and the wood-duck came bowlin' over the meadows as if the old Nick was behind."

David paused and glanced meditatively at the dogs.

"Go on," said Barris in the same strained voice.

"Nothing more sir. The snipe did not come back."

"But that splash in the lake?"

"I don't know what it was sir."

"A salmon? A salmon couldn't have frightened the duck and the snipe that way?"

"No—oh no, sir. If fifty salmon had jumped they couldn't have made that splash. Couldn't they, Howlett?"

"No 'ow," said Howlett.

"Roy," said Barris at length, "what David tells us settles the snipe shooting for to-day. I am going to take Pierpont up to the house. Howlett and David will follow with the dogs,—I have something to say to them. If you care to come, come along; if not, go and shoot a brace of grouse for dinner and be back by eight if you want to see what Pierpont and I discovered last night."

David whistled Gamin and Mioche to heel and followed Howlett and his hamper toward the house. I called Voyou to my side, picked up my gun and turned to Barris.

"I will be back by eight," I said; "you are expecting to catch one of the gold-makers, are you not?"

"Yes," said Barris listlessly.

Pierpont began to speak about the Chinaman but Barris motioned him to follow, and, nodding to me, took the path that Howlett and David had followed toward the house. When they disappeared I tucked my gun under my arm and turned sharply into the forest, Voyou trotting close to my heels.

In spite of myself the continued apparition of the Chinaman made me nervous. If he troubled me again I had fully decided to get the drop on him and find out what he was doing in the Cardinal Woods. If he could give no satisfactory account of himself I would march him in to Barris as a gold-making suspect,—I would march him in anyway, I thought, and rid the forest of his ugly face. I wondered what it was that David had heard in the lake. It must have been a big fish, a salmon, I thought; probably David's and Howlett's nerves were overwrought after their Celestial chase.

A whine from the dog broke the thread of my meditation and I raised my head. Then I stopped short in my tracks.

The lost glade lay straight before me.

Already the dog had bounded into it, across the velvet turf to the carved stone where a slim figure sat. I saw my dog lay his silky head lovingly against her silken kirtle; I saw her face bend above him, and I caught my breath and slowly entered the sun-lit glade.

Half timidly she held out one white hand.

"Now that you have come," she said, "I can show you more of my work. I told you that I could do other things besides these dragon-flies and moths carved here in stone. Why do you stare at me so? Are you ill?"

"Ysonde," I stammered.

"Yes," she said, with a faint color under her eyes.

"I—I never expected to see you again," I blurted out, "—you—I—I—thought I had dreamed———"

"Dreamed, of me? Perhaps you did, is that strange?"

"Strange? N—no—but—where did you go when—when we were leaning over the fountain together? I saw your face,—your face reflected beside mine and then—then suddenly I saw the blue sky and only a star twinkling."

"It was because you fell asleep," she said, "was it not?"

"I—asleep?"

"You slept—I thought you were very tired and I went back—"

"Back?—where?"

"Back to my home where I carve my beautiful images; see, here is one I brought to show you to-day."

I took the sculptured creature that she held toward me, a massive golden lizard with frail claw-spread wings of gold so thin than the sunlight burned through and fell on the ground in flaming gilded patches.

"Good Heavens!" I exclaimed, "this is astounding! Where did you learn to do such work? Ysonde, such a thing is beyond price!"

"Oh, I hope so," she said earnestly, "I can't bear to sell my work, but my step-father takes it and sends it away. This is the second thing I have done and yesterday he said I must give it to him. I suppose he is poor."

"I don't see how he can be poor if he gives you gold to model in," I said, astonished.

"Gold!" she exclaimed, "gold! He has a room full of gold! He makes it."

I sat down on the turf at her feet completely unnerved.

"Why do you look at me so?" she asked, a little troubled.

"Where does your step-father live?" I said at last.

"Here."

"Here!"

"In the woods near the lake. You could never find our house."

"A house!"

"Of course. Did you think I lived in a tree? How silly. I live with my step-father in a beautiful house,—a small house, but very beautiful. He makes his gold there but the men who carry it away never come to the house, for they don't know where it is and if they did they could not get in. My step-father carries the gold in lumps to a canvas satchel. When the satchel is full he takes it out into the woods where the men live and I don't know what they do with it. I wish he could sell the gold and become rich for then I could go back to Yian where all the gardens are sweet and the river flows under the thousand bridges."

"Where is this city?" I asked faintly.

"Yian? I don't know. It is sweet with perfume and the sound of silver bells all day long. Yesterday I carried a blossom of dried lotus buds from Yian, in my breast, and all the woods were fragrant. Did you smell it?"

"Yes."

"I wondered, last night, whether you did. How beautiful your dog is; I love him. Yesterday I thought most about your dog but last night——"

"Last night," I repeated below my breath.

"I thought of you. Why do you wear the dragon-claw?"

I raised my hand impulsively to my forehead, covering the scar.

"What do you know of the dragon-claw?" I muttered.

"It is the symbol of Yue-Laou, and Yue-Laou rules the Kuen-Yuin, my step-father says. My step-father tells me everything that I know. We lived in Yian until I was sixteen years old. I am eighteen now; that is two years we have lived in the forest. Look!—see those scarlet birds! What are they? There are birds of the same color in Yian."

"Where is Yian, Ysonde?" I asked with deadly calmness.

"Yian? I don't know."

"But you have lived there?"

"Yes, a very long time."

"Is it across the ocean, Ysonde?"

"It is across seven oceans and the great river which is longer than from the earth to the moon."

"Who told you that?"

"Who? My step-father; he tells me everything."

"Will you tell me his name, Ysonde?"

"I don't know it, he is my step-father, that is all."

"And what is your name?"

"You know it, Ysonde."

"Yes, but what other name."

"That is all, Ysonde. Have you two names? Why do you look at me so impatiently?"

"Does your step-father make gold? Have you seen him make it?"

"Oh yes. He made it also in Yian and I loved to watch the sparks at night whirling like golden bees. Yian is lovely,—if it is all like our garden and the gardens around. I can see the thousand bridges from my garden and the white mountain beyond—"

"And the people—tell me of the people, Ysonde!" I urged gently.

"The people of Yian? I could see them in swarms like ants—oh! many, many millions crossing and recrossing the thousand bridges."

"But how did they look? Did they dress as I do?"

"I don't know. They were very far away, moving specks on the thousand bridges. For sixteen years I saw them every day from my garden but I never went out of my garden into the streets of Yian, for my step-father forbade me."

"You never saw a living creature near by in Yian?" I asked in despair.

"My birds, oh such tall, wise-looking birds, all over grey and rose color."

She leaned over the gleaming water and drew her polished hand across the surface.

"Why do you ask me these questions," she murmured; "are you displeased?"

"Tell me about your step-father," I insisted. "Does he look as I do? Does he dress, does he speak as I do? Is he American?"

"American? I don't know. He does not dress as you do and he does not look as you do. He is old, very, very old. He speaks sometimes as you do, sometimes as they do in Yian. I speak also in both manners."

"Then speak as they do in Yian," I urged impatiently, "speak as—why, Ysonde! why are you crying? Have I hurt you?—I did not intend,—I did not dream of your caring! There Ysonde, forgive me,—see, I beg you on my knees here at your feet."

I stopped, my eyes fastened on a small golden ball which hung from her waist by a golden chain. I saw it trembling against her thigh, I saw it change color, now crimson, now purple, now flaming scarlet. It was the symbol of the Kuen-Yuin.

She bent over me and laid her fingers gently on my arm.

"Why do you ask me such things?" she said, while the tears glistened on her lashes. "In hurts me here,—" she pressed her hand to her breast,—"it pains.—I don't know why. Ah, now your eyes are hard and cold again; you are looking at the golden globe which hangs from my waist. Do you wish to know also what that is?"

"Yes," I muttered, my eyes fixed on the infernal color flames which subsided as I spoke, leaving the ball a pale gilt again.

"It is the symbol of the Kuen-Yuin," she said in a trembling voice; "why do you ask?"

"Is it yours?"

"Y—yes."

"Where did you get it?" I cried harshly.

"My—my step-fa——"

Then she pushed me away from her with all the strength of her slender wrists and covered her face.

If I slipped my arm about her and drew her to me,—if I kissed away the tears that fell slowly between her fingers,—if I told her how I loved her—how it cut me to the heart to see her unhappy,—after all that is my own business. When she smiled through her tears, the pure love and sweetness in her eyes lifted my soul higher than the high moon vaguely glimmering through the sun-lit blue above. My happiness was so sudden, so fierce and overwhelming that I only knelt there, her fingers clasped in mine, my eyes raised to the blue vault and the glimmering moon. Then something in the long grass beside me moved close to my knees and a damp acrid odor filled my nostrils.

"Ysonde!" I cried, but the touch of her hand was already gone and my two clenched fists were cold and damp with dew.

"Ysonde!" I called again, my tongue stiff with fright;—but I called as one awaking from a dream—a horrid dream, for my nostrils quivered with the damp acrid odor and I felt the crab-reptile clinging to my knee. Why had the night fallen so swiftly,—and where was I—where?——stiff, chilled, torn, and bleeding, lying flung like a corpse over my own threshold with Voyou licking my face and Barris snooping above me in the light of a lamp that flared and smoked in the night breeze like a torch. Faugh! the choking stench of the lamp aroused me and I cried out:

"Ysonde!"

"What the devil's the matter with him?" muttered Pierpont, lifting me in his arms like a child, "has he been stabbed, Barris?"

VII.

In a few minutes I was able to stand and walk stiffly into my bedroom where How-lett had a hot bath ready and a hotter tumbler of Scotch. Pierpont sponged the blood from my throat where it had coagulated. The cut was slight, almost invisible, a mere puncture from a thorn. A shampoo cleaned my mind, and a cold plunge and alcohol friction did the rest.

"Now," said Pierpont, "swallow your hot Scotch and lie down. Do you want a broiled woodcock? Good, I fancy you are coming about."

Barris and Pierpont watched me as I sat on the edge of the bed, solemnly chewing on the woodcock's wishbone and sipping my Bordeaux, very much at my ease.

Pierpont sighed his relief.

"So," he said pleasantly, "it was a mere case of ten dollars or ten days. I thought you had been stabbed——"

"I was not intoxicated," I replied, serenely picking up a bit of celery.

"Only jagged?" enquired Pierpont, full of sympathy.

"Nonsense," said Barris, "let him alone. Want some more celery, Roy?—it will make you sleep."

"I don't want to sleep," I answered; "when are you and Pierpont going to catch your Gold-maker?"

Barris looked at his watch and closed it with a snap.

"In an hour; you don't propose to go with us?"

"But I do,—toss me a cup of coffee, Pierpont, will you,—that's just what I propose to do. Howlett, bring the new box of Panatella's,—the mild imported;—and leave the decanter. Now Barris, I'll be dressing, and you and Pierpont keep still and listen to what I have to say. Is that door shut tight?"

Barris locked it and sat down.

"Thanks," said I. "Barris, where is the city of Yian?"

An expression akin to terror flashed into Barris' eyes and I saw him stop breathing for a moment.

"There is no such city," he said at length, "have I been talking in my sleep?"

"It is a city," I continued, calmly, "where the river winds under the thousand bridges, where the gardens are sweet scented and the air is filled with the music of silver bells——"

"Stop!" gasped Barris, and rose trembling from his chain. He had grown ten years older.

"Roy," interposed Pierpont coolly, "what the deuce are you harrying Barris for?"

I looked at Barris and he looked at me. After a second or two he sat down again.

"Go on, Roy," he said.

"I must," I answered, "for now I am certain that I have not dreamed."

I told them everything; but, even as I told it, the whole thing seemed so vague, so unreal, that at times I stopped with the hot blood tingling in my ears, for it seemed impossible that sensible men, in the year of our Lord 1896, could seriously discuss such manners.

I feared Pierpont, but he did not even smile. As for Barris, he sat with his handsome head sunk on his breast, his unlighted pipe clasped tight in both hands.

When I had finished, Pierpont turned slowly and looked at Barris. Twice he moved his lips as if about to ask something and then remained mute.

"Yian is a city," said Barris, speaking dreamily; "was that why you wished to know, Pierpont?"

We nodded silently.

"Yian is a city," repeated Barris, "where the great river winds under the thousand bridges,—where the gardens are sweet scented, and the air is filled with the music of silver bells."

My lips formed the question, "Where is this city?"

"It lies," said Barris, almost querulously, "across the seven oceans and the river which is longer than from the earth to the moon."

"What do you mean?" said Pierpont.

"Ah," said Barris, rousing himself with an effort and raising his sunken eyes, "I am using the allegories of another land; let it pass. Have I not told you of the Kuen-Yuin? Yian is the centre of the Kuen-Yuin. It lies hidden in that gigantic shadow called China, vague and vast as the midnight Heavens,—a continent unknown, impenetrable."

"Impenetrable," repeated Pierpont below his breath.

"I have seen it," said Barris dreamily. "I have seen the dead plains of Black Cathay and I have crossed the mountains of Death, whose summits are above the atmosphere. I have seen the shadow of Xangi cast across Abaddon. Better to die a million miles from Yezd and Ater Quedah than to have seen the white water-lotus close in the shadow of Xangi! I have slept among the ruins of Xaindu where the winds never cease and the Wulwulleh is wailed by the dead."

"And Yian," I urged gently.

There was an unearthly look on his face as he turned slowly toward me.

"Yian,—I have lived there—and loved there. When the breath of my body shall cease, when the dragon's claw shall fade from my arm,"—he tore up his sleeve, and we saw a white crescent shining above his elbow,—"when the light of my eyes has faded forever, then, even then I shall not forget the city of Yian. Why, it is my home,—mine! The river and the thousand bridges, the white peak beyond, the sweet-scented gardens, the lilies, the pleasant noise of the summer wind laden with bee music and the music of bells,—all these are mine. Do you think because the Kuen-Yuin feared the dragon's claw on my arm that my work with them is ended? Do you think that because Yue-Laou could give, that I acknowledge his right to take away? Is he Xangi in whose shadow the white water-lotus dares not raise its head? No! No!" he cried violently, "it was not from Yue-Laou, the sorcerer, the Maker of Moons, that my happiness came! It was real, it was not a shadow to vanish like a tinted bubble! Can a sorcerer create and give a man the woman he loves? Is Yue-Laou as great as Xangi then? Xangi is God. In His own time, in His infinite goodness and mercy He will bring me again to the woman I love. And I know she waits for me at God's feet."

In the strained silence that followed I could hear my heart's double beat and I saw Pierpont's face, blanched and pitiful. Barris shook himself and raised his head. The change in his ruddy face frightened me.

"Heed!" he said, with a terrible glance at me; "the print of the dragon's claw is on your forehead and Yue-Laou knows it. If you must love, then love like a man, for you will suffer like a soul in hell, in the end. What is her name again?"

"Ysonde," I answered simply.

VIII.

At nine o'clock that night we caught one of the Gold-makers. I do not know how Barris had laid his trap; all I saw of the affair can be told in a minute or two.

We were posted on the Cardinal road about a mile below the house, Pierpont and I with drawn revolvers on one side, under a butternut tree, Barris on the other, a Winchester across his knees.

I had just asked Pierpont the hour, and he was feeling for his watch when far up the road we heard the sound of a galloping horse, nearer, nearer, clattering, thundering past. Then Barris' rifle spat flame and the dark mass, horse and rider, crashed into the dust. Pierpont had the half stunned horseman by the collar in a second,—the horse was stone dead,—and, as we lighted a pine knot to examine the fellow, Barris' two riders galloped up and drew bridle beside us.

"Hm!" said Barris with a scowl, "it's the 'Shiner,' or I'm a moonshiner."

We crowded curiously around to see the "Shiner." He was red-headed, fat and filthy, and his little red eyes burned in his head like the eyes of an angry pig.

Barris went through his pockets methodically while Pierpont held him and I held the torch. The Shiner was a gold mine; pockets, shirt, bootlegs, hat, even his dirty fists, clutched tight and bleeding, were bursting with lumps of soft yellow gold. Barris dropped this "moonshine gold," as we had come to call it, into the pockets of his shooting-coat, and withdrew to question the prisoner. He came back again in a few minutes and motioned his mounted men to take the Shiner in charge. We watched them, rifle on thigh, walking their horses slowly away into the darkness, the Shiner, tightly bound, shuffling sullenly between them.

"Who is the Shiner?" asked Pierpont, slipping the revolver into his pocket again.

"A moonshiner, counterfeiter, forger, and highwayman," said Barris, "and probably a murderer. Drummond will be glad to see him, and I think it likely he will be persuaded to confess to him what he refuses to confess to me."

"Wouldn't he talk?" I asked.

"Not a syllable. Pierpont, there is nothing more for you to do."

"For me to do? Are you not coming back with us, Barris?"

"No," said Barris.

We walked along the dark road in silence for a while, I wondering what Barris intended to do, but he said nothing more until we reached our own verandah. Here he held out his hand, first to Pierpont, then to me, saying good-bye as though he were going on a long journey.

"How soon will you be back?" I called out to him as he turned away toward the gate. He came across the lawn again and again took our hands with a quiet affection that I had never imagined him capable of.

"I am going," he said, "to put an end to his gold-making no-night. I know that you fellows have never suspected what I was about on my little solitary evening strolls after dinner. I will tell you. Already I have unobtrusively killed four of these gold-makers,—my men put them underground just below the new wash-out at the four mile stone. There are three left alive,—the Shiner whom we have, another criminal named 'Yellow,' or 'Yaller' in the vernacular, and the third——"

"The third," repeated Pierpont, excitedly.

"The third I have never yet seen. But I know who and what he is,—I know; and if he is of human flesh and blood, his blood will flow to-night."

As he spoke a slight noise across the turf attracted my attention. A mounted man was advancing silently in the starlight over the spongy meadowland. When he came nearer Barris struck a match, and we saw that he bore a corpse across his saddle bow.

"Yaller, Colonel Barris," said the man, touching his slouched hat in salute.

This grim introduction to the corpse made me shudder, and, after a moment's examination of the stiff, wide-eyed dead man, I drew back.

"Identified," said Barris, "take him to the four mile post and carry his effects to Washington,—-under seal, mind, Johnstone."

Away cantered the rider with his ghastly burden, and Barris took our hands once more for the last time. Then he went away, gaily, with a jest on his lips, and Pierpont and I turned back into the house.

For an hour we sat moodily smoking in the hall before the fire, saying little until Pierpont burst out with: "I wish Barris had taken one of us with him to-night!"

The same thought had been running in my mind, but I said: "Barris knows what he's about."

This observation neither comforted us nor opened the lane to further conversation, and after a few minutes Pierpont said good night and called for Howlett and hot water. When he had been warmly tucked away by Howlett, I turned out all but one lamp, sent the dogs away with David and dismissed Howlett for the night.

I was not inclined to retire for I knew I could not sleep. There was a book lying open on the table beside the fire and I opened it and read a page or two, but my mind was fixed on other things.

The window shades were raised and I looked out at the star-set firmament. There was no moon that night but the sky was dusted all over with sparkling stars and a pale radiance, brighter even than moonlight, fell over meadow and wood. Far away in the forest I heard the voice of the wind, a soft warm wind that whispered a name, Ysonde.

"Listen," sighed the voice of the wind, and "listen" echoed the swaying trees with every little leaf a-quiver. I listened.

Where the long grasses trembled with the cricket's cadence I heard her name, Ysonde; I heard it in the rustling woodbine where grey moths hovered; I heard it in the drip, drip, drip of the dew from the porch. The silent meadow brook whispered her name, the rippling woodland streams repeated it, Ysonde, Ysonde, until all earth and sky were filled with the soft thrill, Ysonde, Ysonde, Ysonde.

A night-thrush sang in a thicket by the porch and I stole to the verandah to listen. After a while it began again, a little further on. I ventured out into the road. Again I heard it far away in the forest and I followed it, for I knew it was singing of Ysonde.

When I came to the path that leaves the main road and enters the Sweet-Fern Covert below the spinney, I hesitated; but the beauty of the night lured me on and the night-thrushes called me from every thicket. In the starry radiance, shrubs, grasses, field flowers, stood out distinctly, for there was no moon to cast shadows. Meadow and brook, grove and stream, were illuminated by the pale glow. Like great lamps lighted the planets hung from the high domed sky and through their mysterious rays the fixed stars, calm, serene, stared from the heavens like eyes.

I waded on waist deep through fields of dewy golden-rod, through late clover and wild-oat wastes, through crimson fruited sweetbrier, blueberry, and wild plum, until the low whisper of the Wier Brook warned me that the path had ended.

But I would not stop, for the night air was heavy with the perfume of water-lilies and far away, across the low wooded cliffs and the wet meadowland beyond, there was a distant gleam of silver, and I heard the murmur of sleepy waterfowl. I would go to the lake. The way was clear except for the dense young growth and the snares of the moose-bush.

The night-thrushes had ceased but I did not want for the company of living creatures. Slender, quick darting forms crossed my path at intervals, sleek mink, that fled like shadows at my step, wiry weasels and fat muskrats, hurrying onward to some tryst or killing.

I never had seen so many little woodland creatures on the move at night. I began to wonder where they all were going so fast, why they all hurried on in the same direction. Now I passed a hare hopping through the brushwood, now a rabbit scurrying by, flag hoisted. As I entered the beech second-growth two foxes glided by me; a little further on a doe crashed out of the underbrush, and close behind her stole a lynx, eyes shining like coals.

He neither paid attention to the doe nor to me, but loped away toward the north.

The lynx was in flight.

"From what?" I asked myself, wondering. There was no forest fine, no cyclone, no flood.

If Barris had passed that way could he have stirred up this sudden exodus? Impossible; even a regiment in the forest could scarcely have put to rout these frightened creatures.

"What on earth," thought I, turning to watch the headlong flight of a fisher-cat, "what on earth has started the beasts out at this time of night?"

I looked up into the sky. The placid glow of the fixed stars comforted me and I stepped on through the narrow spruce belt that leads down to the borders of the Lake of the Stars.

Wild cranberry and moose-bush entwined my feet, dewy branches spattered me with moisture, and the thick spruce needles scraped my face as I threaded my way over mossy logs and deep spongy tussocks down to the level gravel of the lake shore.

Although there was no wind the little waves were hurrying in from the lake and I heard them splashing among the pebbles. In the pale star glow thousands of water-lilies lifted their half-closed chalices toward the sky.

I threw myself full length upon the shore, and, chin on hand, looked out across the lake.

Splash, splash, came the waves along the shore, higher, nearer, until a film of water, thin and glittering as a knife blade, crept up to my elbows. I could not understand it; the lake was rising, but there had been no rain. All along the shore the water was running up; I heard the waves among the sedge grass; the weeds at my side were awash in the ripples. The lilies rocked on the tiny waves, every wet pad rising on the swells, sinking, rising again until the whole lake was glimmering with undulating blossoms. How sweet and deep was the fragrance from the lilies. And now the water was ebbing, slowly, and the waves receded, shrinking from the shore rim until the white pebbles appeared again, shining like froth on a brimming glass.

No animal swimming out in the darkness along the shore, no heavy salmon surging, could have set the whole shore aflood as though the wash from a great boat were rolling in. Could it have been the overflow, through the Weir Brook, of some cloud-burst far back in the forest? This was the only way I could account for it, and yet when I had crossed the Wier Brook I had not noticed that it was swollen.

And as I lay there thinking, a faint breeze sprang up and I saw the surface of the lake whiten with lifted lily pads.

All around me the alders were sighing; I heard the forest behind me stir; the crossed branches rubbing softly, bark against bark. Something—it may have been an owl—sailed out of the night, dipped, soared, and was again engulfed, and far across the water I heard its faint cry, Ysonde.

Then first, for my heart was full, I cast myself down upon my face, calling on her name. My eyes were wet when I raised my head,—for the spray from the shore was drifting in again,—and my heart beat heavily; "No more, no more." But my heart lied, for even as I raised my face to the calm stars, I saw her standing still, close beside me; and very gently I spoke her name, Ysonde. She held out both hands.

"I was lonely," she said, "and I went to the glade, but the forest is full of frightened creatures and they frightened me. Has anything happened in the woods? The deer are running toward the heights."

Her hand still lay in mine as we moved along the shore, and the lapping of the water on rock and shallow was no lower than our voices.

"Why did you leave me without a word, there at the fountain in the glade?"
she said.

"I leave you!——"

"Indeed you did, running swiftly with your dog, plunging through thickets and
brush,—oh—-you frightened me."

"Did I leave you so?"

"Yes—after——"

"After?"

"You had kissed me——"

Then we leaned down together and looked into the black water set with stars,
just as we had bent together over the fountain in the glade.

"Do you remember?" I asked.

"Yes. See, the water is inlaid with silver stars,—everywhere white lilies floating
and the stars below, deep, deep down."

"What is the flower you hold in your hand?"

"White water-lotus."

"Tell me about Yue-Laou, Dzil-Nbu of the Kuen-Yuin," I whispered, lifting
her head so I could see her eyes.

"Would it please you to hear?"

"Yes, Ysonde."

"All that I know is yours, now, as I am yours, all that I am. Bend closer. Is it
of Yue-Laou you would know? Yue-Laou is Dzil-Nhu of the Kuen-Yuin. He lives
in the Moon. He is old—very, very old, and once, before he came to rule the
Kuen-Yuin, he was the old man who unites with a silken cord all predestined couples, after which nothing can prevent their union. But all that is changed since he
came to rule the Kuen-Yuin. Now he has perverted the Xin,—the good genii of
China,—and has fashioned from their warped bodies a monster which he calls the
Xin. This monster is horrible, for it not only lives in its own body, but it has thousands of loathsome satellites,—living creatures without mouths, blind, that move
when the Xin moves, like a mandarin and his escort. They are part of the Xin although they are not attached. Yet if one of these satellites is injured the Xin
writhes with agony. It is fearful—this huge living bulk and these creatures spread
out like severed fingers that wriggle around a hideous hand."

"Who told you this?"

"My step-father."

"Do you believe it?"

"Yes. I have seen one of the Xin's creatures."

"Where, Ysonde?"

"Here in the woods."

"Then you believe there is a Xin here?"

"There must be,—perhaps in the lake—"

"Oh, Xins inhabit lakes?"

"Yes, and the seven seas. I am not afraid here."

"Why?"

"Because I wear the symbol of the Kuen-Yuin."

"Then I am not safe," I smiled.

"Yes you are, for I hold you in my arms. Shall I tell you more about the Xin? When the Xin is about to do to death a man, the Yeth-hounds gallop through the night—"

"What are the Yeth-hounds, Ysonde?"

"The Yeth-hounds are dogs without heads. They are the spirits of murdered children, which pass through the woods at night, making a wailing noise."

"Do you believe this?"

"Yes, for I have worn the yellow lotus——"

"The yellow lotus——"

"Yellow is the symbol of faith——"

"Where?"

"In Yian," she said faintly.

After a while I said, "Ysonde, you know there is a God?"

"God and Xangi are one."

"Have you ever heard of Christ?"

"No," she answered softly.

The wind began again among the tree tops. I felt her hands closing in mine.

"Ysonde," I asked again, "do you believe in sorcerers?"

"Yes, the Kuen-Yuin are sorcerers; Yue-Laou is a sorcerer."

"Have you seen sorcery?"

"Yes, the reptile satellite of the Xin——"

"Anything else?"

"My charm,—the golden ball, the symbol of the Kuen-Yuin. Have you seen it change,—have you seen the reptiles writhe—?"

"Yes," I said shortly, and then remained silent, for a sudden shiver of apprehension had seized me. Barris also had spoken gravely, ominously of the sorcerers, the Kuen-Yuin, and I had seen with my own eyes the graven reptiles turning and twisting on the glowing globe.

"Still," said I aloud, "God lives and sorcery is but a name."

"Ah," murmured Ysonde, drawing closer no me, "they say, in Yian, the Kuen-Yuin live; God is but a name."

"They lie," I whispered fiercely.

"Be careful," she pleaded, "they may hear you. Remember that you have the mark of the dragon's claw on your brow."

"What of it?" I asked, thinking also of the white mark on Barris' arm.

"Ah don't you know that those who are marked with the dragon's claw are followed by Yue-Laou, for good or for evil,—and the evil means death if you offend him?"

"Do you believe that!" I asked impatiently.

"I know it," she sighed.

"Who told you all this? Your step-father? What in Heaven's name is he then,—a Chinaman!"

"I don't know; he is not like you."

"Have—have you told him anything about me?"

"He knows about you—no, I have told him nothing,—ah, what is this—see—it is a cord, a cord of silk about your neck—and about mine!"

"Where did that come from?" I asked astonished.

"It must be—it must be Yue-Laou who binds me to you,—it is as my step-father said—he said Yue-Laou would bind us——"

"Nonsense," I said almost roughly, and seized the silken cord, but to my amazement it melted in my hand like smoke.

"What is all this damnable jugglery!" I whispered angrily, but my anger vanished as the words were spoken, and a convulsive shudder shook me to the feet. Standing on the shore of the lake, a stone's throw away, was a figure, twisted and bent,—a little old man, blowing sparks from a live coal which he held in his naked hand. The coal glowed with increasing radiance, lighting up the skull-like face above it, and threw a red glow over the sands at his feet. But the face!—the ghastly Chinese face on which the light flickered,—and the snaky slitted eyes, sparkling as the coal glowed hotter. Coal! It was not a coal but a golden globe staining the night with crimson flames—it was the symbol of the Kuen-Yuin.

"See! See!" gasped Ysonde, trembling violently, "see the moon rising from between his fingers! Oh I thought it was my step-father and it is Yue-Laou the Maker of Moons—no! no! it is my step-father—ah God! they are the same!"

Frozen with terror I stumbled to my knees, groping for my revolver which bulged in my coat pocket; but something held me—something which bound me like a web in a thousand strong silky meshes. I struggled and turned but the web grew tighter; it was over us—all around us, drawing, pressing us into each other's arms until we lay side by side, bound hand and body and foot, palpitating, panting like a pair of netted pigeons.

And the creature on the shore below! What was my horror to see a moon, huge, silvery, rise like a bubble from between his fingers, mount higher, higher into the still air and hang aloft in the midnight sky, while another moon rose from his fingers, and another and yet another until the vast span of Heaven was set with moons and the earth sparkled like a diamond in the white glare.

A great wind began to blow from the east and it bore to our ears a long mournful howl,—a cry so unearthly that for a moment our hearts stopped.

"The Yeth-hounds!" sobbed Ysonde, "do you hear!—they are passing through the forest! The Xin is near!"

Then all around us in the dry sedge grasses came a rustle as if some small animals were creeping, and a damp acrid odor filled the air. I knew the smell, I saw the spidery crab-like creatures swarm out around me and drag their soft yellow hairy bodies across the shrinking grasses. They passed, hundreds of them, poisoning the air, tumbling, writhing, crawling with their blind mouthless heads raised. Birds, half asleep and confused by the darkness, fluttered away before them in helpless fright, rabbits sprang from their forms, weasels glided away like flying shadows. What remained of the forest creatures rose and fled from the loathsome invasion; I heard the squeak of a terrified hare, the snort of stampeding deer, and the lumbering gallop of a bear; and all the time I was choking, half suffocated by the poisoned air.

Then, as I struggled to free myself from the silken snare about me, I cast a glance of deadly fear at the sorcerer below, and at the same moment I saw him turn in his tracks.

"Halt!" cried a voice from the bushes.

"Barris!" I shouted, half leaping up in my agony.

I saw the sorcerer spring forward, I heard the bang! bang! bang! of a revolver, and, as the sorcerer fell on the water's edge, I saw Barris jump out into the white glare and fire again, once, twice, three times, into the writhing figure at his feet.

Then an awful thing occurred. Up out of the black lake reared a shadow, a nameless shapeless mass, headless, sightless, gigantic, gaping from end to end.

A great wave struck Barris and he fell, another washed him up on the pebbles, another whirled him back into the water and then,—and then the thing fell over him,—and I fainted.

*   *   *   *   *   *

*   *   *   *   *   *

*   *   *   *   *   *

*   *   *   *   *   *

This, then, is all that I know concerning Yue-Laou and the Xin. I do not fear the ridicule of scientists or of the press for I have told the truth. Barris is gone and the thing that killed him is alive to-day in the Lake of the Stars while the spider-like satellites roam through the Cardinal Woods. The game has fled, the forests around the lake are empty of any living creatures save the reptiles that creep when the Xin moves in the depths of the lake.

General Drummond knows what he has lost in Barris, and we, Pierpont and I, know what we have lost also. His will we found in the drawer, the key of which he had handed me. It was wrapped in a bit of paper on which was written:

"Yue-Laou the sorcerer is here in the Cardinal Woods. I must kill him or he will kill me. He made and gave to me the woman I loved,—he made her,—I saw him,—he made her out of a white water-lotus bud. When our child was born, he came again before me and demanded from me the woman I loved. Then, when I refused, he went away, and that night my wife and child vanished from my side, and I found upon her pillow a white lotus bud. Roy, the woman of your dream, Ysonde, may be my child. God help you if you love her for Yue-Laou will give,— and take away, as though he were Xangi, which is God. I will kill Yue-Laou before I leave this forest,—or he will kill me.

"FRANKLYN BARRIS."

Now the world knows what Barris thought of the Kuen-Yuin and of Yue-Laou. I see that the newspapers are just becoming excited over the glimpses that Li Hung Chang has afforded them of Black Cathay and the demons of the Kuen-Yuin. The Kuen-Yuin are on the move.

Pierpont and I have dismantled the shooting box in the Cardinal Woods. We hold ourselves ready at a moment's notice to join and lead the first Government party to drag the Lake of Stars and cleanse the forest of the crab reptiles. But it will be necessary that a large force assembles, and a well-armed force, for we never have found the body of Yue-Laou, and, living or dead, I fear him. Is he living?

Pierpont, who found Ysonde and myself lying unconscious on the lake shore, the morning after, saw no trace of corpse or blood on the sands. He may have fallen into the lake, but I fear and Ysonde fears that he is alive. We never were able to find either her dwelling place or the glade and the fountain again. The only thing that remains to her of her former life is the gold serpent in the Metropolitan Museum and her golden globe, the symbol of the Kuen-Yuin; but the latter no longer changes color.

David and the dogs are waiting for me in the court yard as I write. Pierpont is in the gun room loading shells, and Howlett brings him mug after mug of my ale from the wood. Ysonde bends over my desk,—I feel her hand on my arm, and she is saying, "Don't you think you have done enough to-day, dear? How can you write such silly nonsense without a shadow of truth or foundation?"

The Death of Halpin Frayser

Ambrose Bierce

Frank Long no doubt saw a great deal of himself in the young protagonist of this tale by Bierce: a poetic dandy ill-adjusted to a prosaic career into which relatives assumed he would progress, and finally one who reincarnates the spirit of cherished poets of the past. Both Frayser's life and Long's illustrate that Heideggerian insight that the story itself so well embodies: "thrownness." Heidegger observed that we all find ourselves much in the position of a rock should it become sentient once it had been thrown through the air, in mid-throw. We ask how we happen to be here, hurtling in a particular direction we did not choose, wondering what will become of us when our involuntary trip is done and we crash to the ground. Halpin Frayser begins this story with forgetfulness of his past, at least of his immediate past, and he must infer what little he can from the surprises that blossom around him. And these, to his credit, he uses as fodder for a set of verses. What does Bierce mean when he says Frayser writes to appeal to superior powers? To atone for unknown sins? And then has him write poetry? Perhaps it is because young Frayser can only justify his existence by doing the only thing he could do, what he was born to do, even though merciless fate had conspired against him, and not only lately. For he had been shanghaied away from his true course more than once already.

I cannot help thinking Long borrowed the notion of the forbidden forest filled with fog, in "The Space-Eaters," from Bierce's "The Death of Halpin Frayser." The exposed corpse, lying in a freeze-frame pose of bizarre destruction, in "The Hounds of Tindalos," might have been suggested by the similar scene at the end of Bierce's tale, too, and surely the device of the recorded "famous last words" of Chalmers comes from the notebook verse of Frayser, similarly aborted in mid-sentence.

"The Death of Halpin Frayser" first appeared in the *Wave* (19 December 1891) and was reprinted in Bierce's collection *Can Such Things Be?* in 1893.

I.

For by death is wrought greater change than hath been shown. Whereas in general the spirit that removed cometh back upon occasion, and is

48

sometimes seen of those in flesh (appearing in the form of the body it bore)
yet it hath happened that the veritable body without the spirit hath walked.
And it is attested of those encountering who have lived to speak thereon that
a lich so raised up hath no natural affection, nor remembrance thereof, but
only hate. Also, it is known that some spirits which in life were benign become by death evil altogether.—*Hali.*

One dark night in midsummer a man waking from a dreamless sleep in a forest
lifted his head from the earth, and staring a few moments into the blackness, said:
"Catherine Larue." He said nothing more; no reason was known to him why he
should have said so much.

The man was Halpin Frayser. He lived in St. Helena, but where he lives now is
uncertain, for he is dead. One who practices sleeping in the woods with nothing
under him but the dry leaves and the damp earth, and nothing over him but the
branches from which the leaves have fallen and the sky from which the earth has
fallen, cannot hope for great longevity, and Frayser had already attained the age of
thirty-two. There are persons in this world, millions of persons, and far and away
the best persons, who regard that as a very advanced age. They are the children. To
those who view the voyage of life from the port of departure the bark that has accomplished any considerable distance appears already in close approach to the farther shore. However, it is not certain that Halpin Frayser came to his death by
exposure.

He had been all day in the hills west of the Napa Valley, looking for doves and
such small game as was in season. Late in the afternoon it had come on to be
cloudy, and he had lost his bearings; and although he had only to go always downhill—everywhere the way to safety when one is lost—the absence of trails had so
impeded him that he was overtaken by night while still in the forest. Unable in the
darkness to penetrate the thickets of manzanita and other undergrowth, utterly
bewildered and overcome with fatigue, he had lain down near the root of a large
madroño and fallen into a dreamless sleep. It was hours later, in the very middle of
the night, that one of God's mysterious messengers, gliding ahead of the incalculable host of his companions sweeping westward with the dawn line, pronounced
the awakening word in the ear of the sleeper, who sat upright and spoke, he knew
not why, a name, he knew not whose.

Halpin Frayser was not much of a philosopher, nor a scientist. The circum-
stance that, waking from a deep sleep at night in the midst of a forest, he had spoken aloud a name that he had not in memory and hardly had in mind did not
arouse an enlightened curiosity to investigate the phenomenon. He thought it odd,
and with a little perfunctory shiver, as if in deference to a seasonal presumption
that the night was chill, he lay down again and went to sleep. But his sleep was no
longer dreamless. He thought he was walking along a dusty road that showed white
in the gathering darkness of a summer night. Whence and whither it led, and why
he traveled it, he did not know, though all seemed simple and natural, as is the way
in dreams; for in the Land Beyond the Bed surprises cease from troubling and the

judgment is at rest. Soon he came to a parting of the ways; leading from the high-way was a road less traveled, having the appearance, indeed, of having been long abandoned, because, he thought, it led to something evil; yet he turned into it without hesitation, impelled by some imperious necessity.

As he pressed forward he became conscious that his way was haunted by in-visible existences whom he could not definitely figure to his mind. From among the trees on either side he caught broken and incoherent whispers in a strange tongue which yet he partly understood. They seemed to him fragmentary utterances of a monstrous conspiracy against his body and soul.

It was now long after nightfall, yet the interminable forest through which he journeyed was lit with a wan glimmer having no point of diffusion, for in its myste-rious lumination nothing cast a shadow. A shallow pool in the guttered depression of an old wheel rut, as from a recent rain, met his eye with a crimson gleam. He stooped and plunged his hand into it. It stained his fingers; it was blood! Blood, he then observed, was about him everywhere. The weeds growing rankly by the road-side showed it in blots and splashes on their big, broad leaves. Patches of dry dust between the wheelways were pitted and spattered as with a red rain. Defiling the trunks of the trees were broad maculations of crimson, and blood dripped like dew from their foliage.

All this he observed with a terror which seemed not incompatible with the ful-fillment of a natural expectation. It seemed to him that it was all in expiation of some crime which, though conscious of his guilt, he could not rightly remember. To the menaces and mysteries of his surroundings the consciousness was an added horror. Vainly he sought, by tracing life backward in memory, to reproduce the moment of his sin; scenes and incidents came crowding tumultuously into his mind, one picture effacing another, or commingling with it in confusion and ob-scurity, but nowhere could he catch a glimpse of what he sought. The failure aug-mented his terror; he felt as one who has murdered in the dark, not knowing whom nor why. So frightful was the situation—the mysterious light burned with so silent and awful a menace; the noxious plants, the trees that by common consent are invested with a melancholy or baleful character, so openly in his sight con-spired against his peace; from overhead and all about came so audible and startling whispers and the sighs of creatures so obviously not of earth—that he could en-dure it no longer, and with a great effort to break some malign spell that bound his faculties to silence and inaction, he shouted with the full strength of his lungs! His voice, broken, it seemed, into an infinite multitude of unfamiliar sounds, went babbling and stammering away into the distant reaches of the forest, died into si-lence, and all was as before. But he had made a beginning at resistance and was en-couraged. He said:

"I will not submit unheard. There may be powers that are not malignant trav-eling this accursed road. I shall leave them a record and an appeal. I shall relate my wrongs, the persecutions that I endure—I, a helpless mortal, a penitent, an unof-fending poet!" Halpin Frayser was a poet only as he was a penitent: in his dream.

Taking from his clothing a small red-leather pocketbook, one-half of which was leaved for memoranda, he discovered that he was without a pencil. He broke a twig from a bush, dipped it into a pool of blood and wrote rapidly. He had hardly touched the paper with the point of his twig when a low, wild peal of laughter broke out at a measureless distance away, and growing ever louder, seemed approaching ever nearer; a soulless, heartless and unjoyous laugh, like that of the loon, solitary by the lakeside at midnight; a laugh which culminated in an unearthly shout close at hand, then died away by slow gradations, as if the accursed being that uttered it had withdrawn over the verge of the world whence it had come. But the man felt that this was not so—that it was near by and had not moved.

A strange sensation began slowly to take possession of his body and his mind. He could not have said which, if any, of his senses was affected; he felt it rather as a consciousness—a mysterious mental assurance of some overpowering presence—some supernatural malevolence different in kind from the invisible existences that swarmed about him, and superior to them in power. He knew that it had uttered that hideous laugh. And now it seemed to be approaching him; from what direction he did not know—dared not conjecture. All his former fears were forgotten or merged in the gigantic terror that now held him in thrall. Apart from that, he had but one thought: to complete his written appeal to the benign powers who, traversing the haunted wood, might some time rescue him if he should be denied the blessing of annihilation. He wrote with terrible rapidity, the twig in his fingers rilling blood without renewal; but in the middle of a sentence his hands denied their service to his will, his arms fell to his sides, the book to the earth; and powerless to move or cry out, he found himself staring into the sharply drawn face and blank, dead eyes of his own mother, standing white and silent in the garments of the grave!

II.

In his youth Halpin Frayser had lived with his parents in Nashville, Tennessee. The Fraysers were well-to-do, having a good position in such society as had survived the wreck wrought by civil war. Their children had the social and educational opportunities of their time and place, and had responded to good associations and instruction with agreeable manners and cultivated minds. Halpin being the youngest and not over robust was perhaps a trifle "spoiled." He had the double disadvantage of a mother's assiduity and a father's neglect. Frayser *père* was what no Southern man of means is not—a politician. His country, or rather his section and State, made demands upon his time and attention so exacting that to those of his family he was compelled to turn an ear partly deafened by the thunder of the political captains and the shouting, his own included.

Young Halpin was of a dreamy, indolent and rather romantic turn, somewhat more addicted to literature than law, the profession to which he was bred. Among those of his relations who professed the modern faith of heredity it was well understood that in him the character of the late Myron Bayne, a maternal great-grandfather, had revisited the glimpses of the moon—by which orb Bayne had in his lifetime been sufficiently affected to be a poet of no small Colonial distinction. If not specially observed, it was observable that while a Frayser who was not the proud possessor of a sumptuous copy of the ancestral "poetical works" (printed at the family expense, and long ago withdrawn from an inhospitable market) was a rare Frayser indeed, there was an illogical indisposition to honor the great deceased in the person of his spiritual successor. Halpin was pretty generally deprecated as an intellectual black sheep who was likely at any moment to disgrace the flock by bleating in meter. The Tennessee Fraysers were a practical folk—not practical in the popular sense of devotion to sordid pursuits, but having a robust contempt for any qualities unfitting a man for the wholesome vocation of politics.

In justice to young Halpin it should be said that while in him were pretty faithfully reproduced most of the mental and moral characteristics ascribed by history and family tradition to the famous Colonial bard, his succession to the gift and faculty divine was purely inferential. Not only had he never been known to court the muse, but in truth he could not have written correctly a line of verse to save himself from the Killer of the Wise. Still, there was no knowing when the dormant faculty might wake and smite the lyre.

In the meantime the young man was rather a loose fish, anyhow. Between him and his mother was the most perfect sympathy, for secretly the lady was herself a devout disciple of the late and great Myron Bayne, though with the tact so generally and justly admired in her sex (despite the hardy calumniators who insist that it is essentially the same thing as cunning) she had always taken care to conceal her weakness from all eyes but those of him who shared it. Their common guilt in respect of that was an added tie between them. If in Halpin's youth his mother had "spoiled" him, he had assuredly done his part toward being spoiled. As he grew to such manhood as is attainable by a Southerner who does not care which way elections go the attachment between him and his beautiful mother— whom from early childhood he had called Katy—became yearly stronger and more tender. In these two romantic natures was manifest in a signal way that neglected phenomenon, the dominance of the sexual element in all the relations of life, strengthening, softening, and beautifying even those of consanguinity. The two were nearly inseparable, and by strangers observing their manners were not infrequently mistaken for lovers.

Entering his mother's boudoir one day Halpin Frayser kissed her upon the forehead, toyed for a moment with a lock of her dark hair which had escaped from its confining pins and said, with an obvious effort at calmness:

"Would you greatly mind, Katy, if I were called away to California for a few weeks?"

It was hardly needful for Katy to answer with her lips a question to which her telltale cheeks had made instant reply. Evidently she would greatly mind; and the tears, too, sprang into her large brown eyes as corroborative testimony.

"Ah, my son," she said, looking up into his face with infinite tenderness, "I should have known that this was coming. Did I not lie awake a half of the night weeping because, during the other half, Grandfather Bayne had come to me in a dream, and standing by his portrait—young, too, and handsome at that—pointed to yours on the same wall? And when I looked it seemed that I could not see the features; you had been painted with a face cloth, such as we put upon the dead. Your father has laughed at me, but you and I, dear, know that such things are not for nothing. And I saw below the edge of the cloth the marks of hands on your throat—forgive me, but we have not been used to keep such things from each other. Perhaps you have another interpretation. Perhaps it does not mean that you will go to California. Or maybe you will take me with you?"

It must be confessed that this ingenious interpretation of the dream in the light of newly discovered evidence did not wholly commend itself to the son's more logical mind; he had, for the moment at least, a conviction that it foreshadowed a more simple and immediate, if less tragic, disaster than a visit to the Pacific Coast. It was Halpin Frayser's impression that he was to be garroted on his native heath.

"Are there not medicinal springs in California?" Mrs. Frayser resumed before he had time to give her the true reading of the dream—"places where one recovers from rheumatism and neuralgia? Look—my fingers feel so stiff; and I am almost sure they have been giving me great pain while I slept."

She held out her hands for his inspection. What diagnosis of her case the young man may have thought it best to conceal with a smile the historian is unable to state, but for himself he feels bound to say that fingers looking less stiff, and showing fewer evidences of even insensible pain, have seldom been submitted for medical inspection by even the fairest patient desiring a prescription of unfamiliar scenes.

The outcome of it was that of these two odd persons having equally odd notions of duty, the one went to California, as the interest of his client required, and the other remained at home in compliance with a wish that her husband was scarcely conscious of entertaining.

While in San Francisco Halpin Frayser was walking one dark night along the water front of the city, when, with a suddenness that surprised and disconcerted him, he became a sailor. He was in fact "shanghaied" aboard a gallant, gallant ship and sailed for a far countree. Nor did his misfortunes end with the voyage; for the ship was cast ashore on an island of the South Pacific, and it was six years afterward when the survivors were taken off by a venturesome trading schooner and brought back to San Francisco.

Though poor in purse, Frayser was no less proud in spirit than he had been in the years that seemed ages and ages ago. He would accept no assistance from strangers, and it was while living with a fellow survivor near the town of St. Helena, awaiting news and remittances from home, that he had gone gunning and dreaming.

III.

The apparition confronting the dreamer in the haunted wood—the thing so like, yet so unlike his mother—was horrible! It stirred no love nor longing in his heart; it came unattended with pleasant memories of a golden past—inspired no sentiment of any kind; all the finer emotions were swallowed up in fear. He tried to turn and run from before it, but his legs were as lead; he was unable to lift his feet from the ground. His arms hung helpless at his sides; of his eyes only he retained control, and these he dared not remove from the lusterless orbs of the apparition, which he knew was not a soul without a body, but that most dreadful of all existences infesting that haunted wood—a body without a soul! In its blank stare was neither love, nor pity, nor intelligence—nothing to which to address an appeal for mercy. "An appeal will not lie," he thought, with an absurd reversion to professional slang, making the situation more horrible, as the fire of a cigar might light up a tomb.

For a time, which seemed so long that the world grew gray with age and sin, and the haunted forest, having fulfilled its purpose in this monstrous culmination of its terrors, vanished out of his consciousness with all its sights and sounds, the apparition stood within a pace, regarding him with the mindless malevolence of a wild brute; then thrust its hands forward and sprang upon him with appalling ferocity! The act released his physical energies without unfettering his will; his mind was still spellbound, but his powerful body and agile limbs, endowed with a blind, insensate life of their own, resisted stoutly and well. For an instant he seemed to see this unnatural contest between a dead intelligence and a breathing mechanism only as a spectator—such fancies are in dreams; then he regained his identity almost as if by a leap forward into his body, and the straining automaton had a directing will as alert and fierce as that of its hideous antagonist.

But what mortal can cope with a creature of his dream? The imagination creating the enemy is already vanquished; the combat's result is the combat's cause. Despite his struggles—despite his strength and activity, which seemed wasted in a void, he felt the cold fingers close upon his throat. Borne backward to the earth, he saw above him the dead and drawn face within a hand's breadth of his own, and then all was black. A sound as of the beating of distant drums—a murmur of swarming voices, a sharp, far cry signing all to silence, and Halpin Frayser dreamed that he was dead.

IV.

A warm, clear night had been followed by a morning of drenching fog. At about the middle of the afternoon of the preceding day a little whiff of light vapor—a mere thickening of the atmosphere, the ghost of a cloud—had been observed clinging to the western side of Mount St. Helena, away up along the barren altitudes near the summit. It was so thin, so diaphanous, so like a fancy made visible, that one would have said: "Look quickly! in a moment it will be gone."

In a moment it was visibly larger and denser. While with one edge it clung to the mountain, with the other it reached farther and farther out into the air above the lower slopes. At the same time it extended itself to north and south, joining small patches of mist that appeared to come out of the mountain-side on exactly the same level, with an intelligent design to be absorbed. And so it grew and grew until the summit was shut out of view from the valley, and over the valley itself was an ever-extending canopy, opaque and gray. At Calistoga, which lies near the head of the valley and the foot of the mountain, there were a starless night and a sunless morning. The fog, sinking into the valley, had reached southward, swallowing up ranch after ranch, until it had blotted out the town of St. Helena, nine miles away. The dust in the road was laid; trees were adrip with moisture; birds sat silent in their coverts; the morning light was wan and ghastly, with neither color nor fire.

Two men left the town of St. Helena at the first glimmer of dawn, and walked along the road northward up the valley toward Calistoga. They carried guns on their shoulders, yet no one having knowledge of such matters could have mistaken them for hunters of bird or beast. They were a deputy sheriff from Napa and a detective from San Francisco—Holker and Jaralson, respectively. Their business was man-hunting.

"How far is it?" inquired Holker, as they strode along, their feet stirring white the dust beneath the damp surface of the road.

"The White Church? Only a half mile farther," the other answered. "By the way," he added, "it is neither white nor a church; it is an abandoned schoolhouse, gray with age and neglect. Religious services were once held in it—when it was white, and there is a graveyard that would delight a poet. Can you guess why I sent for you, and told you to come heeled?"

"Oh, I never have bothered you about things of that kind. I've always found you communicative when the time came. But if I may hazard a guess, you want me to help you arrest one of the corpses in the graveyard."

"You remember Branscom?" said Jaralson, treating his companion's wit with the inattention that it deserved.

"The chap who cut his wife's throat? I ought; I wasted a week's work on him and had my expenses for my trouble. There is a reward of five hundred dollars, but none of us ever got a sight of him. You don't mean to say—"

"Yes, I do. He has been under the noses of you fellows all the time. He comes by night to the old graveyard at the White Church."

"The devil! That's where they buried his wife."

"Well, you fellows might have had sense enough to suspect that he would return to her grave some time."

"The very last place that any one would have expected him to return to."

"But you had exhausted all the other places. Learning your failure at them, I 'laid for him' there."

"And you found him?"

"Damn it! he found *me*. The rascal got the drop on me—regularly held me up and made me travel. It's God's mercy that he didn't go through me. Oh, he's a good one, and I fancy the half of that reward is enough for me if you're needy."

Holker laughed good-humoredly, and explained that his creditors were never more importunate.

"I wanted merely to show you the ground, and arrange a plan with you," the detective explained. "I thought it as well for us to be armed, even in daylight."

"The man must be insane," said the deputy sheriff. "The reward is for his capture and conviction. If he's mad he won't be convicted."

Mr. Holker was so profoundly affected by that possible failure of justice that he involuntarily stopped in the middle of the road, then resumed his walk with abated zeal.

"Well, he looks it," assented Jaralson. "I'm bound to admit that a more unshaven, unshorn, unkempt, and uneverything wretch I never saw outside the ancient and honorable order of tramps. But I've gone in for him, and can't make up my mind to let go. There's glory in it for us, anyhow. Not another soul knows that he is this side of the Mountains of the Moon."

"All right," Holker said; "we will go and view the ground," and he added, in the words of a once favorite inscription for tombstones: "'where you must shortly lie'—I mean, if old Branscom ever gets tired of you and your impertinent intrusion. By the way, I heard the other day that 'Branscom' was not his real name."

"What is?"

"I can't recall it. I had lost all interest in the wretch, and it did not fix itself in my memory—something like Pardee. The woman whose throat he had the bad taste to cut was a widow when he met her. She had come to California to look up some relatives—there are persons who will do that sometimes. But you know all that."

"Naturally."

"But not knowing the right name, by what happy inspiration did you find the right grave? The man who told me what the name was said it had been cut on the headboard."

"I don't know the right grave." Jaralson was apparently a trifle reluctant to admit his ignorance of so important a point of his plan. "I have been watching about the place generally. A part of our work this morning will be to identify that grave. Here is the White Church."

For a long distance the road had been bordered by fields on both sides, but now on the left there was a forest of oaks, madroños and gigantic spruces whose lower parts only could be seen, dim and ghostly in the fog. The undergrowth was, in places, thick, but nowhere impenetrable. For some moments Holker saw nothing of the building, but as they turned into the woods it revealed itself in faint gray outline through the fog, looking huge and far away. A few steps more, and it was within an arm's length, distinct, dark with moisture and insignificant in size. It had the usual country-schoolhouse form—belonged to the packing-box order of architecture; had an underpinning of stones, a moss-grown roof and blank window spaces, whence both glass and sash had long departed. It was ruined, but not a ruin—a typical Californian substitute for what are known to guide-bookers abroad as "monuments of the past." With scarcely a glance at this uninteresting structure Jaralson moved on into the dripping undergrowth beyond.

"I will show you where he held me up," he said. "This is the graveyard."

Here and there among the bushes were small inclosures containing graves, sometimes no more than one. They were recognized as graves by the discolored stones or rotting boards at head and foot, leaning at all angles, some prostrate; by the ruined picket fences surrounding them; or, infrequently, by the mound itself showing its gravel through the fallen leaves. In many instances nothing marked the spot where lay the vestiges of some poor mortal—who, leaving "a large circle of sorrowing friends," had been left by them in turn—except a depression in the earth, more lasting than that in the spirits of the mourners. The paths, if any paths had been, were long obliterated; trees of a considerable size had been permitted to grow up from the graves and thrust aside with root or branch the inclosing fences. Over all was that air of abandonment and decay which seems nowhere so fit and significant as in a village of the forgotten dead.

As the two men, Jaralson leading, pushed their way through the growth of young trees, that enterprising man suddenly stopped and brought up his shotgun to the height of his breast, uttered a low note of warning and stood motionless, his eyes fixed upon something ahead. As well as he could, obstructed by brush, his companion, though seeing nothing, imitated the posture and so stood, prepared for what might ensue. A moment later Jaralson moved cautiously forward, the other following.

Under the branches of an enormous spruce lay the dead body of a man. Standing silent above it they noted such particulars as first strike the attention—the face, the attitude, the clothing; whatever most promptly and plainly answers the unspoken question of a sympathetic curiosity.

The body lay upon its back, the legs wide apart. One arm was thrust upward, the other outward; but the latter was bent acutely, and the hand was near the throat. Both hands were tightly clenched. The whole attitude was that of desperate but ineffectual resistance to—what?

Near by lay a shotgun and a game bag through the meshes of which was seen the plumage of shot birds. All about were evidences of a furious struggle; small sprouts of poison-oak were bent and denuded of leaf and bark; dead and rotting leaves had been pushed into heaps and ridges on both sides of the legs by the action of other feet than theirs; alongside the hips were unmistakable impressions of human knees.

The nature of the struggle was made clear by a glance at the dead man's throat and face. While breast and hands were white, those were purple—almost black. The shoulders lay upon a low mound, and the head was turned back at an angle otherwise impossible, the expanded eyes staring blankly backward in a direction opposite to that of the feet. From the froth filling the open mouth the tongue protruded, black and swollen. The throat showed horrible contusions; not mere finger-marks, but bruises and lacerations wrought by two strong hands that must have buried themselves in the yielding flesh, maintaining their terrible grasp until long after death. Breast, throat, face, were wet; the clothing was saturated; drops of water, condensed from the fog, studded the hair and mustache.

All this the two men observed without speaking—almost at a glance. Then Holker said:

"Poor devil! he had a rough deal."

Jaralson was making a vigilant circumspection of the forest, his shotgun held in both hands and at full cock, his finger upon the trigger.

"The work of a maniac," he said, without withdrawing his eyes from the inclosing wood. "It was done by Branscom—Pardee."

Something half hidden by the disturbed leaves on the earth caught Holker's attention. It was a red-leather pocketbook. He picked it up and opened it. It contained leaves of white paper for memoranda, and upon the first leaf was the name "Halpin Frayser." Written in red on several succeeding leaves—scrawled as if in haste and barely legible—were the following lines, which Holker read aloud, while his companion continued scanning the dim gray confines of their narrow world and hearing matter of apprehension in the drip of water from every burdened branch:

> "Enthralled by some mysterious spell, I stood
> In the lit gloom of an enchanted wood.
>   The cypress there and myrtle twined their boughs,
> Significant, in baleful brotherhood.
>
> "The brooding willow whispered to the yew;
> Beneath, the deadly nightshade and the rue,
>   With immortelles self-woven into strange
> Funereal shapes, and horrid nettles grew.
>
> "No song of bird nor any drone of bees,
> Nor light leaf lifted by the wholesome breeze:
>   The air was stagnant all, and Silence was
> A living thing that breathed among the trees.
>
> "Conspiring spirits whispered in the gloom,
> Half-heard, the stilly secrets of the tomb.
>   With blood the trees were all adrip; the leaves
> Shone in the witch-light with a ruddy bloom.
>
> "I cried aloud!—the spell, unbroken still,
> Rested upon my spirit and my will.
>   Unsouled, unhearted, hopeless and forlorn,
> I strove with monstrous presages of ill!
>
> "At last the viewless—"

Holker ceased reading; there was no more to read. The manuscript broke off in the middle of a line.

"That sounds like Bayne," said Jaralson, who was something of a scholar in his way. He had abated his vigilance and stood looking down at the body.

"Who's Bayne?" Holker asked rather incuriously.

"Myron Bayne, a chap who flourished in the early years of the nation—more than a century ago. Wrote mighty dismal stuff; I have his collected works. That poem is not among them, but it must have been omitted by mistake."

"It is cold," said Holker; "let us leave here; we must have up the coroner from Napa."

Jaralson said nothing, but made a movement in compliance. Passing the end of the slight elevation of earth upon which the dead man's head and shoulders lay, his foot struck some hard substance under the rotting forest leaves, and he took the trouble to kick it into view. It was a fallen headboard, and painted on it were the hardly decipherable words, "Catharine Larue."

"Larue, Larue!" exclaimed Holker, with sudden animation. "Why, that is the real name of Branscom—not Pardee. And—bless my soul! how it all comes to me—the murdered woman's name had been Frayser!"

"There is some rascally mystery here," said Detective Jaralson. "I hate anything of that kind."

There came to them out of the fog—seemingly from a great distance—the sound of a laugh, a low, deliberate, soulless laugh, which had no more of joy than that of a hyena night-prowling in the desert; a laugh that rose by slow gradation, louder and louder, clearer, more distinct and terrible, until it seemed barely outside the narrow circle of their vision; a laugh so unnatural, so unhuman, so devilish, that it filled those hardy man-hunters with a sense of dread unspeakable! They did not move their weapons nor think of them; the menace of that horrible sound was not of the kind to be met with arms. As it had grown out of silence, so now it died away; from a culminating shout which had seemed almost in their ears, it drew itself away into the distance, until its failing notes, joyless and mechanical to the last, sank to silence at a measureless remove.

The Space-Eaters

Frank Belknap Long

This is the first and probably still the greatest story to use Lovecraft as a char-acter in a Lovecraftian tale. Simply as a story "The Space-Eaters" is a fine piece of work; it displays a gentle poeticism that I fear too many casual read-ers miss, or Long's reputation would be greater than it is. As an allegory of a horror-writer's inspiration it is unsurpassed. And as a memoir of H. P. Love-craft, "The Space-Eaters" is dead on. We almost feel, at several points, that we have left the fictional page behind and have passed into Long's memoir *Howard Phillips Lovecraft: Dreamer on the Nightside,* or even Lovecraft's own *Su-pernatural Horror in Literature.* In short, though the device of Lovecraft getting a taste of his own medicine also meets us in Bloch's marvelous "The Shambler from the Stars" and Kuttner's entertaining "Hydra," Long alone has really captured Lovecraft in content as well as form.

The story begins with a quote from the abhorred *Necronomicon.* While it is germane to the action of the story, it is not strictly necessary, which may be why August Derleth omitted it from the printing of the story in *Tales of the Cthulhu Mythos.* This epigraph marks the first association, picked up by Love-craft, of John Dee (also mentioned in "The Hounds of Tindalos") with the *Necronomicon.* "The Space-Eaters" first appeared in *Weird Tales,* July 1928.

"The cross is not a passive agent. It protects the pure of heart, and it has often appeared in the air above our sabbats, confusing and dispersing the powers of Darkness."

—John Dee's *Necronomicon*

The horror came to Partridgeville in a blind fog.

All that afternoon thick vapors from the sea had swirled and eddied about the farm, and the room in which we sat swam with moisture. The fog ascended in spi-rals from beneath the door, and its long, moist fingers caressed my hair until it dripped. The square-paned windows were coated with a thick, dewlike moisture; the air was heavy and dank and unbelievably cold.

I stared gloomily at my friend. He had turned his back to the window and was writing furiously. He was a tall, slim man with a slight stoop and abnormally broad shoulders. In profile his face was impressive. He had an extremely broad forehead, long nose and slightly protuberant chin—a strong, sensitive face which suggested a wildly imaginative nature held in restraint by a profoundly skeptical intellect.

My friend wrote short-stories. He wrote to please himself, in defiance of contemporary taste, and his tales were unusual. They would have delighted Poe; they would have delighted Hawthorne, or Ambrose Bierce, or Villiers de l'Isle Adam. They were terrible and somber studies of abnormal men, abnormal beasts, abnormal plants. He wrote of remote and unholy realms of imagination and horror, and the colors, sounds and odors which he dared to evoke were never seen, heard or smelt on the familiar side of the moon. He projected his shameless creations against wormy and shadow-haunted backgrounds. They stalked loathsomely through tall and lonely forests, over ragged mountains, and slithered evilly down the stairs of ancient houses, and between the piles of rotting black wharves.

One of his tales, "The House of the Worm," had induced a young student at a Midwestern University to seek refuge in an enormous red-black building where everyone approved of his sitting on the floor and shouting at the top of his voice: "Lo, my beloved is fairer than all the lilies among the lilies in the lily garden." Another, "The Defilers," had brought him precisely three hundred and ten letters of indignation from local readers when it appeared in the *Partridgeville Gazette*.

As I continued to stare at him he suddenly stopped writing and shook his head. "I can't do it," he said. "I should have to invent a new language. And yet I can comprehend the thing emotionally, intuitively, if you will. If I could only convey it in a sentence somehow—the strange crawling of its fleshless spirit!"

"Is it some new horror?" I asked.

He shook his head. "It is not new to me. I have known and felt it for years—a horror utterly beyond anything your prosaic brain can conceive."

"Thank you," I said.

"All human brains are prosaic," he elaborated. "I meant no offense. It is the shadowy terrors that lurk behind and above them that are mysterious and awful. Our little brains—what do they know of the loathly, crawling things that come down from outer space and suck us dry? I think sometimes they lodge in our heads, and our brains feel them, but when they stretch out horrid tentacles to claw and absorb us we go screaming mad; and of what use are brains then?"

"But you can't honestly believe in such nonsense!" I exclaimed.

"Of course not!" He shook his head and laughed. "You know damn well I'm too profoundly skeptical to believe in anything. I have merely outlined a poet's reactions to the universe. If a man wishes to write ghostly stories and actually convey a sensation of horror to his miserable and unworthy readers he must believe in everything—and *anything*. By *anything* I mean the horror that transcends *everything*, that is more terrible and impossible than *everything*. He must believe that there are things from outer space that can reach down and suck us dry."

"But this thing from outer space—how can he describe it if he doesn't know its shape or size or color?"

"It is virtually impossible to describe it. That is what I have sought to do—and failed. Perhaps some day—but then, I doubt if it can ever be accomplished. But your artist can hint, suggest—"

"Suggest what?" I asked, a little puzzled.

"Suggest a horror that is utterly unearthly; that makes itself felt in terms that have no counterparts on this earth."

I was still puzzled. He smiled wearily and elaborated his theory.

"There is something prosaic," he said, "about even the best of the classic tales of mystery and terror. Old Mrs. Radcliffe with her hidden vaults and bleeding ghosts, Maturin with his allegorical, Faustlike hero-villains, and his fiery flames from the mouth of hell, Edgar Poe with his blood-clotted corpses and black cats, his telltale hearts and disintegrating Valdemars, Hawthorne with his amusing pre-occupation with the problems and horrors arising from mere human sin (as though human sins were of any significance to the things that suck at our brains), and the modern masters, Algernon Blackwood who invites us to a feast of the high gods and shows us an old woman with a harelip sitting before a Ouija board fingering soiled cards, or an absurd nimbus of ectoplasm emanating from some clairvoyant ninny, Bram Stoker with his vampires and werewolves, mere conventional myths, the tag-ends of medieval folklore, Wells with his pseudo-scientific bogies, fish-men at the bottom of the sea, ladies in the moon, and the hundred and one idiots who are constantly writing ghost stories for the magazines—what have they contributed to the literature of the unholy?

"Are we not made of flesh and blood? It is but natural that we should be re-volted and horrified when we are shown that flesh and blood in a state of corrup-tion and decay, with the worms passing over and under it. It is but natural that a story about a corpse should thrill us, fill us with fear and horror and loathing. Any fool can awake these emotions in us—Poe really accomplished very little with his Lady Ushers, and liquescent Valdemars. He appealed to simple, natural, under-standable emotions, and it was inevitable that his readers should respond.

"Are we not the descendants of barbarians? Did we not once dwell in tall and sinister forests, at the mercy of beasts that rend and tear? It is but inevitable that we should shiver and cringe when we meet in literature dark shadows from our own past. Harpies and vampires and werewolves—what are they but magnifica-tions, distortions of the great birds and bats and ferocious dogs that harassed and tortured our ancestors? It is easy enough to arouse fear by such means. It is easy enough to frighten men with the flames at the mouth of hell, because they are hot and shrivel and burn the flesh—and who does not understand and dread a fire? Blows that kill, fires that burn, shadows that horrify because their substances lurk evilly in the black corridors of our inherited memories—I am weary of the writers who would terrify us by such pathetically obvious and trite unpleasantnesses."

Real indignation blazed in his eyes.

"Suppose there were a greater horror? Suppose evil things from some other universe should decide to invade this one? Suppose we couldn't see them? Suppose we couldn't feel them? Suppose they were of a color unknown on the earth, or ra-ther, of an *appearance* that was without color?

"Suppose they had a shape unknown on the earth? Suppose they were four-dimensional, five-dimensional, six-dimensional? Suppose they were a hundred-dimensional? Suppose they had no dimensions at all and yet existed? What could we do?

"They would not exist for us? They would exist for us if they gave us pain. Suppose it was not the pain of heat or cold or any of the pains we know, but a new pain? Suppose they touched something besides our nerves—reached our brains in a new and terrible way? Suppose they made themselves felt in a new and strange and unspeakable way? What could we do? Our hands would be tied. You can not oppose what you can not see or feel. You can not oppose the thousand-dimensional. *Suppose they should eat their way to us through space!*"

He was rapidly talking himself into a frenzy.

"That is what I have tried to write about. I wanted to put into a story the crawling, formless thing that sucks at our brains. I wanted to make my readers, absurd and unworthy fools, feel and see that thing from another universe, from beyond space. I could easily enough hint at it, or suggest it—any fool can do that—but I wanted to actually describe it. To describe a color that is not a color! a form that is formless.

"A mathematician could perhaps slightly more than suggest it. There would be strange curves and angles that an inspired mathematician in a wild frenzy of calculation might glimpse vaguely. It is absurd to say that mathematicians have not discovered the fourth dimension. They have often glimpsed it, often approached it, often apprehended it, but they are unable to demonstrate it. I know a mathematician who swears that he once saw the sixth dimension in a wild flight into the sublime skies of the differential calculus.

"Unfortunately I am not a mathematician. I am only a poor fool of a creative artist, and the thing from outer space utterly eludes me."

Someone was pounding loudly on the door. I crossed the room and drew back the latch. "What do you want?" I asked. "What is the matter?"

"Sorry to disturb you, Frank," said a familiar voice, "but I've got to talk to someone."

I recognized the lean, white face of my nearest neighbor, and stepped instantly to one side. "Come in," I said. "Come in, by all means. Howard and I have been discussing ghosts, and the things we've conjured up aren't pleasant company. Perhaps you can argue them away."

I called Howard's horrors ghosts because I didn't want to shock my commonplace neighbor. Henry Wells was immensely big and tall, and as he strode into the room he seemed to bring a part of the night with him.

He collapsed on a sofa and surveyed us with frightened eyes. Howard laid down the story he had been reading, removed and wiped his glasses, and frowned. He was more or less intolerant of my bucolic visitors. We waited for perhaps a minute, and then the three of us spoke almost simultaneously. "A horrible night!" "Beastly, isn't it?" "Wretched."

Henry Wells frowned. "Tonight," he said, "I—I met with a funny accident. I was driving Hortense through Mulligan Wood—"

"Hortense?" Howard interrupted.

"His horse," I explained impatiently. "You were returning from Brewster, weren't you, Henry?"

"From Brewster, yes," he replied. "I was driving between the trees watching the fog curling in and out of Hortense's ears and listening to the fog-horns in the bay wheezing and moaning, when something wet landed on my head. 'Rain,' I thought. 'I hope the supplies keep dry.'

"I turned round to make sure that the butter and flour were covered up, and something soft like a sponge rose up from the bottom of the wagon and hit me in the face. I snatched at it and caught it between my fingers.

"In my hands it felt like jelly. I squeezed it, and moisture ran out of it down my wrists. It wasn't so dark that I couldn't see it, either. Funny how you can see in fogs—they seem to make the night lighter. There was a sort of brightness in the air. I dunno, maybe it wasn't the fog, either. The trees seemed to stand out. You could see them sharp and clear. As I was saying, I looked at the thing, and what do you think it looked like? Like a piece of raw liver. Or like a calf's brain. Now that I come to think of it, it was more like a calf's brain. There were grooves in it, and you don't find any grooves in liver. Liver's usually as smooth as glass.

"It was an awful moment for me. 'There's someone up in one of those trees,' I thought. 'He's some tramp or crazy man or fool and he's been eating liver. My wagon frightened him and he dropped it—a piece of it. I can't be wrong. There was no liver in my wagon when I left Brewster.'

"I looked up. You know how tall all of the trees are in Mulligan Wood. You can't see the tops of some of them from the wagon-road on a clear day. And you know how crooked and queer-looking some of the trees are.

"It's funny, but I've always thought of them as old men—tall old men, you understand, tall and crooked and very evil. I've always thought of them as wanting to work mischief. There's something unwholesome about trees that grow very close together and grow crooked.

"I looked up.

"At first I didn't see anything but the tall trees, all white and glistening with the fog, and above them a thick, white mist that hid the stars of heaven. And then something long and white ran quickly down the trunk of one of the trees.

"It ran so quickly down the tree that I couldn't see it clearly. And it was so thin anyway that there wasn't much to see. But it was like an arm. It was like a long, white and very thin arm. But of course it wasn't an arm. Who ever heard of an arm as tall as a tree? I don't know what made me compare it to an arm, because it was really nothing but a thin line—like a wire, a string. I'm not sure that I saw it at all. Maybe I imagined it. I'm not even sure that it was as wide as a string. But it had a hand. Or didn't it? When I think of it my brain gets dizzy. You see, it moved so quickly I couldn't see it clearly at all.

"But it gave me the impression that it was looking for something that it had dropped. For a minute the hand seemed to spread out over the road, and then it left the tree and came toward the wagon. It was like a huge white hand walking on its fingers with a terribly long arm fastened to it that went up and up until it touched the fog, or perhaps until it touched the stars of heaven.

"I screamed and slashed Hortense with the reins, but the horse didn't need any urging. She was up and off before I could throw the liver, or calf's brain or whatever it was, into the road. She raced so fast she almost upset the wagon, but I didn't draw in the reins. I'd rather lie in a ditch with a broken rib than have a long, white hand squeezing the breath out of my throat.

"We had almost cleared the wood and I was just beginning to breathe again when my brain went cold. I can't describe what happened in any other way. My brain got as cold as ice inside my head. I can tell you I was frightened.

"Don't imagine I couldn't think clearly. I was conscious of everything that was going on about me, but my brain was so cold I screamed with the pain. Have you ever held a piece of ice in the palm of your hand for as long as two or three minutes? It burnt, didn't it? Ice burns worse than fire. Well, my brain felt as though it had lain on ice for hours and hours. There was a furnace inside my head, but it was a cold furnace. It was roaring with raging cold.

"Perhaps I should have been thankful that the pain didn't last. It wore off in about ten minutes, and when I got home I didn't seem to be any the worse for my experience. I'm sure I didn't think I was any the worse until I looked at myself in the glass. Then I saw the hole in my head."

Henry Wells leaned forward and brushed back the hair from his right temple.

"Here is the wound," he said. "What do you make of it?" He tapped with his fingers beneath a small round opening in the side of his head. "It's like a bullet-wound," he elaborated, "but there was no blood and you can look in pretty far. It seems to go right in to the center of my head. I shouldn't be alive."

Howard had risen and was staring at my neighbor with flaming eyes.

"Why have you lied to us?" he shouted. "Why have you told us this absurd story? A long hand, forsooth! You were drunk, man. Drunk—and yet you've succeeded in doing what I'd have sweated blood to accomplish. If I could have made my idiotic readers feel that horror, know it for a moment, that horror that you described in the woods, I should be with the immortals—I should be greater than Poe, greater than Hawthorne. And you—a clumsy clown, a lying yokel—"

I was on my feet with a furious protest.

"He's not lying," I said. "The man's insane with fever. He's been shot—someone has shot him in the head. Look at his wound. My God, man, you have no call to insult him!"

Howard's wrath died and the fire went out of his eyes. "Forgive me," he said. "You can't imagine how badly I've wanted to capture that ultimate horror, to put it on paper, and he did it so easily. If he had warned me that he was going to describe something like that I would have taken notes. But of course he doesn't know he's an artist. It was an accidental *tour de force* that he accomplished; he couldn't do it again, I'm sure. I'm sorry I went up in the air—I apologize. Do you want me to go for a doctor? That *is* a bad wound."

My neighbor shook his head. "I don't want a doctor," he said. "I've seen a doctor. There's no bullet in my head—that hole was not made by a bullet. When the doctor couldn't explain it I laughed at him. I hate doctors. And I haven't much use for fools that think I'm in the habit of lying. I haven't much use for people who won't believe me when I tell 'em I saw the long, white thing come sliding down the tree as clear as day."

But Howard was examining the wound in defiance of my neighbor's indignation. "It was made by something round and sharp," he said. "It's curious, but the flesh isn't torn. A knife or bullet would have torn the flesh, left a ragged edge."

I nodded, and was bending to study the wound when Wells shrieked, and clapped his hands to his head. "Ah-h-h!" he choked. "It's come back—the terrible, terrible cold."

Howard stared. "Don't expect me to believe such nonsense!" he exclaimed disgustedly.

But Wells was holding on to his head and dancing about the room in a delirium of agony. "I can't stand it!" he shrieked. "It's freezing up my brain. It's not like ordinary cold. It isn't. Oh God! It's like nothing you've ever felt. It bites, it scorches, it tears. It's like acid."

I laid my hand upon his shoulder and tried to quiet him, but he pushed me aside and made for the door.

"I've got to get out of here," he screamed. "The thing wants room. My head won't hold it. It wants the night—the vast night. It wants to wallow in the night."

He threw back the door and disappeared into the fog. Howard wiped his forehead with the sleeve of his coat and collapsed into a chair.

"Mad," he muttered. "A tragic case of manic-depressive insanity. Who would have suspected it? The story he told us wasn't conscious art at all. It was simply a nightmare-fugue conceived by the brain of a lunatic."

"Yes," I said, "but how do you account for the hole in his head?"

"Oh that!" Howard shrugged. "He probably always had it—probably was born with it."

"Nonsense," I said. "The man never had a hole in his head before. Personally, I think he's been shot. Something ought to be done. He needs medical attention. I think I'll 'phone Dr. Smith."

"It is useless to interfere," said Howard. "That hole was *not* made by a bullet. I advise you to forget him until tomorrow. His insanity may be temporary; it may wear off; and then he'd blame us for interfering. It doesn't pay to meddle with lunatics. If he's still crazy tomorrow, if he comes here again and tries to make trouble, you can notify the proper authorities. Has he ever acted queerly before?"

"No," I said. "He was always quite sane. I think I'll take your advice and wait. But I wish I could explain the hole in his head."

"The story he told interests me more," said Howard. "I'm going to write it out before I forget it. Of course I shan't be able to make the horror as real as he did, but perhaps I can catch a bit of the strangeness and glamor."

He unscrewed his fountain pen and began to cover a harmless sheet of paper with curious jeweled phrases—unearthly phrases. I knew that in a moment the paper would become unholy. I knew that it would glow with an unhallowed light; that witch-fires would flicker over it; strange shadows deepen all about it. From his brain strange and monstrous ideas would flow in a continuous stream to the smooth, white paper.

I shivered and closed the door.

For several minutes there was no sound in the room save the scratching of his pen as it moved across the paper. For several minutes there was silence—and then the shrieks commenced. Or were they wails?

We heard them through the closed door, heard them above the moaning of the fog-horns and the wash of the waves on Mulligan's Beach. We heard them above the million sounds of night that had horrified and depressed us as we sat and talked in that fog-enshrouded and lonely house. We heard them so clearly that for a moment we thought they came from just outside the house. It was not until they came again and again—long, piercing wails—that we discovered in them a quality of remoteness. Slowly we became aware that the wails came from far away, as far away perhaps as Mulligan Wood.

"A soul in torture," muttered Howard. "A poor, damned soul in the grip of the crawling chaos."

He rose unsteadily to his feet. His eyes were shining and he was breathing heavily.

I seized his shoulder and shook him. "You shouldn't project yourself into your stories that way," I exclaimed. "Some poor chap is in distress. I don't know what's happened. Perhaps a ship has foundered. I'm going to put on a slicker and find out what it's all about. I have an idea we may be needed."

"We *may* be needed," repeated Howard slowly. "We may be needed indeed. It will not be satisfied with a single victim. Think of that great journey through space, the thirst and dreadful hungers it must have known! It is preposterous to imagine that it will be content with a single victim!"

Then, suddenly, a change came over him. The light went out of his eyes and his voice lost its quaver. He shivered.

"Forgive me," he said. "I'm afraid you'll think I'm as mad as the yokel who was here a few minutes ago. But I can't help identifying myself with my characters when I write. I'd described something very evil, and those yells—well, they are exactly like the yells a man would make if—if—"

"I understand," I interrupted, "but we've no time to discuss that now. There's a poor chap out there"—I pointed vaguely toward the door—"with his back against the wall. He's fighting off something—I don't know what. We've got to help him."

"Of course, of course," he agreed, and followed me into the kitchen.

Without a word I took down a slicker and handed it to him. I also handed him an enormous rubber hat.

"Get into these as quickly as you can," I said. "The chap's desperately in need of us."

I had gotten my own slicker down from the rack and was forcing my arms through its sticky sleeves. In a moment we were both pushing our way through the fog.

The fog was like a living thing. Its long fingers reached up and slapped us relentlessly on the face. It curled about our bodies and ascended in great, grayish spirals from the tops of our heads. It retreated before us, and as suddenly closed in and enveloped us.

Dimly ahead of us we saw the lights of a few lonely farms. Behind us the sea drummed, and the fog-horns sent out a continuous, mournful ululation. The collar of Howard's slicker was turned up over his ears, and from his long nose moisture dripped. There was grim decision in his eyes, and his jaw was set.

For many minutes we plodded on in silence, and it was not until we approached Mulligan Wood that he spoke.

"If necessary," he said, "we shall enter the wood."

I nodded. "There is no reason why we should not enter the wood," I said. "It isn't a large wood."

"One could get out quickly?"

"One could get out very quickly indeed. My God, did you hear that?"

The shrieks had grown horribly loud.

"He is suffering," said Howard. "He is suffering terribly. Do you suppose—do you suppose it's your crazy friend?"

He had voiced a question which I had been asking myself for some time.

"It's conceivable," I said. "But we'll have to interfere if he's as mad as that. I wish I'd brought some of the neighbors with me."

"Why in heaven's name didn't you?" Howard shouted. "It may take a dozen men to handle him." He was staring at the tall trees that towered before us, and I don't think he really gave Henry Wells so much as a thought.

"That's Mulligan Wood," I said. I swallowed to keep my heart from rising to the top of my mouth. "It isn't a big wood," I added idiotically.

"Oh my God!" Out of the fog there came the sound of a voice in the last extremity of unutterable pain. "They're eating up my brain. Oh my God!"

I was at that moment in deadly fear that I might become as mad as the man in the woods. I clutched Howard's arm.

"Let's go back," I shouted. "Let's go back at once. We were fools to come. There is nothing here but madness and suffering and perhaps death."

"That may be," said Howard, "but we're going on."

His face was ashen beneath his dripping hat, and his eyes were thin blue slits. Before the tremendous challenge of his courage I was abashed.

"Very well," I said grimly. "We'll go on."

Slowly we moved among the trees. They towered above us, and the thick fog so distorted them and merged them together that they seemed to move forward with us. From their twisted branches the fog hung in ribbons. Ribbons, did I say?

Rather were they snakes of fog—writhing snakes with venomous tongues and leering, evil eyes. Through swirling clouds of fog we saw the scaly, gnarled boles of the trees, and every bole resembled the twisted body of an evil old man. Only the small oblong of light cast by my electric torch protected us against their malevolence.

Through great banks of fog we moved, and every moment the screams grew louder. Soon we were catching fragments of sentences, hysterical shoutings that merged into prolonged wails. "Colder and colder and colder . . . they are eating up my brain. Colder! Ah-h-h!"

Howard gripped my arm. "We'll find him," he said. "We can't turn back now."

When we found him he was lying on his side. His hands were clasped about his head, and his body was bent double, the knees drawn up so tightly that they almost touched his chest. He was silent. We bent and shook him, but he made no sound.

"Is he dead?" I choked out the question hysterically. I wanted desperately to turn and run. The trees were very close to us.

"I don't know," said Howard. "I don't know. I hope that he is dead."

I saw him kneel and slide his hand under the poor devil's shirt. For a moment his face was a mask. Then he got up quickly and shook his head.

"He is alive," he said. "We must get him into some dry clothes as quickly as possible."

I helped him. Together we lifted the bent figure from the ground and carried it forward between the trees. Twice we stumbled and nearly fell, and the creepers tore at our clothes. The creepers were little malicious hands grasping and tearing under the malevolent guidance of the great trees. Without a star to guide us, without a light except the little pocket lamp which was growing dim, we fought our way out of Mulligan Wood.

The droning did not commence until we had left the wood. At first we scarcely heard it, it was so low, like the purring of gigantic engines far down in the earth. But slowly, as we stumbled forward with our burden, it grew so loud that we could not ignore it.

"What is that?" muttered Howard, and through the wraiths of fog I saw that his face had a greenish tinge.

"I don't know," I mumbled. "It's something horrible. I never heard anything like it. Can't you walk faster?"

So far we had been fighting familiar horrors, but the droning and humming that rose behind us was like nothing that I had ever heard on earth. In excruciating fright, I shrieked aloud. "Faster, Howard, faster! For God's sake, let's get out of this!"

As I spoke, the body that we were carrying squirmed, and from its cracked lips issued a torrent of gibberish: "I was walking between the trees and looking up. I couldn't see their tops. I was looking up, and then suddenly I looked down and the thing landed on my shoulders. It was all legs—all long, crawling legs. It went right into my head. I wanted to get away from the trees, but I couldn't. I was alone in the forest with the thing on my back, in my head, and when I tried to run, the trees reached out and tripped me. It made a hole so it could get in. It's my brain it wants. Today it made a hole, and now it's crawled in and it's sucking and sucking and sucking. It's as cold as ice and it makes a noise like a great big fly. But it isn't a fly. And it isn't a hand. I was wrong when I called it a hand. You can't see it. I wouldn't have seen or felt it if it hadn't made a hole and got in. You almost see it, you almost feel it, and that means that it's getting ready to go in."

"Can you walk, Wells? Can you walk?"

Howard had dropped Wells' legs and I could hear the harsh intake of his breath as he struggled to rid himself of his slicker.

"I think so," Wells sobbed. "But it doesn't matter. It's got me now. Put me down and save yourselves."

"We've got to run!" I yelled.

"It's our one chance," cried Howard. "Wells, you follow us. Follow us, do you understand? They'll burn up your brain if they catch you. We're going to run, lad. Follow us!"

He was off through the fog. Wells shook himself free, and followed with hoarse shrieks. I tasted a horror more terrible than death. The noise was dreadfully loud; it was right in my ears, and yet for a moment I couldn't move. I stared at the blank wall of fog, and gibbered.

"God! Frank will be lost!" It was the voice of Wells, my poor, lost friend.

"We'll go back!" It was Howard shouting now. "It's death, or worse, but we can't leave him."

"Keep on," I shouted. "They won't get me. Save yourselves!"

In my anxiety to prevent them from sacrificing themselves I plunged wildly forward. In a moment I had joined Howard and was clutching at his arm.

"What is it?" I cried. "What have we to fear?"

The droning was all about us now, but no louder.

"Come quickly or we'll be lost!" he urged frantically. "They've broken down all barriers. That buzzing is a warning. We're sensitives—we've been warned, but if it gets louder we're lost. They're strong near Mulligan Wood, and it's here they've made themselves felt. They're experimenting now—feeling their way. Later, when they've learned, they'll spread out. If we can only reach the farm—"

"We'll reach the farm!" I shouted encouragement as I clawed my way through the fog.

"Heaven help us if we don't!" moaned Howard.

He had thrown off his slicker, and his seeping wet shirt clung tragically to his lean body. He moved through the blackness with long, furious strides. Far ahead we heard the maniacal shrieks of Henry Wells. Ceaselessly the foghorns moaned; ceaselessly the fog swirled and eddied about us.

And the droning continued. It seemed incredible that we should ever have found a way to the farm in the blackness. But find the farm we did, and into it we stumbled with glad cries.

"Shut the door!" shouted Howard.

I shut the door.

"We are safe here, I think," he said. "They haven't reached the farm yet."

"What has happened to Wells?" I gasped, and then I saw the wet tracks leading into the kitchen.

Howard saw them too. His eyes flashed with momentary relief. "I'm glad he's safe," he muttered. "I feared for him."

Then his face darkened. The kitchen was unlighted and no sound came from it.

Without a word Howard walked across the room and into the darkness beyond. I sank into a chair, flicked the moisture from my eyes and brushed back my hair, which had fallen in soggy strands across my face. For a moment I sat, breathing heavily, and when the door creaked, I shivered. But I remembered Howard's assurance: "They haven't reached the farm yet. We're safe here."

Somehow, I had confidence in Howard. He realized that we were threatened by a new and unknown horror, and in some occult way he had grasped its limitations.

I confess, though, that when I heard the screams that came from the kitchen, my faith in my friend was slightly shaken. There were low growls, such as I could not believe came from any human throat, and the voice of Howard raised in wild expostulation. "Let go, I say! Are you quite mad? Man, man, we have saved you! Don't, I say—leggo my leg. Ah-h!"

As Howard staggered into the room I sprang forward and caught him in my arms. He was covered with blood from head to foot and his face was ashen.

"He's gone raving mad," he moaned. "He was running about on his hands and knees like a dog. He sprang at me, and almost killed me. I fought him off, but I'm badly bitten. I hit him in the face—knocked him unconscious. I may have killed him. He's an animal—I had to protect myself."

I laid Howard on the sofa and knelt beside him, but he scorned my aid.

"Don't bother with me!" he commanded. "Get a rope, quickly, and tie him up. If he comes to, we'll have to fight for our lives."

What followed was a nightmare. I remember vaguely that I went into the kitchen with a rope and tied poor Wells to a chair; then I bathed and dressed Howard's wounds, and lit a fire in the grate. I remember also that I telephoned for a doctor. But the incidents are confused in my memory, and I have no clear recollection of anything until the arrival of a tall, grave man with kindly and sympathetic eyes and a presence that was as soothing as an opiate.

He examined Howard, nodded and explained that the wounds were not serious. He examined Wells, and did not nod. He explained slowly that Wells was desperately ill. "Brain fever," he said. "An immediate operation will be necessary. I tell you frankly, I don't think we can save him."

"That wound in his head, Doctor," I said. "Was it made by a bullet?"

The doctor frowned. "It puzzles me," he said. "Of course it was made by a bullet, but it should have partially closed up. It goes right into the brain. You say you know nothing about it. I believe you, but I think the authorities should be notified at once. Someone will be wanted for manslaughter, unless"—he paused—"unless the wound was self-inflicted. What you tell me is curious. That he should have been able to walk about for hours seems incredible. The wound has obviously been dressed, too. There is no clotted blood at all."

He paced slowly back and forth. "We must operate here—at once. There is a slight chance. Luckily, I brought some instruments. We must clear this table and—do you think you could hold a lamp for me?" I nodded.

"I'll try," I said.

"Good!"

The doctor busied himself with preparations while I debated whether or not I should 'phone for the police.

"I'm convinced," I said at last, "that the wound was self-inflicted. Wells acted very strangely. If you are willing, Doctor—"

"Yes?"

"We will remain silent about this matter until after the operation. If Wells lives, there would be no need of involving the poor chap in a police investigation."

The doctor nodded. "Very well," he said. "We will operate first and decide afterward."

Howard was laughing silently from his couch. "The police," he snickered. "Of what use would they be against the things in Mulligan Wood?"

There was an ironic and ominous quality about his mirth that disturbed me. The horrors that we had known in the fog seemed absurd and impossible in the cool, scientific presence of Dr. Smith, and I didn't want to be reminded of them.

The doctor turned from his instruments and whispered into my ear. "Your friend has a slight fever, and apparently it has made him delirious. If you will bring me a glass of water I will mix him an opiate."

I raced to secure a glass, and in a moment we had Howard sleeping soundly.

"Now then," said the doctor as he handed me the lamp. "You must hold this steady and move it about as I direct."

The white, unconscious form of Henry Wells lay upon the table that the doctor and I had cleared, and I trembled all over when I thought of what lay before me.

I should be obliged to stand and gaze into the living brain of my poor friend as the doctor relentlessly laid it bare. I should be obliged to stand and stare as the doctor cut and probed, and perhaps I should witness unmentionable things.

With swift, experienced fingers the doctor administered an anesthetic. I was oppressed by a dreadful feeling that we were committing a crime, that Henry Wells would have violently disapproved, that he would have preferred to die. It is a dreadful thing to mutilate a man's brain. And yet I knew that the doctor's conduct was above reproach, and that the ethics of his profession demanded that he operate.

"We are ready," said Dr. Smith. "Lower the lamp. Carefully now!"

I saw the knife moving in his competent, swift fingers. For a moment I stared, and then I turned my head away. What I had seen in that brief glance made me sick and faint. It may have been fancy, but as I stared hysterically at the wall I had the impression that the doctor was on the verge of collapse. He made no sound, but I was almost certain that he had made some horrible, unspeakable discovery.

"Lower the lamp," he said. His voice was hoarse and seemed to come from far down within his throat.

His voice horrified me so that I was guilty of a great treachery. I lowered the lamp an inch without turning my head. I waited for him to reproach me, to swear at me perhaps, but he was as silent as the man on the table. I knew, though, that his fingers were still at work, for I could hear them as they moved about. I could hear his swift, agile fingers moving about the head of Henry Wells.

I suddenly became conscious that my hand was trembling. I wanted to lay down the lamp; I felt that I could no longer hold it.

"Are you nearly through?" I gasped in desperation.

"Hold that lamp steady!" The doctor screamed the command. "If you move that lamp again—I—I won't sew him up. I'll walk out of this room and leave his obscene brain to rot. I don't care if they hang me! I'm not a healer of devils!"

I knew not what to do. I could scarcely hold the lamp, and the doctor's threat horrified me. In desperation I pleaded with him.

"Do everything you can," I urged, hysterically. "Give him a chance to fight his way back. He was kind and good—once!"

For a moment there was silence, and I feared that he would not heed me. I momentarily expected him to throw down his scalpel and sponge, and dash across the room and out into the fog. It was not until I heard his fingers moving about again that I knew he had decided to give even the damned a chance.

It was after midnight when the doctor told me that I could lay down the lamp. I turned with a cry of relief and encountered a face that I shall never forget. In three quarters of an hour the doctor had aged ten years. There were purple caverns beneath his eyes, and his mouth twitched convulsively. There were wrinkles upon his high yellow forehead that I had not seen there before, and when he spoke, his voice was cracked and feeble.

"He'll not live," he said. "He'll be dead in an hour. I did not touch his brain. I could do nothing. When I saw—how things were—I—I sewed him up immediately."

"What did you see?" I half whispered.

A look of unutterable fear came into the doctor's eyes. "I saw—I saw"—his voice broke and his whole body quivered—"I saw—oh, the burning shame of it! Because I have seen a—what man should not look upon—I bear the mark of the beast upon me. I am contaminated forever. I am unclean. I can not stay in this house. I must leave at once."

He broke down and covered his face with his hands. Great sobs convulsed his body.

"Unclean," he moaned. "The old, hideous secret that man has forgotten—a horror to look upon. Evil that is without shape; evil that is formless."

Suddenly he raised his head and looked wildly about him.

"They will come here and claim him!" he shrieked. "They have laid their mark upon him and they will come for him. You must not stay here. This house is marked for destruction!"

I watched him helplessly as he seized his hat and bag and crossed to the door. With white, shaking fingers he drew back the latch, and in a moment his lean figure was silhouetted against a square of swirling vapor.

"Remember that I warned you!" he shouted back; and then the fog swallowed him.

Howard was sitting up and rubbing his eyes.

"A malicious trick, that!" he was muttering. "To deliberately drug me! Had I known that glass of water—"

"How do you feel?" I asked as I shook him violently by the shoulders. "Do you think you can walk?"

"You drug me, and then ask me to walk! Frank, you're as unreasonable as an artist. What is the matter now?"

I pointed to the silent figure on the table. "Mulligan Wood is safer," I said. "He belongs to them now!"

Howard sprang to his feet and shook me by the arm.

"What do you mean?" he cried. "How do you know?"

"The doctor saw his brain," I explained. "And he also saw something that he would not—could not describe. But he told me that they would come for him, and I believe him."

"We must leave here at once!" cried Howard. "Your doctor was right. We are in deadly danger. Even Mulligan Wood—but we need not return to the wood. There is your launch!"

"There is the launch!" I echoed, faint hope rising in my mind.

"The fog will be a most deadly menace," said Howard grimly. "But even death at sea is preferable to *this* horror."

It was not far from the house to the dock, and in less than a minute Howard was seated in the stern of the launch and I was working furiously on the engine. The fog-horns still moaned, but there were no lights visible anywhere in the harbor. We could not see two feet before our faces. The white wraiths of the fog were dimly visible in the darkness, but beyond them stretched endless night, lightless and full of terror.

Howard was speaking. "Somehow I feel that there is death out there," he said.

"There is more death here," I said as I churned at the engine. "I think I can avoid the rocks. There is very little wind and I know the harbor."

"And of course we shall have the fog-horns to guide us," muttered Howard. "I think we had better make for the open sea."

I agreed.

"The launch wouldn't survive a storm," I said, "but I've no desire to remain in the harbor. If we reach the sea we'll probably be picked up by some ship. It would be sheer folly to remain where they can reach us."

"How do we know how far they can reach?" groaned Howard. "What are the distances of earth to things that have traveled through space? They will overrun the earth. They will destroy us all utterly."

"We'll discuss that later," I cried as the engine roared into life. "We're going to get as far away from them as possible. Perhaps they haven't *learned* yet! While they've still limitations we may be able to escape."

We moved slowly into the channel, and the sound of the water splashing against the sides of the launch soothed us strangely. At a suggestion from me Howard had taken the wheel and was slowly bringing her about.

"Keep her steady," I shouted. "There isn't any danger until we get into the Narrows!"

For several minutes I crouched above the engine while Howard steered in silence. Then, suddenly, he turned to me with a gesture of elation.

"I think the fog's lifting," he said.

I stared into the darkness before me. Certainly it seemed less oppressive, and the white spirals of mist that had been continually ascending through it were fading into insubstantial wisps. "Keep her head on," I shouted. "We're in luck. If the fog clears we'll be able to see the Narrows. Keep a sharp lookout for Mulligan Light."

There is no describing the joy that filled us when we saw the light. Yellow and bright it streamed over the water and illuminated sharply the outlines of the great rocks that rose on both sides of the Narrows.

"Let me have the wheel," I shouted as I stepped quickly forward. "This is a ticklish passage, but we'll come through now with colors flying."

In our excitement and elation we almost forgot the horror that we had left behind us. I stood at the wheel and smiled confidently as we raced over the dark water. Quickly the rocks drew nearer until their vast bulk towered above us.

"We shall certainly make it!" I cried.

But no response came from Howard. I heard him choke and gasp.

"What is the matter?" I asked suddenly, and turning, saw that he was crouching in terror above the engine. His back was turned toward me, but I knew instinctively in which direction he was gazing.

The dim shore that we had left shone like a flaming sunset. Mulligan Wood was burning. Great flames shot up from the highest of the tall trees, and a thick curtain of black smoke rolled slowly eastward, blotting out the few remaining lights in the harbor.

But it was not the flames that caused me to cry out in a frenzy of fear and horror. It was the shape that towered above the trees, the vast, formless shape that moved slowly to and fro across the sky.

God knows I tried to believe that I saw nothing. I tried to believe that the shape was a mere shadow cast by the flames. I even managed to laugh, and I remember that I patted Howard's arm reassuringly.

"The wood will be destroyed utterly," I cried. "I know that they will will not escape. They will all perish."

But when Howard turned in his fright and screamed, I knew that the dim, formless thing that towered above the trees was more than a shadow.

"If we see it clearly we are lost!" he shrieked. "Pray that it remains without form!"

"I see nothing!" I groaned. "There is blackness above the trees."

"It has no form," gibbered Howard. "We should not—we must not see it! It is our little brains that give it a form. When it enters our brains it becomes clothed in a form. If it enters our brains we are lost."

"The woods are burning!" I shouted. "There is nothing above the trees. All is blackness and emptiness above the trees."

But even as I stared at the shape with loathing, with furious disbelief, it grew more distinct. Above the burning trees it hovered awfully, and I slowly became aware that it had wings.

"It is like a bat!" I groaned. "It is a great bat with yellow wings brooding over the fire."

"It *is* a bat!" sobbed Howard. "It is dark and very large and almost formless, but it *is* a bat!"

"No, no!" I shrieked. "It is not a bat. We see nothing. There is a great vague form that moves back and forth above the trees, but it is not a bat."

Howard buried his head in his hands and sobbed aloud in an agony of fear. "Our brains will grow cold," he moaned. "They will enter and suck at our brains."

"Oh, not that!" I cried. "I will die first. I will throw myself into the water. That terror is more terrible than drowning."

We stood trembling in the darkness, a prey to the most awful horror. The shape above Mulligan Wood was slowly growing clearer and I did not think anything could save us. And then, suddenly, I remembered that there was one thing that might save us.

"It is older than the world," I thought, "older than all religion. Before the dawn of civilization men knelt in adoration before it. It is present in all mythologies. It is the primal symbol. Perhaps, in the dim past, thousands and thousands of years ago, it was used to—repel the invaders. I shall so use it. I shall fight the shape with a high and terrible mystery."

I became suddenly curiously calm. I knew that I had hardly a minute to act, that more than our lives were threatened, but I did not tremble. I reached calmly beneath the engine and drew out a quantity of cotton waste.

"Howard," I said, "I want you to light me a match. It is our only hope. You must strike a match at once."

For what seemed eternities Howard stared at me incomprehensibly. Then the night was clamorous with his laughter.

"A match!" he shrieked. "A match to warm our little brains! Yes, we shall need a match."

"Trust me!" I entreated. "You must—it is our one hope. Strike a match quickly."

"I do not understand!" Howard was sober now, but his voice quivered hysterically.

"I have thought of something that may save us," I said. "Please light this waste for me."

Slowly he nodded. I had told him nothing, but I knew he guessed what I intended to do. Often his insight was uncanny. With fumbling fingers he drew out a match and struck it.

"Be bold," he said. "Show them that you are unafraid. Make the sign boldly."

As the waste caught fire, the form above the trees stood out with a frightful clarity.

"There is nothing there," I cried. "We see nothing. We are protected. We are invincible."

I raised the flaming cotton and passed it quickly before my body in a straight line from my left to my right shoulder. Then I raised it to my forehead and lowered it to my knees.

In an instant Howard had snatched the brand and was repeating the sign. He made two crosses, one against his body and one against the darkness with the torch held at arm's length. *"Sanctus . . . sanctus . . . sanctus,"* he muttered.

For a moment I shut my eyes, but I could still see the shape above the trees. Then slowly it ceased to resemble a bat, its form became less distinct, became vast and chaotic—and when I opened my eyes it had vanished. I saw nothing but the flaming forest and the shadows cast by the tall trees.

The horror had passed, but I did not move. I stood like an image of stone staring over the black water. Then something seemed to burst in my head. My brain spun dizzily, and I tottered against the rail.

I would have fallen, but Howard caught me about the shoulders. "We're saved!" he shouted. "We've won through."

"I'm glad," I said. But I was too utterly exhausted to really rejoice. My legs gave way beneath me and my head fell forward. All the sights and sounds of earth were swallowed up in a merciful blackness.

II.

Howard was writing when I entered the room.

"How is the story going?" I asked.

For a moment he ignored my question. Then he slowly turned and faced me. His lips opened but no sound came from between them. I noticed that he had aged horribly. He was much thinner (I don't think he weighed more than one hundred and ten pounds) and there were myriads of tiny wrinkles about his eyes.

"It's not going well," he said at last. "It doesn't satisfy me. There are problems that still elude me. I haven't been able to capture *all* of the crawling horror of the thing in Mulligan Wood."

I sat down and lit a cigarette.

"I want you to explain that horror to me," I said. "For three weeks I have waited for you to speak. I know that you have some knowledge which you are concealing from me. What was the damp, spongy thing that landed on Wells' head in the woods? Why did we hear a droning as we fled in the fog? What was the meaning of the shape that we saw above the trees? And why, in heaven's name, didn't the horror spread as we feared it might? What stopped it? Howard, what do you think really happened to Wells' brain? Did his body burn with the farm, or did they—*claim* it? And the other body that was found in Mulligan Wood—that lean, blackened horror with riddled head—how do you explain that?" (Two days after the fire a skeleton had been found in Mulligan Wood. A few fragments of burnt flesh still adhered to the bones, and the skull-cap was missing.)

It was a long time before Howard spoke again. He sat with bowed head, fingering his notebook, and his body trembled horribly, trembled all over. At last he raised his eyes. They shone with a wild light and his lips were ashen.

"Yes," he said. "We will discuss the horror together. Last week I did not want to speak of it. It seemed too awful to put into words. But I shall never rest in peace until I have woven it into a story, until I have made my readers feel and see that dreadful, unspeakable thing. And I can not write of it until I am convinced beyond the shadow of a doubt that I understand it myself. It may help me to talk about it.

"You have asked me what the damp thing was that fell on Wells' head. I believe that it was a human brain—the essence of a human brain drawn out through a hole, or holes, in a human head. I believe the brain was drawn out by imperceptible degrees, and reconstructed again by the horror. I believe that for some purpose of its own it used human brains—perhaps to learn from them. Or perhaps it merely played with them. The blackened, riddled body in Mulligan Wood? That was the body of the first victim, some poor fool who got lost between the tall trees. I rather suspect the trees helped. I think the horror endowed them with a strange life. Anyhow, the poor chap lost his brain. The horror took it, and played with it, and then accidentally dropped it. It dropped it on Wells' head. Wells said that the long, thin and very white arm he saw was looking for something that it had dropped. Of course Wells didn't really see the arm objectively, but the horror that is without form or color had already entered his brain and clothed itself in human thought.

"As for the droning that we heard and the shape we thought we saw above the burning forest—that was the horror seeking to make itself felt, seeking to break down barriers, seeking to enter our brains and clothe itself with our thoughts. It almost got us. If we had seen the shape as clearly as Wells saw the white arm we should have been lost."

Howard walked to the window. He drew back the curtains and gazed for a moment at the crowded harbor and the colossal buildings that towered against the moon. He was staring at the skyline of lower Manhattan. Sheer beneath him the cliffs of Brooklyn Heights loomed darkly.

"Why didn't they conquer?" he cried. "They could have destroyed it utterly. They could have wiped it from the earth—all its incredible wealth and power would have gone down before them. The great buildings would have toppled into the sea, and millions of brains would have fed their lust—their terrible, unearthly lust."

I shivered. "But why didn't the horror spread?" I cried.

Howard shrugged his shoulders. "I do not know. Perhaps they discovered that human brains were too trivial and absurd to bother with. Perhaps we ceased to amuse them. Perhaps they grew tired of us. But it is conceivable that the *sign* destroyed them—or sent them back through space. I think they came once before. I think they came millions of years ago, and were frightened away by the sign. When they discovered that we had not forgotten the use of the sign they may have fled in terror. Certainly there has been no manifestation for three weeks. I think that they are gone."

"Then I have saved the world!" I shouted exultantly.

"Perhaps." He eyed me disapprovingly. "I think I can forgive you for that," he said, "but it is nothing to gloat over."

"And Henry Wells?" I asked.

"Well, his body was not found. I imagine they came for him."

"And you honestly intend to put this—this ultimate obscenity into a story? Oh, my God! The whole thing is so incredible, so unheard of, that I can't believe it. I can't! My friend, my friend, did we not dream it all? Were we ever really in Partridgeville? Did we sit in an ancient house and discuss unmentionable things while the fog curled about us? Did we walk through that unholy wood? Were the trees really alive, and did Henry Wells run about on his hands and knees like a wolf?"

Howard sat down quietly and rolled up his sleeve. He thrust his thin arm toward me.

"Can you argue away that scar?" he said. "There are the marks of the beast that attacked me—the man-beast that was Henry Wells. A dream? My friend, I would cut off this arm immediately at the elbow if you could convince me that it was a dream."

I walked to the window and remained for a long time staring at the stupendous galaxies of Manhattan. "There," I thought, "is something substantial. It is absurd to imagine that anything could destroy it. It is absurd to imagine that the horror was really as terrible as it seemed to us in Partridgeville. I must persuade Howard not to write about it. We must both try to forget it."

I returned to where he sat and laid my hand on his shoulder.

"You'll give up the idea of putting it into a story?" I urged gently.

"Never!" He was on his feet, and his eyes were blazing. "Do you think I would give up now when I've almost captured it? I shall write the most terrible story that the world has ever seen. My readers shall crouch and whimper in awful fear. I shall surpass Poe—I shall surpass all of the Masters."

"Surpass them and be damned then," I said angrily. "That way madness lies, but it is useless to argue with you. Your egoism is too colossal."

I turned and walked swiftly out of the room. It occurred to me as I descended the stairs that I had made an idiot of myself with my fears, but even as I went down I looked fearfully back over my shoulder, as though I expected a great stone weight to descend from above and crush me to the earth. "He should forget the horror," I thought. "He should wipe it from his mind. He will go mad if he writes about it."

Three days passed before I saw Howard again.

"Come in," he said in a curiously hoarse voice when I knocked on his door.

I found him in dressing-gown and slippers, and I knew as soon as I saw him that he was terribly exultant. His eyes shone and he greeted me with a feverish intensity.

"I have triumphed, Frank!" he cried. "I have reproduced the form that is formless, the burning shame that man has not looked upon, the crawling, fleshless obscenity that sucks at our brains!"

Before I could so much as gasp he had placed the bulky manuscript in my hands.

"Read it, Frank," he commanded. "Sit down at once and read it!"

I crossed to the window and sat down on the lounge. I sat there oblivious to everything but the typewritten sheets before me. I confess that I was consumed with an unholy curiosity. I had never questioned Howard's power. With words he wrought miracles; breaths from the unknown blew always over his pages, and things that had passed beyond earth returned at his bidding. But could he even suggest the horror that we had known?—could he even so much as hint at the loathsome, crawling thing that had claimed the brain of Henry Wells?

I read the story through. I read it slowly, and clutched at the pillows beside me in a frenzy of loathing. As soon as I had finished it Howard snatched it from me. He evidently suspected that I desired to tear it to shreds.

"What do you think of it?" he cried exultantly.

"It is indescribably foul!" I exclaimed. "It is terribly, unspeakably obscene!"

"But you will concede that I have made the horror convincing?"

I nodded, and reached for my hat. "You have made it so convincing that I can not remain and discuss it with you. I intend to walk until morning. I intend to walk until I am too weary to care, or think, or remember."

"It is deathless art!" he shouted at me, but I passed down the stairs and out of the house without replying.

III.

It was past midnight when the telephone rang. I laid down the book I was reading and lowered the receiver.

"Hello. Who is there?" I asked.

"Frank, this is Howard!" The voice was strangely high-pitched. "Come as quickly as you can. *They've come back!* And Frank, the sign is powerless. I've tried the sign, but the droning is getting louder, and a dim shape—" Howard's voice trailed off disastrously.

I fairly screamed into the receiver. "Courage, man! Do not let them suspect that you are afraid. Make the sign again and again. I will come at once."

Howard's voice came again, more hoarsely this time. "The shape is growing clearer and clearer. And there is nothing I can do! Frank, I have lost the power to make the sign. I have forfeited all right to the protection of the sign. My soul is corrupt. I've become a priest of the Devil. That story—I should not have written that story."

"Show them that you are unafraid!" I cried.

"I'll try! I'll try! Ah, my God! The shape is—"

I did not wait to hear more. Frantically seizing my hat and coat I dashed down the stairs and out into the street. As I reached the curb a dizziness seized me. I clung to a lamp-post to keep from falling, and waved my hand madly at a fleeing taxi. Luckily the driver saw me. The car stopped and I staggered out into the street and climbed into it. "Quick!" I shouted. "Take me to 10 Brooklyn Heights!"

"Yes, sir. Cold night, ain't it?"

"Cold!" I shouted. "It will be cold indeed when they get in. It will be cold indeed when they start to—"

The driver stared at me in amazement. "That's all right, sir," he said. "We'll get you home all right, sir. Brooklyn Heights, did you say, sir?

"Brooklyn Heights," I groaned, and collapsed against the cushions.

As the car raced forward I tried not to think of the horror that awaited me. I clutched deserately at straws. "It is conceivable," I thought, "that Howard has gone temporarily insane. How could the horror have found him among so many millions of people? It can not be that *they* have deliberately sought him out. It can not be that they would deliberately choose him from among such multitudes. He is too insignificant—all human beings are too insignificant. They would never deliberately angle for human beings. They would never deliberately trawl for human beings—but they did seek Henry Wells. And what did Howard say? 'I have become a priest of the Devil.' Why not *their* priest? What if Howard has become their priest on earth? What if his obscene, loathly story has made him their priest?"

The thought was a nightmare to me, and I put it furiously from me. "He will have courage to resist them," I thought. "He will show them that he is not afraid."

"Here we are, sir. Shall I help you in, sir?"

The car had stopped, and I groaned as I realized that I was about to enter what might prove to be my tomb. I descended to the sidewalk and handed the driver all the change that I possessed. He stared at me in amazement.

"You've given me too much," he cried. "Here, sir—"

But I waved him aside and dashed up the stoop of the house before me. As I fitted a key into the door I could hear him muttering: "Craziest drunk I ever seen! He gives me four bucks to drive him ten blocks, and doesn't want no thanks or nothin'—"

The lower hall was unlighted. I stood at the foot of the stairs and shouted. "I'm here, Howard! Can you come down?"

There was no answer. I waited for perhaps ten seconds, but not a sound came from the room above.

"I'm coming up!" I shouted in desperation, and started to climb the stairs. I was trembling all over. "They've got him," I thought. "I'm too late. Perhaps I had better not—great God, what was that?"

I was unbelievably terrified. There was no mistaking the sounds. In the room above, someone was volubly pleading and crying aloud in agony. Was it Howard's voice that I heard? I caught a few words indistinctly. "Crawling—ugh! Crawling—ugh! Oh, have pity! Cold and clee-ar. Crawling—ugh! God in heaven!"

I had reached the landing, and when the pleadings rose to hoarse shrieks I fell to my knees, and made against my body, and upon the wall beside me, and in the air—the sign. I made the primal sign that had saved us in Mulligan Wood, but this time I made it crudely, not with fire, but with fingers that trembled and caught at my clothes, and I made it without courage or hope, made it darkly, with a conviction that nothing could save me.

And then I got up quickly and went on up the stairs. My prayer was that they would take me quickly, that my sufferings should be brief under the stars.

The door of Howard's room was ajar. By a tremendous effort I stretched out my hand and grasped the knob. Slowly I swung it inward.

For a moment I saw nothing but the motionless form of Howard lying upon the floor. He was lying upon his back. His knees were drawn up and he had raised his hands before his face, palms outward, as if to blot out a vision unspeakable.

Upon entering the room I had deliberately, by lowering my eyes, narrowed my range of vision. I saw only the floor and the lower section of the room. I did not want to raise my eyes. I had lowered them in self-protection because I dreaded what the room held.

I did not want to raise my eyes, but there were forces, hideous and obscene powers at work in the room which I could not resist. I knew that if I looked up, the horror might destroy me, but I had no choice.

Slowly, painfully, I raised my eyes and stared across the room. It would have been better, I think, if I had rushed forward immediately and surrendered to the thing that towered there. It would have consumed me in a moment, consumed me utterly, but what does life hold for me now? The vision of that fetid obscenity will come between me and the pleasures of the world as long as I remain in the world.

From the ceiling to the floor it towered, and it threw off drooling shafts of light. The light was slimy and unspeakable—a liquid light that dripped and dripped, like spittle, like the fetid mucous of loathsome slugs. And pierced by the shafts, whirling around and around, were the pages of Howard's story.

In the center of the room, between the ceiling and the floor, the pages whirled about, and the loathsome light burned through the sheets, and descending in dripping shafts entered—the *brain of my poor friend!* Into his head the light was pouring in a continuous stream, and above, the Master of the Light moved slowly back and forth in awful glee. I screamed and screamed and covered my eyes with my hands, but still the Master moved—back and forth, back and forth. And still the foul light drooled and oozed and ran and poured into the brain of my friend.

And then there came from the mouth of the Master a most awful sound. . . . I had forgotten the sign that I had made three times below in the darkness. I had forgotten the high and terrible mystery before which all of the invaders were powerless. But when I saw it forming itself in the room, forming itself immaculately, with a terrible integrity above the drooling yellow light, I knew that I was saved.

I sobbed and fell upon my knees. The fetid light dwindled, and the Master shriveled before my eyes.

And then from the walls, from the ceiling, from the floor, there leapt flame—a white and cleansing flame that consumed, that devoured and destroyed forever.

But my friend was dead.

The Hounds of Tindalos

Frank Belknap Long

To fend off the most obvious criticism first, is it really thinkable that poor Chalmers would trouble himself to write, with his last breath, "Their tongues! Ahhh . . ."? Okay, probably not. But it may not be quite as ludicrous as I have always supposed. After all, Chalmers had made it clear he wanted a blow-by-blow description of his Liao trip for the sake of scientific record. It is close to believable that he would keep writing as long as possible, even anticipating the death rattle, just as the camera man on the Port Kaituma tarmac in Guyana kept filming right up to the point of being gunned down by Reverend Jim Jones's thugs.

As in "The Space-Eaters," this story's narrator is "Frank." Last time the protagonist was obviously Lovecraft, but is Halpin Chalmers supposed to be Lovecraft, too? I don't think so. Lovecraft would never speak of science and mysticism as Chalmers does here. If anyone, Chalmers's real-life analogue is apparently Ambrose Bierce, since Chalmers is like Bierce but unlike Lovecraft, both a fiction writer and a reporter. However, Lovecraft did like what Chalmers says, since he has Akeley and Wilmarth echo the central thesis in "The Whisperer in Darkness." It is in "The Hounds of Tindalos" that one must look to find the "black truth" concealed in "the immemorial allegory of the Tao." And what is that allegory? Are we to pick up the hint that the great recumbent beast that is the Tao is one of the Hounds of Tindalos? Is it a coincidence that the word "Tindalos" contains the word "Tao"?

Long portrays Chalmers as a mystic, and he makes it ring true with Chalmers's portentous talk of some primordial *deed*, some *choice* made before the world, before right and wrong received their meaning. All this is sublimely redolent of both Gnosticism and Kabbalism, where there is a primordial Fall within the Godhead itself, resulting in the impurity of matter, the *kelipoth*, or shards of fallen light that coalesced into the material world.

"The Hounds of Tindalos" first crept from their kennel in the pages of *Weird Tales*, March 1929.

"I'm glad you came," said Chalmers. He was sitting by the window and his face was very pale. Two tall candles guttered at his elbow and cast a sickly amber light over his long nose and slightly receding chin. Chalmers would have nothing modern about his apartment. He had the soul of a mediaeval ascetic, and he preferred illuminated manuscripts to automobiles, and leering stone gargoyles to radios and adding-machines.

As I crossed the room to the settee he had cleared for me I glanced at his desk and was surprised to discover that he had been studying the mathematical formulae of a celebrated contemporary physicist, and that he had covered many sheets of thin yellow paper with curious geometric designs.

"Einstein and John Dee are strange bedfellows," I said as my gaze wandered from his mathematical charts to the sixty or seventy quaint books that comprised his strange little library. Plotinus and Emanuel Moscopulus, St. Thomas Aquinas and Frenicle de Bessy stood elbow to elbow in the somber ebony bookcase, and chairs, table and desk were littered with pamphlets about mediaeval sorcery and witchcraft and black magic, and all of the valiant glamorous things that the modern world has repudiated.

Chalmers smiled engagingly, and passed me a Russian cigarette on a curiously carved tray. "We are just discovering now," he said, "that the old alchemists and sorcerers were two-thirds *right*, and that your modern biologist and materialist is nine-tenths *wrong.*"

"You have always scoffed at modern science," I said, a little impatiently.

"Only at scientific dogmatism," he replied. "I have always been a rebel, a champion of originality and lost causes; that is why I have chosen to repudiate the conclusions of contemporary biologists."

"And Einstein?" I asked.

"A priest of transcendental mathematics!" he murmured reverently. "A profound mystic and explorer of the great *suspected.*"

"Then you do not entirely despise science."

"Of course not," he affirmed. "I merely distrust the scientific positivism of the past fifty years, the positivism of Haeckel and Darwin and of Mr. Bertrand Russell. I believe that biology has failed pitifully to explain the mystery of man's origin and destiny."

"Give them time," I retorted.

Chalmers' eyes glowed. "My friend," he murmured, "your pun is sublime. Give them *time*. That is precisely what I would do. But your modern biologist scoffs at time. He has the key but he refuses to use it. What do we know of time, really? Einstein believes that it is relative, that it can be interpreted in terms of space, of *curved* space. But must we stop there? When mathematics fails us can we not advance by—insight?"

"You are treading on dangerous ground," I replied. "That is a pitfall that your true investigator avoids. That is why modern science has advanced so slowly. It accepts nothing that it cannot demonstrate. But you—"

"I would take hashish, opium, all manner of drugs. I would emulate the sages of the East. And then perhaps I would apprehend—"

"What?"

"The fourth dimension."

"Theosophical rubbish!"

"Perhaps. But I believe that drugs expand human consciousness. William James agreed with me. And I have discovered a new one."

"A new drug?"

"It was used centuries ago by Chinese alchemists, but it is virtually unknown in the West. Its occult properties are amazing. With its aid and the aid of my mathematical knowledge I believe that I can *go back through time.*"

"I do not understand."

"Time is merely our imperfect perception of a new dimension of space. Time and motion are both illusions. Everything that has existed from the beginning of the world *exists now.* Events that occurred centuries ago on this planet continue to exist in another dimension of space. Events that will occur centuries from now *exist already.* We cannot perceive their existence because we cannot enter the dimension of space that contains them. Human beings as we know them are merely fractions, infinitesimally small fractions of one enormous whole. Every human being is linked with *all* the life that has preceded him on this planet. All of his ancestors are parts of him. Only time separates him from his forebears, and time is an illusion and does not exist."

"I think I understand," I murmured.

"It will be sufficient for my purpose if you can form a vague idea of what I wish to achieve. I wish to strip from my eyes the veils of illusion that time has thrown over them, and see the *beginning and the end.*"

"And you think this new drug will help you?"

"I am sure that it will. And I want you to help me. I intend to take the drug immediately. I cannot wait. I must *see.*" His eyes glittered strangely. "I am going back, back through time."

He rose and strode to the mantel. When he faced me again he was holding a small square box in the palm of his hand. "I have here five pellets of the drug Liao. It was used by the Chinese philosopher Lao Tze, and while under its influence he visioned Tao. Tao is the most mysterious force in the world; it surrounds and pervades all things; it contains the visible universe and everything that we call reality. He who apprehends the mysteries of Tao sees clearly all that was and will be."

"Rubbish!" I retorted.

"Tao resembles a great animal, recumbent, motionless, containing in its enormous body all the worlds of our universe, the past, the present and the future. We see portions of this great monster through a slit, which we call time. With the aid of this drug I shall enlarge the slit. I shall behold the great figure of life, the great recumbent beast in its entirety."

"And what do you wish me to do?"

"Watch, my friend. Watch and take notes. And if I go back too far you must recall me to reality. You can recall me by shaking me violently. If I appear to be suffering acute physical pain you must recall me at once."

"Chalmers," I said, "I wish you wouldn't make this experiment. You are taking dreadful risks. I don't believe that there is any fourth dimension and I emphatically do not believe in Tao. And I don't approve of your experimenting with unknown drugs."

"I know the properties of this drug," he replied. "I know precisely how it affects the human animal and I know its dangers. The risk does not reside in the drug itself. My only fear is that I may become lost in time. You see, I shall assist the drug. Before I swallow this pellet I shall give my undivided attention to the geometric and algebraic symbols that I have traced on this paper." He raised the mathematical chart that rested on his knee. "I shall prepare my mind for an excursion into time. I shall approach the fourth dimension with my conscious mind before I take the drug which will enable me to exercise occult powers of perception. Before I enter the dream world of the Eastern mystics I shall acquire all of the mathematical help that modern science can offer. This mathematical knowledge, this conscious approach to an actual apprehension of the fourth dimension of time will supplement the work of the drug. The drug will open up stupendous new vistas—the mathematical preparation will enable me to grasp them intellectually. I have often grasped the fourth dimension in dreams, emotionally, intuitively, but I have never been able to recall, in waking life, the occult splendors that were momentarily revealed to me.

"But with your aid, I believe that I can recall them. You will take down everything that I say while I am under the influence of the drug. No matter how strange or incoherent my speech may become you will omit nothing. When I awake I may be able to supply the key to whatever is mysterious or incredible. I am not sure that I shall succeed, but if I *do* succeed"—his eyes were strangely luminous—*"time will exist for me no longer!"*

He sat down abruptly. "I shall make the experiment at once. Please stand over there by the window and watch. Have you a fountain pen?"

I nodded gloomily and removed a pale green Waterman from my upper vest pocket.

"And a pad, Frank?"

I groaned and produced a memorandum book. "I emphatically disapprove of this experiment," I muttered. "You're taking a frightful risk."

"Don't be an asinine old woman!" he admonished. "Nothing that you can say will induce me to stop now. I entreat you to remain silent while I study these charts."

He raised the charts and studied them intently. I watched the clock on the mantel as it ticked out the seconds, and a curious dread clutched at my heart so that I choked.

Suddenly the clock stopped ticking, and exactly at that moment Chalmers swallowed the drug.

I rose quickly and moved toward him, but his eyes implored me not to interfere. "The clock has stopped," he murmured. "The forces that control it approve of my experiment. *Time* stopped, and I swallowed the drug. I pray God that I shall not lose my way."

He closed his eyes and leaned back on the sofa. All of the blood had left his face and he was breathing heavily. It was clear that the drug was acting with extraordinary rapidity.

"It is beginning to get dark," he murmured. "Write that. It is beginning to get dark and the familiar objects in the room are fading out. I can discern them vaguely through my eyelids, but they are fading swiftly."

I shook my pen to make the ink come and wrote rapidly in shorthand as he continued to dictate.

"I am leaving the room. The walls are vanishing and I can no longer see any of the familiar objects. Your face, though, is still visible to me. I hope that you are writing. I think that I am about to make a great leap—a leap through space. Or perhaps it is through time that I shall make the leap. I cannot tell. Everything is dark, indistinct."

He sat for a while silent, with his head sunk upon his breast. Then suddenly he stiffened and his eyelids fluttered open. "Got in heaven1" he cried. "I *see!*"

He was straining forward in his chair, staring at the opposite wall. But I knew that he was looking beyond the wall and that the objects in the room no longer existed for him. "Chalmers," I cried, "Chalmers, shall I wake you?"

"Do not!" he shrieked. "I see *everything*. All of the billions of lives that preceded me on this planet are before me at this moment. I see men of all ages, all races, all colors. They are fighting, killing, building, dancing, singing. They are sitting about rude fires on lonely gray deserts, and flying through the air in monoplanes. They are riding the seas in bark canoes and enormous steamships; they are painting bison and mammoths on the walls of dismal caves and covering huge canvases with queer futuristic designs. I watch the migrations from Atlantis. I watch the migrations from Lemuria. I see the elder races—a strange horde of black dwarfs overwhelming Asia, and the Neandertalers with lowered heads and bent knees ranging obscenely across Europe. I watch the Achaeans streaming into the Greek islands, and the crude beginnings of Hellenic culture. I am in Athens and Pericles is young. I am standing on the soil of Italy. I assist in the rape of the Sabines; I march with the Imperial Legions. I tremble with awe and wonder as the enormous standards go by and the ground shakes with the tread of the victorious *hastati*. A thousand naked slaves grovel before me as I pass in a litter of gold and ivory drawn by night-black oxen from Thebes, and the flower-girls scream '*Ave Caesar*' as I nod and smile. I am myself a slave on a Moorish galley. I watch the erection of a great cathedral. Stone by stone it rises, and through months and years I stand and watch each stone as it falls into place. I am burned on a cross head downward in the thyme-scented gardens of Nero, and I watch with amusement and scorn the torturers at work in the chambers of the Inquisition.

"I walk in the holiest sanctuaries; I enter the temples of Venus. I kneel in adoration before the Magna Mater, and I throw coins on the bare knees of the sacred courtezans who sit with veiled faces in the groves of Babylon. I creep into an Elizabethan theater and with the stinking rabble about me I applaud *The Merchant of Venice*. I walk with Dante through the narrow streets of Florence. I meet the young

Beatrice, and the hem of her garment brushes my sandals as I stare enraptured. I am a priest of Isis, and my magic astounds the nations. Simon Magus kneels before me, imploring my assistance, and Pharaoh trembles when I approach. In India I talk with the Masters and run screaming from their presence, for their revelations are as salt on wounds that bleed.

"I perceive everything *simultaneously*. I perceive everything from all sides; I am a part of all the teeming billions about me. I exist in all men and all men exist in me. I perceive the whole of human history in a single instant, the past and the present.

"By simply *straining* I can see farther and farther back. Now I am going back through strange curves and angles. Angles and curves multiply about me. I perceive great segments of time through *curves*. There is *curved time*, and *angular time*. The beings that exist in angular time cannot enter curved time. It is very strange.

"I am going back and back. Man has disappeared from the earth. Gigantic reptiles crouch beneath enormous palms and swim through the loathly black waters of dismal lakes. Now the reptiles have disappeared. No animals remain upon the land, but beneath the waters, plainly visible to me, dark forms move slowly over the rotting vegetation.

"The forms are becoming simpler and simpler. Now they are single cells. All about me there are angles—strange angles that have no counterparts on the earth. I am desperately afraid.

"There is an abyss of being which man has never fathomed."

I stared. Chalmers had risen to his feet and he was gesticulating helplessly with his arms. "I am passing through unearthly angles; I am approaching—oh, the burning horror of it."

"Chalmers!" I cried. "Do you wish me to interfere?"

He brought his right hand quickly before his face, as though to shut out a vision unspeakable. "Not yet!" he cried; "I will go on. I will see what—lies—beyond—"

A cold sweat streamed from his forehead and his shoulders jerked spasmodically. "Beyond life there are"—his face grew ashen with terror—"*things* that I cannot distinguish. They move slowly through angles. They have no bodies, and they move slowly through outrageous angles."

It was then that I became aware of the odor in the room. It was a pungent, indescribable odor, so nauseous that I could scarcely endure it. I stepped quickly to the window and threw it open. When I returned to Chalmers and looked into his eyes I nearly fainted.

"I think they have scented me!" he shrieked. "They are slowly turning toward me."

He was trembling horribly. For a moment he clawed at the air with his hands. Then his legs gave way beneath him and he fell forward on his face, slobbering and moaning.

I watched him in silence as he dragged himself across the floor. He was no longer a man. His teeth were bared and saliva dripped from the corners of his mouth.

"Chalmers," I cried. "Chalmers, stop it! Stop it, do you hear?"

As if in reply to my appeal he commenced to utter hoarse convulsive sounds which resembled nothing so much as the barking of a dog, and began a sort of hideous writhing in a circle about the room. I bent and seized him by the shoulders. Violently, desperately, I shook him. He turned his head and snapped at my wrist. I was sick with horror, but I dared not release him for fear that he would destroy himself in a paroxysm of rage.

"Chalmers," I muttered, "you must stop that. There is nothing in this room that can harm you. Do you understand?"

I continued to shake and admonish him, and gradually the madness died out of his face. Shivering convulsively, he crumpled into a grotesque heap on the Chinese rug.

I carried him to the sofa and deposited him upon it. His features were twisted in pain, and I knew that he was still struggling dumbly to escape from abominable memories.

"Whisky," he muttered. "You'll find a flask in the cabinet by the window—upper left-hand drawer."

When I handed him the flask his fingers tightened about it until the knuckles showed blue. "They nearly got me," he gasped. He drained the stimulant in immoderate gulps, and gradually the color crept back into his face.

"That drug was the very devil!" I murmured.

"It wasn't the drug," he moaned.

His eyes no longer glared insanely, but he still wore the look of a lost soul.

"They scented me in time," he moaned. "I went too far."

"What were *they* like?" I said, to humor him.

He leaned forward and gripped my arm. He was shivering horribly. "No words in our language can describe them!" He spoke in a hoarse whisper. "They are symbolized vaguely in the myth of the Fall, and in an obscene form which is occasionally found engraved on ancient tablets. The Greeks had a name for them, which veiled their essential foulness. The tree, the snake and the apple—these are the vague symbols of a most awful mystery."

His voice had risen to a scream. "Frank, Frank, a terrible and unspeakable *deed* was done in the beginning. Before time, the *deed*, and from the deed—"

He had risen and was hysterically pacing the room. "The seeds of the deed move through angles in dim recesses of time. They are hungry and athirst!"

"Chalmers," I pleaded to quiet him. "We are living in the third decade of the Twentieth Century."

"They are lean and athirst!" he shrieked. *"The Hounds of Tindalos!"*

"Chalmers, shall I phone for a physician?"

"A physician cannot help me now. They are horrors of the soul, and yet"—he hid his face in his hands and groaned—"they are real, Frank. I saw them for a ghastly moment. For a moment I stood on *the other side*. I stood on the pale gray shores beyond time and space. In an awful light that was not light, in a silence that shrieked, I saw *them*.

"All the evil in the universe was concentrated in their lean, hungry bodies. Or had they bodies? I saw them only for a moment; I cannot be certain. *But I heard them breathe.* Indescribably for a moment I felt their breath upon my face. They turned toward me and I fled screaming. In a single moment I fled screaming through time. I fled down quintillions of years.

"But they scented me. Men awake in them cosmic hungers. We have escaped, momentarily, from the foulness that rings them round. They thirst for that in us which is clean, which emerged from the deed without stain. There is a part of us which did not partake in the deed, and that they hate. But do not imagine that they are literally, prosaically evil. They are beyond good and evil as we know it. They are that which in the beginning fell away from cleanliness. Through the deed they became bodies of death, receptacles of all foulness. But they are not evil in *our* sense because in the spheres through which they move there is no thought, no morals, no right or wrong as we understand it. There is merely the pure and the foul. The foul expresses itself through angles; the pure through curves. Man, the pure part of him, is descended from a curve. Do not laugh. I mean that literally."

I rose and searched for my hat. "I'm dreadfully sorry for you, Chalmers," I said, as I walked toward the door. "But I don't intend to stay and listen to such gibberish. I'll send my physician to see you. He's an elderly, kindly chap and he won't be offended if you tell him to go to the devil. But I hope you'll respect his advice. A week's rest in a good sanitarium should benefit you immeasurably."

I heard him laughing as I descended the stairs, but his laughter was so utterly mirthless that it moved me to tears.

II.

When Chalmers phoned the following morning my first impulse was to hang up the receiver immediately. His request was so unusual and his voice was so wildly hysterical that I feared any further association with him would result in the impairment of my own sanity. But I could not doubt the genuineness of his misery, and when he broke down completely and I heard him sobbing over the wire I decided to comply with his request.

"Very well," I said. "I will come over immediately and bring the plaster."

En route to Chalmers' home I stopped at a hardware store and purchased twenty pounds of plaster of Paris. When I entered my friend's room he was crouching by the window watching the opposite wall out of eyes that were feverish with fright. When he saw me he rose and seized the parcel containing the plaster with an avidity that amazed and horrified me. He had extruded all of the furniture and the room presented a desolate appearance.

"It is just conceivable that we can thwart them!" he exclaimed, "But we must work rapidly. Frank, there is a stepladder in the hall. Bring it here immediately. And then fetch a pail of water."

"What for?" I murmured.

He turned sharply and there was a flush on his face. "To mix the plaster, you fool!" he cried. "To mix the plaster that will save our bodies and souls from a contamination unmentionable. To mix the plaster that will save the world from—Frank, they *must be kept out!*"

"Who?" I murmured.

"The Hounds of Tindalos!" he muttered. "They can only reach us through angles. We must eliminate all angles from this room. I shall plaster up all of the corners, all of the crevices. We must make this room resemble the interior of a sphere."

I knew that it would have been useless to argue with him. I fetched the stepladder, Chalmers mixed the plaster, and for three hours we labored. We filled in the four corners of the wall and the intersections of the floor and wall and the wall and ceiling, and we rounded the sharp angles of the window-seat.

"I shall remain in this room until they return in time," he affirmed when our task was completed. "When they discover that the scent leads through curves they will return. They will return ravenous and snarling and unsatisfied to the foulness that was in the beginning, before time, beyond space."

He nodded graciously and lit a cigarette. "It was good of you to help," he said.

"Will you not see a physician, Chalmers?" I pleaded.

"Perhaps—tomorrow," he murmured. "But now I must watch and wait."

"Wait for what?" I urged.

Chalmers smiled wanly. "I know that you think me insane," he said. "You have a shrewd but prosaic mind, and you cannot conceive of an entity that does not depend for its existence on force and matter. But did it ever occur to you, my friend, that force and matter are merely the barriers to perception imposed by time and space? When one knows, as I do, that time and space are identical and that they are both deceptive because they are merely imperfect manifestations of a higher reality, one no longer seeks in the visible world for an explanation of the mystery and terror of being."

I rose and walked toward the door.

"Forgive me," he cried. "I did not mean to offend you. You have a superlative intellect, but I—I have a *superhuman* one. It is only natural that I should be aware of your limitations."

"Phone if you need me," I said, and descended the stairs two steps at a time. "I'll send my physician over at once," I muttered, to myself. "He's a hopeless maniac, and heaven knows what will happen if someone doesn't take charge of him immediately."

III.

The following is a condensation of two announcements which appeared in the Partridgeville Gazette *for July 3, 1928:*

Earthquake Shakes Financial District

At 2 o'clock this morning an earth tremor of unusual severity broke several plate-glass windows in Central Square and completely disorganized the electric and street railway systems. The tremor was felt in the outlying districts and the steeple of the First Baptist Church on Angell Hill (designed by Christopher Wren in 1717) was entirely demolished. Firemen are now attempting to put out a blaze which threatens to destroy the Partridgeville Glue Works. An investigation is promised by the mayor and an immediate attempt will be made to fix responsibility for this disastrous occurrence.

OCCULT WRITER MURDERED BY UNKNOWN GUEST

————

Horrible Crime in Central Square

————

Mystery Surrounds Death of Halpin Chalmers

At 9 A.M. today the body of Halpin Chalmers, author and journalist, was found in an empty room above the jewelry store of Smithwick and Isaacs, 24 Central Square. The coroner's investigation revealed that the room had been rented furnished to Mr. Chalmers on May 1, and that he had himself disposed of the furniture a fortnight ago. Chalmers was the author of several recondite books on occult themes, and a member of the Bibliographic Guild. He formerly resided in Brooklyn, New York.

At 7 A.M. Mr. L. E. Hancock, who occupies the apartment opposite Chalmers' room in the Smithwick and Isaacs establishment, smelt a peculiar odor when he opened his door to take in his cat and the morning edition of the *Partridgeville Gazette*. The odor he describes as extremely acrid and nauseous, and he affirms that it was so strong in the vicinity of Chalmers' room that he was obliged to hold his nose when he approached that section of the hall.

He was about to return to his own apartment when it occurred to him that Chalmers might have accidentally forgotten to turn off the gas in his kitchenette. Becoming considerably alarmed at the thought, he decided to investigate, and when repeated tappings on Chalmers' door brought no response he notified the superintendent. The latter opened the door by means of a pass key, and the two men quickly made their way into Chalmers' room. The room was utterly destitute of furniture, and Hancock asserts that when he first glanced at the floor his heart went cold within him, and that the superintendent, without saying a word, walked to the open window and stared at the building opposite for fully five minutes.

Chalmers lay stretched upon his back in the center of the room. He was starkly nude, and his chest and arms were covered with a peculiar bluish pus or ichor. His head lay grotesquely upon his chest. It had been completely severed from his body, and the features were twisted and torn and horribly mangled. Nowhere was there a trace of blood.

The room presented a most astonishing appearance. The intersections of the walls, ceiling and floor had been thickly smeared with plaster of Paris, but at intervals fragments had cracked and fallen off, and someone had grouped these upon the floor about the murdered man so as to form a perfect triangle.

Beside the body were several sheets of charred yellow paper. These bore fantastic geometric designs and symbols and several hastily scrawled sentences. The sentences were almost illegible and so absurd in content that they furnished no possible clue to the perpetrator of the crime. "I am waiting and watching," Chalmers wrote. "I sit by the window and watch walls and ceiling. I do not believe they can reach me, but I must beware of the Doels. Perhaps *they* can help them break through. The satyrs will help, and they can advance through the scarlet circles. The Greeks knew a way of preventing that. It is a great pity that we have forgotten so much."

On another sheet of paper, the most badly charred of the seven or eight fragments found by Detective Sergeant Douglas (of the Partridgeville Reserve), was scrawled the following:

"Good God, the plaster is falling! A terrific shock has loosened the plaster and it is falling. An earthquake perhaps! I never could have anticipated this. It is growing dark in the room. I must phone Frank. But can he get here in time? I will try. I will recite the Einstein formula. I will—God, they are breaking through! They are breaking through! Smoke is pouring from the corners of the wall. Their tongues—ahhhhh—"

In the opinion of Detective Sergeant Douglas, Chalmers was poisoned by some obscure chemical. He has sent specimens of the strange blue slime found on Chalmers' body to the Partridgeville Chemical Laboratories; and he expects the report will shed new light on one of the most mysterious crimes of recent years. That Chalmers entertained a guest on the evening preceding the earthquake is certain, for his neighbor distinctly heard a low murmur of conversation in the former's room as he passed it on his way to the stairs. Suspicion points strongly to this unknown visitor and the police are diligently endeavoring to discover his identity.

IV.

Report of James Morton, chemist and bacteriologist:

My dear Mr. Douglas:

The fluid sent to me for analysis is the most peculiar that I have ever examined. It resembles living protoplasm, but it lacks the peculiar substances known as enzymes. Enzymes catalyze the chemical reactions occurring in living cells, and when the cell dies they cause it to disintegrate by hydrolyzation. Without enzymes protoplasm should possess enduring vitality, i.e., immortality. Enzymes are the negative components, so to speak, of unicellular organism, which is the basis of all life. That living matter can exist without enzymes biologists emphatically deny. And yet the substance that you have sent me is alive and it lacks these "indispensable" bodies. Good God, sir, do you realize what astounding new vistas this opens up?

V.

Excerpt from The Secret Watchers *by the late Halpin Chalmers:*

What if, parallel to the life we know, there is another life that does not die, which lacks the elements that destroy our life? Perhaps in another dimension there is a *different* force from that which generates our life. Perhaps this force emits energy, or something similar to energy, which passes from the unknown dimension where *it* is and creates a new form of cell life in our dimension. No one knows that such new cell life does exist in our dimension. Ah, but I have seen *its* manifestations. I have *talked* with them. In my room at night I have talked with the Doels. And in dreams I have seen their maker. I have stood on the dim shore beyond time and matter and seen *it*. *It* moves through strange curves and outrageous angles. Some day I shall travel in time and meet *it* face to face.

The Letters of Halpin Chalmers

Peter Cannon

Peter Cannon's present tale is premised upon the fact that even the farthest pond-ripples of the "Lovecraft event" (as we might pretentiously dub it) are no less stranger than fiction than the exploits of the original Lovecraft Circle. In this story, as in his sequence of tongue-in-cheek sequels to "The Thing on the Doorstep" (collected in Cannon's *Forever Azathoth,* Tartarus Press, 1999), Cannon spins out the only barely parodic allegories of the idiosyncrasies and idiocies of the latter-day Lovecraftians, the fortuitous alliance of survivors of the original Lovecraft Circle and their admirers, biographers, and fans who basked in the former's waning light. "The Letters of Halpin Chalmers," as will be obvious to many readers, reproduces with excruciating accuracy the professional, domestic, and marital circumstances of Frank Belknap Long (here assimilated to Frank Carstairs, narrator of "The Hounds of Tindalos") in his declining years as reported in Cannon's nonfiction (but, again, stranger than fiction) memoir *Long Memories.* Ida Carstairs is Lyda Long, though, believe me, only half as maniacal. Halpin Chalmers, doomed star of "The Hounds of Tindalos," is here made to correspond to H. P. Lovecraft. Thus Cannon is retroactively making "The Hounds of Tindalos" an imaginary episode in the friendship of Long and Lovecraft, just as Long himself intended in "The Space-Eaters."

"The Letters of Halpin Chalmers" made its first appearance in *100 Crooked Little Crime Stories,* edited by Stefan Dziemianowicz, Robert Weinberg, and Martin H. Greenberg (Barnes & Noble, 1995), an anthology it hardly fits. I'll bet the editors just liked it so much anyway that they couldn't pass it up!

"I'm glad you've come," said Ida Carstairs. She was sitting by the window beneath the pagoda-shaped bird cage, her face nuzzled by Max, her pet conure. Little had changed in the three years since I had last stopped in, to pick them up for the drive to the Halpin Chalmers centennial conference. About the cluttered living room, displayed on walls or tables, were the dusty souvenirs and tattered testimonials I had come to know over countless visits, the tokens of a long career that had brought its share of recognition but limited financial gain. If anything the place looked tidier and neater than in the past, thanks to the current services of a series of home attendants—and of course emptier. When earlier in the month I had seen the obituary in the *Partridgeville Gazette*, I had decided that it was time to put aside our differences, that I should pay my respects to the widow.

And then there were the letters, the letters of Halpin Chalmers to his best friend, Fred Carstairs, to whom he wrote almost daily during his prolific Brooklyn period. Having recently received the contract for the first critical biography (provisionally titled *Secret Watcher: The Life and Strange Death of Halpin Chalmers*), I was determined at long last to lay my hands on these priceless epistles from the pen of America's foremost author of the occult.

"I knew you'd come, Peter," said Ida Carstairs. "Please sit down." She gestured at Fred's old wheelchair.

For a woman in her late eighties Ida was in remarkably good shape, as strong in body as her husband had been frail. With no sign of strain she rose and lifted Max off her shoulder and into his cage.

"Fred's last months were very difficult," she said. "After he got out of the hospital he wouldn't let anyone touch him. And his language! Such words I had never heard out of his mouth before. He was no longer my sweet little Fredela."

I had known that Fred had been hospitalized, that for a time he had even been placed in the "psycho ward."

"His pain wasn't just physical, Peter. 'Why doesn't anyone come see me?' he'd cry. 'I'm so lonely.'"

Why indeed? Why didn't the fans—and certainly Fred had his own followers, apart from those who cared only about his connection with his more illustrious friend—line up at his bedside to comfort him in his final days? Partridgeville may be off the beaten track, but I believed it when she said no one came. The sad truth is they stayed away, we all stayed away, because of her.

"He was so unworldly, my beloved," she said, mercifully not mentioning my own neglect of Fred, "like Prince Myshkin in Dostoyevsky's *The Idiot*."

As fond as she genuinely was of her late husband, in my experience she could never stand him getting all the attention, even if that attention was motivated out of a regard more for the occult tales of Halpin Chalmers than for the occult tales of Fred Carstairs. I alone of the Chalmersians recognized that the key to Fred lay through Ida. I alone knew of the existence of the Chalmers letters secreted in a musty old trunk I had managed to inspect in Fred's bedroom while pretending to go to the bathroom during one of my earlier visits. So over the years I listened for hours to her wild and fantastic stories of her glamorous youth on the stage and to her grandiose dreams of future travels and triumphs, if only to gain a few minutes with Fred—who might if I was lucky drop a fresh precious nugget or two concerning Halpin Chalmers all those decades ago.

But I could take only so much. My patience ran out in 1991, the year of the Chalmers centennial. I had written Ida a letter politely suggesting that she stay home while I drove Fred to Brooklyn to be the guest of honor at the 100th-birthday celebration weekend. But she didn't take the hint. She had insisted on going too—with her parrot. Those who attended need not be reminded how her antics (and those of her bird) on more than one occasion disrupted the proceedings. She defied me. She had to pay the price. As a consequence I ceased my visits to Fred. I refused to return her phone calls.

"You know, Peter, Fred and I were not all that well matched. My friends, people in the theatre, wondered what I saw in him. He was so shy. At parties he hardly said anything."

As a matter of fact, he hadn't said a whole lot at the centenary either, apart from parroting the same tired anecdotes about Chalmers he'd been repeating for more than sixty years, ever since his fellow author's premature death in 1928. His semi-senile performance there should have been Fred's last bow. No one had expected the venerable occultist to reach his own century or beyond. (While the obituary had reported he died at 100, he was really 101, having shaved a year off his age at some point in his career. To one correspondent Chalmers clearly states that his boyhood pal was born in 1893, not 1894.) But he astonished everyone by surviving another three years. In the meantime, I concentrated on producing shorter critical works for *Chalmers Studies* and other learned journals, knowing that sooner or later I would get my chance at the letters in Fred Carstairs' trunk.

The Chalmers letters to Carstairs! What a trove! A few teasing extracts, a mere fraction of the total, had been published in the *Collected Letters of Halpin Chalmers*. Literally hundreds of virgin pages had yet to meet the feasting eyes of the Chalmers scholar. Why hadn't their recipient sold them? In his declining years, before he fell and couldn't leave their Central Square apartment, Fred had consigned other items in his occult collection to a local second-hand bookdealer, including his copy of *The Secret Watcher*, inscribed by Chalmers himself. I know; I was the one who had picked up this treasure at a price so enviable I forbear from citing the figure. Had he tried to sell off the letters, whether piecemeal or as a lot, my informant, the proprietor of the Angell Hill Bookshop, would have alerted me immediately.

As much as he could have used the money, did Fred deliberately keep the Chalmers letters to himself out of spite? Whenever I hinted at their existence, he pretended not to understand. In face of such coyness I decided early on not to push the matter, instead to adopt a waiting policy, hoping to gain his confidence and eventually the prize that would secure my own name as the world's leading authority on Halpin Chalmers.

"Nobody knew he was a writer. He certainly didn't dress like one. Let me tell you, Peter, before he broke his hip he used to go out in that shabby coat of his and do the shopping. When he sat down to rest, strangers would put a dollar in his hand, thinking he was a homeless person! Can you imagine, Fred Carstairs, the great occult author, mistaken for a homeless person!"

If it can be said that Chalmers died before his time, then Carstairs lived beyond his time—long after his time. At his death Chalmers was at the peak of his powers. His posthumously published work established his reputation as the supreme practitioner of the genre. His heirs are rich today from the royalties generated by the millions of copies of his books still in print. On the other hand, Carstairs in his prime never achieved more than a workmanlike competence. In his old age he was honored more for his longevity than for any lasting contributions to the field. During the occult resurgence of the late 1960s and 1970s he enjoyed a revival of sorts, but by the 1980s and early 1990s he could expect only the rare anthology appearance, or possibly a foreign rights sale, to supplement the monthly social security checks that supported him and his wife and their bird in their golden years.

To be fair to Fred, he could be perfectly candid about his own lack of genius relative to his best friend's. One has only to read that sketchy, rambling, error-riddled, if often charming memoir of his, written in his dotage, *Halpin Chalmers: Voyager of Other and Many Dimensions*, to appreciate the man's modesty. And yet, and yet, there must have been times when he deeply resented his old chum—when the interviewers, their indifference to Fred Carstairs only too evident, asked him just one question too many about Halpin Chalmers.

"He lived in this dump of a town all his life and they completely ignored him. But Fred's big-shot celebrity-author friend, that turd, they named for him that fancy housing development in Mulligan Wood!"

Both writers had grown up in Partridgeville, but Chalmers had left that provincial New England city and settled in Brooklyn to compose the masterpieces on which his fame rests today. As for Carstairs, he had remained in Partridgeville, where nothing newsworthy had occurred since the death of Halpin Chalmers, brutally and mysteriously murdered at age thirty-seven during a short homecoming sojourn. Fred, in fact, had been the last person to see him alive, though he had apparently been no more illuminating when questioned by the police at the time than in 1976 when I first queried him on the subject. (To another correspondent Chalmers records his frustration over his friend's tendency to mix things up—a tendency that did not improve with age.) This was soon after I moved to Partridgeville, where I had been quite fortunate to find a one-bedroom condo in the then newly erected Halpin Chalmers Estates.

"Occult writers, bah! Such people—no class, no culture," Ida continued. "But what did I know? It was only a month after we met that we decided to elope."

Fred and Ida had married late in life, after a brief courtship in New York, he for the first time, she for the fourth or fifth (she was always vague about how many husbands she'd had). Fred had brought his bride back to Partridgeville, a place that she grew to despise and that she loved to abuse almost as much as occult writers. But I had heard the story of their tragicomic marriage a thousand times before. I couldn't care less, especially now. All that mattered was obtaining the letters. At the next pause in the monologue I excused myself and headed down the hall.

Proceeding past the bathroom door I entered Fred's dank, curtained bedroom, hoping to find it unchanged since my last snooping expedition. It was in one essential: the ancient trunk still rested at the foot of the bed. While feigning to listen to Ida, I had conceived a plan—to remove the letters a bundle at a time, to slip them into my jacket or the bookbag I habitually carried. In the coming weeks and months I would visit Ida regularly. I was forgiven; we were, after all, friends again. I wished I had thought of this expedient long before, and wondered at my past scruples. But time had not seemed of the essence, until I received permission from the Chalmers estate for the biography—which would be a lesser thing without ample quotations from the Chalmers letters to Carstairs. I didn't want to disappoint the heirs.

From the living room I could hear Ida conferring heatedly, in French, with the Haitian home attendant. The moment had come to act. As before, no lock secured the rusty clasp of the trunk. My heart in my mouth, I raised the lid. There was the same stale, musty odor I remembered, though somewhat less pungent than previously. I could dimly see—I could see nothing! Or rather, almost nothing. On the bottom lay a few scattered sheets. I seized an envelope, and as I peered closely at the familiar handwritten scrawl, behind me I heard a squawk.

I turned and saw Ida in the doorway, her pet parrot on her shoulder.

"We knew you wanted those letters, Peter. Fred and I often talked about it. It was so obvious. My little 'idiot' said he was going to reward you for your kindness by leaving you the letters after he died. It was to be a surprise. But then, for no good reason, after that horrible trip to Brooklyn, you stopped coming. Then Fredela got ill and I tried to call you and you still wouldn't come. You, the most faithful and loyal of all the Chal*merde*sians!"

I made no apologies. All I could do was stammer something about the letters and their value.

"Oh, yes, I knew we could sell for a pretty penny such dreck. Fools! But at our age, what did we need for cash? Because Fred was a fighter he protested at first when I said I had a better use for them. From his wheelchair, though, he couldn't really go against my will. In the end he went along."

I followed her back into the living room, hoping against hope that she had simply removed the letters of Halpin Chalmers to elsewhere in the apartment.

"The supply has nearly run out, so I'll have to go back to using old newspapers." She placed the conure inside the pagoda-shaped cage and shut the door "There, I bet you didn't realize Max was also a critic!"

The Death of Halpin Chalmers

Perry M. Grayson

It is sad but true that most weird fiction aficionados appreciate Frank Belknap Long mainly as an adjunct to his more famous friend H. P. Lovecraft. Such is the premise of T. E. D. Klein's wonderful story "Black Man with a Horn." Perry Grayson is an exception. An admirer of Long for his own sake, Grayson has dug up forgotten tales of Long and brought them back to light in the small press. He was one of the faithful few gathered with us in Woodlawn Cemetery in 1994 when I delivered the eulogy for his literary idol. As Robert Bloch said he would have crawled on his hands and knees to Lovecraft's bedside had he known he was ailing, Grayson did fly out from his native California to get to Brooklyn on that cold November day.

Grayson has made explicit in his title the debt owed in Long's "The Hounds of Tindalos" to Ambrose Bierce's "The Death of Halpin Frayser." Grayson's story is in turn indebted to Peter Cannon's "The Letters of Halpin Chalmers." Grayson's serves as something of a sequel to Cannon's and maintains a good measure of the latter's wry humor, though the implied horrors are quite effective, too. Cannon himself appears here as a character, one "Peter Hughes," the erstwhile narrator of "The Letters of Halpin Chalmers." The story first appeared in volume 3, number 1 (October–November 1996) issue of *Yawning Vortex*. (All right, perhaps the word "yawning" ought not appear in the title of a fiction magazine.)

"The oldest and strongest emotion of mankind is sarcasm, and the oldest and strongest form of cynicism is sardonic terror of the commonplace."
—Timmeus Gaylord, *Sardonic Terror in Literature* (1926)

An incident regarding a man dead for half a century occurred while I was working on a newspaper article. Before February 1994 I'd never even heard the name Halpin Chalmers. When I'd been given a position with the *Partridgeville Gazette*, I was just a young writer struggling to make a living. I couldn't gripe about the stories I'd been sent out to cover, because no matter how oddball they were it put food in my belly and checks in the landlady's hands. Plus, I believe no one could possibly experience such a singular event slugging it out working at some fast food joint.

But certainly Halpin Chalmers, the occult author of *The Secret Watchers*, was much more than the sort of thing I'd spied pot-smoking pizza delivery boys rambling about. There *was* something in common between those two different types of people. I'd come across the word *narcotics* in a quote from the police officer who spoke to the press about Halpin Chalmers' 1928 death on microfilm in the *New York Herald Tribune* while visiting Miskatonic University by bus on my latest assignment.

The drug was called Liao, and pellets of this substance—similar to nuggets of hash—had been the only thing found aside from the body of Chalmers in a room above Smithwick & Isaac's Jewelry Store. I'd never heard of Liao. I'd assumed it was a rarity piped over the Pacific from China and shuttled across the U.S. by illegal aliens scrambling through Chinatowns in various major cities across middle America. But to me, at first, Halpin Chalmers seemed no different a quack than Aleister Crowley, professing to behold visions of some supreme evil force at the center of the universe while smoking opiates through the snaking tubes of a hookah.

"Funny," I thought to myself, "how they like to imitate the hashish-eaters. They're ancient history and they professed to see not only the future, but through all layers of time and dimension—at once!"

Upon returning to Partridgeville, I decided it was time to check with the police about their records on the subject and ask some questions about *other things*. The station lies on the backside of Angell Hill, and the building hasn't changed in the days since Halpin Chalmers and his friend Fred Carstairs once prowled the same streets in front of Smithwick & Isaac's. I passed the old pharmacy on the corner. In the 1920s and '30s, I'm told it used to be called Korie's "Candy Store" instead of "Pharmacy." The whole idea of Halpin Chalmers' death brought to mind the weird stories that I know filled the pulp magazines on those old candy store racks, with titles like *Strange Tales*, *Thrilling Mystery*, and *Horror Stories*—and suspicious author names on the covers, such as *Justin Case*, *Hugh Speer* and *Peter Held!*

In the bustling stationhouse I walked over the slippery, faded yellow linoleum toward the reception desk.

"Mitch Sonners here to see Sergeant Scholl in narcotics," I told the blue-haired lady whose long acrylic nails were pounding away at a battered computer keyboard. I assumed the thing was once white, but it had taken on a sickly yellow tinge. If it'd been human, you'd think it had Hepatitis-C. The secretary finished squawking into a phone resting in the crook of her neck.

"Oh," harped the old lady, as she brought her pink-tinted bifocals to rest lower on her nose. She craned her neck up from the phone, though her rapid typography continued. "Go right in." One hand continued to type, the other pointed to the swinging partition across from the desk. "He's expectin' ya, sweetie."

She buzzed a switch under the desk and I crossed through into the inner workings of the Partridgeville Police Department.

"Halpin Chalmers . . . Halpin Chalmers . . ." The man in the black uniform flipped his gray head to the side and whispered half to himself.

"That's right, Sergeant, Chalmers was the man's name," I said with a stiff lip.

"Hmm . . . Now let me remember." Scholl pinched the bridge of his nose between his forefinger and thumb and stepped over to a gigantic metal file cabinet taking up the entire wall opposite the Narcotics office.

"Ancient history, isn't it?"

"Uh, yeah. Chalmers, huh? Your boy's Halpin F. Chalmers, one of the strangest cases ever in these parts," answered Scholl, throwing down a legal-sized file folder on his desk. The label was typed in faded pica characters on the flimsy manila folder, which was once canary yellow but now looked like the beige color brush which lined the hills on the sides of the dry Miskatonic River.

"Well—" I began, "is there anything you can tell me that I don't already know from the old *Gazette* article and oh bee? And what about . . ."

"Look, Sonners," the Sergeant fumed, "you've got to keep a lid on this. This case was thrown in here like a mess over fifty years ago. We're talkin' cold case files here. *Dead* cold. We're talkin' Black Dahlia or Jack the Ripper here. Only much weirder. What d'ya want me to do, manufacture an answer out of my ass?"

"But . . . but you're the only ones who could possibly know for sure—"

"Sonners, that old man Chalmers was a kook, a certifiable loon not far above Satan worshipers and religious zealots."

"Why would you say that?"

"Because his book, *The Secret Watchers*, was banned back in the Forties in every library from here to Auburn, California. They added this little update to the file." Scholl slapped a grid-marked piece of paper in front of him.

"You're right. All *but* Miskatonic University."

Scholl paused and ran a wide hand through his gray flat top, shaking his head slightly.

"And about that drug?"

"I've been around here for years, Sonners, but I ain't the one who first took this case, nor would I expect anyone to know much about the whole mess. Chalmers' body was found with some kind of bluish slime all over it. It was like a blue elephant used him for a snot rag. But the coroner did an autopsy"—he kept looking at the old report—"and didn't find much wrong with the cadaver—for most all respects Halpin Chalmers should've been able to walk up from that room and live just like you or I. It was as if everything in his body just stopped dead in its tracks, with no apparent cause. Probably over—"

"Probably related to his drug habit, right?"

"Yeah, that's what they said then—and what I'm telling you now, Sonners. Halpin Chalmers was an old coot who smoked too much out of a bong. He probably got a taste for smack and startin' havin' a real party in his head. Says here the guy plastered up all the goddamn corners in that room he rented above Smithwick and Isaac's, like some kinda paranoid schizophrenic lost in a world of his own.

"They all say it, ya know: 'They're coming to get me. They're coming to get you.' Ya know the deal?"

"And what about Liao—the drug?"

"Well, that's another story. The forensics found only traces of an unknown substance in this guy's bloodstream, and it can't be proven that the substance is the same as in those pellets they found—nor if they're actually what Chinamen call Liao. It's a mythical drug—and if it were really here, then we'd have a hell of a lot of more nut cases to attend to than just these high school kids parading around on crystal meth. Next thing you're gonna tell me there's a craze among queers for shoving Liao suppositories up their asses."

"So what you're saying, Sergeant, is that you can't—"

"Nope. Sorry, kid, this ain't gonna be much, but I really can't help you. The case was never officially closed. The coroner couldn't find a cause of death, and this here file's been sitting here away from the public eye for a while. If you want you can have xeroxes of the whole thing, but it ain't going to tell you much more than I've already said or that your boys at the *Gazette* already knew back in the Thirties, right after Chalmers kicked the bucket. They did a lot of prowling then for a coupla years . . ."

"And I'll do a lot of prowling now, thanks."

"Oh, and Sonners . . . You might wanna track down Fred Carstairs. *If he's still alive*. Says here he never did really talk about the whole thing, even though he was the last person to see Chalmers. He clammed up for years, and the account he did write was fragmentary at best. The inspectors back then *knew* he was holdin' something back—that he wasn't givin' 'em the whole picture.

"*Good luck* finding out any more from him than we already have—he might've left Partridgeville a long time ago. There isn't a peep on him in these reports after the Thirties."

"Okay, Sarge . . ."

He ushered me out into the hall and had me wait at the reception area, while he had a secretary fiddle with the copy machine in the corner. They handed me a sheaf of flimsy papers, smudged because the copier couldn't really make clarity out of the faded type and pulpy paper from a bygone era. Just as I turned to leave two officers came waltzing in dragging a disheveled man with greasy salt and pepper hair and chalky, pale skin in a straitjacket. The man couldn't even stand on his own. The two policemen handled the oil-stained guy with latex gloves, as if he carried the plague. Maybe, I thought, they'd dosed him full of Thorazine.

"Another one for the pen," called one of the officers. "Had to stun him. He was beginning to get violent."

I was heading out the door just as I heard the last bit from the second man in uniform, "May have to call Miskatonic State on this one—he's buck nutty."

I was beginning to feel swamped with all the work the *Gazette* was throwing me, so stopping to ask questions was out of the question. Instead, I decided to return to my apartment and go over what portions of the Chalmers file had been given to me. Somehow I knew another reporter from the *Gazette* would get the scoop on the aggravated, mentally disturbed man who'd been downed with a stun gun.

"Cause of death," I read aloud to myself, "poison. Substance unknown."

The papers were flecked with gray blots and I rustled through them to find a letter and report from James Morton, chemist and bacteriologist for the Partridgeville Chemical Laboratories, to Deputy Sergeant Douglas, then of the Partridgeville Sheriffs. Apparently the blue slime Chalmers was covered with had contained living matter, *cells* which *didn't* contain the 'bodies' known as enzymes.

"But then," I ran my thumb over the stubble on my chin and leaned back on the couch, "most animals secrete enzymes in order to digest or ingest their food—like flies. *Flies?"*

It was like remembering some kind of thing I'd filed away in my head as a kid in elementary school science class: flies throw up on their food in order to ingest it. So, was Chalmers somehow being prepared to be *eaten?* I started to think just how absurd I was becoming just thinking of something so preposterous.

In the morning, back at the *Gazette* office, I spoke with the Book Review editor, Joshua Saint, about what Sergeant Scholl had told me the day before.

"Josh, the Sarge said that there was a chance this occult writer Halpin Chalmers—who I'm doing the article on—had a friend who's still alive today. Granted he might be dead, but if there's a chance that he's out there, I'll *need* to see him. Can you track something down for me on a guy named Fred Carstairs?"

"Sure, Mitch," he nodded. "I should be able to find something out. See ya in a few minutes."

I gave Josh a slap on the back and returned to my little cubicle outside in the main office. I used the time to pore over the photocopied reports again.

"Hey Mitch, found something," came the call from the other room.

"What?" I came running.

"Frederick Carstairs Junior was an occult author, friend and correspondent of Halpin Chalmers, according to the reference book *Modern Scribblers*. He was nicknamed Frank by your boy Chalmers because of his blunt honesty. Carstairs lived in Partridgeville for most of his life, save for a brief few visits to New York. According to this he was born in 1903 and lives on the edge of Mulligan Wood. In other words in the sticks."

"Really? Does it mention anything about his still being *with us*, I mean with the living?"

"No, Mitch—the book's several years old, so you'll have to find that one out by yourself. But it does say that in 1975 he wrote a critical biography of his friend called *Secret Watcher: The Life and Death of Halpin Chalmers*. And his agent is listed as one Peter Hughes, whose address is given as being in New York. Perhaps you might—"

"Look him up?" I asked. "Sure thing."

"It does give a phone number, but again, this is a coupla years old. The publisher of the book, Bloomnote Press, went under about two and a half years back."

"Thanks, Josh. You're a lifesaver," I remarked as I ran out of the building in search of a pay phone.

The booth was marked up with curious graffiti. One pocket knife carving depicted a giant octopus chomping up a tiny stick figure with the words "Yummy humans!!" beneath it.

I dialed the number while chuckling at the little cartoon under my breath.

"Yes," came the voice from the dry throat on the other end.

"Mister Hughes? Peter Hughes?"

"Yes . . ."

"Peter, my name is Mitch Sonners, I'm with the *Partridgeville Gazette*. I'm doing an article on—"

"It wouldn't be about Halpin Chalmers, would it?"

"How did you know?"

"Premonition, you might say. Now, what was it you wanted to ask me?"

"Well, I was told that a Mister Fred Carstairs was Chalmers' best friend and that he might be able to provide some reminiscences and information on his friend for my piece in the *Gazette*."

"I'm afraid that'd be quite impossible. You see, Fred's been dead now for two years."

"That's too bad," I said. "Did he have any relatives, anyone who maybe knew something about Chalmers?"

"Well, I'm afraid that Ida—that's Fred's wife—died about a year after he passed away. That was a year ago, by the way, and since then no one's come forward with anything. Except me. I'm always interested in *Chalmersian* scholarship. In fact, I regularly contribute to *Chalmers Studies*—that's a journal published by Secret Watcher Press in Arkham."

"Carstairs' entry in *Modern Scribblers* said you were his agent . . ."

"Not really *agent*, Mister Sonners. I sold a few things for Fred in his later years when he could no longer really do much work. Maybe a total of four in all, mostly articles rehashing the same old recollections of Halpin Chalmers that he'd made thirty or forty years ago."

"Well, would you mind giving me just a little info?"

"As I said, I'm always interested in Chalmersian studies. You say you're with the *Partridgeville Gazette*? Well, I have to come up there anyway, now that Fred's family monument is to be engraved with his name, so perhaps we could meet later this afternoon."

"Yeah, by all means. I'll give you my address—"

Peter Hughes in person was a man of medium height and middle age, with a receding brown hairline, and crooked teeth. He wore weathered gray corduroy pants and a yellow shirt with a crooked navy blue tie. I led him to the couch and offered him some coffee, and we settled down for a few hours of talk.

"Well, you see, Ida Carstairs was a very artistic—but not entirely sane— woman. You might say that she and Frank, I mean Fred—Halpin used to call him the former because he loathed Fred's taste in realistic literature—was somehow so understanding of her grandiose thoughts of the opera and the stage. But she *hated* people who were interested in Fred solely for his association with Halpin. She used to call them *Chalmerdesians* or degenerates. And she even called Fred her little *idiot* sometimes. You know, like in Dostoyevsky?"

"Really? Sounds pretty sad."

"Yeah, and she actually used, little by little, as time went along, Halpin's letters to Fred to paper the cage of her pet bird! Can you believe it? The most incredible discovery in all of occult author studies and she let her parrot turd on them! It would've meant incredible things to me and the other Chalmers scholars.

"So there you have it, Sonners. It's literally a load of crap. I know really no more than you do. Perhaps a little *more*, as I've read Halpin's *The Secret Watchers* and also Fred's memoir of Ech Cee, as we scholars like to call him."

"There's really no more you can tell me? What about drugs? Did Fred take them, or did he know exactly what Halpin Chalmers was popping?"

"Fred never touched narcotics in his life. An old friend told him he was 'too sensitive an individual' to smoke dope. People thought he did because of what he wrote, but the only thing he ever did was smoke a pipe—tobacco—and drink a lot of Chianti at dinner.

"And I really can't say just what Ech Cee did, because I wasn't there; I never knew him. He died back in 1928, remember."

"Yes, I have the obituary copied from the *Gazette* microfilm."

"Believe it or not, I actually have Fred's personal copy of *The Secret Watchers*, which was inscribed to him by Ech Cee himself. But, pardon me, you're not a collector."

"Perhaps I should be, if it'd help with my article . . ."

"Mister Sonners, it's getting late now, and I really have to get to my hotel room and prepare for the morning trip to the cemetery in Mulligan Wood."

And with that Hughes left behind his drained coffee cup and sauntered off to his car to find a place for the night.

I took the opportunity to visit the Angell Hill Bookshop that afternoon, even though I doubted I'd find precisely what I was looking for. I pawed through bookcases riddled with just as many dust bunnies as paperback books. Most were old, worn, and tattered with yellow, waterlogged and dog-eared pages. The asking price for most was far beyond what I felt someone would pay for such inconsequential and undesirable books. Which is why they'd been sitting there for so long without a buyer. I must've prowled through the place about three times over when I came upon the revelation which caused my pulse to virtually double and the sweat to bead on my forehead. There, amongst the dust-jacketless book club editions of numerous 1970s new wave science fiction novels, was a misplaced copy of *The Secret Watchers* by Halpin Chalmers. My hands automatically rushed to open to the first leaf. $7.50 seems to be the going rate at which books are sold when a dealer has no clue as to what their true value is. So, with a rapid heartbeat and shaky step, I hastily rushed to the counter and paid cash for the black-bound volume that was still in very good shape for its age. I might add it was *the only* copy in the entire store, which I thought of as odd, since Partridgeville was the birthplace of Halpin Chalmers.

While I was putting a ten dollar bill in front of the proprietor, he scrutinized my face, no doubt saying to himself, "What kind of sicko reads this sort of trash? Why, it ought to be banned!" But he couldn't argue with money going into his pocket.

He dug through his beaten register for change. "Oh crap! I'm all out of ones, and I don't even have any silver . . ."

"That's quite all right," I said, trying not to betray the fact that the book could be sold in fine condition for four figures. "Keep the change. Much obliged!"

The book dealer didn't even bob his head in response. I walked out, hearing the lonely chime of the rusty bell hooked to the wooden door.

I took the short distance up Angell Hill to my apartment on Doty Avenue by foot. The afternoon was beginning to dim as I put my key in the lock. Once inside I threw my wallet and keys on the dinner table and unrolled the sofa bed. I brushed the crumbs off the sheets and propped my weary head up on a pillow. Extracting *The Secret Watchers* from the plastic trash bag, I started first by running my fingers over the phosphorescent gold lettering on the spine and boards. I knew this wasn't a cheap book. With the volume open in my hands, I wiped lines of dust from the first leaves and began reading the preface, written by Fred Carstairs.

It seemed to me that no one must've remembered that the foreword to the book was by Carstairs, as if they just blotted him from memory. A short time after I began Section One I must've dozed off. The book fell to rest at my covered knees, my glasses still dangling off my nose.

I awoke around dawn, about 5 A.M. in these parts, feeling as hot as though I'd been left out in the Sahara under the torturous red face of the sun. I hurled the covers off, sending the book clattering to the floor. It snapped closed, resting flat on the threadbare carpet. I had a cold shower while trying to recall just what it was I'd dreamed. It was all so opaque, the dream being lit by dark purples and deep murky blues, until finally all went into blackness. And of course there was that cascade of brilliant flashes, as if I was being bombarded by the explosive force of three white-hot stars revolving around each other. The vague notion struck me as the jets of water hit me. In the dream I'd imagined myself able to at once experience the past, present, and future all as if they were happening at the same moment.

"But that couldn't possibly be," I thought. "It must just be another one of those quirky things Chalmers wrote about."

Breakfasting on a donut, some coffee, and a slice of cheese, I poked diffidently at the morning *Gazette*. It told of an inmate's escape from Miskatonic State Mental Facility's ITU—in other words the violent ward. I only read a fourth of the article before dumping a few things into my briefcase and heading for the door. My curiosity was somewhat piqued by the mention of a break-in at the hardware store on Angell Hill. It said that the only things stolen were two trowels and a couple of plaster canisters.

After reading the few pages of the book that I had, I resolved to pay a visit to Peter Hughes, who I knew I'd find in Mansfield Point Cemetery on the edge of Mulligan Wood. He said he'd be attending to the formalities around having Carstairs' name engraved on the family obelisk—and that he even had Ida Carstairs' ashes to distribute atop Fred's grave.

"Fred was so poor at the time of his death," Hughes had said, "that he was buried in the most thrifty of coffins. Somewhere I've got a picture of me standing beside it. They brought the convicts out from Phillips Island to dig the grave at the height of a storm."

I drove my dented shit-brown Ford Mustang out to the edge of Mulligan Wood, where the road starts to wind and is littered with potholes and caked with dust. I didn't expect to find anyone in the guard shack when I drove up, but a withered, gray-haired man in a plaid flannel shirt greeted me.

"Hiya, sir. Anything I can do?"

"I'm looking for the Carstairs plot, the Fred Carstairs family plot," I responded.

"Carstairs . . . Sure, I've heard the name before, but I don't think there's a Carstairs plot in Mansfield Point. Wait—" he dug into a rusty metal file bin and pulled out a battered map book.

Somehow it didn't surprise me that this combination undertaker and guard hadn't ever heard of Fred Carstairs. It seems not many folks cared to know who he was. But I was amazed to find out that he hadn't talked to Hughes as he passed by the entrance on the way to conduct business matters and visit his one-time acquaintance Mr. Carstairs.

While charting his way on the map, he asked, "Friend o' yours?"

"Nope. Just a wacky old occult writer."

"Ah, that explains it . . ."

"You mean no one's come here asking about visiting the Carstairs plot today?"

"Nope. You're the first one."

Scratching my head, I squinted into the sun and thought that perhaps Hughes hadn't arrived yet. At any rate, I figured I'd meet him at the plot.

"Here we go," he drawled. "Says here that tall monument of da Carstairs family's between Henderson and Symmes up in the far north corner of the cemetery. I've got a photocopy here for you."

The guard nodded as he drew a big "X" in black ink on the blurry sheet.

"Have a good one," dozed the guard, stretching against the back of his chair.

I trudged off in search of the Carstairs plot, and it took a full fifteen minutes to find the damned thing. It was half-hidden by overgrown brush and tall bushes, not to mention a bunch of other monuments in the same area that weren't marked on the map. Finally, after pulling back some dry vegetation from in front of a gravestone, I came upon the name Charles O. Carstairs, marked as having lived from 1859 to 1906.

"That must've been his grandfather." I scratched my right ear. "The one who was in charge of sanitation on Ellis Island when the Statue of Liberty was installed."

I stood for half an hour in front of the Carstairs monument, looking at the newly engraved "Frederick Carstairs (1901–1994)" plaque. Hughes had said that

Fred was a bit coy about his age, but at this point Peter Hughes was becoming more than a little unreliable, as I distinctly recall him having said he'd be at the cemetery by 10 A.M.

"Well, I'll catch up with that flake later. Time for me to hit the road again and do some research."

Part of Carstairs' preface to *The Secret Watchers* had been printed in abridged form in a chapbook distributed to an elite group of aspiring young occult writers, much like an amateur press association, according to the edition I had picked up the day before. So, knowing I'd have a good chance of finding such materials in only a large university library, I set out to take advantage of Miskatonic University, where my *Partridgeville Gazette* ID allowed me all expenses paid access to otherwise costly materials.

That afternoon was mostly spent rifling through an actual old mailing of Chalmers' old cronies' small publications. Their amateur press association was called the Obscure Order of Tindalos, and most of their periodicals contained verse littered with allusions to Satan in one form or another—and far too many exclamation points. I did, however, find an annotation mentioning a semi-legit New England journal called the *Goodberg-Lockwood Weekly*. The librarians scurried around trying to help me out, though a couple of times I was brought the wrong journal or microfilm. Turning through three spools, I finally came upon a single half-page letter from Halpin Chalmers in *Goodberg-Lockwood*. The letter came in defense of Fred Carstairs' first book of verse, *A Man from Krakatoa and Other Poems*, which had been privately printed by another member of the circle of Chalmers correspondents in an apparent limited edition of 25 copies. Turning back to my battered old Mustang in the pay parking lot, I hightailed back to Partridgeville to catch Hughes.

The Miskatonic search had again turned up very little. It might've been just the sort of esoteric find that a Chalmersian scholar would publish in a modern occult journal, using the discovery as their claim to fame. But for me, it was just another indication of Chalmers' bizarre antics—and how his reputation far eclipsed that of his friend Fred Carstairs.

"Perhaps," I thought, "my article should be more about Carstairs than his best friend! That might even spark some comments in *Chalmers Studies*, that mag Hughes mentioned."

More than thirty miles went by on the nearly deserted highway as I made my way back to the office to report in. When I reached my desk around 4:30 P.M. there was a late-afternoon edition sitting smack-dab in the middle of it.

"NY Literary Agent & Editor Hughes Found Dead at the Partridgeville Inn," ran the headline on the front page. I read further along: "Peter Hughes' body was found naked and splattered with traces of a slimy blue substance. Next to the body were found two tiny black and green pellets. The pellets and fluid were sent to the Partridgeville Chemical Laboratories for examination."

"What?" I nearly shouted aloud to myself. "No wonder he wasn't there!"

"Some of the room's furniture was thrown haphazardly into the locked bathroom. A trowel and container of plaster were also found amongst the materials in the back half of Hughes' hotel room," the article went on.

"Sheesh!" I shook my head. "Just as crazy as all the others, huh? What a world!"

On my way out of the double doors in front of the *Gazette* Building I was stopped by Joshua Saint.

"That little headline I threw on your desk ought to add a bit to your article on that Chalmers fellow."

"Right," I said. "Always thinking of your bros, Josh," I said, shaking his hand and heading out to the car.

Josh smiled. "But I don't cater to buffoons!"

On my way up to the apartment, I recalled the headline from the early morning *Gazette*.

"Hmm . . . Hughes isn't the only one who was a bit off his rocker. And what about that guy they had to taze and bring into the pen at the Partridgeville PD Station? He looked like he could've escaped from a state mental ward. Ah well, it takes all kinds these days. All kinds."

I turned the key in the rickety lock and threw my stuff down on the scuffed secondhand coffee table, moving it out from in front of the sofa bed.

"Damn, Chalmers again," I thought as a picked up the black book resting on the table.

"Might as well," I said to the walls.

I rested my head against the cushions and began to peruse the second section of *The Secret Watchers*. The clock had barely struck nine by that time, and I'd only taken a break to wolf down a quick microwave dinner from the freezer. Once back in bed with the Chalmers volume, I leaned one arm against my right temple and continued to deluge my brain with Chalmersian references to beings that might possibly have originated in a fourth dimension beyond what is known to man— and that these entities could see all things on Earth and in the furthest reaches of the cosmos at once. Their native habitat, according to Chalmers, was in some kind of desert abyss in the depths of angular space.

"Bullshit!" I told myself aloud. "Angles and curves exist together on Earth just as much as up where the shuttles go up every few months."

I can remember reading the final paragraph of Section Two before finally blacking out. Three names remained in my head while I had another pitch black dream. "Einstein and John Dee are strange bedfellows," Chalmers had said. "Then, too, we cannot discount the accomplishments of Olaus Wormius and the often quoted Ibn Schacabao, without whom Dee would not have achieved the *English* translation."

Right before falling into an unconscious state I asked myself, "What book is Chalmers referring to here? Did I miss something—did I forget to go to the bottom for a footnote?"

Ibn Schacabao sounded almost vaguely Latin to me, but somehow I couldn't help thinking of how Chalmers' mention of a desert and the intense heat of my apartment the night before conjured up images of the Middle Eastern landscape. Was there another name I'd forgotten—or that I'd seen mentioned in one of Fred Carstairs' prose poems earlier in the day at Miskatonic U.?

My ears are normally sensitive, and I awake frequently some nights to the sound of car alarms going off two miles away on the other side of Angell Hill. From out of the pit of slumber, I cracked an eyelid halfway and thought I heard labored breathing coming from somewhere in the apartment. Somehow, before I'd fallen off to sleep, I must have flicked the switch on the bedside lamp, enveloping the studio apartment in inky darkness.

Carefully, without rustling, I attempted to reach for the light cord and turn the switch on. Just as I was doing that I heard the distinct scuff of shoes on the carpet. Then a fumbling, as if for something that fell on the floor.

The fluorescent light flickered on to reveal the matted, wiry salt and pepper hair of the strange stunned man I'd seen at the police station only two days before. My heart jumped into my throat. I blindly reached for something to help protect myself against the intruder.

Apparently he hadn't noticed me yet. Nor was he taken aback to the light coming on. His arms were stretched out feebly towards the floor as if he were straining against something in order to pick up the book that had tumbled from my chest onto the floor. His pupils were dilated and the whites of his eyes were bloodshot. His gaze was distant, as he ground his filthy, long nails into the volume and shakily put it in his grasp.

"They're coming," he mumbled, but not to me, to himself. "They're almost here!

"I'll have to be quick. I can smell them," the maniac spoke in a hushed tone, as if he were talking to an unseen familiar, resting on his shoulder. "They are lean and athirst!"

I raised the long-necked metal stapler over my head to ward him off in case he tried anything, but apparently the lunatic's eyes just burned right through me and saw past the walls as well. He had opened one palm, in which I noticed was one black pellet, which he brought up to his face, searching direly for his limp mouth.

"Huh? They're watching me, they're playing games with me, like some kind of cat and mouse before the pounce," he raved. "*He's* one of them now. I notice the lines of *his face!*"

I grabbed the cordless phone, dialed the police—and actually received a quick answer. Fortunately, I managed to keep an eye on the intruder's blankly staring eyes while opening the front door and hurling out the trowel and plaster bucket the maniac must've brought with him.

"Right away, Mister Sonners," said the operator on the other end as I dropped the cordless phone and raised the stapler further, in case the intruder made another move.

"This is *his* book," the intruder began rambling again, froth coming to his lips. "And *he* wants to come back. He won't let me have it! *He wrote it.* But *he* seemed human—then."

"What?" I asked to myself silently. "What the hell is he talking about?" I started to hear the sirens approaching. "Jeez, am I lucky I only live down the hill from the police station," was all I could think as I kept glancing from the lunatic to the door, as he began pushing around the room in vain, looking for the stolen hardware that he'd brought with him. I'd thrown them out the door, but he obviously didn't see me do it.

"They're coming, they're right before me now. Must block them out with the *sphere.* I can see *his* angles."

I ducked into the kitchenette.

It was as if the intruder sensed the stolen materials were now outside the open door. He floundered toward it. This happened just as the cops had mounted the stairway to my apartment. Their guns were poised at the ready, I could see, just from leaning out the door after the escaped mental patient. One even had a stun gun raised high. Before the officers could shoot a charge or bullet at the flailing man, his voice capitulated into a high-pitched scream.

"Yaaaaaaaaaaaaaaaaah! *Chaaaaaalmers-s-ss—*"

Suddenly the intruder dropped dead—motionless—to the pavement with a resounding thud. It was as if his heart just stopped functioning. No convulsions, no writhing, nothing.

The police queried me for the reports. And I obliged them by telling precisely what I knew, just in case they might help me in turn with information on the whole sequence of events.

A gloved inspector had opened up the plaster can to find human ashes intermixed with the pasty substance, presumably *Ida Carstairs'*. The next day her urn had been discovered missing from the cemetery.

And the intruder's name? I saw the police confiscate his wallet for evidence—the driver's license read "James Morton II." It was behind celluloid on a faded and torn business card from the Partridgeville Chemical Laboratories.

I could tell more, but it'll all be in a *Partridgeville Gazette* article in another couple of days. I'll have to use a pen name, of course, because all this mingling with occult writers could ruin *my reputation!*

The Madness out of Time

Lin Carter

Lin Carter nursed many grandiose literary schemes. One was an early epic poem about Alexander the Great. Another was the abortive *Khymyrium*. Yet another, and he got closer to finishing this one, was his *Necronomicon*. He had the most fun with the cautionary tales in which Alhazred warned the casual reader away from his own suicidal course of blasphemous delvings. By means of the cautionary tale genre Lin managed to harmonize two otherwise inconsistent portraits of Alhazred running throughout Lovecraftian fiction: that the Mad Arab was at once a practitioner of the Black Arts and a warner against them. "The Madness out of Time" is a rarity: it has Alhazred learning from someone else's mistake. And the moral is a sardonic (not to mention a Sargonic) one: when is it inadvisable to walk the straight and narrow?

"The Madness out of Time" is a title Lovecraft considered using for what became *The Case of Charles Dexter Ward*. Lin figured it was too good not to use, and he went to work thinking what kind of Mythos madness might arrive from out of time's abyss. Naturally he thought of Long's Hounds of Tindalos. Knowing what delight he took in systematizing stray bits of Mythos data, I suggested to him that, as I mentioned in the introduction to this volume, the Hounds of Tindalos ought to be "the Dogs that howl in the Maelstrom of Azathoth" (from "The Horror in the Museum"), whether Lovecraft was thinking of it that way or not. He went for it, and the result is apparent in the present tale, which first appeared in *Crypt of Cthulhu* #39 (Roodmas 1986).

I.

There is a madness beyond Time and a Foulness beyond space, and may Heaven help him who dares arouse the Wrath thereof, and the nameless Doom that ever lies in wait for all who do be rash enough to risk such horror. Know ye that in the ten years that I, Alhazred, did spend in the trackless wastes of Arabia Felix, after what time that I rose up and departed out of the city of the Alexandrians, many and strange were the happenings that befell me, but none there was that was strangelier than this which now I would relate.

In the fullness of time did I betake me to that place in the Waste beknownst unto men as the Valley of Tombs, for that in its desolation there stood the empty fanes and desecrate of an old necropolis abuilded in the days of Ancientry, and by men now forgot save for us sorcerers; ravaged and open stood these tombs, and hewn were they out of the very fabric of the cliffs, which cliffs lined the Vale to either side, like walls; and here it came to pass that I took one of these for mine abode, a tomb that stood up amongst the hills and from which coign had I the broad vantage of the Vale and the oasis that stood amongst the rocks that bestrew the floor of the valley.

And here it was, in solitude and silence, under the wheeling constellations that jewelled the desert night like handsfull of gems strewn on black velvet, that I pondered the Elder Books and scanned the stars, studied the epicycles and meditated upon the arcana of mine Art. Ere long it chanced that I discovered myself not to be the only eremite who dwelt here in the Valley of Tombs, for there was even another: an older man than I was he, and lean and furtive, overgiven to secretive ways, and I but glimpsed him from afar betimes, for we did share the same small oasis amidst the sands, and the fresh, lifegiving waters thereof. Betimes did I observe him as he came and went below the height of my dwelling, as he sought the rich fruit of the date palms and the sweet waters of the pool, but long and long it was to be ere that we exchanged Words, and when at length this came to pass I did learn that he was one Sargon, a Sorcerer who from of old had made his place of abiding within the wastes of that land to the East that was formerly the realm of the famous Chaldaeans, from whose ancient blood was he sprung.

Now in time from the lips of this Chaldaean heard I a frightful Tale of Terrors, but for a while I but watched him as he came and went, and that mostly in the dim gloaming; and I observed of him a curious behavior, in that in these peregrinations he did not progress from point to point in a straight line, as did other men, but in a manner circuitous and serpentine, as meandering in curved paths, which was to me most marvelous strange, as I could imagine no reason for this peculiar mode of locomotion.

And I bethought me then of that which was written of old: that men should tread the Straight and Narrow Path, for the salvation of their Souls; but he was one man whom I have known who trod the same straight and narrow Path to the ultimate and unspeakable Damnation of his soul, whereby had I great cause to Marvel thereat . . .

II.

In the passage of time we became friends, we two lonely Sorcerers who shared betwixt us this barren and bleak Valley of the Tombs; and it was from the lips of this Sargon the Sorcerer that I had the tale which follows.

Now he was gaunt and wasted, this Chaldaean, and it demanded no great shrewdness of mine own to discover that a dreadful Fear rode him as a man bestrideth a Camel, for that Fear thou couldst discern in his shifting and red-rimmed eyes, and in the shaking of his palsied hands, and in the nervous twitching of his Visage. But as to *that* of which he feared I knew not, nor did I care to guess: and the Truth of it all, when at length I gained the knowledge, was strange and strangelier than ever I could have dreamed . . .

Once, O Alhazred (said he unto me), I sought in my rash and imprudent youth to attain to the Vision of the All beknown to Mystics and Philosophers and by such deemed admirable beyond the boundaries of ordinary Experience. The attainment of this Vision I sought by the means of a powerful drug called the Liao, the which is even a derivative of the Black Lotus of much frightful lore and legend; and the drug Liao I in time acquired, purveyed unto mine hands by Divers Ways from the wise and learned apothecaries of Far Cathay. Now it is one of the properties of this drug Liao that it doth dissolve the strictures placed upon the mind of Man by time and space, the both of which cease to exist, thus permitting the Intellect, together with a swift and all-encompassing sense of Perception, to range afar; and when that these strictures of Time and Space are removed there be thus stripped from the eyes of men those Veils of Illusion that time hath thrown over them, the myth of Now and Then, when in reality there be only *forever*.

And thus, having imbibed of the drug Liao, after the prescribed manner, it seemed to me that I did view all Lands and all Ages in one endless and eternal instant, and very wondrous strange was this Marvel: aye, in one and the same flashing Instant of time I saw myself a hairy, bestial creature, squatting in a filthy cave, wrapt about with dirty hides, gnawing on a thigh-bone . . . and a thousand naked slaves grovel before me as I pass in a litter of gold and ivory drawn by a night-black oxen from Thebes; I am a priest, and I exalt with painted palms the beast-headed stony idols of Ægypt . . . and a howling savage from the wind-scoured plains of Parthia, riding to ambush a Roman legion; I am a half-naked Vandal, sacking the desecrated temples of Greece . . . and in India I am an humble acolyte, and I hearken to the teaching of the mystic Masters, and run screaming from their presence, for their revelations are as salt on wounds that bleed . . .

And I am the first man arising from the steaming fens and the quaking bogs of the new-made Earth, and I am fled squealing from between the trampling feet of the vast Reptiles that roved and ruled before the coming of man; and I penetrate further, into the very backward and Abysm of Time, for in the impatience of my Folly I strove to probe even beyond the very bournes of Time and Space, to That which existeth forever, and the which was before ever Time or Space was.

And I, who had lived in all men as all men live in me, I, who had perceived the entirety of human history in one vast moment, one all-pervading Now, sought to go Beyond . . . into that gray and featureless phantasmal bourne that knoweth not the strictures of Where or When, but only Is: and, for a moment (as mere men may measure a moment) I stood upon the pale colourless shore beyond Time, where mist-waves lap at sandless sands, and darkness dwells instead of light; and *They* scented my presence—those shadowy and furtive and implacable Things that dwell in that terrible Realm—That which is begotten of the Madness out of Time and the Foulness that reigneth beyond Space. There, on that dim and hueless shore of shadows, They prowl ever, lean and athirst; and now, O Alhazred, that I have in my folly dared attract Their attention by my uninvited presence in Their realm, They hunt me down all the paths of time and space, and never will I be free of Their unrelenting pursuit.

III.

And I, Alhazred, then roused myself and spake unto this Sargon the Sorcerer from out of the fullness of my daemon-wrested lore, saying: Beware, O hapless Chaldaean, for once in the sealed and hidden Vale of Hadoth beside the immemorial Nile saw I in my youth the likeness of Those you fear; aye, graven it was in an amulet of curious and exotic design, the oddly angular and strangely stylized representation of a winged and couchant Hound, exquisitely and loathsomely carven from a thin wafer of lucent jade. And it was the hand of my Master that held it, the Wizard Yakthoob, for amongst his collection of rare and obscure periapts had he this, that was the ghastly soul-symbol of the corpse-eating cult of forbidden and inaccessible Leng—but of this talisman, of its properties and of the horrible relation of the souls of the dead to That which it symbolizes, I shall speak more fully at another time.

Suffice it to say, O Chaldaean, that stamped upon the semi-canine face of that jade amulet was an expression so repellent in the extreme, savouring at once of death, of bestialism, and of utter malevolence, for that those sinister lineaments were drawn from some obscure manifestation of the souls of those who vexed and gnawed at the dead, that never have I forgotten it, or That which it represents. Aye, I speak of the very Hounds of Tindalos themselves, those Hunters From Beyond that be the Spawn of Noth-Yidik and the effluvium of K'thun, and that howl forever in the maelstrom that is dread and fearsome Azathoth; aye, They be none other than the very minions and servitors of the Daemon-Sultan, under Their ghastly sire and dam, Noth-Yidik and terrible K'thun. Aye, They bay and slaver forever in that shadowy and indistinct realm of Chaos that lieth beyond all bournes of Time or Space, wherein also dwelleth from of old Their Dread Master, Azathoth; and it was writ of old that men awake within Them cosmic hungers: yet are even such as They bound by the Elder Gods with certain strictures, even as be we weak and timorous mortals, for our space is *curved* whilst They move only in *straight lines* or through *right angles,* for such be the limitation of Their nature which are obedient to the biddings of the Elder Gods that rule all that is; wherefore are They hampered in Their pursuit of thee, O Chaldaean; and if thou canst contrive to elude Them long enough, peradventure They will slink back, snarling and ravenous and unsatisfied, to that Foulness wherefrom They came in the beginning, before time and beyond space.

Now somewhat of the import of my words had this Sargon already guessed, which explaineth his circuitous and meandering manner of locomotion, for the Sorcerer well knew of this Difference between curved and angled space; and in the days that followed hard upon the heels of our converse did we extend modes of protection new and novel: with clay dug from the marge of the font amidst the oasis did we smooth into sleek curves the sharply-angled jointures of his stony cell, even the corners of the walls and the roof thereover; and long did we strive with the Exorcisms of Pnom (both the Lesser and the Greater) to free him of this Curse, but, alas! to no avail.

And nightly did I peruse those tomes of the Elder Lore which I had borne hither with me into the fastnesses of the desert for my study, seeking the text of that Great Invocation to Azathoth that might sever the shackles that bound the hapless spirit of my Chaldaean friend to the Hunters from Beyond, who all the while did hunt him down the byways of Time and Space, howling and anhungered. But nowhere in the texts did my perusal disclose this Liturgy and I found it naught, although I searched through those portions of the Pnakotic Manuscripts which may still be deciphered by men. And at length I did despair for the Chaldaean, for many and dread are the Forces that be leagued with those gaunt and famished Hunters from Beyond, and the Dholes may aid Them, and the Little People of the Wood (for these are the servitors of Shub-Niggurath, the Mighty Mother), and by whose aid even the Hounds of Tindalos may move through the Scarlet Circles and encroach upon that region of curved space whereunto be native our mortality.

And yet were all my searchings in vain, for I found not that grand Invocation that was the object of my Quest; and daily, as I consulted with this Sargon the Sorcerer, I could not help but Observe how ever more gaunt and hag-ridden was the unhappy Chaldaean, for that he sensed that the Hunters from Beyond were snuffling at his traces even through his far-wandering Dreams, the which he could not control, no more than may any ordinary man, Sorcerer or shepherd. And there was naught that I could do to succor him in the direst extremity of his Need; and it became apparent to me that some grim doom hovered near unto our dismal Vale, for the skies even of Noon were enshadowed with veils of darkness, through which the stars burned bright as bale-fires at a Witches' Sabbath, and a chill, uncanny breeze, as stenchful as one come panting up from the very Pit, made all that bleak and stony Vale as noisome as an abbatoir.

And then there came a day whereupon all these matters came to a head, as 'twere: a gloaming, when the gibbous Moon rode high in a sky where scudding cloud-wraiths fled before a whining wind, and I shuddered and wrapt more tightly about me the folds of my robe, for as the wind went whistling through the naked fangs of rock over my head, they made a thin, shiversome sound not unlike the howling of hounds, far-off and faint to hear . . . like the baying of those grim Hounds that howl forever at the heart of that black Maelstrom that is even Azathoth, the Daemon-Sultan . . .

Now, as it had chanced, the slumbers of Sargon the Sorcerer had nightly been fitful and much broken, haunted as he was by dire and grisly Dreams, so that he gat of Nights little or no sleep, wherefore had I counselled him to seek his cot during the long afternoons when still the Earth basked in the fullness of the light of day, and Night, and the gruesome creatures that prowl its darksome Deeps, be yet afar-off. But on this very day of days had he sunken deep into the bottomless slumbers of exhaustion, from which he woke asudden, with a fearful start, as the dark shadows crept across the dusty flooring of his stony cell and heralded the Coming of Darkness. And up sprang the Chaldaean, suddenly stricken to the roots of his soul with a nameless Fear, and ran forth from the open portal of the tomb that was his habitation, crying aloud my name, and as I came forth from mine own abode to answer him I beheld beneath me the dark floor of the Valley of Tombs where he fled—and *the gaunt, lean Shapes of darknesses even darker than the shadows that closed upon him from the four points of the compass*—and ripped and tore as I stood, fear-frozen, helpless to do aught.

And I realized that, in his terror, Sargon the Chaldaean had for once forgot to take great care in progressing by curving paths, but had run for mine abode *in a straight line* . . . wherefore do I say that once I have known a man who followed the Straight and Narrow Path to his detriment and very Doom, for all that the Scriptures and the prophets preach . . . aye, ye that scan my words, beware! lest ye incur the wrath of the Hunters from Beyond that are the very Hounds of Tindalos!

The Hound of the Partridgevilles

Peter Cannon

This ingenious follow-up to "The Hounds of Tindalos" and "The Letters of Halpin Chalmers" comes to grips with the inevitable pun. And in so doing Cannon is returning to the fruitful connection he made between Lovecraft, Frank Belknap Long, and Sherlock Holmes in *Pulptime*. One ventures to speculate that the Tindalos theme might have been crossbred with a Doylean tale of an ancestral lycanthropic curse with a good bit more seriousness—had Long not chosen the frivolous name of Partridgeville for his analogue to Providence. But as it is, Cannon has wisely chosen the only proper course.

"The Hound of the Partridgevilles" was first published in Cannon's *Forever Azathoth and Other Horrors* (Tartarus Press, 1999).

"The horror fans came to Partridgeville in a psychedelic fog," said the editor of the *Partridgeville Gazette*. "Thirty years ago anyhow, at the height of the hippie era."

"I wasn't even born then," I said.

"Consider yourself lucky, Linnet."

"You never went through a hippie phase, Mr. Turrow?"

"Well, I did grow my hair long . . . uh, that is, when I had hair."

I chuckled, but stopped as soon as I noticed my boss wasn't smiling.

"You laugh, Linnet, but one day you're going to wonder why on earth you ever wore that godawful ponytail."

"Yes, sir."

"You don't take drugs, do you, Linnet?"

"No, of course not, Mr. Turrow."

"That's good. We all know what happened, uh, to Halpin Chalmers. Now what's this about a special assignment to cover Chalmerscon?"

I didn't wish to antagonize my boss further by being contradictory, but in fact we don't know what happened to Halpin Chalmers, at least not exactly. During the 1980s, one of the more literate Reaganites turned the legendary occult author into a kind of anti-poster boy, an example of how you could wind up—nude, decapitated, smeared with blue pus—if you were so foolish as not to say no to drugs. Chalmers, as stories in the *Gazette* files from 1928 confirmed, had been experimenting with a new drug, one used centuries before by Chinese alchemists. In my view, however, this new-old drug was not the chief cause of Chalmers' brutal slaying. No, there had to be more to it than that, and while you could say the trail had grown a trifle cold I was confident a solution to Partridgeville's crime of the century was not entirely out of the question seventy years later.

Since 1968, the fortieth anniversary of his death, the town has hosted a biennial convention to celebrate the occultist's life and work, over the weekend nearest to July 3. The conflict this choice of date often presents with the nation's birthday has ensured that only the more fanatical Chalmersians have attended, or at any rate those for whom love of country takes a back seat to their favorite author. Many local residents feel ambivalent at best toward Partridgeville's most illustrious native writer, though not I should say the town's leading citizen, Cosmo Hopper Partridgeville VIII—direct descendant of founding father Cosmo Hopper Partridgeville I—who has tirelessly promoted the event for decades.

In truth, Partridgeville is such a backwater that the original family who settled it still runs the place more than three hundred years later. Elsewhere in New England immigrants have overthrown the old Anglo-Saxon oligarchy—Irish, Italians, Portuguese, French-Canadians—but not in Partridgeville, where every elected official—the mayor, the police chief, the school superintendent, the dogcatcher—can proudly claim the first Cosmo Partridgeville as his ancestor. So adept was the Partridgeville clan at weathering the economic tempests of the past that today, in the person of its principal heir, it owns most of the town and much of the surrounding county. Since the nineteenth century the family's wealth has derived mainly from the Glue Works and the Chemical Laboratories, which between them employ the vast majority of ethnic types—Irish, Italians, Portuguese, French-Canadians—who inhabit the blue-collar neighborhoods below Angell Hill.

Cosmo Hopper Partridgeville VIII and his kin occupy of course the fine Federal mansions on the crest of Angell Hill, as well as various country estates. Indeed, "Lord Partridgeville," an honorific title conferred by the press and since come into general use, prefers to spend his leisure hours at his five-hundred acre horse farm near Brewster. For many years he served as Master of Fox Hounds of the Brewster Hunt, the last club in the Northeast still to chase the fox with intent to kill—and if successful to take the bloody tail or bush as a trophy. "Drag-hunting is for sissies," Lord Partridgeville has declared more than once on the editorial page of the *Gazette,* which for the record it's only fair to disclose is part of the family conglomerate, Partridgevilleco.

"Linnet, are you daydreaming again? I asked you a question."

"Huh?"

"Don't lie to me, son—you spaced out on, uh, drugs?"

"No, Mr. Turrow, I most certainly am not—unless you consider the intoxicating atmosphere of an antiquarian's paradise like Partridgeville a drug."

"Linnet, I don't have time for your jokes. I repeat, what's so special about this year's Chalmerscon that you want to cover it?"

"Well, sir, the thing of it is, if you've read Lord Partridgeville's editorial in this morning's edition . . ."

"Yeh, yeh, remind me."

". . . he's given permission for a team of psychics to spend the night at the Central Square apartment where Halpin Chalmers was murdered. Nobody's been allowed inside since the police removed the body in '28. They hope to recreate the exact conditions of that tragic night and thereby learn who or what did him in."

"Does he name these psychics?"

"No, but they're extremely well qualified, according to Lord Partridgeville."

"His lordship's always had a soft spot for the paranormal."

"I'd like to spend the night in Halpin Chalmers' old apartment, too, if it's all right with you, Mr. Turrow."

The editor smoothed back the scattered hairs on his scalp before replying.

"You know, it's one thing for his lordship to sound off in an editorial," he said, "but quite another for a reputable paper to lend legitimacy to dubious claims in a feature story. You're not a bad kid, Linnet, and I'd hate to see you wasting your time on tabloid nonsense."

I tried not to look too disappointed.

"But just to show you what a nice guy I can be, I'm prepared to indulge you this once. Tell you what, if you can get Lord Partridgeville's approval to participate, you've got the assignment. I'll even help arrange an interview. Maybe you can find out who these psychics are his lordship's so keen on."

"Thank you, Mr. Turrow. Thank you very much. I'd knew you'd understand. I—"

"Say, aren't you on your lunch hour, Linnet?"

"Yes, sir."

"Then why don't you do me a favor and go get a haircut."

A few days later I was on the Brewster road, deep within rolling hunt country, headed for my appointment with Lord Partridgeville at his farm, Tindalos Acres. Thanks to a map sent me by his lordship's secretary, I had no trouble finding the Tudor-style gate house. Above the arch was the Partridgeville coat-of-arms—a partridge in a pear tree. I've never been to Hampton Court, but I've seen pictures of it and the stone pile that came into view after creeping a mile or more down the gravel driveway might well have been its twin. A man in livery with an English accent greeted me at the drawbridge. I followed him on foot under a portcullis, through a courtyard, down a dim passage, and into a dark oak-paneled room, where he instructed me to wait while he went to retrieve his master. I passed the time admiring the portrait of a Jack Russell terrier above the walk-in fireplace, the silver cups and blue ribbons in the display cases, the leatherbound sets of *Horse and Hound* in the built-in bookshelves, the crystal decanters with foxhead stoppers on the bar cart, among other totems.

Though I had never met Lord Partridgeville, when he waddled in the room I recognized him at once from his photos in the *Sunday Gazette* society section. A stout man in his late sixties with shaggy eyebrows, red-rimmed eyes, and funny elongated ears, he apologized in the plummy tones of a born aristocrat for making me drive so far but then it was the height of hunting season and wouldn't I like a drink.

"It's Mr. Linnet, isn't it?" he said as he picked up the Scotch bottle.

"Yes, sir."

"We needn't stand on formality, my boy. My friends call me Cozzy."

"Okay, Cozzy. You can call me Doug."

"Okay, Doug. Here's to you. Cheers!"

My host raised his tumbler, gulped about half the amber liquor, then plopped down in a chintz armchair with a satisfied sigh. I took a polite sip from my glass and turned on my tape-recorder before sitting on the loveseat opposite.

"Nice place you have here, Cozzy."

"You like it, do you, Doug?"

"Very homey."

"Not too ostentatious, is it?"

"Not a bit."

"Grand but understated, people tell me. I'll give you a little history. In 1716 my ancestor the first Cosmo Hopper hired the greatest English architect of the day. Do you know who that was, Doug?"

I hesitated.

"I'll give you a hint. He also designed the First Baptist Church in Partridgeville."

"Wait a minute. Are you telling me that Christopher Wren—"

"*Sir* Christopher Wren, Doug. He was knighted in 1675."

"Sorry, Cozzy."

"When I tell you that Sir Christopher Wren designed Tindalos Acres, Doug, I mean he came to America to do the job. Other colonial buildings merely copied the Wren originals in England, but this house and the Baptist Church are the only two actually built under the supervision of the genius who conceived St. Paul's Cathedral."

Mention of the First Baptist Church, whose steeple was demolished during the earthquake of '28 that eerily coincided with the death of Halpin Chalmers, brought the conversation round to the nominal subject of the interview.

"Have you read *The Secret Watchers*, Cozzy?"

"Many times. It's one of my favorite books—other than my usual." He gestured toward the bound volumes of *Horse and Hound*. "Has something of the thrill of the chase in it, wouldn't you say, Doug?"

"If you say so, Cozzy."

"Have you read the authorized biography, Doug?"

"Part of it."

"A pity the Chalmers letters to Fred Carstairs were lost."

"A real shame."

"Fred Carstairs should never have married. You're not married, are you, Doug?"

"No, Cozzy."

"Good fellow. I've been a bachelor all my life—accounts for my longevity."

While Lord Partridgeville refilled his glass at the bar, I wondered if he regretted never having sired a Cosmo Hopper Partridgeville IX.

"So tell me, Cozzy," I said, when my host had resumed his seat, "what's this about a team of psychic investigators spending the night at the spot where Halpin Chalmers met his maker?"

"Ah, you read my editorial. Yes, I admit I was a bit coy in not naming names, but I suppose there's no harm now in revealing it's sort of a family affair. My cousin Nigel, head of the Partridgeville Canine Control department, is working on his mail-order Ph.D. in parapsychology. The Arthur Koestler Institute, of which I'm one of the governors, recently gave him a grant to finish his thesis, on the death of Halpin Chalmers. Being something of a psychic enthusiast myself, I'll be accompanying Nigel—as will be Ken Korey, author of *Spectral Evidence: Who Killed Halpin Chalmers?* Can't have it too much of a family affair."

"Who do you think killed Halpin Chalmers, Cozzy?"

"Haven't the faintest idea, Doug. Ask me again after July 3."

"The apartment at 24 Central Square has been sealed since 1928. Why?"

"Whim of Dad's, I guess. At the time he was managing the realty division of Partridgevilleco, which owns Central Square. Feel free to mention that fact to your readers, Doug."

"Thanks, I will, Cozzy. Say, is there any chance I could join the investigation?"

"What? You want to come along and join the fun, do you, Doug?"

"Yes."

"And report on the results for the *Gazette*, I suppose."

"Yes."

"Hmph."

There was a pregnant pause. At last Lord Partridgeville took a long slug from his glass and declared:

"Well, why not, my boy, why not?" He laughed. "Only understand that I have final editorial say over what goes into your story. Not everything we're apt to learn about the death of Halpin Chalmers may be suitable for a family newspaper."

"That's most considerate of you. I'm sure Mr. Turrow—"

"Never mind that chrome-dome Turrow! You report directly to me on this one, boy!"

After this outburst, to my relief, my host began to reminisce about his parents, in particular his unknown mother who had died when he was an infant. His father, Cosmo Hopper VII, had never remarried, cherishing his late wife's sacred memory to his dying day some fifty years later. By the time the butler returned to announce lunch we were both in tears. Indeed his lordship was too overcome to say goodbye. I switched off the tape-recorder and, guided by another servant, left the palace. On the drive home I reflected that Lord Partridgeville was remarkably open with his feelings for someone of English heritage.

My article headed "Lord Partridgeville to Lead Psychic Probe" was timed to appear in the *Gazette* for July 3. I had interviewed the other two participants by phone—

Nigel Partridgeville and Ken Korey—and was now eager, that Friday of the cele-bratory weekend, to meet these two gentlemen in the flesh.

My opportunity came late that morning at the official Chalmerscon kick-off ceremony, held at Mayor Reginald Partridgeville's office in the neo-Georgian Car-stairs Civic Center, formerly the Adams Civic Center. (The building had been re-named in 1994 in honor of the late Fred Carstairs, Halpin Chalmers' best friend and fellow occult author.) The ceremony included the launch of two new books: a reprint of Ken Korey's *Spectral Evidence: Who Killed Halpin Chalmers?*, billed as a special seventieth-anniversary edition with an added chapter examining the crime in the light of the latest mathematical thinking; and Nigel Partridgeville's *The C Files*, a slick popular account derived from his thesis-in-progress. Both authors cheerfully signed copies for the crowd.

Since the mayor had declared that Friday a local holiday, the lecture halls and conference rooms of the Carstairs Center were free for convention activities. All the important panels would take place the following day, which meant the after-noon was mostly reserved for certain tired Chalmerscon fixtures whom the organ-izers didn't have the heart to deny their turn in the spotlight. Chief among them was L. E. Hancock, a sprightly nonagenarian, who repeated for the nth time how on that fateful day, when he opened his door to take in his cat and pick up the morning edition of the *Gazette*, he had smelt a peculiar odor in the hall of 24 Cen-tral Square. . . . Receiving almost as much sympathetic applause was Detective Ser-geant Douglas's daughter Kim, who spent the bulk of her session flogging tattered copies of her late father's self-published booklet, *Obscure Poisons*. Sad to say, Willy Morton, great-nephew of chemist and bacteriologist James Morton, failed to show. Rumor had it Willy had been arrested for pushing a synthetic version of the drug Liao to an undercover cop he had mistaken for a fan.

The first major event was the cocktail reception that evening, hosted by the school superintendent, Percy Partridgeville, in his private suite. Cosmo Partridge-ville appeared, dressed in white-tie and scarlet tails, about fifteen minutes after he was due to speak. More than a hundred devotees of Partridgeville's most distin-guished author lowered their glasses and ceased munching their canapés. All eyes turned toward his lordship as he stumbled up the temporary dais beneath the crys-tal chandelier.

"Mayor Partridgeville, Superintendent Partridgeville, my fellow Chalmersians," he began, a little breathlessly, "it gives me great pleasure to welcome you all to this, the fifteenth—or is it the sixteenth?—annual, biannual, no, no, sorry, biennial weekend . . ."

"It's the sixteenth, Cozzy, if you count the gathering in '68 as the first," said Ken Korey in a stage whisper.

"Thank you, Ken. Why don't we just call it Chalmerscon '98. Okay?" A chorus of whistles and cheers greeted this suggestion.

"As you've probably all heard, or read in this morning's *Gazette*, this year we're planning something a little different. Ever since that horrible night seventy years ago we Chalmersians have been wondering . . . wondering about the cruel death of our literary hero. At the time most people blamed drugs. But what about booze? After all, it was the depths of Prohibition and Halpin was known to drink a little hooch now and then, not that there was anything wrong with that. Many thirsty law-abiding citizens did the same. Did he owe money to rum runners as one theory has it? Maybe—but as the authorized biography tells us, these were only the first of many rumors.

"Then there's Fred Carstairs. Fred was the last person to see Halpin alive and he had a motive—jealousy. Even back then Fred must have realized that as an occult writer he was always going to play second banana to his more talented pal. You only have to compare the sales of Chalmers titles to Carstairs titles to appreciate this point. Frankly, it's too bad Fred wasn't bumped off in '28 instead. A pity too that Fred attended only one Chalmerscon. Of course we did invite him back, but only if he left his beloved wife Ida at home. I'm afraid we had to be tough after she . . . Well, I just hope it's some posthumous consolation that we've renamed the Civic Center after him.

"Then there are those who believe the federal government iced Chalmers and has been trying to hide the fact ever since. I emphasize the federal government, not the local government. And then there are those who believe the feds didn't do it—it was, ha, ha, if you can believe it, a bungled alien abduction attempt—but the authorities are still trying to cover up the facts. Again, I repeat, our local officials have never been a party to such a conspiracy. Isn't that right, Nigel?"

"That's right, Cozzy," answered the head of the Partridgeville Canine Control department.

"On the contrary, they've done their darndest to discover the truth! And that's what we aim to accomplish tonight, my fellow Chalmersians, discover the truth in the matter of the death of Halpin Chalmers!"

The onlookers erupted in more cheers and whistles.

"To that end I will be joined by two outstanding experts in the field, my cousin Nigel Partridgeville, and Mr. Ken Korey, whom some of you were privileged to meet at the kick-off book signing earlier today."

The applause lasted nearly a minute.

"I'll grant you that each of these fine individuals has his own unique theory," resumed Lord Partridgeville. "They can't both be right. Ken here has taken the abstract route, applying the, the, some Jap—"

"Taniyama-Shimura Conjecture, Cozzy," said Korey. "It all ties in with the proof of Fermat's Last Theorem, the idea that elliptical curves—"

"Right, Ken. Let's not spoil the surprise for your fans, shall we? Nigel, on the other hand, is taking a more practical, down-to-earth approach, using psychic methods which I think it better I not try to explain. You can read his excellent book—and be sure to attend the special panel scheduled for tomorrow evening, when we'll announce the results of our vigil and answer any questions you may have. Thank you."

If Lord Partridgeville had neglected to mention what was happening next it didn't much matter, since anyone aware of the limousine and police escort waiting outside the Carstairs Center could guess that the team would be heading directly to Central Square. That morning his lordship's secretary had phoned to say it would be all right for me to go along for the ride, and accordingly I met the others at the car just as the chauffeur was warming up the engine.

It was less than a mile to Central Square, but we had to proceed almost as slowly as I had along the gravel driveway of Tindalos Acres, owing to the swarms of ethnic folk who clogged the streets in the summer twilight. As the intermittent sound of firecrackers indicated, these locals were not convention goers, but their state of restless excitement reinforced the air of adventurous expectancy we Chalmersians were feeling in the limo.

From an oversized picnic hamper Lord Partridgeville produced a Jeroboam of red wine, which he opened with the corkscrew on his Swiss Army knife. After a glass or two we were all in a convivial mood, though I have to say that the banter between Nigel and Ken soon took on a certain edge. Both authors had reproduced the autopsy photos in their books, but Ken suggested that it was inauthentic for Nigel to have colorized the original black-and-white prints, thus highlighting the blue pus. Nigel replied in so many words that he thought the diagrams and formulas in the new chapter of *Spectral Evidence* would be incomprehensible not only to average readers but also to the mathematics faculty of Partridgeville State. In all fairness, as his lordship hastened to point out, Partridgeville State, being a divinity and agricultural college, had only a third-rate math department. As a trustee of that institution, he was in a position to know.

At last we arrived at Central Square, which had been shut off to motor traffic and was filling with people, many of whom I recognized from the reception at the Carstairs Center. Obviously it had been faster to walk. The police chief, Alasdair Partridgeville, greeted us at the protective barrier set up in front of the former Smithwick and Isaacs jewelry store, since converted to a museum and gift shop dedicated to Halpin Chalmers. He confirmed that a large crowd would be supporting our efforts through the night from the vantage point of the square itself. A detachment of Partridgeville's finest, under his personal command, would ensure everyone's safety.

The super let us into the second-floor apartment, what in today's parlance would be called a studio. The single room was empty, apart from a couple of old bowls in one corner—or what would have been a corner had not every junction of floor and wall and ceiling been rounded off with cracked and crumbling plaster of Paris. Judging from the thick coating of dust and plaster fragments on the floor, it hadn't been entered in some time. The room was also hot and stuffy and with his lordship's permission I opened the window, which looked over the square.

"In Dad's will he insisted the place remain unoccupied in perpetuity," said Lord Partridgeville. "Can't imagine why."

I could see those waiting outside were well equipped with tents and sleeping bags, while we psychic investigators had merely a picnic blanket, which could comfortably accommodate three when spread on the floor. I volunteered to stand—at the window, where I could get some air. I later had reason to be grateful for this choice, though at that moment my prime concern was my stomach. Our only refreshment was the Jeroboam of red wine and I had drunk enough of that. My brain was definitely feeling fuzzy. I wished I had eaten more canapés at the reception.

Ken took some measurements of the room with a small surveyor's tool, then went to work on his pocket calculator. The cousins set up their own apparatus on the blanket and began what they claimed was a test of remote viewing. When it became dark, his lordship lit a candle he had the foresight to bring. It fit nicely in one of the old bowls. The bare bulb hanging by a cord from the ceiling was evidently burnt out.

For the next hour or so my colleagues focused on their tasks, with no discernible results. Only the sound of the occasional firecracker in the distance broke the silence. Out of boredom, or maybe scientific curiosity, I nonchalantly popped the pill I had purchased from Willy Morton that morning, prior to his arrest . . . Yeh, I know what I said earlier about not taking drugs, but in the circumstances I was prepared to make an exception. In my view there was more than one road to Damascus—or was it Samara?

Nigel and Ken were arguing over the efficacy of curves versus angles when the smoke started to pour from a big gap in the plaster of Paris in one of the ceiling corners. The candle flickered, the bare bulb swung on its cord, the light dimmed in the swirling brown smoke. Within seconds a terrific explosion shook the room. Had some fool set off a cherry bomb? Then there was a tremendous thud—and a scream!

Mercifully the candle did not go out, and when the smoke cleared I could see a huge form on top of Lord Partridgeville, prostrate on the picnic blanket, licking his face!

"Your tongue, *ahhh!*" groaned his lordship.

It was an enormous hound, with short chestnut hair, lop ears, and deep mournful eyes—though it could all have been an extremely clever costume. Seams and zippers would have been invisible in the feeble candle glow. When the animal stood upright on its hind legs and began to speak, in correct and idiomatic English, I was sure someone was playing a prank, and yet—

"Well, I knew we were destined to cross paths one of these days," the creature said. "And you do remind me so of your dear father."

"What?!" spluttered Lord Partridgeville, who was now sitting up and mopping his jowls with a handkerchief. "Who—or what—are you?"

"When we first met, Cosmo called me the Hound of Tindalos, but later, after we had . . . Well, I just thought it was more respectable to be known as the Hound of the Partridgevilles."

"Confound it, are you telling me you and Dad were friends?"

"Oh yes, though given certain cosmic limitations we could only meet secretly in our little hideaway. No one knew. If it hadn't been for that unfortunate accident to that writer who used to live here, Cosmo and I might never have . . . He was inspecting the apartment a day or two after the mess was cleaned up. I was still hovering around. He looked so cute I just had to introduce myself. Well, one thing led to another . . . Of course Cosmo was already married, but he confessed early on that his wife had this medical condition, but maybe she could be persuaded to go along and in the end she did, though the poor thing didn't survive the shock. . . . I was very sorry, especially for you . . . son."

"Ma, ma . . ."

"Cosmo and I agreed it was best not to tell you, until you were mature enough to understand . . . to understand for instance why you yourself can't have children. I'm afraid it's the old story of the horse and donkey producing a mule."

"That's why when I first . . . I couldn't . . ."

"Alas, your father died before we felt you were ready to handle the truth. I just hope now you have the courage to forgive us both."

"You and Dad, you . . ."

"He was so proud of you, a natural sportsman! And he was so attentive to me. He always saw to it that I had plenty of food and water when I visited the earthly plane."

I cast a furtive glance at the candle, which continued to flicker in the bowl . . . the dog bowl. Lord Partridgeville sat open-mouthed and wide-eyed on the blanket, evidently dumbfounded.

"This family history of yours is all very well," Nigel said finally, in a tone that suggested he didn't believe a word of it. "But you seem to be evading the real issue."

"That's right," said Ken. "Did you kill Halpin Chalmers?"

"I refuse to answer such a rude question."

""You would be wise to cooperate," continued Nigel. "In my professional capacity I have the authority to detain you at the town pound."

"Say, what kind of hound are you anyway, a blood hound?" added Ken. "A hound that laps up human blood and processes it into blue pus?"

"I've never heard such insults!"

Despite her size, she appeared to be a rather timid soul. (By this point I was ready to accept that the Hound of the Partridgevilles or Tindalos or whatever was a dam.) The two psychic researchers started to move forward, backing her into the gloom. She barked, and her bark was immediately echoed by what sounded like the distant baying of a whole pack of hounds—or was it the noise of the crowd in Central Square, distorted in the rising wind? Leaning out the window I could hear the hitherto quiet hordes mutter and complain, like a theater audience that has waited too long for the opening curtain. I was reassured to hear the police chief warning the more agitated spectators not to cross the barrier below.

A sudden blast of air behind me extinguished the candle. I turned but could see nothing. Amidst the inhuman baying that had by now swollen to nearly deafening levels, however, I could make out a lone human voice, the plummy, aristocratic voice of Cosmo Hopper Partridgeville VIII:

"Yoicks! Tally-ho! After him, lads! The quarry is nigh!"

Did I then actually hear the silvery peal of a hunting horn? Or was the drug driving my brain to produce even wilder hallucinations? Those thundering paws that grew louder and louder sounded only too real. In a panic I realized my only escape was the window, but as I climbed over the sill I was hit from the rear with the force of a locomotive. For an agonizing eternity I thrashed in mid-air, a searing pain at the back of my head. A hundred lights flashed, a thousand throats shouted—then I soared free and the entire universe went black.

"You know, you're a lucky kid, Linnet," said the editor. "Lucky the cops broke your fall before you hit the pavement."

"What about the others, Mr. Turrow?" I asked. It was two days after the episode in Central Square and I had just returned to work from the hospital. No one had told me anything.

"Ken Korey and Nigel Partridgeville are okay, though they seem to have suffered a total memory loss. They can only remember entering the apartment—nothing after that."

"And Lord Partridgeville?"

"His lordship's presently undergoing a rest cure at that sanitarium upstate where he periodically goes to, uh, dry out. I'm afraid he's instructed me to spike the story you were planning to write about the outcome of your psychic investigation. He's sorry."

"Just as well," I said. "We didn't solve the mystery of Halpin Chalmers' murder anyway. Besides, I'm not sure my memories are all that reliable, given my mental state."

"His lordship's also sorry for, uh . . ."

"For what?"

"I guess you haven't seen the front page of Saturday's *Gazette.*" The editor was grinning as he reached under his desk.

"No."

"We put out a special edition. Since so many camera buffs were at the scene we had plenty of high quality photos to chose from. For a night shot the clarity's amazing."

He was positively chortling when he handed me the newspaper. I snatched it open and read the headline: "Lord Partridgeville Bags Big Game." The picture underneath showed me dangling in front of 24 Central Square—held by the ponytail by his lordship, who was sawing at the roots with his Swiss Army knife. You could see the cross, the details were that sharp.

Through Outrageous Angles

David C. Kopaska-Merkel and Ronald McDowell

Eldritch Tales deserves fame as the fan equivalent of *Weird Tales*, sort of a farm club. One can look through old issues and find both stories that represent the baby teeth of since-mature writers and already-vintage works of art (e.g., anything by Tom Ligotti). And we can find filler that would have been bounced instantly back over the *Weird Tales* transom. *Eldritch Tales* is a welcome haven for that unjustly despised subgenre, the fan pastiche. A fine specimen of the fan pastiche is the present story "Through Outrageous Angles." In my opinion, as in this case, the pastiche is about on the same level as the revered tales it emulates, but the originals have since fallen out of favor. Thus, the shadow cast over it comes not from its inherent quality but rather because of changing tastes in the marketplace (or among editors).

"Through Outrageous Angles" obviously builds on two famous Mythos novels, August Derleth's *The Trail of Cthulhu* and Brian Lumley's *The Burrowers Beneath*. This is fitting, as I have always thought of the latter as reading like Colin Wilson's *The Mind Parasites* as it would read if Derleth had written it! The authors, by providing, as it were, a new chapter of *The Trail of Cthulhu*, have filled in a surprising lacuna: why, come to think of it, did Derleth himself never write a tale of the Hounds of Tindalos? One would have sworn he'd have gotten around to them.

"Through Outrageous Angles" initially appeared in *Eldritch Tales* #12, 1986.

(Being an excerpt from the journal of Laban Shrewsbury,
part 2: *The Celaeno Notes*)

"What if, parallel to the life we know now, there is another life that does not die, which lacks the elements that destroy *our* life? Perhaps in another dimension there is a *different* force from that which generates our life. . . . In my room at night I have talked with the Doels. And in dreams I have seen their maker. I have stood on the dim shore beyond time and matter and seen it. It moves through strange curves and outrageous angles. Some day I shall travel in time and meet it face to face."

—Halpin Chalmers, *The Secret Watcher*

I am Laban Shrewsbury. Some weeks ago I directed Andrew Phelan and Nayland Colum to return to Miskatonic from our haven here on Celaeno. They were to carry on our long-standing struggle against the Great Old Ones which was interrupted when we were forced to flee Earth following the murder of two of our comrades, Claiborne Boyd and Abel Keane, and the mutilation of Nayland Colum.

Because of Phelan's powerful and well-trained mind, and because of the enhanced psychic abilities he gained during his stay on Celaeno, he was able to maintain contact with me while he was on Earth. But before I continue further, and lest my narrative prove incomprehensible to the reader unfamiliar with Miskatonic University, myself, or the hideous Old Ones, let me provide some background.

Miskatonic University, situated in Arkham, Massachusetts, is the home of both the Pabodie Library and the Wilmarth Foundation. The former has long been a repository for rare books of forbidden lore. The collection includes such fabled volumes as Von Juntz's *Unaussprechlichen Kulten*, Prinn's *De Vermis Mysteriis*, the pre-Triassic Pnakotic Manuscript, as well as the accursed *Necronomicon* of al-Hazred. These ancient volumes catalogue certain inexplicable happenings, myths, and legends, many of which are older than prehistory. Also housed in the library is the Albert N. Wilmarth collection of New England folklore and his exhaustive nine-volume treatise, "Notes on the Old Ones."

The Wilmarth Foundation (named for Albert Wilmarth) and the Old Ones are intimately related though diametrically opposed in purpose. The Old Ones were and are elemental beings possessing awesome powers that dwarf man's infant technology. The very embodiment of cosmic evil, the Old Ones are completely inimical to human life and constitute the most pressing threat to human existence in the universe. Legend has it that the Old Ones warred against their benign counterparts, the Elder Gods, in Earth's distant past. Fortunately for mankind, the Old Ones lost that conflict and were variously imprisoned by the victors, commonly with the use of the potent star-stones of Mnar. Less fortunately, the servants of the Old Ones, as well as pre-human and, later, human worshippers of the deities, were left relatively unchecked by the Elder Gods and continued to work their masters evil among men.

This brings me, at last, to the Wilmarth Foundation itself. The Foundation was established to combat the minions of the Old Ones whenever and wherever they might be found and to prevent them from gaining the power to free their masters. More recently, the Foundation turned to a direct assault on the Old Ones themselves. The danger of this course was demonstrated all too clearly by the disastrous failure of the attempt to destroy Ithaqua the Wind Walker two years ago.

Since that time, the Foundation has taken a new tack. Certain obscure sources hint that mysterious inhabitants of the gulf beyond time and space, best known as the Hounds of Tindalos or the Dwellers in Angles, may be composed of the same primal substance from which the Old Ones evolved. Wingate Peaslee, the Foundation's director, decided that an indirect study of the Old Ones could be safely undertaken using the Hounds as subjects. To this end, the Tindalos Project had been initiated and was well under way when Andrew Phelan and Nayland Colum returned to Miskatonic University.

I will now set down, exactly as it was related to me by Phelan, an account of the part he played in the experiment recently conducted by Miskatonic. I do so because I am the only living man to know the manner of conclusion of that unhappy affair.

Nayland and I were delivered by the Byakhee birds to the steps of the Library late in the evening on May 5th. We gave your manuscript to Doctor Llanfer, who awaited us, and then checked in with Professor Peaslee. He briefed both of us on the Foundation's latest project: nothing less than an attempt to capture one of the Hounds of Tindalos!

The purpose of the Tindalos Project was to collect a sample of the "flesh" of one of the Hounds for study. Dr. Peaslee explained that the Pnakotic Manuscripts, relic of an enigmatic race that became extinct before the rise of the dinosaurs, hints that the material of which the Hounds are composed is none other than the protean substance from which the Old Ones arose countless millennia ago. A careful study of its chemical and physical characteristics might provide information that could be used to devise a weapon effective even against the Great Old Ones themselves.

Prinn's *De Vermis Mysteriis* contains the hideously enigmatic passage: "Beyond ye time and ye space, on the cold shores, lit by ye dark that is yet light, life hath no place, and evil hath full sway; yet the foulness which came before all good is cloaked in ye horrid beasts of the Tindaloth."

Prinn's remarks, though illuminating, are damnably imprecise, but the researchers at Miskatonic found more useful information in the Pabodie Library's own file of newspaper clippings, probably the most complete collection of newspaper accounts of unexplained events in the world. Two clippings from the *Partridgeville Gazette* for July 1928 describing the mysterious circumstances surrounding the death of the mystic Halpin Chalmers revealed that Chalmers had actually seen, and subsequently been killed by, the Hounds. Further research eventually turned up enough information so that technicians at Miskatonic felt they could construct a trap which would safely imprison one of the Hounds.

The trap they designed consisted of a perfectly spherical room with walls of chrome-steel alloy backed by two layers of reinforced concrete. There was only one door; a section of wall could be slid partway into the chamber by means of a hydraulic mechanism. The movable wall segment was hollow and when traversed all the way into the sphere, it allowed entrance and exit. When partially retracted, the section became a curvilinear projection which interrupted the smooth interior walls of the room. When fully retracted, the section fit perfectly in place, leaving the interior chamber walls as a geometrically precise sphere.

Chalmers demonstrated before his death that the Hounds cannot pass through curves; they can only advance through angles. Chalmers had crudely tried to protect himself from the Hounds by plastering over the corners of his room, but a freak earthquake had shaken the plaster off the walls and they had come for him. It was also known that the Hounds are unable to enter space-time except in pursuit of someone whom they have sighted. Once a person is seen by the Hounds, they can find him anywhere on Earth. Chalmers had traveled through time and seen the Hounds by using the drug Liao, which allows the perception of those realities that exist at other points in time, and as Chalmers discovered to his cost, even *beyond time!* If a man took the drug while standing in the spherical chamber, and sent his mind back through the wide vistas of the past until he crossed the ultimate boundary that separates normal space-time from that non-Einsteinian region of unearthly angles, and saw the things which inhabit it, they would follow him relentlessly. And if the door of the chamber was projecting slightly, interrupting the smooth interior curves with a right angle and allowing the Hounds entrance, then they would pursue him into that room. It would simply remain to close the door completely and they would be trapped. But of course the 'bait' would have no means of escape either, and his body and soul would be devoured by the Hounds. The researchers were still stymied by this problem when Colum and I arrived at Miskatonic. Naturally, Peaslee refused to allow anyone to commit suicide in this most horrible fashion, through there had been several courageous volunteers.

I offered to serve as the bait to attract the Hounds, because of my ability to project my *ka* into the chamber, and thus fool the Hounds into following me there. After luring the Hounds into the chamber, my *ka* would pass through the wall and reinhabit my body in the next room, leaving the Hounds in the trap. I was certain that my twenty years of practice in the controlled projection of my *ka* had given me sufficient expertise to do this in perfect safety. It took some persuading, but I finally convinced Peaslee that I would be in no serious danger. I think he acquiesced more because he knew there was no better alternative than because he really shared my confidence. "If all else fails," I told him, "and the Hounds escape from the trap we set for them, then I will simply return to Celaeno, where they cannot follow me."

The special room had already been constructed, and the laboratory where scientists would study the samples taken from the Hounds had been set up nearby. When the Hounds were securely trapped in the spherical chamber, they would be dissociated with ultrasonics, which would break down their bodies into small clumps of cells. The biologist in charge of this aspect of the project, Dr. Lanier Coursen, did not expect the ultrasonics to kill the Hounds, but the disrupted aggregates of cells would be no threat to humans. It would only take a few moments to collect the tissue samples which the biologists and biochemists needed for their experiments, and they would be finished long before the Hounds could recoalesce. After the samples had been collected, the room would be sterilized with hard radiation from projectors emplaced behind the walls. If this did not prove effective, the room could be flooded with a virulent poison gas.

Chalmers did not record the dosage of Liao which he took, but Miskatonic's pharmacologist prepared several precisely measured doses which she believed would be safe. I have taken the drug and am lying on a cot in a room adjacent to the test chamber. The pharmacologist and a doctor are with me in case something goes wrong. Peaslee and the others are watching the test chamber on closed circuit television. The TV camera is shielded so the Hounds will not be able to destroy it.

I feel a curious apprehension; a vague uneasiness. I suppose it is attributable to my knowledge of the manner of Chalmers' end . . . it was cruel! But he did not have all the safeguards which we have; nothing can go wrong!

The drug is beginning to take effect. It is just as Chalmers described it. Time has stopped and the room is fading. I must move quickly lest I lose my bearings before I project my *ka* into the chamber. God help me if I am not in the chamber when they come for me! I have left my body and passed through the wall, and I just caught a glimpse of the spherical room before it faded from my sight. Chalmers was right! This is fantastic! I perceive simultaneously all of history! I am aware of all the cycles of human history, civilizations rise and as quickly fall, vast migrations of people sweep across Asia again and again. I can actually see the essential cyclic nature of history, it is spread before me in a multifarious pattern that shifts and yet is always the same. I marvel at the first bow, and watch as Nagasaki is destroyed by its awesomely powerful descendent. All this I see simultaneously; I am somehow able to perceive and comprehend each tiniest thread of this impossibly complex skein. I am now looking back into prehistory, before the dawn of our race. Other, prehuman civilizations take man's place, but still the cycle is the same. I see the titanotheres, I observe the death of the last of the dinosaurs, starving in an ecosystem for which they are not suited. This is fascinating! To actually see *Tyrannosaurus rex* stalking his prey! I stand by dark pools out of which crawl the first amphibians. Huge dragonflies buzz through steaming coal swamps and still I gaze back and back! By straining my eyes I can see the entire Paleozoic era at a glance. Now primitive trilobites crawl slowly through the tide pools. Oh, the exhilaration of actually *seeing* all of past time! I stare into the inconceivably vast expanse of Archaean time, into the dead years before the evolution of life. But something makes me hang back from looking farther . . . I am afraid. My God! These angles! I have passed through all of curved space and now I progress through unearthly angles! Soon I will see *them!* I am in the time beyond Time, and now I stand on the hither side of that dread abyss beyond which lies that which both terrifies and fascinates me. You cannot imagine what I am experiencing. My soul quivers with fear but I am drawn irresistibly across the gulf. Oh, the horror of it! Chalmers said nothing of *this!* It cannot be expressed in words! Here is unutterable foulness; cosmic horror. Before time, before the birth of the universe, there was abominable blasphemy! In the beginning a *decision* was made, and the fruit of that decision prowls these hideous angles. Chalmers glimpsed the truth but he did not understand. It is yin and yang. Not good and evil, those are meaningless terms. There are the curves, and the angles which are their antithesis. The curves inherited Einsteinian space-time, but the horror dwells in angles beyond time, and we awaken at our peril. *Yin* eternally desires to be *yang.* All of what we call evil, all foulness, is concentrated in the yin, which moves slowly through unnatural angles in search of *yang,* the curve for which it hungers. All is alien here, sound is not sound, there is light yet it is not light as we know it. Things here are not physical but metaphysical, yet they exist, and if they were to enter normal space-time, then they would take on physical form. I stand on the farther shore and I see *them*. Oh, it has form, the hideous fruit of that awful *choice!* They know I am here, and I am afraid. Slowly their thought crystallizes about me. Their apperceptions and thoughts are alien, and they are utterly foul. I have let them see me clearly and I must flee before they trap me here! I feel the nauseous exhalation of their breath upon me! I flee and they are at my heels!

I know that it has been two days since last I contacted you, but I had a dreadful scare and I am still shaken. I only just escaped, for they nearly caught me, and if they had reached my *ka*, it could never have returned to my body, for they would have devoured it. But I did escape, fleeing through the friendly curved walls of the chamber back into my body, and there on that cot I slept dreamlessly for more than thirty-six hours. While I was thus insensible, others worked furiously.

All this I was told after I awakened. Only one Hound was trapped in the room; the others managed to retreat back through time before the door was fully shut, but one was enough. The ultrasonics functioned perfectly, and a sample of the loathsome ichor which serves them for flesh was collected without incident, though the revolting pungent odor which Chalmers described as being associated with the Hounds filled the building, which is still not quite rid of the stench. The biochemists are studying the stuff now and they are having a field day. They expect fascinating discoveries soon, but there is no breakthrough as yet. The radiation projectors proved to be easily adequate to the task of killing what remained of the Hound, and this was incinerated for good measure. The whole operation went smoothly, yet for some reason I am nervous; but perhaps it is an after-effect of my experience. I have a persistent feeling that I have forgotten something important . . . Well, I will contact you again sometime tomorrow.

I have blundered! Last night I dreamt that *they* still sought me. They moved purposefully through angles, hunting me, following my karmic scent. What a fool I was to forget . . . we trapped only one Hound, what of the others? They fled back to their alien abode, but still they hunger for me, and they do not forget. Even now I feel *their* approach! There is no place on Earth I will be safe, because they can literally *wait forever!* Time does not pass for them, for there is no time as we know it among those outrageous angles. I have only one chance, I must return to Celaeno. They will not be able to follow me there. I shall inform Professor Peaslee of my decision and then summon the Byakhees.

I am speeding toward Celaeno on the back of one of the noxious servants of Him Who is not to be Named. Strange it is that these evil creatures have served us so well for these many years, though their master is one of the accursed Old Ones. My body is safe in the crypt in buried Irem, and soon my *ka* will be with you on Celaeno. Already a wide gulf of space which *they* cannot cross lies behind me.

Something is following me!!! No, it can't be! For . . . for a minute I thought I sensed their lean shapes behind me. But I must have been mistaken. My fear makes me imagine all manner of things. Surely they cannot range at will through *all* space and time in pursuit of their prey?!

After this experience I do not think I will have the courage ever to return to Earth again! The battle against the cosmic evil of the Old Ones is a lonely one, and for those of us caught up in it there can never be any rest. Sometimes I wish I had never . . . They are coming!!! Fool that I am! To believe I could ever escape their unutterable foulness! That I could ever hope to thwart their insatiable hunger once it had been aroused! They draw closer; if only these accursed Byakhees would fly faster! But that would avail me nought, for if the space I have already crossed is no barrier, then they could easily follow me all the way to Celaeno. There are angles in space, Shrewsbury, angles exist everywhere, and the Hounds of Tindalos can progress through angles! I can feel my mind succumbing to hysteria! Slow, slow as corrupt death was their movement in that alien land beyond the past, but swift is their pursuit now that they have sighted me, their quarry! God, Shrewsbury . . . I, I feel their noisome paws upon my back, the foetor of their stinking breath! They are . . .

Those were the last words Andrew Phelan spoke to me. I have waited a sufficient time for him to have reached Celaeno if he were able and he is not here, so I can only conclude that he was overtaken by the Tind'losi in the black spaces between Earth and Celaeno. His material body was of course unharmed, but they have eaten his soul, and his body will lie eternally in the City of the Calusians, for there is nothing to inhabit it. Too often we have underestimated the power and malice of those whom we fight, yet still we persist. Perhaps it was ordained that to achieve this victory Andrew Phelan must die; perhaps his death could have been averted. I do not know. I do know that whatever the cost we shall continue the battle until the last trace of the Old Ones has been eradicated.

Firebrands of Torment

Michael Cisco

In the introduction to this collection I ventured a theory about the origin and meaning of the word "Tindalos." This story embodies another educated guess, this time by Michael Cisco. As many have observed, "Tindalos" sounds kind of Greek. Long himself evidently wanted us to think it a Greek name, even though you will find it in no lexicon: "The Greeks had a name for it." Apparently it was a new coinage for an esoteric phenomenon, known only to Greeks like, let's say, the Byzantine monk Carnamagos. So what would it mean? Comparing possible roots, Cisco has come up with a distinct possibility: "Firebrands of Torment," which is a pretty good candidate for a horror story title, if you ask me.

In a sense, Cisco here recapitulates the adventure of Halpin Chalmers in that he goes back in time, into the time of Chalmers himself, to present an alternate take on the events of "The Hounds of Tindalos." You thought you knew what happened? Think again.

Cisco, a major new talent in the field of the macabre and the surreal, writes, as one critic said of Nikos Kazantzakis, "near-hallucinatory prose." You know this if you have read previous work of his including *The Divinity Student*, "The Reliquaries," "The Water Nymphs," "*He* Will be There," and others. This one appears in Cisco's collection *Secret Hours* (2007).

From the *Tuey Monthly Occult Index* #137 (August 1948), entry by Arthur Hennepin Tuey:

CHALMERS, Halpin—He who gave us so much in life left us less than nothing in death. Despite the lapse of twenty years, the mind still reels at Douglas's ham-fisted 'investigation'. But where has the common outrage of our community found expression in action? Finally, it is left to Tuey to put aside his infirmities and probe the matter personally.

How many of our number have been dismissed and ignored as 'unstable'? How many persecuted outright as lunatics? The memory of Halpin Chalmers has been slandered and his work belittled almost as a matter of course. His stature in the field and the significance of his discoveries need no defense here.

But the recurrent question of madness, especially with regard to the Liao drug, does demand our attention. Was Chalmers 'slipped a mickey'?

An associate of mine, whose haunts include the Chinese neighborhoods of New York City, agreed to run this matter to ground for me. He visited as many traditional Herbalists as he could find, and I append here his account of a typical exchange:

"I asked about the Liao drug—a half-concealed snicker was the only reply.

"'What's funny?' I asked.

"Grinning, he exchanged a few words with a colleague somewhere at the back of the shop, a man I could hear but not see. The one at the counter seemed to be asking—should I tell him?

"'I don't understand,' I said.

"He smiled and said, 'Mister, you don't know what you're talking about.'

"There was a pause. He kept on smiling.

"'Well are you going to tell me?' I asked.

"He snickered again and held up a finger. 'Wait. I'll make you some Liao.'

"He went down to the end of the aisle where the least expensive items were, and without taking his eyes off me took down five bottles. He brought them back, mixed some of the contents without weighing them, and pushed the blend toward me on a fold of paper.

"'Liao,' he said.

"Then, he went back to the end of the aisle, still looking at me and smiling, took down five other things at random, mixed them, and pushed the blend toward me on the counter, next to the first.

"'Liao,' he said. 'Four thousand!'

"Then he leaned forward and said, 'Confidentially, "Liao" is Chinese Herbalist for snake oil. For tourists only.'"

———

"Don't be an asinine old woman!" Chalmers was saying. He wore a mildly disappointed and superior expression. "Nothing that you can say will induce me to stop now. I entreat you to remain silent while I study these charts."

Frank remained silent and stared at the clock on the mantel. Chalmers remained motionless and bored into his papers with his eyes. There were a series of primer images, designed to advance him in regular steps to the last, operative diagram of a single four-dimensional figure. He felt the iciness of its abstraction stitched in silver blazes behind his eyes—he cleared his mind and settled into a null state, the lines of the figure turning into sight-lines and then into time-lines. How long he had stared he did not know. He was breathing long vapor trails in time. The box with the Liao pellets seemed to twist into view off to one side of the desk—it was open. With a convulsive gesture he plucked up one of the pellets and swallowed it; it grated against his dry throat, his Adam's apple pressed against his high collar. The clock, whose sound seemed to emanate from somewhere behind him, suddenly fell silent.

He looked up to see Frank coming toward him with a solicitous, disapproving look. Frank's body yawed weirdly in the direction he had come, as if he were still in the intervening space.

"The clock has stopped," Chalmers said. His voice boomed in his ears. A sudden vertigo seized him and he spoke again, his voice rapid and quiet, to distract himself. The room rolled like the deck of a swiftly-tilting ship.

". . . It is beginning to get dark and the familiar objects in the room are fading out." He willed himself to keep talking; he tried to orient himself according to the protocols of the experiment. He had not failed to anticipate some disorientation—to some extent the pretense of dictation was to be his anchor in the present. Dimly aware of Frank shaking his pen and the thunderous loudness of its nib.

". . . Everything is dark, indistinct."

Something crashed over him like a wave of liquid air and an impalpable metallic cold—Chalmers' form was an icy mold in space, he felt his outline become something tangible in transparent layers of sucking cold. In suspended time he felt that outline gradually pass into him as if he were ballooning out in all directions, a sense of rising above the horizon of time. He was sitting at his desk, and Frank sat across the room bent—motionless—over his pad.

————

From the memoirs of A. N. Burton, forensic expert and consultant to the Providence police department from 1927 to 1931:

> Regarding the murder of Halpin Chalmers, there was no evidence to corroborate the so-called "cult" theory, although this remains among the more likely explanations. Sidney [county coroner at the time] asked me to look into the possibility of insanity, given the character of Chalmers' books and the circumstances surrounding is death; viz the plastered room, the notes found around the remains, etc.
>
> My first task was to read Chalmers' books. In my opinion, they were clearly the work of a psychotic, although not necessarily a dangerous one. From what few accounts of his character there are, I am not inclined to say that he was a violent or hysterical man, regardless of the circumstances of his death.
>
> Lacking much firsthand evidence, I resorted to genealogical research. I have always been a firm believer in the importance of hereditary factors in the development of mental disease. It was here that I made the most interesting discoveries. Chalmers had been raised in Providence by Hetty and Boone Chalmers of Waterman Street, but, owing to my association with the police department and the nature of my investigation, I was given access to city records of adoption proceedings dated 1898. Halpin Chalmers' real parents were a pair of Dutch immigrants named Helstrup, who lived in Providence for a time before moving to New York.

. . . as far as forensic evidence of insanity was concerned, there was almost nothing to go on. I was able to discover only that Chalmers' mother, Ada, died in Bellevue in 1901. The cause of death was 'general paresis.' In those days, that was sort of a "code phrase" for tertiary syphilis, although I would hasten to point out that, lacking any medical records or documentation from the autopsy, it is impossible to say precisely what disease she had. However, the fact that she died in a mental hospital is suggestive: syphilis, in the final stages, attacks the tissues of the brain, producing symptoms of insanity including hallucinations and paranoia.

If Ada Helstrup did have syphilis, it is not out of bounds to propose that she may have had the disease as early as 1890, when she gave birth to Chalmers, and, in that case, she would almost certainly have passed it on to him. The plot thickens when we consider that Georg Helstrup, whose autopsy records I uncovered, was completely free from any trace of the disease when he died in an accident in the fall of 1905. He had remarried, and when his widow, Sylvia, née Bishop, died a few years ago (April 1930), she also exhibited no signs of the disease.

Whether or not Ada Helstrup had syphilis or something else, she evidently contracted it outside of her marriage.

———

A conscious element in a still life, Chalmers was facing the door; unable to move his eyes, his range of vision was fixed, with Frank's downturned face barely visible in the periphery. With an uncanny feeling of coming to himself after an unknown interval, Chalmers again returned in his mind to the protocols of the experiment and tried to orient himself. Chalmers had nowhere yet to go. He was there, now to go. Frozen, with no physical sensation, he felt a cold bodiless panic, as if his mind were panting and groping in the dark—his panic had driven the diagrams out of his head; with a great effort he brought them up in his mind now as if on a movie screen. The dimensions of the room around him began to alter and he seemed to be teetering on the brink ready to slide off, his will to remain where he was manifesting as a kind of increased friction or adherence to the chair.

Chalmers sat frozen against the tilt of the space he was in and stared at the room, at Frank's absurdly calm face, and at once understood that the fall opening in front of him was where he was going. He could either pull back or fall forward. He could not remain clinging to the margin with an effort that was exhausting him.

Chalmers released himself and slid forward, the room around him veered past and disappeared into nothing.

There was no way to close his eyes. Open or closed, or eyes at all, there was no light, nothing but the sensation of a kind of angular momentum. Chalmers rambled faster and faster in his mind—where space is angular, it will converge at fixed vertices. Motion down an incline. The room had opened in concentric series in parallel, each one like a frame in a film. His eyes had wanted to focus on each at once. Rising above the horizon of time. His body was present to him but it seemed to recede to a vanishing point in the depth, which was all around him. Was he still dictating to Frank?

There was a wrenching sensation, another scene took shape around him, turning the corner he saw his mother as he remembered her, sitting in a print dress on the front steps. The street was dark, there were no lights in the street or on the porch, only moonlight. She sat smiling at him, resting one hand on her rounded stomach where she was pregnant with him. Above her on the porch he could see his father almost completely invisible in the shadows leaning against the wall between the door and the window with his head tilted back, motionless, and there was, Chalmers suddenly knew, another presence there on the porch in the dark by the wall where his father was but coming from the other side from his father, moving low and curling round his mother where he started forward to get it away, it was something. He shook and saw it was almost a huge flayed dog, in the pale light he could see it—a dripping carcass rolling a long black tongue in its mouth and reeking like an open sewer, the stink hit him in palpable waves and he felt his body recoiling—even looking at it made his eyes feel infected, his face and hands were scummed over, and this beast nuzzled around his mother familiarly and where its body touched her dress it left a smear, and it left a smear on her bare arm. His mother let it come near and smiled at it—Chalmers' stomach convulsed so hard he nearly fell forward and he was still watching, he watched as the beast pressed his paw on his mother's belly, the beast did it with a proprietary air—the beast laid its paw on his mother's belly with an obscenely proprietary air—it touched her belly and looked up into her face and she smiled at it and glanced up at Chalmers with uncannily bright and vivid brown eyes, her everyday brown eyes were uncannily bright and vivid and laughing and Chalmers saw a light on the porch, a little glow from his father's face as he gazed down with laughing brown eyes which were uncannily bright and vivid; because of course Chalmers' eyes were as blue as the blue eyes this beast laughingly turned toward him—Chalmers made a sound and choked at once on blue bile as his limbs and body erupted like a bursting cadaver, falling to his knees he split down his spine, his face screwed up with anguish as if it were being crushed by an invisible hand, the muscles locked and the eyes burned hot, his crying voice bayed, his eyes popped open in his reeking face out of a halo of spiraling blue talons and he saw the blissful family smiling at him—still jackknifing uncontrollably at the waist he lunged at his mother wanting to claw that gobbet out of her belly, and to gouge the grin off of his father's face—before he reached the porch the beast and his unbearable blue eyes was there between him and them—all the strength flowed out of him and seemed to puddle on the ground; the spiraling cloud of his body stopped, helpless and staring at the scene which refused to fade.

————

From Burton's memoir:

> The last piece in the puzzle—not the solving piece, just the last one—was a photograph I uncovered of the Helstrups. There was a very strong family re-

semblance between Chalmers and his mother, but none at all to his father. We can only conclude that Halpin Chalmers, and almost certainly the disease that killed Ada Helstrup, was the result of an extramarital affair. As to the identity of Chalmers' real father, no clue remains. We may only say with confidence that he had blue eyes.

But we must lay alongside the question of hereditary predisposition or even brain disease the equally important question of the extent of Chalmers' own knowledge of this case. Needless to say, the devastating potential of these facts, the adoption, the affair, the possible profligacy of Ada Helstrup, the possibility of an inherited taint, might drive an already delicately-balanced mind over the brink. From the point of view of the forensic psychologist, the most crucial question of all remains unanswered: how much of this, if any, was known to Halpin Chalmers?

———

Struggling through a dark morass—as he had been for infinite time. Streaks reflected from nowhere on the surface, the only light. Weighted down and exhausted with an eternity of floundering and useless wandering to no ready goal, relentlessly pulled along by no will of his own, through a slough of filth that closed over his head and swallowed him the moment he stopped. He would watch the dim surface rising away from him and in panic claw his way out again, breathing and choking and swallowing filth. Burdened with an exhaustion that ground down into his perforated bones he had to fight at every moment the desire to let himself go, release his grip, relax his body, and allow himself to be swallowed once and for all time, sink to the bottom and disappear in the mire. His body was spent, rotted through and hanging in rags, a nearly formless clot of corrupted flesh, cold and lifeless, animated only by its decay. He could feel the powerful, alien life of the decay in his arms and legs that convulsively dragged him forward and kept his head above the surface. The decay rode him like an animating parasite, satisfying itself endlessly on what was left of his flesh and vitality. Despite the fatigue there was only a sweet toothache pain in his bones; an abominable, mocking pleasure warming his rotting flesh as it bloated and sloughed off in thin sheets, with a little ooze of viscous blood.

There before him—strange empty white room with rounded corners, and a figure inside—a familiar little man. He watched that little man pacing self-importantly around the room and he flung himself forward, screaming and clawing he flung himself again and again against the tiny room. Suddenly a gap appeared and he was through.

———

Chalmers stood just inside the corner of the room, in a half-space protruding into the room from the corner. He looked at his hands and they were hands and they were clean. A moment before things had been different. He had plucked off the offending organ, not the eye in this case he had done the Bible one better, and had paused a moment to redecorate the old place. Now he placed his head in his hand and gazed at Frank sitting frozen on the other side of the room—what a face! Pink and credulous and empty as a store for rent. Chalmers ambled to his chair and leaned over the back with his forearms crossed looking at Frank with sardonic pity. Well, well.

Chalmers resumed his seat and leaned back. After a moment he stiffened and opened his eyes, fluttering the lids. "God in heaven!" he cried. "I see!"

"Chalmers—Chalmers, shall I wake you?" came Frank's voice.

Chalmers ranted and raved, an inspired performance, to say the least. At the end, he crawled on the floor and spat lather from his lips. Frank grabbed his shoulders shouting. Rather a bit over the top but Chalmers barked jerkily to cover the spasms of laughter that were convulsing in his stomach; he snapped at Frank's wrist and nearly gave himself the hiccoughs trying to contain himself. Frank kept shaking and chiding, and Chalmers gradually relaxed, allowing himself to collapse on the floor, hiding his face.

Chalmers asked for whisky. He raved for sheer pleasure. "They are lean and athirst! The Hounds of Tindalos!" 'Tindalos' was the piece de la resistance, a Greek flourish meaning 'Firebrands of Torment'!

Frank's scientific education had not included Greek: "A week's rest in a good sanitarium should benefit you immeasurably."

And there Chalmers simply let his head hang back and the laughter pour out. And after Frank was gone, he went on, helpless, breath after breath of laughter filling up a mouth that distorted and distorted and distorted . . .

———

". . . I did not mean to offend you." Chalmers was saying. "You have a superlative intellect, but I—I have a superhuman one. It is only natural that I should be aware of your limitations."

"Phone if you need me."

The door closed behind Frank. Chalmers sat in the middle of the floor, then curled into a ball, eyebrows raised, exhausted and helpless in his hilarity tears streaked down his face.

"The Hounds of Tindalos!"

He had tried to put a stop to it all when he first knew and lunged, but had been stopped instead. He had found his second chance in future time, but he would need to complete the gesture from this end, to bring both ends of the same story to meet, or should it be said, to bring together both rays at a common vertex. But there must be no interference from the family quarter so to speak. The family might not understand so to speak. That one would try to stop him again. He looked at the now weirdly-rounded room.

"Now I'm safe," he thought, and rolled on the floor again.

Chalmers watched the night fall through the newly oval windows. Some people bicycled by the window. The day's clouds swept by in much the same way. He enjoyed waiting. After it got completely dark he lay on the floor and doodled—what would they make of these? He scribbled note after note, frantically exaggerating his handwriting and collapsing in little fits with increasing regularity.

Suddenly the earth shifted, the ground bucked and the whole building shifted violently—Chalmers had never felt an earthquake before, but smiled up at the cracks that snaked in the plaster. When the quake was over, not a piece had fallen. He'd seen to it.

Chalmers rushed to the wall, where the edge would be, and as if inside it he felt the heat and onrush and the futile ragings—

"Sorry, but this is my room!" Chalmers said with a razory grin.

Not for long, but long enough. Calm returned, the onslaught was over, the gap in time had opened. Chalmers sat in the middle of the floor. His head began to nod, chortling bobbed up his throat, he took a sheet and wrote—

"Good God, the plaster is falling! A terrific shock has loosened the plaster and it is falling. An earthquake perhaps! I never could have anticipated this. It is growing dark in the room. I must phone Frank. But can he get here in time? I will try. I will recite the Einstein formula. I will—God, they are breaking through! They are breaking through! Smoke is pouring from the corners of the wall. Their tongues—ahhhh—"

—and at the last he flung it into the air on spiraling gales of hysterics rolling on the floor and clutching his stomach with both arms. Then, grinning, he got to his feet and casually stripped himself, throwing his clothes—well, not into a corner perhaps but away at any rate. He took up his hammer, and knocked away the plaster here and there, where the mood took him. The fragments he arranged on the floor, where he will wait, where he had seen himself waiting. Chalmers paced the unlit room.

Something is glinting in one corner. Chalmers looks more closely—the lines of the ceiling and the upright angle of the wall drop away, sight-lines into a deep distance, and where they converge there is a minuscule figure, loping on all fours, racing toward him with shining eyes. As Chalmers continues to look, the figure grows larger bit by bit, seeming to accelerate—when the eyes are near enough to recognize and the abyss before him has become a mirror, he gazes back at himself, Chalmers calmly moves to the center of his triangle to wait.

The Shore of Madness

Ann K. Schwader

A number of H. P. Lovecraft's stories grew from plot germs first recorded in his *Fungi from Yuggoth*. If we didn't know better, we might guess that Frank Long's "The Hounds of Tindalos" grew from the evocative lines penned here by Ann K. Schwader. The abstraction is fully as powerful, in the manner of its chosen genre, as the full-blown tale.

On wings of alchemy I chased the past
Through ebb and flow of all humanity,
Beheld Atlantis vanquished by the sea,
Then backward further still—until at last
The simplest single cells winked out of sight
As angled time replaced the purer curve
Of mundane being. Stricken to the nerve,
I glanced about in light that was not light
And found myself upon the *other side:*
That ghost-gray shore where silence writhes and shrieks,
Where there is never anywhere to hide.
A wind is rising now that steams and reeks
Like daemon's breath . . . dear God, I know those sounds . . .
The nightmare baying of Tind'losi Hounds!

Gateway to Forever

Frank Belknap Long

Frank Long's "Gateway to Forever" was one of the high points in the hundred-plus issue history of *Crypt of Cthulhu*, my own fanzine. Just as Ed Wood couldn't allow the aged Bela Lugosi, once he had the surprising good fortune to meet him, to pass from this world without making at least one more movie ("You! vill! become! . . . *bride of the atom!*"), neither could I allow the venerable Frank Belknap Long to let sleeping dogs lie. I felt it my duty to persuade the master to write another tale of Tindalos, and it appeared in *Crypt of Cthulhu* #25 (Michaelmas 1984). There is a strange irony about the ending of the two stories, for, if "The Hounds of Tindalos" ends too abruptly, the protagonist writing his own death-rattle, "Gateway to Forever" ends too late, anticlimactically, with the protagonist retiring to a monastery to think things over.

It had taken Thomas Granville less than three months—it took longer perhaps in the case of many others—to discover how insecure a man could be made to feel by a desperate kind of loneliness. The big house with its costly furnishings, and the leisure he needed for his widely-known research in the realm of consciousness-expansion were his by right of inheritance and could not be taken from him. But the death of his wife in a motor accident, and the departure of his closest friend for a teaching job in England had left him with no one he could depend on for encouragement and understanding.

No one, that is, until, quite by happenstance, a near-miracle happened. He'd been drifting about in a singles bar neighborhood—there were four within walking distance of his residence—and had just entered his usual tavern of choice, with its oak-paneled decorum and lack of clatter, when he saw the girl.

The hour was an early one, and she was sitting alone at the far end of the bar, toying with a drink, and the instant their eyes met the strange feeling swept over him that he had known her from childhood. Granville was aware that at some time in their lives few people have failed to experience such a feeling on meeting someone new for the first time—often more than once. But in this instance—

Well, just by shutting his eyes he could visualize her beautiful adult face, with its deepset, haunted eyes, high cheekbones, and sensuously curving lips, as changing to that of a little girl with very much the same expression. And at almost the same instant he had a vision of himself as a boy of seven or eight, sitting opposite her in a grade school classroom, and reaching out from his desk to hers to clasp her fingers tightly, and stroke her hair in a secret caressment.

Quickly, quickly . . . lest Miss Someone-or-other at the blackboard—he could only remember her stiffly starched aspect—outraged by such an occurrence should come striding down the aisle toward him with fury in her eyes. Yes . . . oh, yes. He could almost hear the crack of the descending ruler, and feel the pain.

It was all nonsense, of course. It had to be, because at that period in his life he had been in an *all boys* private school just two or three stages above kindergarten.

He had opened his eyes and was staring at her again when she smiled abruptly, as if in amusement, and pointed at her empty glass. The invitation to join her could not have been more direct, but somehow just the fact that it was lacking in subtlety meant nothing at all to him. It was as if she realized that they would have to meet, and shared his dislike of circumlocutions of a trivial nature when a bond had been established in other ways.

He gestured to the bartender as he crossed to where she was sitting and drew an empty chair to her side, placing his nearly empty glass next to hers as he sat down. Quick refills followed before he could say a word, with the robotlike efficiency which often follows pickups in good singles bars. But this wasn't an ordinary pickup, and the bartender seemed to sense it, for his look said as plain as words: "You've got yourself a respect-rating, mighty serious kind of date. She won't appreciate a pawing, so be careful not to get the wrong ideas."

She spoke the instant he had turned and was distant enough to keep their conversation from being overheard. "You're in great need of someone to talk to," she said. "I can usually tell. Please don't ask me how. I get so tired of explaining to the few people I make a mistake about."

"You mean—the ones you're *not* mistaken about should know without asking?"

"That pretty well covers it," she said, smiling. "Not completely, but well enough."

Her drink had been a pale pink one, very tall and garnished with a lime. It seemed to become her somehow. Granville's had been a Scotch and soda. He dawdled with the spindle of the refill before they began to talk. He introduced himself in a quiet, earnest way and talked continuously for several minutes. He knew that he should have asked her more about herself first, and that his failure to do so would have seemed unforgivable to some women. But he had the strange feeling that she cared not at all about his self-centeredness in that respect.

Everything he said, he felt, was of importance to her, and she would pass no judgments, quick or otherwise, until she knew almost as much about him as he knew himself at that particular moment in time. He had never needed the meditative assistance of a think tank to become convinced that men and women could only know themselves to a certain extent, and in a certain way, at any single moment in time, and he had the incredible feeling, at least while he talked, that sitting at his side was someone he could transfer all of that inner knowledge to as he might have done with a computer—with one vital difference. Not only did computers lack all capacity for departures in thinking, apart from the data fed into them, but human emotions—or the emotions of a gnat or great ape, for that matter—were alien to their functioning.

Granville could not avoid feeling that there might well be an element of absurdity in such a notion. But absurd or not, there was a warmth, a depth of understanding in the way she kept looking at him as he talked that made it seem far more than just a wish-fulfillment fantasy.

She began to talk about herself as soon as he fell silent, and it was all so much more than a simple get-acquainted kind of conversation that it was hard for him to realize that he had paid the check and left the tavern, and she was still talking at his side as they walked along a pedestrian-crowded crosstown street in what she'd told him was the direction of her home. Her home, not his—an unexpected reversal of the way such evenings were most likely to terminate, if the patrons of a singles bar had some kind of permanent relationship in mind. But what they had talked about had made the bar's ceaseless hum of other conversation seem remote, and the direction they were taking inevitable.

He'd told her about his big, lonely brownstone, and his research, and the consciousness-raising experiments he'd been conducting since his post-graduate years at Brown University, and his one brief year as an associate professor. And she had told him about her uncle. He, too, had engaged in studies and experiments of a closely similar, almost parallel nature, particularly in the realm of time transcendence. Even as a child she had been preoccupied with such matters, and for five years she had been her uncle's secretary and co-worker.

He was also a man of independent means, and possessed his home—it had become hers now as well—by right of inheritance. He was away now on a brief trip, but would soon return. She had not mentioned the nature of the trip, and had seemed slightly reluctant to talk about it. She had hastened to add that there could be no better time than the present evening, to show Granville some of her uncle's books and papers, and the most unusual research materials he'd been making use of.

Before leaving the tavern they had dwelt for a moment on consciousness-raising, and time transcendence in relation to more than one challengingly insightful theory of the past century and a half, including Nietzsche's Eternal Return, and the much later speculations of Dunne which H. G. Wells had taken seriously enough to discuss at some length, their premise being that every human life repeats itself over and over, with only minor variations at each recurrence. It was a reassuring premise, for the most part, but what had always troubled Granville was Dunne's failure to rule out the possibility that even such minor variations could, on occasion, be sanity-threatening and catastrophic.

Long experience in discussing ideas and thoughts which were of great importance to him with someone he felt was gifted with an exceptional kind of understanding had taught Granville the value of a few moments of silence, and they traversed three long blocks without speaking at all.

Even in Manhattan there are still a few streets where all the buildings are smallish, and the pavements still cobblestoned, and so dimly lighted they would not seem in any way out of place to a wandering ghost from the gaslight era.

It was along such a street that they walked, and came at last to a three-story brownstone surviving in the midst of several small warehouses with night shields of corrugated metal, securely lowered and bolted.

The front door was on street level and in a moment she had a key out, and was unlocking it, turning once slightly to press his hand, as if she felt he might be in need of reassurance on entering a house so run down and deserted-looking. She had left no lights on, but the globular street lamp near the corner, dim as it was, provided sufficient illumination to enable him to make out exactly how chipped and weather-worn the façade had become.

"For as long as I can remember," she said, "Uncle has never given a thought to the look of this place from the outside, all apart from the fact that there are no longer neighbors to impress. I'm afraid I haven't either. There's a kind of delight in just knowing that the ugliest exterior has no importance when you've passed beyond it."

Beyond it? For a moment Granville felt she was speaking in riddles, but he knew what she meant the instant they were inside, and had passed down a long, oak-paneled hall with framed lithographs on both of its walls, and entered one of the strangest-looking rooms he had ever seen, large or small.

It was quite large, and each of the four walls was adorned with a painting in a cinematic kind of three-dimensional perspective, lighted in a different way. One was bathed in a rosy radiance, another in pale blue, and the one facing him was as dun-colored as the desert landscape it depicted, which seemed to stretch out almost featurelessly for miles.

The other wall was filled from floor to ceiling with a huge, built-in bookcase, containing what appeared to be close to three hundred volumes, all bound in calfskin, but differing greatly in height and thickness.

There were only two articles of furniture in the room. The largest, in almost its precise center, was a couch which, Granville could see at a glance, could be converted into a bed by the simple lowering of its top. The other was a small, circular table which could hardly have contained more medical-looking accessories if it had stood at the bedside of a hospitalized patient under emergency nursing care.

"Drugs?" Granville wondered, and for an instant a feeling of unease took hold of him. In all his consciousness-raising research he had shunned the use of the ordinary sensation-distorting drugs, even LSD, for the simple reason that they seemed to him to contribute nothing to the kind of time transcendence he had been hoping to achieve.

She tapped him gently on the shoulder, as if she had followed the direction of his gaze, and had guessed at his thoughts.

"Do not be misled by what that table contains," she said. "The powders and fluids in those bottles are not medicinal in an ordinary, prescription-drug sense. You may think of them as drugs, if you wish. But all of them are of a very ancient, far-

Eastern nature, their effects untested by anyone but Uncle—and to a lesser extent myself through long hours of patient experimentation. Right in this very room—"

She broke off abruptly, and paused an instant, as if abandoning one thought to take up another of greater, more immediate importance.

"There must always be, as you know, some prearranged locality, some definite starting point, for experiments of a certain kind. As for the chemicals in those phials, none of them are difficult to obtain. It is the mixture alone that can produce quite startling changes in our mastery of what would otherwise be barriers to the few—there are basically not more than three—altered states of consciousness that are in direct contact with hyperdimensional space-time."

"The mixture?" Granville heard himself asking. "You mean—the precise way each of the chemicals is combined? The actual formulae?"

"Yes, of course," she replied, smiling a little as if to relieve the tension she felt he might be laboring under.

"But you said they are of a very ancient, far-Eastern nature," he reminded her.

"Years ago, when I was still a child, Uncle's scholarship was just as remarkable as it is now. When he had some all-compelling purpose in mind, when his emotions were deeply stirred and his heart was set on something, his capacity for unusual research was almost beyond belief. He deciphered some faded Chinese parchments that went back to the end of the Chou dynasty and could well have been studied and pondered before the founding of Taoism three centuries later by Lao-Tse himself."

"But parchments so ancient would have long ago crumbled to dust," Granville protested.

She shook her head. "I'm afraid you're mistaken," she said, easing the harshness of her challenge to his scholarship with another slight smile. "As I'm sure you know, there are hundreds—no, thousands—of Egyptian papyri in existence that haven't even begun to disintegrate. And ancient China was the first to manufacture thin sheets of paper with an actual, close to time-resistant fibre content."

Something happened then that startled him by its suddenness. She had taken firm hold of his arm, and was drawing him toward the couch with an intention that could not have been otherwise than unmistakable. It was made to seem doubly so by what had happened in the tavern, when she had looked directly at him and pointed at her empty glass, indicating that she could never have been faulted for making slow decisions.

"You told me as we were walking," she said, "that when you left your home tonight, returning within a short while would be impossible. You intended to walk and walk until you brought yourself to a state bordering on exhaustion. When we met I knew that some such feeling had made you go into the tavern, in the hope that you would be spared the need of returning alone to a house that has ceased to symbolize, to a man like yourself, anything to treasure and take pride in. There is nothing so destructive to human values as total loneliness."

As she continued to draw him toward the couch her voice changed to such a tender, beguilingly seductive whisper that he was seized by a mad desire to do what he had wanted to do from the first—take her into his arms and crush her to him, raining passionate kisses on her lips, and entangling his fingers in her hair. But he managed to restrain himself with a tremendous effort of will, fearing to cut her off in mid-speech when her every spoken word had become so important to him.

"There are more than a dozen drugs to choose from," she went on, as if their very thoughts had entered into a kind of marriage. "Several are comparatively mild, if you think of them in terms of safety only—there is nothing mild about moments of rapture—and they will take us on brief, happy journeys, quite unlike the long and dangerous one from which Uncle has not as yet returned."

The trembling began before they had quite reached the foot of the couch. It was barely perceptible at first, but it swiftly spread to the entire room and increased in violence until the ceiling and floor began to shake and the walls to sway, as if the house were being buffeted by a suddenly arising gale.

In another moment—or it could have been at the same instant, since in moments of great and sudden shock time's sequence blurs a little in most minds—Granville saw that the desolate desert landscape in the wall painting had taken on a look of even greater depth and begun to brim with a brighter, almost fiery kind of radiance.

Across the desert waste a human figure was running. It was wavering back and forth, stumbling and falling and getting up again. It was clearly in the grip of fear and appeared to be fleeing from something, although no pursuing figure, man or animal, was visible on the empty sands at its back.

It was so distant at first that it could have been either a man or a woman, but in a matter of seconds all that changed, and it loomed so large and near that its fright-convulsed face, darkly bearded, and with eyes that had gone wild—in what appeared to be mindless or close to mindless panic—left no doubt in Granville's mind that he was staring at someone he had once met and talked to with no clear remembrance of exactly when or where.

The woman at his side must have shared the way he felt, for her fingers clawed at his wrist and she had begun to scream. But it was not her screams alone that he heard. Deep in his mind another voice seemed to rise higher than hers, blotting it out for a moment, as inner voices can sometimes do when the veils that cloak transcendence are ripped to shreds by some brief, shattering revelation that can seldom be repeated or explained.

"They are lean and athirst! *The Hounds of Tindalos!*"

All at once the fleeing man ceased to remain within the confines of the painting, as if it had never been more than a symbolically constructed portal, a necessary but arbitrary point of departure for a journey that transcended it. He was lying on the floor at its base. His clothes and beard had burst into flame, and a spiral of thick, black smoke was arising from his sprawled out body.

Deep in Granville's mind the voice spoke again. "They move through angles in dim recesses of time, and men awaken in them cosmic hungers."

Across the desert landscape five monstrous shapes were now moving, with a rapidity that seemed in some quite terrible way unnatural. In aspect they were vaguely wolflike, with blazing eyes and clashing jaws. But their contours kept shifting as they advanced, as if all the evil in the universe were reshaping them, from instant to instant, to make them increasingly more frightful in their destructiveness.

Before Granville's suddenly confused awareness could return to the full, immediate horror of what he saw, or remember that he was not alone in backing away from something that made all his research seem like mere surface-skimming, a flood of other memories took possession of his mind.

Somewhere at some time, on some level of awareness that he could not relate in any clear way to his present journey from his cradle toward his grave he had met and talked with—in fact, known as a friend—a man who had no niece, but had otherwise gone as far as the fire and smoke-enveloped figure on the floor had on a journey through time and space.

On that same level of still-existent awareness from some vast ocean of time the figure could hardly have been a different man, for his age, height, and features were exactly the same. The room itself—yes, there was a difference there, but not so great, for that other room had contained a library of unusual books, and drawings and diagrams that had much in common with the wall paintings in a general way.

It was the voice that seemed to come from deep in his mind that had told him the most about the journey itself, and now it seemed to be speaking again, relating how the centuries had fallen away until first human and then continuously more primitive forms of life had vanished from the earth, and more primal mysteries had begun to reveal themselves, taking on a frightful form and substance in boundless regions of space and time.

The figure seemed to be speaking to him directly now, but he was sure that it was his own inner voice he still heard, repeating as if he were himself the speaker, what he had once heard from his friend's own lips.

"For a moment I stood on the *other side*. I stood on the pale gray shores beyond time and space, and in an awful light that was not light, amidst a silence that shrieked, I saw the Hounds. I heard them breathe. They turned toward me, and I fled screaming. I fled screaming through time. I fled down quintillions of years."

For an instant that had seemed like an eternity, but could hardly have been more than a few seconds, for the smoke arising from the figure on the floor still had a just-starting look, Granville had lost all awareness of the woman at his side. But no sooner did that awareness come sweeping back than it ceased to be a reality.

Not only had she left *his* side, she had rushed to her uncle's side and was trying desperately to smother and stamp out the flames, seemingly oblivious to her own deadly peril.

For another moment, brief this time *both* subjectively and objectively, he remained motionless, helplessly staring. His every muscle seemed frozen.

Gradually at first, and then more swiftly the entire room became suffused with a light that streamed down from the ceiling and all four of the walls, continuing to increase in brightness until it became almost blinding.

An invisible something in it could not have possessed more strength and firmness if it had been a steel brace clamped to Granville's shoulders. It lifted him up and hurled him backwards.

Back and back, amidst cascading spirals of radiance that slowly began to grow dim again until they vanished, like the light from a shattered sun in the interstellar gulfs.

He was told later that he had been found lying in a crumpled heap on a cobblestoned street before a row of warehouses that had been built on the site of four or five rooming houses, converted brownstones, one of which had maintained its single-family integrity until it had been gutted by a still-remembered four-alarm blaze a half-century ago.

In the months that followed, by the strength of his will alone, Granville managed to rebuild his life and to find some measure of peace and contentment by joining one of the many monastic and semimonastic orders dedicated to contemplation and the journey inward. Though in the one he chose almost absolute silence was enjoined, he achieved protection at least from the destructiveness of absolute loneliness.

The Gift of Lycanthropy

Frank Belknap Long

A genre unique, I dare say, to fandom is the round-robin. We love to write 'em and to read 'em. And we love to pester professional writers to join them because it's like watching an all-star game. Imagine a team-up, not just of two favorite writers (King and Straub on *The Talisman*) but a whole gang of them! Everyone knows of "The Challenge from Beyond," both versions, in which Julius Schwartz, then (1935) editor of *Fantasy Magazine,* prevailed upon five fantasy writers (A. Merritt, C. L. Moore, H. P. Lovecraft, Robert E. Howard, and Frank Belknap Long) and five scientifiction authors (Stanley G. Weinbaum, Donald Wandrei, E. E. "Doc" Smith, Harl Vincent, and Murray Leinster) to write a tale to fit the title "The Challenge from Beyond." Necronomicon Press performed the great service of collecting and reprinting both these stories in 1990. Seven years later, and with much greater difficulty, it managed to assemble a far more ambitious project initiated back in 1977 by Jonathan Bacon, editor of *Fantasy Crossroads.* You see, this fanzine was one of many at the time devoted to the work of Robert E. Howard, and it occurred to Bacon to publish one of the fragments Howard wrote about his much-reincarnated hero James Allison, called "Genseric's Fifth-Born Son," and to invite a whole Hyborian legion of writers to continue it, no doubt way beyond anything Howard himself ever envisioned. A dozen chapters were published over time, but the magazine finally folded in 1979 with five chapters to go. Glenn Lord, to whom all Howard fans have been indebted for decades, had a copy of the whole epic and shared it with Marc Michaud, who published it in 1997 as *Ghor, Kin-Slayer: The Saga of Genseric's Fifth Born Son.* The authors were, after Howard himself, Karl Edward Wagner, Joseph Payne Brennan, Richard L. Tierney, Michael Moorcock, Charles R. Saunders, Andrew J. Offutt, Manly Wade Wellman, Darrell Schweitzer (who, I'm guessing, as a studied gesture of disrespect to the whole genre, had the hero's arm hacked off), A. E. van Vogt, Brian Lumley, Frank Belknap Long, Adrian Cole, Ramsey Campbell, H. Warner Munn, Marion Zimmer Bradley, and Richard A. Lupoff—there's a galaxy for you! We reproduce three chapters here, as they feature none other than the Hounds of Tindalos.

I knew not what guided me through the maze of unfamiliar streets, past dimly lit wineshops, with the raucous shouts of drunken revelers drifting out into the night.

Never before had I felt quite so much like a wolf as my breath came and went, as if its intake was slowed by the fierce clashing of my teeth. Never once could I remember stopping to stand erect like a man, for some deep-seated instinct prevented me from drawing myself up to my full height.

I made half-growling sounds deep in my throat which seemed as natural to me as breathing, as natural as they would have been if I had been the leader of a wolf pack bent on slaying and dismembering the self-deceiving creature called "Man."

What wolves did men did also, but with more cunning and guile, pretending always to possess, deep in their minds, another self they could summon forth in battle attire at will, to fight for what they liked to call justice and mercy. In some strange way, it made the slaying of their own kind less troublesome to them. But always the slaying went on and on, just as it did with wolves. Was it not better then to *be* a wolf, totally untroubled by guilt?

There is nothing strange or unnatural about what wolves do when they slay, and whenever I felt I was becoming more like a man I was assailed by rage and self-reproach and I made haste to put all such thoughts from my mind.

The narrow streets twisted and turned and some ended in blind alleys as they had in the border kingdoms of Nemedia, particularly in the city of Belverus, which seemed as remote to me now as was Argos and Shem and the tropical rain forests of Keshan, forcing me to circle back to escape from the sea-bordering maze that was Zaporakh. I have said that I knew not what was guiding me. But that would not have been strictly true if I could have given more thought to everything that I knew or suspected.

I never for a moment doubted that I was still under the spell of the Ice Bitch, however remote she may have been from me in space at that particular time, and that her powers remained so great that I would soon be loping inland, straight as an arrow, toward the habitation of the White Magician. I knew as well that she was implanting in my mind images, however nebulous, that would unfailingly guide me when I left Zaporakh, and passed into the surrounding countryside, if a desert waste without flowering shrubs or animal life of any kind could be thought of as a countryside.

I even knew that the habitation I sought would be of stone, a tower perhaps on an almost featureless plain, or some rock-walled chamber deep underground.

I was sure that Ythillin's guidance would not fail me. Had she not come to me out of the sea, swimming up out of the depths, awesome in her beauty, when I had come close to perishing, saying things that had made me think of her, once again, as both bitch and the goddess she had proclaimed herself to be? So sure was I that if she had chosen to preserve me then, when my eyes had been clouding in death, her purpose in guiding me now would remain steadfast.

Exactly what that purpose was I did not know—only that meeting and talking with the White Magician was as important to her as it had now become to me.

And that was why I endured with patience retracing my course a dozen times within the boundaries of Zaporakh, knowing I would soon be on its outskirts and loping onward until its white towers, silvered by moonlight, became a receding blur in the distance.

But that, too, proved no more than a mind's gaze image, for when once Zaporakh was actually behind me and the desert waste stretched out before me with only a few scattered boulders arising, as far as my eyes could see, in a monotonous expanse of sand, my urge to make haste was so great that I did not turn to glance back until the city had vanished from view.

The horizon ahead seemed to blend with the plain in a featureless glimmering, but a vast cliff wall soon appeared in the distance as I continued on. When I drew near to it I saw that the rock had been hollowed out to create a tunnel-like cave in direct line with my approach. It appeared to be lighted from deep within by a dull, reddish glow that seeped out upon the plain, forming a luminous, blood-red figure of a configuration I had never seen before.

Its half-triangular, half-circular shape made me feel for an instant it might be a sorcerer's talisman in luminous form which it would be dangerous for me to cross. But nothing happened as I passed through it and entered the cave.

It was a very large cave and for a moment my wolfish eyes saw only a number of vague shadow-shapes that seemed to be leaping up and down.

Then the light seemed to grow a little brighter and I saw—

I had split the skulls of many enemies. I had sliced off their arms and legs and plunged my sword deep into their vitals. I had eviscerated them by slicing downward from their chests to their groins sending them crashing with a wolf's merciless howl.

But the skeletons that dangled from the walls impaled on iron hooks had endured mutilations that would have made anyone less capable than I was of surmounting all fear back away quickly and go fleeing from the cave, for what had happened to intruders in the past could happen again, and seemed infinitely more akin to black sorcery than white.

For an instant the skeletons seemed clothed once more in human flesh as they swayed back and forth with the light playing over them. In the red gleaming it was as if they were still being ripped and torn asunder in a hundred hideous ways, for enough flesh still adhered to the bones to make it clear that what had been done to them had seldom been duplicated. No, not even by the dwarfed human ghouls, cannibals all, that crowded around campfires in far Keshan, and muttered and mumbled low, as they tossed into campfires, one by one, every sliced-off part of what had once been a man.

He came toward me out of the shadows, the hairiest creature on two legs I had ever seen, with the features and carriage of a man. His chest, which was barrel-shaped, was covered with hair so thick it seemed almost furlike, and his huge, muscular arms would have made an ape feel an instant kinship, despite the slight difference between human hair, however thick, and the body covering of an ape.

"Don't let my small trophy collection alarm you," he said, without preamble and in a surprisingly soft-spoken voice. "Those were Ythillin's enemies—and mine. It is necessary to be harsh in dealing with men whose every instinct is hostile. It serves as a warning; it keeps rumors flying in all directions over land and sea, and in every crevice there are deadly vipers who must be discouraged from venturing forth."

He paused an instant, then went on quickly. "Ythillin has assured me you seek my aid as a friend. And although I am entirely human I have only the warmest of friendly feelings toward wolves and their kith and kin."

He nodded and his lips split in a toothless grin. "You have no doubt heard that I am myself part beast and often turn into one and run savagely through the night. But that is wholly untrue. I am a magician and a magician can transform himself in outward appearance in any way that suits his fancy. But that outward appearance is an illusion which exists solely in the eyes of the beholder. It would not mean that I would cease to be as I am now, even if I seemed to transform myself into a crocodile, which I could easily accomplish at this moment, right before your eyes."

I spoke then for the first time, but I hardly recognized the half-wolf sounds that came from my lips until, with a supreme effort, I found myself forming words that I felt would be comprehensible to him. Or was I mistaken? He seemed to understand what I was trying to say before I regained my mastery of the human tongue.

"I do not need to transform myself in any way," I said. "In your eyes or the eyes of others. I am far more of a wolf than a man and the men and women who know me find that out quickly enough, with no need of magic to create meaningless illusion."

"You have always thought of yourself as a wolf," he said. "And that is understandable. You were raised by wolves, and it was as a wolf you watched your own mother being torn apart by wolves. But that is an illusion in your mind. I think it comes and goes. I am sure you know at times that I speak only the truth, painful as it may be for you to confess your human kinship, even to yourself."

I said nothing, for his words were as salt on a wound that bled.

"What if I made you a true wolf?" he said. "In every fiber of your being, whenever you wished to become one? Then you would become what no man could ever be, whenever the need arose for you to join forces with and secure the aid of all the great powers that are far older than Man, and can only communicate with those who share their primal impulses, both on earth and in the gulfs between the stars. In the vastness of those cosmic gulfs there is a sharing and a kinship. Yes, even with wolves who run savagely through the night in the full of the moon."

"You could make me—"

"A true wolf," he reiterated, before I could go on. "It is within my power to bestow upon you the priceless gift of Lycanthropy. There are only a few words that you must say. They would be dangerous ones for me, but not for you. Ythillin will protect me when I utter them, as I must, and I will not be changed in any way. But at any other time—

"No matter. My safety is assured, and for you the transformation will take only a moment or two and will last as long as you wish it to endure. Then, whenever you so desire, you may regain your human form, simply by repeating the words in reverse. You need finger no talisman. You need take no magic brew. I will see to all of that, with Ythillin's aid."

"Is that her wish?" I asked. "That cold and merciless—"

"No, no, you do her an injustice," he said. "In the depths of her mind she is attracted to you. But all amorousness she puts aside when she has some great purpose in mind that even I have not fully fathomed."

"There may be truth in what you say," I told him. "Very well. Tell me the words that I must speak—"

"It is not as simple as that," he said. "I must go into a trance first and summon all my inner strength to make the words truly magical. And I must summon as well Ythillin's now distant presence to aid me."

"Distant?" I asked. "It was almost as if I heard her voice guiding me to you."

"Her guiding presence was no more than an aura to which she had given instructions," he replied. "It was implanted in your mind that last time you saw her. I will still need more of her assistance."

He was staring at me very steadily, and his way of moving his arms when he spoke was, I suddenly realized, no more abrupt than the quick responses which came from his lips when he saw I was troubled by some still unspoken thoughts.

"You are telling yourself that no one would bestow a priceless gift and expect nothing in return," he said. "You would regard with mistrust anyone whose generosity exceeded all bounds in that respect, and your mistrust would be justified. But the favor I shall ask of you is a small one, as favors go. Have you ever heard of Lamaril?"

I shook my head, puzzled.

"Lamaril the Invincible," he said. "He is coming down from the North to lay waste to the coastal plains and bind into slavery everyone lucky enough to survive his barbarous onslaught. Or perhaps I should say, unlucky enough. But he will destroy me through nights and days of slow torture, because we were in conflict once and he bears me an undying enmity."

He paused an instant, still staring at me steadily. "He leads a mighty army of thousands of heavily armed men," he went on slowly. "But he always rides ahead of his legions, a full league ahead to establish his recklessness and courage, in the eyes of all men everywhere. He is like a savage child in his self-love, but not like a child otherwise. Destroy him and his legions will scatter in panic and despair, since they worship him as a god."

"Although I have never heard of him," I said, "he must be brave beyond most men to take so great a risk. To ride alone when men of every breed—pirates and human flesh eaters who would just as soon kill as look at you, merchants who would kill as readily to protect their wares from the rapacity of an invading army, tavern roisterers with long, sharp knives who will go out into the desert at night by twos and threes to waylay any stranger to gain the price of one more drink—"

"You have never before seen such a man," the White Magician said before I could finish. "He is huge of girth and well over seven feet in height, protected both by the magic spells known to his people, and armor forged by the most skillful of weapon makers. He bears me, as I have said, an enmity that would make him take delight in seeing me impaled above the ramparts of Zaporakh, dangling from an iron spike."

"Whether the favor be a large or small one," I said, "I promise you that I will hold it a small enough recompense for the gift of Lycanthropy."

He looked pleased. "That is all that I could ask."

If his motions had seemed abrupt before, they were more so now, for without saying another word he sat down upon the floor of the cave and folded his legs in front of him.

I watched him closely as he sat cross-legged on the floor, no longer staring at me, the fur cape that hung from his shoulders—it was fastened in the middle of his chest by a jeweled clasp of intricate design—seeming almost to blend with the hairiness of his unclothed arms and legs and the bulging expanse of wrinkled grey flesh in the region of his navel. Not once did he lower his eyes in contemplation to where he had been cut at birth from his mother, as did the shaven-headed priests of Nemedia, but stared straight ahead into vacancy.

It was not the first time I had seen a man pass into a deep trance through his own willing. It has been said that such states can be dangerous and that a journey undertaken in the dark of the mind may turn the body corpselike and stop its breathing.

I have never seen anyone, man or woman, go mad or die in convulsions on awakening from such a trance. But occurrences of that nature have been reported too often to be thought of as fabrications.

But it was not that so much as what he had told me about the power that could be gained from such an inward journey that I chose to dwell on now, since no other possible outcome was of such vital and immediate concern to me.

I had no great knowledge of magic. But that a few spoken words or a simple hexagram traced in the sand after the undertaking of such a journey could shatter the swords of a thousand advancing warriors and send them into the wildest kind of battle disarray I had once confirmed with my own eyes, though the magician who had wrought that spell had been unknown to me.

As the memory of what had happened on that never-to-be-forgotten day came sweeping back into my mind I did something I was later to regret. I detached Genseric's sword and my new weapon arm with its screw-onable hook, fumed about and set both down a short distance from me.

I had remembered something else that it might have been better not to have recalled, or to have blotted from my mind with a deliberate effort of will. When an act of magic is about to be performed, whether for good or ill, it was thought wise not to tempt fate by arming one's self with a deadly weapon.

Sorcery I had never feared, as men do, or allowed it to stay my hand in battle, even though I had seen with my own eyes a thousand swords shattered and the weapon wielders destroyed, but I had been told, many times, by men familiar with the darkest secrets of sorcery, that a flashing sword in a human hand invites destruction. Genseric's deadly blade and my new arm were both more a part of me than any ordinary weapon, though I could detach them at will. Wisdom and fearlessness in battle are things apart, and I saw no reason to abandon all caution in the presence of a White Magician who practiced black magic as well, as the skeletons that dangled on the cave wall had made abundantly clear.

I knew that I could regain my weapon arm quickly enough should the need arise. Was I matching my wolf cunning against a man who had promised me a gift it seemed well within his power to bestow? I did not know, could not be sure. A wolf as well as a man does things at times that are foolish and unwise, but to abandon all caution is a greater risk.

There was more to it than that. If any transformation was to take place in me, if the gift of Lycanthropy was a reality, it might well have been better if I had experienced the change nude. But an artificial limb that served as a weapon might prove a handicap indeed. How could I make use of it as a true wolf? And would it not delay and handicap such a change?

It was almost as if the seated figure facing me, in the depths of his trance, knew the strange conflict that was taking place in my mind and wanted me to put my new weapon arm aside. I was firmly convinced it would have been a mistake to trust him completely as far as the promise he had made and I had made to him in return. But not to have trusted him at all seemed unwise also, for Lycanthropy was a gift which he alone, with Ythillin's aid, could bestow. It was a gift to be prized, for once I possessed it I might even find a way to rescue Shanara, my lost love, and restore her to my arms, after I had fulfilled my promise to him.

I was still watching the White Magician closely and suddenly his expression became less vacant. His nostrils quivered, as if like an animal excited by a strange and unfamiliar scent, his inward journey had aroused in him an emotion which, even in his trancelike state, was mirrored in his features.

I, too, had known such excitement when my wolfish instincts had taken complete possession of me, and even so small a thing as a faint odor had made me sniff the air and grind my teeth in a frenzy of anticipation.

Just between sleeping and waking I have traveled great distances, across grey wastes and frozen tundras, for dreams and the state into which he had passed were alike in many ways and I had no way of knowing how long his trance would last.

I only knew I experienced no surprise when it was over, in as short a time as it would have taken me to cross to the opposite wall of the cave and return again to where he was sitting.

He got to his feet slowly, drawing his fur cape more firmly around him, and looked at me with no trace of agitation in his gaze. I knew at once that he had not failed to complete the task he had set himself before sinking into a trance, for there can be no mistaking the difference—in calmness and assurance—between a man who has succeeded in a difficult task and one who has failed.

I thought for a moment he was going to speak the words then and there, but he took a slow step backwards, and continued to look at me, very thoughtfully now.

"We must both be careful to avoid mistakes," he said. "There are spells that are not easy to cast, simple as they may seem in superficial ways. The slightest mistake in what must be done can have dangerous, even fatal consequences. Do you understand?"

I nodded, impatient for him to go on but knowing that I must not let my attention stray for an instant from what he felt he must tell me.

He did not speak again for a full minute, as if he wanted me to know that he was aware of my impatience, and was relieved that I had made no attempt to interrupt him by asking questions.

"The words are quite simple ones," he said, finally. "They are in a tongue unknown to you, but that is of no importance. They are harsh, short words without sibilants, and if you can say, 'Tit tat,' you can say them also. It does not matter if you cannot speak them exactly as I am about to do. They are so laden with magic now that even if you spoke them crudely and stammeringly the Lycanthropic transformation would start instantly.

"As I have said before, Ythillin has made certain that I will be protected when I utter them. If she had not done so, I, too, would become a wolf."

"You would have me speak them now?"

He shook his head. "That is the last thing that I or Ythillin would want you to do," he said. "You must leave this cave as you are now, if you are to keep the promise you made me, and what she may later ask of you, for she has earned your gratitude. You will know when the right time comes. It will be when you see Lamaril riding alone in the desert . . ."

"But if I do not speak the words after you—"

"You must memorize them," he said, cutting me short. "Simply listen attentively. Four words, no more—all of one and two syllables. I will speak them slowly."

"My memory—"

Again he cut me short. "They will be deeply engraved on your memory the instant you hear them. You will never forget them. That, too, is part of the magic."

He waited, but when I said nothing went on quickly: "You must banish from your thoughts the widely held but mistaken belief that Lycanthropy must await the rising of the moon or a change in its phases as it passes from crescent to round. You may repeat the words at any time, whenever you wish the transformation to occur. And when you repeat them in reverse, the last word first, you will regain your human form as swiftly as you fell to all fours. Just listen now. I ask no more."

He drew himself up to his full height and what I had thought might be incredible words seemed as commonplace as the gibberish of some drunken reveler struggling homeward in the night.

I memorized the words the instant he fell silent, repeating them three or four times in my mind and taking care to guard against so much as moving my lips. The faintest of murmurs might have escaped me, and tight-lipped silence was, I felt, the only absolute safeguard,

I had lowered my eyes for an instant to avoid the slightest distraction and was only aware that a sudden shuffling sound had replaced the White Magician's harsh breathing.

I thought he had simply taken a few more steps backward, as a man will often do when he has been standing close to someone with an exacting task completed. Alert as I am to small sounds ordinarily I gave it no heed until the harsh breathing began again with something chillingly different about it. It seemed more like a panting.

I looked up abruptly then, and saw that there was no longer a human figure facing me. A huge furry shape with pointed ears, bared teeth and savagely gleaming eyes was backing slowly away from me, saliva dripping from its black-rimmed jaws.

It was backing away, I knew instantly, only far enough to enable it to hurl itself straight at me in a flying leap and bear me to the floor of the cave with the rapacious howling of a hunger-maddened wolf. A gigantic wolf, the largest I have ever seen or gone loping with through forests of the night, feeling myself to be more than the equal in strength of the breed that had nurtured me and claimed me as their own. But never before had I set eyes on a wolf such as this.

In two or three more seconds, at most, I was sure that the monstrous beast would be at my throat. Not only was it between me and the weapon arm I had made the mistake of detaching, but it was certain to leap the instant I moved in that direction, or in any direction. If I had been cursed with human stupidity at its worst, I might have been foolish enough to believe otherwise. But I was not so cursed.

There was a long pikestaff hanging on the wall within reach of my hand, with shreds of blackened flesh still clinging to its pointed iron head, which was two-thirds unsheathed.

I ripped the weapon down just as the great beast leapt and struck out at him as he came hurtling toward me. I struck out with all my strength, and the point of the terrible blade pierced him in the eye and passed deep into his skull with a bone-splintering crunch.

He rose on his hind limbs, clawing at the air, and I tugged at the weapon till it came loose, leapt backwards and stabbed him twice, the second thrust carrying the blade so deep into his vitals that the entire weapon was torn from my clasp and carried with him as he thudded to the floor of the cave.

Shaken a little by the suddenness of his leap, but otherwise as calm as I always remained when a killing went smoothly and without injury to myself and the pure joy of slaying was kept within bounds by circumstances of an unusual nature, I watched the great beast become a man again.

The White Magician's body was twisted in a half-loop and became continuously more twisted as he thrashed up and down, tearing frenziedly at his chest in a futile effort to dislodge the iron shaft that had impaled him. The grey wolf tail had shriveled and vanished and his animal hairiness had taken only a moment longer to become once more a human hairiness, so encrimsoned where it was most dense that his chest seemed covered with tiny, threadlike blood worms from a tidal pool as the dark wetness swelled and spread.

Suddenly a convulsive trembling seized him, and he arched himself twice, the long wolf snout, already greatly shortened, turning slowly into a human nose and a spreading flatness that was quickly transformed into the other lineaments.

For the barest instant, just before he flattened out on the cave floor and lay still, with a thin trickle of blood running from his mouth, he trained on me a look which made me remember the times when a killing rage had overcome me and I had felt myself to be driven by forces over which I had no control. At such times I had felt myself to be wholly a wolf and yet, when the madness passed, a strange, almost tormenting doubt had taken hold of me, although I could still have killed in a totally remorseless way, unshaken by the gushing forth of an adversary's blood or the dismemberment of his limbs.

But not to be completely sure of anything, to be torn by uncertainty as to what the totally unexpected might mean was like being caught in a raging flood at the brink of a precipice, with no rocks or overhanging boughs to cling to as the torrent rushed on.

I had spoken the transforming words only in my mind. My lips had not moved. It was the White Wizard who had spoken them aloud, after assuring me, more than once, that his instructional utterance would be of no danger to himself. If he had wanted to destroy me from the first, could he not have done so without deceiving me in so contrived and complicated a way? A single blow while my back was turned would have felled me, or a sword-thrust the instant I was inside the cave.

Had the Ice Bitch deceived and betrayed him with a false promise? Had she wanted him to become a wolf, knowing that no counter spell she could cast in advance would stop the Lycanthropic change when once he had spoken the words?

Had she wanted him to leap upon me and tear out my throat? Or to slay himself, knowing that if I attacked him with a pikestaff it would be the same as if he had chosen to die by impaling himself upon it? Perhaps she had been certain, with her precognitive powers, that I would do exactly that, since in an act of folly I had detached my new arm and set it down a short distance from me.

The blade of a pikestaff could grind and tear and rend as a sword could not, rupturing and mangling the vital organs in an even more savage way. It is thought that a stake, driven through the heart of a vampire, can put an end to his nightly wanderings forever. Might not the mangling inflicted by a pikestaff destroy the magical powers of a sorcerer in much the same way, denying him the slightest chance of defeating death? Had he earned the Ice Bitch's undying hatred in some way unknown to me, and brought that kind of retribution upon himself? Might it not be possible that such a retribution could only be accomplished through Lycanthropy? A werewolf, like a vampire, was an unnatural creature and if slain in his transformed state might well remain forever dead. It would matter not at all if he regained his human form again before all the breath left his body. He would crumble into dust and never rise again.

They were wild thoughts, perhaps wholly untrue, and I put them from me. I was only sure of one thing. I was in the deadliest kind of danger as long as I remained in the cave. I walked quickly to where my new weapon arm was lying, picked it up and re-attached it. Upon sheathing Genseric's sword, I passed out into the night.

The desert which stretched out before me was still silvery with moonlight. Miles upon miles of nothing but sand, with only a few scattered boulders to break its monotony from the cave to an horizon so distant that it seemed to blend with a wilderness of stars.

I began to walk, swaying a little, still assailed by doubts, but determined not to falter or turn back toward the coast. If the slumped, lifeless figure I had left lying in the red-lit cave had spoken the truth I now had the gift of Lycanthropy and was following some course that was too predetermined to alter in any way. Knowing that I could become a wolf in outward form was more important to me than anything else, and there was no weapon, however miraculous, I would have traded for a gift so priceless. I was now walking erect like a man, but for the moment walking seemed, for some strange reason, easier than loping. Perhaps it was because I was more contemptuous of men than ever before, and could adopt their ways for purposes of convenience without any loss of my wolf pridefulness.

For a long time I continued on over the grey waste, feeling a need simply to keep walking, in search of a figure I felt I would eventually encounter if I did not abandon all thought of pursuing a course I no more than obscurely understood. I only knew that the Ice Bitch was still guiding me, and her guidance was not lacking in purpose. Even if that purpose was cold and remorseless and linked with acts of betrayal, I could not believe she actually sought my destruction. The prophecy she had made to me on our first meeting had angered me, almost beyond endurance, for she had told me that danger and strife would be mine for all the years of my life, and I would never find peace and my years would be few in number.

But she had also made it plain that she had no wish to side with my enemies and that it would be my destiny to save a civilization, in fact all civilization, in some crucial future conflict. Hence I had no choice but to follow her guidance cautiously, for I was in a new land, a strange land, and a wolf without allies in such a land would be certain to find his survival endangered.

I lost track of time as I continued on over the desert. I only know that the minutes lengthened into hours and that the present darkness was replaced by the brightness of another sunrise and then by the coming of another night, with the moonlight flooding down.

He came into view at first as no more than a jogging dot on the far horizon. But swiftly the dot grew larger and became a mounted human figure, crossing the plain in my direction, the moonlight glimmering on his breastshield and helmet.

His mount alone was astonishing, for he rode a creature I had never set eyes on before, striped like a zebra, and with the general aspect of a horse. But its head was reptilian and flattened, and kept bobbing to the right and left as it carried him swiftly across the plain. I had heard of such creatures, mythical beasts of legend from far northern lands, but such accounts I had never taken seriously. Magic can work strange miracles, and I was almost sure that the head of the beast was illusionary, created by some sorcerer's spell, the better to strike terror in the eyes of a beholder when Lamaril the Invincible rode coastward ahead of his legions and entirely alone, as the White Magician had informed me was his wont.

As he drew nearer everything the White Magician had told me about him was fully confirmed. He was the hugest man I had ever seen, apart from actual giants, who are ill-proportioned and ungainly of aspect. He had the look of a proud warrior whose every sinew had been strengthened by battle, and he bore himself like some legendary prince whose right to command had not been questioned from birth, even when he had been no more than an infant mewling and puking in his nurse's arms.

His helmet and breastshield were of intricate design, but the sword he carried was without ornamentation of any kind, a naked blade, long and sharp, which he held aloft in his hand as he rode, as if his decimations had already begun. Or perhaps as a warning to any desert ghoul mad enough to leap from behind a boulder in a wild attempt to bring him down.

His sudden appearance on the desert rim had taken me by surprise and a decision I might have made earlier I was forced to make at once. How binding was the promise I had made to the White Magician now that he was dead, and the slaying of Lamaril could mean nothing to him?

How binding when I knew so little as to why he had perished and the part the Ice Bitch might have played in his destruction? The answer came quick and certain. Even if the Ice Bitch had betrayed us both for purposes of her own, the pledge would still have to be kept. Otherwise I would know nothing. The gift of Lycanthropy was in some way linked to my destiny, and some instinct told me that, for good or ill, I must now pursue that destiny to the utmost. It would have been dangerous to do otherwise, for the thread of one's destiny can seldom be cut and I lacked all positive knowledge as to the wisdom of attempting it.

I removed my new arm for the second time, and set it down along with Genseric's blade on the sand. I stood very straight for a moment, precisely as the White Wizard had done before pronouncing the four words that had brought destruction upon him. I pronounced them slowly and clearly.

For a moment nothing happened. Then, when I looked down over myself, I saw that my body had begun to lengthen and change shape, becoming much narrower from my chest to my hips.

Coarse white hair had started to appear on my torso and thighs, and it spread so quickly that even before I dropped to all fours I knew that my clothes had disappeared as my new arm might possibly have done if I had not taken it off. I gave it hardly a thought, for it was well in accord with what has been said about the Lycanthropic change. Garments vanish in some strange way, and regain their substance when the need for them returns. I only knew as I bounded forward across the plain that the howl that came from my throat was more savage than it had ever been before, and my jaws had become so completely the jaws of a wolf that the clash of my teeth jerked my head to right and left and streaked the sand with a whitish froth.

Lamaril's mount was less than eighty feet distant from me now, but he had seemingly not seen me. He was staring straight ahead with a preoccupied air, as if meditating on his coming conquests.

Without waiting for him to come any nearer I loped out across the sand directly in his path, so swiftly that when his vision centered on me it was too late for him to do anything but rein in his mount and raise his great sword in self-defense. He had need for such defense, for in another moment I had left the ground and was leaping straight for his throat.

It was a sudden flash of moonlight on his sword that saved him. It was too late for him to have run me through, but the flash so distorted his aim that the sword struck me flatside on the right flank, hurling me to the sand.

He dismounted instantly, with a bellow of rage so loud that it echoed back from some distant crag or cave, and let his mount gallop on. He faced me again with his sword upraised, advancing upon me with a string of oaths in a language unknown to me. I knew they were oaths by the fierce look in his eyes and the rigid set of his jaw.

His hugeness alone would have cowered most men, formidably armed as he was, but hugeness in a figure as vulnerable as a man means nothing to a wolf.

It was only his reputed skill at swordplay, which the White Wizard had extolled, which made me cautious for an instant and kept me from leaping straight at him again.

I circled about him instead, so swiftly that twice he lunged at me and missed. My chance came at last, when he turned for the barest instant to determine the source of what was probably no more than an imagined sound at his back or one made by the wind ruffling the sand.

I leapt at his right leg, sank my teeth into it, and tore and ripped at the flesh until he began to scream, his sword falling to the sand. It was a pitiful thing to hear such a scream coming from a man of fabled and heroic mold. But I showed him no mercy and I am sure he expected none.

I did not stop with his leg and went on and on with the slaughter, until the sand about him was darkly sodden and glistening, and his throat torn out.

I turned abruptly, rejoicing in what I saw and not in any way sickened by it, as a man might well have been. I turned because regaining my human form had suddenly become of vital concern to me. I had to know if the Lycanthropic transformation could be reversed at will, as the White Magician had said. If not, if he had lied to me, the new land at which I had arrived might prove hostile and dangerous to such an extent that I could not hope to survive for long with my belly hugging the ground and wolf cries coming from my throat.

A stout warrior in human form may be hated and feared, but a wolf running through the night is looked upon as ferocity incarnate, and becomes an instant target for hurled javelins and poison-tipped arrows.

I went loping back across the sand to where I had left my weapons, and in my haste to get arm and sword securely in my clasp again I spoke the words in reverse the instant I came in sight of them.

More swiftly than I could have anticipated I found myself arising to an almost upright position. I had no doubt that I remained for a moment longer almost entirely a wolf in bodily form, still half-crouching on my haunches. But the change that was making me rise was accompanied by a lessening of the fur on my back and thighs. I could distinctly feel the loss of its heaviness, and there was a faint rustling sound as the skin beneath became enveloped in the slight tightness of a returning garment. It was as if the substance of my clothing had dissolved and been held in suspension by magic, hovering over me all the while like an aura. It puzzled me less when I remembered how ice could turn into moist air, and then become ice again.

The instant I had arisen to full human height my new arm seemed almost to leap into my hand. I had no clear recollection of even bending and picking it up, but I must have done so. As I stared down at it swaying a little, a voice spoke to me in the wind-swept, moon-brightened waste. Whence it came I did not know, only that it was clear and bell-like, as if the Ice Bitch had broken through all barriers of space and time to bring me a message that was straining her powers to the utmost. A tinkling accompanied the syllables of her speech, as if millions of tiny ice crystals were swirling around and around inside a jar of glass as large as the earth, dissolving, reforming and beating against the glass until it became resonant with the faintest of musical sounds.

"You have done well," the voice said. "It is only with your human form cast off, only with the great gift of Lycanthropy yours to summon at will . . . that you can be sure of triumph in the struggles which must still be waged, against enemies more fearsome than any you have yet met. Blood must flow freely, for the danger is great that all life will otherwise vanish from the earth.

"You have slain many times before without pity and without remorse. But just thinking of yourself as a wolf in human form was not enough. What is true of wolves is just as true of a lion or a bear or some small furry creature of the wild that must slay to survive. They alone can draw strength from the great Old Ones, who sway in the timeless winds that blow cold upon us from the depths of space. The Old Ones have not yet awakened and still lie dreaming, and they sway in a way that men would think mindless, for Man can possess no knowledge of what that kind of mindlessness can mean. They are far more ancient, stronger, wiser than the Ice Gods, whose first daughter I am, in ways that would be incomprehensible to Man. Only when you run savagely through the night as a true wolf will their still half-somnolent strength flow into you, for men cannot communicate with them except in fugitive dreams, vague and terrifying, which they blot from their minds on awakening, in dread of going mad.

"A day will come when the Old Ones will awaken and earth will quake with their unchained rage, for they were cast into outer darkness by an accident of Time. But that day is far in the future and it would be unwise to dwell upon it now, for there is no certainty that the earth will someday be destroyed. It is enough to know that Yog-Sothoth and ocean-dreaming Cthulhu can strengthen you now as you run through the night as a true wolf, and that if you strain your ears you can hear the far-off baying of the Hounds of Tindalos."

In all my wanderings I had never heard anyone speak of such gods. But it was well in accord with what she had said. There were gods so fearsome that men blotted all knowledge of them from their minds, lest madness overtake them.

Strangely enough, it was a matter less awesome but of more immediate importance to me that made me raise my own voice in sudden anger and fierce protest.

"Why did you betray the White Magician?" I asked. "Was it necessary for him to be transformed into a true wolf and be slain by me? Did he lie when he told me that he could speak the transforming words without endangering himself in any way? Did you not promise him he would be protected by the powerful magic you helped him summon to his aid in the deep trance into which he passed? Did you secretly hate him and wish him to be destroyed?"

"How can you hate a miserable worm?" she replied. "And what are promises given to a worm? He was a wretched, deceitful creature, willing to aid me only to gain my favor, in the hope of draining away some of my magical powers to his own advantage. His destruction was of no importance. It was all part of the testing I wished you to undergo, to make sure the gift of Lycanthropy would be worthily bestowed.

"In human form you slew a monstrous beast, instantly alert to the peril you were in, quick to seize a weapon that served you well. Then, as a true wolf, you slew again, and there was no more formidable warrior chieftain in all this new land than Lamaril the Invincible. You did well to follow my guidance and in your slaying you did well also.

"Together we will do better still. Our destinies are now joined and I will henceforth never be wholly absent when you slay again. But your strength will come from the Old Ones as well."

"But there is much that I do not understand," I said. "If the Old Ones you speak of are utterly malignant and hostile, not only to man, but to the guardians of Earth's civilization—yes, even to the Ice Gods—how can they defend and protect us in the struggle that must still be waged? Are they not both your enemies and mine? And has it not been predicted that I am destined to save Nemedia?"

"Save Nemedia you will," she said, "for now, when you run as a true wolf through the night, the inscrutable powers of the Old Ones will strengthen you in more than one way. Those powers will become so much a part of you that you will now be able to *bend them to our purpose.*"

"To our purpose?" I persisted. "I still do not quite understand. Are you saying the Old Ones can be made either to defend or to destroy us?"

"I may seem to speak in riddles, but it is not really so," Ythillin said. "The Old Ones themselves cannot be swayed by man or wolf. Neither can they be swayed by the Ice Gods. They are beyond and above all such swaying. But their powers can be drawn into every fiber of your being whenever you become a true wolf—

inscrutable powers, which even then you will not completely understand, but which can be bent to defend and protect you, and aid you in the destruction of Nemedia's enemies."

Ythillin paused, then went on swiftly, her voice becoming even more persuasive because of its increasing earnestness. "As I have said, even the lowliest of animals, the small furry creatures of the forest, can become more formidable and dangerous through their instinctive use of those powers. In a very primitive way even they can bend such powers to their use in a struggle for survival."

"But man, too, is an animal," I said. "Why does he not share with a wolf—"

Before I could say more she answered my incomplete question with a persuasiveness that carried total conviction. Knowing man as I did, there was no need for me to question her further.

"Man's vaunted reason—a pitiful thing, really, a cloak for ignorance—prevents him from bending to his purpose the powers which he does, to some extent, possess. Every living creature can draw strength from the Old Ones in moments of deadly peril.

"A few men, perhaps because of their rapaciousness and barbaric near-madness may go far in making use of such powers, but never as successfully as can a wolf or a tiger. Mentumenen, for instance, has deluded himself into believing that the powers of the Old Ones can be bent to serve the enemies of Nemedia. In his near-madness he even thinks that it is the Old Ones themselves he has summoned to his aid. In the first surmise he is not entirely mistaken. He can bend the powers to some extent but you can defeat him by bending them more strongly in defense. In the second surmise he is entirely mistaken. In both he is now courting defeat and disaster."

The War among the Gods

Adrian Cole

Ythillin's last words to me out in that cold desert fortified my purpose. "You must find Shanara. She is closer than you think. Follow Lamaril's beast north." The revelations the Ice Bitch had made had filled my head with strange images, confusing as much as enlightening me. I spat a curse for her but loped northward, following the clear spoor of the reptilian horse that had been Lamaril's. As I crossed the rolling dunes, I was deeply aware of the beast within me now, scarcely beneath my crust, and the urge to take upon me the shape of the wolf grew more urgent with each mile. In that feral state I had been closer than ever to the pulsing wilds.

Topping another of the endless dunes, I saw before me in a natural hollow an oasis, or what I took to be one. The thought of water spurred me downwards to those still shadows, but something else about the place instinctively cautioned me. A wolf smells sorcery even more readily than a man. That animal in me sniffed at the brooding atmosphere, for something undefined lurked in that place. But I must have water. I bared my teeth in a snarl and clutching my sword moved stealthily into the first of the trees.

The hair from my neck to the base of my spine stiffened; I had known the aura of the supernatural times enough, but here something awesome seemed to stir. I thought of the grim island in the Vilayet Sea. But this place was dissimilar. These trees, though, were not of the desert. Their trunks were too gnarled to be palms, their leaves were like sprawling canopies. As I moved through them to the pool at the heart of the oasis, it was as though the trees whispered to themselves and then pressed in like great sheaves of grass. I growled like a predator at its kill watching for jealous rivals. I dipped my face to the water. It was like heady wine and I took my fill.

As I rose from the water, I stared up at the night sky. Here in the desert it is ablaze with a million stars, scattered like jewels over a velvet cloak—and yet now I saw none! Above me all was black, as though a colossal shadow had shut me into that place of mystery. Something rustled the trees, as if they breathed and would bend down to enfold me.

"Ghor!" hissed a voice. "Child of the earth!"

Both Genseric's sword and the blade in Dar'ah Humarl's weapon flashed. The killing mood was on me—I needed but a lead. Something moved among those thick leaves.

"We are your brothers. Be guided by us." As they spoke, three figures dropped to the sand and stood before me openly. They were unarmed and too diminutive to offer a real threat. Their skin was the texture of tree bark, their grotesque arms like slender branches. As they faced me, I heard the gentle creaking of their bodies.

"Who are you?" I growled.

"Elementals," they breathed as one. "Our purpose is to serve you, though we serve one greater. We must take you to her." They approached me and still I was cautious, distrustful. They made a circle around me. I readied my blades, but when the movement came it was from an unexpected quarter. The ground beneath me rippled. Then it moved distinctly and began to subside. I had heard of such phenomena in the desert, but this was no natural thing, I was certain. It was too late to attack the elementals, or indeed move, for I was being swallowed up by the earth.

"Beshrew your fears, Ghor," whispered the elementals, peering down at me. "Your enemies are far away. Take what blessings you shall find below and be strengthened."

To my horror the sand began to fall in on me. I was being buried alive! Too late I screamed out a stream of abuse at the gods and whatever things had trapped me, for the soft, reassuring voices of the elementals did nothing to calm me. The sky blotted out; sand crushed me to my knees. It squeezed in on me from all sides, pressing me down, down, into the cold earth below. It filled my eyes, my ears, my mouth. Everything—all my fire, my trapped bestiality—all shut off as though I had died.

What followed was more like a dream than reality. I knew that I had been entombed, deep down in the earth. There was nothing around me for vast distances but solid earth and sand—somehow I knew that. And yet I did not writhe in mental anguish. Warmth suffused me, and then peace, and last a feeling of unique awareness. I was one with the earth, the womb that had bred me.

Her voice drifted into my dream of peace like a soft tide, so calm and still that even the raw violence of the beast was subdued for a time. I knew it was the very earth that spoke to me, just as I sensed her every fibre stretching away from me in a vast circle that embraced all her creations, animate and inanimate.

"You are a child of the earth, Ghor. Draw strength from me."

I wanted to speak, to question, but I could not. My mind was like a vessel into which she would pour the dizzy wine of truth. I tasted the earth, smelled it, heard it whisper around me.

"I have drawn you far into me that the gods hear nothing of what I must tell you. The gods—how they use my poor children!" she said. "How they are using you, Ghor, in this endless war. And they have told you so little—hinted at pieces of a broken mirage, no more. Fed you images that draw you on to the destiny they have already woven for you. And yet you have the power to carve your own path, even if it should lead to the goals they have chosen for you.

"Long has this war among gods racked me, who am forced to fight against them! Gods of Order and Gods of Chaos! Forever they will strive, embroiling not one universe but all! How I despise them, for they tear me and my true children like wolves at a carcass. The Gods of Order—they such as the Ice Gods whom Ythillin serves—seek to build civilization up to great heights, for they believe that men and the gods can only coexist if man climbs up from barbarism. They seek to bind together all the internecine nations of your world, Ghor—bind them together under a new empire that will be greater than any other that has gone before. Nemedia!

"But as ever, the Chaos Lords oppose them, as they oppose all life. Once before they embroiled themselves in a cosmic war that destroyed the very fabric of the world. I almost died and became no more than a sterile rock, but I found the strength to go on. I grew strong again, as you can see; I gave my children new power. Yet those vile Chaos Lords still seek to disrupt and destroy the works of Order and of me and completely rework the fabric of life to their own debased cause, perverting and disjointing this world and all others—even those of the future.

"Thus they clash eternally. Many are the deities that strive and countless their pantheons. Innumerable are the demigods and demons, the spirits and the beings in the dark places that contend, for this dreadful celestial war sucks into its voracious maw all things living.

"I despise them for it! Gods of Order and Gods of Chaos! I was never a part of them, for they have abused me and molded my children to their ends, not mine! I will oppose them, for I must if my body is to survive. I will cast them out, god by god, demon by demon.

"There are others here, too. Aeons ago there were monstrous beings that swam amongst the stars of the many universes. They served not the Chaos Lords, but their own heinous whims, no less terrible. They, too, took of my life force and made from it offspring of their own. For this blasphemy they were enchained by other gods and forced into eternal banishment. Now they slumber, immortal but incarcerated. Many of them are embedded deep in me. I hold these Old Ones and keep them stilled in their fretful dreaming. Ythillin has spoken to you of them. Beware of using their powers! There will be a price if you do.

"You, Ghor, are not as other men. You have sensed this from your very birth—just as Gudrun, your mother, sensed it. When she had you left for the wolves, it was not your crippled leg that prompted her; she knew you were a child of the earth. More beast than man, whom nature would look after. Have I not done so? Did you ever marvel at your wild life, your ability to survive where other men would have perished?

"There are men and men, Ghor—my true children, and those that the gods have warped to their schemes. It was the elemental in you that singled you out in the eyes of the Ice Gods. To establish Nemedia as all-powerful, fountain of civilization, they have to wreak violence and havoc, for only then can they subjugate all others. They need a man who is more than a man (and they have used such men before, as they did with the pink-eyed albino sorcerer and the Cimmerian colossus). This time you are that man. No one is closer to the rawness of nature than Ghor the Strong! You are destined to save their civilization and build its foundations in blood! Yet civilization is against your nature, so you defy them.

"But what of my desires, Ghor? I say again—I oppose them all, who would rape me and taint me with their spawn! I oppose these Gods of Order, for they seek to enforce an unnatural order on my randomness that will lead to total destruction. I oppose the Chaos Lords, who seek to change all things and create new universes that have no place for sanity, only pain.

"Thus I say to you, earth child, go forth and establish this Nemedian empire as has been prophesied. Subjugate the other ravening nations. I will bend this to my own scheme of things, for know this—I will bring it down. Not through fire and flood and earthquake and storm, but through these very chattels of the Ice Gods! I will drive them south: Cimmerian, Vanir, Æsir—drive them shivering before the wall of *ice*. The very gods that they seem to worship will seem to have turned against them. There will be wars and more wars, but the Ice Gods will pass away! Oh, they will be replaced, for the Gods of Order are as imperishable as those of Chaos, and I will oppose them once more.

"So follow your destiny, Ghor! Establish Nemedia, even if it is not for yourself. If you fail in this, it will be to the benefit of the Chaos Lords. If they change the future we have seen for one of their making, we are all lost. You have been given weapons and powers to aid you—Chaos took away your arm and Ythillin has given you a new one, as she has given you, through the White Magician, the gift of Lycanthropy. Use that gift with care, for it will bring you closer to me. You have another weapon, the powers of which I have masked from the Ice Gods since first it came into the world. Genseric's sword. It was forged by fire elementals deep within my bosom when I was young. If you call upon the dreaming powers of the Old Ones, the sword will protect you from the consequences, for without it you would sink into the depths of their will, as men have done ere now and will again.

"Above all, beware of Mentumenen! That demigod seeks power and sovereignty over the world and that before all else. Yet he is the tool of Set and the Chaos Lords, though he does not realize how they use him! He schemes to put Tashako on Nemedia's throne, for he has corrupted the youth and stolen his wits. He will use Shanara against you, too, Ghor. How heartless the gods are! They have used her as bait to ensnare you from the first, goading you on with her loveliness. But they will never let you win her. Did the Ice Bitch not tell you you would die without seed? Have you not wondered that Shanara's belly remains fallow after so long with you? Aye, seedless you will be, for you are to have no future claim to the kingship of Nemedia. The Ice Gods will use the elemental in you to win a throne for them, but ultimately they seek to destroy that part of man and make man their own. I will be a mother without children when they have done. No, earth child, Hialmar is to be king of Nemedia. Mentumenen plays on that, too, for he knows that if Shanara and Hialmar become lovers, there will be much hate between you and your friend. This rift will split Nemedia in twain and leave her powerless to rise to glory.

"You must not let Mentumenen destroy the empire before it is born! Chaos and its future must be thwarted! Accept that Shanara is not for you. Accept Hialmar's destiny, his glory; it is he that will slay the Pictish sovereign, Gorm. Do not oppose Hialmar, for in so doing you serve Chaos. And Chaos has already sought to trick you into serving it and abandoning me. On the island in the Vilayet you awoke from a dream of winged, bronze monsters and found your men slain—for a time you thought it was by your bloody hand they had died. I heard you shout out that you would fight all mankind, all gods and all demons. And that you would flatten the earth with your sword. In your vision, the shades of the dead—your family and all you had slain—taunted you. *All nature, all the earth and things beyond the earth revile thee,* they laughed. Such are the twisted lies of Chaos! Beware, for Chaos would use you. Turn not against the elemental in you, Ghor, for all nature and all the earth are your real hope. We are your allies. Grasp firmly your convictions that you speak for the wilderness, for it is so! You are my voice, my sword, my champion!"

My mind was a cauldron, seething with visions, bubbling with the numerous images I had been shown in this dream. The whole of the cosmic tapestry was at last before me, as though, until now, I had been staring at mere sections of it. Ythillin had not lied to me, no! Yet she had cheated me. I had been right to mistrust her. She had shown me and told me just enough to make me go on. Teasing me, using Shanara to goad me. Shanara! Was it true what the earth oracle had told me? That I could never win her? I had no time to think on that, for the voice came to me anew.

"Chaos has become violently active since Mentumenen unwittingly drew upon those absolute, destructive forces he cannot control. His dealings with Set and other blasphemous Southern entities has presaged a number of irruptions of evil, like pestilences upon the earth. Lamaril and his army was one such plague. He was a Chaos minion. The White Magician who served Ythillin, Telordric, tried to destroy Lamaril and what followed him, but failed. Telordric fled here from the north, with Lamaril sworn to destroying him. In his battle, Telordric had been corrupted by Chaos and so earned the wrath of Ythillin, whom he served. It was because of that wrath that he died—through you, Ghor. Ythillin could easily have destroyed Telordric herself, but she left it to you and did not tell you the real reason why. The elemental in you purified Telordric as he died, and his soul went not to Chaos, but into the earth womb. Had Ythillin destroyed him, she would have sent him to Chaos, and she would never send so much as a mote of dust to her hated enemies! So once more you were deceived.

"Telordric told you that Lamaril's legions would scatter in panic and despair if you killed Lamaril. They should have. But Mentumenen has reorganized them. Even now, with Tashako and the captive Shanara, the black sorcerer is preparing to take the army across the Vilayet Sea. He will unleash it wherever it suits him. I cannot say where. I cannot read what is in Mentumenen's heart, for it is so corrupted by Chaos that what small part of him was once of the earth is dead within him.

"You, Ghor, must go north. Find the army and a way to destroy it! Aye, and the sorcerer, too, if you can. Take Shanara back to Belverus if you triumph, in spite of what I have said of her destiny. But destroy Lamaril's army. If you do not, Chaos will grow bolder and will likely spawn even greater horrors. The fabric between dimensions is so thin! Know, Ghor, that a titanic struggle is imminent, not only here on your world, but across the cosmos. There have been upheavals and cataclysms before, but the outcome of this conflict will decide the fate, not only of me, but of all universes and all times. The conflict between you and Mentumenen is the fulcrum on which the Cosmic Balance rests."

A great sigh followed this, as though the earth had tired herself. Silence surrounded me and from it I drew new strength: the earth nourished me as I had never been nourished before. The earth had said all she would say to her child. She had unlocked the mysteries that had puzzled me. Now I must choose a path.

Mentumenen and Shanara were near. I must find them. I would bring whatever powers I could down on the sorcerer's head. He was the vent through which Chaos would spill out onto the earth.

I shook my head and found myself standing once more beside the pool. The elementals had gone and the trees were no longer the strange growths they had been, but palms. Beside me I found raw meat, freshly killed, and I wasted no time asking myself how it had got there. I sank my teeth into it and tore chunks from it, chewing like a ravenous beast. Such would I be. If I was to win anything, I now knew, I must reject the last remnants of civilized man that clung to me. I was an earth child, a beast of the wild, and only through my untamed spirit could I take what was mine and the earth mother's.

The sky was clear again, shot with stars, and an immense full moon rode the heavens. I threw back my head and bayed at it, the sounds that came from my throat purely those of a wolf. I sucked in the night air, scenting out the spoor of Lamaril's beast. I looked north. Somewhere there, at the edge of the Vilayet, they would be. Finishing my feast, I loped on across the dunes.

For two days and nights I tracked the Chaos beast, pausing only to hunt for food, a predator of the desert more deadly than the jackals. I tore my kills apart and drank the hot blood from their jugulars, delighting in the beast blood singing in my veins. James Allison was never further from me, for I had truly reverted to my primeval self. All modern man's complexes and phobias were gone. I was a child of the earth, my heart, my veins pulsing with the same raw energy that sang in the vitals of the planet beneath me. Telordric's strange gift had opened up my mind to the earth mother as he could never have realized.

At last I reached a place, high on a scarp of broken rocks, where I could look down at a valley. There, a few miles from the moonlit waters of the Vilayet, I saw the host of Lamaril. Darkness obscured those minions at this distance, but I knew they were not of this dimension. Spawn of some deep abyss they must be, for they were ranked like men risen from graves, and were as silent as the mummies I had seen beneath the ruins of northern cities. Above them flapped creatures whose form I could not see, even by the glare of that immense moon, but I guessed that they were Chaos-born, too. Set there by Mentumenen, ever watchful.

There were tents in the distance—tents where perhaps Shanara would be, and the brat, Tashako. I would claw him to earth and tear out his throat before the night was out. The earth mother had told me I must destroy this horde. Yet how was I to do that? Become a werewolf and run amok? But there were thousands of beast beings below me, arranged like statues. If I attacked, would they become animate?

No, I must attack Mentumenen directly. He could not know I was here, so close. I would become a wolf, though, and slink about the perimeters of the camp. I was loathe to hide Genseric's sword, now that I knew its true purpose, but decided to bury it with my false arm. I marked the spot in my mind, then uttered Telordric's mystic words. At once my transformation began. I was a white wolf, silvered by moonlight, prowling through the dunes at the edge of the vast encampment. I made for the tents.

There were hound-like beasts tethered outside—three-headed horrors that were not spawned on this world. Their scarlet eyes flashed out at the night as they got my scent. As one they leapt up and began snarling, rattling their chains. I loped back into shadow. Men came to the tent flaps and my hackles rose, for Tashako was with them. They held high their torches, searching the night landscape, but saw me not. Yet the hound-beasts snarled on. Let the men unleash them! I would rip them to shreds and toss their carcasses back into the camp! But the men quelled them.

If Mentumenen was here, I would not be able to get to him without being detected. I could not risk a direct attack, even though I could bring utter havoc on the camp. Sheer numbers weighed against me. I thought hard on the words of Ythillin—and of the earth mother. The powers of the Old Ones were not of Chaos, but they were within my reach. Telordric had spoken grim names—Yog-Sothoth, Cthulhu, and the Hounds of Tindalos. Hounds! Somewhere in the back of my wolf-mind I could hear their baying, as if from some point far out among the stars—or *behind* them. Would the Hounds not aid a werewolf? I would see.

Searching deep inside myself, I found the hidden keys that would bring the Hounds to me. The earth mother had told me that she kept the Old Ones imprisoned; now I sensed that she was draining off something of their powers to aid me, for I knew what I must do. I found a place of flat sand and with my claws scratched out two squares, one inside the other. I then urinated at the four points of the inner square and stood within it. I raised my head to the moon and the waiting stars. The Hounds of Tindalos would come to me through the angles of the outer square. I began to bay, and it seemed as though the very earth shook.

At once the camp exploded with life. A terrible wailing broke out amongst the zombie-like beings of the army. The hound creatures shrieked in madness. It was as though Chaos strained at its own leash, sensing that some terrible force was arriving.

The ground at my feet was slick with saliva as I bayed. The stars seemed to me to ripple and blur as if seen through a disturbed pool. I heard a deep, soul-shaking growl and turned. Behind me, within the first square, stood a lean, shaggy monster, tall at the shoulder as a man. It had eyes that would turn a sane man mad, and teeth that flashed like knives; from them dripped sizzling saliva, more deadly than any poison, for I knew that one drop spelled utter corruption. Creatures of the first evil of creation, they pressed forward in a pack, a dozen of the horrors, sniffling and snarling at my urine. The sound of their dreadful breathing blew over me like a wave from the depths of any cosmic hell, but they kept off me. These were the Hounds of Tindalos, and terrible was their hunger.

With an insane shriek of joy, I leapt from my inner square and burst through the Hounds, charging down upon the camp where bedlam now reigned. At once the Hounds behind me set up such a baying and slavering as no mortal ears have heard. As a unified pack, we burst into the camp, tearing and slashing at all living things in our way. How I controlled the hellish pack I cannot say, but the Hounds of Tindalos did my killing as well as their own. They set upon Lamaril's army, gorging themselves ferociously, ripping apart all those that stood before them. No beast of earthly realms ever knew such hunger.

Now I saw the hell-spawn that made up this Chaos army. Awful beings, parodies of humanity and bestiality, some more reptile than man, shrieked and hissed before us. Some were clawed, some flicked curling tentacles; some crawled, some hopped. Here was proof enough that Chaos had ripped its way into this dimension. I would feel no remorse in shredding this vile gathering. Such things that flapped in the air, multi-headed and with razor claws, screamed as they swooped upon us. I caught one leathery beast and sank my teeth into its wing, pulling it down on top of me. I was a whirlwind, a volcano of savagery. It was as though some dark, preternatural force had filled me and blotted out everything but the killing mania. Slick with blood, I tore off the head of the Chaos being, tossing the body far from me. I ripped out the throats of other monsters, thinking that I would raise the very Old Ones themselves if I had to!

Time was suspended while that madness vented itself. Then the first of the tents was before me. I barely controlled my frenzy enough to rip its hangings aside. Therein, Tashako stood behind his human guards. With a feral roar, I rushed upon them. They cut at me with their blades, but I moved like quicksilver. I was too fast for them and knocked them to the sand, tearing out their throats in a welter of blood. I was up before Tashako could bolt and smashed him to the ground. I placed a claw upon his throat. He was screaming. Now I could see how Chaos had corrupted him, for he was more tainted by Chaos than humanity; his skin had changed, as if the very fabric of his body had been remoulded into something repellent to this world.

I could not speak, beast that I was, but I growled out the words that again made me Ghor, the half-man. Tashako fell deathly silent, studying my terrible visage.

"Ghor?" he croaked. "Can it be you? Has Chaos corrupted you also?"

I felt no pity for one who had betrayed me and who had sought my death. With my one bare hand I gripped his thin neck and twisted it like the dried stem of a plant. It was a merciful death. I wiped away the thick blood from my face and went outside. The Hounds had unleashed chaos on Chaos. As far as the eye could see there was an ocean of bloodshed. The noise was frightful.

I rushed to the other tents, ripping them down, but they were empty, save for the mangled corpses of Mentumenen's human acolytes. But where was the sorcerer?

From overhead came the sound of thick wings, beating at the night sky frenetically. A Hound leapt up and barely missed those rising claws. It was the huge flying creature I had seen before—the last time upon the island in the sea.

"Ghor!" shrilled a voice. High-pitched, full of terror, it was that of Shanara. I stood helplessly as the bird monster (which I knew to be the metamorphosed Mentumenen) rose upwards towards the moon. Again he had escaped me. But I thought not of him, only Shanara. My longing for her gushed back like the hot blood I had spilled. She had shouted but one word, my name, but in that shouting had been a world of meaning. Love? Aye, it was there. Whatever the gods had decreed—whatever the earth mother had confirmed—I knew Shanara loved me. That one thought kept me from insanity.

I stifled my bestial rage. I must organize my pursuit. I looked at the pandemonium before me. It must stop. I would not destroy the Chaos spawn of Lamaril. I would use it!

I bayed at the moon, calling off the Hounds of Tindalos. As before, they obeyed me. They dropped to their bellies in the sand, thick black tongues lolling, licking the blood and ordure of the dead from their lean bodies. They waited. The army was like a wounded beast, groaning with terror and pain. I would use it. If I must win Nemedia, I would need allies. I had used the dark horrors of the Hounds—I would use these. Aye, and any that would aid me. I would be the instrument of destruction, just as Mentumenen sought to be. To the abyss with all gods! Once I had used this grim army, I would destroy it, just as the earth mother had insisted.

Quickly I went up into the dunes to find the sword of Genseric and my mechanical arm. I moved more like a wolf now than ever, by pure instinct. Was there a dividing line between man-wolf and werewolf? If so, it grew thinner by the hour. I took up the sword and bayed again at the heavens. Let all the gods hear me! I was their toy no longer. Let them clash and bring about the downfall of man, I would survive! I and my brothers of the wild—we would survive and we would seed the earth anew.

I called off the Hounds. They slinked off into the desert, and though they were out of sight, the sound of their rasping breathing still reached me like a hot desert wind. Tomorrow I would begin the long march that would eventually bring me upon the rear of the Hyrkanians. The Hounds of Tindalos would patrol the flanks of my unearthly army, and those that broke ranks they would devour, Fear would be my whip. I would smash aside any who stood in my way.

Let the gods meet, let the earth shake, let the stars tremble. The children of the earth scorned them.

The Ways of Chaos

Ramsey Campbell

At dawn the army reached the steppes. Hard earth the colour of baked dung, interrupted only by tussocks of grass like spiky yellow scalps, spread monotonously to the horizon. The sky was more bare than the land; not a cloud relieved its glaring. Already the horizon was blurred by heat and roving dust. I scanned it constantly, alert for patrols. Though my sight was keen as any wolf's, I had to strain to penetrate the haze—yet I was glad of that, for it helped me not to dwell on the troops I presumed to command.

All the humans save one had died in the attack. Perhaps some of the things which marched before me had once been human. Their unnaturally regular tread, monotonous as the stamping of a gigantic mechanical hammer, veiled them in clouds of dust, but I had only to glance about me to glimpse horrors.

Here was a swollen lip that dangled lower than the chin, here a head which kept rising from a moist pit between shoulders, there a giant figure on whose left jowl, quivering and blinking as he marched, simpered a rudimentary face. A shape which trudged on the left of my mount might almost have been a shaggy warrior, except that his eyes, whenever the dust stung them, withdrew like snail's horns into his flesh. Often I was near to falling on these creatures, to rend them to death in revulsion, in clean animal rage. But I must not, for they were leading me to my prey.

Mentumenen had erred. Remembering, I grinned savagely. Last night, as he had escaped bearing Shanara, the heads of his army had turned to watch him. When the worst of his creatures had begun to struggle in the direction he had taken, I was ready to slaughter them until I saw how they would aid me. In their mindless way, the troops of Chaos were still loyal to Mentumenen, and would follow him as best they could. Since their compulsion was leading them also toward the Hyrkranians, I was doubly right to follow.

The one human who had survived the attack, I had spared. The smell of his fear had led me to the dune behind which he had been cowering. His dark skin and his shaven crown showed him to be one of Mentumenen's acolytes, though it was weedy with stubble now. About to tear out his gulping throat, I had reconsidered: what might he tell me of his master's plans? I had bound his hands—a distasteful task, for his left arm was corrupted by Chaos, the finger-tips bloated and gelatinous—and now he rode beside me.

His gratitude disgusted me. I thought of a beaten mongrel, snuffling and licking his master's feet. More intolerably, he seemed to think I had spared him because he was human, as though we were brothers. Nor did he seem likely to prove useful; something—his alliance with Chaos, or Mentumenen's power—had robbed him of the memory of his own name. When we made camp, I was determined that I would pry his secrets from him by whatever means were necessary.

By noon I could bear him no longer: neither his fawning gaze nor his silence. Now the steppes were a featureless sea of parched grass, the colour of senile skin, which rustled harshly beneath the marchers. A pall of brownish clouds seemed to weigh down the air. Infrequent breezes raised shapeless ghosts of dust that hissed through the grass. At the edge of the army, where long angular shapes formed in the grass, the hiss had a slobbering quality, and I knew the Hounds of Tindalos were vigilant. Yet I felt alone with the suffocated landscape, the horizon which appeared to be receding, the clouds of flies which rose from stagnant gullies to feed on the horde. I was growing desperate for action. When several wild horses thundered by on the horizon, it was minutes before I could be sure they were not a patrol.

My gaze was drawn to a marcher ahead of me, his fattened head swollen almost to the breadth of his shoulders. A swarm of flies was feasting there. As I watched, a dozen moist holes gaped in the hairless head and swallowed the flies. I could bear no more; I must act or run amok. Drawing Genseric's sword, I pricked the throat of the bound acolyte. "Tell me of Mentumenen," I snarled. "Enlighten me, or rot here, feeding the flies."

The Stygian's face crumpled; he looked ready to blubber. "The Master," he whispered fearfully. "Mustn't sleep. He is waiting for me in my dreams. He wants to—" He fell silent, shuddering.

Did the wretch fear more than nightmares? I remembered how Mentumenen had appeared to me on the island of the massacre. Seizing the rein of his mount, I drew blood from the Stygian's throat with my sword. "Speak, or there will be no wakening."

"Set is waiting," he babbled. Perhaps the threat of death had reminded him. "Once I saw his snout. He stands always at the Master's shoulder, listening . . ."

I was tired of his ravings, and barely able to prevent my sword from thrusting deep. Perhaps he sensed this, for all at once he grew perfectly calm, as though he knew he was doomed whatever he might say. "I know what the Master intends," he whispered.

"Tell me quickly," my sword-point said for me.

He glared about, fearing perhaps that the deformed horde might fall on him to silence him. "The chiefs of the Hyrkranians and of the Picts will dream of him. He will persuade them to unite against Nemedia—he has ways to persuade them even of that. He will offer them allies beside which this army is as naught. But when they have conquered Nemedia, the chiefs will be his puppets and he will be emperor."

His calm was brief. His eyes began jerking wildly, his bloated fingertips pinched shut his lips. If he had known that Mentumenen was himself a puppet of Chaos, how much worse his fear of the horde might have been! But my sour grin tightened, dragging savagely at my teeth. If Mentumenen was a puppet, what was I?

I glared across the endless fields of scorched grass. Nothing seemed to move out there but dust, groping feebly into the yellowish air, then sinking back. I was alone with my brooding, for I felt estranged from both humanity and gods. The Ice Gods would rob me of a throne, the earth goddess who claimed to have borne me would steal my mate. Only Chaos had aided me, leading me unwittingly toward my goal.

How I craved the taste of blood, the cries of battle, the moans of the wounded and vanquished—anything rather than the dust that coated my tongue, the ceaseless thirsty rustling of the grass! How I yearned to cut down Shanara's captors, to bear her away—but for whom?

The Stygian acolyte flinched, but I was not snarling at him. By all the gods—if any were to be trusted enough to be so invoked—I would not give up Shanara again. The Lord Garak had stolen her to present to the oily emir; now Hialmar sought to win her. Would he fight for her tooth and claw, as I already had? No, he would seduce her with soft words; he was too weak to gain her otherwise from me—too human.

Perhaps my mind was parched and suffocated, that I thought these things of my friend; yet who could say that they were not true? Could I truly call any man friend? Was not the dead landscape proof that the earth goddess had deserted me until she had a use for me once more? Balked of a victim, my lust to savage could only turn inward.

Then I glimpsed a blur on the horizon which neither drifted nor changed, only stood and grew more solid. It was a small forest, the first I had seen all day. My surge of gratitude soured at once, for it was the horde of Chaos, not the earth goddess, that had led me here. Nevertheless I knew that the infrequent forests of the steppes were to be found on the banks of lakes or rivers. My thirst was a harsh ache in my throat as I followed the horde.

The foremost of the creatures had almost reached the lake when a small mounted troop of Hyrkranians came into view beyond the trees. They had been making for the water. Now, no doubt aghast at the size and nature of the army, they turned and fled. The chorus of abominable sounds with which the army set off in pursuit was no more savage than my own roar of glee; at last I had adversaries. Unsheathing Genseric's sword, I spurred my mount onward.

Red rage filled me. I bore down on the Hyrkranians' left flank. I disdained to use the artificial arm—not only was it difficult to operate while I held the sword, but it was a product of civilization, hence loathsome—yet it saved me from an arrow which my shield failed to deflect, as the Hyrkranians took a desperate stand. Then I was on them, and they must have seen their deaths glaring out of my eyes.

The first of them was distracted by the things that followed me. My sword plunged through his guts and out beyond them, thrust there as much by the force of my ride as by my instincts; I felt the blade scrape his spine. As I wrenched the blade free he toppled, limp as his spilling entrails.

A warrior taller than I chopped down my shield with a blow that should have lopped my arm—but that arm was metal, and his blade recoiled, ringing. Its edge cut into my upper arm. Maddened, I smashed his shield away, and my sword cleaved deep into his side, which opened like a dyke full of blood.

Somewhere within the hot crimson mist I thought that I was serving the earth goddess, after all; the thirsty ground was drinking deep of blood, the parched grass was wet now, crimson. I hurled down a warrior with a blow of my shield, which was still clamped fast by my metal arm. As he fell, my sword split his skull and almost scalped him.

A fourth warrior was trying to flee two creatures which resembled men, except that their arms were long as their bodies. These arms they had wrapped about the hindquarters of his mount, which they were struggling to topple. Something besides rage made me cut him down; though he must die, at least he deserved a warrior's death. My blow almost scythed his head from his shoulders. The two creatures still clung to the screaming horse, one of whose legs they had now bitten off. Sickened, I killed the beast.

The Hyrkranians were vanquished. My rage was fading, sated, and I was able to survey the battlefield. At once I began to tremble with a new rage; bile rose to my throat. This had not been a battle, for the things I had thought to command fought neither like men nor like animals. Their savagery was perverted, distorted, the antithesis of life.

Some of the Hyrkranians still lived. One creature was reaching a tentacle down the throat of a victim to disembowel him. Two leathery men were dismembering and eating a dying warrior. A screaming naked Hyrkranian was being dragged through razor-sharp grass. Everywhere I looked the inhuman army was satisfying its unnatural lusts on the wounded, the dying, and even the dead.

And this was the army I had thought to wield! My revulsion against them was no more violent than my disgust with my own stupidity. Had Mentumenen hoped that I would choose not to destroy the army, and that the forces of Chaos would corrupt me as they had Tashako? Might he have foreseen that I would delude myself that I could control the army, whereas I could only follow? Had my growing hatred of all life been the first symptom of my corruption?

Mentumenen had not reckoned with my new powers. My face a grim mask, I rode away from the carnage, toward the lake. The Stygian acolyte was cowering behind the trees. At least he had taken no part in the carnage, and for the moment I was loath to kill him. When I had made certain that his bonds were secure, I rode to the far side of the lake. Once my mount had drunk its fill I tethered it, then I hid my sword and my metal arm among the exposed roots of trees.

Merely to loose the Hounds of Tindalos on the army would not be enough. I had participated in their atrocities against the Hyrkranians, however inadvertently; now I must lead the pack against them, to clean myself of their corruption. I spoke the words of changing, and at once my pelt was hot and thick, my fangs and claws were sharp, eager to tear. I could barely restrain my animal rage long enough to perform the ritual of the squares.

The Hounds came loping through the lattices of trees and shadows. Why did they seem more scrawny, more angular? Was I growing able to see them clearly? In a dreadful way their slavering faces seemed almost human, as humanity might have looked if it had evolved from something unimaginably alien, toward an intelligence dark and distant as the rim of the universe. But I had no time for such reflections now. Howling, I led the pack to the abominable horde.

Some of the creatures were too intent on their perversions even to glimpse their oncoming doom. Those which fled were outrun effortlessly by the pack. I ran down horror after horror, ripping their throats with my teeth, spitting out the gelatinous flesh. Its taste and texture maddened me with disgust, with a fury that could not bear to leave one of the monsters alive. Their cries—squeals, moist gobbling, thick jellied roars—drove me to greater frenzy.

When the last of them was destroyed I lay panting, licking my wounds. Around me in the grass, beyond the wide patch that glistened with blood and inhuman liquids, lay the pack, yet this reminiscence of my childhood among the wolves less heartened than dismayed me: the angular limbs of the Hounds at rest reminded me of the bunched legs of spiders, ready to seize prey. Nevertheless I was too exhausted by the slaughter to move away.

All at once my mind, purged of thought and attuned to the pack by the shared slaughter, seemed to glimpse the dreaming of the Hounds. They were one mind, and their thoughts were the dreams of their masters, the Old Ones. I glimpsed eyes large as a man's head, opening far beneath sea and stone. Something shapeless and black as liquescence bubbled amid limitless darkness; the bubbles seemed to dance to the rhythms of an atrocious piping, or to become misshapen objects which crawled about the pitchy surface with a kind of life before sinking back into the depths. A great dark shape—leathery wings, or webbed claws, or something beyond words—loomed toward the world.

I jerked into full consciousness. The eyes of the Hounds—which I could call eyes only because they were located where those organs should be—watched me unreadably. What forces had I wakened by calling on the pack? How could I be sure of withstanding those utterly alien powers? I had no words nor ritual to dismiss the Hounds, but I must beware of calling on them often, for what else might I unleash?

And so I had nothing: neither an army nor the Hounds. I could only trust that Genseric's sword would arm me against Mentumenen. I must follow the route that the horde had been pursuing, and trust that would lead me to him. Muttering the words of change, I made for the lake.

Once more I found my human aspect difficult to regain. My skin felt stubbled, and I had to make a conscious effort to rise from all fours. Had the change affected my vision? For a moment I scanned the gloom beneath the trees. Shadows slithered over trunks, dimness swayed beneath them; I felt I was trying to peer deep into mud. Then I ran forward, roaring. My horse had gone.

Even before I reached the tree I knew that Genseric's sword had been stolen. The Hounds had not alerted me; why should they, when it served to protect me from their masters? The metal arm still lay beneath the roots; the double burden must have proved too heavy for the thief.

As I seized the arm and thrust my stump viciously into the socket, I saw him. The Stygian acolyte, his hands unbound now, was fleeing toward the horizon in the direction the horde had been following. He was crouched low over his horse, as if praying to remain unseen. The sword of Genseric gleamed dully in his arms, the left of which looked boneless. Chaos had helped him struggle free.

I was about to call the Hounds, whatever the consequences, when I saw my horse. He stood at the far edge of the forest, and I had taken him for a shaking mass of branches and foliage. Had he snapped his reins for fear of the Hounds? At least the thief had been unable to catch him.

I paced toward him through the tangle of roots and sparse undergrowth, and struggled to suppress my blood-lust, lest it panic him. Though I had ridden him only since the battle by the Vilayet, he seemed to have sensed the animal in me, and to know that it meant him no harm. Though he tossed his head and backed away, snorting, he suffered me to stroke him while I murmured sounds I knew instinctively rather than understood, and eventually to mount him.

Still murmuring, I coaxed him out of the forest; then my rage would be contained no longer. With an inarticulate shout that was more of wolf than of man, I spurred the horse in pursuit of the Stygian, who had almost reached the horizon. Already the horse was foaming, its flanks were beginning to sweat—but I would ride it until its heart burst, so long as I retrieved the sword.

The sky had darkened, and was rumbling. A shower of rain dashed into my face, both refreshing and frustrating me; I was thirsty now not for water but for the Stygian's blood. Already I was gaining on him. When the bald head turned and saw me, he began to kick wildly at his horse's flanks.

The shower was over, having scarcely relieved the oppression. Feeble gleams of lightning tried to part the clouds. The sky was a slate cliff tilted close to the browned landscape, and about to topple. There was nothing but the miniature horse and rider ahead, apparently suspended between the changeless landscape and sky but in fact growing nearer. I gripped the metal wrist. Soon my prey would be in range.

The landscape was not quite changeless. Another small forest sprang into view on the horizon, and seemed to be the acolyte's goal. Before long my wolfish gaze spied the reason. A figure was perched in one of the foremost trees. Above the bat-wings that cloaked its body its face was vaguely human, insofar as it resembled anything even faintly wholesome. It was Mentumenen.

Why had he not flown to meet his acolyte? Perhaps it amused the sorcerer to play us both. Though I could not be sure that the acolyte was yet in range, I could wait no longer. Gripping my steed with both legs, I steadied my aim as best I could with my remaining hand before I loosed the metal bolt.

At first it seemed that the bolt would fly over the acolyte's head. Then it curved down, too low, too far, losing impetus. My gasp was as loud as my victim's when it struck him at the base of his spine.

Though it failed to penetrate, it knocked him from his horse. Genseric's sword was hurled from his arms, to impale the ground several yards away.

When I heard the unfurling of leathery wings I grinned viciously, for I was sure that I would be first to reach the sword. The acolyte lay stunned, face gaping at the sky. As I spurred my mount into a final effort, I realised that the bat-winged creature had not even taken flight. Let him venture within my reach once I had Genseric's sword!

Moments later I saw why he was biding his time. From behind the trees, a dozen Hyrkranians rode out at me.

By the gods, I would battle them too. I was nearer the sword than they were, and my horse seemed as frenzied as I. Let me only grasp the sword, and whatever the outcome, more of their blood than of mine would be spilled on this field. But I was nowhere near the sword when the first arrow ploughed into my thigh.

Though it felt as though a red-hot poker had been plunged into my flesh, I might still have reached the sword had not a second arrow pierced my steed's eye. When I crashed to the ground, which was hard as stone, the beast fell on top of me, pinning my metal arm. Now I was weaponless, and unable to struggle free, for my arm was caught almost up to the shoulder.

My death was riding at me, two Hyrkranian horsemen with swords raised to chop me like meat. But their commander shouted behind them, "Take him alive!"

In the moments before they reached me, as I dragged wildly at my trapped stump and tried vainly to heave the corpse away with my free arm, I saw the bat-winged creature rise flapping from the trees. It swooped down on the acolyte, and its claws ripped out a handful of his upturned throat. His usefulness, or his ability to amuse, was finished.

When the Hyrkranians dismounted I kicked out wildly, snarling like a trapped beast. I had kicked aside one sword when the hilt of the other struck me a blow that would have caved in a lesser man's skull. I thought my skull had broken too, for darkness flooded in. Just before it blinded me I saw the thing that was Mentu-menen sailing triumphantly toward the zenith, Genseric's sword in its claws.

Juggernaut

C. J. Henderson

C. J. Henderson has garnered a legion of fans by updating the venerable tradition of the psychic detective, changing the prototype from Sherlock Holmes to Philip Marlowe. Some of his various novels featuring supernatural sleuth Teddy London pit him and his amazing crew against the like of Great Qatulu. There were six of these books, and Henderson then followed them up with a series of story-length London adventures. This one first appeared in 2000, in *Imelod* #17.

It's a gruesome thing, from what I'm told. An unstoppable monster—all legs and claws and molten muscle that fangs down on a man like water cascading across pavement. Everywhere at once, always coming, always from every direction, relentlessly. As endless as water, as patient as the mountains. They say it can't be killed, can't be turned, can't be avoided. Inevitable as tomorrow, final as judgment. That's what they say, anyway.

Circles confuse them. Spheres, the very thought of bending frightens them like a shadow that isn't cast by anything in sight, and yet is still there crawling across the ground toward you. Curves are their unknown, and they fear them. But it's never been quite understood that curves cannot block them forever—nothing is so fearful of anything that it can be held in check forever. Creatures of sufficient intelligence can figure anything out sooner or later. And despite what most people believe, the Hounds of Tindalos can think. Trust me, I know.

My name's Teddy London. I used to be just a simple New York City private detective. Then I died. It wasn't long after that initial revelation, the first time I walked the dream plane—just removed my physical form from out of time and space for a moment to avoid dying, or more to the point, dying by being dragged off to some nether dimension by something or other that would torture me for my arrogance from now unto eternity—that I decided that perhaps it was time to change my line of work. Or at least, how I went about it. Since then I've spent a lot of time learning new tricks. A bit of on-the-job training, so to speak.

"So, boss—what'dya think these things look like anyway?" The question was from my partner, Paul Morcey. Balding, a bit overweight, but as loyal and sharp as you could want in the person watching your back. He's seen most everything I have, and he's still around, which says a lot. People don't tend to last long in this business.

"Well, some reports," I told him, indicating the papers on my desk, "say they're greenish, hairless dogs with blue tongues. Some describe them as black, formless shadows. Then there's a layer of the dream plane where they're seen as mercury-like creatures whose bases glide smoothly over anything at lightning speeds, but the surface, due to contact with the air, is a constant boil of unbreakable spines . . ."

"So, in other woids, they're tough to get a positive I.D. on before it's too late."

"No I.D.," I admitted, "but we got an M.O. for them. Why don't you explain a little about them, Doc."

Professor Zachary Goward took center stage. The Doc's always been good for background on this or that beyond-the-edge nasty that I've run into. I've gotten help from all manner of people along the way, just trying to stay alive, which is really all I've been doing since I got my first peek behind the curtain and learned there really are things out there going bump in the night. You see, the problem with stumbling into something like this is . . . well, basically, just what do you do once you know about these things?

Most of the world thinks beings like vampires and dimensional shamblers and the walking dead and all are just stories. Oh, a part of their mind believes, but ultimately they're too intelligent for all that—don't you know. And so, when they finally do stumble across something—something all teeth and tentacles—they freeze. It's the slightest of moments, that infinitesimal split second they need to adjust to what's being seen, to run through the files in their brains to find some kind of label for the horror for which they have no immediate designation. Of course, by the time they do find a name for it, they're usually dead.

"These things, the Hounds of Tindalos," said the professor, "aren't really dogs of any kind, of course. They're creatures of immense power possessed of the ability to travel through time itself. Millions of years ago, the reports say, they dwelled in a city of corkscrew towers somewhere here on Earth. Where this was, what has happened to the city, where the hounds are now, what's become of them, et cetera, all unknown. Not even any guesses worth mentioning, although I do have a theory."

"Spill them beans, Doc," said Paul. My partner has a way of cutting through the red tape that has to be admired. He's the only person I've ever come across who wears his enthusiasm for this work openly. Most of the rest of us could leave it behind, permanently, without a second thought. I know I could. Not Paul, though. Smiling, he added, "It's been a while since I've wrestled with something beyond me comprehension."

The problem with getting mixed up with this "from beyond" stuff is that there's just too much of it. The concepts are all big and overwhelming. Little is known for sure, and what is known is wrong half the time, or insufficient. For instance, there really are vampires, but they aren't afraid of religious icons. Or sunlight. And they don't drink blood, either. They simply pull the energy out of you. There's no sexual thirst, no entrancing kiss—that's romantic bullshit cobbled together by a century of hacks to trick money out of the gullible. Real vampires just break your legs or your back and then strip away your remaining years while you claw the ground in pain.

"If the hounds are anything we know of already," Goward told those assembled, "it would be the fallen angels of the Christian Bible, actually, the rebels who followed Lucifer when he attempted to overthrow the Heavens."

"Angels?" asked Cat, an electronics expert still willing to gamble her life now and again on one of my stunts.

"Sometime in prehistory," answered the professor, "there was a great upheaval between two powers. If you like 'God and his angels,' fine. If you want other labels, I'm not opposed. These Tind'losi appear to be the basis for the legend of the fallen angels. Whatever they and their masters were, are, whathaveyou, they seem to have rebelled and then been sealed away in their city outside of normal time as a punishment. You see—the hounds cannot navigate curves—"

"Oh, but excuse me, doctor," asked Pa'sha, a weapons maker from the Caribbean whom I've known longer than anyone else in the room, "but if you could explain that concept even just a tiny bit more thoroughly."

Goward sighed. I didn't blame him. That's what this game is like—you're just constantly shattering people's notions of what is and isn't real or permanent or whatever. And worse yet, once someone who's just gotten a taste of the beyond finds out you've stopped something—something that's weird, supernatural, paranormal, ultradimensional—whatever, suddenly you're supposed to be able to do anything, stop anything. Hey, Marge, ain't that the guy who killed a rat with a shotgun? Let's give him a Bowie knife and point him at Godzilla.

"As briefly as possible," Goward answered Pa'sha, "Tind'losi occupy the angles of time, while mankind, as well as every other living thing, I imagine, live within the curves of time. I know this is a difficult concept to grasp, I'm not really comfortable with it myself, but it does make a certain mathematical sense. You see, if the hounds were pulled outside of normal time as a punishment, they would have to be bound away from humanity by some sort of cosmic geometry. This notion of them being Lucifer's troops—why not? The hounds of Tindalos are the only creatures in all arcana which are described as existing under such conditions. Perhaps Tindalos is Hell. It would explain a great deal—why there is no trace of their city on Earth today, why they hate humanity so . . ."

"How's it explain that?" asked Paul.

"Tind'losi can only come after human beings whom they have seen. Which, because of their unique situation in the universe, means that humans have to make the first contact."

"But how could a person contact these things if they exist outside normal time and space?" asked Cat.

"There are ways," said the professor. "For instance, a man by the name of Harvey Walters once found a gemstone which, when meditated upon, allowed him to look into the far past. When he did so, he was seen by a Tind'losi which apparently, once it had made visual contact with him, was able to track him through the millennia, traveling through the angles of time until it . . ." Goward paused for a moment, then composed himself, finishing with, "Anyway, it's from Mr. Walters we have so many of the descriptions of Tindalos and the hounds, et cetera."

"Okay, okay," said Morcey. "So, dese things is tough to kill and they come after ya worse than the IRS. So what's all this got to do with us?"

A while back I'd thought that maybe we might have finally seen it all. I mean, as a group, we'd tangled with vampires and succubi, werewolves and winged lizardmen, cast the abomination known as Lilith back into the pit and thwarted the rapacious desires of more than one interdimensional traveler.

"Ah, you see . . ." answered Goward with hesitation, "the reason I know about Mr. Walters' gem is . . . it was sent to me for study. I didn't know what it was when I first began to examine it. But, after I looked into it under a microscope and saw that terrible face leering back at me across the endless tracts of history . . ."

The professor paused to remove his glasses, wiping away imaginary grime as he said, "Anyway, according to the best information available, the hound should arrive here somewhere between four and five days from now. At which time, I imagine, it will destroy my physical being and then return to Tindalos with my soul which it will keep, and torment, throughout eternity."

Seen it all, I asked myself. We hadn't seen anything yet. But we were about to. And it wasn't going to be pretty.

We put the next few days to good use. Knowing that a sphere would keep the professor safe, our first priority was to come up with a safe house. Pa'sha solved that problem for us by taking us out to the Brooklyn docks. New York's shipping industry used to be one of the greatest in the world. Times change, though, and over the years more and more of the city's harbor area had been allowed to drift into disrepair.

What Pa'sha knew about was a foundry that at one time had worked in die casting wrecking balls. The firm had sold all its molds to the Japanese just before World War II. When hostilities broke out, the massive casting blocks had been stored rather than shipped out to the enemy. Too bulky to move, they'd simply been warehoused, then forgotten. The die stood some fifteen feet in height. When Cat noted that the sphere inside was rather cramped, Paul quipped that it was a lot more roomy than a coffin. Goward agreed. That closed that deal.

Our plan was simple. As the final moments arrived, Goward would enter the spherical interior of the mold through the pour hole in the top. After that, we would wait for the arrival of the hound. As soon as we got a fix on it, a second mold would be lowered on top of the other to eliminate the entrance and keep the Tind'losi at bay. The only things we stocked the sphere with were water and scuba gear. There wasn't any use in wasting space on food or a chemical toilet or most of the other things that got suggested. Oxygen tanks are fairly bulky for the amount of breathable atmosphere they can hold. The professor was going to run out of air long before he got very hungry.

After the defense was set, it was time to work on the offense. This was where Cat and Pa'sha came in. Cat, of course, worked on our sensors, setting up a relay system that would drop the second mold atop the first as soon as we had confirmation that the hound had arrived. She also worked out a few other tricks to help give us an edge.

We were stymied for a while on how to aim our weapons, but Goward himself gave us the answer to that one. Not knowing from which angle in the warehouse the creature would appear, he suggested we simply eliminate all but one of them and then concentrate our fire power there. We did. The entire warehouse was lined with chicken wire and then sprayed with plaster foam. As the foam set, we carved the corners into pockets. None of them were perfect, but that didn't matter. As long as we didn't leave any angles steeper than forty-five degrees, the Tind'losi would be denied entrance. Only one corner, the one farthest from the mold in which we would hide Goward, was left untouched. In that space we concentrated our bombs and nets and everything else we had to throw against the monster.

We didn't, however, expect any of this to stop it. We would happily accept a miracle, obviously, but if Coward's research was accurate we pretty much knew nothing we were doing there in the warehouse was actually going to stop the beast. Bullets, electricity—petty annoyances like these were only going to enrage the thing. Madden it beyond reason. Which, of course, was our plan.

The last night before the Tind'losi was supposed to arrive, I sat up with my fiancée, Lisa Hutchinson. I couldn't sleep and neither could she. Lisa is a partner in my agency. We met when I saved her from an experience that didn't do either of our mental states much good. I spent a long time in the hospital after it was over. Lisa was there every day at my bedside, refusing to let me just slide into the madness that beckoned so comfortingly from the edges of my mind. Since then she's done her best to keep me sane. I try not to let on what a crummy job I think she's doing.

"What're you thinking about?" she asked me. I told her.

"Tomorrow, mostly. How I'm going to . . . um, handle this whole mess."

"Translation . . . 'how you're going to live through it' . . . was that more what you meant to say?"

"Well, something on that order, I guess." I stared into Lisa's eyes, drinking in the shining blue of them, concentrating on their color, letting blinding nuisances like thought and reality fall aside into disrepair.

"You want to talk?" she asked, knowing I didn't, but that I had to. I'm the kind of person who thinks well on his feet, but I'm not much of a planner.

"Like to," I admitted, "but there isn't much to say. Sometime tomorrow this thing is going to show up. We'll seal Zach in the mold and then we'll try to get rid of whatever it is that wants to get him."

"And if you can't?" Her voice was tense. Not tearful or threatening, she covered herself well. But there was no getting around the fact that she was worried. Then again, why shouldn't she be? I was worried, too. "What then?"

"Then," I told her, "I guess people are going to die."

Her fingers tightened around mine, her body falling in closer to me, pushing us deeper into the couch cushions. She didn't start crying, or asking foolish questions like why was I the one who had to face this thing. She knew why. For some reason when Lisa had been in trouble a few years back, fate had shoved her in my direction, made me her protector whether I wanted to be or not. A lot of people didn't live through the experience. I did, though—barely. I survived with the knowledge that these things are powerful and fearsome and evil. Some will try to tell you that these creatures are so cosmically almighty that they're beyond good and evil, but that's a crock.

Everybody acts with intent. Everything has motivation. Nothing is random, and that means the actions of gods, monsters, and heroes are no exception. Surviving that first attack moved me up a square, made me more visible. After that, stuff just kept finding its way to my doorstep—faster and faster. For me to turn away from any of it would be to surrender. Not facing this Tind'losi, whatever it turned out to be, would be a death sentence for the professor. If I didn't try to stop it, I might as well just put a gun to Zach's head and pull the trigger myself. Certainly it would be more merciful than leaving him to it.

Lisa knew all that, though. She knew I had to play the hand I'd been dealt, as we all do. I could have turned my back on her when we'd met. If I had, of course, she would have died and shortly thereafter the entire world would have been nothing much more than a cosmic cinder. But I didn't. I faced what was after her and managed to stop it. I ended up with four broken ribs, a shattered leg, pneumonia and scores of gashes and burns. I also went somewhat insane. But I was rewarded with Lisa's love, a pure and guiding comfort that in the end seemed worth a thousand such conflicts. Feeling her next to me on the couch, the pattern of her breathing, the rhythm of her heartbeat, the anxiety that had been digging its silver nails under my skin began to dissolve—dissipated by the care of a loving woman's heart.

I was counting down the minutes to when I would be forced to face a creature that was, for all intents and purposes, quite literally straight out of Hell. In a matter of hours I would pit my few score pounds of flesh and brain against a monster every source available to us considered unkillable—unstoppable by any means. Looking into Lisa's eyes once more, however, I simply couldn't find it within myself to worry any further. I had no illusions about my chances.

Most likely, a voice from the back of my brain told me, there is no way we can survive.

Nodding in unconscious agreement, I smiled at my beautiful Lisa and then bent toward her. Our lips touched and the next day was forgotten. Eventually one of us turned out the lights, but for the life of me I can't tell you who it was.

"So," called out Paul, grinning as he stood in the center of the foundry, hands on his hips, "are we all ready to kick a little monster ass?"

"Oh, ho," answered Pa'sha, "and tell me, my friend, what is it that leads you to believe this approaching monster has small buttocks?"

"Dis guy," complained Paul, grinning as he did so, "he's so stupid he's makin' me look smart."

"Now, now, Morcey-mon," answered Pa'sha with feigned indifference, "you know full well there's none in all this wide world quite that stupid."

The two laughed, coming together for their ritual drink. Pa'sha's been known to toss down more than his share of alcohol, true enough, but Paul isn't that much of a drinker. The pair of them always get together before things get started, though, to knock back a couple of shots together. Pulling his usual silver and glass flask from inside his jacket, Pa'sha handed it to Paul, telling him warmly,

"A coconut rum from my father's own home town. Fiery and dangerous, but a true flash of lightning, you shall see."

Paul unscrewed the cap and took a whiff.

"Whooo—" he exclaimed. "Some strong stuff here. Kind that puts hair on your chest." As he hoisted the flask in a momentary salute, then moved it to his mouth to take a drink, Pa'sha answered him, saying,

"This one does not put hair on the chest, Morcey-mon . . . it burns it off."

The two laughed and drank, Pa'sha waving various members of his crew over to join them. His "Murder Dogs," as he calls them, were happy to oblige. The heat in the foundry was punishing and after the grueling preparations we'd readied during the previous few days, there weren't any of us who weren't primed to take a break. All of Pa'sha's troops set aside their weapons, crowding forward to partake in their boss's bounty.

While they did, I turned away for a moment, needing to complete a ritual of my own. Opening my bag, I began the process of slipping into my shoulder holster. I already had my ankle sheath in place, my stiletto, Veronica, secure inside. With a shrug and a twist I had my holster on, my .38 Betty snug under my arm.

Don't ask me why I named my weapons after the girls from the Archie comics. For some reason, a very long time ago, I thought it was funny. Don't ask me what I thought either one of them was going to accomplish in a battle with a Tind'losi, either. I knew neither weapon would be of much use considering what I was going up against, but there're things we do that make us feel prepared, relaxed—more confident. It was a morning for such rituals. Those who didn't have any were advised to start making some up.

Professor Goward was smoking his pipe—maybe not a ritual, but certainly a relaxant. All things considered, the Doc looked to be holding up pretty well. Sure, he was worried, being the one directly in the line of fire—who wouldn't be? But still, he was calm enough on the outside to help keep the tension level down, which is always a good thing. Wiping a handful of sweat from my brow, I crossed the room to check on him. I made sure all the rebreathers that had been loaded into the dye with him were full, then I reviewed how to use one properly with him. He reached out while I spoke, catching hold of my shoulder. Grasping it firmly, he said in a low voice,

"You know, I never really have thanked you for taking all this on."

"Don't thank me yet, Zach," I answered him honestly. "We've got a long way to go before we see who lives through this."

"True enough, Theodore," he told me. "But you know what they say about 'thoughts and deeds' and such. I just didn't want to appear ungrateful—especially considering the fact that I might not get a chance to say it later on at all."

"Jeez," I answered, only half in jest, "and they call me a cynic."

The professor extended his hand toward me. Although the angle was difficult given how high off the ground he was situated, I reached out to take his hand when suddenly a burning, acrid scent pushed its way into and through the room. It was an unbelievably pungent odor, one so nauseous that for a split-second everyone's attention was frozen. We sprang into action, however, as Cat's voice bellowed through the speakers we'd strung throughout the foundry.

"Incoming!"

I snapped my hand back as the top half of the spherical mold began to lower into place. The professor flipped his pipe outside the dye and then began fumbling into his breather. Above, the second mold followed the top half of the first, weighing the first down and sealing it shut. Racing across the room, Paul threw himself upward forcibly, climbing the ladder to the control room where Cat was waiting two rungs at a time. Pa'sha and his men scattered as well, each man heading for his prearranged station. Gas masks and ear plugs were hurriedly slipped into place. The muffled sounds of footfalls and weapons being cocked filled the large room, echoing off the cold concrete walls and floor and ceiling.

All eyes stared at the entry point. The one remaining corner in all the building gushed with a thick, purplish billow. Tendrils of it lurched awkwardly upward and outward, looking more like one liquid forcing its way into another than smoke filling the air. The impenetrable haze grew heavier, crimson sparks flashing randomly within its spreading body. Then, suddenly, something solid emerged from the depths of the cloud.

"It's here!"

An awkward, almost crablike paw stepped down out of the putrid swirl of gases and scratched along the concrete floor. A bulbous snout followed, red and hard, masking a jaw possessed of multiple layers of needling teeth and fangs. What we could see so far indicated a being roughly the size of a large cow, or perhaps a rhinoceros. Bluish pus dripped from the creature's sides, splattering the floor, burning into the poured stone wherever it landed. Another paw followed the first, striding forward, pulling more of the loathsome body into view. It was long, like a hound, but the comparison was strained—like describing a hand grenade by saying it was oval-shaped, like an egg.

The thing's mouth opened, and a black and yellow mix of gases shrieked out into the room. As hands cocked weapons, I stepped back farther away from the stacked molds, my eyes firm on the creature's advance. Then, once I was certain its entire mass had exited onto our plane, I dropped my hand. In the control room Cat flipped a massive connecting toggle, electrifying the steel mesh net we had spread across the floor.

The beast howled as current filled its body. Hundreds of thousands of volts shot into the thing's massive frame. Its screams were ghastly, bright gray things, darts of sound that shattered glass throughout the building. At the same time, Paul threw a second toggle. This dropped a reinforced mesh net from the ceiling, one layered with thick, but sharp, metal hooks, each of them covered with scores of wicked barbs. The Tind'losi, bucking and straining against the current, only succeeded in snarling itself totally in the two nets, a score of the hammer-sized hooks tearing into its body. In addition, the barbs were coated with every available poison—hemlock, arsenic, strychnine, everything we could find. The hounds of Tindalos might be power incarnate within their own realm, but to walk amongst men they had to take on flesh of one form or another, and in that one tiny weakness we'd put our hopes. For a moment, it seemed as if our hopes might not be vain ones.

The horror in the nets screeched and bellowed, sizzling pus and bile flying from its body as it writhed in electrical pain. In the control room, Cat targeted the creature with a ringed battery of white sound cannons, blasting the demon with high frequency noise. As she guided both attacks, she also watched over the power meters, making certain we stayed at maximum output without going into overload. While she did, Paul started setting things into motion for the second part of our plan. We'd selected the Tind'losi's entrance point carefully, making certain it brought the beast directly beneath the foundry's pour bucket. As the nets below began to smoke and spark, Paul prepared to drop the load of molten metal we had waiting.

"The power's topping out," shouted Cat. "We've got to slice it or we're going to burn down the neighborhood."

Paul nodded, his hands gliding through the routine he had practiced a thousand times over the last few days. As the power to the nets was cut, we all prayed the poison had had a chance to have some kind of effect as the pour bucket released its contents. Ironically, the Tind'losi looked up just as the molten metal dropped down onto it.

New screams lashed through the building, the force of them etching scattered cracks in the walls and ceiling. The smell of burning bone and organs filled the room. Combining with the smell of the creature's arrival, the stench grew almost overpowering, easily reaching us through our gas masks. As the pour bucket emptied, the entire room hued over in reflected oranges and reds. A torrent of molten splash was flung everywhere, hot metal burning the floor, melting the nets, searing the alien flesh of the Tindalos hound. Not ready to leave anything to chance, however, I gave Pa'sha the high sign from my hiding place. He cued his men. Explosions filled the air.

The Murder Dogs targeted the glowing, thrashing figure in the center of the room, pumping hundreds of bullets a second into the monstrous thing. A two-man team fired anti-tank missiles into the burning form, blowing out successively larger chunks of the creature with each fearsome strike. Shotguns and flamethrowers were added to the mix, our redundant efforts hoping to enrage and confuse as much as to weaken. It was amazing how little good any of it seemed to do.

With a hissing whisper the Tind'losi stood erect once more. Poison gas canisters were released by Pa'sha and his men, as well as chemical burners and flash bombs. More miniature missiles were launched. Grenades followed. Even though every man fought from behind a steel-reinforced lead shield of considerable thickness, three of the Murder Dogs were already out of action, one felled by an unfortunate ricochet, two hit by molten slag thrown off by the screaming monster in the center of the foundry.

And then, suddenly it seemed as though we were getting somewhere. For a moment it had appeared that the creature was rallying, but then the moment passed and the Tind'losi sank to its knees, crippled beyond repair. Pa'sha and his Murder Dogs kept firing, throwing everything they had left into their attack. Thousands of rounds were launched, enough firepower slamming into the burning thing on the floor to pierce the side of a battleship. And still, somehow the terrible form threw itself up off the floor, its front legs pawing the air violently.

But then, the unbelievable happened. Another massive howl, an almost sonic blast of hate and fear, erupted from the creature. Lashing through the room, the horrid screech shook the entire building, piercing our ear plugs and gas masks, even moving the five-ton mold we'd used to seal in Goward by several inches.

The thing fell to the ground completely then. Its burning head slammed into the concrete, cracking it open to the depth of eighteen inches. Its massive legs kicked brutally against the air, sending more molten slag and superheated bits of netting flying through the air. But as each second passed its thrashing grew less and less violent. And then, suddenly, the unstoppable beast simply ceased moving.

In the control room, Cat switched on the massive roof fans. We hadn't dared run any power equipment while trying to electrocute the beast, but the moment for caution seemed to have passed.

"We did it!" shouted Paul. Dancing a victory shuffle in the control room, he pulled Cat from her chair, laughing as he twirled her around the room. "We killed it! Ding, dong—the humpin' bastard is dead!"

A part of my brain was amazed at how easy it had all been. Another voice from within my mind snickered at my naïveté. We had gone through enough power to keep Time Square lit up for several months. We had fired some fifteen thousand projectiles into the thing—followed by several hundred compressed pounds of various gases and chemical poisons. All told, we had spent nearly a million and a half dollars of the company's money. The rest of my brain told the single dissenter to shut up, though. Yes, we had thrown everything we had against the creature. If it had lived another few minutes we'd have been reduced to hurling rocks at it. But it hadn't. We'd beaten it. The battle was over. The professor was safe.

Or . . . so we thought.

"Hey," called out one of the Murder Dogs, "what the hell be dot, mon?"

From the initial entry point, once more there came a gushing, thick, purplish billow. Once more tendrils of it lurched awkwardly into our dimension, the same heavy, crimson sparks flashing through the mounting haze, the same vague solid stirring moving forward from deep within the depths of the cloud.

"Sweet bride of the night!" screamed Paul. "There's two of them!"

Again, an awkward, almost crablike paw stepped down out of the newly forming swirls of smoke and gas stretching through the foundry. But, unlike the first attack, this time there was a substantial difference. This time, there was more than one of the creatures. As everyone around the room simply stared in amazement, a second bulbous snout moved out of the haze, followed by another, and then another. Behind them, receding down the corridors of time, stretching off through some unbelievable chain of right-angled space, waited an infinite number of the pus-dripping creatures, all of them straining to pass through into this world.

My eyes darted throughout the room, time splitting into micro-seconds as I checked on everyone. Cat had fallen back into her chair, stunned into immobility. Even through her gas mask her eyes showed wide and unblinking. One of her hands was raised to her face, her forefinger upheld, the entire hand trembling.

Paul was still standing, his shoulders stiff and tight. He had already pulled his Auto-Mag from his shoulder holster and was headed for the control room door. The same held for Pa'sha and his men. None of them had more than a few rounds of ammunition available to them. Most had nothing left, but they were ready to fight nonetheless. If only one more of the creatures had arrived it might have been different. One more might have inspired terror within us—or a sense of futility. But there were so many coming toward us that fear became useless.

So was throwing away lives, however. Knowing there was no sense in everyone dying, I stepped forward into the room, drawing as close to the volcanic heat of its still molten center as I dared. Hoping the fans had already completed their job, I tore off my gas mask and addressed the Tind'losi in the lead.

"And just what the fuck do you want?"

The creature was taken aback for a moment. It sniffed the air between us, its cautious movements halting its massed fellows. The thing stared at me with interest, like a child wondering exactly what kind of bug it was that stood on its hind legs and dared bark so. There was no fear in the thing—its curiosity was borne more of an awesome delight, the joy in finding an unexpected treat. Some of the Tind'losi behind it began to snarl and jabber, bucking to push their way forward into the foundry. The leader silenced them with a tearing hiss that blew bloody steam from its nostrils. Then, returning its attention to me, it spoke.

"To step into the world once more, and to find man so utterly unchanged." Its voice was a harsh yet elegant sound. The clattering growl of a cultured cement mixer. "As if a hundred billion revolutions round the center were but a yawning brief pause."

The creature smiled, horrible rows of devilish teeth grinding against one another in its terrible jaw. Taking another step into the foundry, the thing reared upward, then sat down on the floor, its body towering over us all. Looking down at me, it announced,

"You may call me Belial. It means . . ."

"It means," I cut the thing off, "'without a master.'"

"Why—what a clever puny you are." Turning to its fellows, Belial snarled contemptuously, "You see—I told you. There will be more sport here than simply slaughtering them all."

"You're not going to slaughter anyone."

A great angry barking arose through the crowding horde. Their master silenced them with another steaming shriek. It turned languidly, its torso twisting unnaturally, and then struck the two closest Tind'losi devastating blows with its forepaws. As it did, I bent my head slightly, trying to corral my runaway nerves. I knew what I had to do next.

You do, do you? A voice from the back of my consciousness, some ancestor from the early recesses of my racial memory, shouted at me. *This isn't what you expected—is it? No—things have gone far beyond anything you imagined, haven't they?*

We still have a plan.

You had a plan for dealing with one of these things—ONE! screamed another, albeit less stable, one of my forefathers. *This is more than ONE!*

SILENCE, I thought darkly, flooding the single word throughout my consciousness. Several other dissident voices were trying to speak up, but the creature had turned back toward me and I had to be ready for it. The struggle for power between us was about to commence and it wouldn't do if I was too busy comforting myself to play its game.

"So, my little puny, you are the one called 'the Destroyer'—yes?"

"There are some who call me that," I admitted.

"Well then, tell us, Destroyer, how is it that we are not going to do that which we have come to do—that which we have dreamed of since a trillion centuries before you had form?"

"Because you're all going to turn around—right now—and go back to where you come from. And then you're going to stay there."

Clearing my mind, pushing panic and all her sisters away from me, crushing terror and fear, I sent my senses out beyond my body, feeling my way into the city beyond. On any given day there are at the very least well over five million people in New York City. Gently, from each one of them, from their pets and all the trees and plants of every shape and size—from every living thing in every direction I began the siphoning of tiny bits of power.

"And why would we do this, my puny?"

"Because I'll destroy you all if you don't."

Globs of mucused spittle spat from a thousand throats, yellow-brown fangs clattering in raucous glee. I got the feeling the Tind'losi didn't believe me. Not that I cared. The longer they allowed me to stall, the better my chances got. Unfortunately, they didn't give me all that long.

"Anduscias," snapped the creature, "attend to my puny."

As the thing to Belial's left moved forward, I continued stealing what power I could—the energy to run up a flight of stairs, a week's life here and there, the power to mix a pan of batter, a toss of a bowling ball, five minutes' walking, et cetera—storing it all in an ever-tightening clutch as I casually asked,

"This Anduscias, not a close friend, is he?"

The second Tind'losi stared at me, taking my measure for a split second. The right side of its maw curling in a wicked sneer, it dug a claw into the foundry's floor, flicking brick-sized chucks of concrete this way and that.

"Why do you ask?"

Anduscias sprang, his motion a blur. My hand shot up of its own volition, releasing a huge blast of the energy I had stolen. The Tind'losi was torn in two, its organs splattering across the floor, a length of its spine splashing up through its back, shattering against the ceiling, various bits of it clattering back to the foundry floor. My nerves tingled throughout my body from the release, burning flashes tearing at my flesh, unraveling my tendons, grinding my bones one against the other. I kept my face calm, somehow, and answered Belial.

"I just hate to break up happy couples." I gave the words a second to penetrate, then tried my bluff again. "Be that as it may, that's all the time we have. I want to thank you for playing with us. Be sure to pick up a copy of our home game on your way out. You know where the exit is. Don't let the door smack you while you're leaving."

"I do not believe you understand the situation, my puny." Leaning forward, Belial bent its massive head downward until it was within a few feet of my own. "We were locked away from this world for not bowing. We chose to be the lords of Tindalos rather than to bend our knees to others—to be told we were not the equal of what was to come. Of you."

"My heart's bleeding, pal. Tell it to someone who cares. Now are you going calm, or do we have to have trouble?"

"Thrown from this world," snarled Belial, "we were refused entry to it, unless called by human voice. Only a handful of times have you punies reached out so far as to touch us. We have always come. But when puny blood has cooled our throats, back always have we been flung. Until now."

I followed the creature's eyes as it looked at its fallen comrades. Knowing where it was going next, I prepared myself for the inevitable.

"No anchor would we have in this world. One puny found allowed one of us to escape, but contact was always fatal, and fatality always sent us back. But you, Destroyer—you have ended that. You have spilled Tind'losi blood. You have given us our anchor here. Now, this world is ours. We shall scatter across the face of it, and everything shall be consumed. Beginning with you."

I threw myself back just as Belial threw itself forward, its wicked fangs snapping the air where my head had been. Instantly those others behind the monster pushed their way into the foundry. As they turned their attention this way and that, their master commanded—

"No! None other than the Destroyer! He dies—then we live!"

I threw a mental challenge out to all the Tind'losi, driving it straight into their brains, daring them to come after me. Then I turned tail and ran, heading for the outside. I didn't bother to waste time looking over my shoulder. The sound of walls being smashed, of the ground itself being ripped asunder as the monsters tore through everything in their path, let me know I had no worries about being followed. Diving into my waiting car, I punched the ignition and headed for the gate.

My rearview mirror was filled with the sight of scores of slavering monstrosities galloping down the road after me. Even over the roar of the car's engine I could hear the screams of those people who spotted the horde tearing through the streets. Did any of the monsters stop, changing targets, gobbling down those innocents who just happened by? They did. I couldn't see them, but I could feel each strike—each stopped heart and silenced brain—all of them cutting through me like thrusts from wide, dull knives.

I couldn't worry about that, though. We had miscalculated—badly. Seeking only to save our friend, we had unleashed a Hell throng upon the Earth, one that would wipe out every last living soul if they were not turned or stopped. Luckily, we had a plan that might just do the trick. It had been our last-ditch reserve, a dodge we'd cooked up in case our more conventional weapons failed. It had seemed a foolproof fail-safe—for taking care of the single hound we had expected. As for hundreds of thousands . . . that I didn't know.

What I did know, however, was that the trap we'd come up with was the only chance we had, and that I'd better concentrate on springing it.

With a lurch I threw my car into a hard right, sending it flying down a broken side street. The Tind'losi piled up on each other, clawing and biting their own, giving me a chance to get a few blocks ahead of the pack. I gunned the motor, ignoring red lights, laying on the horn, chasing cars out of my way, using any lane I needed to, or even the sidewalk, to keep moving forward. Behind me the monsters charged headlong, crashing into buildings, tearing storefronts away with glancing blows of their bodies.

People staggered in the street, reeling with disbelief at what they were seeing. Fangs and claws tore them apart without compunction—practically without notice. A bus ground its brakes, screeching to a halt as the wave of Tind'losi filled the street behind me. I swerved around it, crashing against the minivan behind. Caroming off the damaged vehicle, I reached out with my mind toward the souls in the bus, even as I fought with the steering wheel to straighten out my car. As I found each pulse on the bus I extinguished it, seconds before the Tind'losi could tear the fragile steel and iron to shreds.

"After him!" came the great, growling shriek. "Kill the Destroyer—kill him! *Only him!*"

I'd led the attack that destroyed one of their own. I'd killed another right before their eyes. Now, whenever they tried to take the souls of the humans that crossed their paths, I reached out and stole those first, as well. I was hoping this tactic would outrage the monsters. From what I could see in my rear view mirror, it was working. Praying that it was working well enough, I floored the gas and threw my car onto the ramp exit leading down to the Battery Tunnel. Breaking through the toll barrier, I shot down into the descending opening. Behind me, Tind'losi tore great gashes in each other trying to be the first to enter the tunnel after me.

Reaching a point beyond the monsters' line of sight, I slammed on the brakes and stopped the car. Leaping out as fast as I could, I concentrated deeply, working to open a doorway to the dream plane. I knew where I wanted to go, I knew when I wanted to arrive. I just had to make certain my timing was perfect. Sensing the approaching Tind'losi, I closed my eyes and stepped forward, disappearing into the dimensional rift I had opened. Behind me, I could hear the creatures running forward, screeching over what I had done. They had seen me, had figured out what I was doing, and were following me through the gateway.

Excellent, I thought. Now if I can just get them all there on time.

I used nearly half the energy I had gathered from the dying to cut a swath across the dream plane. I needed to take the Tind'losi to another location on Earth. Opening the doorway there in the tunnel in Brooklyn, I opened another into a tunnel in Switzerland—in Geneva to be exact. The Cern Facility is built in a tunnel some three hundred feet underneath Geneva. It is a circular burrow twenty-seven kilometers in length. I didn't open the gateway exit into that tunnel, however, but rather into the metal pipe suspended in the center of that tunnel. The Cern Facility is the world's largest particle accelerator, a massive, city-sized machine scientists use to split atoms and create new elements. It is a perfect cylinder, designed to keep radioactive particles—which can only travel in straight lines—from escaping its confines.

"Good God," exclaimed one of the control technicians. "There's some massive build-up in the core pipe."

"Yeah," I snapped. Stepping into the control room, from out of thin air for all the scientists there knew, I ordered, "Start it up, now."

"You're mad—there are hundreds of thousands of alien particles in the cyclotron chamber. They're simply appearing from nowhere. The vacuum isn't . . ."

"Don't even talk to him," interrupted an older man. Snapping his fingers at another, he ordered, "Call security. Get someone in here right away."

They were all speaking Swiss, of course. I was talking to them by thought, putting words directly into their brains, which they translated themselves. Not having time to argue, I started putting orders in instead of suggestions.

"You've got plutonium tests scheduled all day today. I know the rail gun is loaded and waiting. Fire it—now!"

The man's hands moved to obey my orders even as his conscious brain protested. It didn't matter. I had influenced the day's schedule when we'd first decided on this plan. By leading the Tind'losi into the tunnel, I'd hoped to trick them into not noticing they were being moved from one type of tunnel into a vastly different one. I wanted them to think I was trying to escape them so they would rush in after me. Once in the gateway, our relative size would become unmeasurable. There would be no way for them to notice they were being shrunk by the exit portal to sub-atomic size. Sidedooring on them, I had led them into the particle accelerator while I dropped into the control room.

The rail gun was primed to fire an atom of plutonium into the accelerator. We had assumed, if this was done with the Tind'losi that was coming after the professor inside, that the thing would be atomized—split asunder in a nuclear reaction that would create a new element with a half-life of a millisecond. That was one Tindalos hound, of course. What would happen with hundreds of thousands was anyone's guess. But it was the only chance the world had. If the Tind'losi escaped, billions would die. Casting aside the seductive pleasure of doubt, I pushed my anger into the operator's brain and squeezed his soul until his hands did my bidding. The single atom of plutonium was fired into the accelerator tube. And then, their world ended.

As the technicians screamed, the entire control room began to vibrate. One by one the monitors covering the accelerator tunnel glowed, then exploded. The curving atom's merging with the angles of the Tind'losi set off a chain reaction that shattered the central tube, incredible explosions ripping along the miles of subterranean passages. In seconds vast sections of the city began tumbling into the ground. Gas lines erupted, flames shooting hundreds of feet into the air. Buildings crashed against each other, falling into the vast, mile-wide cracks opening everywhere throughout the city.

In my head, I could feel thousands dying all around me. Those in the control room had gone first. I'd plucked the energy of their wills to power my escape, feeling them curse me with their dying moments. Fine by me, I thought. They weren't the first.

Sliding into the dream plane, I gathered what force I could from the legions of the dying below. Staring down into the city from the safety of my ethereal vantage point, I steeled myself against the wail of sorrow I could feel drenching my soul. Thousands dead. Crushed, ripped apart by shrapnel, burned, asphyxiated, atomized in nuclear-force blasts. I was as staggered by the enormity of what I'd done as by the reason I'd done it.

An accident had brought a friend under the sights of a thing from Hell which meant to wear his soul for lunch. Determined to save him, I had put together a group that stood up to the beyond-thing and annihilated it. Which, it turned out, was exactly what the horrors had wanted us to do. Simply trying to save a friend's life had resulted in a staggering loss of life—blood spilled and souls consumed on both sides of the world—thousands sacrificed so that billions could live.

Was it worth it?

The question came from the back of my brain, not one of the sneering voices I so often have to argue with, but one of my calmer ancestors, one given to asking direct questions without any ulterior motives. I looked at the horrible welter of black clouds rising up out of the billowing rage of fire consuming Geneva, and I wondered—was it?

Should I have let the Tind'losi consume the Earth rather than risk having the tragedy below on my conscience? Should I have simply told Goward he'd sealed his own fate and allowed him to be taken away?

No, I thought, it had to be done. Whatever they were, whatever force had sealed them away in the dark origins of the Earth, the denizens of Tindalos had waited eons to attack mankind. If they hadn't been stopped now, they would have had to have been dealt with later. Coldly, I looked out at the horror spreading across the face of Geneva and decided that, as monstrous a measure as it had been, it had been worth doing if it stopped the Tind'losi.

The only problem was, they hadn't been stopped.

As I watched in blank and numbing horror, scores of the nightmare beasts began to pull themselves up out of the burning wreckage of the city. Many of them were gone—most of them. But still, thousands had survived. Thousands of immortal Hell beasts. Thousands of supremely powerful agents of chaos. Thousands of . . .

"Destroyer!" Belial's voice growled clear and harsh across the dark madness of the blazing havoc. "There will be now a reckoning!"

I hadn't stopped them. Some of them—yes. Their forces were crippled—certainly. But, stopped? No. Were they still a force to be reckoned with? Could they still end all life on the planet? Had Armageddon finally arrived? Before I could decide on an answer, I turned and ran instead.

I didn't return to Geneva, but stayed on the dream plane. Not that it mattered. I had led the Tind'losi to that separate dimension beyond man's normal consciousness and now given the monsters free rein within it. It wouldn't take them long to realize its many uses. Indeed, with access to the powers it gave its users over the dreamers of Earth, there was no telling what insanity they might visit on the planet. Running straight across the vast open plane before me, I taunted the Tind'losi madly, doing everything I could to keep them concentrating on me.

"There is no escape this time, Destroyer."

"You might be right," I agreed truthfully. Playing off the honesty Belial could sense in my voice, I added, "But then again, maybe I'm just toying with you."

"I've read you now, my puny," the thing answered, its galloping strides dragging it quickly across the dream plane. Red dust splashing up around its great legs, Belial growled, "That was your big plan. You've nothing left. You're finished. And we are coming for you."

"You come right along, pal," I shouted back. Something was stirring within my memory, one last place I might be able to take the remaining Tind'losi. I had learned to twist space on the dream plane, to make it do my bidding, to open doorways to here and there at the slightest whim. It took power, of course, life force stolen from the world about me, so it was not a skill I utilized often. Still, if I could mold space . . . why not its cousin?

What was that date, I whispered to myself, begging my brain for the answer. When? When do I want to be?

"We are coming for you, Destroyer!"

I reached the base of a staggering orange and purple mountain range. Throwing myself upward, I clawed at the brilliant rocks, my hands tearing on the glass-sharp facets. I ignored the pain, though, ignored the blood, ignored the baying of the creatures behind me and the mindless screams of the thousands of dead Swiss still howling in my brain. I ignored everything, demanding of my memory one simple thing. A date and a time.

April 26, 1986, came a whisper. 1:23.

A smile crossed my lips. I had them now. With the horrors clawing their way up the mountain after me, I knew they would now follow me anywhere. To anytime. So I took them where I wanted. To the Soviet Union, and the nuclear reactor at Chernobyl.

My memory had given me the exact time of the accident that had shocked the world. I would open a doorway into the reactor core at the top of the mountain. It would take the Tind'losi and me directly to that moment and place when the world was presented with its first nuclear meltdown.

Giddy with anticipation, I threw myself up and over the top of the summit's edge. As I did so, I found myself in the main generator room. All around me people stood staring. People with clipboards. People who did not look as if they were in the middle of the most terrible man-made disaster of all time. Not knowing how many seconds I had before the Tind'losi crossed the threshold into the same reality, I grabbed the nearest person I could. Shaking him, I screamed a thought into his brain.

"What're you doing? Don't you know the reactor is melting down?!"

The technician looked at me as if I were a lunatic. Mostly, he was correct. I was dirty and bleeding, my clothing in tatters, my hair soaked with sweat and blood, my eyes wild and stained with tears. Others approached to free their friend, but I knocked them away with a sonic blast of energy. The man I had seized was stammering, confused by my presence, frightened by my urgency. I probed his brain with a thought, forcing him to answer me. Suddenly coherent, he said,

"There is no meltdown. We are only carrying out tests today. We need to prove that the coasting turbine can provide sufficient power to pump coolant through the reactor core while waiting for electricity from the diesel generators. The circulation of coolant, you see, will be sufficient to give the reactor an adequate safety margin while we wait for . . ."

Because I had ordered him to explain, he continued to speak even after I no longer needed him. Looking around myself, I began to laugh. Suddenly, everything had been made clear to me.

"Destroyer—now you will learn what it means to dare the wrath of Tindalos."

I turned and stared at Belial. The thing was burned and scarred, but hardly injured. Scores of Tind'losi were already in the massive generator room. Hundreds more were cramming in behind them. My laughter had now turned into a wild cackling. Belial and his fellows stopped their forward progress for a moment, staring in wonder at my antics.

All the workers from the generator station had fled the area. Searching my mind, I remembered that the only thing the investigating authorities could agree upon about the Chernobyl disaster was that there had been an unexpected fall in power. Knowing what had to come next, I reached into my shoulder holster and pulled out Betty. Aiming her at the reactor's main control panel I fired, squeezing off round after round. A warning siren sounded as suddenly the control rods began sliding back into their slots. This set into operation additional pumps that began removing heat from the core, causing the spontaneous generation of steam. Almost instantly, the reactor's power rose to more than one hundred times its design value. Inside, fuel pellets started shattering, fuel channels ruptured, and while monsters howled, the explosions began.

As always, I lived. How many died, I don't know. Think what you want, but at this point I don't even care. Somehow I managed to slide back through the dream plane to New York, right back to the foundry. The others bundled me up and took me home. It was only a week before I was coherent again.

The professor, of course, is very grateful. He says it was something that had to be done. Knowing what we know now, it's certain the Tind'losi would have found a way to invade the Earth sooner or later. They'd been waiting a long time. They'd have found a way. Everyone else agrees. Hell, maybe they're right.

But then again, they didn't sink a score of square miles of Geneva under the mantle of the Earth. They didn't decide it was all right to set off mankind's only nuclear disaster and let a bunch nobody particularly liked take the rap for it. And they don't have to live with the screaming in their ears of the souls they harvested, using their life energy as a marathon runner uses pasta—pounding them down without a second thought, all sacrificed for some overwhelming goal.

Of course, we don't even know if the Tind'losi are gone for good. Yes, as best I can tell they sank into the ground, trapped in the molten core of the Chernobyl reactor. But what are we supposed to do—gaze into the professor's goddamned gem once more and pray we don't see anything? Not bloody likely.

And that's the other problem with investigating this stuff. You never really kill any of these things off. Maybe you disperse one, stall it for a while, shut a door in its face. But end one of these things for good? Not really.

The only things that ever die permanently are human beings. I should know, I've killed plenty of them. All in the name of protecting humanity.

Oh yeah, the hounds of Tindalos—gruesome things—unstoppable monsters—all legs and claws and molten muscle that fangs down on a man like water cascading across pavement. Everywhere at once, relentless—unkillable, unturnable, unavoidable. Inevitable as tomorrow, final as judgment. That's what they say, anyway, about the Tind'losi.

I wonder what it is they whisper about me?

Scarlet Obeisance

Joseph S. Pulver, Sr.

During my fondly remembered years in the Episcopal Church I became quite interested in liturgy. And eventually I wondered what sort of liturgical chants and hymns might have accompanied the worship of the Lovecraftian Old Ones. Their cult ceremonies cannot have been *all* orgies, live organ donations, and frenzied mouth-foaming. There must have been intricate incantations aplenty. And I have found Joseph S. Pulver, Sr., to be a liturgist extraordinaire! Much of his pious verse appears in the Chaosium collection *The Book of Eibon*. Here is a bit of Tindalosian liturgy to enable you to put into practice some of what you have learned in the rest of the present collection. For the record, another page from the same missal appears in Anton LaVey's *The Satanic Rituals* (Avon Books, 1972), under the title "Die Elektrischen Vorspiele."

For Frank Belknap Long, Poet at the Gates of Wonder

When he comes from his sleep in the dusky havens
To the squat foothills of Tsang
At the base of the dolorous mountain
Ringed-heavy with moisture and green and silence,
To laugh, to feast—that insatiable visitation upon opulent flesh,
The poems, the music
Will be as a hurricane
Penetrating from life to life to life.
Only bones and dim stains—the truth of dark chaos
Shall he leave upon the rocks.

In the empty space of his temple,
Cluttered with dust the winds have not swept away
And deranging secrets from moments long ago
His immortality measures, and remeasures in dreams like illnesses,
Images, tainted by time's grave,
Of lustrous, dark red currents of reluctant fragile things
Rampant with ruin's lesson.

*   *   *

In the primal forest, dense of teakwood and bamboo,
Where stalking shadows like serpentine coils weave undulant textures,
And even the great cat painted in orange and night-line stripes
Fears to pad,
All lesser creatures are loath
To summon up their voices or breathe,
As the vapors of his inexorable hunger arise
From the ebon caverns beneath.

> O Elephantine-headed Father
> Of the Miri Nigral and Tcho-Tcho man-demon,
> What doom-destined om sounds in thy vast webbed ears?
> What cosmic wheel spins,
> And in its ageless dervish rotations
> Brings the days closer
> To the call to swift running harvests unending?

> O Chaugnar Faugn,
> Bloated Feaster of jet-tusks and conduit trunk,
> Fattened on oceans of claret red,
> What darkling meditations dost thou beguile in,
> Sitting, lotus-poised, before the scarlet mandalas
> So long ago employed as stepping stones
> To ford the cold heavens?

> O Grim Legend of the East,
> Slumbering on thy pedestal of foulsome dreams aflame,
> Awaiting the White Acolyte's coming
> And thy journey from cold, far corners,
> Wake from thy unbending contemplations,
> For the ripe fruit of your garden gleams.
> Rise from that perfect darkness
> To the dense woods of confused blood dreaming of escape.
> Rise up, Idle One—
> Multitudes, phantoms of nothingness though they know it not,
> Await thy taking of softness and fear with particular pleasure.

Come to me now, Irresistible Mountain,
> *bring Thy new day of barren, terrible night!*
Come to me, Sleeping Emperor,
> *Refresh Thyself.*
Hear Thy acolyte, Chaunger Faugn,
> *meditate no longer in Thy exile of inanimate solitude,*

come laugh the Conqueror's Laugh that rends all asunder—
Lose Thy roar, full sore, that all may become omnipresent silence.
   Open Thy great hand—man's grave,
   so that all may see the vicissitude illuminated
Here is the map drawn of my passions,
   come from the labyrinth of Hell
   and collect Thy accounts due.
Take their wits and ingenuity and emblems,
Take their memoirs and melancholies,
Come Immutable Triumph—
   bind all to thy maw of annihilation
   for clemency has been irrevocably damned.
Come with the ferocious tools of Thy Holy Frenzy blazing,
   and overturn their vulgar wisdom.
Come, Lord of Desolation,
   Thy brides despairing, bloom!

O Swollen One,
Vast in thy abandonment so like a dance,
When the Night of all nights,
That perfect nothingness after thy feasting,
That void as barren as the very beginning, is the All—
Will you then, reclining in repose, be contented,
Or will you, Elemental-Predator, once again beset by wounding thirsts, dream
Of bones and dim stains upon the rocks?

The Horror from the Hills

Frank Belknap Long

Frank Belknap Long was inspired to write this novella by the startling sight of a statue of the Saivite deity Ganesha. (One wonders if a similar impetus did not lie behind Robert E. Howard's cosmic Conan tale "Rogues in the House.") As originally planned, the tale would have been at least a bit different, as he had planned to call it "The Elephant God of Leng." As it now reads, Chaugnar Faugn is instead the elephant god of Tsang, an occult plateau down the road from Leng. Long invented his own race of swarthy Asian devils, counterparts to August Derleth's Tcho-Tcho People of the Plateau of Sung. Long's are known as the Miri Nigri, which is Latin and means "wondrous dark folk." Perhaps they retained this name from their earlier sojourn in Roman Europe, from whence Chaugnar's cult emigrated to Inner Asia. What, pray tell, were they doing in Europe? Well, Frank Leng, er, Long expressed his appreciation for a record Lovecraft had set down of a vivid "Roman dream" (as it came to be known) and asked his friend's permission to incorporate it bodily into a piece of fiction he planned to write. This turned out to be "The Horror from the Hills." I have always thought the dream episode would have fit much more naturally into something like Robert Bloch's "The Power of the Druid" (included in the Arkham House Bloch collection *Flowers from the Moon and other Lunacies*) or even Lovecraft's own "The Rats in the Walls."

"The Horror from the Hills" first appeared in *Weird Tales*, January and February/March 1931.

---

1. The Coming of the Stone Beast

In a long, low-ceilinged room adorned with Egyptian, Graeco-Roman, Minoan and Assyrian antiquities a thin, careless-seeming young man of twenty-six sat jubilantly humming. As nothing in his appearance or manner suggested the scholar—he wore gray tweeds of Ivy League cut, a pin-striped blue shirt with a buttoned-down collar and a ridiculously brilliant necktie—the uninitiated were inclined to regard him as a mere supernumerary in his own office. Strangers entered unannounced and called him "young man" at least twenty times a week, and he was frequently

208

asked to convey messages to a non-existent superior. No one suspected, no one dreamed until he enlightened them, that he was the lawful custodian of the objects about him; and even when he revealed his identity people surveyed him with distrust and were inclined to suspect that he was ironically pulling their legs.

Algernon Harris was the young man's name and post-graduate degrees from Yale and Oxford set him distinctly apart from the undistinguished majority. But it is to his credit that he never paraded his erudition, nor succumbed to the impulse—almost irresistible in a young man with academic affiliations—to put a Ph.D. on the title page of his first book.

It was this book which had endeared him to the directors of the Manhattan Museum of Fine Arts and prompted their unanimous choice of him to succeed the late Halpin Chalmers as Curator of Archeology when the latter retired in the fall of the previous year.

In less than six months young Harris had exhaustively familiarized himself with the duties and responsibilities of his office and was becoming the most successful curator that the museum had ever employed. So boyishly ebullient was he, so consumed with investigative zeal, that his field workers contracted his enthusiasm as though it were a kind of fever and sped from his presence to trust their scholarly and highly cultivated lives to the most primitive of native tribes in regions where an outsider was still looked upon with suspicion, and was always in danger of bringing down the thunder.

And now they were coming back—for days now they had been coming back—occasionally with haggard faces, and once or twice, unfortunately, with something radically wrong with them. The Symons tragedy was a case in point. Symons was a Chang Dynasty specialist, and he had been obliged to leave his left eye and a piece of his nose in a Buddhist temple near a place called Fen Chow Fu. But when Algernon questioned him he could only mumble something about a small malignant face with corpsy eyes that had glared and glared at him out of a purple mist. And Francis Hogarth lost eighty pounds and a perfectly good right arm somewhere between Lake Rudolph and Naivasha in the Anglo Egyptian Sudan.

But a few inexplicable and hence, from a scientific point of view, unfortunate occurrences were more than compensated for by the archeological treasures that the successful explorers brought back and figuratively dumped at Algernon's feet. There were mirrors of Graeco-Bactrian design and miniature tiger-dragons or tootiehs from Central China dating from at least 200 B.C., enormous diorite Sphinxes from the Valley of the Nile, "Geometric" vases from Mycenaean Crete, incised pottery from Messina and Syracuse, linens and spindles from the Swiss Lakes, sculptured lintels from Yucatan and Mexico, Mayan and Manabi monoliths ten feet tall, Paleolithic Venuses from the rock caverns of the Pyrenees, and even a series of rare bilingual tablets in Hamitic and Latin from the site of Carthage.

It is not surprising that so splendid a garnering should have elated Algernon immoderately and impelled him to behave like a college junior at a fraternity-house jamboree. He addressed the attendants by their first names, slapped them boisterously upon their shoulders whenever they had occasion to approach him, and went roaming haphazardly about the building immersed in ecstatic reveries. So far indeed did he descend from his pedestal that even the directors were disturbed, and it is doubtful if anything short of the arrival of Clark Ulman could have jolted him out of it.

Ulman may have been aware of this, for he telephoned first to break the news mercifully. He had apparently heard of the success of the other expeditions and hated infernally to intrude his skeleton at the banquet. Algernon, as we have seen, was humming, and the jingling of a phone-bell at his elbow was the first intimation he had of Ulman's return. Hastily detaching the receiver he pressed it against his ear and injected a staccato "What is it?" into the mouthpiece.

There ensued a silence. Then Ulman's voice, disconcertingly shrill, forced him to hold the receiver a little further from his ear. "I've got the god, Algernon, and I'll be over with it directly. I've three men helping me. It's four feet high and as heavy as granite. Oh, it's a strange, loathsome thing, Algernon. An unholy thing. I shall insist that you destroy it!"

"What's that?" Algernon raised his voice incredulously.

"You may photograph it and study it, but you've got to destroy it. You'll understand when you see what—*what I have become!*"

There came a hoarse sobbing, whilst Algernon struggled to comprehend what the other was driving at.

"It has wreaked its malice on me—on me . . ."

With a frown Algernon re-cradled the receiver and began agitatedly to pace the room. "The elephant-god of Tsang!" he muttered to himself. "The horror Richardson drew before—before they impaled him. It's unbelievable. Ulman has crossed the desert plateau on foot—he's crossed above the graves of Steelbrath, Talman, McWilliams, Henley and Holmes. Richardson swore the cave was guarded night and day by hideous yellow abnormalities. I'm sure that's the phrase he used—abnormalities without faces—subhuman worshippers only vaguely manlike, in thrall to some malign wizardry. He averred they moved in circles about the idol on their hands and knees, and participated in a rite so foul that he dared not describe it.

"His escape was a sheer miracle. He had displayed extraordinary courage and endurance when they had tortured him, and it was merely because they couldn't kill him that the priest was impressed. A man who can curse valiantly after three days of agonizing torture must of necessity be a great magician and wonder-worker. But it couldn't have happened twice. Ulman could never have achieved such a break. He is too frail—a day on their cross would have finished him. They would never have released him and decked him out with flowers and worshipped him as a sort of subsidiary elephant-god. Richardson predicted that no other white man would ever get into the cave alive. And as for getting out . . .

"I can't imagine how Ulman did it. If he encountered even a few of Richardson's beast-men it isn't surprizing he broke down on the phone. 'Destroy the statue!' Imagine! Sheer insanity, that. Ulman is evidently in a highly nervous and excitable state and we shall have to handle him with gloves."

There came a knock at the door.

"I don't wish to be disturbed," shouted Algernon irritably.

"We've got a package for you, sir. The doorman said for us to bring it up here."

"Oh, all right. I'll sign for it."

The door swung wide and in walked three harshly-breathing, shabbily dressed men staggering beneath a heavy burden.

"Put it down there," said Algernon, indicating a spot to the rear of his desk.

The men complied with a celerity that amazed him.

"Did Mr. Ulman send you?" he demanded curtly.

"Yes, sir." The spokesman's face had formed into a molding of relief. "The poor guy said he'd be here himself in half an hour."

Algernon started. "What kind of talk is that?" he demanded. "He doesn't happen to be a 'guy' but I'll pretend you didn't say it. Why the 'poor'? That's what I'm curious about."

The spokesman shuffled his feet. "It's on account of his face. There's something wrong with it. He keeps it covered and won't let nobody look at it."

"Good God!" murmured Algernon. "They've mutilated him!"

"What's that, sir? What did you say?"

Algernon collected himself with an effort. "Nothing. You may go now. The doorman will give you a dollar. I'll phone down and tell him."

Silently the men filed out. As soon as the door closed behind them Algernon strode into the center of the room and began feverishly to strip the wrappings from the thing on the floor. He worked with manifest misgivings, the distaste in his eyes deepening to disgust and horror as the massive idol came into view.

Words could not adequately convey the repulsiveness of the thing. It was endowed with a trunk and great, uneven ears, and two enormous tusks protruded from the corners of its mouth. But it was not an elephant. Indeed, its resemblance to an actual elephant was, at best, sporadic and superficial, despite certain unmistakable points of similarity. The ears were *webbed and tentacled*, the trunk terminated in a huge flaring disk at least a foot in diameter, and the tusks, which intertwined and interlocked at the base of the statue, were as translucent as rock crystal.

The pedestal upon which it squatted was of black onyx: the statute itself, with the exception of the tusks, had apparently been chiseled from a single block of stone, and was so hideously mottled and eroded and discolored that it looked, in spots, as though it had been dipped in sanies.

The thing sat bolt upright. Its forelimbs were bent stiffly at the elbow, and its hands—it had human hands—rested palms upward on its lap. Its shoulders were broad and square and its breasts and enormous stomach sloped outward, cushioning the trunk. It was as quiescent as a Buddha, as enigmatical as a sphinx, and as malignantly poised as a gorgon or cockatrice. Algernon could not identify the stone out of which it had been hewn, and its greenish sheen disturbed and puzzled him.

For a moment he stood staring uncomfortably into its little malign eyes. Then he shivered, and taking down a woolen scarf from the coatrack in the corner he cloaked securely the features which repelled him.

Ulman arrived unannounced. He advanced unobtrusively into the room and laid a tremulous hand on Algernon's shoulder. "Well, Algernon, how are you?" he murmured. "I—I'm glad to get back. Just to see—an old friend—is a comfort. I thought—but, well it doesn't matter. I was going to ask—to ask if you knew a good physician, but perhaps—I—I . . ."

Startled, Algernon glanced backward over his shoulder and straight into the other's eyes. He saw only the eyes, for the rest of Ulman's face was muffled by a black silk scarf. "Clark!" he exclaimed. "By God, but you gave me a start!"

Rising quickly, he sent his chair spinning against the wall and gripped his friend affectionately by the shoulders. "It's good to see you again, Clark," he said, with a warm cordiality in his voice. "It's good—why, what's the matter?

Ulman had fallen upon his knees and was choking and gasping for breath.

"I should have warned you not to touch me," he moaned. "I can't stand—being touched."

"But why . . ."

"The wounds haven't healed," he sobbed. "*It* doesn't want them to heal. Every night it comes and lays—the disk on them. I can't stand being touched."

Algernon nodded sympathetically. "I can imagine what you've been through, Clark," he said. "You must take a vacation. I'll have a talk with the directors about you tomorrow. In view of what you've done for us I'm sure I can get you at least four months. You can go to Spain and finish your *Glimpses into Pre-History*. Paleontological anthropology is a soothing science, Clark. You'll forget all about the perplexities of mere archeological research when you start poking about among bones and artifacts that haven't been disturbed since the Pleistocene."

Ulman had gotten to his feet and was staring at the opposite wall.

"You think that I have become—irresponsible?"

A look of sadness crept into Algernon's eyes. "No, Clark. I think you're merely suffering from—from non-psychotic, very transitory visual hallucinations. An almost unbearable strain can sometimes produce hallucinations when one's sanity is in no way impaired, and considering what you've been through . . ."

"What I've been through!" Ulman caught at the phrase. "Would it interest you to know precisely what they did to me?"

Algernon nodded, meeting the other's gaze steadily.

"Yes, Clark. I wish to hear everything."

"They said that I must accompany Chaugnar Faugn into the world."

"Chaugnar Faugn?"

"That is the name they worship *it* by. When I told them I had come from the United States they said that Great Chaugnar had *willed* that I should be his companion.

"'It must be carried,' they explained, 'and it must be nursed. If it is nursed and carried safely beyond the rising sun it will possess the world. And then all things that are now in the world, all creatures and plants and stones will be devoured by Great Chaugnar. All things that are and have been will cease to be, and Great Chaugnar will fill all space with its Oneness. Even its Brothers it will devour, its Brothers who will come down from the mountains ravening for ecstasy when it calls to them.' They didn't use precisely that term, because 'ecstasy' is a very sophisticated word, peculiar to our language. But that's the closest I can come to it. In their own aberrant way they were the opposite of unsophisticated.

"I didn't protest when they explained this to me. It was precisely the kind of break I had been hoping for. I had studied Richardson's book, you see, and I had read enough between the lines to convince me that Chaugnar Faugn's devotees were growing a little weary of it. It isn't a very pleasant deity to have around. It has some regrettable and very nasty habits."

A horror was taking shape in Ulman's eyes.

"You must excuse my levity. When one is tottering on the edge of an abyss it isn't always expedient to dispense with irony. Were I to become wholly serious for a moment, were I to let the—what I believe, what I know to be the truth behind all that I'm telling you coalesce into a definite construction in my mind I should go quite mad. Let us call them merely regrettable habits.

"I guessed, as I say, that the guardians of the cave were not very enthusiastic about retaining Chaugnar Faugn indefinitely. It made—depredations. The guardians would disappear in the night and leave their clothes behind them, and the clothes, upon examination, would yield something rather ghastly.

"But however much your savage may want to dispose of his god the thing isn't always feasible. It would be the height of folly to attempt to send an omnipotent deity on a long journey without adequate justification. An angered god can take vengeance even when he is on the opposite side of the world. And that is why most barbarians who find themselves saddled with a deity they fear and hate are obliged to put up with it indefinitely.

"The only thing that can help them is a legend—some oral or written legend that will enable them to send their ogre packing without ruffling its temper. The devotees had such a legend. At a certain time, which the prophecy left gratifyingly indefinite, Chaugnar Faugn was to be sent out into the world. It was to be sent out to possess the world to its everlasting glory, and it was also written that those who sent it forth should be forever immune from its anger.

"I knew of the existence of this legend, and when I read Richardson and discovered what a vile and unpleasant customer the god was I decided I'd risk a trip across the desert plateau of Tsang."

"You crossed on foot?" interrupted Algernon with undisguised admiration.

"There were no camels available," assented Ulman. "I made it on foot. On the fourth day my water ran short and I was obliged to open a vein in my arm. On the fifth day I began to see mirages—probably of a purely hallucinatory nature. On the seventh day"—he paused and stared hard at Algernon—"on the seventh day I consumed the excrements of wild dogs."

Algernon shuddered. "But you reached the cave?"

"I reached the cave. The—the faceless guardians whom Richardson described found me groveling on the sands in delirium a half-mile to the west of their sanctuary. They restored me by heating a flint until it was white-hot and laying it on my chest. If the high priest hadn't interfered I should have shared Richardson's fate."

"Good God!"

"The high priest was called Chung Ga and he was devilishly considerate. He took me into the cave and introduced me to Chaugnar Faugn.

"You've Chaugnar there," Ulman pointed to the enshrouded form on the floor, "and you can imagine what the sight of it squatting on its haunches at the back of an evil-smelling, atrociously lighted cave would do to a man who had not eaten for three days.

"I began to say very queer things to Chung Ga. I confided to him that Great Chaugnar Faugn was not just a lifeless statue in a cave, but a great universal god filling all space—that it had created the world in a single instant by merely expelling its breath, and that when eventually it decided to inhale, the world would disappear. 'It also made this cave,' I hastened to add, 'and you are its chosen prophet.'

"The priest stared at me curiously for several moments without speaking. Then he approached the god and prostrated himself before it. 'Chaugnar Faugn,' he intoned, 'the White Acolyte has confirmed that you are about to become a great universal god filling all space. He will carry you safely into the world, and nurse you until you have no further need of him. The prophecy of Mu Sang has been most gloriously fulfilled.'

"For several minutes he remained kneeling at the foot of the idol. Then he rose and approached me. 'You shall depart with Great Chaugnar tomorrow,' he said. 'You shall become Great Chaugnar's companion and nurse.'

"I felt a wave of gratitude for the man. Even in my befuddled state I was sensible that I had achieved a magnificent break. 'I will serve him gladly,' I murmured, 'if only I may have some food.'

"Chung Ga nodded. 'It is my wish that you eat heartily,' he said. 'If you are to nurse Great Chaugnar you must consume an infinite diversity of fruits. And the flesh of animals. Red blood—red blood is Chaugnar's staff. Without it my god would suffer tortures no man could endure. It is impossible for a man to know how great can be the suffering of a god.'

"He tapped a drum and immediately I was confronted with a wooden bowl filled to the brim with pomegranate juice.

"'Drink heartily,' he urged. 'I have reason to suspect that Chaugnar Faugn will be ravenous tonight.'

"I was so famished that I scarcely gave a thought to what he was saying and for fifteen minutes I consumed without discrimination everything that was set before me—evil-smelling herbs, ewe's milk, eggs, peaches and the fresh blood of antelopes.

"The priest watched me in silence. At last when I could eat no more he went into a corner of the cave and returned with a straw mattress. 'You have supped most creditably,' he murmured, 'and I wish you pleasant dreams.'

"With that he withdrew, and I crawled gratefully upon the mat. My strength was wholly spent and the dangers I still must face, the loathsome proximity of Great Chaugnar and the possibility that the priest had been deliberately playing a part and would return to kill me, were swallowed up in a physical urgency that bordered on delirium. Relaxing upon the straw I shut my eyes, and fell almost instantly into a deep sleep.

"I awoke with a start and a strange impression that I was not alone in the cave. Even before I opened my eyes I knew that something unspeakably malign was crouching or squatting on the ground beside me. I could hear it breathing in the darkness and the stench of it strangled the breath in my throat.

"Slowly, very slowly, I endeavored to rise. An unsurpassably ponderous weight descended upon my chest and hurled me to the ground. I stretched out my hand to disengage it and met with an iron resistance. A solid wall of something cold, slimy and implacable rose up in the darkness to thwart me.

"In an instant I was fully awake and calling frantically for assistance. But no one came to me. And even as I screamed the wall descended perpendicularly upon me and lay clammily upon my chest. An odor of corruption surged from it and when I tore at it with my fingers it made a low, gurgling sound, which gradually increased in volume till it woke echoes in the low-vaulted ceiling.

"The thing had pinioned my arms, and the more I twisted and squirmed the more agonizingly it tightened about me. The constriction increased until breathing became a torture, until all my flesh palpitated with pain. I wriggled and twisted, and bit my lips through in an extremity of horror.

"Then, abruptly, the pressure ceased and I became aware of two unblinking, fish-white eyes glaring truculently at me through the darkness. Agonizingly I sat up and ran my hands over my chest and arms. My fingers encountered a warm wetness and with a hideous clarity it was borne in on me that the thing had been feasting on my blood! The revelation was very close to mind-shattering. I was on my feet in an instant, trying desperately not to succumb to panic, but knowing, deep in my mind, that it would be a losing battle.

"A most awful terror was upon me, and so unreasoning became my desire to escape from that fearsome, vampirish obscenity that I retreated straight toward the throne of Chaugnar Faugn.

"It loomed enormous in the darkness, a refuge and a sanctuary. The wild thought came to me that if I could scale the throne and climb upon the lap of the god the horror might cease to molest me. Malignant beyond belief it undoubtedly was. But I refused to credit it with more than animalistic intelligence. Even in that moment of infinite peril, as I groped shakingly toward the rear of the cave, my mind was evolving a conceit to account for it.

"It was undoubtedly, I told myself, some cave-lurking survival from the age of reptiles—some atavistic and predatory abnormality that had experienced no necessity to advance on the course of evolution. It is more than probable that all backboned animals above the level of fishes and amphibians originated in Asia, and I had recklessly conveyed myself to the hoariest section of that primeval continent.

Was it after all so amazing that I should have encountered, in a dark and inaccessible cave on a virtually uninhabited plateau, a reptilian predator endowed with the rapacity of that most hideous of blood-sucking animals—the vampire bat of the tropics?

"It was a just-short-of-destructive conceit and it sustained me and made my desperate groping for some kind of certainty seem the opposite of wasted until I reached the throne of Great Chaugnar. I fear that up to that instant my failure to suspect the truth was downright idiotic. There was only one adequate explanation for what had occurred. But it wasn't until I actually ascended the throne and began to feel about in the darkness for the body of Chaugnar that the truth rushed in upon me.

"Great Chaugnar had forsaken its throne! It had descended into the cave and was roaming about in the darkness. In its vampirish explorations it had stumbled upon my sleeping form, and had felled me with its trunk so that it might satisfy its thirst for blood with quick and hideous ferocity.

"For an instant I crouched motionless upon the stone, screaming inwardly, feeling the darkness tightening about me like a shroud. Then, quickly, I began to descend. But I had not lowered more than my right leg when something ponderous collided with the base of the throne. The entire structure shook and I was almost hurled to the ground.

"I refuse to dwell on what happened after that. There are experiences too revolting for sane description. Were I to tell how the horror began slowly to mount, to recount at length how it heaved its slabby and mucid vastness to the pinnacle of its throne and began nauseatingly to breathe upon me, the slight uncertainty I now entertain as to my sanity would be dispelled in short order.

"Neither shall I describe how it picked me up in its corpse-cold hands and began detestably to maul me, and how I nearly fainted beneath the foulness which drooled from its mouth. Eventually it wearied of its malign sport. After sinking its slimy black nails into my throat and chest until the pain became almost unbearable, it experienced a sudden access of wrath and hurled me violently from the pedestal.

"The fall stunned me and for many minutes I lay on my back on the stones, dimly conscious only of a furtive whispering in the darkness about me. Then, slowly, my vision cleared and under the guidance of some nebulous and sinister influence my eyes were drawn upward until they encountered the pedestal from which I had fallen and the enormous, ropy bulk of Chaugnar Faugn loathsomely waving his great trunk in the dawn.

"It isn't surprising that when Chung Ga found me deliriously gibbering at the cavern's mouth he was obliged to carry me into the sunlight and force great wooden spoonfuls of revivifying wine down my parched throat. If there was *anything* inexplicable in the sequel to that hideous nightmare it was the matter-of-fact reception which he accorded my story.

"He nodded his head sympathetically when I recounted my experiences on the throne, and assured me that the incident accorded splendidly with the prophecies of Mu Sang. 'I was afraid,' he said, 'that Great Chaugnar would not accept you as

its companion and nurse—that it would destroy you as utterly as it has the guardians—more of the guardians than you might suppose, for a god is not motivated by
our kind of expediency.'

"He studied me for a moment intensely. 'No doubt you think me a superstitious savage, a ridiculous barbarian. Would it surprize you very much if I should
tell you that I have spent eight years in England and that I am a graduate of the
University of Oxford?'

"I could only stare at him in stunned disbelief for a moment, but so unbelievable and ghastly had been the coming to life of Chaugnar Faugn that lesser wonders made little impression on me and my incredulity passed quickly. Had he told
me that he had an eye in the middle of his back or a tail twenty feet long which he
kept continuously coiled about his body I should have evinced little surprize. I
doubt indeed if anything short of a universal cataclysm could have roused me from
my dazed acceptance of revelations which, under ordinary circumstances, I should
have dismissed as preposterous.

"'It astonishes you perhaps that I should have cast my lot with filthy primitives
in this loathsome place and that I should have so uncompromisingly menaced your
countrymen.' A wistfulness crept into his eyes. 'Your Richardson was a brave man.
Even Chaugnar Faugn was moved to compassion by his valor. He gave no cry
when we drove wooden stakes through his hands and impaled him. For three days
he defied us. Then Chaugnar tramped toward him in the night and set him at liberty.

"'You may be sure that from that instant we accorded him every consideration. But to return to what you would undoubtedly call my perverse and atavistic
attitude. Why do you suppose I chose to serve Chaugnar?'

"His recapitulation of what he had done to Richardson had awakened in me a
confused but violent resentment. 'I don't know,' I muttered. 'There are degrees of
human vileness—'

"'Spare me your opprobrium, I beg of you,' he exclaimed. 'It was Great
Chaugnar speaking through me that dictated the fate of Richardson. I am merely
Chaugnar's interpreter and instrument. For generations my forebears have served
Chaugnar, and I have never attempted to evade the duties that were delegated to
me when our world was merely a thought in the mind of my god. I went to England and acquired a little of the West's decadent culture merely that I might more
worthily serve Chaugnar.

"'Don't imagine for a moment that Chaugnar is a beneficent god. In the West
you have evolved certain amiabilities of intercourse, to which you presumptuously
attach cosmic significance, such as truth, kindliness, generosity, forbearance and
honor, and you quaintly imagine that a god who is beyond good and evil and hence
unamenable to your 'ethics' can not be omnipotent.

"'But how do you know that there *are* any beneficent laws in the universe, that
the cosmos is friendly to man? Even in the mundane sphere of planetary life there
is nothing to sustain such an hypothesis.

"'Great Chaugnar is a terrible god, an utterly cosmic and unanthropomorphic god. It is akin to the fire mists and the primordial ooze, and before it incarned itself in Time it contained within itself the past, the present and the future. Nothing was and nothing will be, but all things are. And Chaugnar Faugn was once the sum of all things that are.'

"I remained silent and a note of compassion crept into his voice. I think he perceived that I had no inclination to split hairs with him over the paradoxes of transcendental metaphysics.

"'Chaugnar Faugn,' he continued, 'did not always dwell in the East. Many thousands of years ago it abode with its Brothers in a cave in Western Europe, and made from the flesh of toads a race of small dark shapes to serve it. In bodily contour these shapes resembled men, but they were incapable of speech and their thoughts were the thoughts of Chaugnar.

"'The cave where Chaugnar dwelt was never visited by men, for it wound its twisted length through a high and inaccessible crag of the mysterious Pyrenees, and all the regions beneath were rife with abominable hauntings.

"'Twice a year Chaugnar Faugn sent its servants into the villages that dotted the foothills to bring it the sustenance its belly craved. The chosen youths and maidens were preserved with spices and stored in the cave till Chaugnar had need of them. And in the villages men would hurl their first-borns into the flames and offer prayers to their futile little gods, hoping thereby to appease the wrath of Chaugnar's mindless servants.

"'But eventually there came into the foothills men like gods, stout, eagle-visaged men who carried on their shields the insignia of invincible Rome. They scaled the mountains in pursuit of the servants and awoke a cosmic foreboding in the mind of Chaugnar.

"'It is true that its Brethren succeeded without difficulty in exterminating the impious cohorts—exterminating them unspeakably—before they reached the cave, but it feared that rumors of the attempted sacrilege would bring legions of the empire-builders into the hills and that eventually its sanctuary would be defiled.

"'So in ominous conclave it debated with its Brothers the advisability of flight. Rome was but a dream in the mind of Chaugnar and it could have destroyed her utterly in an instant, but having incarned itself in Time it did not wish to resort to violence until the prophecies were fulfilled.

"'Chaugnar and its Brothers conversed by means of thought-transference in an idiom incomprehensible to us and it would be both dangerous and futile to attempt to repeat the exact substance of their discourse. But it is recorded in the prophecy of Mu Sang that Great Chaugnar spoke *approximately* as follows:

"'"Our servants shall carry us eastward to the primal continent, and there we shall await the arrival of the White Acolyte."

"'His Brothers demurred. "We are safe here," they affirmed. "No one will scale the mountains again, for the doom that came to Pompelo will reverbcrate in the dreams of prophets till Rome is less to be feared than moon-dim Nineveh, or Medusa-girdled Ur."

"'At that Great Chaugnar waxed ireful and affirmed that it would go alone to the primal continent, leaving its Brothers to cope with the menace of Rome. "When the time-frames are dissolved I alone shall ascend in glory," it told them. "All of you I shall devour before I ascend to the dark altars. When the hour of my transfiguration approaches you will come down from the mountains cosmically athirst for That Which is Not to be Spoken of, but even as your bodies raven for the time-dissolving sacrament I shall consume them."'

"'Then it called for the servants and had them carry it to this place. And it caused Mu Sang to be born from the womb of an ape and the prophecies to be written on imperishable parchment, and into the care of my fathers it surrendered its body.'

"I rose gropingly to my feet. 'Let me leave this place,' I pleaded. 'I respect your beliefs and I give you my solemn word I will never attempt to return. Your secrets are safe with me. Only let me go—'

"Chung Ga's features were convulsed with pity. 'It is stated in the prophecy that you must be Chaugnar's companion and accompany it to America. In a few days it will experience a desire to feed again. You must nurse it unceasingly.'

"'I am ill,' I pleaded. 'I can not carry Chaugnar Faugn across the desert plateau.'

"'I will have the guardians assist you,' murmured Chung Ga soothingly. 'You shall be conveyed in comfort to the gates of Lhasa, and from Lhasa to the coast it is less than a week's journey by caravan.'

"I realized then how impossible it would be for me to depart without Great Chaugnar. 'Very well, Chung Ga,' I said. 'I submit to the prophecy. Chaugnar shall be my companion and I shall nurse it as diligently as it desires.'

"There was a ring of insincerity in my speech which was not lost on Chung Ga. He approached very close to me and peered into my eyes. 'If you attempt to dispose of my god,' he warned, 'its Brothers will come down from the mountains and tear you indescribably.'

"He saw perhaps that I wasn't wholly convinced, for he added in an even more ominous tone, 'It has laid upon you the mark and seal of a flesh-dissolving sacrament. Destroy it, and the sacrament will be consummated in an instant. The flesh of your body will turn black and melt like tallow in the sun. You will become a seething mass of corruption.'"

Ulman paused, a look of unutterable torment in his eyes. "There isn't much more to my story, Algernon. The guardians carried us safely to Lhasa and a fortnight later I reached the Bay of Bengal, accompanied by half a hundred ragged, gaunt-visaged mendicants from the temples of obscure Indian villages. There was something about our caravan that had attracted them. And all during the voyage from Bengal to Hongkong the Indian and Tibetan members of our crew would steal stealthily to my cabin at night and look in on me, and I had never before seen human faces quite so distorted with superstitious terror.

"Don't imagine for a moment that I didn't share their awe and fear of the thing I was compelled to companion. Continuously I longed to carry it on deck and cast it into the sea. Only the memory of Chung Ga's warning and the thought of what might happen to me if I disregarded it kept me chained and submissive.

"It was not until weeks later, when I had left the Indian and most of the Pacific Ocean behind me, that I discovered how unwise I had been to heed his vile threats. If I had resolutely hurled Chaugnar into the sea the shame and the horror might never have come upon me!"

Ulman's voice was rising, becoming shrill and hysterical. "Chaugnar Faugn is an awful and mysterious being, a repellent and obscene and lethal being, but how do I know that it is omnipotent? Chung Ga may have maliciously lied to me. Chaugnar Faugn may be merely an extension or distortion of inanimate nature. Some hideous *process*, as yet unobserved and unexplained by the science of the West, may be noxiously at work in desert places all over our planet to produce such fiendish anomalies. Perhaps parallel to protoplasmic life on the earth's crust is this other aberrant and hidden life—the revolting sentiency of stones that aspire, of earth-shapes, parasitic and bestial, that wax agile in the presence of man.

"Did not Cuvier believe that there had been not one but an infinite number of 'creations', and that as our earth cooled after its departure from the sun a succession of vitalic phenomena appeared on its surface? Conceding as we must the orderly and continuous development of protoplasmic life from simple forms, which Cuvier stupidly and ridiculously denied, is it not still conceivable that another evolutionary cycle may have preceded the one which has culminated in us? A non-protoplasmic cycle?

"Whether we accept the planetesimal or the three or four newer theories of planetary formation it is permissible to believe that the earth coalesced very swiftly into a compact mass after the segregation of its constituents in space and that it achieved sufficient crustal stability to support animate entities one, or two, or perhaps even five billion years ago.

"I do not claim that life *as we know it* would be possible in the earliest phases of planetary consolidation, but is it possible to assert dogmatically that beings possessed of intelligence and volition could not have evolved in a direction merely parallel to the cellular? Life as we know it is complexly bound up with such substances as chlorophyll and protoplasm, but does that preclude the possibility of an evolved sentiency in other forms of matter?

"How do we know that stones can not think; that the earth beneath our feet may not once have been endowed with a hideous intelligence? Entire cycles of animate evolution may have occurred on this planet before the most primitive of 'living' cells were evolved from the slime of warm seas.

"There may have been eons of—experiments! Three billion years ago in the fiery radiance of the rapidly condensing earth who knows what monstrous shapes crawled—or shambled?

"And how do we know that there are not survivals? Or that somewhere beneath the stars of heaven complex and hideous processes are not still at work, shaping the inorganic into forms of primal malevolence?

"And what more inevitable than that some such primiparous spawn should have become in my eyes the apotheosis of all that was fiendish and accursed and unclean, and that I should have ascribed to it the attributes of divinity, and imagined in a moment of madness that it was immune to destruction? I should have hurled it into the depths of the seas and risked boldly the fulfillment of Chung Ga's prophecy. For even had it proved itself omnipotent and omniscient by rising in fury from the waves or summoning its Brothers to destroy me I should have suffered indescribably for no more than a moment."

Ulman's voice had risen to a shrill scream. "I should have passed quickly enough into the darkness had I encountered merely the wrath of Chaugnar Faugn. It was not the fury but the forbearance of Chaugnar that has wrought an uncleanliness in my body's flesh, and blackened and shriveled my soul, till a furious hate has grown up in me for all that the world holds of serenity and joy."

Ulman's voice broke and for a moment there was silence in the room. Then, with a sudden, convulsive movement of his right arm he uncloaked the whole of his face.

He was standing very nearly in the center of the office and the light from its eastern window illumed with a hideous clarity all that remained of his features. But Algernon didn't utter a sound, for all that the sight was appalling enough to revolt a corpse. He simply clung shakingly to the desk and waited with ashen lips for Ulman to continue.

"It came to me again as I slept, drinking its fill, and in the morning I woke to find that the flesh of my body had grown fetid and loathsome, and that my face— my face . . ."

"Yes, Clark, I understand." Algernon's voice was vibrant with compassion. "I'll get you some brandy."

Ulman's eyes shone with an awful light.

"Do you believe me?" he cried. "Do you believe that Chaugnar Faugn has wrought this uncleanliness?"

Slowly Algernon shook his head. "No, Clark. Chaugnar Faugn is nothing but a stone idol, sculptured by some Asian artist with quite exceptional talent, however primitive he may have been in other respects. I believe that Chung Ga kept you under the influence of some potent drug until he had—had cut your face, and that he also hypnotized you and suggested every detail of the story you have just told me. I believe you are still actually under the spell of that hypnosis."

"When I boarded the ship at Calcutta there was nothing wrong with my face!" shrilled Ulman.

"Conceivably not. But some minion of the priest may have administered the drug and performed the operation on shipboard. I can only guess at what happened, of course, but it is obvious that you are the victim of some hideous charlatanry. I've visited India, Clark, and I have a very keen respect for the hypnotic endowments of the Oriental. It's ghastly and unbelievable how much a Hindoo or a Tibetan can accomplish by simple suggestion."

"I feared—I feared that you would doubt!" Ulman's voice had risen to a shriek. "But I swear to you . . ."

The sentence was never finished. A hideous pallor overspread the archeologist's face, his jaw sagged and into his eyes there crept a look of panic fight. For a second he stood clawing at his throat, like a man in the throes of an epileptic fit.

Then something, some invisible force, seemed to propel him backward. Choking and gasping he staggered against the wall and threw out his arms in a gesture of frantic appeal. "Keep it off!" he sobbed. "I can't breathe. I can't . . ."

With a cry Algernon leapt forward, but before he reached the other's side the unfortunate man had sunk to the floor and was moaning and gibbering and rolling about in a most sickening way.

2. The Atrocity at the Museum

Algernon Harris emerged from the B.M.T. subway at the Fifty-ninth Street and Fifth Avenue entrance and began nervously to pace the sidewalk in front of a large yellow sign, which bore the discouraging caption: "Buses do not stop here." Harris was most eager to secure a bus and it was obvious from the expectant manner in which he hailed the first one to pass that he hadn't the faintest notion he had taken up his post on the wrong side of the street. Indeed, it was not until four buses had passed him by that he awoke to the gravity of his predicament and began to propel his person in the direction of the legitimate stop-zone.

Algernon Harris was abnormally and tragically upset. But even a man trembling on the verge of a neuropathic collapse can remain superficially politic, and it isn't surprising that when he ascended into his bus and encountered on a conspicuous seat his official superior, Doctor George Francis Scollard, he should have nodded, smiled and responded with an unwavering amiability to the questions that were shot at him.

"I got your telegram yesterday," murmured the president of the Manhattan Museum of Fine Arts, "and I caught the first train down. Am I too late for the inquest?"

Algernon nodded. "The coroner—a chap named Henry Weigal—took my evidence and rendered a decision on the spot. The condition of Ulman's body would not have permitted of delay. I never before imagined that—that putrefaction could proceed with such incredible rapidity."

Scollard frowned. "And the verdict?"

"Heart failure. The coroner was very positive that anxiety and shock were the sole causes of Ulman's total collapse."

"But you said something about his face being horribly disfigured."

"Yes. It had been rendered loathsome by—by plastic surgery. Weigal was hideously agitated until I explained that Ulman had merely fallen into the hands of a skillful Oriental surgeon with sadistic inclination in the course of his archeological explorations. I explained to him that many of our field workers returned slightly disfigured and that Ulman had merely endured an exaggeration of the customary martyrdom."

"And you believe that plastic surgery could account for the repellent and grue-some changes you mentioned in your night-letter—the shocking prolongation of the poor devil's nose, the flattening and broadening of his ears . . ."

Algernon winced. "I must believe it, sir. It is impossible sanely to entertain any other explanation. The coroner's assistant was a little incredulous at first, until Weigal pointed out to him what an unwholesome precedent they would set by even so much as hinting that the phenomenon wasn't pathologically explicable. 'We would play right into the hands of the spiritualists,' Weigal explained. 'An offi-cer of the police isn't at liberty to adduce an hypothesis that the district attorney's office wouldn't approve of. The newspapers would pounce on a thing like that and play it up disgustingly. Mr. Harris has supplied us with an explanation which seems adequately to cover the facts, and with your permission I shall file a verdict of nat-ural death.'"

The president coughed and shifted uneasily in his seat. "I am glad that the co-roner took such a sensible view of the matter. Had he been a recalcitrant individual and raised objections we should have come in for considerable unpleasant public-ity. I shudder whenever I see a reference to the Museum in the popular press. It is always the morbid and sensational aspects of our work that they stress and there is never the slightest attention paid to accuracy."

For a moment Doctor Scollard was silent. Then he cleared his throat, and reca-pitulated, in a slightly more emphatic form, the question that he had put to Algernon originally. "But you said in your letter that Ulman's nose revolted and sickened you—that it had become a loathsome greenish trunk almost a foot in length which continued to move about for hours after Ulman's heart stopped beating. Could—could your operation hypothesis account for such an appalling anomaly?"

Algernon took a deep breath. "I can't pretend that I wasn't astounded and ap-palled and—and frightened. And so lost to discretion that I made no attempt to conceal the way I felt from the coroner. I could not remain in the room while they were examining the body."

"And yet you succeeded in convincing the coroner that he could justifiably render a verdict of natural death!"

"You misunderstood me, sir. The coroner *wanted* to render such a verdict. My explanation merely supplied him with a straw to clutch at. I was trembling in every limb when I made it and it must have been obvious to him that we were in the presence of something unthinkable. But without the plastic surgery assumption we should have had nothing whatever to cling to."

"And do you still give your reluctant assent to such an assumption?"

"Now more than ever. And my assent is no longer reluctant, for I've suc-ceeded in convincing myself that a surgeon endowed with miraculous skill could have effected the transformation I described in my letter."

"Miraculous skill?"

"I use the word in a merely mundane sense. When one stops to consider what astounding advances plastic surgery has made in England and America during the past decade it is impossible to disbelieve that the human frame will soon become more malleable than wax beneath the scalpels of our surgeons and that beings will appear in our midst with bodies so grotesquely distorted that the superstitious will ascribe their advent to the supernatural.

"And we can adduce *more* than a surgical 'miracle' to account for the horror that poor Ulman became without for a moment encroaching on the dubious domain of the super-physical. Every one knows how extensively the ductless glands regulate the growth and shape of our bodies. A change in the quantity or quality of secretion in any one of the glands may throw the entire human mechanism out of gear. Terrible and unthinkable changes have been known to occur in the adult body during the course of diseases involving glandular instability. We once thought that human beings invariably ceased to grow at twenty-one or twenty-two, but we now know that growth may continue till middle age, and even till the very onset of senility, and that frequently such growth does not culminate in a mere increase in stature or in girth.

"Doubtless you have heard of that rare and hideously deforming glandular malady acromegaly. It is characterized by an abnormal over-growth of the skull and face, and the small bones of the extremities, and its victims become in a short time tragic caricatures of humanity. The entire face assumes a more massive cast but the over-growth is most pronounced in the region of the jawbones. In exceptional cases the face has been known to attain a length of nearly a foot. But it is not so much the size as the revolting primitiveness of the face which sets the victims of this hideous disease so tragically apart from their fellows. The features not only grow, but they take on an almost apelike aspect, and as the disease advances even the skull becomes revoltingly simian in its conformation. In brief, the victims of acromegaly become in a short while almost indistinguishable from very primitive and brutish types of human ancestors, such as *Homo neanderthalensis* and the unmentionable, enormous-browed caricature from Broken Hill, Rhodesia, which Sir Arthur Keith has called the most unqualifiedly repulsive physiognomy in the entire gallery of fossil men.

"The disease of acromegaly is perhaps a more certain indication of man's origin than all the 'missing links' that anthropologists have exhumed. It proves incontestably that we still carry within our bodies the mechanism of evolutionary retrogression, and that when something interferes with the normal functioning of our glands we are very apt to return, at least physically, to our aboriginal status.

"And since we know that a mere insufficiency or superabundance of glandular secretions can work such devastating changes, can turn men virtually into Neanderthalers, or great apes, what is there really unaccountable in the alteration I witnessed in poor Ulman?

"Some Oriental diabolist merely ten years in advance of the West in the sphere of plastic surgery and with a knowledge of glandular therapeutics no greater than that possessed by Doctors Noel Paton and Schafer might easily have wrought such an abomination. Or suppose, as I have hinted before, that no surgery was involved, suppose this fiend has learned so much about our glands that he can send men back and back through the mists of time—back past the great apes and the primitive mammals and the carnivorous dinosaurs to their primordial sires! Suppose—it is an awful thought, I know—suppose that some creature closely resembling what Ulman became was *once* our ancestor, that a hundred million years ago a gigantic batrachian shape with trunk-like appendages and great flapping ears paddled through the warm primeval seas or stretched its leathery length on banks of Permian slime!"

Mr. Scollard turned sharply and plucked at his subordinate's sleeve. "There's a crowd in front of the Museum," he muttered. "See there!"

Algernon started, and rising instantly, pressed the signal bell above his companion's head. "We'll have to walk back," he muttered despondently. "I should have watched the street numbers."

His pessimism proved well-founded. The bus continued relentlessly on its way for four additional blocks and then came so abruptly to a stop that Mr. Scollard was subjected to the ignominy of being obliged to sit for an instant on the spacious lap of a middle-aged stout woman who resented the encroachment with a furious glare.

"I've a good mind to report you," he shouted to the bus conductor as he lowered his portly person to the sidewalk. "I've a damn good mind . . ."

"Let it pass, sir." Algernon laid a pacifying arm on his companion's arm. "We've got no time to argue. Something dreadful has occurred at the Museum. I just saw two policemen enter the building. And those tall men walking up and down on the opposite side of the street are reporters. There's Wells of the *Tribune* and Thompson of the *Times,* and . . ."

Mr. Scollard gripped his subordinate's arm. "Tell me," he demanded, "did you put the—the statue on *exhibition?*"

Algernon nodded. "I had it carried to Alcove K, Wing C last night. After the inquest on poor Ulman I was besieged by reporters. They wanted to know all about the fetish, and of course I had to tell them that it would go on exhibition eventually. They would have returned every day for weeks to pester me if I hadn't assured them that we'd respect the public clamor to that extent at least."

"Yesterday afternoon all the papers ran specials about it. The *News-Graphic* gave it a front-page write-up. I remained at my office until eleven, and all evening at half-minute intervals some emotionally-overcharged numbskull would ring up and ask me when I was going to exhibit the thing and whether it really looked as repulsive as its photographs, and what kind of stone it was made of and—oh, God! I was too nervous and wrought-up to be bothered that way and I decided it would be best to satisfy the public's idiotic curiosity by permitting them to view the thing today."

The two men were walking briskly in the direction of the Museum.

"Besides, there was no longer any necessity of my keeping it in the office. I had had it measured and photographed and I knew that Harrison and Smithstone wouldn't want to take a cast of it until next week. And I couldn't have chosen a safer place for it than Alcove K. It's roped off, you know, and only two paces removed from the door. Cinney can see it all night from his station in the corridor."

By the time that Algernon and Mr. Scollard arrived at the Museum the crowd had reached alarming proportions. They were obliged to fight their way through a solid phalanx of excited men and women who impeded their progress with elbow-thrusting aggressiveness, and scant respect for their dignity. And even in the vestibules they were repulsed with discourtesy.

A red-headed policeman glared savagely at them from behind horn-rimmed spectacles and brought them to a halt with a threatening gesture. "You've got to keep out!" he shouted. "If you ain't got a police card you've got to keep out!"

"What's happened here?" demanded Algernon authoritatively.

"A guy's been bumped off. If you ain't got a police card you've got to . . ."

Algernon produced a calling-card and thrust it into the officer's face. "I'm the curator of archeology," he affirmed angrily. "I guess I've a right to enter my own museum."

The officer's manner softened perceptibly. "Then I guess it's all right. The chief told me I wasn't to keep out any of the guys that work here. How about your friend?"

"You can safely admit him," murmured Algernon with a smile. "He's president of the Museum."

The policeman did not seem too astonished. He regarded Mr. Scollard dubiously for a moment. Then he shrugged his shoulders and stepped complacently aside.

An attendant greeted them excitedly as they emerged from the turnstile. "It's awful, sir," he gasped, addressing Mr. Scollard. "Cinney has been murdered—knifed, sir. He's all cut and mangled. I shouldn't have recognized him if it weren't for his clothes. There's nothing left of his face, sir."

Algernon turned pale. "When—when did this happen?" he gasped.

The attendant shook his head. "I can't say, Mr. Harris. It must've been some time last night, but I can't say exactly when. The first we knew of it was when Mr. Williams came running down the stairs with his hands all bloodied. That was at eight this morning, about two hours ago. I'd just got in, and all the other attendants were in the cloak room getting into their uniforms. That is, all except Williams. Williams usually arrives about a half-hour before the rest of us. He likes to come early and have a chat with Cinney before the doors open."

The attendant's face was convulsed with terror and he spoke with considerable difficulty. "I was the only one to see him come down the stairs. I was standing about here and as soon as he came into sight I knew that something was wrong with him. He went from side to side of the stairs and clung to the rails to keep himself from falling. And his face was as white as paper."

Algernon's eyes did not leave the attendant's face. "Go on," he urged.

"He opened his mouth very wide when he saw me. It was like as if he wanted to shout and couldn't. There wasn't a sound came out of him."

The attendant cleared his throat. "I didn't think he'd ever reach the bottom of the stairs and I called out for the boys in the cloak room to lend me a hand."

"What happened then?"

"He didn't speak for a long time. One of the boys gave him some whisky out of a flask and the rest of us just stood about and said soothing things to him. But he was trembling all over and we couldn't quiet him down. He kept throwing his head about and pointing toward the stairs. And foam collected all over his mouth. It was ghastly."

"'What's wrong, Jim?' I said to him. 'What did you see?'

"'The worm of hell!' he said. 'The Devil's awful mascot!' He said other things I can't repeat, sir. I'm a God-fearing man, and there are blasphemies it's best to forget you ever heard. But I'll tell you what he said when he got through talking about the worm out of hell. He said: 'Cinney's upstairs stretched out on his back and there ain't a drop of blood in his veins.'

"We got up the stairs quicker than lightning after he'd told us that. We didn't know just what his crazy words meant, but the blood on his hands made us sure that something pretty terrible had happened. They kind of confirmed what we feared, sir—if you get what I mean."

Algernon nodded. "And you found Cinney—dead?"

"Worse than that, sir. All black and shrunken and looking as though he'd been wearing clothes about four sizes too large for him. His face was all *gone*, sir—all eaten away, like. We picked him up—he wasn't much heavier than a little boy—and laid him out on a bench in Corridor H. I never seen so much blood in my life—the floor was all slippery with it. And the big stone animal you had us carry down to Alcove K last night was all dripping with it, 'specially its trunk. It made me sort of sick. I never like to look at blood."

"You think some one attacked Cinney?"

"It looked that way, Mr. Harris. Like as if some one went for him with a knife. It must have been an awful big knife—a regular butcher's knife. That ain't a very nice way of putting it, sir, but that's how it struck me. Like as if some one mistook him for a piece of mutton."

"And what else did you find when you examined him?"

"We didn't do much examining. We just let him lie on the bench till we got through phoning for the police. Mr. Williamson did the talking, sir." A look of relief crept into the attendant's eyes. "The police said we wasn't to disturb the body further, which suited us fine. There wasn't one of us didn't want to give poor Mr. Cinney a wide berth."

"And what did the police do when they arrived?"

"Asked us about a million crazy questions, sir. Was Mr. Cinney disfigured in the war? And was Mr. Cinney in the habit of wearing a mask over his face? And had Mr. Cinney received any threatening letters from Chinamen or Hindoos? And when we told them no, they seemed to get kind of frightened. 'If it ain't murder,' they said, 'we're up against something that ain't natural. But it's got to be murder. All we have to do is get hold of the Chinaman.'"

Algernon didn't wait to hear more. Brushing the attendant ungratefully aside he went dashing up the stairs three steps at a time. Mr. Scollard followed with ashen face.

They were met in the upper corridor by a tall, loose-jointed man in shabby, ill-fitting clothes who arrested their progress with a scowl and a torrent of impatient abuse. "Where do you think you're going?" he demanded. "Didn't I give orders that no one was to come up here? I've got nothing to say to you. You're too damn nosy. If you want the lowdown on this affair you've got to wait outside till we get through questioning the attendants."

"See here," said Algernon impatiently. "This gentleman is president of the Museum and he has a perfect right to go where he chooses."

The tall man waxed apologetic. "I thought you were a couple of newspaper Johns," he murmured confusedly. "We haven't anything even remotely resembling a clue, but those guys keep popping in here every ten minutes to cross-examine us. They're worse than prosecuting attorneys. Come right this way, sir."

He led them past a little knot of attendants and photographers and fingerprint experts to the northerly part of the corridor. "There's the body," he said, pointing toward a sheeted form which lay sprawled on a low bench near the window. "I'd be grateful if you gentlemen would look at the poor lad's face."

Algernon nodded, and lifting a corner of the sheet peered for an instant intently into what remained of poor Cinney's countenance. Then, with a shudder, he surrendered his place to Mr. Scollard.

It is to Mr. Scollard's credit that he did not cry out. Only the trembling of his lower lip betrayed the revulsion which filled him.

"He was found on the floor in the corridor about two hours ago," explained the detective. "But the guy who found him isn't here. They've got him in a straitjacket down at Bellevue, and it doesn't look as though he'll be much help to us. He was yelling his head off about something he said came out of hell when they put him in the ambulance. That's what drew the crowd."

"You don't think Williams could have done it?" murmured Algernon.

"Not a chance. But he saw the murderer all right, and if we can get him to talk . . ." He wheeled on Algernon abruptly. "You seem to know something about this, sir."

"Only what we picked up downstairs. We had a talk with one of the attendants and he explained about Williams—and the Chinaman."

The detective's eyes glowed. "The Chinaman? What Chinaman? Is there a Chinaman mixed up in this? It's what I've been thinking all along, but I didn't have much to go on."

"I fear we're becoming involved in a vicious circle," said Algernon. "It was your Chinaman I was referring to. Willy said you were laboring under the impression that all you had to do to solve this distressing affair was to catch a Chinaman."

The detective shook his head. "It's not as simple as that," he affirmed. "We haven't any positive evidence that a Chinaman did it. It might have been a Jap or Hindoo or even a South Sea Islander. That is, if South Sea Islanders eat rice!"

"Rice?" Algernon stared at the detective incredulously.

"That's right. In a bowl with long sticks. I'm no authority on etymology, but it's my guess they don't use chopsticks much outside of Asia."

He went into Alcove K and returned with a wooden bowl and two long splinters of wood. "All those dark spots near the rim are blood stains," he explained, as he surrendered the gruesome exhibits to Algernon. "Even the rice is all smeared with blood." Algernon shuddered and passed the bowl to Scollard, who almost dropped it in his haste to return it to the detective.

"Where did you find it?" the president spoke in a subdued whisper.

"On the floor in front of the big stone elephant. That's where Cinney was killed. There's blood all over the elephant—if it's supposed to be an elephant."

"It isn't, strictly speaking, an elephant," said Algernon.

"Well, whatever it is, it could tell us what Cinney's murderer looked like. I'd give the toes off my left foot if it could talk."

"It doesn't talk," said Algernon decisively.

"I wasn't wisecracking," admonished the detective. "I was simply pointing out that that elephant could give us the lowdown on a mighty nasty murder."

Algernon accepted the rebuke in silence.

"There ain't no doubt whatever that a Chinaman or Hindoo or some crazy foreigner sneaked in here last night, set himself down in front of that elephant and began eating rice. Maybe he was in a church-going mood and mistook the beast for one of his heathen gods. It kind of looks like an oriental idol—the ferocious-looking kind you sometimes see in Chinatown store windows."

Algernon smiled ironically. "But unquestionably unique," he murmured.

The detective nodded. "Yeah. Larger and uglier-looking, but a heathen statue for all that. I bet it actually was worshipped once. Hindu . . . Chinese . . . I wouldn't know. But it sure has that look."

"Yes," admitted Algernon, "it is indubitably in the religious tradition. For all its hideousness it has all the earmarks of a quiescent Eastern divinity."

"There ain't anything more dangerous than interfering with an Oriental when he's saying his prayers," continued the detective. "I've been in Chinatown raids, and I know. Now here's what I think happened. Cinney is standing in the corridor and suddenly he hears the Chinaman muttering and mumbling to himself in the dark. He's naturally frightened and so he rushes in with his pocketlight where an angel would be fearing to tread. The light gets in the Chinaman's eyes and sets him off.

"It's like putting a match to a ton of TNT to throw a light on a Chinaman when he's squatting in the dark in a worshipful mood. So the Chinaman goes for the kid with a knife. He feels outraged in a religious way, isn't really himself, thinks he's avenging an insult to the idol."

Algernon nodded impatiently. "There may be something in your theory, sergeant. But there's a great deal it doesn't explain. What was it that Williams saw?"

"Nothing but Cinney lying dead in the corridor. Nothing but Cinney looking up at him without a face and that awful heathen animal looking down at him with blood all over its mouth."

Algernon stared. "Blood on its mouth?"

"Sure. All over its mouth, trunk and tusks. Never seen so much blood in my life. That's what Williams saw. I don't wonder it crumpled the kid up."

There was a commotion in the corridor. Someone was sobbing and pleading in a most fantastic way a few yards from where the three men were standing. The detective turned and shouted out a curt command. "Whoever that is, bring him here!"

Came an appalling, ear-harassing shriek and two plainclothesmen emerged around a bend in the corridor with a diminutive and weeping Oriental spread-eagled between their extended arms.

"The Chinaman!" muttered Scollard in amazement.

For a second the detective was too startled to move, and his immobility somehow emboldened the Chinese to break from his captors and prostrate himself on the floor at Algernon's feet.

"You are my friend," he sobbed. "You are a very good man. I saw you in green-fire dream. In dream when big green animals came down from mountain I saw you and Gautama Siddhartha. Big green animals all wanted blood—all very much wanted blood. In dream Gautama Siddhartha said: 'They want you! They have determined they make you all dark fire glue.'

"I said, 'No! *Please,*' I said. Then Gautama Siddhartha let fall jewel of wisdom. 'Go to *museum.* Go to big *museum* round block, and big green animal will eat you quick. He will eat you quick—before he make American man dark fire glue.'

"All night I have sat here. All night I said: 'Eat me. *Please!*' But big green animal slept till American man came. Then he moved. Very quickly he moved. He gave American man very bad hug. American man screamed and big green animal drank all American man's blood."

The little Oriental was sobbing unrestrainedly. Algernon stooped and lifted him gently to his feet. "What is your name?" he asked, to soothe him. "Where do you live?"

"I'm boss big laundry down street," murmured the Chinaman. "My name is Hsieh Ho. I am a good man, like you."

"Where did you go when—when the elephant came to life?"

The Chinaman's lower lip trembled convulsively. "I hid back of big white lady."

In spite of the gravity of the situation Algernon couldn't repress a smile. The "big white lady" was a statue of Venus Erycine and so enormous was it that it occupied almost the whole of Alcove K. It was a perfect sanctuary, but there was something ludicrously incongruous in a Chinaman's seeking refuge in such a place.

One of the detectives, however, confirmed the absurdity. "That's where we found him, sir. He was lying on his back, wailing and groaning and making faces at the ceiling. He's our man, all right. We'll have the truth out of him in ten minutes."

The chief sergeant nodded. "You bet we will. Put the bracelets on him, Jim."

Reluctantly Algernon surrendered Hsieh Ho to his captors. "I suggest you treat him kindly," he said. "He had the misfortune to witness a ghastly and unprecedented exaggeration of what Eddington would call the random element in nature. But he's as destitute of criminal proclivities as Mr. Scollard here."

The detective raised his eyebrows. "I don't get it, sir. Are you suggesting we just hold him as a material witness?"

Algernon nodded. "If you try any of your revolting third-degree tactics on that poor little man you'll answer in court to my lawyer. Now, if you don't mind, I'll have a look at Alcove K."

The detective scowled. He wanted to tell Algernon to go to hell, but somehow the inflection of authority in the latter's voice glued the invective to his tongue, and with a surly shrug he escorted the group into the presence of Chaugnar Faugn.

Sanguinary baptism becomes some gods. Were the gracious figures of the Grecian pantheon to appear to us with blood upon their garments we should recoil in horror, but we should think the terrible Mithra or the heart-devouring Huitzilo-pochitli a trifle unconvincing if they came on our dreams untarnished by the ruddy vintage of sacrifice.

Algernon did not at first look directly at Chaugnar Faugn. He studied the tiled marble floor about the base of the idol and tried to make out in the gloom the precise spot where Cinney had lain. The attempt proved confusing. There were dark smudges on almost every other tile and they were nearly all of equal circumference.

"Right there is where we found the corpse," said the detective impatiently. "Right beneath the trunk of the elephant."

Algernon's blood ran cold. Slowly, very slowly, for he feared to confront what stood before him, he raised his eyes until they were level with the detective's shoulders. The detective's shoulders concealed a portion of Chaugnar Faugn, but all of the thing's right side and the extremity of its trunk were hideously visible to Algernon as he stared. He spoke no word. He did not even move. But all the blood drained out of his lips, leaving them ashen.

Mr. Scollard was staring at his subordinate with frightened eyes. "You act as though—as though—good God, man, what is it?"

"It has moved its trunk!" Algernon's voice was vibrant with horror. "It has moved its trunk since—since yesterday. And most hideously. I can not be mistaken. Yesterday it was vertical—today it is in a slightly upraised position.

Mr. Scollard gasped. "Are you sure?" he muttered. "Are you absolutely certain that the trunk wasn't in that position when the god arrived here?"

"Yes, yes. Not until today. In the excitement no one has noticed it, but if you will call the attendants—wait!"

The president had started to do that very thing, but Algernon's admonition brought him up short. "I shouldn't have suggested that," he murmured in Scollard's ear. "The attendants mustn't be questioned. It's all too unutterably ghastly and inexplicable and—and mad. We've got to keep it out of the papers, seek a solution secretly. I know some one who may be able to help us. The police can't. That's obvious."

The detective was staring at them pityingly. "You gentlemen better get out of here," he said. "You aren't used to sights like this. When I was new at this game I made a lot of mistakes. I could hardly stand the sight of a dead man, for instance.

Used to hurry things along when there was no real need for haste, which is just about the worst mistake you can make at the preliminary examination stage."

With an effort Algernon mastered his agitation. "You're right, sergeant," he said. "Mr. Scollard and I realize that this business is a little too disturbing for sane contemplation. So we'll retire, as you suggest. But I must warn you again that you'd better think twice about treating poor Hsieh Ho as a convicted murderer."

In the corridor he drew Mr. Scollard aside and conversed for a moment urgently in a low voice. Then he approached the detective and handed him a card. "If you want me within the next few hours you'll find me at this address," he said. "Mr. Scollard is returning to his home in Brooklyn. You'll find his phone number in the directory, but I hope you won't disturb him unless something really grave turns up."

The detective nodded and read aloud the address on Algernon's card. "Dr. Henry C. Imbert, F.R.S., F.A.G.S."

"A friend of yours?" he asked impertinently.

Algernon nodded. "Yes, sergeant. The foremost American ethnologist. Ever hear of him?"

To Algernon's amazement the sergeant nodded. "Yes. I got kind of interested in etymology once. I was on a queer case about two years ago. An old lady got bumped off by a poisoned arrow and we had him in for a powwow. He's clever all right. He gave us all the dope soon as he saw the corpse. Said a little negro had done it—one of those African pigmies you read about. We followed up the tip and caught the murderer just as he was giving the little fellow a cyanide cigarette to smoke. He was a shrewd Italian. He got the pigmy in Africa, hid him in a room down on Houston Street and sent him out to rob and bump off old ladies. He was as spry as a monkey and could shinny up a drainpipe on the side of a house in ten seconds. If it hadn't been for Imbert we'd never have got our hands on the guy that owned him."

Mr. Scollard and Algernon descended the stairs together. But in the vestibule they parted, the president proceeding down the still crowded outer steps in the direction of a bus whilst Algernon sought his office in Wing W.

"When Imbert sees this," Algernon murmured, as he extracted a photograph of Chaugnar Faugn from his chaotically littered desk, "he'll be the most disturbed ethnologist that this planet has harbored since the Pleistocene Age."

3. An Archeological Digression

"The figure is totally unfamiliar," said Doctor Imbert. "Nothing even remotely resembling it occurs in Asian or African mythology."

He scowled and returned the photograph to his youthful visitor, who deposited it on the arm of his chair.

"I confess," he continued, "that it puzzles and disturbs me. It's preposterously archeological, if you get what I mean. It isn't the sort of thing that one would—imagine."

Harris nodded. "I doubt if I could have imagined it from scratch. Without imaginative prompting or guidance from someone who had actually set eyes on it, it would be very difficult to conceive of anything so—so—"

"*Racial,*" put in Doctor Imbert. "I believe that is the word you were groping for. That *thing* is a symbolic embodiment of the massed imaginative heritage of an entire people. It's a composite—like the Homeric epics or the Sphinx of Giza. It's the kind of art manifestation you would expect a primitive people to produce collectively. It's so perversely diabolical and contradictory in conception that one can scarcely conceive of a mere individual anywhere in the world deliberately sitting down and creating it out of his own imagination. I will concede that an unusually gifted artist might be *capable* of imagining it, but I doubt if such an obscenity would ever form in the human brain without a *raison d'être*. And no individual living in a civilized state would experience the need, the desire to imagine such a thing, and least of all, to give it objective expression.

"Mental illness, of course, might account for it, but the so-called interpretative reveries of psychotics are nearly always of predictable nature. Grotesque and absurd as they may sometimes be, certain images occur in them again and again and these images are definitely meaningful. They follow prescribed patterns, are crude and distorted representations of familiar objects and people. The morbidities out of which they arise have been studied and classified and a psychiatrist who knows his business can usually decipher them. If you have ever examined a batch of drawings from a mental institution you will have noticed how the same motifs occur repeatedly and how utterly *unimaginative* such things are from a sane and sophisticated point of view.

"It is of course true that the folk creations of primitive peoples usually embody or symbolize definite human preoccupations, but more boldly and imaginatively, and occasionally they depart from the predictable to such an extent that even our expert is obliged to throw up his hands.

"I have always believed that most of the major and minor monstrosities that figure so conspicuously in the pantheons of barbarian races—feathered serpents, animal-headed priests, grimacing sphinxes, etc.—are synthetic conceptions. Let us suppose, for instance, that a tribe of reasonably enlightened barbarians is animated by the unique social impulse of co-operative agriculture and is moved to embody its ideals in some colossal fetish designed to suggest both fertility and brotherhood—in, let us say, a great stone Magna Mater with arms outstretched to embrace all classes and conditions of men. Then let us suppose that co-operative agriculture falls into disrepute and the tribe becomes obsessed by dreams of martial conquest. What happens? To an obbligato of tomtoms and war drums the Mother Goddess is transfigured. A spear is placed between her extended arms, the expression of her face altered from benignity to ferocity, great gashes chiseled in her cheeks, red paint smeared on her arms, breasts and shoulders and her ears lopped off. Let another generation pass and the demoniac goddess of war will be transformed into something else—perhaps into a symbol of the most abandoned kind of debauchery.

"In a hundred years the original fetish will have become a monstrous caricature, a record in stone of the thoughts and emotions of generations of men.

"It is the business of the ethnologist and the archaeologist to decipher such records, and if our scientist is sufficiently learned and diligent he can, as you know, supply a reason for every peculiarity of configuration. Competent scholars have traced, in a rough way, the advance or retrogression of racial groups in ethical and esthetic directions merely by studying and comparing their objects or worship and there does not exist a more fruitful science than idolography.

"But occasionally our ethnologist encounters a nut that he cannot crack, a god or goddess so diabolical or grotesque or loathsome in conformation that it is impossible to link it associatively with even the most revolting of tribal retrogressions. It is a notorious fact that human races are less apt to advance than circle back on the course of evolution, and that idols and fetishes that were originally conceived in a comparatively noble spirit very often become, in the course of time, embodiments of the bestial and the obscene. Some of the degraded objects of worship now employed by African bushmen and Australian aborigines may conceivably have been considerably less revolting ten or fifteen thousand years ago. It is impossible to predict the depths to which a race may descend and the appalling transformation which may occur in its 'sacred' imagery.

"And so occasionally we encounter shapes that we scarcely like to speculate about, shapes so *complicatedly* vile that they haven't even analogous counterparts in comparative mythology. Your fetish is of that nature. It is, as I say, preposterously archeological and it differs unmistakably—although I am willing to concede a superficial resemblance—from the distorted dream images conjured up by psychotics and surrealistic artists. Only racial dissolution and decay extending over wide wastes of years could, in my opinion, account for such a ghastly anomaly."

He learned forward and tapped Algernon significantly upon the knee. "You haven't told me its history," he admonished. "Reticence is an archeologist's prerogative, and in our work it is always an asset, but for a young man you're almost abnormally addicted to it."

Algernon blushed to the roots of his hair. "I'm seldom actually reticent," he said. "At the Museum they all think I talk too much. I've an exuberant, officious way at times that positively appalls Mr. Scollard. But this affair is so—so outside all normal experience that I've been dreading to tax your credulity with a resume of it."

Doctor Imbert smiled. "Your books reveal that you are a very cautious and honest scholar," he said. "I don't believe I'd be inclined to question the veracity of whatever you may choose to tell me."

"Very well," said Algernon. "But I must entreat that you suspend judgment until you've heard all the evidence. One can adduce rational explanations for each of the incidents I shall describe, but when one views them in the sequence in which they occurred they resolve themselves into a devastatingly hideous enigma."

Very tersely, without self-consciousness or affectation, Algernon then related all that he knew and all that he surmised and suspected about the thing whose image spread defilement on the paper before him.

Doctor Imbert heard him out in silence. But his eyes, as he listened, grew bright with horror.

"I doubt if I can help you," he said, when Algernon was done. "This thing transcends all my experience."

There ensued a silence. Then Algernon said in a tone of desperate urgency, "But what *are* we to do? Surely you've something to suggest!"

Doctor Imbert rose shakingly to his feet. "I have—yes. I know some one who can, perhaps, help. He's a recluse, a psychic—a magnificent intellect obsessed by mysteries and mysticisms. I put little faith in such things—to me it's a degradation. But I'll take you to him. I'll take you anyway. God knows you're in trouble—that is obvious to me. And this man may be able to suggest something. Roger Little is his name. No doubt you've heard of him. He used to be a criminal investigator. A good one—a psychologist—discerning, erudite, shrewd—no mere detective-novel sleuth."

Algernon nodded understandingly. "Let us go to him at once," he said.

4. The Horror on the Hills

It was while Algernon and Doctor Imbert were journeying in the subway toward Roger Little's residence in the Borough of Queens that the Horror was announced to the world. An account of its initial manifestation had been flashed from Spain at midday to a great American news syndicate and all the New York papers had something about it in their evening editions. The *News-Graphic's* account was perhaps the most ominously disturbing in its implications. A copywriter on that enterprising sheet had surmised that the atrocities were distinguished by something outré, something altogether inexplicable, and by choosing his diction with unusual care he had succeeded in conveying to his unappreciative readers a tingling intimation of shockingness, of terror.

Beneath half-inch headlines which read: HIDEOUS MASSACRE IN THE PYRENEES, he had written:

"The authorities are completely baffled. Who would wish to assassinate fourteen simple peasants? They were found at sundown on the mountain's crest. All in a row they lay, very still, very pale—very silent and pale beneath the soft Spanish sky. All about them stretched new-fallen snow and beside them on the white expanse were marks, peculiar and baffling. Men do not make footprints a yard wide. And why were all the victims laid so evenly in a row? What violence was it that could deprive them of their heads, drain the blood from their bodies and lay them stark and naked in a row upon the snow?"

5. Little's Dream

"Some one has been murdered and so you wish my advice," murmured Roger Little wearily. "You wish the advice of a retired and eccentric recluse, well on in years, who has ceased to traffic with crime. I am quoting from a profile which did not appear in the *New Yorker.*" He was staring into the fire and the bright radiance which streamed roomward from the grate so illumed the sharp outlines of his profile that Algernon was struck silent with awe.

"A positively Satanic presence," he murmured, to himself. "The exact facsimile of a sorcerer from the *Malleus Maleficarum.* They would have burned him in the Fifteenth Century."

"Murder," resumed Little, "has become a shabbily synthetic art and even the most daring masterpieces of the contemporary school are composed of inferior ingredients clumsily combined. Men no longer live in fear of the unknown, and that utter and abysmal disintegration of soul which the wise still call psychic evil no longer motivates our major atrocities. Anger, jealousy, and a paltry desire for material gain are pitiful emotional substitutes for the perverse and lonely egoism which inspired the great crimes of the Twelfth, Thirteenth and Fourteenth Centuries. When men killed with the deliberate certainty that they were jeopardizing their immortal souls and when the human body was regarded as a tabernacle for something more—or less—than human the crime of murder assumed epic and unholy proportions. The mere discovery of a mutilated cadaver in an age when men still believed in something—at least in *something*—filled every one with terror and with awe. Men, women and children took refuge behind barricaded doors and the more devout fell upon their knees, crossed themselves, lighted candles and chanted exorcisms.

"But in this decadent age when a human being is assassinated society merely shrugs its shoulders and relinquishes the sequel to the police. What have the police to do with a sacrament of evil in our midst? The sense of virtually immitigable evil, of stark unreasoning fear which murder once left in its wake, and the intense esthetic enjoyment which certain individuals derived from merely studying such crimes as works of perverse and diabolical art have no parallels in contemporary experience. Hence it is that all modern murderers commit commonplace crimes— kill prosaically and almost indifferently without any suspicion that they are destroying more than the lives of their unfortunate victims. And people go calmly about their business and are apparently not displeased to rub shoulders with the unholy ones in theaters, restaurants and subways!"

Algernon shifted excitedly in his chair. "But the problem we bring to you is enmeshed in the supernatural more hideously than any atrocity of the Ages of Faith. It transcends normal experience. If you will listen while I . . ."

Little shook his head. "I have written books—many books—describing dozens of instances of possession, of return, of immolation, of divination, and of transformation. I have confirmed the reality of the *concubitus daemonum;* have proved incontestably the existence of vampires, succubi and lamias, and I have slipped not too unwillingly into the warm and clinging arms of women five centuries dead."

He shuddered. "But what I have experienced in this very room is no more than a flickering shadow, swift-passing and obscurely glimpsed, of the horror that lurks godlessly in undimensioned space. In my dreams I have heard the nauseous piping of its glutinous flutes and I have seen, terribly for an instant, the nets and trawls with which it angles for men."

"If you are convinced that such a horror exists . . ." Algernon began, but Little would not let him finish.

"My books have left most of my readers totally unconvinced, for it would disturb them to believe that I am not mentally unbalanced," he went on quickly.

"Erudite and brilliant, but as mad as Bruno when he was burned at the stake for refusing to keep his speculations about the nature of the physical universe to himself."

He rose passionately to his feet. "So I've definitely renounced the collection and correlation of facts," he said. "Hereafter I shall embody my unique convictions in the eloquent and persuasive guise of a fable. I shall write a novel. The art of fiction as a purveyor of essential truth has innumerable advantages which detached and impersonal utterance must of necessity lack. The fictioneer can familiarize his readers *gradually* with new and startling doctrines and avoid shocking them into a precipitous retreat into the shell of old and conventional beliefs. He can prevent them from succumbing to prejudice before they have grasped one-quarter of the truths he is intent upon promulgating. Then, too, the artist can be so much more persuasive and eloquent than the scientist, and it can never be sufficiently emphasized that eloquence is never so effective in convincing men that certain things which are obviously false are momentarily true as it is in inducing them to discover that which is ultimately true beneath all the distortions of reality which can leave reason stranded in minds dominated by wishful thinking and a deep-seated fear of the unknown. Human wishes and desires are so eloquent in themselves that certainly some eloquence must be used in combating them. And that is why the mere scientist is so hopelessly at a loss when he seeks to convert others to what he himself believes to be the truth.

"He doesn't perceive that new truths must be presented to the human mind vividly, uniquely, as though one were initiating a mystery or instituting a sacrament, and that every failure to so present them decreases the likelihood that they will gain proponents, and that an entire civilization may pass away before any one arises with sufficient imagination and sufficient eloquence to take truths which have been enunciated once or twice coldly and forgotten because of the repugnance with which the common man regards fact barely recited and to clothe them in garments of terror and splendor and awe and so link them with far stars and the wind that moves above the waters and the mystery and strangeness that will be in all things until the end of time."

Little's eyes were shining. "I have determined," he said, "to thrust aside the veil as fearlessly as Blake must have done when he wrote of a new heaven and a new earth, to fashion a garment so mind-beguiling in its beauty that the ultimate revelation will remain cloaked until a spell has been cast which will permit of no drawing back, no craven surrender to fear."

He stopped suddenly, as if sobriety and an awareness of his surroundings had returned with a blood-rush to his entranced brain. "I have raved, no doubt. Like

Blake, like Poe, like Gerard de Nerval I am always dreaming dreams, seeing visions. And to worldly men, calm and objective toward everyday realities, skeptical of all else, such visions, such glimpses are wholly incomprehensible. And you, no doubt, are inwardly pitying me and wondering how offended I would be if you should get up abruptly and plead a pressing engagement elsewhere. But if you only knew.

"There are things from *outside* watching always, secretly watching our little capers, our grotesque pranks. Men have disappeared. You're aware of that, aren't you? Men have disappeared within sight of their homes—at high noon, in the sunlight. Malignant and unknowable entities, *fishers* from outside have let down invisible tentacles, nets, trawls, and men and women have been caught up in a kind of pulsing darkness. A shadow seems to pass over them, to envelop them for an instant and then they are gone. And others have gone mad, witnessing such things.

"When a man ascends a flight of stairs it does not inevitably follow that he will arrive at the top. When a man crosses a street or a field or a public square it is not foreordained that he will reach the other side. *I have seen strange shadows in the sky.* Other worlds impinging on ours? I know that there are other worlds, but perhaps they do not *dimensionally* impinge. Perhaps from fourth-, fifth-, sixth-dimensional worlds things with forms invisible to us, with faces veiled to us, reach down and take—instantaneously, mercilessly. Feeding on us perhaps? Using our brains for fodder? A few have glimpsed the truth for a terrifying instant in dreams. But it takes infinite patience and self-discipline, and years of study to establish waking contact, even for an instant, with the bodiless shapes that flicker appallingly in the void a thousand billion light years beyond the remotest of the spiral nebulae.

"Yet I—can do this. And you," he laughed, "come to me with a little mundane murder."

For an instant there was silence in the room. Then Algernon stood up, his face brightened by the flames that were still crackling in the grate. "You say," he exclaimed, "a little mundane murder. But to me it is more hideous, more alien to sanity and the world we know than all of your cosmic trawlers, and 'intrusions' from beyond."

Little shook his head. "No," he said. "I cannot believe that you are not exaggerating. It is so easy for men of exceptional intelligence to succumb at times to the fears, dreads, forebodings of ordinary men. Imaginative in a worldly sense, but blinder and dumber than clods cosmically. I am sure that I could unravel your puzzle with the most superficial layer of my waking mind, the little conscious mind that is so weak, so futile to grapple with anything more disturbing than what the body shall eat and drink and wear."

"If I had not seen," said Algernon, speaking very deliberately, "a stone thing shift its bulk, doing what the inanimate has never done in all the ages man has looked rationally upon it, I would have seriously doubted your sanity. It would be dishonest for me to pretend otherwise."

"A stone, you say, moved?" For the first time Little's interest quickened and a startled look came into his eyes.

"Yes, in the shape in which something—nature primeval perhaps, in eons primeval—shaped it. Moved in the night, unwatched by me. When Chaugnar Faugn . . ."

He stopped, was silent. For from his chair Little had sprung with a cry, his face bloodless, a cry of terror issuing from his thin lips.

"What is the matter?" gasped Doctor Imbert, and Algernon turned pale, not knowing what to make of so strange an occurrence. For Little seemed wholly undone, a mystic gone so completely mad that a violent outburst was only to be expected and might well be repeated, if he were not placed under immediate restraint. But at last he sank again into the chair from which he had so shockingly arisen, and a trace of color returned to his cheeks.

"Forgive me," he murmured brokenly. "Letting go like that was inexcusable. But when you mentioned Chaugnar Faugn I was for an instant mortally terrified."

He drew a deep breath. "The dream was so vivid that my mind rejected instantly a symbolic or allegorical interpretation. That name especially—Chaugnar Faugn. I was certain that something, somewhere, bore it—that the ghastliness that took Publius Libo on the high hills was an actuality, but not, I had hoped, an actuality for us. Something long past, surely, a horror of the ancient world that would never return to . . ." He broke off abruptly, seemingly lost in thought.

"Tell me about it," he entreated, after a moment.

With bloodless lips Algernon related once again the history of Chaugnar Faugn as it had been related to him by Ulman, enhancing a little its hideousness by half-guesses and surmises of his own. Little listened in tight-lipped silence, his face a mask, only the throbbing of the veins on his temples betraying the agitation which wracked him. As Algernon concluded, the clock on the mantel, a tall, negro-colored clock with wings on its shoulders and a great yellow ocean spider painted on its opalescent face, struck the hour: eleven even strokes pealed from it, shattering the stillness that had settled for an instant on the room. Algernon shivered, apprehensive at the lateness of the hour, fearful that in his absence Chaugnar Faugn might move again.

But now Little was speaking, striving painfully to keep his voice from sinking to a whisper.

"I had the dream last Halloween," he began, "and for detail, color and somber, brooding menace it surpasses anything of the kind I have experienced in recent years. It took form slowly, beginning as a nervous move from the atrium of my house into a scroll-lined library to escape the sound of a fountain, and continuing as an earnest and friendly argument with a stout, firm-lipped man of about thirty-five, with strong, pure Roman features and the rather cumbersome equipment of a *legatus* in active military service. Impressions of identity and locale were so nebulous and gradual in their unfoldment as to be difficult to trace to a source, but they seem in retrospect to have been present from the first.

"The place was not Rome, nor even Italy, but the small provincial municipium of Calagurris on the south bank of the Iberus in Hispania Citerior. It was in the Republican age, because the province was still under a senatorial proconsul instead of a *legatus* of the Imperator. I was a man of about my own waking age and build. I was clad in a civilian toga of yellowish color with the two thin reddish stripes of the equestrian order. My name was L. Caelius Rufus and my rank seemed to be that of a provincial quaestor. I was definitely an Italian-born Roman, the province of Calagurris being alien, colonial soil to me. My guest was Cnaeus Balbutius, *legatus* of the XII Legion, which was permanently encamped just outside the town on the riverbank. The home in which I was receiving him was a suburban villa on a hillside south of the compact section, and it overlooked both town and river.

"The day before I had received a worried call from one Tib. Annaeus Mela, edile of the small town of Pompelo, three days' march to the north in the territory of the Vascones at the foot of the mysterious Pyrenees. He had been to request Balbutius to spare him a cohort for a very extraordinary service on the night of the Kalends of November and Balbutius had emphatically refused. Therefore, knowing me to be acquainted with P. Scribonius Libo, the proconsul at Tarraco, he had come to ask me to lay his case by letter before that official. Mela was a dark, lean man of middle age, of presentable Roman features but with the coarse hair of a Celtiberian.

"It seems that there dwelt hidden in the Pyrenees a strange race of small dark people unlike the Gauls and Celtiberians in speech and features, who indulged in terrible rites and practices twice every year, on the Kalends of Maius and November. They lit fires on the hilltops at dusk, beat continuously on strange drums and horribly all through the night. Always before these orgies people would be found missing from the village and none of them were ever known to return. It was thought that they were stolen for sacrificial purposes, but no one dared to investigate, and eventually the semi-annual loss of villagers came to be regarded as a regular tribute, like the seven youths and maidens that Athens was forced to send each year to Crete for King Minos and the Minotaur.

"The tribal Vascones and even some of the semi-Romanized cottagers of the foothills were suspected by the inhabitants of Pompelo of being in league with the strange dark folk—*Miri Nigri* was the name used in my dream. These dark folk were seen in Pompelo only once a year—in summer, when a few of their number would come down from the hills to trade with the merchants. They seemed incapable of speech and transacted business by signs.

"During the preceding summer the small folk had come to trade as usual—five of them—but had become involved in a general scuffle when one of them had attempted to torture a dog for pleasure in the forum. In this fighting two of them had been killed and the remaining three had returned to the hills with evil faces. Now it was autumn and *the customary quota of villagers had not disappeared*. It was not normal for the Miri Nigri thus to spare Pompelo. Clearly they must have reserved the town for some terrible doom, which they would call down on their unholy Sabbath-night as they drummed and howled and danced outrageously on the mountain's crest. Fear walked through Pompelo and the edile Mela had come to Calagurris to ask for a cohort to invade the hills on the sabbath night and break up the obscene rites before the ceremony might be brought to a head. But Balbutius had laughed at him and refused. He thought it poor policy for the Roman administration to meddle in local quarrels. So Mela had been obliged to come to me. I enheartened him as best I could, and promised help, and he returned to Pompelo at least partly reassured.

"Before writing the proconsul I had thought it best to argue with Balbutius himself, so I had been to see him at the camp, found him out and left word with a centurion that I would welcome a call from him. Now he was here and had reiterated his belief that we ought not to complicate our administration by arousing the resentment of the tribesmen, as we undoubtedly would if we attempted to suppress a rite with which they were obviously in ill-concealed sympathy.

"I seemed to have read considerable about the dark rites of certain unknown and wholly barbaric races, for I recall feeling a sense of monstrous impending doom and trying my best to induce Balbutius to put down the sabbath. To his objections I replied that it had never been the custom of the Roman people to be swayed by the whims of the barbarians when the fortunes of Roman citizens were in danger and that he ought not to forget the status of Pompelo as a legal colony, small as it was. That the good-will of the tribal Vascones was little to be depended upon at best, and that the trust and friendship of the Romanized townsfolk, in whom was more than a little of our own blood after three generations of colonization, was a matter of far greater importance to the smooth working of that provincial government on which the security of the Roman imperium primarily rested. Furthermore, that I had reason to believe, from my studies, that the apprehensions of the Pompelonians were disturbingly well-founded, and that there was indeed brewing in the high hills a monstrous doom which it would ill become the traditions of Rome to countenance. That I would be surprized to encounter laxity in the representatives of those whose ancestors had not hesitated to put to death large numbers of Roman citizens for participation in the orgies of Bacchus and had ordered engraved on public tablets of bronze the *Senatus Consultum de Bacchanalibus.*

"But I could not influence Balbutius. He went away courteously but unmoved. So I at once took a reed pen and wrote a letter to the proconsul Libo, sealing it and calling for a wiry young slave—a Greek called Antipater—to take it to Tarraco.

"The following morning I went out on foot, down the hill to the town and through the narrow block-paved streets with high whitewashed dead-walls and gaudily painted shops with awnings. The crowds were very vivid. Legionaries of all races, Roman colonists, tribal Celtiberi, Romanized natives, Romanized and Iberized Carthaginians, mongrels of all sorts. I spoke to only one person, a Roman named Æbutius, about whom I recall nothing. I visited the camp—a great area with an earthen wall ten feet high and streets of wooden huts inside, and I called at the *praetorium* to tell Balbutius that I had written the proconsul. He was still pleasant but unmoved. Later I went home, read in the garden, bathed, dined, talked with the family and went to bed—having, a little later, a nightmare *within the dream* which centered about a dark terrible desert with cyclopean ruins of stones and a malign presence over all.

"About noon the next day—I had been reading in the garden—the Greek returned with a letter and enclosure from Libo. I broke the seal and read: 'P. SCRIBONIVS L. CAELIO. S. D. SI. TV. VALES. VALEO. QVAE. SCRIPSISTI. AVDIVI. NEC. ALIAS. PVTO.'

"In a word, the proconsul agreed with me—had known about the Miri Nigri himself—and enclosed an order for the advance of the cohort to Pompelo at once, by forced marches, in order to reach the doom-shadowed town on the day before the fatal Kalends. He requested me to accompany it because of my knowledge of what the mysterious rites were whispered to be, and furthermore declared his design of going along himself, saying that he was even then on the point of setting out and would be in Pompelo before we could be.

"I lost not a second in going personally to the camp and handing the orders to Balbutius, and I must say he took his defeat gracefully. He decided to send Cohors V, under Sextus Asellius, and presently summoned that *legatus*—a slim, supercilious youth with frizzed hair and a fashionable fringe of beard-growth on his under jaw. Asellius was openly hostile to the move but dared not disregard orders. Balbutius said he would have the cohort at the bridge across the Iberus in an hour and I rushed home to prepare for the rough day and night march.

"I put on a heavy paenula and ordered a litter with six Illyrian bearers, and reached the bridge ahead of the cohort. At last, though, I saw the silver eagles flashing along the street to my left, and Balbutius—who had decided at the last moment to go along himself—rode out ahead and accompanied my litter ahead of the troops as we crossed the bridge and struck out over the plains toward the mystic line of dimly glimpsed violet hills. There was no long sleep during all the march, but we had naps and brief halts and bites of lunch—cakes and cheese. Balbutius usually rode by my litter in conversation (it was infantry, but he and Asellius were mounted) but sometimes I read—M. Porcius Cato *De Re Rustica*, and a hideous manuscript in Greek, which made me shudder even to touch or look at but of which I can not remember a single word.

"The second morning we reached the whitewashed houses of Pompelo and trembled at the fear that was on the place. There was a wooden amphitheater east of the village, and a large open plain on the west. All the immediate ground was flat, but the Pyrenees rose up green and menacing on the north, looking nearer than they were. Scribonius Libo had reached there ahead of us with his secretary, Q. Trebellius Pollio, and he and the edile Mela greeted us in the forum. We all— Libo, Pollio, Mela, Balbutius, Asellius and I—went into the curia (an excellent new building with a Corinthian portico) and discussed ways and means, and I saw that the proconsul was with me heart and soul.

"But Balbutius and Asellius continued to argue and at times the discussion grew very tense. Libo was an utterly admirable old man, and he insisted on going into the hills with the rest of us and seeing the awful revelations of the night. Mela, ghastly with fright, promised horses to those of us who were not mounted. He had pluck—for he meant to go himself.

"It is impossible even to suggest the stark and ghastly terror which hung over this phase of the dream.

"Surely there never was such evil as that which brooded over the accursed town as the sinking sun threw long menacing shadows amidst the reddening afternoon. The legionaries fancied they heard the rustling of stealthy, unseen and ominously deliberate presences in the black encircling woods. Occasionally a torch had to be lighted momentarily in order to keep the frightened three hundred together, but for the most part it was a dreadful scramble through the dark. A slit of northern sky was visible ahead between the terrible, cliff-like slopes that encompassed us and I marked the chair of Cassiopeia and the golden powder of the Via Lactea. Far, far ahead and above and appearing to merge imperceptibly into the heavens, the lines of remoter peaks could be discerned, each capped by a sickly point of unholy flame. And still the distant, hellish drums pounded incessantly on.

"At length the route grew too steep for the horses and the six of us who were mounted were forced to take to our feet. We left the horses tethered to a clump of scrub oaks and stationed ten men to guard them, though heaven knows it was no night nor place for petty thieves to be abroad! And then we scrambled on— jostling, stumbling and sometimes climbing with our hands' help up places little short of perpendicular. Suddenly a sound behind us made every man pause as if hit by an arrow. It was from the horses we had left, and it did not cease. They were not neighing but *screaming*. They were screaming, mad with some terror beyond any this earth knows. No sound came up from the men we had left with them. Still they screamed on, and the soldiers around us stood trembling and whimpering and muttering fragments of a prayer to Rome's gods, and the gods of the East and the gods of the barbarians.

"Then there came a sharp scuffle and yell from the front of the column which made Asellius call quaveringly for a torch. There was a prostrate figure weltering in a growing and glistening pool of blood and we saw by the faint flare that it was the young guide Accius. He had killed himself because of the sound he had heard. He, who had been born and bred at the foot of those terrible hills and had heard dark whispers of their secrets, knew well why the horses had screamed. And because he knew, he had snatched a sword from the scabbard of the nearest soldier—the centurio P. Vibulanus—and had plunged it full-length into his own breast.

"At this point pandemonium broke loose because of something noticed by such of the men as were able to notice anything at all. *The sky had been snuffed out.* No longer did Cassiopeia and the Via Lactea glimmer betwixt the hills, but stark blackness loomed behind the continuously swelling fires on the distant peaks. And still the horses screamed and the far-off drums pounded hideously and incessantly on.

"Cackling laughter broke out in the black woods of the vertical slopes that hemmed us in and around the swollen fires of the distant peaks we saw prancing and leaping the awful and cyclopean silhouettes of things that were neither men nor beasts, but fiendish amalgams of both—things with huge flaring ears and long waving trunks that howled and gibbered and pranced in the skyless night. And a cold wind coiled purposively down from the empty abyss, winding sinuously about us till we started in fresh panic and struggled like Laocoön and his sons in the serpent's grasp.

"There were terrible sights in the light of the few shaking torches. Legionaries trampled one another to death and screamed more hoarsely than the horses far below. Of our immediate party Trebellius Pollio had long vanished, and I saw Mela go down beneath the heavy caligae of a gigantic Aquitanian. Balbutius had gone mad and was grinning and simpering out an old Fescennine verse recalled from the Latin countryside of his boyhood. Asellius tried to cut his own throat, but the sentient wind held him powerless, so that he could do nothing but scream and scream and scream above the cackling laughter and the screaming horses and the distant drums and the howling colossal shapes that capered about the demon-fires on the peaks.

"I myself was frozen to the helplessness of a statue and could not move or speak. Only old Publius Libo the proconsul was strong enough to face it like a Roman—Publius Scribonius Libo, who had gone through the Jugurthine and Mithridatic and social wars—Publius Libo three times praetor and three times consul of the republic, in whose atrium stood the ancestral forms of a hundred heroes. He and he alone had the voice of a man and of a general and triumphator. I can see him now in the dimming light of those horrible torches, among that fear-struck stampede of the doomed. I can hear him still as he spoke his last words, gathering up his toga with the dignity of a Roman and a consul: '*Malitia vetus—malitia vetus est—venit—tandem venit . . .*'

"And then the wooded encircling slopes burst forth with louder cackles and I saw that they were slowly moving. The hills—the terrible living hills—were closing up upon their prey. The Miri Nigri had called their terrible gods out of the void.

"Able to shriek at last, I awoke in a sea of cold perspiration.

"Calagurris, as you probably know, is a real and well-known town of Roman Spain, famed as the birthplace of the rhetorician Quintilianus. Upon consulting a classical dictionary I found Pompelo also to be real, and surviving today as the Pyrenean village of Pampelona."

He ceased speaking, and for a moment the three men were silent. Then Algernon said: "The Chinaman had a strange dream too. He spoke of the horror on the mountains—of great things that came clumping down from the hills at nightfall."

Little nodded. "Mongolians as a rule are extremely psychic," he said. "I have known several whose clairvoyant gifts were superior to a yoga adept's often astounding feats of precognition."

"And you think that Hsieh Ho's dream was a prophecy?" whispered Imbert.

"I do. Some monstrous *unfettering* is about to take place. That which for two thousand years has lain somnolent will stir again and the 'great things' will descend from their frightful lair on the Spanish hills drawn cityward through the will of Chaugnar Faugn. We are in propinquity to the primal, hidden horror that festers at the root of being, with the old, hidden loathsomeness which the Greeks and Romans veiled under the symbolical form of a man-beast—the *feeder, the all.* The Greeks knew, for the horror left its lair to ravage, striding eastward in the dawn across Europe, wading waist-deep in the dark Ionian seas, looming monstrous at nightfall over Delos and Samothrace and far-off Crete. A nimbus of starfoam engirdled its waist; suns, constellations gleamed in its eyes. But its breath brought madness, and its embrace, death. The feeder—the all."

The telephone bell at Little's elbow was jangling disconcertingly. Stretching forth a tremulous hand he grasped the receiver firmly and laid it against his cheek. "Hello," he whispered into the mouthpiece. "What is it? Who is speaking?"

"From the Manhattan Museum." The words smote ominously upon his ear. "Is Mr. Algernon Harris there? I phoned Doctor Imbert's house and they gave me this number."

"Yes, Harris is here." Little's voice was vibrant with apprehension. "I'll call him."

He turned the instrument over to Algernon and sank back exhaustedly in his chair. For a moment the latter conversed in a low tone; then an expression of stunned incredulity appeared on his face. His hand shook as he put back the receiver and tottered toward the fireplace. For an instant he stood staring intensely into the coals, his fingers gripping the mantel's edge so tightly that his knuckles showed white. When he turned there was a look of utter consternation in his eyes.

"Chaugnar Faugn has disappeared," he cried. "Chaugnar Faugn has left the museum. No one saw him go and the idiot who phoned thinks that a thief removed him. Or possibly one of the attendants. But *we* know how unlikely that is."

"I'm afraid we do," Little said, grimly.

"I am to blame," Algernon went on quickly. "I should have insisted they patrol the alcove. I should have at least explained to them that some one might try to steal Chaugnar Faugn, even if Ulman's story had to be kept from them."

He shook his head in helpless frustration.

"No . . . no . . . that would have done no good. A watchman would have been utterly impotent to cope with such a horror. Chaugnar Faugn would have destroyed him hideously in an instant. And now it is loose in the streets!"

He walked to the window and stared across the glittering harbor at the darkly looming skyline of lower Manhattan. "It is loose over there," he cried, raising his arm and pointing. "It is crouching in the shadows somewhere, alert and waiting, preparing to . . ." He broke off abruptly, as if the vision his mind had conjured up was too ghastly to dwell upon.

Little rose and laid a steadying hand on Algernon's arm. "I haven't said I couldn't help," he said. "Though Chaugnar Faugn is a very terrible menace it isn't quite as omnipotent as Ulman thought. It and its brothers are incarnate manifestations of a very ancient, a very malignant hyperdimensional entity. Or call it a principle, if you wish—a principle so antagonistic to life as we know it that it becomes a spreading blight, as destructive as a nest of cancer cells would be if cancer could be transplanted by surgical means into healthy tissue, and continue to grow and proliferate until every vestige of healthy tissue has been destroyed. But it is a cancer whose growth I can at least retard. And if I am successful I can send it back to its point of origin beyond the galactic universe, can cut it asunder forever from our three-dimensional world. Had I known that the horror still lurked in the Pyrenees I should have gone, months ago, to *send it back*. Yes, even though the thought of it now fills me with a loathing unspeakable, I should have gone.

"I am not," he continued, "a merely theoretical dreamer. Though I am by temperament disposed toward speculations of a mystical nature, I have forged a very concrete and effective weapon to combat the cosmic malignancies. If you'll step into my laboratory I'll show you something which should restore your confidence in the experimental capacity of the human mind when there is but one choice confronting it—to survive or go down forever into everlasting night and darkness."

6. The Time-Space Machine

Roger Little's laboratory was illumed by a single bluish lamp imbedded in the concrete of its sunken floor. An infinite diversity of mechanisms lined the walls and sprawled their precise lengths on long tables and dangled eerily from hooks set in the high, domed ceiling; mechanisms a-glitter in blue-lit seclusion, a strange, bizarre foreglimpse into the alchemy and magic of a far-distant future, with spheres and condensers and gleaming metal rods in lieu of stuffed crocodiles and steaming elixirs.

All of the contrivances were arresting, but one was so extraordinary in size and complexity that it dominated the others and riveted Algernon's attention. He seemed unable to drag his gaze from the thing. It was a strange agglomeration of metallic spheres and portions of spheres, of great bluish globes surrounded by tiny clusters of half-globes and quarter-globes, whose surfaces converged in a most fantastic way. And from the globes there sprouted at grotesque angles metallic crescents with converging tips.

To Algernon's excited imagination the thing wore a quasi-reptilian aspect. "It's like a toad's face," he muttered. "Bulbous and bestial."

Little nodded. "It's a triumph of mechanical ugliness, isn't it? Yet it would have been deified in Ancient Greece—by Archimedes especially. He would have exalted it above all his Conoids and Parabolas."

"What function does it perform?" asked Algernon.

"A sublime one. It's a time-space machine. But I'd rather not discuss its precise function until I've shown you how it works. I want you to study its face as it waxes non-Euclidean. When you've glimpsed a fourth-dimensional figure you'll be prepared to concede, I think, that the claims I make for it are not extravagant. I know of no more certain corrective for an excess of skepticism. I was the *Critique of Pure Reason* personified until I looked upon *a skinned sphere*—then I grew very humble, reverent toward the great *Suspected*.

"Watch now." He reached forward, grasped a switch and with a swift downward movement of his right arm set the machine in motion. At first the small spheres and the crescents revolved quickly and the large spheres slowly; then the large spheres literally spun while the small spheres lazed, and then both small spheres and large spheres moved in unison. Then the spheres stopped altogether, but only for an instant, while something of movement seemed to flow into them from the revolving crescents. Then the crescents stopped and the spheres moved, in varying tempo, faster and faster, and their movement seemed to flow back into the crescents. Then both crescents and spheres began to move in unison, faster and faster and faster, until the entire mass seemed to merge into a shape paradoxical, outrageous, unthinkable—a sphenoid with a non-Euclidean face, a geometric blasphemy that was at once isosceles and equilateral, convex and concave.

Algernon stared in horror. "What in God's name is that?" he cried.

"You are looking on a fourth-dimensional figure," said Little soothingly. "Steady now."

For an instant nothing happened; then a light, greenish, blinding, shot from the center of the crazily distorted figure and streamed across the opposite wall, limning on the smooth cement a perfect circle.

But only for a second was the wall illumed. With an abrupt movement Little shot the lever upward and its radiance dimmed, and vanished. "Another moment, and that wall would have crumbled away," he said.

With fascination Algernon watched the outrageous spheroid grow indistinct, watched it blur and disappear amidst a resurgence of spheres.

"That light," cried Little exultantly, "will send Chaugnar Faugn back through time. It will reverse its decadent *randomness*—disincarnate and disembody it, and send it back forever."

"But I don't understand," murmured Algernon. "What do you mean by *randomness?*"

"I mean that this machine can work havoc with entropy!" There was a ring of exaltation in Little's voice.

"Entropy?" Algernon scowled. "I'm not sure that I understand. I know what entropy is in thermodynamics, of course, but I'm not sure . . ."

"I'll explain," said Little. "You are of course familiar with the A B C's of Einsteinian physics and are aware that time is *relatively* arrowless, that the sequence in which we view events in nature is not a cosmic actuality and that our conviction that we are going somewhere in time is a purely human illusion conditioned by our existence on this particular planet and the limitations which our five senses impose upon us. We divide time into past, present and future, but in reality an event's sequence in time depends wholly on the position in space from which it is viewed. Events which occurred thousands of years ago on this planet haven't as yet taken place to a hypothetical observer situated billions and billions of light years remote from us. Thus, cosmically speaking, we can not say of an event that it has happened and will never happen again or that it is about to happen and has never happened before, because 'before' to us is 'after' to intelligences situated elsewhere in space and time.

"But though our familiar time-divisions are purely arbitrary there is omnipresent in nature a principle called entropy which, as Eddington has pointed out, equips time with a kind of empirical arrow. The entire universe appears to be 'running down.' It is the consensus of astronomical opinion that suns and planets and electrons are constantly breaking up, becoming more and more *disorganized*. Billions of years ago some mysterious dynamic, which Sir James Jeans has likened to the Finger of God, streamed across primeval space and created the universe of stars in a state of almost perfect integration, welded them into a system so highly organized that there was only the tiniest manifestation of the random element anywhere in it. The random element in nature is the uncertain element—the principle which brings about disorganizations, disintegration, decay.

"Let us suppose that two mechanical men, robots, are tossing a small ball to and fro, to and fro. The process may go on indefinitely, for the mechanical creatures do not tire and there is nothing to make the ball swerve from its course. But now let us suppose that a bird in flight collides with the ball, sends it spinning so that it misses the hand of the receiving robot. What happens? Both robots begin to behave grotesquely. Missing the ball, their arms sweep through the empty air, making wider and wider curves and they stagger forward perhaps, and collapse in each other's arms. The random, the uncertain element has entered their organized cosmos and they have ceased to function.

"This tendency of the complex to disintegrate, of the perfectly-balanced to run amuck, is called entropy. It is entropy that provides time with an arrow and, disrupting nebulae, plays midwife to the birth of planets from star-wombs incalculable. It is entropy that cools great orbs, hotter than Betelgeuse, more fiery than Arcturus through all the outer vastnesses, reducing them to sterility, to whirling motes of chaos.

"It is the random element that is slowly breaking up, destroying the univere of stars. In an ever widening circle, with an ever increasing malignancy—if one may ascribe malignancy to a force, a tendency—it works its awful havoc. It is analogous to a grain of sand dropped into one of the interstices of a vast and intricate machine. The grain creates a small disturbance which in turn creates a larger one, and so on *ad infinitum*.

"And with every event that has occurred on this earth since its departure from the sun there has been an increase of the random element. Thus we can legitimately 'place' events in time. Events which occurred tens of thousands of years ago may be happening *now* to intelligences situated elsewhere, and events still in the offing, so to speak, may exist already in another dimension of space-time. But if an earth-event is very disorganized and very decadent in its contours even our hypothetical distant observer would know that it has occurred very late in the course of cosmic evolution and that a series of happier events, with less of the random element in them, must have preceded it in time. In brief, that sense of time's passing which we experience in our daily lives is due to our intuitive perception that the structure of the universe is continuously breaking down. Everything that 'happens,' every event, is an objective manifestation of matter's continuous and all-pervasive decay and disintegration."

Algernon nodded. "I think I understand. But doesn't that negate all that we have been taught to associate with the word 'evolution'? It means that not advancement but an *inherent* degeneration has characterized all the processes of nature from the beginning of time. Can we apply it to man? Do you mean to suggest . . ."

Little shrugged. "One can only speculate. It may be that mediaeval theology wasn't so very wrong after all—that old Augustine and the Angelic Doctor and Abelard and the others surmised correctly, that man was once akin to the angels and that he joined himself to nature's decay through a deliberate rejection of heaven's grace. It may be that by some mysterious and incomprehensibly perverse act of will he turned his face from his Maker and let evil pour in upon him, made of himself a magnet for all the malevolence that the cosmos holds. There may have been more than a little truth in Ulman's identification of Chaugnar with the Lucifer of mediaeval myth."

"Is this," exclaimed Imbert reproachfully, "a proper occasion for a discussion of theology?"

"It isn't," Little acknowledged. "But I thought it desirable to outline certain— possibilities. I don't want you to imagine that I regard the intrusion of Chaugnar Faugn into our world as a scientifically explicable occurrence in a facilely dogmatic sense."

"I don't care how you regard it," affirmed Algernon, "so long as you succeed in destroying it utterly. I am a profound agnostic as far as religious concepts are concerned. But the universe is mysterious enough to justify divergent speculations on the part of intelligent men as to the ultimate nature of reality."

"I quite agree," Little said. "I was merely pointing out that modern science alone has very definite limitations."

"And yet you propose to combat this . . . this horror with science," exclaimed Imbert.

"With a concrete embodiment of the concepts of transcendental mathematics," corrected Little. "And such concepts are merely empirically scientific. I am aware that science may be loosely defined as a systematized accumulation of tendencies and principles, but classically speaking, its prime function is to convey some idea of the nature of reality by means of an inductive logic. Yet our mathematical physicist has turned his face from induction as resolutely as did the mediaeval scholastics in the days of the Troubadours. He insists that we must start from the universal assumption that we can never know positively the real nature of anything, and that whatever 'truth' we may deduce from empirical generalities will be chiefly valuable as a kind of mystical guidepost, at best merely roughly indicative of the direction in which we are travelling; but withal, something of a sacrament and therefore superior to the dogmatic 'knowledge' of Nineteenth Century science. The speculations of mathematical physicists today are more like poems and psalms than anything else. They embody concepts wilder and more fantastic than anything in Poe or Hawthorne or Blake."

He stepped forward and seized the entropy-reversing machine by its globular neck. "Two men can carry it very easily," he said, as he lifted it a foot from the floor by way of experiment. "We can train it on Chaugnar Faugn from a car."

"If it keeps to the open streets," interjected Algernon. "We can't follow it up a fire-escape or into the woods in a car."

"I'd thought of that. It could hide itself for days in Central Park or Inwood or Van Cortland Park or the wider stretches of woodland a little further to the north but still close to the city. But we won't cross that bridge until we come to it." His expression was tense, but he spoke with quiet deliberation. "We could dispense with the car in an emergency," he said. "Two men could advance fairly rapidly with the machine on a smooth expanse.

"We must make haste," he continued, after a moment. "It's my chauffeur's day off, but I'll take a taxi down to the garage and get the car myself." He turned to Algernon. "If you want to help, locate Chaugnar Faugn."

Algernon stared. "But how . . ." he gasped.

"It shouldn't be difficult. Get in touch with the police—Assistance and Ambulance Division. Ask if they've received *any* unusually urgent calls, anything of a sensational nature. If Chaugnar has slain again they'll know about it."

He pointed urgently toward a phone in the corner and strode from the laboratory.

7. A Cure for Skepticism

When Algernon had completed his phone call he lit a cigarette very calmly and deliberately and crossed to where Doctor Imbert was standing. Only the trembling of his lower lip betrayed the agitation he was having difficulty in controlling. "There have been five emergency calls," he said, "all from the midtown section—between Thirty-fifth and Forty-eighth Streets."

Imbert grew pale. "And—and deaths?"

Algernon nodded. "And deaths. Two of the ambulances have just returned."

"How many were killed?"

"They don't know yet. There were five bodies in the first ambulance—three men, a woman and a little girl—a negress. All horribly mutilated. They've gone wild over there. The chap who spoke to me wanted to know what I knew, why I had phoned—he shouted at me, broke down and sobbed."

"God!"

"There's nothing we can do till Little gets back," Algernon said.

"And then? What do you suppose we can do then?"

"The machine . . ." Algernon began and stopped. He couldn't endure putting the way he felt about Little's machine, and the doubts he had entertained concerning it into words. It was necessary to believe in the machine, to have confidence in Little's sagacity—supreme confidence. It would have been disastrous to doubt in such a moment that a blow would eventually be struck, that Little and his machine together would dispose, forever, of the ghastly menace of Chaugnar Faugn. But to defend such a faith rationally, to speak boldly and with confidence of a mere intuitive conviction was another matter.

"You know perfectly well that Little's mentally unbalanced," affirmed Imbert, "that it would be madness to credit his assertions." He gestured toward the machine. "That thing is merely a mechanical hypnotizer. Ingenious, I concede—it can induce twilight sleep with a rapidity I wouldn't have thought possible—but it is quite definitely three-dimensional. It brings the subconscious to the fore, the subconscious that believes everything it is told, induces temporary somnolence while Little whispers: 'You are gazing on a fourth-dimensional figure. You are gazing on a fourth-dimensional figure.' Such deceptions aren't difficult to implant when the mind is in a dreamlike state."

"I'd rather not discuss it," murmured Algernon. "I can't believe the figure we saw was wholly a deception. It was too ghastly and unbelievable. And remember that we both saw the same figure. I was watching you at the time—you looked positively ill. And mass hypnotism is virtually an impossibility. You ought to know that. No two men will respond to suggestion in the same way. We *both* saw a four-dimensional figure—an outrageous figure."

"But how do you know we both saw the same figure? We may easily have responded differently to Little's suggestion. Group hypnotism is possible in that sense. I saw something decidedly disturbing and so did you, but that doesn't prove that we weren't hypnotized."

"I'll convince you that we weren't," exclaimed Algernon. "A time-space machine of this nature isn't theoretically inconceivable, for physicists have speculated on the possibility of reversing entropy in isolated portions of matter for years. Watch now!"

Deliberately he walked to the machine and shot the lever upward.

8. What Happened in the Laboratory

Algernon raised himself on his elbow and stared in horror at the gaping hole in the wall before him. It was a great circular hole with jagged edges and through it the skyline of lower Manhattan glimmered nebulously, like an etching under glass. His temples throbbed painfully; his tongue was dry and swollen and adhered to the roof of his mouth.

Some one was standing above him. Not Imbert, for Imbert wore spectacles. And this man's face was destitute of glitter, a blurred oval faultlessly white. Confusedly Algernon recalled that Little did not wear spectacles. This, then, was Little. Little, not Imbert. It was coming back now. He had sought to convince Imbert that the machine wasn't a mechanical hypnotizer. He had turned it on and then— Good God! what had happened then? Something neither of them had anticipated. An explosion! But first for an instant they had seen the figure. And the light. And he and Imbert had been too frightened—too frightened to turn it off. How very clear it was all becoming. They had stood for an instant facing the wall, too utterly bewildered to turn off the light. And then Little had entered the room, and had shouted a warning—a frenzied warning.

"Help me, please," exclaimed Algernon weakly.

Little bent and gripped him by the shoulders. "Steady, now," he commanded, as he guided him toward a chair. "You're not hurt. You'll be all right in a moment. Imbert, too, is all right. A piece of plaster struck him in the temple, gave him a nasty cut, but he'll be quite all right."

"But—what happened?" Algernon gestured helplessly toward the hole in the wall. "I remember that there was an explosion and that—you shouted at me, didn't you?"

"Yes, I shouted for you to get back into the room. You were standing too close to the wall. Another instant and the floor would have crumbled too and you'd have had a nasty tumble—a tumble from which you wouldn't have recovered."

He smiled grimly and patted Algernon on the shoulder. "Just try to calm down a bit. I'll get you a whiskey and soda."

"But what, precisely happened?" persisted Algernon.

"The light decreased the wall's *randomness*, sent it back through time. I warned you that the wall would crumble if the light rested on it for more than an instant. But you had to experiment."

"I'm sorry," muttered Algernon shamefacedly. "I fear I've ruined your apartment."

"Not important, really. It's eery, of course, having all one's secrets open to the sky, but my landlord will rectify that." He gazed at Algernon curiously. "Why did you do it?" he asked.

"To convince Imbert. He said the machine was merely a mechanical hypnotizer."

"I see, Imbert thought I was rather pathetically 'touched'."

"Not exactly. I think he wanted to believe you . . ."

"But couldn't. Well, I can't blame him. Five years ago I would have doubted too—laughed all this to scorn. I approve of skeptics. They're dependable—when you've succeeded in convincing them that unthinkable and outrageous things occasionally have at least a pragmatic potency. I doubt if even now Imbert would concede that this is an entropy-reversing machine, but you may be sure his respect for it has grown. He'll follow my instructions now without hesitation. And I want you to. We must act in unison, or we'll be defeated before we start."

Algernon began suddenly to tremble. "We haven't an instant to lose," he exclaimed. "I got in touch with the police just before you came back—they're sending out ambulance calls from all over the city. "Chaugnar has begun to slay—" Algernon had risen and was striding toward the door.

"Wait!" Little's voice held a note of command. "We've got to wait for Imbert. He's downstairs in the bathroom dressing his wound."

Reluctantly Algernon returned into the room.

"A few minutes' delay won't matter," continued Little, his voice surprisingly calm. "We've such a hideous ordeal before us that we should be grateful for this respite."

"But Chaugnar is killing now," protested Algernon. "And we are sitting here letting more lives . . ."

"Be snuffed out? Perhaps. But at the same instant all over the world other lives are being snuffed out by diseases which men could prevent if they energetically bestirred themselves." He drew a deep breath. "We're doing the best we can, man. This respite is necessary for our nerves' sake. Try to view the situation sanely. If we are going to eradicate the malignancy which is Chaugnar Faugn we'll need a surgeon's calm. We've got to steel our wills, extrude from our minds all hysterical considerations, and all sentiment."

"But it will kill thousands," protested Algernon. "In the crowded streets . . ."

"No," Little shook his head. "It's no longer in the streets. It has left the city."

"How do you know?"

"There has been a massacre on the Jersey coast—near Asbury Park. I stopped for an instant in the *Brooklyn Standard* office on my way up from the garage. The night staff's in turmoil. They're rushing through a sensational morning extra. I found out something else. There's been a similar massacre in Spain! If we hadn't been talking here we'd have known. All the papers ran columns about it hours ago. They're correlating the dispatches now and by tomorrow every one will know of the menace. What I fear is mass hysteria."

"Mass hysteria?"

"Yes, they'll go mad in the city tomorrow—there'll be a stampede. Unreasoning superstition and blind terror always culminate in acts of violence. Hundreds of people will run amuck, pillage, destroy. There'll be more lives lost than Chaugnar destroyed tonight."

"But we can do something. We must."

"I said that we were merely waiting for Doctor Imbert." Little crossed to the eastern window and stared for a moment into the lightening sky. Then he returned to where Algernon was standing. "Do you feel better?" he asked. "Have you pulled yourself together?"

"Yes," muttered Algernon. "I'm quite all right."

"Good."

The door opened and Imbert came in. His face was distraught and of a deathly pallor, but a look of relief came into his eyes when they rested on Algernon. "I feared you were seriously hurt," he cried. "We were quite mad to experiment with—with that thing."

"We must experiment again, I fear."

Irnbert nodded. "I'm ready to join you. What do you want us to do?"

"I want you and Harris to carry that machine downstairs and put it into my car. I'll need a flashlight and a few other things. I won't be long . . ."

9. The Horror Moves

"We must overtake it before it reaches the crossroads," shouted Little.

They were speeding by the sea, tearing at seventy miles an hour down a long, white road that twisted and turned between ramparts of sand. On both sides there towered dunes, enormous, majestic, morning stars a-glitter on the dark waters intermittently visible beyond their seaward walls. The horseshoe-shaped isthmus extended for six miles into the sea and then doubled back toward the Jersey coast. At the point where it changed its direction stood a crossroad, explicitly sign-posted with two pointing hands. One of these junctions led directly toward the mainland, the other into a dense, ocean-defiled waste, marshy and impregnable, a kind of morass where anything or anyone might hide indefinitely.

And toward this retreat Chaugnar fled. For hours Little's car had pursued it along the tarred and macadamized roads that fringe the Jersey coast—over bridges and viaducts and across wastes of sand, in a straight line from Asbury Park to Atlantic City and then across country and back again to the coast, and now adown a thin terrain lashed by Atlantic spray, deserted save for a few ramshackle huts of fishermen and a vast congregation of gulls.

Chaugnar Faugn had moved with unbelievable rapidity; from the instant when they had first encountered it crouching somnolently in the shadows beneath a deserted bathhouse at Long Branch and had turned the light on it and watched it awake to the moment when it had gone shambling away through the darkness its every movement had been ominous with menace.

Twice it had stopped in the road and waited for them to approach and once its great arm had raised itself against them in a gesture of malignant defiance. And on that occasion only the entropy machine had saved them. Its light Chaugnar could not bear, and when Little had turned the ray upon the creature's flanks the great obscene body had heaved and shuddered and a ghastly screeching had issued from its bulbous lips. And then forward again it had forged, its thick, stumpy legs moving with the rapidity of pistons—carrying it over the ground so rapidly that the car could not keep pace.

But always its tracks had remained visible, for a phosphorescence streamed from them, illuming its retreat. And always its hoarse bellowing could be heard in the distance, freighted with fury and a hatred incalculable. And by the stench, too, they trailed it, for all the air through which it passed was acridly defiled—pungent with an uncleanliness that evades description.

"It is infinitely old," cried Little as he maneuvered the car about the base of a sea-lashed dune. "As old as the earth's crust. Otherwise it would have crumbled. You saw how the bathhouse crumbled—how the shells beneath its feet dissolved and vanished. It is only its age that saves it."

"You had the light on it for five minutes," shouted Algernon. His voice was hoarse with excitement. "And it still lives. What can we do?"

"We must corner it—keep the light directed at it for—many minutes. To send it back we must decrease the random element in it by a billion years. It has remained substantially as it is now for at least that long. Perhaps longer."

"How many years of earth-time does the machine lop off a minute?" shouted Imbert.

"Can't tell exactly. It works differently with different objects. Metals, stone, wood all have a different entropy-rhythm. But roughly, it should reverse entropy throughout a billion years of earth-time in ten or fifteen minutes."

"There it is!" shouted Algernon. "It's reached the crossroads. Look!"

Against a windshield glazed with sea-mist Imbert laid his forehead, peering with bulging eyes at the form of Chaugnar, phosphorescently illumed a quarter-mile before them on the road, and even as he stared the distance between the car and the loathsome horror diminished by fifty yards.

"It isn't moving," cried Little. He had half risen from his seat and was gripping the wheel as though it were a live thing. "It's waiting for us. Turn on the light, sir. Quick! for God's sake! We're almost on top of it!"

Algernon fell upon his knees in the dark and groped about for the switch. The engine's roar increased as Little stepped furiously upon the accelerator. "The light, quick!" Little almost screamed the words.

Algernon's fingers found the switch and thrust it sharply upward. There ensued the drone of revolving spheres. "It's moving again. God, it's moving!"

Algernon rose shakingly to his feet. "Where is it?" he shouted. "I don't see it!"

"It's making for the marshes," shouted Little. "Look. Straight ahead, through here." He pointed toward a clear spot in the windshield. Craning hysterically, Algernon described a phosphorescent bulk making off over the narrowest of the bisecting roads.

With a frantic spin of the wheel Little turned the car about and sent the speedometer soaring. The road grew narrower and more uneven as they advanced along it and the car careened perilously. "Careful," Algernon called out warningly. "We'll get ditched. Better slow up."

"No," cautioned Little, his voice sharp with alarm. "We can't stop now."

The light from the machine was streaming unimpeded into the darkness before them.

"Keep it trained on the road," shouted Little. "It would destroy a man in an instant."

They could smell the mud flats now. A pungent salty odor of stagnant brine and putrescent shellfish drifted toward them, whipped by the wind. A sickly yellow light was spreading sluggishly in the eastern sky. Across the road ahead of them a turtle shambled and vanished hideously in a flash.

"See that?" cried Little. "That's how Chaugnar would go if it wasn't as old as the earth."

"Be ready with the brakes," Algernon shouted back.

The end of the road had swept into view. It ran swiftly downhill for fifty yards and terminated in a sandy waste that was half submerged at its lower levels. The illumed bulk of Chaugnar paused for an instant on a sandy hillock. Then it moved rapidly downward toward the flats, arms spread wide, body swaying strangely, as though it were in awe of the sea.

Little steered the car to the side of the road and threw on the brakes. "Out—both of you!" he shouted.

Algernon descended to the ground and stood for an instant shakingly clinging to the door of the car. Then, in a sudden access of determination, he sprang back and began tugging at the machine, whilst Imbert strove valiantly to assist him.

There came a bellow from the great form that was advancing into the marsh. Algernon drew close to Little, and gripped him firmly by the arm. "Hadn't we better wait here?" he asked, his voice tight with strain. "It seems to fear the sea. We can entrench ourselves here and attack it with the light when it climbs back."

"No," Little's reply was emphatic. "We haven't a second to waste. It may—mire itself. It's too massive to flounder through the mud without becoming hopelessly bogged down. We'll drive it forward into the marsh."

Resolutely he stopped and beckoned to his companions to assist him in raising and supporting the machine. Dawn was spreading in the east as the three men staggered downward over the sandy waste, a planet's salvation in the glittering shape they carried.

Straight into the morass they went, quaking with terror but impelled by a determination that was oblivious to caution. From Chaugnar there now came an insistent screeching and bellowing, a noise that smote so ominously on Algernon's ear that he wanted, desperately, to drop the machine and head back toward the car. But above the obscene bellowings of the horror rose Little's voice in courageous exhortation. "Don't stop for an instant," he cried. "We must keep it from circling back to the road. It will turn in a moment. It's sinking deeper and deeper. It will have to turn."

Their shoes sank into the sea-soaked marsh weeds, while luridly across the glistening morass streamed the greenish light from the machine, effacing everything in its path save the mud itself, which bubbled and heaved, made younger in an instant by ten thousand years. And then, suddenly, the great thing turned and faced them.

Knee-deep in the soft mud it turned, its glowing flanks quivering with ire, its huge trunk malignly upraised, a flail of flame. For an instant it loomed thus terribly menacing, the soul of all malignancy and horror, a cancerous cyclops oozing fetor. Then the light swept over it, and it recoiled with a convulsive trembling of its entire bulk. Though half mired, it retreated swayingly, and its bellows turned to hoarse gurglings, such as no animal throat had uttered in all earth's eons of sentient evolution.

And then, slowly, it began to change. As the light streamed over and enveloped it, it began unmistakably to shrivel and darken.

"Keep the light steady," Little cried out, his voice tremulous with concern, his features set in an expression of utter revulsion.

Algernon and Imbert continued to advance with the machine, as sickened as Little was by what they saw but supported now by the disappearance of all uncertainty as to the truth of Little's claims.

And now that which had taken to itself an earth-form in eons primordial began awfully to disincarn and before their gaze was enacted a drama so revolting as to imperil reason. A burning horror withdrew from its garments of clay and retraced in patterns of unspeakable dimness the history of its enshrinement. Not instantly had it incarned itself, but by stages slow and fantasmal and sickening. To ascend, Chaugnar had had to feast, not on men at first, for there were no men when it lay venomously outspread on the earth's crust, but on entities no less malignant than itself, the spawn of star-births incalculable. For before the earth cooled she had drawn from the skies a noxious progeny. Drawn earthward by her holocaust they had come, and relentlessly Chaugnar had devoured them.

And now as that which had occurred in the beginning was enacted anew these blasphemies were disgorged, and above the dark wrack defilement spread. And at last from a beast-shape to a jelly Chaugnar passed, a jelly enveloped in darting filaments of corpse-pale flame. For an instant it moved above the black marsh, as it had moved in the beginning when it had come from beyond the universe of stars to wax bestial in the presence of Man. And then the flames vanished and nothing remained but a cold wind blowing across the estuary from the open sea.

Little let out a great cry and Algernon released his hold on the machine and dropped to his knees on the wet earth. Imbert, too, relinquished the machine but before doing so he shot back the lever at its base.

Only for an instant did the victory go unchallenged. For before the spheres on the machine had ceased to revolve, before even the light had vanished from the gleaming waste, the malignancy that had been Chaugnar Faugn reshaped itself in the sky above them.

Indescribably it loomed through the gray sea-mists, its bulk magnified a thousandfold, its long, dangling trunk swaying slowly back and forth.

For an instant it towered above them, glaring venomously. Then, like a racer, it stooped and floundered forward and went groping about with its monstrous hands for the little shapes it hated. It was still groping when it dimmed and vanished into the depth of the hazy, dawn-brightened sky.

10. Little's Explanation

It was the fifth day since Chaugnar Faugn had been sent back through time. Algernon and Little sat in the latter's laboratory and discussed the destruction of the horror over cups of black coffee.

"You think, then, that the last manifestation we saw was a kind of spectral emanation, without physical substance."

"Not wholly, perhaps," replied Little. "An odor of putrefaction came from it. I should regard the phenomenon as a kind of tenuous reassembling rather than an apparition in a strict sense. Chaugnar had been incarnate for so long in the hideous shape with which we are familiar that its disembodied intelligence could reclothe itself in a kind of porous mimesis before it returned to its hyperdimensional sphere. So rapidly did our machine reverse entropy that perhaps tiny fragments of its terrestrial body survived, and these, by a tremendous exercise of will, it may have reassembled and, figuratively, *blown up*. That is to say, it may have taken these tiny fragments and so increased their porosity beyond the normal porosity of matter that they produced the cyclopean apparition we saw. All matter, you know, is tremendously porous, and if I could remove all the 'vacuums' from your body you would shrink to the size of a pin-head."

Algernon nodded, and was silent for a moment. Then he stood up, laid his coffee cup on the windowsill and crossed to where Little was sitting. "We agreed," he said, "that we wouldn't discuss Chaugnar further until . . . well, until we were in a little calmer frame of mind than we were a few days ago. It was a wise decision, I think. But I'm now so certain that what we both witnessed was not an illusion that I must insist you return an *honest* answer to two questions. I shall not expect a comprehensive and wholly satisfying explanation, for I'm aware that you are not completely sure yourself as to the exact nature of Chaugnar. But you have at least formed an hypothesis, and there are a good many things you haven't told me which I've earned the right to know."

"What do you wish to know?" Little's voice was constrained, reluctant.

"What destroyed the horror in the Pyrenees? Why were there no more massacres after—after that night?"

Little smiled wanly. "Have you forgotten the pools of black slime which were found on the melting snow a thousand feet above the village three days after we sent Chaugnar back?"

"You mean . . ."

Little nodded. "Chaugnar's kin, undoubtedly. They accompanied Chaugnar back, but left like their master, a few remainders. Little round pools of putrescent slime—a superfluity of rottenness that somehow resisted the entropy-reversing action of the machine."

"You mean that the machine sent entropy-reversing emanations half across the world?"

Little shook his head. "I mean simply that Chaugnar Faugn and its hideous brethren were *joined together* hyperdimensionally and that we destroyed them simultaneously. It is an axiom of virtually every speculative philosophy based on the newer physics and the concepts of non-Euclidean mathematics that we can't perceive the real *relations* of objects in the external world, that since our senses permit us to view them merely three-dimensionally we can't perceive the hyperdimensional links which unite them.

"If we could see the same objects—men, trees, chairs, houses—on a fourth-dimensional plane, for instance, we'd notice connections that are now wholly unsuspected by us. Your chair, to pick an example at random, may actually be joined to the window-ledge behind you or . . . to the Woolworth Building. Or you and I may be but infinitesimally tiny fragments of some gigantic monster occupying vast segments of space-time. You may be a mere excrescence on the monster's back, and I a hair of its head—I speak metaphorically, of course, since in higher dimensions of space-time there can be nothing but analogies to objects on the terrestrial globe—or you and I and all men, and everything in the world, every particle of matter, may be but a single fragment of this larger entity. If anything should happen to the entity you and I would *both* suffer, but as the monster would be invisible to us, no one—no one equipped with normal human organs of awareness—would suspect that we were suffering because we were parts of *it*. To a three-dimensional observer we should appear to be suffering from different causes and our invisible hyperdimensional *solidarity* would remain wholly unsuspected.

"If two people were thus hyperdimensionally joined, like Siamese twins, and one of them were destroyed by a machine similar to the one we used against Chaugnar Faugn, the other would suffer effacement at the same instant, though he were on the opposite side of the world."

Algernon looked puzzled.

"But why should the link be invisible? Assuming that Chaugnar Faugn and the Pyrenean horrors were hyperdimensionally joined together—either because they were parts of one great monster, or merely because they were *one* in the hyperdimensional sphere, why should this hyperdimensional connecting link be invisible to us?"

"Well—perhaps an analogy will make it clearer. If you were a *two-* instead of a three-dimensional entity, and if, when you regarded objects about you—chairs, houses, animals—you saw only their length and breadth, you wouldn't be able to form any intelligible conception of their relations to other objects in the dimension you couldn't apprehend—the dimension of *thickness*. Only a portion of an ordinary three-dimensional object would be visible to you and you could only make a mystical guess as to how it would look with another dimension added to it. In that, to you, unperceivable dimension of thickness it might join itself to a thousand other objects and you'd never suspect that such a connection existed. You might perceive hundreds of flat surfaces about you, all disconnected, and you would never imagine that they formed one object in the third dimension.

"You would live in a two-dimensional world and when three-dimensional objects intruded into that world you would be unaware of their true objective conformation—or relatively unaware, for your perceptions would be perfectly valid so long as you remained two-dimensional.

"Our perceptions of three-dimensional world are only valid for that world—to a fourth-dimensional or fifth- or sixth-dimensional entity our conceptions of objects external to us would seem utterly ludicrous. And we know that such entities exist. Chaugnar Faugn was such an entity. And because of its hyperdimensional nature it was joined to the horror on the hills in a way we weren't able to perceive. We can perceive connections when they have length, breadth and thickness, but when a new dimension is added they pass out of our ken, precisely as a solid object

passes out of the ken of an observer in a dimension lower than ours. Have I clari-
fied your perplexities?"

Algernon nodded. "I think—yes, I am sure that you have. But I should like to
ask you another question. Do you believe that Chaugnar Faugn is a transcendent
world-soul endowed with a supernatural incorporeality, or just—just a material entity? I mean, was Ulman's priest right and was Chaugnar an incarnation of the Oneness of the Brahmic mysteries, the portentous all-in-all of theosophists and occultists,
or merely a product of physical evolution or a plane incomprehensible to us?"

Little took a long sip of coffee and very deliberately lowered his head, as
though he were marshalling his convictions for a debate. "I believe I once told
you," he said at last, "that I didn't believe Chaugnar Faugn could be destroyed by
any agent less transcendental than that which we used against it. It certainly wasn't
protoplasmic or mineral, and no mechanical device not based on relativist concepts
could have effected the dissolution we witnessed. An infra-red ray machine, for
instance, or a cyclotron would have been powerless to send it back. Yet despite the
transcendental nature of even its carnate shell, despite the fact that even in its
earth-shape it was fashioned of a substance unknown on the earth and that we can
form no conception of its shape in the multidimensional sphere it now inhabits, it
is my opinion that it is inherently, like ourselves, a circumscribed entity—the
spawn of remote worlds and unholy dimensions, but a creature and not a creator, a
creature obeying inexorable laws and occupying a definite niche in the cosmos.

"In a way we can never understand it had acquired the ability to roam and
could incarn itself in dimensions lower than its own. But I do not believe it possessed the attributes of deity. It was neither beneficent nor evil, but simply amo-
rally virulent—a vampire-like life form from beyond the universe of stars strayed
by chance into our little, walled-in three-dimensional world. One unguarded gate
may be standing ajar . . ."

"But do you believe that it actually made a race of men to serve it—that the
Miri Nigri were fashioned from the flesh of primitive amphibians?"

Little frowned. "I don't know. Conditions on the cooling earth two billion
years ago may once have been such that creations of that nature antedated the
process of biological evolution with which we are familiar. And we may be sure
that Chaugnar Faugn with its inscrutable endowments could have fashioned men-
shapes had it so desired—could have fashioned them even from the planktonlike
swarms of small organisms which must have drifted with the tides through the ancient oceans."

Little lowered his voice and looked steadily at Algernon. "Some day," he
murmured, "Chaugnar may return. We sent it back through time, but in five thousand or a hundred thousand years it may return to ravage. Its return will be presaged in dreams, for when its brethren stirred restlessly on the Spanish hills both I
and Hsieh Ho were disturbed in our sleep by harbingers from beyond. Telepathi-
cally Chaugnar spoke to sleeping minds, and if it returns it will speak again, for
Man is not isolated among the sentient beings of earth but is linked to all that
moves in hyperdimensional continuity."

Pompelo's Doom

(a dream of Chaugnar Faugn)

Ann K. Schwader

Ann K. ("Ankh") Schwader is one of the tiny tip-top group of Lovecraftian poets writing today, breathing the very same foetid tomb-exhalations Lovecraft expelled. Here is a verse-version of Lovecraft's Roman dream, used by Long in "The Horror from the Hills." I only wish Lovecraft himself could have read it.

Before Rome's restless eagles worked their will
To claim the cursed and craglost Pyrenees;
Before, indeed, its storied seven hills
Were more than mud beneath primordial seas;
A thing of Chaos twisted time and space
To manifest Itself among our race.

The Greeks and those before them knew It well
As feeder, man-beast, eater of the all,
As shadows in the dawn, or sudden pall
Across the stars at midnight . . . shape of Hell
Incarnate, yet with contours ill-defined
To any but a wise and troubled mind.

At length It and Its lesser brethren came
To plague Iberia's high wilderness
With toad-spawned servitors by loathsome name
Of *Miri Nigri,* shaped as men but less
Than puppets for each horrid act and thought
That Its inhuman chaos-mind had wrought.

Each Kalends of November brought such rites
As nightmare shrieks of on the mountain crests
Above Pompelo: all that life detests
Was danced and drummed of in those black delights,
Until great Rome, in sickened sympathy,
Sent aid to its beleaguered colony.

One cohort of the finest marched that day
Against a foe no Roman blade could mark—
In pride and ignorance they wound their way
Amid strange hills until the falling dark
Revealed too late what made their horses scream
Brute terror at the madness of this dream.

What howled and gibbered on those hellish peaks,
No man returned alive and sane to know . . .
What roused the hills themselves to prey below,
Pompelo's colonists could never speak
Without a rolling eye, a mouth of foam:
Dread Chaugnar Faugn, who broke the mind of Rome!

[after Frank Belknap Long's "The Horror from the Hills"]

Confession of the White Acolyte

Ann K. Schwader

We read in this statement of rueful helplessness the same conscience-damned impotence that greets us in every episode of Lovecraft's "Herbert West—Reanimator." The narrator of this poem is the protagonist of Long's "The Horror from the Hills." Why is he a "white" acolyte? Two reasons: he is not one of the Asiatic Miri Nigri, but a Westerner. And he is blanched, drained dry by someone's vampiric proboscis. Take your pick.

———————

From storied Tsang to Lhasa's ancient gates,
I bore the bane of Mu Sang's prophecy,
Soul-bound since time forgotten to one fate:
To nurse Great Chaugnar over land and sea.
I dared not hurl my burden to the waves
In dread of sacramental vengeance . . . cursed
Indeed my coward's life! for courage saves
Us not from death itself, but from the worst
Which lurks beyond that vale. Damnation deep
As any traitor's is my portion now—
Unspeakable, unhealed, I rise from sleep
To rue the mirror's verdict on my vow,
And read within the ruins of my face
The dissolution of the human race.

[after Frank Belknap Long's "The Horror from the Hills"]

When Chaugnar Wakes

Frank Belknap Long

Long was not quite done with Chaugnar Faugn once he finished "The Horror from the Hills." Perhaps he felt a narrative sequel would spoil the effect of the original. But he did indulge himself with one more Chaugnar appearance, something of a verse prequel to the novella. In what might pass for a stray *Fungi from Yuggoth* stanza, Long's "When Chaugnar Wakes" seems to provide a glimpse of the god's career before he came down from the stars.

You will note the simplification of the entity's name. No "Faugn" this time. Why? Maybe on second thought it sounded too redolent of the gentle and Disneyesque satyrs of Greek mythology. Maybe it was just to make the poem scan easier. But it is worth noting that Frank once complained that Ron Goulart had somewhere mixed up "Chaugnar Faugn" with Lovecraft's "Cthulhu fhtagn." Maybe he wanted to avoid that possibility.

What is the origin of the name "Chaugnar"? I don't claim to know, but it does sound appropriately Indian, as befits the Ganesha connection. It recalls the divine name Juggernaut or Jagganath, two versions of one of Krishna's names. The word "juggernaut" suggests something unstoppable, an irresistible force. This is because, as Krishna's image passed through the crowded streets at festival time, atop a gigantic wagon, some of the frenzied faithful would throw themselves as sacrifices of devotion beneath the wheels of the passing Juggernaut.

"When Chaugnar Wakes" first appeared in *Weird Tales* for September 1932.

A billion miles beyond the suns
　　Which gild the edge of space,
Great Chaugnar dreams, and there is hate
　　And fury on its face.

Beyond the universe of stars
　　Where red moons wane and swim,
Great Chaugnar stirs, and heaves its bulk
　　Upon a crater's rim.

Its ropy arms descend to suck
    Dark nurture from the deeps
Of lava-pools within a cone
    That shines whilst Chaugnar sleeps.

Explorers from the outer stars
    Have glimpsed that glowing cone;
Have glimpsed the vast and silent shape
    Asleep upon its throne.

Explorers from the world we know
    Have seen that shape in dreams;
Have watched its shadow fall and spread
    On dim, familiar streams.

When Chaugnar wakes, its mindless hate
    Will send it voyaging far;
It may set Sirius adrift,
    Or seek a humbler star.

A humbler star with satellites,
    Small planets in its train:
And that is why I kneel and kneel
    Before Great Chaugnar's fane.

The Elephant God of Leng

Robert M. Price

Dazzled by the prospect of sharing an authorial by-line with the great Frank Belknap Long, I once approached him with the idea of collaborating on a new Chaugnar tale. He agreed readily enough at the time, seeing my plot outline, but later, as I learned many years afterward from Peter Cannon's memoir *Long Memories,* he had second thoughts and decided to bow out. All I had known was that he never got around to it. But I did, and dedicated it to his memory. You will have no trouble recognizing Frank and Lyda Long in what follows. The story turned out not to be a sequel to "The Horror from the Hills," but rather something of an update. It was first published in my short story collection, *Blasphemies & Revelations* (2008).

———————————

(Dedicated to the shade of Frank Belknap Long)

It seems to me I once read in Plutarch that the only difference between the atheist and the superstitious man is that while the first believes there is no god, the second believes there is but wishes there wasn't. Then it struck me as something of a joke. But now that I recall the remark, it seems to me truer words were never spoken. I have read something else, seen something else, in the intervening years that brought the ancient quip home to me with genuine force. I used to be an atheist. Now I guess you could call me superstitious.

It was winter back home but felt like summer as I crossed the great steppes of Siberia, headed for an obscure destination in the secret heart of Central Asia. It's possible that Aeroflot once ran an occasional plane out this way, but I doubt it, and since the Union of Soviet Socialist Republics fell, there was no route out here except the ancient one: camelback. I felt like Haliburton himself with my hired retainers, a ragtag bunch of bearded mutterers, most of whom had drifted (or been pursued) for so long that they'd probably forgotten what dusky national origin they once had. There were, thankfully, a few other Westerners with me, mostly technicians along to operate the film equipment for the PBS documentary we were shooting.

The whole thing had seemed the wildest of goose chases from the start. I'd never have taken on the assignment if my job with the production company weren't already hanging by a thread. Well, if the rumors proved out, we'd get plenty of ratings on this one, by God, public TV or no. It started when one of the directors, a typical limousine liberal given to the delusions of the affluent, described a conversation she'd had with a member of her Theosophist group. Somewhere in the jungle of Blavatsky's *The Secret Doctrine* there was a reference to ancient Cyclopean ruins in Asia, supposedly left over from a colony of ancient Mu or Lemuria, or maybe it was Oz. As the network exec described it, it didn't matter who built them, but if there really was a neglected set of ruins out there, maybe a city, the Theosophical thing would make a good hook for an otherwise dull archaeological documentary.

Trouble was, there was absolutely no solid evidence. Everybody who has studied it knows that Blavatsky was at least half-charlatan, and that half of what she wrote she made up. But how would we know for sure if we didn't go take a look? That's what we were doing under the blazing sun, in the exact middle of nowhere: taking a look.

We found nothing—except, that is, for some lost Afghan rebels who didn't seem to know their war was over and thought we were the enemy. Lucky for us, some of our bearers, who turned out to be Afghan themselves, were able to calm them down. As the drift of their parlay became evident, chiefly by the lowering of gun barrels, a bright idea occurred to me. So I emerged from cover and sauntered out to where the men stood, still talking. Once there, I asked our man Achmet to ask the other man if he and his compatriots had spotted anything like what we were looking for. After all, I figured, they must be pretty well used to all manner of secret paths and shunned quarters after years of skulking and guerrilla warfare.

The news was both good and bad. First, there was nothing else, nothing at all, the way we were headed. But there was indeed something, possibly an old hermitage, that sounded kind of like the name of Blavatsky's Brigadoon. But whatever it was, it involved a hike up to the top of a plateau some leagues in a completely different direction. The trouble was, I knew good and well that if I returned to the States with this job left hanging, I'd be finished in the business. No one would consider mitigating circumstances. That's the only reason we decided to keep going. I knew what Moses felt like wandering in the wilderness for all those forty years.

We traded the camels for donkeys at a bazaar along the way. Better for the climb. Weeks passed, and we came in sight of the place, the Plateau of Tsang. It wasn't on any map I could find. So I guess that made it a good enough candidate for the site of a lost city. Or temple, or whatever.

Finally we had to leave the donkeys with one or two of the bearers on a lower ledge and get out the climbing gear. It was clear that if there'd been some sort of monastery up there, the monks weren't kidding about isolation from the world. At the top, we found ourselves so exhausted, even the hardy hill men in our number, that we all decided to take a siesta before striking across the surprisingly small surface of the plateau. It appeared to extend for not much more than an acre. At the far end there was a visible structure, or the remains of one, but unless it extended underground, it didn't look like much. It would wait.

I was awakened by the sounds of gunfire. It seemed a couple of our men just couldn't wait to get a look at whatever valuables the plateau might conceal. Thinking there'd be a treasure, or maybe a leftover cache of Soviet weapons, a pair of them had snuck off. And they'd found something. Something worth fighting over. I jumped to my aching feet and ran for where the shots had echoed. I didn't hear any more of them, so I hoped the coast was clear.

Everyone now was awake, and the others, hardier specimens, beat us Americans to the spot. By the time we caught up with them, we were greeted by a cacophony of wailing gibberish. It seemed these men, many of them kneeling, were calling on Allah, perhaps in mourning, perhaps asking for protection. I elbowed my way through the suddenly pious crowd to get a good look at the two bodies.

There had been shooting, all right, but they hadn't been shooting at each other after all. A later scrutiny of the scene would show bullets having knocked some chips from the stone ruins that loomed over them. But what had the men been shooting at? I had to assume, at whatever killed them. But filling in that blank did not look to be an easy matter. The dust of the ground had been stirred and disturbed by the footprints of the panicked bearers as they had first surrounded the corpses of their fallen comrades, then sprung away in panic. But between the troop of footprints, I thought I made out fragments of a broad sweeping motion, as if huge ropes or snakes had dragged the ground in a semicircular motion.

But the corpses, carcasses really, of the two poor bastards were the most mystifying. The throats and wrist of one had been torn away, possibly scraped away, while the other's heart had been pulled out of his chest. His chest hung wide like an opened clam. I didn't call on Allah, but as soon as I could reach a place with a ham radio I did call the network office to tell them that we were headed home. Needless to say, the documentary was as dead as the two guides. And the network was fretting, last time I heard, about possible suit from the survivors of the two men.

I arrived home in New York free of two worries: I wasn't going to die parched in the desert, and I still had my job. At least for now. Nobody could say I had botched the project, so at least I had a reprieve—until another batty exec had a fool's errand to send me and my crew on. But maybe it wouldn't come to that. For, you see, the trip wasn't entirely a waste after all.

I said we were wrong in our first guess that the two bearers had killed each other. But we were right about them having discovered something before they died. It was lying there between them on the ground, only partly stained by their flying blood. They had dug up a stone box, even opened it. It was nothing that interested either of them, couldn't have been, not that they had the time to do much calculating before whatever it was took them by surprise.

It was a book, and after my first decent hot shower in many weeks, I settled down in a nice soft robe with a glass of Scotch and opened its covers. Not that I could really read it, mind you. But I knew what it was, and it was something to look at. The thing was an elaborate wooden codex, varnished boards enclosing bound pages of some tough parchment. The characters seemed something between Sanskrit and Tibetan, maybe that Senzar language Blavatsky had written about. Maybe she wasn't lying. She hadn't been lying about the ruins, that's for sure.

The text was block-printed the way they do it in Tibet and Nepal. The volume might be valuable as an artifact, and if worse came to worst, I could try to sell it, though I suspected the network would claim possession of it as soon as they heard of its existence, which, thanks to me, they hadn't yet. But then it occurred to me that if I could get the thing translated, it might hold the clues to future archaeological digs that would ensure my reputation for years to come. I could see myself not only on PBS, but the Discovery Channel, too—hell, maybe even at a university post. It wasn't out of the question.

About this time I was jarred from my boozy musings by the sound of someone out in the hall. I put my slippers on and went to the door. No one was there anymore. But then from the corner of my eye I could have sworn I saw someone out on the fire escape. Again, no one. By now I was plenty spooked. Could someone be trying to break in? Or was I under surveillance? New York began to seem to me altogether as creepy as the shunned Plateau of Tsang. Hell, maybe I'd be safer there. I double-locked the doors and windows, then searched the apartment, every square foot, all the while assuring myself it was just jet-lag and the jitters. I wanted to believe this, and I had just about got myself believing it till I took another look over in the foyer area and saw something sitting on the mail table.

It was an unmarked videocassette, no box either. I held the cool plastic of thing, puzzled, my tired mind somehow failing to connect it with the suspicious noises and glimpses I'd just been investigating. Instead, I tried to remember if I'd rented the tape before going away and considered what a hell of an overdue fee I must owe by now. But I didn't think I'd rented anything. Could somebody have dropped a home video through my mail slot? Might I have absent-mindedly picked it up on the way in from the airport? Didn't recall that either. But by now, my relaxing was ruined anyway. I was tense and edgy, both from the long trip and from my probably imaginary suspicions. So I popped the video into the machine and reached for another Scotch. Maybe between the two of them, they'd put me to sleep.

No such luck. The tape had no trailer, no intro, and, as it developed, no real plot either. I began to wonder if what I was watching had been taped starting halfway through a sci-fi movie on late night TV. But there was no dialogue, no voiceover. The film was grainy, but the effects were, I had to admit, quite well done, maybe computer graphics? Anyway, first there was just the expanse of space. One star grew slowly larger (far too slowly for good cinematic pacing) until you could see it was a spacecraft. A queer combination, from what you could see of it, of egg-shaped pods and a central disk. They didn't make the stars move behind the ship, a common but scientifically inaccurate gimmick. Without any transition you could see into a viewport. The scene was bouncy but it seemed as if the helmets worn by the pilots were strangely oblong. But who said they were supposed to be from NASA?

Another long shot. Now you could see this ship wasn't landing, just floating, orbiting I guess, with the planetary disk well below them. But then you could see closer to the surface. There was a kind of ghostly light or lambence, just enough to show the texture of the world, again amazingly well simulated. The terrain was parched, crumbling into dust. There were interlocking webs of impact craters. But, off center on the screen, you could see a large body different in color from the rest, and, yes, more regular, a geometric shape: a broken cone or pyramid. Was it supposed to be the last building left standing, or some natural formation? A volcano of some type? I suddenly caught myself taking it for reality.

And from the drifting pall of desolation on this barren surface, there was suddenly motion, too fast for the eye to follow. The transition back to the orbiting craft was abrupt, painful to watch since the camera seemed to quickly follow whatever had moved, dizzying and confusing the viewer. Somebody needed some direction help here. Now what was happening on board the ship? You saw agitation inside the viewport, and the whole craft began to bob and dip. It was as if it had been lassoed. And then a wider shot showed that it had been. The silver bulk of the thing, confusing to the eye even when moving smoothly, was apparently trying to escape what looked like a fleshy web or rope that entangled it and tugged powerfully.

But this was the most ridiculous thing of all: how were you supposed to believe a lariat could extend from the planet's surface into outer space? Next the camera backed up, letting you see the space ship nearing the planet, falling out of the sky and bursting into flame. No transition this time, but now you could see the opening of that cone—yes, it was a cone. The debris of the ship was being swallowed, like dust bunnies going into a vacuum cleaner. And now you could see a little bit of the rope up close. It seemed almost to be flexing and shifting like a living appendage. And there might have been suckers on it.

All this abruptly stopped and something else began—also in the middle, by the look of it. I guessed that someone had taped what I just saw over this, some footage of a ritual some relative of the guy with the camera must have been involved in. It was Buddhist or Hindu. I couldn't see any faces through the thick, clinging smoke. People had red robes, tasseled hats. Some held banners or standards aloft. Some bowed down before an idol, which I thought I could recognize. The elephant head—let's see, who would that be? I'd seen it plenty of times in a local Indian restaurant. The Hindu god Ganesha, I was pretty sure. But somehow different in detail. And then, for the first time, there was sound. Coming up gradually, it seemed, not surprisingly, religious chanting. Reminded me momentarily of the terrified bearers up on the Tsang Plateau. What were they saying? A foreign language; I just tried to remember the sound of syllables: *Chaugnar fhtagn.*

The tape was over. I hit eject, and out it came. Like the old automat sandwiches, I thought. Had one when I was a kid. A glance at the clock showed nearly two hours had gone by. That didn't seem possible. I couldn't have been watching it that long. It was kind of engrossing, I had to admit, but I couldn't have lost track of time to that extent, could I?

Well, that could wait till tomorrow. The tape had worked; I was drowsy and headed for the bed. I wasn't sure I could stay awake long enough to get under the covers. I slept like the dead. If I dreamed at all, I don't remember it.

Next day I dropped by the studios, said hello to a few friends who'd heard of the strange deaths and were worried about me. I told them I couldn't do much by way of satisfying their curiosity about the two mangled men. There had been no question of keeping the bodies with us on the journey back, and so we had the Asians bury them on the plateau, which they did with amazing efficiency. Guess they didn't want to look at them any longer than they had to.

The execs were waiting to see me. But really there was nothing any of us could say, no questions I could answer. I was relieved that they did at least credit me with the effort to make it across that hostile terrain. Maybe we'd even be able to work some of the footage shot on the way into some other project. I told them I doubted it, since there had been no way to stabilize the cameras on camelback for very long. Most of it no doubt looked as clumsy as that video I'd viewed last night. And then it occurred to ask whether any of the execs had sent someone to drop that cassette off. Was it supposed to be part of someone's trial project? I didn't think we were in the business of sci-fi entertainment. But, no, no one professed to know anything about it.

I checked in at a couple of my favorite bars, to say hello to a few people, and a few martini glasses, that hadn't seen my face for a while. Time passed, and I returned to the apartment. Sending my hat across the couch like a Frisbee, I began loosening my tie and looked over to see if the message machine wanted to talk to me. For once, nothing. There was a movie I wanted to catch on cable, but that wouldn't be on for an hour or so. I went to get the book from where I'd secured it. Suddenly thinking of the strange things I half imagined I'd seen and heard the previous night, I got worried it might not be there. After a moment's panic, the way I get when I feel for my keys and think I've lost them, I reached around the interior of the lock-box and was relieved when I felt the smooth surface of the lacquered boards.

I thought a closer look at the thing wouldn't hurt. Clearing some space on the kitchen table (the book was pretty large), I opened the covers, intending to take a good look at the illuminations, which I remembered as showing fine workmanship. My eye followed the margins, the colored inks still quite brilliant, until I happened to pause on a square inch of text. I felt instantly confused, felt maybe I was seeing double. A headache exploded out of nowhere, and I found myself falling back against the cushion of my chair. What had happened? I was afraid to look at the page again. Was there something written on it that was somehow just too terrible for my brain to let me see? No, that was absurd—I couldn't even read the language!

I was wrong. When my eyes rested on the page again, with only a mild wave of disorientation this time, I could read it! Now let me tell you, I had forgotten the little Spanish I'd had to take in high school. On the trip to Asia I couldn't read a sign for an airport restroom unless somebody translated it. And now I could read and comprehend a language which only the night before I could not even recognize.

My nerves were calm in the face of it. The impossible sat before me like an impenetrable block. All I could do was to stare dumbly at it. My eyes slowly gravitated to the page again. What it would have said had it been in English was "The Testament of Mu Sang." I didn't read any more. I somehow felt as if I were reading someone else's mail. By rights I should never be able to read it, and so I was afraid to. I got up, got myself a drink, paced. Turned on the TV and stared at it blankly. I guess my cable program came on, but I never knew it.

Finally it occurred to me to phone up Joey Aronson, a pal from the network who designed foreign language programs, concentrated language learning programs for adults. Luckily he was home. I interrupted him watching the same show I had planned to see. He didn't mind. It took me some minutes to figure out how to ask my question, a few more for him to realize just what I meant. It seemed so absurd. Yes, overnight I learned a language, and yes, without even trying.

Joey had never heard of anything like it, but on second thought, he suggested maybe some sort of sleep-learning program. But I dismissed that: wouldn't I remember having taken it? Not remembering something . . .? Ironically, that rang a bell somewhere. Joey hung on, probably more convinced by the minute that I had gone crazy over there in Central Asia.

"Look, Joey, come to think of it, last night, something strange did happen. Somebody left me an unmarked video. I watched it, some confusing movie footage. But when it was over, I was missing at least an hour and a quarter by the clock. Is there any way the tape could have . . . hypnotized me? And while I was under, fed me knowledge of this language?"

"To be honest, Ed, it sounds impossible, but I don't know. We have language immersion weekends for people to pick up a language before they go abroad. And then there's sleep learning, like you mention. I've never heard of the pace being accelerated like this, though. Listen, I just thought of something. Ed, can you speak this language? Get the book and try reading something to me."

I reached over for the book and opened it at random. Again, it made sense to me. I started reading as if it were the morning newspaper.

"Hold on, Ed, you're reading me English. I don't want you to translate. Just read it."

I gazed at the page.

"Sorry, I wouldn't have the faintest guess how you'd say any of this stuff. It's like it just comes right into my mind what it means."

"Try this: what's the word in this language for 'book'?"

"Can't tell you. Doesn't that beat the hell out of you!"

"Tell you what, Ed. Bring the book down to my office tomorrow, and . . ."

I interrupted him. "Sorry Joey, but for reasons of my own, I'm not sure I want anybody seeing it just yet. Would it work if, say, I just traced a page or so of it?"

"Okay, whatever. I'd like to take it to somebody I know at the Museum. If it's a known Asian language, he'll be able to read it or know someone who can."

"Fine, but, Joey, that's not the trouble. I can read the damn thing. I just don't know how come!"

"Yeah, I understand, but let's do it my way for now. Get copying." He hung up. I got out some onionskin paper and started tracing, trying not to read much of it as I went. I was still wary of it. This wasn't my mail; whose was it?

Bright and early the next morning, I stepped out of the taxi in front of the network building. Joey was waiting for me at the curb and suggested we bundle ourselves right back into the cab for the ride over to the Museum. It was a cold day, our breath steaming even within the confines of the car. We tried to talk about in-house gossip. Somebody was about to be fired for sexual harassment, but I couldn't remember who. I could sense Joey shared my eagerness. Traffic was fairly light given the New York snow mounds, and we made it there in no time.

A knock on the pebble glass window of Dr. Harding's office fetched a quick response. As the genial man extended his hand, I realized I'd met him before in connection with one or another documentary I'd assisted on. He was in his late fifties, heavyset, graying, ruddy face, few wrinkles. Surprisingly, he remembered me, too. I was happy to let Joey do what explaining he could, all the time thinking to myself that it was probably a psychiatrist's office, not a linguist's, I should be sitting in.

The professor interrupted my encouraging train of thought. "This all sounds most intriguing! And now may I see the text?" I unfolded the sheet and began to read. Even though it was in English, it still sounded like outlandish gibberish, even to me. Then I handed Professor Harding the paper. Donning a pair of reading glasses, he regarded the cryptic symbols in silence for some time. Finally, he looked up and spoke.

"Mr. Banning, I am afraid there is no Senzar language, any more than Joseph Smith's Reformed Egyptian was a genuine language, ancient or modern. But this," he shook the paper, "is a real language. It is a sort of primitive Pali, an earlier stage of what Gautama Buddha would have spoken. Linguists have hypothesized such a tongue, but until now, no actual examples have ever been found. Whatever manuscript you have discovered will be of great scientific interest."

"Wait a minute, Professor Harding. Are you saying that this book is pre-Buddhist?"

"That I cannot judge without seeing it; of course, it may be a more recent copy, though still quite old, of a very ancient literary work. But yes, that work would have to antedate the birth of the Buddha, unless the primitive Pali continued alongside the more developed version, which I would have to judge unlikely."

"I assumed it was an artifact of some Central Asian Buddhist monastery."

"If not for the peculiar dialect, that would be a good guess. Many such manuscripts were buried by monks to keep them safe against the advance of the Mongol armies."

Joey interposed, "Is it something you can read, professor?"

"Yes, there is little problem there. It is close enough to standard Pali for me to make out most of it. But naturally there is far too little in this copied fragment for me to understand just what is going on in the passage. Perhaps if you would let me see the complete manuscript . . . ?"

"Tell me one thing. How good was my translation?"

The professor removed his reading glasses again and paused, looking at Joey who seemed to know what he was going to say next: "I am sorry to say that your reading bears absolutely no relation to this piece of text. Of that I feel sure."

If there is some square before square one, that's where I'd been left standing. Having crumpled up the onionskin sheet, I tossed it and rose, taking my hat and coat, leaving the others protesting as I slammed the door and sought the steps. Making for the subway, I knew there was one thing left for me to do. Read the whole manuscript. Or, since apparently I was not exactly reading it, I guessed I would simply be picking up the receiver and letting someone talk.

Once home, I retrieved the great wooden volume and placed it before me. I turned on every light in the place and disconnected the phone. Then I opened the covers and began to "read." This is what I thought I read.

The Testament of Mu Sang

This is the oracle of the one born of Hanuman's womb. These are the words to confirm what has gone before and what is to follow. Blessed is the one who grasps their inner meaning, for only the inner eye may read.

In the fifth month of the Year of the Badger, my office was that of first attendant to the Feeble One, the century-old master of our sect, and his bloated viceregent, the Mad Prophetess. For many generations we had occupied the forlorn lamasery of Tsang, whereupon no worldly man may enter. Our chief task was the keeping and copying of scrolls, which were housed in abundance. Many were written in scripts none could any longer read. Most were traced upon parchment dried from the skins of High Lamas, stripped from them on their deathbeds.

When on occasion one of the brethren might dare to read what was contained within certain carefully guarded scrolls, dangerous doctrines might arise within our ranks. But such heresies as reared their heads were quickly dispatched by means of the tortures which were our other inherited trade. By these two arts, the copying of scrolls, and the slow flaying of human hides, was the lamasery much enriched over many generations. Many of the mountain chiefdoms required copies of the scriptures as well as discipline for their prisoners.

We went along peacefully in this fashion year after year until the return of one brother, Zinxong, who had spent many years away from the community while serving as the court torturer for Qwon-ling, the most powerful of the mountain chieftains. At first he was received back with great rejoicing, as for a long-lost relative. Little we knew that, even as the traitor sat at table with the aging Lama and us, his attendants, the warriors of the chieftain he had lately served and still did serve were swarming over the low walls of the lamasery, quietly slaying all who opposed them.

As the sounds of fighting were heard in the dining hall, we rose to our feet, all but the Feeble One who was past rising and indeed had to be carried from place to place. And our false brother went to greet his brethren in perfidy, the chieftain himself as well as his shaman. It was now all too clear that his tribe had made alliance with our traditional rivals, the Brotherhood of Leng. Their silken yellow caps glowed in the soft light of the butter lamps. Their very presence here was blasphemy. I clutched my robes of holy crimson, the true color of enlightenment, and sought egress as the sword of the traitors unerringly found the brittle breastbone of our revered master the Feeble One. A second stroke silenced forever the raving mouth of the Mad Prophetess who was ever at his side.

In truth, I confess I mourned not greatly at the passing of the Feeble One. His voice had not been heard in many a season, since the Mad One had grown to dominate him. And her dispatching I greeted with positive elation. She had abused us for the last time. But this meant I stood next in line for the pontificate of our sect, the Red Hats of Tsang.

Thus it was that I resolved that the heretical Yellow Hats of Leng should by no means usurp our holy monastery and its riches for their own. As the attendant of the High Lama, I knew well the secret paths of escape, that might even that day have availed the Feeble One had he not been so palsied and under the fell dominion of the Mad Raving One. But secure behind thick tapestries I made my way silently down hidden stairs to the Inner Adytum far below the surface.

There I knew that I must call on the aid of our gods to vindicate and protect those few remaining Red Hats from the bloody hands of the blasphemers.

None had dared approach the hall of shrines in many a year, as the curtains and ropes of cobwebs made manifest. I bent and peered close at the writing upon the bases of the statues. Legend had it that the divine images had been brought here from the stars and were themselves older far than the monastery, which had been later erected over this very cave. Genuflecting, I passed quickly by the squat representations of Nug and Yeb, of Lloigor and Zhar. I shuddered and lingered not at the chapel of Dark Han. The image I sought was that of elephant-headed Yag-Kosha, whom our forbears had worshipped in ancient Khitai. Alone among the brethren I had been given access to the antique scrolls of summoning and now sought to call out of the dimensions the terrible form of Yag-Kosha, that his righteous fury might take vengeance upon the usurping devils of the Yellow Hat.

At last I saw that I had reached a web-festooned image which seemed clearly to bear the outlines of the mighty elephant, the chosen avatar of the blessed Yag-Kosha. There were the flaring ears, the gracefully bending trunk. The engraved nameplate at the base of the statue had been too much corroded with verdigris to be legible, but no matter. I knew I had found our savior. Setting down my butter lamp, I prostrated my form, casting aside my crimson habit so that my naked form might be seen to be covered with penitential scars and tattoos as offerings to the divine Yag-Kosha whose epiphany I sought.

So absorbed with mystic rapture was I in calling upon the deity that I scarce marked it when the sound of sandaled footfalls approached. It seemed that a few of my surviving brethren had surmised my destination and made to rejoin me. At once they prostrated themselves around me and sought as best they might to repeat the ancient vocables after me.

The musty air began to stir. The sole butter lamp flared like a torch, and from somewhere we all alike heard the slow grating of stonework being forced apart. Dared we hope that our supplications had found a receptive ear? We regained our feet and stared about in the lightening gloom.

For a moment we yielded to faithless fear as we saw the villainous Yellow Hats and their retainers pouring into the far end of the chamber. They had discovered, no doubt with the aid of the traitor Zinxong, our place of refuge. They lost no time in locating us and sending armed men, their scimitars already upraised, to finish their slaughter. This they did, sparing only my own humble person so that I might guide them to the treasury of the Red Hats.

The devil Zinxong approached me and warned his master Qwon-ling that it would not be easy to torture the secret out of me, as I myself was as expert in the art as he and knew secrets of resistance that few could break. As for me, I rejoiced at the prospect of silent triumph over the white-hot sitting spike, the drill of the eye, the slow nibbling of the flesh.

But this contest was not to be mine. The flabby, debauched faces of Zinxong and Quon-ling alike were drawn in terror by the terrible bellow that now sounded through the chamber like a thousand bone trumpets. The flaggings of the floor beneath us began to spew forth like froth from the cataract. As many of the godless Yellow Hats succumbed to the rain of stones, the two traitors released me and sought futile shelter. More Red Hats, having procured their own weapons, rounded the corner into the hall and stood transfixed at the sight that greeted them.

Where moments ago only cringing and fleeing human forms had stood now towered the form of a god. Its massive bulk rolled with surprising speed over the piles of bodies now collecting on the floor. With fleshy tendrils and ropy coils it grasped hapless monk and heretic alike, as a frog might retrieve a juicy fly. Even for the steeled eye of a master of torment it was not easy to look upon men's skulls as they crumbled from within, sucked empty of all contents. Once-firm limbs shrank and bonelessly rolled up like emptied sleeves and stockings.

Why, I wondered in pious horror, did the blessed Yag-Kosha not distinguish between the righteous and the wicked? I stood aghast, panting in terror against the base of one of the support columns. So far the swinging tentacles had not sought me out. For this I could not account, except it be that the great lord understood that I had summoned him and had mercy on me alone.

Then it was that I beheld the half-torn form of the perfidious Zinxong being slowly borne by a mighty arm toward the ravening maw of the feaster. "Fool!" he gasped. "It is not who you think! It is Chaugnar you have summoned, the doom of us all!" And with that his skull snapped like a cracked almond.

And now I perceived that the terrible form before me bore but faint resemblance to the noble lines of the mighty elephant. What had seemed the fan-like ears were in fact rudimentary membranous wings. What seemed an elegant trunk was a central proboscidian tentacle. All else was madness with no comprehensible form. Now at last I understood the ancient parable of the blind men and the elephant. The form of Chaugnar was such that no mortal eye could grasp it and retain sanity.

When it was over, I, Mu Sang, stood alone and vindicated as the keeper of the sacred monastery of Tsang. Mine was the honor to have opened the portal of worlds to Great Chaugnar, to have awakened him from his sated sleep of ages, and to have summoned him from that distant world where he alone remained alive, all its creatures having fed his eternal hunger.

And now I was chosen. My task it is to serve him as he sleeps content and full. But the ages must pass, and one day he shall awaken again, when the gnawing pangs grow too great.

This is my prophecy, and now I go to seal it up for the day that he shall find it whom Chagnar has chosen to succeed me.

Iä! Chaugnar fhtagn!

I read and reread the thing. Dawn came up. Noon passed. Realization grew upon me. I not only understood what the strange manuscript meant, I also understood what it meant that I understood it. It was I who had brought the party of men to the Plateau of Tsang and disturbed its dust of ages. In fact, I guess it was I who provided bloody Chaugnar with his breakfast after his long sleep. Where was he now? From what I had read, I knew he could hardly be confined to space as we are. Maybe Madame Blavatsky would have known how to explain it. I didn't. But I knew it had to be waiting.

I took some pills and finally got some sleep. The next day I began wondering what might have happened to all the rest of the bearers. Did their wailings to Allah protect them in the end? There's no way to trace them. I didn't even know most of their names. But I did make some calls to my camera men. The tearful wife of one of them told me he had been inexplicably mauled in Central Park. When people rushed to the scene there had been no sign of the assailant. None of the others could be reached, but I had a hunch I'd be hearing similar stories soon. All these poor bastards had actually trespassed on Chaugnar's sacred ground, where the priest Mu Sang had brought him. I was the only one to get away. Maybe now it would be over. Maybe I was able to flee the destiny after all. But what if I hadn't?

I got a sick feeling when I thought of Joey. Haven't got up the nerve to call his wife yet. I'm hoping Professor Harding's okay, but I shouldn't kid myself, I guess. I had, I now realized, randomly chosen to copy and then read aloud the part of the manuscript which includes the prayer of summoning for Chaugnar. He must have made the trip. I guess it'll go on till he's satisfied again and sleeps like I do after Thanksgiving dinner. It took only a few dozen before. Maybe it won't be many more this time.

But what about old Mu Sang? Did he finally escape? How do I know how long he lived after he finished his manuscript? I'm just about done with mine. For all I know, I may be next on the menu.

Death Is an Elephant

Robert Bloch

It came as a shock to me, when putting together the Arkham House collection *Flowers from the Moon and Other Lunacies,* that Robert Bloch had written a tale featuring Chaugnar Faugn. I knew I would have to reprint it here. Bloch returns to the ultimate origin of Chaugnar in the mytheme of the Sacred Elephant in India and plays up that angle. The story shares with Long's "The Horror from the Hills" the basic *fabula* of supernatural vengeance wreaked upon thick-headed Westerners who dare make a public spectacle of the Elephant God of the East. It is also the basic plot of *King Kong,* though the divine monster there is a gorilla. Come to think of it, the same plot forms the basis of *Horton Hatches the Egg,* too. You don't suppose Dr. Seuss's elephant could be yet another avatar of Chaugnar? And then what about Babar . . .?

"Death Is an Elephant" made its debut in *Weird Tales,* February 1939. Bloch wrote it based on ideas supplied him by Nathan Hindin, and the story appeared under Hindin's name, not Bloch's.

"Death is an elephant
Torch-eyed and horrible
Foam-flanked and terrible."
—Vachel Lindsay, "The Congo."

It's not the easiest job in the world, this being press agent for a circus. The ordinary routine is bad enough, what with temperamental stars and equally temperamental newspaper men to deal with. There are a thousand angles to every story, and a thousand tricks to play in order to get that story printed.

But the very devil of it is, the best stories are those which can never be printed: fascinating, mysterious, incredible stories set against the background of circus glamour—stories which I can never write—that's the worst side of this business.

Of course, there's a way out, and I'm taking it. The queer business about the animal trainer, Captain Zaroff, has already seen publication; with radical changes in the names of the principals involved.

I have an itch to see the yarns in print; there's ink in my blood, as the boys say.

Particularly when the tales are true; then there comes a time when I can no longer suppress the urge to reveal them to the world.

Such a story and such a time is here again. Hence this document, with names, dates, and slight details altered—but with a strange story, to the truth of which my eyes can testify; for I was there to see it all. I saw the horror when first it crept from its lair in the jungle hills; I saw it stalk and strike. Sometimes I wish I could forget that striking, but still I dream. I dream of an elephant with blazing eyes, and feet that are blood-red. Blood-red. . . . But this is the tale.

In the fall of '36, Stellar Brothers Circus went into winter quarters and plans were begun for the following year, and a new show. The old man and I knew what we wanted and what the public always wants—novelty. But where to find that novelty? It's the perennial question which drives the entertainment world mad. Clowns, animals, acrobats—these are the eternal backbone of the circus's attraction; but novelty is the drawing-card.

Two weeks of planning, pondering, and bickering got us no place. The question of a novel star feature remained unsettled. To add to the confusion, the old man was in bad shape physically. As a result he left the whole situation in the balance, threw up the work, and sailed for a six-weeks' trip abroad.

Naturally, I accompanied him. I managed to see that the papers played it up in the right way; the boss was traveling to secure a mysterious foreign attraction for next year's show—an attraction so important that he personally would handle the affair.

This sounded pretty good, but it left us in a spot. We had to come back with something that lived up to expectations, and I swear neither of us had the faintest ideas as to what it could be. It was up to Fate to deal the aces.

A Pacific crossing took us to Honolulu; thence to the Philippines. Gradually the old man's temper improved, and my own spirits were raised. After all, we were heading for the Orient, and there's plenty of circus material there. The best jugglers, acrobats, tumblers and freaks are found in the East, and as for animals and natural oddities, the woods are full of them.

Acting on a hunch, I cabled George Gervis in Singapore. Gervis is an animal man; a trapper and collector of circus beasts who knows the tropics like a book. I felt confident that he'd have something new for us, and arranged to meet him.

And that's how we got the Sacred White Elephant of Jadhore.

Gervis explained the situation carefully that first afternoon as we sat in his hotel room. I've known George for a number of years, and never have I seen him so excited. He tried hard to speak casually of the matter, and emphasize the fact that we had only an outside chance, but enthusiasm fairly oozed from him.

Briefly, the situation as he outlined it was this. Jadhore is one of the smaller principalities of the Malay States, under British protectorate. The natives are ruled by their own hereditary rajah; for unlike the majority of the Straits Settlements, the inhabitants are more Hindoo than Moslem. They have their own priesthood, their own government—under British jurisdiction. For years it had been the custom of the English government to pay the rajah an annuity; this, in turn, maintained the dignity and splendor of his court.

At this time, however, the annuity had for some reason been discontinued, and the present rajah was in sore straits for money. If his splendor as a potentate diminished, he would lose face before the eyes of his own people and neighboring kingdoms. And this rajah, in accordance with the tenets of his faith, had a Sacred White Elephant. Now if we could tactfully broach the matter in such a way as not to offend the religious scruples of the rajah or his priests; well—there was our attraction!

It sounded like a natural to me. Evidently the old man felt the same way, for he immediately gave Gervis *carte blanche* in the matter and sent him off to Jadhore to negotiate the transaction.

It was nearly a week later that he returned—a very anxious and fretful week for the old man and myself, for we were fighting against time.

Gervis had not brought the Sacred Elephant with him, but he had come to terms. These he now outlined for us.

The rajah definitely refused to sell the animal. His religious principles absolutely forbade the sacrilege. After consultation with the priests, however, he offered to rent the beast to the show for one season, provided that certain stipulations be made.

The animal must not be trained nor molested in any way. It must not be decorated, nor allowed to mingle with common pachyderms. It could, however, be placed on exhibition, and take part in any parades or processionals that were a feature of the performance. Special food and quarters would have to be provided as a matter of course. In addition, the rajah himself must be allowed to travel with the show, as guarantor of the Sacred Elephant's safety to the priests. Native attendants would be provided by the priests as well, and certain religious ceremonials must not be interfered with.

Such were the terms Gervis had agreed to. He had inspected the animal, and pronounced it to be a splendid specimen of its kind—abnormally large for the Indian elephant, and quite handsome.

At the conclusion of this report the old man blew up.

"Animal be damned!" he shouted. "I can't buy it, I can't train it, can't use it in the regular show. Can't even handle it myself—got to let a two-bit rajah and a gang of nigger priests feed it and burn incense in front of its trunk! What's the use? Special quarters, too—a gold freight car, I suppose. How much did you say?—seventeen hundred a week rental and expenses? Of all the———"

Here the boss demonstrated his restored health by going off into one of the profane tirades for which he is justly famous. I waited for him to cool a bit before I stuck my oar in.

Then I quietly pointed out certain obvious facts. These terms—they sounded difficult, but really were just what we wanted. Novelty—we'd play up the restrictions ourselves. "The Sacred White Elephant of Jadhore—Accompanied by the Priests of Worshipping Millions! See the Sacred Rites of the Jungle Temples! Personally Accompanied by the Illustrious Char Dzang, Rajah of Jadhore!" And so on.

I recalled for his benefit the success of the old white elephant importation of other days, which resulted in the famous Barnum-Forepaugh feud. Barnum's white elephant was a great success, and Adam Forepaugh, a rival circus-owner, thereupon took an ordinary beast and whitewashed its hide. The subsequent exposure of this hoax and the resultant publicity attendant had made fortunes for both men.

I showed the old man how the religious angle would pack them in. We'd play up the sanctity, the restrictions, the priests and attendants. And imagine a circus with a real rajah! Why, this was an attraction that would sell itself—no other build-up was needed.

When I had finished I knew from the look on the old man's face that my case was won.

"How soon can you arrange to get the animal down here?"

"Within two days," the animal-man promptly replied.

"Get going," said the old man, lighting a fresh cigar. Then to me, "Come on. We're heading for the steamship office."

II.

True to his promise, Gervis returned on the third morning. We were already on the dock, waiting, for the boat sailed at noon. Passage had been arranged, quarters for the beast made ready; cables had been sent ahead to winter quarters. And I had just released a story that met with instant success. It was therefore with an air of pleased anticipation that we greeted the arrival of our prize and regal guests.

Nor was our first glimpse disappointing. Today, in view of the sinister aftermath of the whole affair, it seems almost incredible that we so blithely accepted our acquisitions; that we did not realize even then the curious and disturbing features of the itinerary. But that morning, as the procession came down the dock, I felt quite proudly satisfied with our work.

Two swarthy Hindoos led the way—little, turbaned, bearded men, clad in robes of purple and gold. Their hands held silvered chains, for they were leading the Sacred Elephant.

The mighty beast lumbered into view—I gasped a bit, I confess. Never had I seen an elephant like this! Fully ten feet tall was the White Elephant of Jadhore; a giant among the East Indian pachyderms. It had long, gleaming white tusks that swept outward from its massive jaws like twin sabers. Its trunk and hooves were enameled in gold, and on its back rested a howdah of hammered brass. But the color!

I had expected, from what I'd read, that a white elephant was a sort of sickly gray-skinned creature. This beast was almost silver; a leprous silver. From its oiled body glinted little shafts of scintillating light. It looked unreal, unearthly, yet magnificent.

At a word of command the beast halted and surveyed us with smoldering little eyes that rested like red rubies in a silver skull.

The occupants of the howdah dismounted and came forward, and again I was astonished. The rajah of Jadhore wore an ordinary business suit, and his face was clean-shaven in contrast to the bushy beards of the attendants. He wore a green turban that seemed utterly incongruous in comparison to the modern attire. It seemed even more incongruous when he greeted us in perfect English.

"Are we ready, gentlemen?" he inquired. "Have arrangements been made to take this—er—sacred tub aboard ship? My men want to handle it, of course; there are certain religious restrictions against crossing water, y'know."

I stared at him, and I saw the old man's eyebrows rise in surprise as the rajah lit a cigarette and calmly tossed the match beneath the Sacred Elephant's gilded feet. He took charge of the situation.

"It was stipulated in the agreement, gentlemen, that the beast was to have a permanent religious attendant. Allow me to present her—the High Priestess of the Temple of Ganesha."

He beckoned the figure in the background to come forward. Out of the shadow cast by the elephant's body stepped a girl. And for the third time that morning I uttered a low murmur of surprise.

Now I understood the meaning of that beauty of which Oriental poets sing. For this woman was lovely past all understanding or describing. She was dressed in a robe of white, but the lissome curves of her perfectly molded body shone through her garments and caused all memory of them to be forgotten. Her hair was ebon as the jungle night, but it was coiled like a crown above a face of such bewitching perfection as to render powerless even a press-agent's powers of portrayal.

Was it the ripe scarlet blossom of her mouth, the gem-like facets of her high bronze cheeks, the creamy marble of her sweeping brow that so blended into a blaze of indescribable beauty? Or was it her eyes—those great green jewels with tawny flecks glittering in a serpent stare? There was icy wisdom here as well as loveliness; the woman had the look of Lilith about her. Woman, girl, priestess; she was all three as she gazed at us, acknowledging all introductions in calm silence.

"Leela speaks no English," the rajah explained.

Leela! Lilith! Green eyes—priestess of mystery. For the first time I was aware of an inner disturbance. I sensed now the reality of what we were doing; we were dabbling in sacred spheres. And I knew that this woman did not like us; that she scorned and hated this prostitution of her religion. We had made a dangerous opponent, I mused.

The truth of my surmise was soon to be horribly revealed.

In due time the elephant was hoisted aboard the ship and deposited in special quarters within the hold. The attendants and Leela accompanied the animal; the rajah joined us. At noon, we sailed from Singapore.

The old man and I found the rajah a likable fellow. He was, as I suspected, educated in England; his present life frankly bored him. We found it easy to converse with him about our plans for the circus, and told him how we intended to use the elephant in the procession and build quarters in the menagerie tent. I even proposed that the High Priestess be a member of the Grand Entry number, riding in the howdah on the beast's back.

Here the rajah looked grave. No, he declared, the idea was out of the question. Leela was sacred; she would never consent. Besides, she had opposed the entire venture, and the priests had upheld her. It was best not to cross her, for she had mystic powers.

"Well," I interjected. "Surely you don't believe all that Oriental bosh."

For the first time the rajah of Jadhore lost his carefully-acquired British aplomb.

"I do," he said slowly. "If you were not ignorant of my people and their ways, you would also know that there are many things in my religion which you of the West cannot explain. Let me tell you, my friend, what the High-Priestess means to our faith.

"For thousands of years there has been a temple of Ganesha, the Elephant-God, in our land. The Sacred White Elephant holds His Divine Spirit, bred through generations of the animals. The White Elephant is not like others, my friends. You noticed that.

"The God of my people is more ancient than your Christian one, and master of darker forces which only the jungle peoples know and can invoke. Nature-demons and beast-men are recognized today by your scientists; but priests of my simple people have controlled strange forces before ever Christ or Buddha trod the earth. Ganesha is not a benevolent god, my friend. He has always been worshipped under many names—as Chaugnar Faugn, in the old places of Tibet; and as Lord Tsathoggua aforetime. And He is evil—that is why we treat His incarnation in the White Elephant as sacred. That is why there have always been High Priestesses in his temple; they are the holy brides and consorts of the Elephant One. And they are wise; bred from childhood in the black arts of worship, they commune with the beasts of the forest and serve to avert the wrath of the evil ones from their people."

"You believe that?" laughed the old man.

"Yes," said the rajah, and he was no longer smiling. "I believe. And I must warn you. This trip, as you must have heard, is against the wishes of my priesthood. Never has a Sacred Elephant crossed the great waters to another land, to be gaped at by unbelievers for a show. The priests feel that it is an insult to the Lord Ganesha. Leela was sent with the elephant by the priests for a purpose—she alone can guard it. And she hates you for what you're doing; hates me, too. I—I don't like to speak of what she can do. There are still human sacrifices in our temples at certain times, of which the Government knows nothing. And human sacrifices are made with a purpose—the old dark powers I spoke of can be invoked by blood. Leela has officiated at such rites, and she has learned much. I don't want to frighten you—it's really my fault for consenting to this—but you should be warned. Something may happen."

The old man hastened to reassure the rajah. He was smugly certain that the man was nothing but a savage beneath his veneer of superficial culture, and he spoke accordingly.

As for me, I wondered. I thought again of Leela's eery eyes, and imagined easily enough that they could gaze on bloody sacrifice without flinching. Leela could know evil, and she could hate. I remembered the rajah's final words, "Something may happen."

I went out on deck, entered the hold. The elephant stood in his stall, placidly munching hay. Leela stood stolidly beside him as I inspected the animal's chains. But I felt her eyes bore into my back when I turned away, and noticed that the Hindoo attendants carefully avoided me.

Other passengers had got wind of our prize, and they filed into the hold in a steady stream. As I left, a fellow named Canrobert strolled up. We chatted for several minutes, and when I went up on deck he was still standing there before the beast. I promised to meet him in the bar that evening for a chat.

At dinner a steward whispered to me the story. Canrobert had come up from the hold late in the afternoon, walked to the rail in plain view of several passengers, and jumped overboard. His body was not recovered.

I took part in the investigation which followed. During the course of it we ventured down into the hold. The elephant still stood there, and Leela was still keeping watch beside him. But now she was smiling.

III.

I never did learn about the death of a man named Phelps on the third day out. But it was a hoodoo voyage for certain, and I was glad when we disembarked at last and headed for winter quarters.

I am a practical man, but I get occasional "hunches." That is why I avoided the rajah during the rest of our homeward journey. I fled when he approached, because I felt that he would have an explanation for the deaths of the two men—an explanation I did not care to hear. I didn't go near Leela nor the elephant either, and spent most of my time doping out the show with the old man.

It was good to see winter quarters again. A handsome stall had been built for the Sacred Elephant, and Ganesha (for so we had christened the beast) was quartered therein.

No greater compliment could have been paid to my advance publicity than the attention shown the beast by our hardened circus folk. Stars and supers alike, they crowded around the stall, eyed the mighty animal, gazed at the silent bearded attendants, and stared in speechless admiration at Leela. The rajah struck up an immediate acquaintance with Captain Dence, our regular elephant-keeper.

I immediately plunged into work with the old man, for the show opened shortly.

Therefore it wasn't until several weeks later that I began to hear the disquieting rumors that floated around the lot concerning our star attraction.

The restlessness of the other elephants, for example—how, in rehearsal for the Grand Entry, they shied away from the Sacred Ganesha, and trumpeted nightly in their picket line. The queer story of how the foreign woman *lived* in the stall with the animal; ate and slept there in stolid silence. The way in which one of the clowns had been frightened while passing through the animal barn one evening; how he had seen the two Hindoos and the girl bowing in worship before the silver beast, who stood amidst a circle of incense fires.

Even the old man mentioned a visit from the rajah and Captain Dence during which both men pleaded to break the contract and allow the animal and its attendants to return to Jadhore before the show opened. They spoke wildly of "trouble" to come. The proposal was of course rejected as being out of the question; our publicity was released, and both men were evidently under the influence of liquor at the time.

Two days later Captain Dence was found hanging from a beam behind the elephant-line. It was a case of suicide beyond question, and there was no investigation. We had a show funeral, and for a while a gloomy shadow overcast our lot. Everyone remarked about the shocking look of horror on poor Dence's death-distorted face.

About this time I began to wake up. I determined to find out a few things for myself. The rajah was almost always intoxicated now, and he seemed to avoid me purposely; staying in town and seldom visiting the lot. I know for a fact that he never again entered the menagerie barn.

But I learned that others did. Perhaps it was morbid curiosity; but the show-folk, even after their first trips of inspection, seemed to spend much of their time around the elephant lines. Shaw, our new keeper, told me that they were continually before the stall of the Sacred Elephant. In his own opinion many of the men performers were stuck on that "pretty foreign dame." They stared at her and at the elephant for hours on end; even the big stars came.

Corbot, the trapeze artist, was a frequent visitor. So was Jim Dolan, the acrobatic clown, and Rizzio, our equestrian director.

Another was Captain Blade, our knife-thrower in the sideshow. What they found in the woman he couldn't say, for she never spoke and they were silent.

I could make nothing of this report. But I determined to watch the beautiful High Priestess for myself.

I got into the habit of sauntering through the menagerie at odd hours and glancing at the Sacred Elephant. Whatever the time of day, there was Leela, her emerald eyes burning into my back. Once or twice I saw some of the performers gazing raptly at the stall. I noticed that they came singly at all times. Also I saw something which proved the keeper's theory to be wrong.

They were not infatuated with the woman, for they looked only at the elephant! The gigantic beast stood like some silver statue; impassive, inscrutable. Only its glistening oiled trunk moved to and fro; that, and its fiery eyes. It seemed to stare mockingly in return, as though contemptuous of attentions from the puny creatures before it.

Once, when the place was deserted, I saw Leela caressing its great body. She was whispering to it in some low and outlandish tongue, but her voice was ineffably sweet and her hands infinitely tender. I was struck by a curious and somewhat weird thought—this woman was acting toward the beast as a woman in love acts toward her lover! I remembered how the rajah spoke of her as the bride of Ganesha, and winced. When the animal's serpentine trunk embraced the lovely girl she purred in almost blissful satisfaction, and for the first time I heard the beast rumble in its massive throat. I left, quickly so as to be unobserved.

Opening day loomed, and once again I was forced to turn my mind to other things. The cars were loaded for Savannah; the dress rehearsal was performed; I sent the advance men on the night before we left, and the regular routine got under way.

The old man was pleased with the show, and I must admit that it was the best we'd ever turned out. Corbot, the trapeze artist, was a good drawing card; we got him from the big show through sheer good fortune. Jim Dolan, the chief clown, was always a draw. We had some fine animal acts, and many novelty features as well. And the Sacred Elephant of Jadhore was bidding fair to become a household name before the public had ever seen it.

We had a private car for the animal and its three attendants; the two Hindoos smiled happily when they saw it, and even Leela was slightly taken aback with its splendor. On our arrival under canvas the beast was installed in a superb new station atop a platform in the center, and with its hide newly oiled and decorated it looked superb.

The menagerie crowd on the opening day was highly impressed. They stared at the impassive Hindoos and positively gaped at Leela in her white ceremonial gown. The rajah they did not see—he was shaking drunk in his own quarters, behind locked doors.

I didn't even have time to think of the superstitious coward. I'm like a kid when a new show opens each year, and the old man is no different. We sat in our box and positively beamed with joyous excitement as the trumpet blasts announced the Grand Entry.

Our procession was Oriental—Arabian riders, Egyptian seers on camels, harem beauties on elephants, califs and sultans in jeweled litters. At the very last came the Sacred White Elephant of Jadhore; the mightiest of them all. The great silver beast moved with a sort of monstrous beauty; in regal dignity Ganesha padded on to the beat of thundering drums. The two Hindoos led the way, but Leela was not present. The great spotlight followed every step; so did the eyes of the crowd. I can't explain it, but there was *something* about the animal which "clicked." It had beauty—and that unearthly majesty I had noticed. It was the Sacred Elephant indeed.

The procession vanished. The show was on. Sleek black ponies galloped into the rings, and whips cracked in merry rhythm with their hooves. The music altered its tempo; the clowns strutted in to do the first of their walk-arounds. Applause, laughter, and the ever-beating rhythm of the band. Excitement, as the jugglers vied with a troupe of seals in dextrous competition.

The star acts were coming up, and I nudged the old man to attract his special attention.

With a flurry of drums the big spot in the center ring blazed forth as the other lights dimmed. Alonzo Corbot, the trapeze star, raced in. His white body bounded across the ring to the ropes beneath the main pole where his partner waited.

The snare-drums snarled as the two performers mounted up—up—up—sixty feet in the air to the platform and the trapeze rings.

Out they swung now, silver bodies on silver rings; out into the cold clear light that bathed the utter emptiness of the tent-top. Swing—swoop—soar; rhythmically rise, unfalteringly fall. Tempo in every movement of the clutching hands; timing even in the feet that danced on empty air.

Corbot was a marvel; I'd seen him work in rehearsal many times and was never tired of watching the perfection of motion he displayed. He trained rigorously, I knew; and he never slipped. He caught his partner by the hand, the wrist, the elbow, the shoulder, the neck, the ankle. Feet suspended from the rings, he shot to and fro like a human pendulum while his partner somersaulted through space into his waiting hands. At precisely the exact fraction of a second they met in midair; an error in timing meant certain death. There were no nets—that was Corbot's boast.

I watched, the old man watched, the audience watched, as two men fluttered like tiny birds so far above. Birds? They were demons with invisible wings now in the red light that flashed on for the climax of the act. Now came the time when Corbot and his partner would both leave the rings, leap out into that dizzying space and turn a complete somersault in midair, then grasp the rings on the opposite side of their present position.

The drums went mad. The red light glared on that little hell of high space where two men waited, their nerves and muscles tense.

I could almost feel it myself—that moment of dread expectancy. My eyes strained through the crimson haze, seeking Corbot's face so far above. He would be smiling now; he was preparing to leap . . .

Drums, cymbals crashed. The waiting figures sprang. Corbot's arms were ready to grasp his partner in whirling space—or were they? Good God, no—*they were stiff at his side!*

There was a streaking blur crossing that empty scarlet expanse of light, and then it was gone. Something struck the center ring with a heavy thud. Somebody screamed, the band blared a desperate march, and the lights went up. I saw that Corbot's partner Victoire had saved himself by catching a ring just in time, but my eyes did not linger above. They centered themselves on the ground; on the center ring where something lay in a pool of crimson that came from no light.

Then the old man and I were out of our box and running across the tent with attendants at our side. And we stared for a sickening second at that boneless pulpy red thing that had once been Alonzo Corbot the trapeze star. They took him away; fresh sawdust covered the spot where he had fallen, and the band, the lights, the music covered the audience's panic until their fears were forgotten. The clowns were out again as the old man and I left, and the crowd was laughing—a bit weakly, perhaps, but laughing nevertheless. Corbot's hail and farewell was typical; the show went on.

Victoire, the partner, staggered in as we gathered by the body in the dressing-room. Pale, limp, badly shaken, he wept convulsively when he saw—it—lying there.

"I knew it!" he gasped. "When he stood on the other platform just before he leaped, I saw his eyes. They were dead and far away. Dead . . . No, I don't know how it happened. Of course he was all right before the show. I hadn't seen him much lately; between rehearsals he spent a lot of time some place. . . . His eyes were dead. . . ."

We never learned anything more from Victoire. The boss and I hurried through the menagerie to the main office. As we passed the big platform where the Sacred Elephant was quartered, I noticed with a shock that it was empty of attendants. Something brushed against me in the dark as I hurried on. It was Leela, the High-Priestess, and she was smiling. I had never seen her smile before.

That night I dreamed of Leela's smile, and Corbot's redly ruined face. . . .

IV.

There's only a little more to tell. For that I'm thankful, because the rest is even now a nightmare I would rather forget. We learned nothing of Corbot's death from anyone. It created a flurry, of course, and the performers' nerves were shattered. After all, an opening-day tragedy like that is disquieting.

The old man raved, but there was nothing to do. The show went on; the morbid public swarmed in that second day, for despite my efforts publicity was released.

Nor was the morbid public disappointed. For on the second night, our fourth show—Jim Dolan died.

Jim was our acrobatic clown, and a star in his own right. He'd been with us twelve seasons, always doing his regular routine of juggling and pantomime.

We all knew Jim and liked him as a friend. He was a great kidder; nothing of the pagliaccio about Dolan. But on that second evening he stopped for a moment in his routine before the center ring, put down his juggling-clubs, pulled out a razor, and calmly slit his throat.

How we got through that night is still a mystery to me. "Jinx" and "hoodoo" were the only two words I heard. The show went on, the boss raved, and the police quietly investigated.

The following afternoon Rizzio, our equestrian director, walked into the line of the bareback routine, and a horse's hoof broke his spine.

I'll never forget that twilight session after the show, in the old man's tent. Neither of us had slept for two days; we were sick with fear and nameless apprehension. I've never believed in "curses," but I did then. And so I looked at the official reports and the headlines in the papers, glanced at the old man's gray face, and buried my own in my arms. There was a curse on the show.

Death! I'd walked with it for weeks now. Those two chaps on the boat, then Captain Dence, the elephant man, then Corbot, Dolan, Rizzio. Death—ever since we had taken the Sacred White——

The rajah's words! His story about curses and queer rites; the vengeance of the god and his priests! The Priestess Leela, who smiled now! Hadn't I heard stories about the performers visiting the elephant's stall?—why, all three of the men who died here in the show had done that! The rajah knew—and I had thought him a drunken coward.

I sent a man off to find him. The old man, utterly collapsed, slept. I spent an anxious hour waiting.

The rajah entered. A glance at my face told him the story.

"You know now?" he said. "I thought you would never come to your senses. I could do nothing without your belief, for *she* knows I understand, and she hates me. I have tried very hard to forget; but now men die and this thing must be stopped. Ganesha may send me to a thousand hells for this, but it is better so. It is magic, my friend."

"How do you know?" I whispered.

"I know." He smiled wearily, but there was black despair in his eyes. "I watched from the beginning. She is cunning, that Leela, so very cunning. And she knows *arts*."

"What arts?"

"You of the West call it hypnotism. It is more than that. It is transference of will. Leela is an adept; she can do it easily with the elephant as medium."

I tried vainly to understand. Was the rajah crazed? No—his eyes burned not with derangement but with bitter hatred.

"Post-hypnotic suggestion," he breathed. "When the fools came to watch the Sacred Elephant, she was always there. Her eyes did it; and when they watched the gleaming trunk of the beast it acted as a focal point. They came back again and again, not knowing why. And all the while she was willing them to act; not then, but later. That is how the two men died on the boat. She experimented there; told them to drown themselves. One went immediately, the other waited several days. All that was needed was for them to see her once at the time she willed for them to die. Thus it was. And here, in the menagerie, it has been the same way. They stare at the silver elephant. She willed them to die during the performance. At the proper time she stood in the entrance-way; I have seen her there. And the men died—you saw that.

"She hates the show, and will ruin it. To her the worship of Ganesha is sacred, and she is wreaking vengeance. The old priests that sent her must have instructed this, and there must be an end. That is why I dare not face her."

"What's to be done?" I found myself asking. "If your story is true, we can't touch her. And we can't give up the show."

"I will stop her," said the rajah slowly. "I must."

Suddenly, he was gone. And I realized with a start that the show was almost ready to begin. Quickly I roused the old man from his slumber. Then I dashed out. Collaring a roustabout, I ordered him to find the rajah at once. There would be a showdown tonight; there must be.

I had two guards with guns secretly posted at the side entrance to the tent, where the performers came in. They had orders to stop anyone who loitered there during the show. There must be no Leela watching and commanding that night.

I dared not incarcerate her at once for fear of a row while the show was on. The woman was evidently capable of anything, and she must not suspect. Still, I wanted to see her for myself. A half-hour before the menagerie opened I hurried in. The elephant's stall was again untended!

I ran around to the side entrance. There was no one there. Out on the midway I raced, mingling with the crowd. Then it was that I noticed the excited throng before the side show. Elbowing through, I came upon two men and the barker as they emerged from the tent carrying a limp form in their arms. It was the girl assistant of Captain Blade, the knife-thrower. He had missed.

Leela passed me in the crowd, smiling. Her face was beautiful as Death.

When I rushed back to the boss tent, I found the roustabout and the rajah. The latter was trembling in every limb.

Hastily I collared the potentate and dragged him through the crowd toward the main tent.

"I believe you now," I whispered. "But you're not going to do anything rash. Give me your knife."

I'd guessed correctly. He slipped a dirk out of his sleeve and passed it to me unobserved.

"No more bloodshed," I muttered. "I have two men at the side entrance. She'll not watch *this* show and cast any spells. When the performance is over, I'll have her behind bars on your testimony. But no disturbance before the crowd."

I shouldered my way into my regular box and he followed after me.

The big tent was crowded. There was an air of grim waiting, as if the spectators were *expecting* something. I knew what they expected; hadn't the papers been full of "the Hoodoo Circus" for the past three days? There was a low murmur as of massed whispering voices. I thought of a Roman amphitheater and shuddered.

The big drums rolled. The parade swept into view, and I cast an anxious glance at the side entrance when it cleared. There were my two guards, armed with efficient-looking guns. No trouble tonight! And the rajah was safe, with me.

The Sacred Elephant swept into view; serene, majestic, lumbering gigantically on ivory hoofs. There was only one Hindoo leading him tonight and—the howdah was on his back!

In it sat—Leela, the High Priestess of Ganesha.

"She knows," breathed the rajah, his brown face suddenly animal-like with convulsed terror.

Leela was smiling. . . .

Then horror came.

The lights flickered, failed, blinked out. The vast tent plunged into nighted darkness and the band ceased. There was a rising wail of sound, and I rose in my seat with a scream on my lips.

There in the darkness glowed the silver elephant—the Sacred White Elephant of Jadhore. Like a leprous monster, its body gleamed with phosphorescent fire. And in the darkness I saw Leela's eyes.

The elephant had turned now, and left the parade. As shrieks rose in a thousand throats it thundered forward—straight for our box.

The rajah broke from my grasp and vaulted over the railing to the ground. My hand flew to my pocket and I cursed in dismay. The knife he had given me was gone. Then my eyes returned to the hideous tableau before me.

The elephant charged with lifted trunk, tusks glistening before it. There was a shrill trumpeting from its silver throat as it bore down on the slight figure of the man who raced toward it.

He ran to death, but his head was high. He was seeking that black figure in the howdah on the beast's back.

In a moment everything was over. A gleaming arc in the air as something long and thin and silver whizzed up to the elephant's back. A woman's shrill scream and gurgling sob. A mighty bellowing of brutish, berserk rage. A thud of massive feet as the silver giant trampled on. The crunching . . . the screams, the shots, and the great shock as the great body turned and fell.

And then the audience rose and fled. When the lights went on once more, there was nobody in the tent but the performers and the roustabouts.

In the center of the areaway lay the gigantic Ganesha, silver sides streaked with scarlet in death. The crumpled howdah held all that remained of Leela the High Priestess. The rajah's knife had struck home, and her torn throat was not a pretty sight.

As for the rajah himself, there was only a slashed red horror dangling on the end of those ivory tusks; a mashed and pulpy thing.

Thus ended the affair of the Sacred White Elephant. The police accepted our story of the animal's running amok during the show when the lights failed.

They never learned of the Hindoo who had so horribly short-circuited the connection with his own body, and we buried his seared remains in secret.

The show closed for two weeks and we re-routed it for the rest of the year. Gradually, the papers let the story die and we went on.

I never told the truth to the old man. They're all dead anyway, and I'd like to forget it myself. But I have never liked novelty acts since, nor visited the Orient; because I know the rajah's story was true, and Leela had killed those performers as he had explained it. Those priests and priestesses have secret powers, I am convinced.

I've figured it all out—Leela found out that the rajah had told me the facts; knew she'd be exposed, and acted accordingly.

She sent the Hindoo to fix the lights, then arranged to have Ganesha the elephant charge our box and kill the rajah as she'd planned.

I have it all figured out, but I'd never tell the old man. There's one other fact I know which I must not reveal.

The rajah's knife did not kill Leela as she rode on the elephant's back. It could not, for she was already dead; dead before she entered the tent.

One of the two guards I stationed had shot her two minutes before at the side entrance as she rode past in the howdah of Ganesha, the Sacred White Elephant.

It seems that she must have hypnotized the beast, too—or did she? The Soul of Ganesha inhabits the body of the Sacred Elephant, the rajah said. And Ganesha wreaks a vengeance of his own.

The Dweller in the Pot

(OR, THE PASTA OUT OF SPACE EATERS)
by Frank Chimesleep Short

Robert M. Price

The premise of this story I owe to two colleagues. The use of Long and Lovecraft as fictional characters continues a tradition begun by Long himself in "The Space-Eaters," though my immediate model was Peter Cannon's *Pulptime* (available in his collection *The Lovecraft Papers*, Guild America Books, n.d.). C. J. Henderson once told me he had an idea involving a kitchen chancing to lie astride an interdimensional nexus. He thought he might use it for an informal tale set in a sequence of "Adventures in Gluttony." These began as tall tales spun around the table during Italian feasts shared between Henderson and the late great artist Roy Krenkel. He never did, so I stole it.

"The Dweller in the Pot" first appeared in the much-lamented British fanzine *Dagon* #27 (June 1990) and was reprinted with one additional joke in *Crypt of Cthulhu* #74 (Lammas 1990).

―――――――――――

Since my friend and longtime correspondent Howard had moved to that "Babylonish Burg" New York City—a relocation, he had sworn months before when the proposition was merely theoretical, he could never be constrained to make under the direst circumstances—it was not uncommon for me to pick up the ringing telephone at well-nigh any hour and hear his high-pitched tones at the other end of the line, summoning me either to a barely affordable expedition through the city's bookstalls or to some adventure in gluttony (this latter may surprise the reader in view of Howard's well-known stature: tall, somewhat stooped—and almost cadaverously thin). On the particular afternoon of which I will write, it was the latter to which Howard's excited, nasal tones beckoned me.

I see I have neglected to tell you how my remarkable friend had chanced to move to the "pest zone," as he fondly called it. What could have motivated this staunch Novanglian Yankee to leave his beloved Providence to plunge into New York's "sewer of ethnic excretions," to swim upstream against the "foetid tides of rat-faced mongrel hordes," as he lightheartedly called them? In fact it was the non-

Aryan charms of a colleague in amateur journalism, his beloved Sonya. Having somehow managed to prompt Howard to break his once-adamantine bond to bachelorhood, she went on to dissolve his tie to his native Providence as well.

It seemed that just now, Sonia was out of town on a buying trip for her fledgling hat business, and Howard found himself left for a week to function in his old bachelor mode. As if to celebrate "the cat's being away," Howard intended to splurge with a big pot full of his favorite spaghetti. This preference in food was itself surprising in view of Howard's aforementioned distaste for any racial group that hailed from without the radius of Northwestern Europe. As the temperature of one's homeland rose, so proportionately did Howard's esteem for one's pedigree plummet. In fact, Howard did not hesitate to broadcast his racialist sentiments, wholly unmoved by my attempts at moderation, at every opportunity. True, he rarely wore his immaculately lettered INFERIOR RACES GO HOME sandwichboard in public, but other avenues for propaganda were ready to hand, amateur journalism being one. Though few readers will be aware of the fact, equally few will be surprised to learn that the title of Howard's famous tale "Dagon" had been shorter by one letter (I leave the reader to imagine which one) and in its first draft depicted the fevered reactions of a shipwrecked mariner beached on the Italian mainland as he witnesses a stout native emerging from the sea to hug the Leaning Tower of Pisa. Here I was able to persuade my friend to a greater degree of subtlety in a second and better-known draft.

But let me cease to linger and press on to linguini. No doubt I hesitate to face the memory of the eldritch events of that evening of eating.

It was with a distinct sense of foreboding that I wended my way, with many an over-the-shoulder glance, through the squalid Red Hook section of Brooklyn close to where Howard lived. I had once wagered that even Howard's febrile imagination could not wrest a truly cosmic spectral tale from what I then viewed as the purely mundane urban decay that formed the environs of his Clinton Street address. Now I was not so sure.

I breathed easier as Howard opened the door promptly to my customary three-two knock.

"Chimesleepius!" he greeted me, simultaneously pumping my hand and patting me on the back, as might a doting grandfather welcoming back his prodigal grandson not seen for years. In fact Howard's proprietary interest in my writing career was genuinely parental though he was only a handful of years my elder.

"Just let your olfactories partake of the bewitching aroma that your old Grandpa has conjured! I make bold to guarantee they've never sniffed the like!"

Indeed they had not. Though I had been party to many of Howard's spaghetti feasts in the past months, this collection of smells was unprecedented. Neither unpleasant nor altogether inviting, the fumes of the bubbling pot seemed almost to awaken a hitherto-dormant sense that nature in her wisdom had long since judged best to breed out of the race. It was only by analogy that it could be called a smell at all.

As Howard doffed his bulbous chef's hat, so disturbingly reminiscent of some bloated, detestable fungus, and his KISS THE COOK apron, he motioned me to take a seat. I complied, rapidly becoming aware of some disquieting sense of cosmic dislocation in the close quarters of the scent-filled apartment. Did I catch the haunting tones of cracked flutes wailing some malignant dirge as if gloating over the impending heat-death of the universe? But then the common sense of the self-blinded earth-gazer reasserted itself, and I recognized the music as proceeding from Howard's much bemoaned Syrian neighbor upstairs.

Howard ladled out a clenched mass of pasta tendrils, dumping them in a smoking heap on the plate in front of me. As I reached for the meat sauce, he strode over to the kitchen counter and took up a large black volume. Holding the folio-sized tome propped against his chest for my perusal, he announced triumphantly, "The recipe comes from this curious cookbook I discovered last evening when some whim moved me to take a late stroll down toward the harbors. When the old Levite who ran the shop saw my interest in gustatory antiquarianism he parted with the volume for a ridiculously small sum. Yes, don't strain yourself, Chimesleepius, it's in Latin all right, but the ingredients are readily enough decipherable for one of my classical erudition."

I could barely make out the faded lettering imprinted on the spine: *De Vermicelli Mysteriis*. I shuddered involuntarily, and my amply laden fork hesitated in its progress to my mouth. Yet offend my enthusiastic host I dared not. I chewed in silence for some moments, considering whether to identify the peculiar taste as surpassingly delicious or unspeakably repugnant. Howard in the meantime had fallen to with gusto. The quizzical look written across his grotesque lantern-jawed visage, now stuffed with pasta and tomato sauce, made clear that he harbored the same cryptical doubts as I.

Howard dished up another platter of the seething stuff, while I reached for coffee (my teetotaling friend would not stock wine even for such an occasion as this) to wash it down.

It seemed that Howard had decided what he thought of the doubtful dish and was about to make some pronouncement to that effect—*when suddenly silenced by one whipping tendril of spaghetti* which unreeled from the spoonful he held ready and wound itself with lightning speed around his head like a gag stopping his open mouth! His eyes started from their sockets; his bony arms began to flail like the wings of a windmill. His chair legs scraped across the floor; momentarily I thought he had leapt back from the table in a gesture of escape. In fact, his gaunt form was being repelled from the table by more animate tentacles seeking to defend themselves against this human devourer.

Myself, I had lost no time in leaping clear of the table, now become an interdimensional gate for trans-cosmic forces so reminiscent of Howard's famous tale "The Call of Calimari." The narrow dimensions of the room afforded little refuge, especially as Howard had cooked up a great mass of the stuff, unwittingly providing more than enough rope to hang himself—and me!

It was clear by now that we were dealing with no recipe ever devised by sane mortals. Poor strangling Howard began to turn purple; I had bare moments to think as I dodged the snapping feelers of extra-cosmic spaghetti. From the corner of my eye I spotted the worm-eaten binding of the cookbook which had become the source not merely of a meal but now, as it seemed, our soul-blasting doom. With a sidewise lunge, I snatched up the evil volume and let it fall open to the place Howard had last opened it.

Holding the place with my finger and trying not to stain the page with sauce (I knew how particular Howard was about the condition of his books), I sought egress via the window and climbed out onto the rusting grate of the fire escape. Slamming the window on a fugitive strand of the evilly sentient pasta, I was revolted to see the severed stalk wiggle like a maggot and fall into the alley below.

I stood shaking with exertion, newly aware of the dropping night temperature, my threadbare overcoat lying useless inside the apartment. I fumbled the book open again, and my eye scanned the page. A quick glance back inside revealed Howard, somehow having freed himself from the gag, perhaps by taking a vicious bite, fencing with his salad fork, in retreat from the questing bands of that amoeboid cluster of living pasta.

My Latin was none too proficient, but I dared hope I might chance to discover some antidote, some counter-recipe that might send the malevolent meal back into its harmless components. Alas, with mocking conciseness the relevant page closed with the epigram, roughly translated. "Do not cook up what you cannot keep down."

I cast the useless volume aside as another idea came to me: Where one book did not serve, another might. As Howard had said between mouthfuls, he was something of an authority on ancient cookery, and more than likely his study contained other volumes which might yield the secret that alone could save us from being ourselves the main course for the ravishing noodles from beyond. I dashed across the fire escape to where it extended under the next window, which opened upon Howard's makeshift study. Kicking in the glass, I jumped heavily into the room, sending the book-laden ottomans and end tables flying. As Howard had often generously pressed upon me the use of his private library for my youthful studies, I had a fair idea of the lay of the land. As my eyes adjusted to the gloom, I quickly found the shelf of cookbooks and squinted at their spines. I knew that Miss Murray's *The Sandwich Cult in Western Europe* would be of little use, as would *Cultes des Goulash*. With but a glance at the all-but-unreadable blackletter pages of the *Unaussprechlichen Kuchen*, I hastened to the one volume that might hold my answer—the abhorred *Home Economicon*.

The sounds of crashing vases and toppling furniture assured me that in the next room Howard continued his valiant struggle, but I knew that unless my own efforts bore fruit very soon, all would be lost.

Luck was with me! Thumbing through the musty pages feverishly, I quickly determined that Howard had used a most potent ingredient, the Cheese of the Goat with a Thousand Young. But, thank God! the solution was a simple one! So simple in fact, that I cursed my stupidity for not thinking of it as soon as I had noticed the lack of a customary ingredient in any Italian recipe. The text, again roughly translated, ran as follows: "Garlic is not a passive agent, but has oft-times appeared in belches in the midst of our covens, scattering all present with its power." If it worked on vampires, why not on sentient spaghetti? I slammed the book shut.

Now, of course, the challenge was to reach Howard's spice cabinet across the room in which he fought tooth and nail with the vague cloud of spaghetti-tentacles. As I cocked my ear to listen for the direction of the struggle, better to aim the headlong plunge for which I had already begun bracing myself, I noticed the sudden echo of silence.

Dread crushed me like a *Weird Tales* rejection slip. Surely my beloved mentor was dead, flayed to a crimson ruin by the threshing stalks of the pasta out of space!

I began to weep, dropping to my knees, cushioning my forehead against my folded arms. Then I heard—and *smelled*—the *belch!* Of course! Howard must have known the contents of his own library! He must instantly have inferred what I had had to discover.

As I rose and entered the kitchen, my suspicions were thankfully confirmed. The struggle had in fact been one rather more of tooth than nail! A bloated Howard, half-empty garlic can in hand, stood by the emptied vessels of a hasty and desperate feast. His apology punctuated by a series of scarcely diminishing gastric explosions, Howard wiped sauce from his mouth and shrugged, "Well, Chime-sleepius, one can't *always* play the gentleman!"

The Dweller in the Pot was vanquished, the pasta out of space consumed. Howard broke out the ice cream.

But It's a Long Dark Road

Joseph S. Pulver, Sr.

What Joe Pulver provides us here is not really a story, though for various reasons we have to pretend it is. I'm doing a pretty bad job of keeping that secret. Actually, as you can see, it is a transcript of a fateful conversation containing some very bad, fatally bad, advice for someone who has a fire in his belly to sing the blues (and have the drugs, the women, and all the other fringe benefits) even if it costs him his soul. The advice is not not to. The whole thing is chilling, a brief crack-opening of the door of the cosmic refrigerator. And the cold truth is the well-known fact that merit alone is anything but a ticket to success. Passage in that direction costs something much more.

Pulver's "tale" (wink, wink) raises an interesting theoretical point about verisimilitude in the Cthulhu Mythos. One thing's for sure: the Mythos entities are supposed to be unknown factors. This is aesthetically important so their appearance can have the effect of a total incursion of the Wholly Other. On the other hand, their mentions in stories usually have them riding piggyback on more familiar mythologies, usually pretty strange to Western readers in their own right. Lovecraft himself did this when he gave his alien gods' names an Egyptian, Arabic, or Tibetan ring (as he explicitly admitted in his letters). Pulver does something similar here by knitting the horror of the Hounds of Tindalos into the damp, coarse fabric of swampland Obeah. Why is this? Doesn't the association of the Mythos with conventional deviltry and occultism blunt its edge? Steal its thunder? Dilute its pungency?

No, I think not. You see, Lovecraft also said that the shocker, the alien assault has to ride in on the tide of convincing mundane detail, hence all the linguistic, archeological, and scientific minutiae Lovecraft's narrators supply. We only find out too late what has hitched a ride and is about to make mincemeat of our reality. Well, "traditional" occultism and diabolism are part of that detail. Oddly, in comparison to, in relation to, the Mythos revelations, even these horrors are only connective tissue. It's just there to soften you up. It's the syrup that makes the foul medicine go down. Remember, Lovecraft realized that the old horrors like vampires and ghouls had to be pepped up by something new, and this was where his "science fiction as horror" innovation made so much sense. The terrors of the Mythos are the unimagined real thing that lurks beneath the folklore with which the human race has cu-

shioned its apprehension of the true horror. Once you experience the dark
epiphany of Tindalos, you wish voodoo were the worst of it!

―――――――――――

Say why ya come, Boy? Ta bring back hellfire? That's a long dark road. Pain an'
voices fill ya . . . Troubles. Awls bad troubles, leaves ya a-crawlin' 'cross da floor—
begging . . . Ya wan know? After that, ya never talk to Good God again. He don'ts
want to know those tetched by da Black Hand.

Just further up da road a-ways. Don't needs no chart, Boy. Just heart ta walk it . . .

Where Old Man Huey's fields comes together. Them crows sit on that post-
sign on da Northside of da Crossroads an' watch . . . I tells ya, Boy, thems perni-
cious eyes seen fire come out the Obeah man's mouth and seen what his three-
finger'd hand brewed in da pot. Seen when da Obeah man put da hair an' bones
an' teeth in there ta boil. And he put other things in that pot, *peculiar things*. My
pappy told me them crows first come one day when he was a chile. Come like
theys church revelers callin', but there ain't no church there less'n it be da church
of walkin' dead mens. An' ya know what's strange? Theys ain't never left. Not even
on da night when da dead mens speak in da voice of a frog. Devils theys be. Devils
come home to roost on them dark corners.

Don'ts cares what theys tell ya, Boy. No spell never tamed the volcanoes at
that Crossroads. Some says theys done-did, but theys didn't.

There's no lobby at da Corners. Eshu's house be dry leaves an' arteries cracked
open. Time out of straight lines, bent wrong ya-know. Recipes for erosion written
in pictures on da Goodbye Road. But no lobby. An' ya don't has to wait on midnight. Just da settin' sun. It bleeds out an' things, hungry things, smudged with
curses or black impurities, comes out to dance . . . an' to prey.

Da moon come up in the sky of mandala clouds. Da stars rattle an' them long
arms comes down from them dark hills. Theys come to open da gates. Ya pour in
woe an' blood—go ahead, spit it right there, right on da worm, an' theys drink that
small hot ocean like it's tea.

Ain't gonna need no compass. Don't need no black robes or roots. Fire-wings
an' guitar-breath do the trick. Ya call, theys comes.

Ya see. Bright as fire in the dead man's eye theys come. Leave lip prints an' paw
prints on skin. The Strays From da Outer, full of nightlines . . . Runnin'. Bad, rollin'
an' tumblin' out da mouth of Hell. Like theys snake bit an' pullin' Ba Doom from
that black bottle. Tell ya, Boy, Old Nontooth Mag Zelma told me when I was nothin' but a chile, theys Hell hounds walk on splinters gilded wit diff'rent . . . Comes
down from da patchs of blackness forgotten in da Unmaking to thems a callin'.

Back in double-ought an' two Zye gots lost, then that boy he comes back . . .
Come back with devil water. Comes back to play them Blues. Phantom blues, cold
as theys Devil's own hands. The gutbucket delta flow of spirit songs from Out
There. Fat bedtime stories of quasars an' torture cloaked in zombie skin. Had da
night an' devils in his fingers. Made awl them wimmens scream. But made them
come to his bed. That's whys he goes Out There. For wimmen, an' *The Power*.

Skinny ones, tall, fat as plump cushions, theys awl rushed to him. Tender birds to da door, an' there was a cat inside. An Zye ate. Told his raw stories an' it was like lookin' through a magic glass. Ya could see it.

Every night them wimmens comes 'round. Brought him eats an' paid for his whiskey. Awl da young brown biscuits comes a-struttin' to give him what delights they had. Rich or dry wimins, crawlin' fer his love, forgets they Sunday preachin' for that backdoor man. They'd steal an' black-lie to be wit that boy. An' Zye took like a fat possum eatin' neckbones an' chicken scraps off da trashpile. Put da devil in them wimmens, made theys wild, awl turned 'round an' out. Dat chickenhead boy took an' he took. Like he was fillin' a empty barrel. But nothin' grow in da dead blackness that Zye brought back from da Crossroads. It's awl hollow, dead. No man-root get it teeth in da game of da ancients. Won't grow. But ya go try. Let yer harp sing out. Theys come. Those stray dogs that run wild in da Outer. Theys hear ya call, them black Hell hounds comes. Comes likes Hell-bound trains, bellowin' lonesome an' mean.

So ya wants to play da Blues. Ya got *da Eye,* I sees them hot desires in it. That flood in ya, fillin' ya wit brimstone-hoodoo knockin'. Then go. Sell what ya got ta sell to Old Nontooth Mag Zelma for yer ticket. Say, let me in, an' she gon give ya Da Adorned Hand . . . Da Hand That Stretches Back . . . An' when time comes ya pay what ya owes . . . An' if'n ya comes back, no remedy gon help ya. So forget sun an' awl them fields ya know an' take up moon an' herb. Go. Draw yer scarlet circles at da Crossroads . . . Fold yer desire back on da Legends—go back to them ugly, iron days when da Old Kings tended the Bone Music, devour awl ya can hold before da Tinlows comes down from the empty spaces an' lay theys tongues on ya. Ya gots firevision burnin' in *Yer Eye,* ya go see what they dead man's eye see.

'Course da Tinlows is real. No folktale that, real trouble I gon tell ya. Ain't no washer wimins jawin'. Theys bad juju up in that there place. Bad as anything crawlin' or flitin' down in Craney Swamp . . . Theys like da death-worms in gumbo when theys comes to da croaker-chant rattlin' old ills. Bad as black cats oil . . .

Ya ever look up there? Up in that sky when midnight's flowin. Up 'tween the stars in that desert of black there's a window an behind it theys laugh, waitin' on fools to kiss theys rottin' towers of sin wit their need. When the church saints whispered 'bout da Mysteries, that's when I heard 'bout it. Heard 'bout da end of this world.

I know what's plain, Boy. I'm blind, but I see. An' I remember it. Ya don't forgets when da Black touches yer heart wit it's firepoison—no shovel buries that harm. Never heard of a remedy to put it back in the cold ground. Plead for mercy from da awful breath, but it don't come. Some learnin' can't be undid, no, Sir . . .

I knows it. Got tetched by it da first time I heard that fool Zye sing them songs he learned at the feet of da Old Kings. Sat right there wit my soul burnin' when Zye played. Back then had da itch in my heart an' da fire lickin' my fingers . . . Had it strong, like whiskey gesturin' in the bottle. Ain't gon lie, I wanted them hot biscuits for me. Wanted theys magic-eyes hungerin' for *me,* wanted them girls in my bed likes crops offerin' me da harvest sweet . . . I was there the night he begged for mercy an' that cat-eyed girl stuck him. That's when I got blind. His devil-blood splashed in my eyes . . . Poison. Pure poison . . . Last sight I seen in this world was Zye bled out like a Easter hog right on them boards. An' then da whole big world went black. Ya never want ta see what lives in Da Black. Never. Remember that, there's a price for desires.

Zye was a layin' there, callin' out to da Old Kings to save 'em from death and damnation. He was a-bleedin', an' there was screamin' an' peoples talkin' 'about da Old Kings an' their troubles a-way back then, an' Zye was a holdin' his guts from a fallin' out . . . An' Zye said he could see da Old Kings waitin' on him to Come Over, said theys was a standin' right there—I couldn't see them, but he said theys was there an' that's when smoke started comin' out da corners of that chicken shack and you could hear those hounds bellowin' like damnation's bells. Zye reached up to grabs me and that's when his blood gots in my eyes. Don'ts knows what went on after that 'cause someone drags me outta there an' we's awl hear Zye screamin'. When I gots someone to takes me back there da next day weren't no signs of Zye. Said they's weren't no blood neither.

Ya hearin' any of this, Boy? I'm a guessin' no . . .

I can see how's theys chains of trouble lay on yer mind, Boy. I see that need to sing, an' da rain an' blood an' da hunger that eats inside a man at midnight wit that knife tongue. But bones an' muscle ain't nothin' when da Fury come. An' they comes. Came fer Zye twelve months and a day after he made that pact. That worth it? One fat year of pleasure fer yer soul?

Pride's a thorn that'll kick ya faster then a goodbye an' it's twice as hard to handle as a big, mean woman grow'd up thick as a mule's mind. Stings ya everytime. An' leads most to losin', losin' it awl. Seen crazy go 'cause theys had jealous hard in theys heart. Ate 'em until even theys bad luck was gone.

But even right words ain't gon stop ya. Will they?

See that shack just yonder? I hid Zye's gitar in there day after he gone on. Ya go take it. Let it pull ya . . . Play it likes ya a cock on fire wit morning light. Go out on da firey sea an' see whatcha can grow in that hollow bottom ya call yer soul. Fill it wit whiskey, wimmens, an' coin. Won't saves ya from that demon howlin' an' gnawin' inside yer gut. Yer mortal clay can't never satisfy his spoon. He keep diggin' an' diggin' until yer liferoot wither an' die.

That's awl da tellin', now git, Boy. Go ring yer bell, but dontcha bring anything unnatch'l back here, 'nuff souls been stole by what passed by before. Don't want any foul troubles 'round here no more. Now git yer boots down off'n my porch for ya brings Judgment a-callin'.

An', Boy, take that lonesome moonshine wit ya. It hurts my eyes.

(after Robert Johnson's "Hell Hound on My Trail" & "Cross Roads Blues")

Nyarlatophis:
A Fable of Ancient Egypt

Stanley C. Sargent

When pulp-era writers used to refer to professional "occultists," their contemporary readers had a somewhat clearer idea of what they meant. In our day, we might substitute "New Age gurus," though it wouldn't be quite correct. Henry Kuttner, Robert Bloch, and the rest were picturing individuals, I think, like Charles Leadbeater and Rudolf Steiner, people with one foot in the Theosophical Society and the other in parapsychological research. Someone like Dr. Van Helsing, whether in the Universal or the Hammer Films. It was not yet clear enough that these were fields of crank science and pseudohistory. The only genuine "occultist" to survive with reputation justifiably intact was Carl Jung. He practiced a technique he called "active imagination," something on the order of lucid dreaming. In it one could visit dangerous depths of the primordial Unconscious. Rudolf Steiner, by contrast, practiced much the same discipline, but he believed he was literally seeing into the past, like the characters in Colin Wilson's fascinating novel *The Philosopher's Stone.* Wilson's was a fiction in which such powers of "retrovoyance" were real. Steiner was writing fiction in his reports of ancient civilizations, trips of the Buddha to Mars, etc., only he didn't know it. If you ask me, Stan Sargent does much the same thing Steiner and Jung did, and without having to sink into a trance state. Though his fictional creation is always supported by the good strong skeleton of careful, even exhaustive research, that erudition is almost like a magic carpet carrying him into centuries lost to the rest of us. He writes as if at home in them. He has a genuine grasp of the way the ancients, as opposed to moderns, thought, acted, reacted, and expressed themselves. There is little more painful in fiction, to me at any rate, than when a writer does *not* have a sure grasp of these things. That is what makes Stan's tales set in exotic times and climes such a pleasure to read. This one first appeared in his collection *The Taint of Lovecraft* (Mythos Books, 2002).

"He swallowed up the White Crown and the Red, . . .
Lo! he devoured the mind of every god,
And so shall live forever and endure
Eternally, to do as he desires."

(excerpt from "Orion in Egypt," portion of Old Kingdom papyrus
known as *The Burden of Isis*, Dennis translation.)

". . . and everyone felt that the world and perhaps the universe had passed
from the control of known gods or forces to that of gods or forces that
were unknown."

—H. P. Lovecraft, "Nyarlathotep"

The still-rolled and sealed papyri lay unnoticed and forgotten in a drawer labeled simply "Ches-
ter" in the back-basement storage area at Miskatonic University for nearly a hundred years before
I inadvertently stumbled upon them. After an exhaustive search of the University's files and corre-
spondence, as well as references to Chester and a throne recorded in the expedition diaries of the
first true Egyptologist, Flinders Petrie, I finally mapped out the following best scenario for the
provenance of the papyrus sheets. In all likelihood, these scrolls had been acquired as part of a
ramshackle lot of artifacts smuggled out of Egypt by the unscrupulous Reverend Greville Chester,
an antiquarian and collector who often traveled to Luxor and Cairo during the late nineteenth
century to buy antiquities that he would later sell in London to the highest bidder.

After lengthy negotiations with a dealer in Luxor, Chester apparently had, in 1887, pur-
chased a throne thought to be part of the funerary furniture of the legendary Queen Hatshepsut.
He buried his dismantled prize beneath a plethora of more ordinary antiquities, the Scrolls among
them, before shipping everything off to London where the entire lot was sold at public auction mi-
nus, of course, the priceless throne, which he kept for himself. The remaining lot was purchased on
behalf of the Miskatonic University of Arkham, Massachusetts; once received in Arkham, over-
worked university archivists carefully catalogued the relics before storing them away without further
scrutiny.

A graduate student of Miskatonic University, I was granted permission to be the first to
study the contents of the papyrus manuscript (hereinafter the "Scrolls") I had unearthed there. I
enlisted the aid of Hans von Hagen, a highly talented graduate student with a degree in epigraphy.
Hans and I had been a couple for many years, having met during our senior year at Miskatonic.
This proved an optimal situation for us as we not only worked together at the university during
the day, but at home during the evenings as well, consultations thus being quite convenient.

Together we spent several months transcribing the contents of what we came to call the Ame-
nemhat Scrolls. The author claimed to have been not only the Chief Vizier of Mentuhotep
("Montu is pleased") IV, the mysterious final pharaoh of Egypt's 11th Dynasty, but further
identified himself as Amenemhat ("Amun shall lead") I, the founder of a new dynastic line (now
referred to as the 12th Dynasty), established upon the death of Mentuhotep IV in 1991 B.C.E.
Of course, we had no means of proving or disproving beyond doubt the actual identity of the au-
thor, but we set out to do our best. Our initial approach involved the creation of general profiles,
one for a king's Chief Vizier, the other for the author. They matched extremely well.

While it is generally held that few pharaohs bothered to learn to read or write, literacy would have been absolutely mandatory for a man holding the position of the king's Chief Vizier. The Chief Vizier served as the eyes and ears of the king, plus he was expected to closely monitor the royal accounts of foreign tribute as well as, in this case, the taxes of the forty-two recently reunited nomes (provinces) that were collectively known as Ta-Wy, the "Two Lands" comprising the united Upper and Lower Egypt. As stated in one ancient inscription, a good Vizier knew "all that is and is not."

Hans and I were amazed that the text before us was not, as we expected, the usual bragging, exaggerated account of a king's piety, building accomplishments, and prowess in war. Instead, this self-declared man of common birth had produced an intimate, eyewitness chronicle of his personal thoughts and emotions as he partook in the supernatural events that culminated in his being crowned pharaoh. Such an intimate diary of events was absolutely unique, dramatically differing from all other extant literature of ancient Egypt.

Little is known of the shadowy final years of Egypt's 11th Dynasty. The Pyramid Age had ended nearly half a millennium earlier, and the reigns of Tutankhamun and Ramses II were still hundreds of years in the future. The official kings lists at Saqqara and Abydos indicate Mentuhotep III as the last king of that dynasty, while the fragmentary Royal Canon of Turin papyrus describes a seven-year continuation of that dynasty after the death of Mentuhotep III. This fits perfectly with our author's claim that a fourth Mentuhotep ruled Egypt for those seven years. The only concrete evidence we have is a royal cartouche of Mentuhotep IV, together with that of Amenemhat I, which occur on a fragment of a slate bowl found at Lisht, near the new capital city founded by the latter, that has been dated to the final years of the latter's reign as the founder of the 12th Dynasty. If we accept the premise that Mentuhotep IV actually existed, we are forced to conclude that something most shameful occurred during his short reign, the overall blame for which was attributed to him. Thereby, his very memory became anathema to those who succeeded him. What disgrace could he have incurred to warrant the purging of not only the mention of his name but the very acknowledgment of his existence? We know the same punishment was doled out some 630 years thereafter when the pharaoh and priests of Amun-Re worked together to expunge every mention of the 18th Dynasty pharaoh Amenophis/Amenhotep IV (the suffixes "-ophis" and "-hotep" actually being verbs which both translate as "is pleased," the former being of Greek derivation), the so-called "heretic king" who changed his name to Akhenaten ("Useful to the Aten" or the "Essence of the Aten").

✳   ✳   ✳

[Translator's note: For the benefit of lay readers, familiar names are used herein in place of the ancient designations. Thus, Ta-Wy or the Two Lands = Egypt, Waset = Thebes, Ipet-isut = Karnak, Ipet-rasyt = Luxor, etc. The title of "pharaoh" has been used despite the fact that it derives from "per-o" ("Great House [of Egypt]") as mispronounced in the Levant; the word "pharaoh" was never used as a royal title in ancient Egypt.]

Although my lord Mentuhotep was a weak man, too young and unsuitable for the immense power bestowed upon a pharaoh, I had sworn to serve him to the best of my ability, both as vizier and advisor, that *maat* be ever maintained throughout the land.

✳   ✳   ✳

The Scrolls describe the arrival of a superhuman being called Nyarlatophis ("Nyarlat [meaning unknown] is pleased") and a resulting series of events so horrendous that they culminated in the death of a pharaoh and a dynasty. A major dilemma facing us was where to draw the line between historical fact and supernatural trappings. As scientists, we could not, of course, accept at face value the author's implausible claim that an ultimate evil had intruded upon and altered the course of history.

*   *   *

Out of the blackness of the barren wastes of *Manes* (the desert waste southwest of Egypt) He came, a flickering flame of scarlet burning brightly across the landscape. His appearance coincided with that of *Sopdet* [Sirius] in the sky at the beginning of *Akhet*, the season of inundation. From that land beyond Nubia, where it is said the sky Nile descends in a cascade to source its life-giving earthly counterpart, He followed the course of the sacred valley directly north toward the capital city of *Waset* (Thebes). At times He performed miracles, exciting wonder in the populace; soon, however, He proved to be no agathodemon as he changed, leaving a trail of senseless desolation and death in His wake. Wherever He strode, the land turned dry and lifeless; whenever He directly encountered people, their bodies grew weak and wasted away. What or who He was, none could say; certainly He was neither man nor god, but something far more dangerous and foreign to mankind.

*   *   *

We shared our initial rough translation of the manuscript with several colleagues, all experts in one or more facets of Egyptology. Although we could and did confirm the proximate date of the Scrolls with radiocarbon dating, as well as a few associated shards of pottery using thermoluminescent techniques, our fellow scientists scoffed at us, deigning the manuscript a hoax, albeit one perpetrated by a highly educated and creative prankster or madman in the distant past. Pharaohs simply did not leave personal records of their lives, we were reminded again and again; they recorded only that for which they wished to be remembered. No pharaoh wanted to be remembered for the failures and defeats he suffered, and it was not uncommon for them to exaggerate their prowess, frequently crediting themselves with triumphant conquests that were actually accomplished by others long before their own reigns began. Never did they record their weaknesses or the details of their personal lives or thoughts. Such texts even avoided any outright mention of a pharaoh's death, preferring instead to state the great one had gone on to Amenti, the land of the dead that lay to the West.

*   *   *

On foot and by boat He rampantly traversed the countryside like a ravenous jackal stalking its prey. In passing, He casually desecrated the temples of the gods, denouncing them as useless fabrications created by the few as a means to control the many. Upon His vocal command, the great sanctuaries of the most revered pharaohs collapsed, their roof-supported columns buckling as the earth gave way beneath them. He despoiled the tombs of the ancient kings, revealing their hidden locations beneath the soil and causing doors sealed for centuries to burst open. With taunting and cajoling words, He encouraged onlookers to plunder the rich booty of those tombs and burn the mummified remains of the honored rulers within, thus forever destroying the souls of those divine monarchs.

At my urging, my lord Mentuhotep dispatched a troop of soldiers to restore order and kill the sacrilegious fiend who called himself Nyarlatophis. Without fail, however, all of those sent out were ruthlessly massacred, some slain by unseen demonic forces, while others were incinerated before they could lay a hand upon the unholy intruder. And still He pushed on toward the royal seat.

*   *   *

Discounting the more fantastic aspects contained in the text, the underlying theme of the document is concerned with the age-old struggle between good and evil. It is vital, however, that one realize the concept of good held a different meaning for the ancient Egyptians than it holds for us today. We usually consider good to involve doing the right thing and treating others as we ourselves wish to be treated, concepts that were taken for granted in ancient times. Additionally, we generally consider good as establishing and retaining freedom and equality for all men, something that did not occur to the people of four thousand years ago. The best world of which they conceived was one in which life went on as usual, free of unexpected change and unwelcome disasters. Thus, good to the ancient Egyptian mind was conceived as harmony, balance and, above all, divine order. This grand orderliness they termed maat, *a word often inadequately translated as "truth," "justice" or "peace."*

The gods, they believed, resided in a perfectly harmonious reflection of Egypt high in the sky above this world, in a celestial paradise. The star-studded stream of the Milky Way was viewed as a mirror-image in the firmament of their own life-giving Nile. The sun god Re carried the dead in his solar barque across the starry waters in the sky, eventually delivering them to various lands of eternal paradise. In an effort to make earthly Egypt resemble the celestial world more closely, the ancients erected the trio of Great Pyramids to represent the three brightest stars they observed on the banks of the heavenly Nile, the triad comprising the starry belt of the constellation Orion. The pyramids were sized and aligned in exact mathematical imitation of their stellar counterparts, a practical application of the "as above, so below" concept.

Temples were considered pathways to the divine, oases of order in the chaotic ocean of the cosmos, and thus essential for the maintenance of maat. *They functioned as portals through which the gods in the sky disseminated power to their earthly counterparts.*

As the gods assured maat *in the heavens, the ultimate duty of the pharaoh, the issue of the gods and thus himself divine, was to maintain* maat *in Egypt. His subjects individually participated in this process by worshipping the gods and remaining loyal and obedient to their divine leader. A pharaoh's role did not end with his death, for even after his spirit had risen to join the gods in heaven, he was expected to curry favors for his former kingdom far below. Without maat, the Nile would cease to bestow life upon Egypt via its biennial flooding, and chaos would ensue in the form of famine, insanity, pestilence and foreign conquest. Thereby chaos became synonymous with the epitome of evil.*

*   *   *

Descriptions of Nyarlatophis' disquieting physical appearance varied tremendously, although certain aspects remained constant. At first it was claimed He wore robes of brilliant red, beneath which lay a perfect specimen of the male human body in its prime. He soon chose, however, to abandon the robes, taking a common white linen kilt as primary adornment for His slender, swarthy form. He brazenly donned the striped cloth *nemes* headscarf as well, which only a pharaoh may wear. As further insult, He soon thereafter attached to His headwear the image of the *uraeus* serpent, the traditional symbol of pharaonic vigilance in the form of a cobra poised to spit venom in the face of Egypt's enemies.

Later reports concerning Nyarlatophis' countenance varied more radically. Some said He bore the visage of a man, while others claimed His head resembled that of a ram, a serpent or, at times, that of a toad. Most often, however, it was said His excessively large and billowing *nemes* concealed His face in shadow altogether. So deep was the shadowing that some swore He was possessed of no face at all and that those who dared gaze directly saw naught but a vast and star-filled abyss where a face should reside.

No one saw Him eat, drink or consume anything that might provide mortal sustenance, and He apparently never slept. Thus were we deprived of any obvious means of causing Him harm via these simplest of means.

Such stories struck no end of fear in the heart of my lord Mentuhotep, who was at a loss as to how he should deal with the approaching menace. More often than not, he would go boating on the artificial lake his father had built at *Ipet-isut* (Karnak temple complex), conscripting the prettiest girls in his harem as rowers, that he might for a time forget his fear. It was not until news arrived of a ghastly occurrence in a village near *Abu* (Elephantine) that Pharaoh was forced to contemplate further action.

The men of that village, believing Nyarlatophis' arrival impending, conspired to protect the temple of the city's patron goddess, Satis. Leaving their families alone and unguarded, the men took arms and gathered to stand guard about the structure. Unbeknownst to the would-be guardians, the sly Nyarlatophis avoided the temple and, instead, approached the unsuspecting and unguarded village. When the men were finally alerted to His treachery, they rushed to protect their homes and loved ones. They arrived in time to witness a most terrible scene; their wives, sisters and adult daughters had cast their own offspring into the waters of the Nile where the innocent infants and children were devoured by swarming crocodiles. When confronted with their crime, the women seemed entranced and could provide no reason for their actions. Moreover, once they came to full realization of the evil deed they had committed, the women flung themselves as well into the waiting jaws of the insatiable wedge-nosed reptilians.

*   *   *

Hans and I did our utmost to further establish the authenticity of the Scrolls via every possible avenue. As previously noted herein, the author described an era about which very little is actually known today, as almost no records have survived from the closing years of the 11th Dynasty. We do know, however, that Thebes had replaced Memphis as the political and cultural center of Egypt by that time. The 11th Dynasty kings had struggled to consolidate all the forty-two nomes (provinces) that the country might once again come together under a single monarch. Once the Nile-divided city of Thebes was established as the new political and cultural center of Egypt, many of the nomarchs (provincial governors) of the more rebellious nomes were replaced one by one by officials deemed loyal to the Theban government.

To the west of Thebes lay the mortuary complex of Nebhepetre Mentuhotep (Mentuhotep I) in the cemetery region. The adjacent funerary temple of Hatshepsut, as well as the grand burials in the Valley of the Kings and the Valley of the Queens, were still far in the future, but great strides were being made to insure the burgeoning temple complex at Karnak on the northeastern edge of Thebes would become the principal religious center of Egypt. Although little is presently known about the layout of the temple center at Karnak at that time, since the temples were later either destroyed or their stones reused for later constructions, the Scrolls offer a great insight into this aspect of Egyptian history. They provide an overview of the then extant colossal temple of Montu, not to mention that which would, centuries later, become the largest religious structure the world has ever known, the temple complex of Amun.

Luxor, a mile to the south of Karnak, would not reach prominence as a religious site until centuries later due to the massive construction carried out during the reigns of Amenophis ("Amun is pleased") III and, much later, Ramses ("Re has fashioned him") II. The text of the Scrolls, if proven reliable, would provide a wealth of heretofore unknown, invaluable knowledge of both Karnak and Luxor during the earliest stages of their development.

* * *

Despite my protests, my Lord Mentuhotep insisted on dispatching an emissary to intercept and placate Nyarlatophis before He could come any nearer to Waset. At the king's order, the most talented artist of the court fashioned an intricately carved scarab from soapstone inlaid with jewels, faience and precious metals as a gift for the approaching intruder. The scarab was sent, along with a written message bearing Pharaoh's greetings and a plea that Nyarlatophis pause in His journey long enough to be Pharaoh's guest in a plush and comfortable villa of his choosing anywhere along the route to Waset. The gift and missive reached their destination within a fortnight when the emissary encountered the one he sought just outside *Ta-sny* (Esna).

The tall, sunburned figure sat in the dust like a common laborer as He bid the emissary attend Him. The man extended greetings and stated his mission, before cautiously drawing near enough to proffer the scarab and papyrus to the commanding figure. Ignoring the gift at first, Nyarlatophis glanced briefly at the glyphs inscribed upon the scroll, which began: "Health, strength and plenty be thine, most honorable traveler." The messenger, assuming Nyarlatophis was unable to decipher the Pharaoh's words, was about to offer a translation when the stranger spoke.

"Tell your master I appreciate his offer of comfort and fine lodgings, but my mission will not be delayed," He calmly intoned. For one fleeting moment, a wry, unsettling smile disturbed His otherwise complacent features as He tossed the papyrus and scarab irreverently into the dirt. He then turned to pluck a brown dung beetle from its burrow in the hot sand. With a flourish, He popped the hardshelled insect, its legs squirming wildly, into His mouth and closed His lips tightly to curtail its escape. An instant later, He disgorged a glittering scarab of solid gold, identical in size and shape to the living creature He had just swallowed. "Deliver him this as a token of my esteem," He hissed as He placed the unmoving insect in the quaking messenger's outstretched hand.

"What manner of being is this Nyarlatophis?" Mentuhotep later demanded as he casually fondled the golden amulet the emissary had presented to him. Staring more intently at the scarab's inscribed underside, he scoffed, "And this cryptic message, pray tell what is the meaning of 'I am the beginning and the end'?"

None could descry the meaning of the wizard's strangely worded inscription. Turning to me, Pharaoh shouted in irritation, "I must know what the oracle has to say! Obtain for me the advice of the prophet of Montu on this matter immediately!"

*   *   *

The religion of ancient Egypt developed haphazardly over more than three thousand years; during that time many of the originally independent forty-two nomes of Egypt promoted their own patron god or goddess. In later efforts to peacefully unite the country, the pharaohs strove to appease all by consolidating the countless conflicting cults and divinities of their subjects into one loosely knit state religion. Modern efforts to define this ever-changing pantheon in simple, one-line progression have only led to confusion and consternation.

In keeping with the standard of the day, the kings of the 11th Dynasty introduced their own religious beliefs at Thebes when they established that city as Egypt's new capital. They chose to promote Montu, a warrior god of human form often depicted with the head of a falcon or ram, above all other gods without denying or outlawing any of Thebes's pre-established divinities. Thus Montu's temple quickly came to dominate the newly established sacred area of Karnak. The worship of Thebes's more traditional deities, including Khonshu and Amun, continued on a greatly reduced scale throughout the reigns of the several 11th Dynasty kings.

It was not until Amenemhat established the 12th Dynasty that Montu's popularity waned drastically. Almost overnight, Amun was elevated to the rank of the national god, despite his former status as a minor wind deity. The Amun cult continued to grow and flourish in Egypt for many hundreds of years until eventually the priesthood blended Amun and Ra, two of Egypt's most powerful gods, creating Amun-Ra, a god whose authority would eventually rival and overthrow that of the pharaohs themselves. By the time of Rameses III, it has been calculated that the estate of the Theban Amen-Re alone owned one-fifth of the inhabitants and one-third of the farmlands of Egypt.

*   *   *

I hastened to obtain Montu's advice for my master, petitioning the prophets of Montu for counsel on behalf of His Majesty. That very afternoon, I sauntered by the less-impressive temples of Khonshu and Amun and strode directly into the far more awe-inspiring sanctuary of Montu, to which commoners are forbidden entry. I was escorted through the outer court and lush gardens into the silence of the expansive but dimly lit hypostyle hall that comprised the greater part of the edifice. Once there, I was told to spend time in contemplation amidst the forest of giant, round, lotus-crowned pillars while the priests awakened Montu and begged consultation. The silence struck me as rather eerie, for whenever I had previously been in the temple, it had been filled with singers, dancers and the tinkling sound of the *sistra* used to ward off evil spirits.

I passed the time of waiting in study of the magnificent, colorfully bedizened walls and the life-size paintings of divine events, processions and appointments thereon. I was somewhat saddened, however, at the realization that such exquisite craftsmanship was meant to be seen by kings and priests alone.

When signaled, I reverently progressed to the innermost chamber, where I was confronted by three gigantic sandstone images of the warrior god Montu depicted in his theophany as a falcon-headed man. Maneuvering carefully through the stifling gloom to a space directly behind these figures, I found myself surrounded by solemn-faced priests, the personal attendants of the divine idol. The dim glow of isolated oil lamps offered the only illumination. The robed forms cut through the pungent smoke of burning incense before bowing and stepping aside to reveal the small, richly vested golden image within which Montu is said to reside. Set within the *naos* (wooden enclosing shrine), the idol's features were realistically portrayed with bits of inlaid faience and precious stones. Atop its head rose an elaborate crown of solid gold.

I prostrated myself before the gleaming effigy and reverently prayed aloud that Montu might see fit to guide Pharaoh in dealing with the approaching demon Nyarlatophis. An eerie silence ensued for many minutes, during which time I failed to experience the slightest sense of awe or divine mystery one would expect to feel in the presence of a god. I did not ponder the peculiarity of this for long, as the muffled, echoing tones of an unnaturally loud, deep voice abruptly filled the room, its source apparently the shadow-enveloped image of Montu. I raised my head slightly above the masonry that I might clearly hear all that was said; the oraculation had begun.

"Though the worrisome intruder be naught but a trickster," pronounced the disembodied voice, "Pharaoh must bid Him welcome in Waset and provide Him haven within the walls of the Southern Palace. Through deceit and subtle prying, the secrets of the intruder's magical powers must be pried from Him. That knowledge must then be related to my servants and them alone."

Peering at the previously immobile idol, I noted that emphasis was lent to particular phrases by the stiff and jerky raising and lowering of its arms. The god's lips remained absolutely fixed and unmoving even when speaking.

"Only by such means," the disembodied voice continued, "can the threat to the united lands be safely dispelled."

It was over that quickly. A pair of wooden doors I had not previously noticed slammed closed without warning, separating me from the holy image of Montu. For a second time I was abandoned in total darkness.

I confess I harbored grave misgivings as I left the temple with what were purported to be divine instructions. Would that I had not discerned the fraud of the priests in the form of wires by which they manipulated the lifeless image of the god and not clearly recognized the distinct speech mannerisms of the high priest in what supposedly was Montu's voice. In spite of all this, however, I had no doubt whatsoever that Mentuhotep would obediently comply with the oracle's instructions without thought or further consideration.

Not only was I proven correct in my assumption concerning Mentuhotep's reaction to the deceptive prophecy, but by the time I returned he had become so enamored of the golden scarab of Nyarlatophis that he ordered an elaborate gold and faience pectoral be designed to display the gaudy trinket. He would proudly wear it, he said, when he and the fantastic sorcerer finally met face-to-face.

Unhesitantly, he sent a message to Nyarlatophis inviting Him to enter the great southern gate of Waset just two days hence at noon. Pharaoh promised to greet Him there. Thereafter, lavish lodgings in the residence of the Southern Palace would be provided for Nyarlatophis, where He would be welcome to remain and commune with Pharaoh and his officials for as long as He desired.

Nyarlatophis provided no response to this second missive, which Pharaoh took as acceptance. Thus he was taken aback when, the very next day, the sorcerer unexpectedly altered the course of his desert march, turning due north toward the royal cemeteries located on the western bank across the Hep-ur (Nile River, literally "Great Hapi") from Waset. He was, of course, followed at a distance by Pharaoh's spies. Even more puzzling, He made a detour to the great Mansion of Millions of Years (mortuary temple) of Mentuhotep I immediately upon arrival in the necropolis. That complex, an ambitious three-story stone conglomeration, consisted of an approach via an inclined causeway that rose above a pillared ground level to provide access to an open terrace surrounding a second tier of pillars. These in turn upheld a third level tier which upheld a small pyramid.

Mentuhotep I's body was actually entombed in a much smaller construct located behind and beneath the dominant temple. The awesome complex attracted a vast number of pilgrims year-round as hundreds of offerings were made to the deceased god-king in hope of receiving his blessing.

It was at this very site that Nyarlatophis performed a puzzling ritual. He was observed to traverse the perimeter of the main temple, stopping every few feet to poke and prod at the earthen foundation of the superstructure's outermost walls. He rebuffed those who attempted to fawn over Him and caused no disturbance of any kind. Having completed this inexplicable ritual, He immediately departed, doubling back on His earlier route that He might enter Waset from the south as Pharaoh had requested.

Promptly at noon the following day, Nyarlatophis emerged from the uninhabitable waste of the desert only to be spotted from the high walls that sheltered the city from attack. To our surprise, He was accompanied by a black, heavily maned lion that vied for attention and licked its master's outstretched palm each time it was proffered.

Pharaoh sat perched high upon a royal palanquin borne by ten sturdy men. While we waited, the king's favorite pygmy did his utmost to keep the monarch entertained with tricks and jests involving an ape and a mongrel dog.

Mentuhotep scoffed aloud at the sorcerer, feigning confidence by declaring too loudly that Nyarlatophis and His obviously domesticated pet impressed him but little. Despite the king's outward show of confidence, those of us who attended him closely noted how intensely his pale and trembling fingers clasped the glittering token sent to him by Nyarlatophis, the amulet of heavy gold now prominently displayed as the centerpiece of the gaudy and oversized pectoral adorning his chest. I confess I too harbored anxious reservations concerning the imminent meeting of my master and the redoubtable sorcerer.

As the preternatural pair drew near, it became possible to better distinguish the details of the intruder's appearance. His bearing was most regal compared to the overweight and pampered Mentuhotep. The haughty, self-possessed figure of Nyarlatophis displayed an unusual magnificence, almost an elegance, beyond even the ideal the royal artists tried so hard to depict in idealized images of the king.

Apart from the black lion, Nyarlatophis sported a second companion, an elemental rear guard in the form of a squalling, gray-brown wall of churning sand that howled and raged just a few feet behind Him. The unexplainable phenomenon obscured the landscape beyond the sorcerer to the extent that His outline as well as that of His bestial companion seemed to float effortlessly just above the dun, shimmering surface of desert sea.

A dip in the uneven dunes caused Nyarlatophis and his attendants to drop out of sight for what should have been only a moment. We waited for them to reach the dune's crest, but when the strange pair and their devilish sand curtain failed to reappear, Mentuhotep grew impatient. He ordered a troop of royal guards to discover the reason for the sorcerer's delay. Yet no sign of Nyarlatophis or His bestial companion was found; their tracks ended abruptly near the apex of the obstructing desert mound. It was as if they had simply ceased to exist. I shuddered to hear jackals howling eerily in the distant hills to the West, for it was but midday and jackals are known to howl only during the darkest hours of night.

Furious over Nyarlatophis' seeming deception, Pharaoh, with the royal party in attendance, decided to return to the primary residence at the Northern Palace. Yet the entourage had traversed but a short distance before a cry rang out. A commoner came running toward the king's entourage, breathlessly calling that he bore news of great import for Pharaoh.

"Divine one," the exhausted man stuttered, falling to his knees before the royal palanquin, "the sorcerer, Nyarlatophis . . . He is at *Ipet-rayst* (Luxor temple complex), having taken shelter in the ruined temple there."

Mentuhotep bristled at the insolence of the sorcerer; why had there been no mention of Ipet-rayst in Montu's prophecy?

"Such audacity!" he hissed. "And does He expect the divine Pharaoh of the Two Lands to attend Him there?"

"No, no, My Lord," the messenger continued breathlessly, fear becoming apparent in the trembling of his voice, "Nyarlatophis insists He wants for nothing and can not, must not, be disturbed under any circumstances whatsoever until He is ready to receive guests. Forgive me, but no one, not even you, Great Sire, may approach Him at present for . . . He absolutely forbids it."

Outraged, Pharaoh strained to regain his aplomb. "Then," he shrieked an invective, "by all the gods, may He rot in that dung hole He has chosen for His burrow!" Without further ado, Mentuhotep ordered his followers onward to the palace.

Once there, he commanded that I send a corps of spies to Ipet-rasyt that he might be kept fully apprised of Nyarlatophis' every move, whether it be by light of day or during the night. Beyond this, he vowed that he would personally consult the oracle of Montu that very night. Having said this, his royal temper began to cool somewhat. Still, it was obvious to all that he dared not defy Nyarlatophis' order that He not be disturbed.

I must digress for a moment to confess I was deeply troubled by these events. The look in Pharaoh's eye as I had initially repeated Montu's counsel to him had not spoken of his desire to acquiesce to the god's wishes, but of an unwholesome desire to acquire the secrets of the sorcerer's power for himself. It struck me that not only common sense but the king's sacred duty as guardian and preserver of his kingdom dictated that this superhuman enemy should never have been offered welcome among us. And now that the advice of Montu's power-hungry priests had brought the enemy into our camp, it became vital that plans be immediately devised to protect Ta-Wy!

Everywhere Nyarlatophis traveled, pestilence had broken out in His wake. Despite prayers and offerings meant to curry the favor and support of Sekhmet, goddess of pestilence and destruction, hundreds were soon stricken. The disease ran its course within a few days, causing its victims to lose weight rapidly due to lack of appetite and excessive vomiting. Hundreds died, many of them succumbing to illnesses that heretofore had proven lethal only to young children. The foremost physicians were utterly powerless to check the spread of this terrible plague, and now its foul harbinger resided on the outskirts of the capital.

Focusing exclusively on the plan to gain the powers of the impertinent stranger, Mentuhotep ignored the ensuing revolts in the outlying territories of Ta-Sety (Nubia), Assyria (northern Iraq), and Mitanni (Babylon and Lebanon, approximately), as well as the threat of invasion by fearsome forces of Hatti (the Hittites). The stability his forbears had struggled for decades to establish was allowed to deteriorate to the extent that even serious rumors of imminent uprisings within the kingdom itself failed to capture Mentuhotep's attention.

A brooding sense of ensuing danger overcame the populace. Unexplained, sinister phantasms were seen throughout the city, particularly on hot, moonless nights. Soon even the bravest citizens were barricading themselves behind securely locked doors.

It was abundantly clear to me that it portends naught but disaster when a people and their leader become obsessed with fear. Although this king was but twenty-two years of age, four years my junior, I would have gladly given my life for him. He had raised me through the ranks to highest station despite my common birth, and although I am not a soldier by trade or training, he had enough faith in my abilities to appoint me the leader of his army during several campaigns against the

Pedjet ("Nine Bows"—general term for the enemies of Egypt). I am proud to say all the campaigns I led ended in great victories for the Two Lands. But beyond all this, I must admit that above all I harbor a greater allegiance to my beloved Ta-Wy than to its ruler, thus I could not simply stand idly by as disaster descended upon my country. I was determined to prevent such disaster at any cost.

I contemplated the place in which Nyarlatophis had taken shelter. Ipet-rasyt was a shunned cemetery of evil reputation, a dry and dusty plain at the city's south-ernmost limit. The site was crowned with the dead shell of an archaic temple once dedicated to the profane worship of Set, the eternally restless spirit of chaos and confusion. The enemy of all other gods, Set, it is claimed, was the first god man worshipped. From the infernal breath of that chthonic entity, legend claimed, worms had first emerged from the red desert sands.

The princes who had originally divided the Two Lands in their ploys for terri-tory and power had bowed to Set as Sutekh, after that terrible deity of Hatti, and set him above all other gods. When those usurpers were overthrown and the Two Lands reunited by Pharaoh's ancestor, the images of both Set and Sutekh were de-stroyed throughout the land, his name forbidden to be recorded or voiced. His children were said to be the pig, the hippopotamus, and the crocodile, although his erstwhile companions were a pack of impossibly monstrous jackals or hounds that hailed from an opposing universe known as Thindahloos.

Should Nyarlatophis decide to ally Himself with Set, what power of heaven or earth could stand against Him?

The next day, as I wandered along a crowded street with this implacable conun-drum in my mind, a message was stealthily forced into my hand. I caught only a fleet-ing glimpse of a young boy who may well have been the message bearer, but before I could apprehend and question him, he disappeared into the sea of pedestrians.

On a crumpled leaf of papyrus was written: "The fate of the Ta-Wy lies in your hands; Amun alone has the power to save us."

I puzzled over the curious message for an entire day and night before making the decision to visit Amun's temple, a humble sanctuary located at the foot of the Ipet-isut plateau. Amun was not a popular god with either Pharaoh or the people of Waset at that time, thus his temple was not afforded a place on the higher ground of the sacred plateau proper. Only those structures dedicated to the wor-ship of Montu and his wife Mut and son Khonshu were deemed worthy of occu-pying the enclosed sacred area, Montu's temple being the largest construction by far as within its walls lay not only a magnificent temple but many attendant struc-tures, all possessing a grand view of the king's artificial lake.

I waited until the royal court was distracted with the making of plans for a great celebration to be held at Mentuhotep, Nebhepetre's pyramid-capped mortu-ary temple west of Waset. It struck me as more than coincidence that this was the very same temple at which Nyarlatophis had performed His curious ritual before coming to Waset. Pharaoh, along with his firstborn son and heir, Mentunosis ("Born of Montu"), and Princess Merytmentu ("Beloved of Montu") planned to sail the Hep-ur in the royal barque for the short trip from the eastern to the western bank. Pharaoh and his children would then be borne upon a litter for the final journey to the desert temple complex. Once there, Mentuhotep was to lead a joyous celebration honoring the accomplishments of his illustrious, divine ancestor. Nefertmentu ("Beautiful is Montu"), who was not only Pharaoh's Chief Wife but his elder sister as well, declined to accompany the family on this particular occasion for reasons never explained.

Without a doubt Pharaoh would have been outraged had he known I sought Amun's counsel, thus it was necessary for me to travel under cover of darkness, a wig covering my shaved head as I donned the apparel of a common craftsman. To my amazement upon arrival at Amun's humble temple, a lector priest ushered me into the forbidden areas of the holy house immediately, as if I were expected. He abandoned me in a small dimly lit room where I believed myself alone until a feeble voice pierced the shadows behind me.

"So you have finally arrived, Amenemhat the Vizier!" the unseen speaker whispered. "Amun is pleased and bids you welcome."

When I turned, I beheld the outline of a slight figure, a white-haired man with a long beard, draw near.

Cautiously, I mumbled, "Do you speak for the god, old priest?"

The bent and hoary servant chuckled, "Indeed I do, for I am his First Prophet. Amun uses me as the tool through which he can express his wishes directly. Through me, he will show you the way to save the country and people we both love so much."

Before I could respond, the spry old priest spun around and, with a giggle and a wave of the hand, bid me follow him through an even darker passage and into the most sacred of the temple's inner sanctums. Our path slanted downward, taking us far beyond the outermost perimeter of the small temple above. After a time, we entered secret chambers far beneath the surface that were known to none but the god's most trusted initiates.

As my eyes adjusted to the faint flicker of the priest's lamp, I spied the silhouette of a small figure stationed at the far side of the room. As we drew near, I recognized the dwarfed form as a graven image of Amun shimmering in the dim light of altar lamps placed at its base. The divine image struck a regal pose, the left foot extended forward, a *was* scepter clutched in the left hand; upon its head sat a solar disk supported by two tall symbolic plumes, the symbols of the sun and the wind. Unlike Montu's statue of solid gold, Amun's image consisted of little more than carved wood gilded with a thin layer of electrum. Faience inlays gave the viewer the eerie impression that Amun stared directly at him from some unfathomable space.

I studied the immobile idol for a time before hazarding, "It seems, First Prophet, that Lord Amun has naught to tell me after all."

My silent companion smiled indulgently. "The very word 'amun' means 'hidden,' just as in your own name, but it is difficult for people to believe in a god they cannot see." Gesturing to indicate the figure of the god, he added, "That is why we servants of the god oblige the masses by providing the image before you. "

As I considered the truth of his comments, the priest began to sway as if he were about to swoon. I reached out to offer him support just as he steadied himself, closed his eyes and began to breathe deeply and regularly. His right hand shot out suddenly and snatched the staff from the idol's grasp.

I jumped back, taken by surprise, as some unseen mechanism within the stone flooring ground into action beneath my feet. The shimmering idol was slowly dragged aside, allowing a full view of the rear wall. The monolithic profile of a human face, a face bearing features similar to that of the idol, had been carved into the wall. I gazed breathlessly upon the beauty of the relief, fascinated by the magnificence of the image incised in stone.

As I looked to the old priest for explanation, the shadow he cast upon the great relief caught my eye. It did not define the bent and feeble body of the elderly priest but the physique of a well-muscled youth, and yet it moved in perfect tandem with the priest's body.

When my host opened his mouth, it struck me that the voice seemed to come from far away, as if the priest's throat were but a vehicle for transmitting the words of another, someone millions of miles away. The words carried an echo as inhumanly deep tones declared, "Suffer that which I reveal to you now, Amenemhat, for you alone can save the Two Lands of Ta-Wy . . . and the world."

Moving closer to the countenance carved into the stone wall, the priest pressed a hand upon an oversized eye of stone. The very substance of it magically dissolved, leaving only an ebony hole where the pupil had formerly been.

The transformed priest muttered, "You must bind yourself to my service without question, Amenemhat. You must do as I dictate perfectly and without hesitation, though you find the immediate result offensive." With great intensity, he added, "Behold the future that will come to pass should you refuse or fail!"

He directed my attention to the round void he had accessed in the wall so that there, in the very eye of god, I might gaze upon a vile and horrific future.

At first I did not recognize what proved to be the festering remains of my beloved Waset. No single structure remained intact; every public building, palace and temple lay shattered and crushed as if the earth itself found their presence repellent. Clouds of blackened smoke partially obscured my view, but with their passing, it became clear that the rotting carnage of countless men and beasts littered the rubble.

My point of vantage altered then, broadening to embrace a wider vista. My eyes traced the dry, scar-like trench of black mud through which the cool, blue life-giving waters of the Hep-ur once flowed. The very breath caught in my throat as one lifeless community after another passed before my eyes. Nothing had escaped the unearthly devastation as one by one Egypt's teeming metropolises were reduced to unattended slaughterhouses, the nauseating stench of which rose up to sear my nostrils.

Barely recognizable too was the holy plain at Rostau (Giza). Where once the titanic triad of superb pyramids had proudly pointed heavenward, nothing remained but smashed and ravaged heaps of loose, broken stones. Instinctively, I winced, realizing the rest of the world surely fared no better.

With every ounce of strength, I struggled to turn away from these pathetically painful scenes. But despite the certainty that I could bear no more, I was held fast by unseen hands that I might not turn away.

Mercifully, the stone-ringed portal slowly blurred, the terrible images becoming less distinct. But the eye had only blinked, for it cleared just moments later to focus once again upon the view of decimated Waset. Out from the sprawling graves and rubble of temples crawled those pathetic versions of our proud gods, now smitten and battered by a relentless rain that tainted all with the dark crimson of coagulated blood.

The fallen, dishonored gods and goddesses staggered, slipping and stumbling, in the gelatinous sanguine grue, their grotesque and pain-riddled features weighed down with their individual, tremendously elaborate crowns, crowns that had long since forsaken all meaning. Their human shoulders heaved under the burden of the grotesque visages of jackals, lions, falcons, crocodiles, felines, ibis and all variety of beasts. Ta-Wy's once great divine pantheon had been deplorably transformed, reduced to little more than a collection of dishonored, pitiful travesties of their former adored selves. Deprived of their temples, the mechanisms that had served as portals through which great surges of vitality flowed from the stars to the earthly manifestations of the gods, the immortals grew weak and starved for celestial renewal. Without the heaven-sent sustenance, the immortal monstrosities were doomed to endless torment devoid of even the promise of death's eventual release.

Sickened to the depths of my soul, I buried my face in my arms, praying that the visual barrage cease least my *ka* (aspect of the soul able to travel great distances) and *ba* (aspect of the soul which remains near the body in the tomb after death) abandon me. Only when I tumbled backward, slamming upon the cold stone floor in the midst of a thrashing fit, did the eye of Amun cloud over to end the apocalyptic scene.

I must have lost consciousness for a time, for when I awoke, I lay on the hard masonry gasping for air and unsure of my surroundings. From somewhere amidst the enclosing shadows, the priest hailed me gently in more natural, human tones.

"Amenemhat," he whispered, "now you have seen the destiny of this world should you fail to intercede. This decision, this terrible responsibility, is yours alone to bear. Leave now and allow that which you have seen come to pass, or pledge before Amun that, upon the infinite aspects of your soul, you will do all within your power to carry out Amun's will. Should you choose to withhold your pledge of absolute and unwavering loyalty to Amun, everything and everyone you know will be swallowed by the catastrophic forces of eternal Chaos. You must decide now, without further delay."

Confused and half-stunned, I struggled and staggered to regain my footing as I pleaded, "How can Nyarlatophis alone decimate the world and cast down its gods?"

"Nyarlatophis is neither man nor god, but the tool of primal *Isfeh* (Chaos). The universe was born of Isfeh and to Isfeh it will eventually return. Your mission is to suspend the culmination of that inevitability. By intervening now, you offer mankind a few millennia more to prepare for its inevitable demise."

"How can this be?" I begged. "What can I do alone against such incomparable power?"

Without pause, the priest responded, "You must lead the forces Pharaoh has abandoned, the very troops you have led to victory repeatedly. They know, trust and admire you, thus they will overwhelmingly welcome the return of their much-loved general. They will eagerly follow you, for they know you hold your love for the Two Lands above all else."

"What," I queried, "does Amun demand in exchange for the knowledge by which Nyarlatophis may be defeated?"

The priest smiled a final time. "Only that you declare your debt to Amun before all the world, proclaiming him the greatest of gods, the creator of all gods and savior of mankind. In Ipete-isut and Ipet-rasyt you must initiate the construction of the largest and most beautiful temples man shall ever know, though they take a millennium to complete. That is the payment required."

As confused, overwhelmed and terrified as I was, there could be but one choice. And thus did I swear upon my very *ka* to obey Amun's instructions to the letter and without hesitation no matter what they might be. Only later was I to realize the irony of my very name, Amenemhat, for, as though preordained from the day of my birth, it proclaims "Amun, the Hidden One, Shall Lead."

He then dismissed me with, "When your presence here is again required, look for the sign of Amun's ram."

*   *   *

I assumed I had only been within the temple for two or three hours at most, so I was shocked to learn I had been gone an entire night and day. Pharaoh had been frantically searching for me, for, as I should have foreseen, the plague that paced Nyarlatophis had struck Waset with a vengeance.

When I came before Pharaoh once again, he said he had feared me dead. He was so relieved to find me alive that he failed to ask where I had been. It had been difficult without my advice, he said, but he had made one fateful decision in my absence. The only way to stop the plague, he had decided, was to order all forty-two *nomarchs* to kill anyone within the limits of their *nomes* who displayed the slightest sign or symptom of infection. All the corpses were to be burned but for those of certain wealthy and influential individuals whom the king would not deprive of an afterlife by destroying their remains. They too would be slaughtered with the rest but their corpses would be mummified and treated with due ceremony and given proper burial.

I protested avidly. Pharaoh had always been a just man deserving of the love of his people, but this cleansing he had prescribed, I asserted, would prove a tragic error. Hundreds, perhaps thousands, of innocent persons would be murdered at the whim of the *nomarchs'* officials; this, I explained, was the perfect means for them to rid themselves of their political enemies. At the very least, I insisted, it must be proven beyond doubt that those accused actually carried the infection before they were executed. It was tragic enough that the sick should die by the sword, but the wholesale murder of citizens on a nationwide basis, I argued, was unthinkable. When confronted with the horror of this widespread injustice, the *nomarchs* would surely place blame for their crimes upon Pharaoh, which could lead to a series of revolts in the more unstable districts. His father, grandfather and especially his great-grandfather had spent their entire reigns doing everything possible to unite the discordant *nomes*, yet Mentuhotep now risked throwing the entire country into revolt. Finally, I advised that the corpses of the infected should universally be burned if contagion was to be curtailed entirely.

But Pharaoh assured me the order had already been given and would not be retracted. Nothing could be done to halt the ensuing bloodshed.

Thus it was that a plethora of black, acrid smoke rose in streams toward heaven from innumerable makeshift crematoriums.

I also learned that the residence where Nyarlatophis had established temporary habitation had mysteriously changed and "grown" overnight, almost as if it were a living entity feeding on the very stones themselves. Nyarlatophis had been seen in the streets of Waset the previous night by many, although those watching His lair swore no one had entered or exited the premises. Still, those who observed Him in the city streets agreed that He kept the company of a large black lion as He tossed golden ingots to those who dared attend him. Some even bragged that He had summoned them to His side and spoken to them, although none could recall what had been said.

Such reports struck me as particularly foreboding. Pharaoh, however, dismissed them as fabrications contrived by attention seekers. Unlike me, Pharaoh had not gazed into the future Nyarlatophis was creating.

The king was far more interested in the plans for a forthcoming grand ceremony celebrating his ancestor, Mentuhotep I. In Pharaoh's absence, I was to be in charge of policing the city with ready authority to act on my own. Pharaoh was so preoccupied that, when a rash of suspicious fires broke out in Waset, he instructed me to deal with the problem.

From the start, it was clear the fires were being deliberately set in homes, workshops and even a section of the Southern Palace. Unfortunately, the facilities for fire fighting in Waset were all but nonexistent. There had never been a real conflagration in the mudbrick city, so we were totally unprepared for a sudden rash of such outbreaks. Although much loss of property was incurred and countless lives lost before the end of the week, we had the problem under control, but not until a foul black smoke rose heavenward from the city.

My utmost priority was to guarantee the security of Pharaoh's entourage as it maneuvered through the crowded streets from the palace to the harbor. My worries were unfounded, however, as my troops cleared a safe path for the royal party, which subsequently arrived at the harbor without incident. Still, I heaved a sigh of relief upon receiving word that the royal barque had safely reached the river's western shore.

Yet I continued to brood, wondering just what form Nyarlatophis' next assault would take. I could not accept, as did the king and his advisors, that the recent fires had been set as protests over the killing of the plague bearers. I was tempted to return to Amun for counsel, but recalled the priest's assurance that Amun would send his ram as a sign should the need arise for a further meeting. In the meantime, I had to deal with any intervening crises on my own. Understandably, the people were miserably frightened; an unknown wizard had suddenly appeared in their town, snubbing their king and afflicting the town with plague and fire. Yet these afflictions were only the beginnings of the more horrendous calamities that were to follow.

*   *   *

Mentuhotep and his party arrived at their destination, the mortuary temple some distance across the desert waste. The main structure of the complex consisted of a huge solid, square platform faced with rows of columns that supported a second, smaller platform. A lengthy inclined causeway of stone led from the harbor, rising as it traversed the temple's tree-filled terrace to the forecourt of the second tier. That level's many columns in turn supported an even smaller platform that would serve as a podium from which Mentuhotep planned to address the celebrants. A red mud-brick pyramid twice the height of a man not only crowned the edifice but provided a dramatic backdrop for the king.

*   *   *

The description of Mentuhotep I's mortuary temple appears valid in light of the present-day ruins to be found in Deir el-Bahri. The main edifice was set against the bay of the natural cliff face, while the actual burial chambers were carved from the bedrock of the cliff itself. No evidence remains today of a pyramidion atop the great temple; however, its existence was documented by foreign authors who visited the West Bank of Thebes in ancient times. More than half a century later, Queen Hatshepsut of the 18th Dynasty was so inspired by the layout of Mentuhotep's mortuary temple that she would erect a much grander version of that temple, calling hers the Djeser-djeseru ("Sacred of Sacreds"), in direct abutment to the earlier structure.

*   *   *

The celebration, an elaborate event replete with dancers and musicians, was unfortunately somewhat out of control by the time Pharaoh and his children, the royal guard, and over a hundred aristocrats, court officials and favorites made their way across the stone causeway, through the tamarisk and fig groves of the second-level terrace forecourt, and into the actual temple itself, where a lavish banquet had been laid out. Pharaoh alone proceeded to the third level as a frenzied horde of pilgrims proceeded to flood the platform of the second tier. More and more of the clamorous throng pushed their way onto the structure until every inch of space was jammed beyond reasonable capacity.

Stationing himself at the base of the pyramidion that capped the temple, Pharaoh prepared to praise his divine great-grandsire for driving the last of the rebel princes to their knees and reuniting the Two Lands once more. From his high perch, he raised his arms in a call for silence. The dull murmur of the crowd died out slowly, only to be replaced by another, more foreboding sound.

The tortured moan of stone heaving against stone grew piercingly louder and louder to the dismay of all present. Nervous murmurs of earthquake were mouthed, despite the fact that such things are more than rare in that area; it soon became apparent that a tremor could not be the cause of the disruption.

Suddenly the entire face of the platform abruptly broke away from the rear portion, sinking at an angle several feet into the rocky ground. The banquet terrace above immediately followed suit, buckling and splitting, its teetering stone roof splaying row after row of columns amidst the panicked assemblage. Thrashing human bodies tumbled and slid from the forecourt as if being flung and tossed by invisible hands.

As the rear of the base platform began a similar but more slowly paced descent into the earth, the massive stone roof of the banquet hall divided, raining tons of splintered limestone slabs down upon hundreds of screaming, terror-stricken revelers. The victims had no opportunity for escape as the world simultaneously collapsed under their feet and toppled down upon their heads. The vast majority of them died instantly, their bodies mangled and crushed by the colossal avalanche of unforgiving stone.

The third-level podium bearing Pharaoh fared better only because it was not roofed over, but still the masonry heaved and tilted threateningly beneath the king. Half falling, half sliding, he struggled to find purchase amidst the moving jumble of stonework. The dislodged mass of mudbrick of the structure's pyramidal capstone rained down upon the helpless monarch, pelting him with bricks as he tumbled headlong into the collapsing, gore-splattered rubble of the ruined banquet hall below.

It would thereafter take the engineers weeks to explain what happened that day. They eventually concluded that a subterranean void had mysteriously been created beneath the structure, possibly as the result of a fluke underground waterflow that dissolved the limestone. This, they claimed, had made the edifice unstable and thus unable to bear the tremendous additional weight of the throng of human bodies crowding onto the second level. The building's foundation, they explained, had broken through the rocky surface of the plain before sinking several feet below the surface. I could not, however, accept this as the complete explanation, for I knew better.

At the time, no one could convince the battered and bruised Mentuhotep that the calamity had been anything but a deliberate attempt upon his life by Nyarlatophis. This was understandable considering the fact that the sorcerer had gone out of his way to visit that very temple before entering Waset and, once there, had performed some nefarious ritual as he circumvented the structure.

The king suffered multiple injuries, including heavy blows to his head and chest, but his physicians were convinced none of these were life-threatening or permanently debilitating. Still, he expressed remarkably little concern when informed that all the court officials accompanying him that day had died, wiped out in an instant along with hundreds of elite citizens. His self-involved terror was so intense that he failed to inquire after his children until hours after he had been hauled, half-conscious, from the wreckage. He merely nodded when informed that both children had miraculously survived the grisly catastrophe. Reports of the disaster and its aftermath reached me that very night.

Mentuhotep, it seemed, remained so shaken by the ordeal that he chose not to accompany his children on their return boat trip to the royal residence. Instead, he planned to stay on the western side of the Hep-ur until completely recovered. When I learned of this, I suspected that, in truth, he was afraid to place himself in close proximity to Nyarlatophis again so soon. It would not be long before his fears proved justified, for another tragic incident occurred almost immediately.

Although Pharaoh declined to return to Waset, Prince Mentunosis and Princess Merytmentu returned to the royal barge and set out for home across the Hep-ur, being but seven and five years old respectively, they longed for the safety and comfort of home after their ordeal. They and a small number of guardians boarded the twenty-five-foot boat, the prow of which was carved in the likeness of a shrewmouse, and set out in early evening for what should have been an uneventful trip. But the ship ran aground on a sandbar while maneuvering through a boggy papyrus marsh just offshore from their destination. Two crewmen and three of the six oarsmen jumped in the neck-deep water to try and free the vessel and, in so doing, disturbed a family of hippopotami. The enraged adult hippos, assuming their young ones were being attacked, turned in rage upon the men and boat.

The children were thrown from the small wood-frame cabin on the boat's deck and, in the ensuing struggle between man and beast, Mentunosis, the heir to the throne, was crushed to death by one of the enormous bulls. His sister, Merytmentu, was drowned. Only three crewmen survived to relate the details of the incident to the officials who eagerly awaited the royal party's arrival.

It fell upon me to alert Pharaoh by letter to the tragic deaths of his heir and his daughter. I understand he went berserk upon receipt of the grim news, his grief only outweighed by his ever-increasing fear of Nyarlatophis. He was unshakably convinced that the black sorcerer was responsible for the death of his children and that *he* had actually been the target. His return message stated that he was going into hiding in his House of Eternity. By this he meant the unfinished tomb being fashioned for him in the valley beyond the rock cliff face that cradled the body of his great-grandfather. He would remain ensconced there, he insisted, until I had rid the city of the damnable hierophant.

The impact of the dual tragedies upon the population of Ta-Wy, and Waset in particular, was dramatic. Yet by hiding, the king deprived his people of the very assurance of security the presence of their leader lent; his sudden and complete absence only compounded the increasing air of unease.

In an effort to bolster public confidence, I deployed the whole of the policing force at my command as well as several squadrons of soldiers, placing them prominently throughout the city in hope their presence might lend a sense of well-being. Privately, however, I braced myself for whatever form the next assault would take.

Two days passed without further complication. During that time, I spent many hours brooding over the surveillance reports of those sent to watch Nyarlatophis' lair. Despite my absolute confidence in the accuracy of the reports, I was baffled;

the descriptions of the ever-changing sanctuary of Nyarlatophis confounded all logic.

Each night since Nyarlatophis' arrival, the fortress had grown by leaps and bounds from the scattered blocks of the long-shunned ruin, certainly by means of some abominable sorcery. Unlike the original temple, the new structure was round and had only one detectable means of access, a strange oval window or doorway set so far above ground-level that it could not be reached even by ladder. After sunset, the walls glowed with a ghostly indigo luminosity most unsettling to behold. In little more than a week the monstrosity had risen nearly three stories above the surface of the plain.

The roof itself was an anomaly. It appeared to be composed of a great mass of plantlike stalks of great length, randomly wound and interlaced to cover the structure. They looked like flexible logs woven together, but these were unlike anyone had ever seen.

The very substance of the construct defied every attempt at analysis, and samples obtained from the structure's walls confounded our most learned men. The material resembled the extraordinarily tough hide of some impossible hippopotamus but for certain unique qualities. All attempts to displace more than the most minute bit of material from the walls' surface failed; wounds inflicted by blades "healed" even before the blade could be completely withdrawn. Massive blows had no effect whatsoever on the walls. How could such a diabolic structure be penetrated should the need arise? I was at a maddening loss.

As I sat alone in my quarters, pondering such questions, something unexpectedly seized my attention. Among the papyri spread across the top of my bench, I spotted a foreign object that had not been there a moment earlier. I plucked the thing from its resting-place and, recognizing it, heaved a sigh of relief. It was a small ram carved of wood, a ram bearing the singularly long, curved and downturned horns of Amun's sacred beast. This was the long-awaited sign promised by the priest. I vowed to seek the god's counsel at first light.

Yet, in the middle of the night I was awakened by Mersu, my trusted, ebonyskinned assistant, who bore news of great import. A sullen courier had presented himself at the Northern Palace with an urgent request for Mentuhotep, inviting him to Nyarlatophis' abode. When Sihathor, my representative at the palace, informed the courier that Mentuhotep was not currently in Waset proper, the courier demanded to know the whereabouts of the king as he had been ordered by his master to fetch the monarch without fail. He was, of course, refused that information. The courier's previously brash manner was instantly betrayed by a look of abject fear. Owl-eyed, he produced a rolled sheet of papyrus before falling to his knees. He begged Sihathor to deliver this written message to me alone and without delay. Once assured his request would be granted, the quaking man turned and fled as though pursued by a demon.

With no little trepidation, I broke the seal and unrolled the papyrus. Addressing me by title and name, it read: "Your master cannot long conceal himself from me. I warn you, should he not arrive at my abode by noon tomorrow, I will send my Amit Hounds for him."

As I read the ominous words, a coil of dread bored through my gut. All pretense of friendly relations had finally given way to a demand and a threat. What would He do to or with Pharaoh were He to capture him, I wondered? And could the Amit ("Destroyer") Hounds mentioned be the legendary beasts of Thindahloos?

Unable to wait until dawn, I abandoned my dressing gown to don my white linen robe and golden collars of office before setting out for Amun's temple.

*   *   *

One of the god's lesser servants greeted me cordially at the temple entrance. He then guided me through various shadowed chambers to a small chapel. Once there, he advised me that Master Ipi, the elderly priest I had spoken to previously, would join me shortly. I rested upon a stone bench and waited, the darkness around me dispersing slowly as the first rays of dawn penetrated the clerestory windows high above my head. Finally, I rose to the sound of shuffling feet.

Approaching, Ipi hailed me as "Lord Amenemhat," a title above my station.

Returning salutation, I quickly launched into an account of the disturbing recent events. With a gesture, however, Ipi bade me be silent, assuring me he already knew all, including the contents of Nyarlatophis' missive. Noting my amazement, he smiled before reminding me that nothing was "hidden" from Amun.

"Tell me, then," I begged, "why is Nyarlatophis suddenly so intent on seeing Pharaoh?"

Ipi clicked his tongue despairingly. "It is not the seeing of Pharaoh that He desires, my friend, but the possession of Pharaoh that He craves. He knows full well that although He plunge all of Ta-Wy into havoc and turmoil, as I can assure you He will try to do, a small measure of hope will always abide in the hearts of the people so long as they know their divine king leader remains safe. On the other hand," he added, "should Pharaoh become the sorcerer's prisoner, the populace would be left without a shred of hope to which they might cling."

I interjected, "But surely some means to thwart this plot must exist!"

Nodding patiently, old Ipi responded, "Like freshly made bricks of mud and straw set to dry in the burning heat of day, the future, even that revealed by Amun himself, is not completely hardened and set. Your presence here is proof of this. Unfortunately, as you will soon discover, you stand entirely alone in your resolve. Painful as it may be, you must be prepared for the fatal blindness of those to whom you have sworn most sacred allegiance. Your only haven is your unshakable love for and devotion to the preservation of the Two Lands."

The ancient priest's admonition troubled me deeply. After a time, I managed to sigh, "But Teacher, I am but a mortal man after all."

As Ipi leaned to embrace me tenderly, he whispered into my ear, "For the present, that is true."

Before I could descry the meaning of his words, the hoary figure whirled away from me, suddenly instilled with an air of new authority. "Now," he declared, "you must listen with utmost intensity to the following instructions.

"Nyarlatophis is neither demon nor god; instead, He represents the essence of the black, sentient force that resides at the heart of all creation. This force is ageless, a gibbering lunacy dead-set on unraveling the very fabric of the universe. Approximately every thousand years by our reckoning, the stars align to a specific configuration, allowing Nyarlatophis to emerge from hibernation in a liminal existence. It is His aim to serve as the catalyst to quicken the process of Isfeh. Yet each time He has attempted to destroy this world, He has been checked, once by men, once by the gods, and initially by alien monstrosities that first colonized this world. Now you, with Amun's assistance, must stop Him once again."

"But how can I defeat such an inhuman force?" I inquired.

"The Hounds to which Nyarlatophis alludes are indeed the abominable Hounds of Thindahloos, just as you feared. They are not truly hounds in the familiar sense, for they are formless and immaterial beasts never meant for this reality. Those who encounter them see only an abstraction that their confounded minds translate as giant, slavering, flesh-eating jackals. These incomprehensible creatures travel through space and time along the planes of angularity, appearing wherever two surfaces intersect at an angle. They will eventually discover Mentuhotep's hiding place, no matter where it may be, and they will fetch him back to Nyarlatophis' despicable lair, unless . . ."

"Yes?" I agitatedly cried.

"Unless he barricades himself within a chamber, every angle of which has been obliterated." He went on to describe, in detail, the means for creating such a sanctuary. The joinings of ceiling, walls and floor, even the corners of doorways, must be smoothed to cover all angles with plaster, that the entire room be round and curved in every way. Even though the Hounds might scent Mentuhotep in his hiding place, such measures would keep them at bay. These instructions," he admonished, "must be carried out to the letter, for even a slight deviance will allow the fearsome mongrels entry.

"It is your sacred duty to maintain *maat*," he ominously announced, "for panic will overtake the people once they hear of the Hounds' bloody attacks. Nyarlatophis' evil influence will cause otherwise decent citizens to commit terrible crimes upon each other and their families; for this you must be prepared."

Continuing, Ipi confided the secret of the golden scarab the dark sorcerer had sent to Mentuhotep, the bauble now so proudly displayed upon his breast. In truth, it was an assassin's tool set to foully murder Pharaoh upon verbal command. His twitching fingers traced the form of hieroglyph for the word representing that command so I might know it without it being spoken aloud. He indicated in the softest of whispers that this word was the true name of the abominable lord of Isfeh to whom Nyarlatophis owed allegiance. Once that name was spoken in the presence of the golden scarab, the king's life would be irretrievably forfeit. He assured me, Nyarlatophis would never find occasion to use this weapon, yet I be aware of the word.

I listened, puzzled, but I dared not question Ipi's wisdom. Then I pleaded, "Are there no means by which I might release Mentuhotep?"

In the gentlest of voices, Ipi answered, "With your aid, Pharaoh will find release."

Finally, he instructed me to dispatch a number of troops to the site of the fallen mortuary of Mentuhotep's forebear. Once there, the men were to dig beneath the foundations of the ruin, through rock, dirt and sand until they encountered a large deposit of finely ground dust shot through with veins of red, iron-gray and gold. As much of this deposit was to be collected in baskets numbering three dozen and brought to Ipet-isut. There, under cover of darkness, the troops were directed to spread the dust generously along the outer perimeter of Montu's temple.

He scoffed at the look of worry that crossed my face and swore that Montu himself had granted permission for this seeming blasphemy. At present, he stated, it was not necessary for me to know the precise purpose of these acts.

"Take heart, Amenemhat, Amun has faith in you," he said. Then, almost as an aside, he cryptically added, "Remember, my son, Amun is the wind and the very air we breathe. Even the ferocious grip of Isfeh itself must fail should it beset itself against this god."

Though I begged him to explain his words further, he would not, assuring me I would understand in the fullness of time. Should more instruction be required, he confided, Amun himself would come to me.

With that the audience ended. I departed ready to complete the duties assigned to me to the best of my ability.

*   *   *

In a subsequent communication to Mentuhotep, I informed him of Nyarlatophis' threat and begged him to institute the exotic protective measures described by Ipi, confessing they had been revealed to me by the god Amun. He scoffed in reply, asking if I had taken leave of my senses; he considered the eradication of angles in his surroundings a ridiculous suggestion, especially as the idea had come from a lesser god. In a display of false bravura, he reminded me that as Pharaoh he was divine. My warning that the Hounds could find him anywhere reawakened his need to display at least the pretense of courage in the face of such dire danger. I immediately wrote again, begging him to follow my advice. Once loosed, I assured him, the voracious Hounds would have little regard for the divine status of their intended victim. To my great despair, he offered no response at all to this, my final warning.

The deadline came and went quickly; that very night saw the Hounds' first bitter assault. Eyewitnesses among the few survivors stated that all appeared well in the Northern Palace until, without warning, a strange mist seeped into the central audience hall that housed Pharaoh's throne. The attendant guards and royal staff later insisted they had experienced an unnatural wooziness, vertigo and distortion of time, as if they had suddenly become drunk. A great icy wind pervaded the hall, overturning the throne and furnishings; those persons present were slammed bodily against the walls. One survivor, who had observed the attack from a connecting room, told me it was as if a yawning portal to the infernal underworld had opened. He interpreted the Hounds' vague materialization as the coming of formless demons that took the shape of huge canine attackers. The descriptions of these nearly transparent, monstrous dogs bore an uncanny resemblance to the aforementioned Set animal—upright forked tails, elongated downturned muzzles, almond-shaped eyes, and long pricked-up ears with flat tips. The lead beast was said to bear a dagger deeply imbedded in its head, an age-old sign of evil. The beasts rampaged through the corridors of the palace in frantic search of Pharaoh before unleashing their frustration and inhuman wrath upon the palace's occupants.

Despite the creatures' insubstantial appearance to the human eye, their vengeance proved deadly; the unlucky victims were rent limb from limb, their still-beating hearts wrenched from their chests and shredded by slavering jaws. None of those attacked escaped beheading.

The ordeal lasted only a few brief moments, for as quickly as the slaughter had begun, it was over and the monsters gone. Despite an overwhelming barrier of haziness both physical and mental, the royal guard had responded gallantly in spite of the fantastic circumstances. Of the thirty persons who died that night, I personally had trained more than half of them.

No members of the royal family were in the palace at the time of the onslaught, thank the gods. The King's Chief Royal Wife was safely sequestered at a secret residence in Waset where she privately mourned the loss of her children. I had convinced the mother of Pharaoh's one remaining child, Pharaoh's true love and Foremost of the Secondary Wives, that she and her two-year-old daughter, Princess Neith, must leave Waset for the time being to ensure their well-being; they escaped just hours before the arrival of the murderous Hounds.

Still, there were difficulties beyond even these, just as Ipi had predicted. Trouble erupted within the very heart of the capital city. Respected, decent citizens suddenly went mad for no apparent reason, murdering entire families before committing suicide. The first of these tragic events occurred within hours of the Hounds' assault. In an effort to instill a sense of order, I posted the whole of my policing force conspicuously throughout the streets. Yet, as the frequency of such berserk incidents increased during subsequent evenings, an insidious terror began to spread through the citizenry despite our efforts. Their fear was most understandable, for who among their own family and neighbors could be trusted to remain sane? I found myself feigning confidence, assuring the people that the situation was under control, as my men hastily cleared the carnage as inconspicuously as possible. It was not until much later that we were to realize that, in every instance, the persons running amok were among those to whom Nyarlatophis had spoken directly at one time or another. I could only assume that the vile monster had somehow implanted the seed of madness in their minds, instilling fiendishly lethal suggestions set to erupt during the subsequent days or weeks.

With the setting of the sun each eve, a deep-seated fear overcame the citizenry of Waset, the only sounds periodically despoiling the chilling silence being the nightmarish shrieks of madmen and their tormented victims. Sleep frequently was nigh impossible until the earliest hours of dawn.

Luckily, no one realized that I not only acted as their absent Pharaoh's representative, but had actually taken nearly all his duties and responsibilities upon myself. Had the people learned their leader hid quivering in terror within the confines of his unfinished tomb, the resulting loss of faith would certainly have led to nationwide panic and mindless havoc.

As the frightful rampage of Nyarlatophis' fearsome Amit Hounds continued, every palace was attacked and many innocent people died gruesome deaths, rent to bits in the Hounds' insatiable jaws. Having exhausted that avenue of pursuit, the Hounds began to invade the homes of high royal officials, including my own residence. For once I was grateful to the gods that I am a widower without offspring; considering the extreme pressure of my situation already, I could not have borne the added stress of losing those I loved the most.

I prayed the damnable Hounds would not discover Pharaoh's place of concealment, but when I received report that his favorite scribe's headless corpse had been found in his home on the city's west bank, my confidence began to dwindle.

Throughout this time, my persistent communiqués to Mentuhotep went unheeded. The only information I could glean concerning his activities or state of mind was derived from the men who delivered my messages. From them I learned Mentuhotep had in no way altered his surroundings to eradicate the angles, which led me to conclude his capture, and probable demise, would not be long in coming.

Thus when it did come, I was somewhat prepared for the catastrophic news. The Hounds had finally infiltrated Pharaoh's sanctuary, leaving its brilliantly adorned walls awash with the blood of the noble royal bodyguard. A subsequent search of the premises confirmed my belief that the royal person was nowhere to be found among the human carnage. I could only conclude my worst fear had been realized; the Hounds had spirited the still-living Mentuhotep off to the unholy clutches of Nyarlatophis's lair.

When it seemed events could get no worse, one of my watchmen informed me that Chief Royal Wife Nefertmentu had covertly entered Nyarlatophis' lair. The unnatural sanctuary had by then expanded to a height of four stories and engulfed a tremendous area of land as well. My informants explained that the singular access to that immense citadel, an entryway suspiciously reminiscent of an anus, had slowly crept downward from its unreachable position to provide the Nefertmentu ease of access. They swore no one other than the royal consort had entered or left the lair. Should Mentuhotep be immured within, the Hounds could only have transported him through the unfathomable portals of angular space.

My first thought was that Nefertmentu had been taken there by the heinous Hounds, but I soon learned the Chief Royal Wife had entered the pesthole of her own volition.

Why would her majesty surrender herself so easily to that which could only be a deathtrap? Her purpose in so doing struck me as suspect. When word got out, no doubt it would be generally presumed that she had chosen to sacrifice herself in an attempt to free her lord. But anyone gullible enough to accept such a selfless act as her motive did not know the dear lady.

Nefertmentu was her husband/brother's senior by two years and, sad though it be, their only true emotional bond was naught but jealousy and animosity. Their union was dictated by tradition alone, and it was nothing less than a miracle that the marriage produced two offspring, although Mentuhotep once confided in me his doubts that he had truly sired Princess Merytmentu. Nonetheless, the royal couple continued to present themselves as happily allied for the benefit of an unsuspecting public.

The Nefertmentu I had come to know was a cold and scheming, headstrong woman who longed to sit alone upon the throne of the Two Lands in her brother's stead. Mentuhotep had no choice but to tolerate his bride and sister, for her position was secured by the birth of their two children, one of whom had been, until his recent demise, heir apparent to the throne. With the death of her children, however, Nefertmentu justifiably feared being replaced by one of the king's lesser wives, whereupon she would be banished to the dull existence of life in the royal harem. Because of these considerations, I questioned the integrity of her intentions in voluntarily entering Nyarlatophis' realm. Yet, whatever her motivations were, I could only do my utmost to deliver her as well as my king from the confines of the sorcerous fortress.

I was convinced a direct siege upon Nyarlatophis' den would prove both futile and costly in terms of human lives. Also, despite the lack of any tangible proof, I strongly believed there was a connection between the queer nature of the ever-expanding construct and the several reported disappearances of both livestock and men, two of my best observers among them, from the proximate area. All had vanished without trace on moonless nights. Still, I could not for the life of me contrive a possible motive for these inexplicable abductions.

That night, the most urgent of my questions found answer in the form of a lucid dream in which Amun in the guise of Master Ipi visited me in my quarters.

"Do not despair, Amenemhat," began the vessel of the god, "for so long as you continue to follow my instructions, *maat* will certainly prevail.

"Have little concern for Nefertmentu," he added after a short pause, "that foolish cow has chosen her own fate. As to the Hounds, they have retreated once more to their black realm, the hunt having been successfully concluded. As you have dared to hope, your pharaoh has indeed survived the Hounds' onslaught, but as you feared, he has become the prisoner of the crawling chaos Nyarlatophis. Be forewarned, however, that Mentuhotep is changed; the merciless Hounds dragged him through the incomprehensible empty places that exist between space and time. His *ka* has fled, abandoning his body, although his *ba* remains trapped within his earthly form. He is thus deprived of self-will, his mind enslaved by his captor."

"What can I do to free him?" my dreaming self begged.

The shadowy figure hung his head, then mumbled softly, almost sadly, "The means of Mentuhotep's release will be made known to you only at the precise moment of that release."

I felt a sense of uneasy relief at the deity's words.

Ipi then divulged the exotic circumstances that had led to the collapse of Mentuhotep I's mortuary temple. He spoke of a life form so infinitely small that it was completely invisible to the human eye. Nyarlatophis, he said, lured a previously unknown form of life from its native realm deep within the earth's bowels, a thing so elemental that it actually survives without air or water by eating and breathing rock, minerals and soil!

Nyarlatophis directed this life form's bizarre ability to consume the very earth itself by implanting large numbers of the minute creatures all around the outer perimeter of Mentuhotep's marvelous temple. By use of His inhuman willpower, He altered the mindless things' natural habits and inclinations, causing the colony to multiply a thousand times faster than normal in order that it might consume the foundational bedrock beneath the temple. Solid stone was thereby transformed into a dust-like compatible substance. So undermined, the great structure was set to disintegrate and plunge into the hollow beneath once burdened with the excessive burden of too many celebrants.

"If this be the case," I inquired, "why would you have my men inflict this same destructive life form on Montu's temple?"

"In the fullness of time," he assured me, "you will fully comprehend Amun's infinite wisdom. Until then, be patient."

Ipi next provided me with a detailed plan for an all-out assault on Nyarlatophis' citadel, to be launched at my discretion. By such means, I was told, the sorcerer's living lair could be savaged, driving its creator to undertake "an immense transformation" that would lead to His ultimate undoing. Having adopted a new and frightening form, the First Prophet explained, Nyarlatophis would then seek to sever Montu's heaven-sent flow of empowering energy by obliterating his temple. Should He succeed in this, the sanctuaries of all the gods and goddesses of the Two Lands and beyond would be targeted, thereby depriving the world of all prospect of supernal aid. The world would be helpless and at the mercy of this servant of chaos.

Upon waking, I found I could barely come to terms with the ominous import of this wondrous dream when, to my amazement, I was alerted that a message from Pharaoh himself had been delivered by one of the men who had vanished while keeping watch on Nyarlatophis' lair.

The messenger, one Ahmose, had appeared, seemingly from nowhere, a short distance from the sorcerer's citadel. When my men brought him before me, it was clear the poor fellow's mind was gone, to the extent that my feeble attempts to question him proved utterly fruitless. His glassy eyes reminded me of the lifeless stare of a statue.

On his person, however, a papyrus scroll was found. It bore Mentuhotep's official seal. The contents were short and succinct: "Attend, Vizier, that you may know my wishes. At the mid-hour of night, the portal of Nyarlatophis' temple will admit you and only you to my presence."

The cold and impersonal tone of the message was unlike that to which I was so well accustomed from my monarch, and I was taken aback as well that he referred to the sorcerer's hellish lair as a "temple."

There could be no question but that I would present myself at the appointed place and time, alone and weaponless; I had sworn allegiance to Mentuhotep, therefore I was honor-bound to attend him. If nothing else, I hoped to obtain inside knowledge of the enemy's quarters and defenses. Better yet, I recalled, Ipi had assured me that only through me might Mentuhotep find release. I considered it likely, and acceptable, that I would be required to forfeit my life in exchange for the life of my god-king, thus I steeled myself for whatever was to come.

I watched in awe as the palely glowing wall before which I stood trembled and rippled like the water of a lake. The peculiar portal slowly crept and floated down to the level of the plain on which I stood. The edges of the crude opening slowly splayed outward, reminding me again of an extended anus, this time offering me dark, penetrating entry.

Squeezing through the sparse opening, I was struck by the fetid odor of the bowel-like tunnel I faced. The walls, floor, and the ceiling above my head were composed of a soft, spongy substance unfamiliar to me. Once fully inside, the moist and slimy surroundings caressed my body as I progressed onward; I felt as if the walls yearned to consume my flesh. A subtle light, emitted by the pale glowing veins of an unknown substance embedded in the gelatinous walls, described the choked pathway ahead. A repetitious sound like the heaving of enormous lungs accompanied me as I continued.

I threaded my way through the winding intestinal morass until I found myself standing at the threshold of a great, spacious gallery. My glance upward was rewarded with a dizzying view of what appeared to be the multi-storied interior of a tremendous cylinder of living, throbbing tissue. The walls of this shaft were intermittently pierced by the gaping mouths of caverns accessible only by means of a series of precariously thin ledges molded from the walls themselves. To my surprise, I could not detect the slightest sign of defense in my surroundings.

Beyond the spongy lip of the ledge on which I found myself lay a lake-sized basin filled with a foul and vomitous liquid. Floating upon the foamy surface of the sloshing liquid were the worm-riddled, rotting remains of sheep, fowl and . . . human beings. I could now account for the men and livestock that vanished in the proximity of the damnable place.

A bright illumination lit a cavernous gap in the expansive wall opposite and somewhat above me. As my eyes adjusted, I was able to distinguish two backlit figures poised side-by-side within that large opening. As I had seen Him previously, I immediately recognized the bold visage of the hateful Nyarlatophis.

At His side stood Mentuhotep, dressed in a kilt of the finest linen, robes and sandals, with the double crown of the Two Lands perched on his head. Splayed across his chest was an elaborately bejeweled pectoral with the infamous golden scarab nestled at its heart. So far as I could determine, his eyes were closed.

On the other side of Nyarlatophis, reclining in a somewhat shadowed corner, crouched another familiar form, that of the sorcerer's night-dark leonine companion.

Decorum prevented me from being the first to speak. As I waited in silence, Pharaoh's eyes slowly opened, as if he only really awoke when Nyarlatophis touched his shoulder.

Mentuhotep stared into the nothingness straight ahead, his expression completely vacant. Only at the sorcerer's command did he loudly declare, "Hear me, my Vizier, and obey your lord without hesitation!" His tone and inflection were devoid of emotion.

I bowed respectfully, then as I rose, I responded, "Yes, My Lord!"

As if in a trance, Mentuhotep recited a stream of shocking orders. In monotonous tones, he declared, "Henceforth, there shall be no god other than Nyarlatophis, for He is divine Isfeh incarnate. His commands must be obeyed instantly, upon pain of death."

Aghast at Pharaoh's blasphemous words, I froze at attention.

"Every temple, altar and image of any other so-called god or goddess is to be completely obliterated without delay," he continued. "The various priesthoods shall be disbanded entirely and the total assets of every temple confiscated and delivered here to Nyarlatophis, the only true god."

He ended his speech as abruptly as he had begun.

Rage filled my entire being. It was not only the intent of Pharaoh's blasphemous words that infuriated me, for I knew them to be Nyarlatophis' words simply being parroted for my benefit. Did the sorcerer take me for a fool? Nothing about the king was normal, neither the total absence of inflection in his voice, the lack of body mannerisms, nor the artificial, puppet-like way he remained motionlessly poised beside his nemesis.

"Are these truly your wishes and yours alone, My Lord?" I challenged. "Do you swear you speak freely and of your own volition rather than at the behest of this fiend?"

Mentuhotep remained transfixed, unmindful of his surroundings, as if he had not heard my questions. After a moment, the sorcerer leaned and whispered into the king's ear. Stiffly, his gaze still focused unseeingly ahead, Pharaoh turned and retreated to an area to the rear of his controller.

Nyarlatophis glared down at me. "You have sworn absolute allegiance to your Pharaoh," He calmly reminded me. Then, in more brazen tones, "Your master has given you orders, now carry them out without delay!"

Infuriated, I shouted, "Black demon! Release my master! Remove this bewitchment at once! I obey only my worthy lord Mentuhotep, not this mockery into which you have converted him."

The sorcerer paused, considering response. Then, in an almost patronizing voice, He said, "So, Amenemhat, you do recognize this small pretense for what it is. Yet, should you dare defy your regent, you will find you stand alone. You, of course, know this poor idiot of a Pharaoh personally and intimately, but do you sincerely believe anyone else will sense enough of a change in their king to refuse his explicit commands?

"Have you forgotten that in the minds of the people, this man"—He gestured to indicate the living puppet behind him before continuing with His usual aplomb—"is not only Pharaoh but one who has achieved divine apotheosis as well? He is the holy protector of your beloved Two Lands. Without him the Hep-ur will not flood in the vital season and the people of Ta-Wy will starve! Do you believe for an instant that your challenge, your doubts, could ever overcome such firmly entrenched faith? I think not!

"Of course, the priests will cry out desperately against the looting and the suspension of their lavish lifestyles, but the ignorant poor will happily flock to assist in the downfall of the gods, driven by the promise of rich spoils.

"Would you set yourself against the greedy masses? As long as Pharaoh moves and speaks, though he be manipulated like a child's toy, his people will obey his every direction." Then, almost as an aside, He taunted, "Should you or anyone else protest this course of events, you will be deftly silenced . . . forever."

I knew the fiend was right in all that He had said, but still I refused to give up. I spat back at Him, "Then I will find a means to free Mentuhotep from your despicable possession!"

Had Nyarlatophis had the capacity for laughter, I would surely have heard it then, but instead He calmly responded, "Should you find such means, it would not serve you well. Do you not understand I have annihilated this pathetic creature's mind? What you see here is the animated shell of an irretrievably deceased man."

Again I instinctively knew He spoke the truth. My master truly was lost, beyond all salvation. An irrational, boiling fury welled up within me; I had to find a way to salvage something from this catastrophe.

"And what of the royal consort? What of the Nefertmentu?" I demanded.

"You may take her," said the sorcerer, "for she is of no further use to me." Pointing, he indicated a crevice not far to my left in which a shadowed figure lay prone and unmoving.

"Go on," He urged, "take her. She is not dead, merely *indisposed*."

With infinite care I edged my way along the narrow, slippery ledge. One careless step and I would plunge my form into the churning brine that lapped so near my precarious perch. Further, despite the nearness of the neighboring niche, I did not trust Nyarlatophis enough to know if there might be a trick or trap awaiting me.

Having established a firm footing within the unnatural alcove, I knelt beside what I prayed truly was Nefertmentu. I was appalled to see the wretched woman's nude form was frightfully abused. From head to foot, her blood-streaked skin displayed the ravages of cruel, vicious bites and relentless clawing.

Sickened and enraged, I turned to the solemn observer above and shouted accusation, "You have tortured this innocent woman beyond all comprehension! To what possible end?"

Without pause, Nyarlatophis sneered, "It was she who came to me. Knowing her brother-husband was no match for me, this 'innocent woman' hoped to ingratiate herself by seducing me. She was very confident that by bewitching me, she could retain high position after I have usurped Mentuhotep's throne. When she failed to elicit any promise from me, she disrobed and approached me."

He proceeded to describe their sexual liaison. Nefertmentu's error, it seemed, was her naïve assumption that she was dealing with a powerful human being, which the sorcerer definitely was not. Nyarlatophis confessed that, in throes of passion, He had given in to His animal instinct. To her horror, Nefertmentu had suddenly found herself coupling with the dog-headed ape into which her lover had transformed himself. In this mutated form, the sorcerer had bitten and mauled her mercilessly.

A brief examination of the despondent victim revealed that the detestable experience had been more than her mind could bear. She lay perfectly still in my arms, her empty eyes staring at naught. As unaware as a child's doll, her mind had fled the torment of her ordeal. Despite my lack of respect for the woman, I could not help but feel pity for the miserable wretch.

Rising, I gathered her limp form in my arms. Then, in an instant storm of rage and disgust, I recalled that Nyarlatophis meant to devastate the whole of the Two Lands just as he had done to the royal couple. This I could never allow.

A unique clarity of mind settled upon me. I knew precisely what must be done, though I knew it would pain me very deeply.

The sorcerer interrupted my stream of thought with a final, loud demand, "Will you bow in abeyance to your Pharaoh or must I destroy you here and now?"

Gathering my wits, I responded that my loyalty to Nefertmentu required I attend her before all else. I would, I swore, take her outside to safety, then return with my answer. This was a declaration, not a proposal, so I did not await Nyarlatophis' permission before proceeding and, to my great relief, He made no move to stop me.

The exit journey was even more difficult with the added strain of toting the dead weight of the unconscious wife of the king, but my strength seemed renewed once I passed her along to my compatriots waiting outside. I bid them cover her warmly and rush her to the royal physicians without delay. Then, with a wave of my hand, I dismissed their urgent inquiries by announcing, "Should any of you care to wait, I will return soon."

With unblinking determination, I strode back into the stinking bowels of that deplorable place until once again I defiantly faced the enemy.

Mentuhotep, or rather his sad remnant, stood stiffly at attention to the immediate right of the recalcitrant sorcerer. I addressed the latter fearlessly, "You offer me two choices: either I cooperate in bringing about the destruction of the world or refuse to cooperate. The first option means the death of my soul in exchange for the short time you would allow me to live before proving of no further use. The second choice means my instant eradication. As neither of these choices appeals to me, I propose a third solution."

The stone-faced sorcerer stood fast without comment, so I boldly continued. "I propose that the conquest of the Two Lands would be of greater interest if it were an actual challenge."

No reaction was immediately forthcoming, so I steadied myself, prepared for a painful death.

Instead, Nyarlatophis stated flatly, "I am completely invulnerable to any form of resistance you may offer."

I quickly countered, "Would You allow me to leave here unharmed if I were able to demonstrate my worthiness as an opponent?"

Nyarlatophis repeated His previous declaration of invulnerability word for word.

"That is no answer," I jeered. "Will You let me leave this place unharmed if I can prove myself a worthy opponent?"

Shaking his head with disgust, Nyarlatophis replied, "Very well, should you defeat me in even the slightest manner here and now, I guarantee your safe exit."

He surely expected me to make some move to rescue Mentuhotep. But that was not my goal, for I knew Pharaoh was already irrevocably lost. I could not have done what I did next had I not been thoroughly convinced no means of saving my king existed.

I stepped forward, announcing, "You would plunge the Two Lands into lethal chaos under the leadership of this, our Pharaoh transformed. I cannot allow that tragic scenario to reach fruition."

"Words," sneered the sorcerer, "you dare challenge me with naught but words?"

"Never underestimate the strength of words, Powerful One!" I sarcastically retorted. Half turning, I made as if to depart. As if it were but an afterthought, I suddenly did an about-face. With fists tightly clinched in anticipation of dire result, I screamed, "Azathoth!" at the top of my lungs.

I had initially closed my eyes as I called out the dread name Ipi had entrusted to me, but despite my morbid fear I could not help but look moments later. Nothing appeared to have changed, as if my verbal gesture had no effect whatsoever. The two figures remained immobile above me, poised on the brink of the cavernous gulf that separated us. For an instant stark terror seared up and down my spine as I stared in open-mouthed disbelief. Had Ipi and his god played me for a fool?

I would have fled at that point had my body allowed. I glanced from Mentuhotep to Nyarlatophis, then back again. I could feel the wave of pure, limitless hatred the sorcerer was directing at me.

Only when a flutter of movement caught my attention did I chance to believe the priest had not betrayed me after all. Breaking the hold of the sorcerer's insidious glare, I beheld an unexpected motion at the center of the gaudy pectoral adorning Pharaoh's breast.

The scarab, no longer gold and glittering, grew larger and larger as I watched. The dark outline of its shell heaved and swelled as it encompassed more and more of the royal chest.

Without warning, six reed-thin, black jointed limbs shot with lightning speed out from beneath the body of the beetle's swelling shell. The chitinous legs extended to grasp Pharaoh by the shoulders, arms and wrists, binding his torso in an embrace so ferocious that blood spurted and oozed from his flesh.

To my great relief, Mentuhotep gave no indication that he felt the insect's murderous grasp; his face remained absolutely without expression and wholly devoid of awareness.

Nyarlatophis continued to fix His terrible, unflinching gaze on me, infinite hatred obviously overriding any concern He might have for His victim's altering situation.

A pair of saw-toothed pinchers slowly emerged from the underside of the growing scarab. The gigantic, serrated pinchers encircled Mentuhotep's naked throat and, as I caught my breath, the merciless blades clamped brutally down on both sides of his neck. With my raised forearms, I tried to blot the unbearable sight from my view, but nothing could shelter me from the ensuing sound of the grinding of bones. When I finally dared look again, the demonic beetle had dropped from the teetering body of Mentuhotep. As his body collapsed, the terrible insect rolled its prize, Pharaoh's severed head, back into the dark recesses of the cavern, as if it were a common ball of dung.

To my eternal shame it was by means of such a heinous act that I was able to prove myself an opponent of worth. Shocked and sickened beyond all measure at the cost of Mentuhotep's "release," I shot a final glance at the unyielding countenance of Nyarlatophis before turning to retreat through the noxious labyrinthine tunnel once again.

After a seemingly endless time, I stumbled out into the arms of my patient companions. Nothing could compare to the sweetness, the cool, fresh nectar of that clean night air. Sipping the fresh water offered me, I learned that I had been within the confines of Nyarlatophis' pest hole for several hours. Still weak from my ordeal, I gladly allowed my loyal friend and aide Mersu to offer me the physical support required to return to headquarters.

I had only time to sit down for a moment before I was bombarded with news of the disastrous state into which the kingdom had further deteriorated during my absence. In order to avoid complete and hopeless panic, I shared the secret of Pharaoh's terrible demise with dark-skinned Mersu.

Still, it soon became obvious that the people of Egypt sensed the impending doom about to envelop their world, and they reacted accordingly. Revolution stalked the land and, in fear, many turned to violence. Blood flowed in the streets and alleys of every city of Ta-Wy; so many died that the great river offered the only means to dispose of the plethora of rotting corpses.

Vermin overran the country as the restless desert encroached unnaturally on the fertile farmlands. Foreign hordes made preparations for descent on our borders from the every direction. It was as if the whole world had begun to whirl insanely on a potter's wheel.

I allowed myself a rest of but a few short hours, during which I vainly attempted to come to terms with the fact that it had been necessary for me to initiate my Pharaoh's execution. Only then could I bring myself to order not only the police but the whole of the king's standing royal army to assemble. Without doubt, the time for action had arrived.

With the implication that I acted at the direct order of the absent Pharaoh, I instructed the men to prepare a siege. The source of the crises consuming the country, I entreated them, must be obliterated.

I directed a number of men to comb the city and suburbs in search of as much raw and lamp oil as could be located; it was all collected and stored in one specific place near Ipet-rasyt. Cattle-drawn wagons were gathered along with large earthen jars for transporting the oil. All was accomplished within two days despite the interference provided by the rampant violence and confusion that rapidly spread throughout the town; we were ready to fight with all our strength to save our world.

The caravan of commandeered wagons converged on the target later that very afternoon. The coming of night did not deter us, for we knew the sky above Ipet-rasyt would be bright with light soon enough.

After surrounding the base of Nyarlatophis' tower, we began to unload the carts and remove the stoppers from half the oil jars. The next step was to drench the tower walls to as great a height as possible with our black liquid cargo. To our surprise, no attempts were made to interfere or prevent us from dousing the structure.

Once that task had been accomplished, I called to the men to draw back a safe distance. A line of troops brandishing flaming torches advanced to form a ring around the tower. Then, at my signal, the burning torches went coursing through the evening air. The oil caught fire easily, instantly transforming the sorcerer's stronghold into a dazzling inferno. And still there came no resistance from within.

The burning edifice emitted a gas so noxious that we were forced to move upwind. Still, we savored the sight of the walls as they buckled and squirmed in the flames, praying we had managed to inflict irreparable damage. I prayed the structure suffered just as had the victims whose remains I had seen in its inner pool.

We moved downwind from the surging fire to avoid the great billowing clouds of dark, acrid smoke. Whenever it appeared the flames were dying down, we flung more fuel onto the spasming structure. I could only assume that Nyarlatophis would be impervious to the oven-blast of heat, but I was determined to deprive Him completely of His necrophagous abode.

As the orange and yellow flames reached the upper portions of the tower, the tendrils we had interpreted as a roof covering began to unravel, drooping downward like the wilting stalks of a dying plant. The largest were thick as the trunks of trees and long enough to dangle limply all the way to the ground. We paid these no particular notice until one of the larger stalks curled like a snake around one of my men, holding him fast until the tip suddenly opened and stifled his screams by swallowing his head. The helpless, thrashing man was quickly and silently swept upward until he disappeared in the darkness, apparently dragged down into the interior through some unseen opening above. At the success of that stalk, the others displayed nefarious stirrings. Why had Ipi not warned me of this devious method of defense? I certainly could not have been expected to anticipate it on my own.

Without a moment to lose, I frantically called for those poised within the zone of danger to run for their lives. I then had others cast burning, oil-drenched spears and firebrands at the writhing, unearthly strands. The stalks caught fire easily, their subsequent whipping and thrashing through the air only serving to enhance the flames. Thoroughly entangled, the tendrils inadvertently ignited their squirming neighbors until, in the end, the last of the stalks drooped and fell lifelessly to the ground. Unfortunately, two more men were caught and whisked away before the last stalks charred and snapped off.

By that time, the tower was entirely engulfed in the conflagration. I was tempted to rejoice at the sight of the tower being slowly reduced to glowing red and white-hot embers, despite the fact that our victory over insufferable evil was far from complete. But the rivers of foul black smoke that rose heavenward for a third time reminded me that the battle was far from over.

A few minutes later I was forced to set aside any further rumination as a messenger arrived bearing news of unanticipated activity on and around the plain of Ipet-isut. The townspeople could not help but see the firestorm we had created at Ipet-rasyt, and thus they raced *en masse* through smoke-filled streets to the temple of their patron god, Montu. The sacred *temenos* was filled, actually clogged to overflowing, with hundreds of frantic, torch-bearing pilgrims petitioning Montu for salvation.

I faltered momentarily, unsure of the proper course of action. It struck me as vital that I be present when the "transformed" Nyarlatophis emerged from the fiery ruins of His lair. Simultaneously, I had no doubt that those who were gathering at Montu's temple were unknowingly in the very gravest of danger, for surely Amun's intention was to lure the altered sorcerer to that very place for a final, titanic confrontation.

In the end, I was spared the difficult decision by the clangorous disintegration of the white-hot tower. With a mournful sigh the roasted walls were slowly and relentlessly rent asunder. Like bloodless wounds, two immense parallel fissures appeared in the midst of the structure to the accompaniment of an ear-shattering scream. The very fabric of the tower began to stretch and distort unnaturally as we watched. Some incredibly tremendous bulk was undermining the very integrity of the building from within!

When the walls could expand no further, great chunks commenced to break free of the main structure, the slabs teetering precariously for a moment before careening headlong outward. Those nearest the rupturing tower ran for their lives, while others simply retreated a few paces to avoid the threat of raining debris.

At that point, we noted a queer whimpering or purring moan emanating from deep within the flickering glow of the wreckage. Mesmerized, I felt myself being drawn toward the eerie sound to the extent that my fellow listeners had to draw me back forcibly lest I unwittingly offer myself up to the incinerating blast of heat radiating from the yawning ruin.

It was Mersu who steadied me when a deafening roar burst forth from the deepest recesses of the crumbling edifice. Together we watched in fearful awe as a mammoth four-legged beast extricated itself from the ash and fire of Nyarlatophis' lair. It was, I knew, the transformed sorcerer Himself, but I could not immediately determine what brand of horrific creature He had become.

The behemoth boldly strode from the fiery wreckage, causing us to retreat even further. We found ourselves facing the deformed image of a colossal lion, a new horror surely the product of Nyarlatophis having physically intermingled with His dark familiar, the black lion He brought from the desert. But it was the head, framed within the striped folds of the beast's *nemes* headgear, that defied all logic, for the lion bore the face of Nyarlatophis Himself! The monster's vile appearance mocked that of the great stone Sphinx, the guardian of the gateway that leads to the trio of mighty pyramids at Rostau. It even sported the false beard of that archaic, monumental sculpture.

I could readily see my own fear and confoundment reflected in the faces of the others. I cried out for everyone to disperse and seek shelter, unaware that Mersu was no longer by my side.

As if He recognized my voice, the looming sphinx sought to discover my whereabouts among the throng of scattering bodies. I made no effort to conceal myself, so the haughty beast lumbered over to confront me. He emitted a low growl that may well have indicated satisfaction, then assumed a couchant, catlike pose identical to that of His limestone twin at Rostau. He remained motionless and only the bellows-like sound of His breathing broke the silence as He tilted His great head from side to side, assessing me as an opponent. I stood my ground defiantly, determined to conceal the chilling terror within my heart. The standoff ended when a gurgle emerged from the chimera's throat, a chuckle-like gurgle surely meant to ridicule me before my own troops, whom I signaled the fall back.

I too studied my enemy, realizing the hideousness of the mad amalgam was equaled only by the sheer splendor of its mesmerizing beauty. Had this towering monster, I wondered, served as model for ancient sculptors who carved the guardian image of the protector of the pyramids?

In a somewhat distorted human voice, the sphinx hailed me as a suitable foe.

Purring tones added, "Although you have reduced my lair to a mere pile of ash, you have failed to vanquish me." When I did not respond, He continued boastfully, "That is something you could never achieve, even with the aid of your petty gods."

I started, then held my breath in anticipation. If Nyarlatophis had realized my pact was with Amun rather than Montu, all would have been lost.

"I will avenge myself on your god lending you aid. I shall grind asunder the stones of his temple until nothing remains but dust," He sneered. "How will he help you when he grows weak, deprived of life giving sustenance from the stars?

Thereafter, one by one, I shall trample and smash every temple across the face of Egypt and beyond, regardless to which god or goddess the temples belong. Then and only then will this land behold the true strength of Isfeh."

My spirits were dashed as all hope bled from my soul. What chance could there be to stop this abomination should Amun be deprived of his source of power? And still the chimera ranted on.

"I spare you for the time being, Amenemhat, only that you may witness the unfolding of my great victory. You shall accompany me to Ipet-isut to witness the obliteration of the temple of your great Montu."

I had to struggle not to display any signs of the incredible relief I felt at these final words. All was not lost after all! Not only was Nyarlatophis still unaware that Amun rather than Montu was my benefactor, but His great hubris was leading Him directly into Amun's finely tuned trap!

The bragging man-beast rose up on His haunches. I prepared to be torn apart by His terrible claws.

All this changed, however, when a piercing cry broke from somewhere behind me. A dark-skinned figure, whom I quickly recognized as my friend Mersu, hurled past me, arms flailing, directly at the bewildered beast. Without consideration for his own safety, Mersu stopped just long enough to fling a large object at the monster before retreating. I heard the shatter of ceramic as the thrown object smashed upon the sphinx's face. Hot upon Mersu's heels, yet another man charged forward to toss a flaming faggot at the identical target. The broken container had contained a quantity of black oil that instantly ignited, engulfing the whole of Nyarlatophis' face in a brilliant flash of orange.

The Nyarlatophis sphinx reared up on His hind legs, mewling, thrashing and pawing frantically in a futile attempt to extinguish the flesh-searing flames. His deafening roars of agony assaulted our ears as the three of us raced for cover beyond the reach of the sphinx run amok. From safe vantage, we stared in wonder as the four-legged terror tumbled and writhed in the relentless grip of merciless hideous burning until, with a final bloodcurdling wail, the wretched beast turned and fled into the desert. None of us moved until the last of the eerie glow had completely vanished into the nighted distance.

The others threw their arms about one another in celebration, laughing and hooting uncontrollably as they pranced a congratulatory dance. Although aware that our seeming victory was but temporary, I joined the rejoicing until eventually we collapsed, exhausted but smiling, on the ground.

The preternatural sphinx of Nyarlatophis could not, I knew, die of these or any injuries inflicted by mere mortals. And when He returned, He would present an even more deadly menace.

Nyarlatophis' goal went far beyond the obliteration of Montu's sanctuary at Ipet-isut, despite the fact that He still seemed to maintain the erroneous belief that Montu alone presented any tangible threat to his insidious campaign. His final goal was to destroy Montu's temple so as to plunge the Two Lands and then the entire world into the madness of Chaos's mephitic abyss. So if the earlier report was accurate, His first victims were now amassing at that very sanctuary; my fellow countrymen were unwittingly offering themselves up for slaughter.

Wasting no time, I dispatched the troops, authorizing them to proceed to Ipet-isut without delay by whatever means possible. I sent Mersu to fetch the raiment of my office that he might meet me at the docks as quickly as possible.

The rest of us hurried to the riverbank where we seized every available seaworthy craft, the Hep-ur providing the most expedient route to the harbor nearly a mile to the north.

We made good time but were not encouraged by the sight that greeted our makeshift flotilla as we neared Ipet-isut. The sun was just rising as we entered the harbor, providing us a view of the thousands of men, women and children jamming the temple's outer courtyard, their numbers flowing far beyond the perimeter walls of the temple. We disembarked and assembled, proceeding up the causeway toward the crowd. I encouraged the men to display an air of confident authority as they approached the terrified pilgrims as brandishing their weapons certainly would incite panic amongst the already frightened mob.

My troops opened a path through the befuddled mass that I might pass between the temple's banner flags directly to the massive first pylon. As I approached the double-towered entryway, I paid silent salute to the seated pair of larger-than-life-size stone figures set on either side, the smaller a portrait of the Pharaoh Mentuhotep, the larger of Montu. I proceeded through the magnificently decorated pillared courts to the inner sanctum.

There I came upon an appalling scene. Sickening as it was, I experienced a sense of familiarity, as if it were something I recalled from a half-remembered dream, the remnants of which still lingered in my mind. Although I thought myself emotionally prepared for anything, the sight of such widespread human carnage so close at hand affected me greatly, the impact enhanced by this normally being a place of worship. I was again reminded that should I fail to avert the eternally dark future Ipi had shown me, the entire world would soon suffer a similar fate.

Solemnly, I retraced my steps, returning to the hushed crowd that breathlessly awaited me just beyond the initial pylon. Upon arrival, I instructed a number of my men to drag the corpses from the holy-of-holies and stack them before the pylon in a sturdy heap. They were extremely reluctant to enter such a holy place that had always been forbidden them, but as Mersu led the way the others obediently followed.

I had the corpses piled one upon the other so as to create an impromptu platform. From this bloody construct, I planned to address a shocked audience gathered close that they might stare in stunned silence. As I climbed the pile of dead bodies, I recognized my name being whispered by the onlookers, which reassured me for, if they knew me, they also knew I spoke for Pharaoh. The tense murmuring waned to a nervous hush as I gazed across the sea of anxious faces from atop the heap of fly-beset corpses.

Taking a deep breath, I shouted, "Citizens of Waset, hear me! On the horizon, you see the glare of the flames which engulf our enemy's lair, and you have come here to this sacred place to seek sanctuary in the house of Montu. It is right that you should fear the invader Nyarlatophis, for truly He brings evil beyond imagining to our beloved capital." Gesturing to the stack of dead bodies that served as my podium, I added, "It is proper too that you seek the protection of the gods for, as these priests before you have already learned, the gods do not tolerate those who bear false witness in their name.

"These men betrayed their vows; they lied to Pharaoh, assuring him it was Montu's wish that the harbinger of Isfeh be made welcome in our city. When they realized the consequences of their blasphemy, they chose to take their own lives, praying this atonement might spare them from the devouring monsters awaiting them in the land of the dead. I assure you, however, those monsters are unforgiving and eagerly await their tainted souls!"

A flurry of shock and outrage stirred my listeners, causing many to step back and away from the offending compilation of bodies.

I stated further, "The help you seek, however, cannot be found here. Montu has retreated, greatly offended by the deeds of his trusted priesthood. But do not despair, for Amun has vowed to save us by delivering the Two Lands from the clutches of this inhuman menace! He alone possesses the means to defeat this malefic sorcerer, and he has entrusted me with the knowledge to achieve that goal. Already my men have driven Nyarlatophis from his fortress with fire.

"Yet we cannot allow ourselves to be lulled into a false sense of security! Nyarlatophis has undergone a most terrible transformation! He has, it is true, fled into the desert wastes, but be warned, His infernal return is imminent! It is to this very place He will come, for only here can He be vanquished!"

Irrepressible panic surged through my audience. I was relieved to note that my words caused many swiftly to abandon the closely packed sea of confused and frightened faces.

"I beg you, my people," I screamed at the top of my lungs, "run from this place at once if you wish to live! Hurry to the safety of your homes, for this place is doomed, as you will be if you become caught up in the ensuing battle!"

I was prepared to argue further but, praise the gods, a frantic cry suddenly rang out from beyond the outer wall of the temple complex. "Vizier, something approaches from the south," insisted the straining voice. "It's huge, more massive than two houses set atop each other!"

A nightmare of hysteria and madness ensued. Many were killed or injured in the crazed crush of bodies as terrified men, women and children raced to distance themselves from the sacred enclosure. To their great credit, my troops did their utmost to preserve some semblance of order, but they were outnumbered to such a degree by the rampaging crowd that their efforts were of little avail.

Although appalled by the response to the coming danger, I forced myself to focus on preparing myself for the imminent arrival of the sphinx. I sent Mersu and two others back into the inner sanctuary to collect linen sheets to obscure the true nature of the charnel platform from the approaching Nyarlatophis. I deemed it imperative that He should continue to believe it was Montu alone who encouraged the resistance against Him.

Having concealed the pile of dead with drapery, my men proceeded to escort stragglers to a safe distance. I then ordered the troops to retreat as well. I knew I must stand alone within the confines of the sanctuary, a lure to draw the abomination into Amun's trap.

In the distance, I descried the four-legged horror's menacing approach as He bounded across dunes stained orange and red by morning sunlight. An indescribable dread permeated my consciousness, encouraging me to surrender to fear and thus flee. But what refuge might I find that could shelter me from this avatar of chaos?

Larger and nearer loomed the mute silhouette of the preternatural fiend, His face obscured within the shadows of a nemes headscarf. Despite the abject terror in the pit of my gut, I struggled to maintain a defiant stance atop the shrouded mound of putrefying carcasses, disregarding the muffled mutterings of those unseen observers foolish enough to remain in the temple's proximity.

I held my breath as the gigantic cat set the first of His taloned paws to the raised surface of the plateau. As He reached the western wall of the sacred enclosure, the great sphinx paused to survey the area carefully, sniffing the air briskly as He cautiously made His way across the bounds of the sanctuary walls.

His path strayed somewhat out and away as He neared the statue-guarded pylon of the temple entrance. Looking around, He chose a path with great care, purposely crushing those foolish spectators who remained within the *temenos* of the sanctuary. Those who fled their hiding places were quickly caught and torn to pieces in the intruder's ferocious jaws; the temple grounds became littered with the shredded bits of human gore.

I confronted Nyarlatophis at the foot of the mudbrick pylon. He momentarily surveyed the oversized stone figures to either side of me before swinging an overgrown paw through the air far above my head. The powerful paw flew harmlessly over me, but it struck and decapitated Mentuhotep's statue. Montu's statue, however, remained unscathed.

At the exact instant, a gentle stirring of air not only brought the chimera's noxious stench to my senses, but also sent the folds of His nemes billowing. The greatly intensified horror of the creature's countenance was revealed to all!

Although the scarf was merely blackened here and there, all but the merest vestiges of skin had been scored from His features, exposing the pallid skull beneath. Occasional bits of singed and blackened skin still clung to the bone around the scorched cavities that bore the vestiges of His eyes and nose. Deprived of lips, Nyarlatophis' full-toothed grimace intimidated me more than I care to recall as He focused his full attention upon me.

Assuming a couchant pose, the great beast continued to leer at me insolently as He struggled to speak. Not only were His words slow, slurred and guttural, but certain sounds were particularly difficult for Him to vocalize in the absence of the lips I had helped sear from bone.

"Amenemhat," He growled, "as I have stated, you have indeed proved a worthy foe, but you must know you cannot win this war. For the moment, we share this world, but you are still but a fragile mortal set against an unnatural, relentless, immortal force. I am the humble messenger of the mindless, gurgling abyss out of which every thing is born and to which all things must return. Isfeh is incontrovertible, a universal law that can absolutely never be altered, not even by the gods."

I shouted a challenge, "What you say may well be true, that all must eventually be swallowed by the eternal void, but the human spirit will not surrender to destiny! This world is young, young and full of potential. Though the chaotic end of which you speak be inevitable, we will find a way to postpone its coming, for it is the nature of man to struggle perpetually against the inevitable. Though our efforts be futile, we will fight to the death against the fate you intend to impose upon us."

Surprised by these brave words, Nyarlatophis nodded His savage head gravely, as if in contemplation.

"So be it," He mumbled gravely through bloodstained teeth. "You must fail, but I salute your courage." He remained silent for a moment, having so solemnly intoned the final verdict.

He proceeded to march directly into the temple, His tremendous legs passing over the adjoined towers of the grand pylon, leaving them unscathed. As that colossal form passed directly over my head, I could only gawk mutely, awed at the wonder of such a fabulously grotesque being. As the sandy-brown, leonine brisket slowly passed overhead, the fur-tipped tail twitched as if in anticipation of the coming destruction. I prayed in silent desperation, realizing that the fate of the world now lay exclusively in Amun's hands.

The purring hulk strode onward, marching boldly through the large open court of the holy structure. With one careless stroke of His great tail, He toppled row after row of columns lining both sides of the court. I hesitantly followed as He tramped unmindingly through the lush green and flowering plants of the sacred garden, despoiling their beauty, until, with a gentle leap, He attained the flat surface of the roof that covered the main hypostyle hall. Nothing could bar or even slow the progress of the shambling abomination as He slammed heavy paws through the ceiling and walls of the gaily painted corridor. He halted only when confronted by the double doors of Montu's innermost holy-of-holies.

A single massive paw smashed through the carved bronze doors, only to emerge a moment later with the god's sacred image of gold, the image in which he is believed to dwell, clutched in one paw. Nyarlatophis raised the shimmering prize skyward as if it were a trophy.

I had until that moment considered myself alone in defying the intruder, but the shocked gasps of several of my loyal men revealed their proximity.

Time itself slowed as I anxiously watched as the fabulous golden image was cast violently down from a great height and onto the burnished temple floor where it lay shattered and ruined not far from where I stood.

Nyarlatophis crouched and drew back on his heavy haunches. In an effort to perform the ultimate sacrilege of depriving the dishonored Montu of celestial power, the sphinx lunged at the innermost shrine like a starving lion pouncing on a defenseless victim.

Upon the application of the beast's tremendous weight, the shrine rent in half, its floor cracking and crumbling. Yet it was the sound that immediately followed, the deep-rooted, agonized moan of splintering bedrock, which stands out most clearly in my memory. Sourced somewhere beneath the foundation of the deteriorating structure, a terrific rumbling and grinding announced the condensing of tons of what had previously been solid stone. Total silence followed the deafening roar; it was as if the whole of the world had come to a sudden, abrupt halt.

For what seemed an eternity, the defiant beast stood frozen, incapable of disengaging His legs from the embrace of the crumbled shrine. His head slowly revolved, turning to glower at me with a hatred beyond imagining radiating from His hideously skeletal face. It had finally dawned on Him that the great undefeatable crawling chaos, the stalker of the empty space between the stars, had again been bested. With that, He dropped from sight, His entire body tumbling into the chasm along with the sinking debris!

I fell to my knees; Amun's mysterious plan had succeeded! In transporting the earth-consuming invisibles from the wreck of Mentuhotep I's mortuary complex to the boundaries of Montu's sanctuary, my men had unknowingly sown the seeds of Nyarlatophis' downfall. The invisible ones had weeks to undermine the temple's foundation, rendering the entire edifice too unstable to support the added weight of Nyarlatophis' raging aberration. I had not fully comprehended the brilliance of Amun's plan until that moment. Our nemesis had been undone with His own device!

At the same time, I realized that those of us who had pursued the demon into the temple were now in grievous jeopardy. Large sections of the temple's foundation continued to drop from sight as the superstructure tumbled into the newly formed subsurface void. Recognizing the vulnerability of our position, I did an immediate about-face, ordering all to run, lest they join Nyarlatophis in the ever-expanding crevice. No second warning was required.

I, however, again stationed myself between the towers of the main pylon, the destruction having ceased just before reaching its twin towers. Bolstering my courage, I dared to peer into the shadowy abyss, then jumped back as a deafening roar assaulted my ears. Despite my earnest hopes to the contrary, Nyarlatophis was far from dead.

The outraged anomaly appeared completely unharmed as He paced furiously back and forth within the dust-choked depths of His crude prison. He repeatedly lunged at the soft sides of the enclosure in a desperate attempt to free Himself. Again and again, the shrieking creature thrashed and hurled Himself wildly against the earthen slope in hope of finding some purchase by which He might haul His great bulk out of the hole. Although the eroded walls merely crumbled when assailed, it was inevitable that Nyarlatophis sooner or later would attain a foothold and extricate Himself from what I swore would be His grave. Should He escape, there could be no further opportunity for redemption.

My worst fears were realized as an enormous paw suddenly cleared the hole, locking vicious claws solidly into the disrupted masonry. Slowly, painstakingly, Nyarlatophis continued to hoist His smoky-gray body up and over the edge of the crevice.

At a loss, I turned to the polished eidolon Montu transmogrified as Amun. Desperate, I screamed at the changed but unmoving deity, "You cannot allow this! The world cannot end in such a miserable, tormented way! Lord Amun, save your children from Isfeh's mad embrace!" I ranted. "I beg you!"

I threw my body onto the plinth that served as base for the statue that now bore the likeness of Amun and covered my face, sure that I had somehow failed. Thus, before the very god whose name I share, I openly wept . . . but not for long.

Alerted by the painful screech of talons raking across smooth stone, I looked up, startled. I found myself staring into the osseous face of the huge villainous feline, the forepart of His body already dragged up from the depths to the safe, flat surface. Something far worse than death glared hatefully at me from somewhere within the black, soulless void of those raging eyes.

As the creature struggled, finally raising its heavy hindquarters from the hole, I noted a small whirlwind forming in the space between the twin towers of the pylon near where I still lay sprawled at the feet of the statue. That seemingly insignificant cloud of dancing dust and dirt was all that stood between myself and my grotesque nemesis.

I rose slowly, watching the churning sprite grow larger with each passing moment until, finally, my heart nearly leapt from my chest. I clearly recognized the impalpable, divine likeness of Amun coalescing within the swirling bounds of the mysterious storm. It was not long before his features were perfectly duplicated by the shifting dust and spiraling sands. When the insubstantial effigy opened its divine eyes, I dropped to my knees, heartfelt praises pouring profusely from my throat.

The demonic chimera that was Nyarlatophis studied the sandy figure momentarily before rearing up on its hind legs. He unleashed a piercing shriek of unbearable intensity that struck me as not only an acknowledgment that He had been played for a fool but also an admission of vulnerability.

The fiendish amalgam repeatedly struck out with its mammoth forepaws, battering the divine image with all His strength in an attempt to dissipate it. To the utter frustration of the infuriated creature, however, Amun's divine phantom immediately re-formed each time it was dispersed.

It was only when the beast began to display signs of exhaustion that the windwrought figure of Amun became truly animated. Reaching out, it cupped the air with outspread arms and hands as if drawing and gathering an invisible force from the atmosphere.

Befuddled, Nyarlatophis paused long enough to assume an intensely guarded pose, His rope-like tail swaying nervously to and fro in mocking caricature of a common housecat.

Intuition commanded me to seek shelter at once, lest I be caught up in the ensuing battle of inhuman titans. Rushing to the larger statue, that of Amun, I grap-
pled and climbed the rough-carved legs that I might observe the impending clash
from the relative safety of the stone figure's more than ample lap. Nestled in my
hiding place, I watched with fascination as the phantom god opened wide his
mouth, releasing a searing torrent of breath so powerful that his opponent was
tossed over and onto His back. For a time the half-stunned Nyarlatophis lay still
until, having regained a certain degree of sensibility, He regained His footing and
charged His windswept opponent.

Never was there a gale to match the lethal force of Amun's blasting breath.
The continuous bombardment of searing sand focused on the sphinx. The ruthless
barrage assailed the hapless creature's furry carcass mercilessly, slicing through
flesh like ground glass. Before long, great gouts of dark blood filled the air surrounding the torn and bleeding monster.

The hail of wind-blown sand caused me to huddle further within the limestone
lap of Amun's statue. Had the stony figure faced the battle rather than away, I too
would have been ripped to pieces and buried alive. I finally lost consciousness,
buried beneath a suffocating bed of fine powder and dust created by the maelstrom. Only later did I learn the torrent attained such a velocitous pitch that the
entire temple complex was leveled, reduced to little more than rubble and sand
flush with the surrounding plain.

My only regret is that I did not witness the actual consummation of the confrontation between Amun and Nyarlatophis. The weakened messenger of chaos was
completely driven back into the pit before mounds of sand covered and buried him.

Despite the consensus that no one could possibly have survived the vicious
onslaught, a few of my faithful compatriots stubbornly insisted on sifting through
the dunes that now blanketed the ground around the sand-battered pylon and its
weathered guardians. However, it was Mersu who eventually spied my right hand
extending from the deposit of accumulated sand cradled in the lap of one of the
remaining statues. He hurriedly scaled the chipped and battered legs of the colossus and released me from what nearly became my grave.

The gathered group of onlookers rejoiced to see me, though I was more dead
than alive.

Once revived, I learned that my eyes alone had beheld the miracle of Amun's
presence within the heart of the mechanism of Nyarlatophis' defeat.

*   *   *

The Queen lived only long enough to give her blessing to my subsequent marriage to Princess Neith, Mentuhotep's daughter by his second wife. This formality
permitted me to assume the throne officially, although the sight of my body being
retrieved from the sand-covered lap of the god's graven image had been more than
enough to win me the adoration of the populace. They cheered uproariously,
shouting that Amun himself had miraculously resurrected me from the dead that I
might found a new dynasty of god kings. Thus they say I was reborn, sprung di-

rectly from the very loins of Amun, savior of all Ta-Wy! I neither confirm nor deny that claim as ruler of the Two Lands and reborn offspring of the divine Amun.

Yet I know in my heart that Nyarlatophis cannot truly be dead; He cannot die as we mortals define the term. I pray He will remain securely entombed beneath the rock-littered plain of Ipet-isut forever, but I fear that sometime, in some distant aeon yet to come, He will again find release.

*　　*　　*

I have done my utmost to be a just, wise and strong ruler of the Two Lands. As pharaoh, I have taken Wehemmesut ("Repeating of Creation") as my Horus name to proclaim the new and glorious beginning I hope to bestow upon Egypt. I made Mersu my Chief Vizier of the entire country in appreciation of his bravery and the infinite loyalty he repeatedly demonstrated during the calamity. Together we have made every effort to institute a glorious rebirth of *maat* throughout all our beloved realm.

I have kept my word to Amun as well, proclaiming him the greatest of all gods and causing splendid temples to be built in his honor at Ipet-rasyt as well as at Ipet-isut. Enhancements are made to these already sprawling edifices every year. Smaller shrines dedicated to Montu and other lesser gods are contained within the confines of the holy enclosure that they too may receive the honor they deserve. Additionally, I have restored Mentuhotep's temple complex in the West as well as possible, considering the grave damage it suffered.

After a while, I found I could no longer abide the sight of Waset due to the tragic memories it still holds for me. For this reason and in order to promote the establishment of a new era in the land, I moved the capital city to Itjtaw near the country's geographical center.

Cases of the terrible plague brought to us by Nyarlatophis were reported for a time after the sorcerer's defeat, but I am pleased to say no further instances have occurred within the last five years. The outbreak extended as far north as Mennefer (Memphis), but the last of the infections occurred among the priests of Serapis and the baboons sacred to his shrine on the western bank adjacent to Mennefer. It is over, for now.

*　　*　　*

It should be noted that Amenemhat I's thirty-one-year reign brought a greater degree of stability to Egypt than the kingdom had known for more than two centuries. Despite this, two attempts were made upon his life, both stemming from conspiracies born within his own harem. The second attempt to assassinate Amenemhat unfortunately succeeded; the sleeping sovereign was murdered in the middle of the night in his private sleeping chamber. His oldest son and co-regent, Senusret I, revenged the regicide and thereafter ruled Egypt wisely for fifty years.

*　　*　　*

Although the above manuscript speaks for itself, my companion and cohort, Hans von Hagen, feels it is vital to point out two related factual items that may someday shed some light on some of the deeper challenges presented by the contents of the scrolls. Therefore, in deference to my colleague's wishes, and in light of the generally accepted theory that most legends are based, at least in part, upon historical fact, the following factual and easily verifiable information has been appended to the above document:

1) It is well known that monkeys of several species carry viruses that appear to be closely related to the outbreak of AIDS in the late twentieth century. It seems likely the HIV virus and/or its forerunner(s) existed for thousands of years before its/their resurgence in modern Africa. One theory proposes that the reappearance of this virus may even be the result of accidental simian and purposeful human intrusion into ancient tombs, the preserved mummies of which might still harbor dormant stains of the disease.

From pre-dynastic times through the Late Period of Egyptian history, baboons were considered sacred animals at Saqqara, Egypt, and thus were mummified and entombed in collective burials. In 1993, a collaborative research project was established between the Egyptian-Dutch Research Project on Ancient DNA, the Institute of Virus Evolution and the Environment, the National Museum of Antiquities at Leiden, and the Egyptian Exploration Society of Great Britain. The purpose of this ongoing project is the examination of the remains of ancient monkeys and apes, as well as any viruses found in their remains, and the study of the possible impact such viruses have had upon contemporary humanity. The project is currently focusing on the Baboon Galleries of North Saqqara, its goal being to gather enough samples from the mummified baboons to create a cross-section of DNA that can be analyzed to identify any viruses present. The more long-term aim is to discover any information that might allow scientists to pinpoint the origin of the AIDS retrovirus and thereby add to the ongoing search for a cure.

2) In 1994, geologist T. C. Onstott of Princeton University, while working with the U.S. Department of Energy and the Texaco Corporation near Washington D.C., discovered a form of anaerobic bacteria in exploratory core samples taken from a natural gas well located 1.7 miles beneath the earth's surface. These so-called "living fossils" apparently survived and thrived despite the very harshest of conditions including oxygen deprivation and extreme heat, taking hundreds or even tens of thousands of years to procreate. The strain has been named Bacillus infernus, *"the bacterium from hell."*

Subsequently identified deep-earth bacterial strains collected in a South African mine by Onstott and others appear to "breathe" not oxygen but ferric iron, sulfate, nitrate, nitrite, uranium, and other minerals. In 1995, a team at the Department of Energy's Hanford Reservation in Washington also reported the discovery of what they termed "rock-eating" microbes.

FINIS

Respectfully dedicated to Simson Najovits, Egyptian scholar extraordinaire

Mind-Pilot

William Laughlin

This neglected tale appeared first in an on-line zine called *The Black Book* #3, 2003. It is of a particular type that I happen much to enjoy. It may be a sequel to Frank Belknap Long's "The Hounds of Tindalos," or it may be a kind of modernized remake, taking advantage of greater scientific progress since Long's day. It is not some sort of "daring" New Wave contraption, seeking to subvert the traditional horror genre upon which it is a mocking hypertext. No, it modernizes in a different sense, almost a latter-day reincarnation of the original. I love reading both the prototype and the antitype side by side. It makes me appreciate each one better. You know Frank Long would have been proud of this one! I'm only sorry the author has joined Frank in the Great Beyond, safe at last from the lean and thirsty hounds. I did not know him, but I am happy to publish this fine adventure as a memorial to William Laughlin, a talented fellow indeed.

>   But the man who comes back through the Door in the Wall will never be quite the same as the man who went out.
>   —Aldous Huxley, *The Doors of Perception*

Mandelbrot mandalas faded to a rainbow of holo-ghosts as the monitor slowly restored light to the room. Shea watched the centrifuge dissipate, pulsing a final few translucent patterns—fractal phantoms that vanished into the grid. Shea sighed. He was dead-dry exhausted.

After three long hours in the chair, the test-run for L-13 was finally over.

"Thank you, Mr. Hoffmann—good shift. See you in three days." Chalmers' voice resonated through the test-room. As he got up, Shea rubbed the nape of his neck and steadied himself on the chair. He spoke to Chalmers through the microbead on his Chalmers-Reardon work-togs:

"I'm having some memory trouble, Doctor, in fact, most of the last two hours are a total blank."

Chalmers chuckled. "A short-term memory loss is a normal side-effect of L-13, I'm afraid—something I hope to alleviate in future refinements. I'll see you on Thursday, Mr. Hoffmann. Good day."

After two green-smocked lab-techs plucked tubes and removed wires from his torso and arms, Shea impatiently shrugged off his togs, donned a smock, and headed for the door. He hated working with Chalmers. As he left he glanced at the mirrored rectangle of the monitor room. There was always something in Dr. Winston Chalmers' tone that he didn't trust. . . . The door slid open and after waving at his ochre reflection in the monitor room window, Shea headed for the main spiral of the Chalmers-Reardon Complex. A late Mozart symphony seeped gently from discreet intercoms as he made his way down the sloped corridor to the elevator and his quarters on the third floor. Once more, Shea Hoffmann rubbed the back of his neck. His scalp felt like a film of putty. Yawning, he passed his card-key through the swipe-slot. As Shea headed for the shower, he dreaded the purge-pattern for the next few days—things tasting too sweet or salty; a few peripheral twitters or peripatetic conversation, then it'd be over—just in time for Thursday—and another dose of the drug. For the first forty-eight hours, he had to remain on the Western Pennsylvania campus of the international pharmaceutical giant, then, after an examination, he was free to go back to his condo located nearby in the small town of Mullencroft. A reminder blinked on his wall monitor; wondering what his employers had made the media say, Shea had keyed up a government-sanctioned documentary on the Mind-Pilot Program on the Science Channel this morning. It was bound to be pure propaganda, but he had a morbid curiosity. Maybe because, deep down, he didn't want to believe the truth—

Mind-Pilots weren't heroes. They were shaved Rhesus monkeys.

But just as he stepped into the shower, Shea heard the bell chime—an urgent message. Drying off and yoking the towel around his shoulders, he put on his wall screen and checked his message. It was from Akono Kai, friend and fellow pilot—they had gone through psych-evaluation together. Replaying the message, Shea munched a Pro-bar and hastily dressed.

As he buttoned up, the doorbell sounded—Akono was here. Something was wrong—Shea opened the door.

"So how urgent is urgent?" Wiping his eyes, he gasped.

His colleague looked as though he had aged a decade in the last two weeks. His dreadlocks were shot with gray and his expression road-haggard as though he hadn't slept in days. Shea took a breath. Hadn't bathed either. Glancing furtively behind him, Akono pushed past Shea, and collapsed on his sofa.

"Would you like a cup of tea? Water—" Akono waived off his niceties.

"Shea, we've got to get off-campus—I don't feel safe discussing this here."

Hoffmann shook his head, "You know that I've got to be under observation for a day." Akono pulled out his palm-top and plugged it into Shea's entertainment console. His speakers hissed and crackled.

"This will generate white noise." Akono began to pace across the floor, frantically gesticulating with his hands as he spoke:

"The L-13 test. Chalmers isn't telling you, us, the full truth—"

"What do you mean?"

"We're both testing the same drug; that is, I'm testing L-12, but it's the same strain—" Shea cut him off.

"Listen, Akono, calm down! So what if the drug is the same—?" Akono whirled around and grabbed him by his tee shirt, stretching the corp-logo into a smear.

"No, Shea, this drug, it's synthesized from an eastern plant called Liao. There are strange side effects. Ten pilots have gone paranoid-critical at Chalmers-Reardon research plants around the world. One is dead—disappeared! I got this from a rogue site that was shut down almost as soon as I downloaded the data."

Suddenly, Akono swayed back and forth.

"Oh, no! I'm—I'm losing control—" As his friend staggered, groping for the wall to steady himself, Shea broke Akono's enfeebled grip.

"OK, I believe you—so what do you want to do?" Clutching at his collar, Akono furtively glanced around him again, Lorre-like, showing all the signs of early para-crit neurosis. Still, he was a friend. If there were anything he learned after all of these years—mind-pilots took care of their own.

"This disc has everything," Akono whispered. "Open it tomorrow, at home, behind a firewall—read it as soon as possible. Then we can act!" Shea nodded, palming the file, hoping to pacify Akono till he could sort it all out.

The door chime sounded. Shea answered. There were two guards in the video monitor. "Mr. Hoffmann? This is Richards from Security. Have you seen Akono Kai?"

Shea looked at Kai, gog-eyed, sweating with palpable fear

"He stopped by, but I was in the shower—what's up?"

"He attacked a guard—he should be considered dangerous. Please, inform us immediately if you should contact him. Thank you, Mr. Hoffmann." The guard turned and left. Shea shut the door. Shea was surprised—they hadn't even bothered to search his room. From behind him, Akono Kai sighed with relief. Shea cursed under his breath and went to his cooler and poured himself a glass of tea. Kai broke the uneasy silence.

"I, uh, didn't attack that guard, Shea. He tried to stop me. I broke free and ran—" Shea waived off the explanation and sipped his tea.

"I believe you, Akono. You're in no condition to hurt anyone."

"So, what are you going to—*ah!*" Convulsively, Kai clutched his temple, staggering back to the couch. Shea steadied him, dropping his cup. The glass shattered, the raspberry tea spreading a bloody blot on the beige carpeting.

"Akono, what is it?" Kai gaped in terror—pressing deep into the vinyl cushions.

"No—no! I'm still here! I still control. God—they're drilling into my brain!" Kai thrashed in silence.

"Akono—" Shea began to regret sending the guard away. Then, abruptly, Kai seemed to shake off his hallucination, regain his composure, and suddenly become perfectly lucid. The effect was eerie, as though his friend had been momentarily "possessed."

"I know you're humoring me. God, it's getting worse. Shea, listen to me! Chalmers has found it—something that takes the mind into the deep subconscious, penetrating into the collective memory. But—but we've gone too far. I've seen the shapes *before*, the archetypes, the *sounds* before words! Creatures darting in the corner of my eye!"

"Akono, you've just got to clam down. Drain out."

"No! No doctors! Please, Shea, just scan this disc, I'll meet you at the planetarium in two days—" And with that, Akono whipped out a long nylon rope, swiftly attached it to the balcony, and, after tying off—rappelled down the side of the building. Kai landed safely and, ninja-like, disappeared into the hedges below. Suddenly, Akono was completely his old self. Determined, athletic, logical. Searchlights snaked across the walls. Shea ducked below the window.

Minutes later, still stunned, cleaning up his spilled tea, Shea half-watched the documentary, while trying to figure out what sort of scandal he'd stumbled into.

THE SCIENCE CHANNEL PRESENTS
THE MIND-PILOT PROGRAM:
AMERICA'S METAPHYSICAL MANIFEST DESTINY

(Red White and Blue waves watermark on Phrenologist's brain-map)

NARRATOR: THE VAN ALLEN BELT.

(Animated globe-map against starscape. A white highlighted "atmospheric" halo encircling the earth: 360-degree rotation shot.)

LITTLE DID THE MINDS OF NASA SUSPECT THAT THIS WOULD BE THE GRAVEYARD OF AMERICA'S MANNED SPACE PROGRAM.

(Video file footage of numerous shots of missiles being launched from various worldwide locations. Newscasters and world leaders smiling.)

THE FAMOUS "PEACE LAUNCH" OF 2075 WOULD CHANGE EVERYTHING. A UNITED NATIONS EFFORT TO RID THE WORLD OF NUCLEAR WEAPONS, BY LAUNCHING THEM INTO THE SUN, WOULD HAVE DISTASTROUS CONSEQUENCES FOR YEARS TO COME.

(File-footage of launching of nuclear weapons around the globe.)

AFFECTED BY THE NUCLEAR DETONATIONS, PROLONGED SOLAR FLARE ACTIVITY WOULD RAISE THE BACKGROUND RADIATION OF THE BELT TO OVER TEN TIMES THE ORIGINAL AMOUNT—THE RESULT:

(Photo of solar corona before/after shot.)

AN IMPENETRABLE BARRIER TO THE OUTER SOLAR SYSTEM THAT WOULD TAKE DECADES TO ATTENUATE.

(Graphic of new halo around earth representing increased radiation.)

THE CITIZENS OF THE UNITED STATES SOON LOST INTEREST IN UNMANNED EXPEDITIONS. AND THUS CAME THE END OF JOHN KENNEDY'S NEW FRONTIER.

(NASA base in Florida overgrown and rusted with disuse.)

THEN, IN 2085, "THE NEXT FRONTIER" CAPTURED THE IMAGINA-TION OF A NEW GENERATION OF PIONEERS, AND THE MIND-PILOT PROGRAM WAS BORN!

(A montage of chemists with alembics and shots of pharmaceutical plants inter-cut with encephalographic readings and close-ups of computer-enhanced schematics of the brain.)

THE CULMINATION OF A DOZEN HIGH-TECH PHARMACEUTICAL RESEARCH PROJECTS, UNITED TO FORM A SINGLE GOVERNMENT AGENCY, THE SO-CALLED "PSYCHONAUT" OR "MIND-PILOT" PRO-GRAM DISCOVERED AND TESTED DRUGS THAT WOULD LEAD TO INCREDIBLE BREAKTHROUGHS IN MEMORY ENHANCEMENT, ALZHEIMER'S DISEASE, BIPOLAR DISORDERS, AND OTHER NEURO-CHEMICAL CHALLENGES.

(Montage of drugs being administered to a series of patients, charts, and close-ups of syringes and pills interspersed with shots of mind-pilots in control rooms.)

HUNDREDS OF BRAVE SOULS, RIGOROUSLY TRAINED TO OBSERVE AND PERFORM COMPLEX MENTAL CALISTHENICS, HAVE TESTED THOUSANDS OF UNKNOWN CHEMICAL AGENTS FOR THE BENEFIT OF MANKIND AND AMERICA'S "*METAPHYSICAL MANIFEST DES-TINY*"! BASED UPON THE "BERKELEY MODEL" OF A CENTURY AGO, A RESEARCHER OR "CONTROL" WILL INTRODUCE A SERIES OF VIS-UAL CUES IN THE FORM OF GEOMETRIC PATTERNS DISPLAYED UPON A WALL-SIZED MONITOR.

(Series of resmers displayed on video; basic shapes cones, swirls, and rods.)

THESE PATTERNS OFTEN ACHIEVE A HYPNOTIC EFFECT UPON THE "MIND-PILOT," AND PROVIDE THE RESEARCHER WITH A MEANS OF ESTABLISHING A PATTERN OF "BASE READINGS" TO USE AS A WAY OF "MIRRORING" OR "AMPLIFYING" THE VARYING MENTAL STATES THAT WILL ACCOMPANY THE TESTING OF A PSY-CHOACTIVE AGENT. WE INTERVIEWED—

Flipping off the monitor with disgust, Shea shook his head and stretched out on the floor trying to unclench the taut muscles in his lower back. America's meta-physical manifest destiny! What a joke!

Shea smirked to himself—the Mind-Pilot initiative had as many secret casual-ties as the Russian Space Program! Hidden, top-security files with the real stories—madness, suicides, irreparable brain damage, strokes, hundreds of tales of psychic collisions and incompetent overdoses. The real stories were considered too demor-alizing to the nation, and only passed as oral tradition from m-pilot to m-pilot through the years. Now *that* would make a good special—*Secrets of the Paranoid—Critical!* Men forgotten by official history: men like Akono Kai.

Suddenly exhausted, Shea went back to his bedroom and, dialing a slow hypnospin on his wall monitor, stretched out on his fluid-form cloud-couch. His head whirled with questions as he dropped into sleep—

*   *   *

Four o'clock in the morning—

Shea woke bleary-eyed to darting vermin-like shadows creeping at the edge of his living room—a crouched shadow at his side—the disc!

With a snarl, he leapt upon the figures, kicking out at one intruder, but the silent enemies just stunned him with a shock-gun and Shea lost consciousness with the bitter knowledge that he had so easily and carelessly lost the precious data that Akono Kai had risked his life to deliver.

*   *   *

The Stellarium sat on a hillside overlooking Mullencroft. Designed to be a library, the domed building had been converted into a planetarium in the latter half of the previous century—and now was almost abandoned. Shea's friend, ex-mind pilot Rob Rostack, had assumed the custodianship as a pay-off from a para-crit incident caused by pharmacological negligence. The work involved was minimal, a few school planetarium shows and tours, and Rostack's livelihood was secured, another mind-pilot put quietly out to pasture in a remote, controlled location, to limit his exposure to others. Given a small vocation to calm his nerves, ease his bitterness.

This tactic of course hadn't worked with Rostack.

Rostack hated the mind-pilot initiative, hated what it had done to him, and collected all the subversive, hidden history of the program—he was also connected to the underground network of para-crit vets.

But Robert Rostack wasn't all hatred and bile—far from it.

Shea met Rob while taking a summer Observational Astronomy course—with Rostack as instructor. A complete astro-nut, Rostack really believed in the stars. And Shea had been rapidly infected by Rostack's quixotic dream, sitting with his new friend in the vast expanding starscapes of the Stellarium. He marveled at Rostack's patience—measuring the radiation levels in the Van Allen Belt for the slightest incremental decline, examining the data from the last few unmanned probes, dreaming of future "safe-levels" that would be decades past his own lifespan.

Shea climbed up the hillside, still aching from the previous night's assault and battery. It had to have been M-R security. No wonder they didn't search his apartment. Now he was implicated. He needed some advice.

Sliding his card-key into the slot, Shea entered the domed neo-gothic structure, searching for his friend in its curved expanse.

A voice came from behind him. Shea jumped.

"You're early."

"I wish you wouldn't do that, Rob." Shea swore at him. Rostack laughed.

"Sorry. You know that the outer walls are seamed with passages. After all these years with so few visitors, it's really second nature. You're awfully jumpy. Anyway, what's going on?"

"Akono Kai's gone para-crit. He says there's a problem with the new drug we're testing: L-13. Kai gave me this disc with the backstory—but security broke in and took it from me."

"Interesting. Surprised that you haven't been detained for questioning. They really must be up to something with that drug. They obviously don't want to jeopardize losing you for research—otherwise they'd detain you. This is clearly something the Feds don't know about. Who's the control on the project?"

"Chalmers."

Rostack nodded. "Why did I have to ask? C'mon, let's go into the booth and talk this over." Shea nodded, following his friend into a secret hatchway in the sidewall connected to a room in the domed building that housed the circuit board and controls for the planetarium and doubled as a workshop. On the walls were four neo-psychedelic holo-portraits of Galileo, Hawking, Kepler, and Copernicus made to look like Richard Avedon's Beatles photos. As they entered Rostack sighed.

"So, Kai is on the loose—another para-crit. You know, it took them twelve hours to find me and strap me to a stretcher."

Shea nodded. "Bad time to remind me. What I'd like to know is what was on that file that Akono was trying to give me." Scratching his chin. Rostack sat at his workstation.

"Let's see if I can find it through another rogue site. What was the drug?"

"L-13. Synthesized from an opiate called *Liao*." Rostack grunted.

"I've heard of it. That is one strong hallucinogen." Rostack typed a few commands, and then gasped. "Look. Here we go—there's this group called the Biblioweb Guild, some of my psych-vet friends get filtered info through them." Shea looked at the downloaded data.

Scrolling on the twin screens came the data from the hidden shadow-site. Shea recognized from the diagrams and chemistry that *Liao* was some sort of psychoactive agent that worked naturally at the molecular level.

"Hey, look, this stuff is highly illegal. Six para-crit incidents, and the Feds discontinued testing." Rostak turned to look at Shea, creased features blue and grim in the half-light. "Chalmers is in deep here; this isn't a sanctioned R&D project."

Suddenly a gunshot sounded, and at the east fire exit the double doors flew open—it was Akono Kai. Immediately, he slammed the doors shut as best as he could, then leaned back against them.

Kai was screaming. "They're coming! Dear god!"

Shea and Rob Rostack looked at each other. Akono fired a shot into the floor.

"Get back! All of you—"

"Yup," said Rob, with the weary voice of a man who had expected this insanity. Shea bit his lower lip. Kai was barricading the door with folding chairs and a table.

"Security must be on the way," said Shea. Rob snorted.

"What makes you think so? He could be hallucinating—" Rob began to flip switches, gradually rotating the planetarium.

"That'll disorient him a bit. He can't see us, but this wall isn't bulletproof. I think we ought to do something, Shea."

"Like what? He's freakin' nuts!"

"Like maybe disarm him—you're a lot younger than I am."

Shea stared at Rostack in disbelief. "So, I attack armed with what, a telescope? Christ, Rob!"

"Look!" Rob pointed at Akono, who had slumped down in a heap by the double door, pistol dangling in his right hand. Shea instantly ran for the door

Akono Kai fell onto the ground clutching his head, then curled into a fetal position—convulsing with spasms of pure agony. Crouching low, Shea raced down into the rows of seats in the silent planetarium. Above them the projected stars whirled and spun, constellations outlined like glowing paper dolls. As he drew closer, Shea heard Kai muttering—his wan, unshaven face blank with panic.

"Th—They can't get in, they can't break the circle—the circle by and by, Lord, by and by—they're still trying, though, howling behind my eyes! They want to swallow my self—my soul!"

Gently, Shea grabbed the gun from Kai's hand. Kai didn't seem to care—eyes fixed on the barricaded door, staring as if in expectation of a cataclysm. Suddenly, Shea heard Rob's voice through the PA system:

"Shea, we've got company. Security. They've crashed the gate."

Kai reacted as though he'd been hit with a cattle-prod and with a shriek he fell to the floor. "No! The Hounds! They'll break the circle—"

"Akono—wait!" But as the security guards forced through his flimsy barrier, Shea paused. Something shimmered in the air above them. At first Shea thought that it was a leftover mirage from L-13, but then he saw something solidify above Kai—as if the air itself had become gelatinous.

Kai crab-crawled back against the curved wall like a trapped insect as the strange opaque shape hovered sinuously toward him. Shea froze, unable to act.

Kai pointed at the sundered entranceway. "Shea—the circle!"

And that was the last thing that Akono Kai ever said to him.

The amoebic wraith swallowed him as though he were suddenly immersed in churning water, there was no escape from it—Kai's flailing body was permeated with the clear plasma.

Then, with eyes rollback white, mouth foaming, Kai began to croak—to *bark*—

It was a hoarse, guttural sound, deathly, like a man choking—and the sound had a horrifying effect on Shea. Because it wasn't as if it were Kai's voice at all, but as if Kai's vocal chords were now simply a vehicle, a marionette for another creature trying vainly to approximate its own voice through a hopelessly inadequate and alien instrument.

"Shea, what's going on down there?" Rob's concerned, half-hysterical voice carried through the planetarium speakers. The security guards shouted inane warnings at him. But everything, all the actions in the room, had been rendered arbitrary by the sight before them.

Akono Kai was floating.

Suspended in mid-air, Kai's levitating body was jerking spastically, as though electric shocks were running through his veins. Then a thick, bluish fluid began to form around him, and Kai's clothing began to melt away into the jellied mass.

Shea sank to his knees as the first wave of the nauseating scent stung his nostrils.

It was an acrid, sulfurous gas that seemed to permeate the room, as if the air itself were being changed by the process taking place before them. In the corner of his eye, Shea vaguely noticed more guards queueing up at the entranceway. It didn't matter. Akono Kai was dead. But whatever had seized him had yet to finish what it had started.

Kai's skin began to roil and undulate, bubbling, stretching till it burst; then the horrible sounds of breaking bone—and Shea understood.

Whatever it was that had seized Akono Kai was trying to alter him into some kind of form that would serve as a suitable host or atmosphere for itself.

But Kai's poor violated flesh had reached its breaking point.

With a sickening burst of stretched tendons, Kai's head fell from his shoulders, and his corpse fell unceremoniously to the ground, the cloud dispersing into the immaterial air, leaving only a shredded husk and a foul stench permeating the room. Overcome with nausea, Shea buried his head in his hands.

And that was all that M-R security needed. The intercom barked.

"Shea—" Then, two gunshots rang out. From above him, the speakers gave a *brap* of static. Now two of his friends were dead. Shea heard heavy footfalls behind him.

And that was all Shea Hoffmann heard or saw.

* * *

Floating deepblack in cold numb untime . . .

"**u *r* *n a* a**u***n*e"

A spike of light, ghost voices calling—

"*ou *re *n a* a**ul***n*e"

Louder now, urging, wakeupwakeupWAKEUP—

"—you are on an ambulance!"

Shea blinked blurred, gray shadows, straining against restraints, unable to move.

"OK, he's responsive. Give him the sedative—"

"But he's a mind-pilot—it could kill him!"

"Chalmers gave us a special mix—look, he said to get him conscious, then hit him."

"He's the boss."

Shea heard cloth tearing, the sound of traffic, ambulance banshee, horns—the sight of the Chalmers-Reardon Complex swimming up at him.

And then, he disappeared from himself awhile . . .

* * *

Echoes of echoes, his name came from the end of a twenty-mile tunnel, repeated like a mantra.

Shea rubbed his eyes. It was Dr. Winston Chalmers.

"Mr. Hoffmann. Good. We have much to discuss—"

Shea pulled against Mylar restraints. He was on a gurney in the control room. His neck was collared. A sickening feeling of fear bled ice in the pit of his stomach.

"You killed my friends, you fucker—"

"I'm sorry. It was completely unintentional—"

"How can you *unintentionally* murder someone? You're insane, Chalmers." The pale, short man with the black monk-cut hair leaned over him, grinning.

"Oh, the old 'mad scientist' canard! As Einstein was, or Hawking or Newton?" Chalmers walked swiftly across the room, then returned into his restricted sight, waving a handful of brown, stained, burned papers and printouts.

"This, Mr. Hoffmann—*this* is what we have been working for—a breakthrough! One that philosophers, physicists, alchemists and scientists have been trying to make for thousands of years—"

"And what would that be, O tragically misunderstood genius?"

"Spare me your sarcasm, Hoffmann, you can't deny it—you've seen them!"

"Seen who?"

"The inner demons—the eternal creations of Jung's collective unconscious, creatures that are palpable manifestations of every-man's fears, desires, hatreds."

Shea watched Chalmers raving, and was terrified. He'd never seen the controlled, dispassionate researcher behaving in this erratic manner. Unable to contain himself, Hoffmann exploded.

"You idiot! Those are not *inner* demons. They are *outer* ones, Chalmers! They are some kind of creatures. I mean, what moves as fast as the speed of light—the speed of thought! And what makes the speed of thought reach the velocity of these conceptual boundaries? L-13! Chalmers, these things are some kind of . . . aliens!"

Chalmers chuckled. "Well, that is why you are my ace mind-pilot—you are the most imaginative. However, you are wrong. They are just deep psychological constructs. Chimeras, nothing more."

"Look at the tape, man. Didn't you see Akono?" Hoffmann pleaded.

"A seizure after an over-aggressive assault."

"They didn't touch him. No one did! Chalmers, please listen to me—"

"Nonsense. Mr. Hoffmann, you have been chosen. You are my Balboa, my Armstrong. You will make contact with these imaginary creatures in their realm in your deep subconscious and bring back a report, a catalog of their properties and characteristics."

"Chalmers, these aren't psychological constructs—look at the two EKG's, for Chrissakes!"

"Schizophrenics can produce two sets of brainwaves upon occasion, Hoffmann, you know that."

"They ripped his goddamn head off! Everyone who takes your damn drug dies at the hands of these things!" Shea screamed.

"No, no—that is merely a dosage problem, I've made further refinements. You'll see."

"A dosage problem? This is only a dosage problem?" Shea laughed tonelessly.

Chalmers didn't notice. "Trust me. It won't be like that this time. The dosage must be exact and the setting must be perfect. L-14 only creates seconds of precise attunement so that you cannot succumb to these figments, these shadows." Chalmers held his syringe to the light.

Shea sickened. "Chalmers, don't do this—I'm warning you. This is insanity."

"Yes. Yes it is, Mr. Hoffmann. By definition, I believe it *has* to be. Good luck."

And blithely Chalmers plunged the needle in—

Shea before
the gray walls
of logic then bent
and folded between
sanity's sorted piles
his finitude shattered
an eternal second caught

Another than
itself, it smells
in the outer edges
trembling thoughts
float though the sharp
cornered angels of night
sundered into fragments

in the gridded intersecting in the nexus
of merged consciousness each touch
the barriers of the other's self reaches
every limit of I-ego then passes
far across a cross across a
cross across a cross
crossing across
a crossed x
across
x crossed a
crossing across
cross across a cross
across a cross across far
reaches of this other-self passes
limits and I-ego barriers moves out of
touch of the nexus consciousness unmerge
out of the gridded intersecting out of the gridded

fragments and hungers
back in night's corner
sharp with desire for
fearful thoughts
in the outer edges
it can smell
the Other

seconds caught in eternal
infinitely re-assembled in
sorted piles of sanity
folded unevenly
logic fractured
back in walls
of Shea

The creature had brushed against his consciousness—

"Hoffmann! Mr. Hoffmann, respond!"

Shea heard Chalmers through the intercom. His arms ached. His throat hurt—he'd been screaming. Shea looked up to see Chalmers standing over him. Shea realized that he was on the floor—he'd pulled off the restraints and in the process probably had dislocated a shoulder. Chalmers kneeled beside him. Shea blinked.

Then, without hesitation, he flung himself onto his captor.

Chalmers was stunned by the suddenness of the attack and fell almost immediately, his head colliding with the wall as he fell. With his mind working at preternatural speed, Shea noticed the room, his surroundings, and the syringe of L-14.

Grabbing the needle, Shea pinned the sprawled researcher to the ground and swiftly injected him with the drug.

Then, Shea Hoffmann bundled up the concussed scientist and his thumb-worn documents, and fled for the Stellarium, hearing the alien creatures scrabbling in his back-brain.

Then, listening to Chalmers' screams as the L-14 took hold, Shea felt the abject, all-consuming fear of Akono Kai ripple in the walls as the beings approached

*   *   *

(Six months later . . .)

"More plaster! Where is the architect, you idiots—these rooms must be completely *round!*" Shea cringed behind his palmtop as Chalmers shrieked at the contractors through his telecom bead. The Stellarium, as usual, was in perpetual transformation around him. Modified and altered with a series of circular passages, it has become a building without corners, without angles, a bizarre edifice that has been compared by the local reporters to the old Winchester Mystery House, built by the mad moneyed American heiress fearful of a thousand murdered ghosts. Chalmers, in one of his more lucid ravings, had theorized that the circles and tunnels somehow confuse these beings and proceeded to erect crenellated walls with religious fervor.

Hoffmann shivered, his hand bleached white leaning against the wet plaster in the hall.

Shea prayed it was a good theory; Hoffmann could feel the mind-hunters again, the Hounds drawing nearer each day, squirming behind his eyes.

Chalmers had missed the point—these beings were explorers, too. They traversed space-time looking for new homes, new frontiers: the minds, the bodies of men were only terra incognita, blank slates to be re-formed into habitable hosts, as casually as we might plow a field or build a fence.

Manifest destiny.

Though the animosity remained, he and Chalmers were now allies of necessity. The vast fortune of Chalmers' company at their disposal, the Stellarium was rapidly being transformed into a permanent base of operations—a fortress—but already there were questions. The media was comparing Chalmers to a latter-day Howard Hughes. The Board of Directors was demanding the heir explain himself. Shea sighed, staring up at the artificial stars, the pages of Chalmers's latest research, coffee stained, spread open on his lap.

They were training a squadron of Mind-Pilots now, adepts, aces—psychic warriors primed for mental combat against these new invaders. Chalmers was designing an arsenal of psychotropic weapons, brain-warpers, mind-bombs for a new, unknown realm of warfare.

The first salvo had been fired. The doorway had been blown open by the Liao tests. It was only a matter of time—

Now caged in a widening gyre, their brains chewed and bitten by L-14, licked by the slavering, outer dark—how long would it be before those creatures poked through the veil once more, found them, penetrated the tissue of their minds, and worse—

After all this, could either of them still be safely called "human"?

Acknowledgments

Robert Bloch, "Death Is an Elephant," *Weird Tales* (February 1939), as by Nathan Hindin); copyright © 1939 by Popular Fiction Publishing Co.; in *Flowers from the Moon and Other Lunacies* (Arkham House, 1998), copyright (c) 1998 by Eleanor Bloch. Reprinted by permission of Ralph Vicinanza Agency.

Ramsey Campbell, "The Ways of Chaos," in *Far Away and Never* (Necronomicon Press, 1996), copyright © 1996 by Ramsey Campbell; in *Ghor, Kin-Slayer: The Saga of Genseric's Fifth-Born Son* (Necronomicon Press, 1997), copyright © 1997 by Necronomicon Press. Reprinted by permission of the author.

Peter Cannon, "The Hound of the Partridgevilles," copyright © 2010 by Peter Cannon. Printed by permission of the author.

Peter Cannon, "The Letters of Halpin Chalmers," in *100 Crooked Little Crime Stories,* ed. Robert Weinberg, Stefan R. Dziemianowicz, Martin Greenberg (Barnes & Noble, 1994), copyright © 1994 by Barnes & Noble, Inc. Reprinted by permission of the author.

Lin Carter, "The Madness out of Time," *Crypt of Cthulhu* No. 39 (Roodmas 1986), copyright © 1986 by Cryptic Publications. Reprinted by permission of the author's literary executor, Robert M. Price.

Michael Cisco, "Firebrands of Torment," in *Secret Hours* (Mythos Books, 2007), copyright © 2007 by Michael Cisco. Reprinted by permission of the author.

Adrian Cole, "The War among the Gods," in *Ghor, Sin-Slayer: The Saga of Genseric's Fifth-Born Son* (Necronomicon Press, 1997), copyright © 1997 by Necronomicon Press. Reprinted by permission of the author.

Perry M. Grayson, "The Death of Halpin Chalmers," *Yawning Vortex* 3, No. 1 (1996), copyright © 1996 by Perry M. Grayson. Reprinted by permission of the author.

C. J. Henderson, "Juggernaut," in *Imelod#*17, copyright © 2000 by C. J. Henderson. Rerinted by permission of the author.

David C. Kopaska-Merkel and Ronald McDowell, "Through Outrageous Angles," *Eldritch Tales* #12, copyright © 1986 by Crispin Burnham. Reprinted by permission of the authors.

William Laughlin, "Mind-Pilot," *The Black Book* No. 3 (2003), copyright © 2003 by William Laughlin. Reprinted by kind permission of Lynne Laughlin, agent for the Author's Estate.

Frank Belknap Long, "Gateway to Forever," *Crypt of Cthulhu* No. 25 (Michaelmas 1984), copyright © 1984 by Cryptic Publications. Reprinted by permission of copyright holder Robert M. Price.

Frank Belknap Long, "The Gift of Lycanthropy," *Fantasy Crossroads* (January 1979), copyright © 1979 by Jonathan Bacon; in *Ghor, Kin-Slayer: The Saga of Genseric's Fifth-Born Son* (Necronomicon Press, 1997), copyright © 1997 by Necronomicon Press. Reprinted by permission of the Pimlico Literary Agency.

Frank Belknap Long, *The Horror from the Hills, Weird Tales* (January and February–March 1931), copyright © 1931 by Popular Fiction Publishing Co.; Arkham House, 1963, copyright © 1963 by Frank Belknap Long. Reprinted by permission of the Pimlico Literary Agency.

Frank Belknap Long, "The Hounds of Tindalos," *Weird Tales* (March 1929), copyright © 1929 by Popular Fiction Publishing Co. Reprinted in *The Hounds of Tindalos* (Arkham House, 1946), copyright © 1946 by Frank Belknap Long. Reprinted by permission of the Pimlico Literary Agency.

Frank Belknap Long, "The Space-Eaters," *Weird Tales* (July 1928), copyright © 1928 by Popular Fiction Publishing Co.; in *The Hounds of Tindalos* (Arkham House, 1946), copyright © 1946 by Frank Belknap Long. Reprinted by permission of the Pimlico Literary Agency.

Frank Belknap Long, "When Chaugnar Wakes," *Weird Tales* (September 1932), copyright © 1932 by Popular Fiction Publishing Co.; in *In Mayan Splendor* (Arkham House, 1977), copyright © 1977 by Frank Belknap Long. Reprinted by permission of the Pimlico Literary Agency.

Robert M. Price, "The Dweller in the Pot," *Crypt of Cthulhu* No. 74 (Lammas 1990), copyright © 1990 by Cryptic Publications. Reprinted by permission of the author.

Robert M. Price, "The Elephant God of Leng," in *Blasphemies & Revelations* (Mythos Books, 2008), copyright © 2008 by Robert M. Price. Reprinted by permission of the author.

Joseph S. Pulver, Sr., "But It's a Long Dark Road," copyright © 2010 by Joseph S. Pulver, Sr. Printed by permission of the author.

Joseph S. Pulver, Sr., "Scarlet Obeisance," copyright © 2010 by Joseph S. Pulver, Sr. Printed by permission of the author.

Stanley C. Sargent, "Nyarlatophis: A Fable of Ancient Egypt," in *The Taint of Lovecraft*, copyright © 2002 by Stanley C. Sargent. Reprinted by permission of the author.

Ann K. Schwader, "Confession of the White Acolyte," "Pompelo's Doom," and "The Shore of Madness," copyright © 2010 by Ann K. Schwader. Printed by permission of the author.

CPSIA information can be obtained
at www.ICGtesting.com
Printed in the USA
BVHW01s0328150318
510162BV00002B/143/P